Praise for David Anthony Durham
and the Acacia Trilogy

"Provides the best of both worlds: epic world-changing conflict and touching character-centered story. What else could you possibly want?"
—Patrick Rothfuss, author of *The Wise Man's Fear*

"A fascinating world. . . . All [of the characters] are gratifyingly multidimensional, flawed, gifted, and conflicted in their makeup and motivations, and capable of change."—*USA Today*

"A big, fat, rich piece of history-flavored fantasy. . . . Imagined with remarkable thoroughness."
—Lev Grossman, *Time*

"Excellent. . . . A multi-layered, page-turning series that pushes the envelope of epic fantasy."
—*Contra Costa Times*

"Extraordinary. . . . One of the best books, fantasy or otherwise . . . in recent memory. . . . A work of pure genius."
—*The Free-Lance Star*

"Distinctive, idiosyncratically meditative, politically topical. . . . Rarely has medieval epic been quite this pertinent."
—*Locus* magazine

"Something genuinely new. . . . Strong echoes of Homer and Virgil, Tolkien, Norse mythology's Twilight of the Gods and America's compromised history as a republic built on slavery fuse into an enthralling, literate and increasingly suspenseful narrative."
—*Kirkus Reviews* (starred)

"Brilliant. . . . Astonishing. . . . Durham has made the leap from contemporary to historical to fantasy/allegorical with formidable ease." —*Black Issues Book Review*

"A deeply political vision of the fantastic that exposes the humanity at the heart of every ruthless machination. . . . *Acacia* isn't just a vastly entertaining epic. With its symbolism, pathos, and penetrating examination of political motives, it's downright literary." —*Strange Horizons*

"David Anthony Durham's story confounds expectations at almost every turn, creating a novel that leaves you waiting for the next installment with great expectations." —*SFSite.com*

"A huge, sprawling epic that manages to weave together history, politics, intrigue and thunderous action scenes without ever losing track of the multitudes of finely drawn characters. . . . *Acacia* has wonders in store both for those who love epic fantasy and for those who think it's old hat." —*Revolution SF*

"Poised writing, rich characterization, and world-building. . . . Wonderfully [reflects] the cultural and racial diversity of our own world." —*Fantasyliterature.com*

"Excellent. . . . Great writing, complicated characters, moral and social woes that echo our own world in an imaginative fashion—this is what fantasy is all about."—*The Agony Column*

David Anthony Durham

The Sacred Band

David Anthony Durham received the 2009 John W. Campbell Award for Best New Writer of Science Fiction for *Acacia* and *The Other Lands* (the first two volumes of the Acacia Trilogy). Author of the historical novels *Gabriel's Story*, *Walk Through Darkness*, and *Pride of Carthage*, he was handpicked by George R. R. Martin to write for his Wild Cards series of collaborative novels. Durham lives with his wife and children in western Massachusetts.

www.davidanthonydurham.com

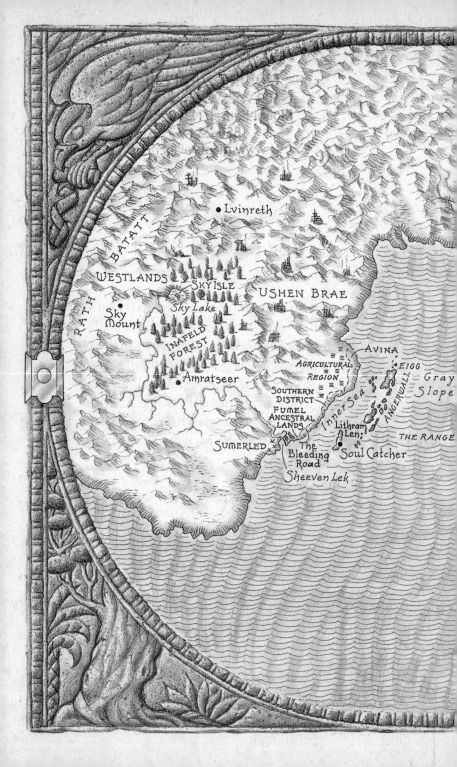

The
Sacred Band

The Sacred Band

Book Three
of the Acacia Trilogy

David Anthony Durham

Anchor Books
A Division of Random House, Inc.
New York

FIRST ANCHOR BOOKS EDITION, APRIL 2012

The Library of Congress has cataloged the Doubleday edition as follows:
Durham, David Anthony, 1969–
The sacred band / David Anthony Durham.—1st ed.
    p. cm.—(Acacia trilogy ; bk. 3)
            I. Title.
        PS3554.U677S24 2011
        813'.54—dc22   2011006736

Anchor ISBN: 978-0-307-94715-4

Book design by Maria Carella
Map illustration by David Cain

www.anchorbooks.com

Printed in the United States of America
10 9 8 7 6 5 4 3 2 1

For Sorley, Beth, Gudrun, and Jamie

Contents

The
Sacred Band

The Story So Far

The *Other Lands*, the second book of the Acacia trilogy, begins with a prologue that dates back to the time of Hanish Mein's rule. League slavers have caught the twins Mór and Ravi, in a mass roundup of quota children. On a remote beach in rural Candovia, Ravi tries to stir the other youths into rebellion. When he is captured, a leagueman spares his life, saying that a different fate awaits him—and his soul—in the Other Lands.

The story proper begins some nine years after the events in *Acacia: The War with the Mein*. Corinn Akaran, now the undisputed queen of Acacia, keeps tight control of her power. She trusts few people beyond her assistant, Rhrenna, a Meinish woman she had been friendly with during Hanish Mein's reign. Corinn has commissioned experiments on a new distillation of the mist—called the vintage—that can be added to wine. The vintage is being created in partnership with the league, which she appeased after Hanish's war. She has let them expand their operations on the Outer Isles. The league is now running those islands like a private fiefdom, with the aim of producing quota children on large plantations. Outside of the duties of her office, Corinn has a softer, more maternal side. She dotes on her eight-year-old son, Aaden. He is the only one who knows Corinn is studying *The Song of Elenet*.

Corinn's two younger siblings are busy as well. Mena Akaran

begins the novel on the plains of Talay, where she is in charge of exterminating the foulthings, the mutated creatures that resulted from the corrupted magic the Santoth unleashed when they destroyed the Meinish army after Aliver's death. Foulthings vary in form, size, and dangerousness, but Mena—along with her husband, Melio, and Aliver's friend Kelis Umae—defeats them one by one. Her brother, Dariel Akaran, has been assuaging the guilt he harbors about allowing Aliver to duel Hanish by overseeing reconstruction projects across the empire.

The main storyline begins with the arrival of Sire Dagon and Sire Neen with news for Corinn of a mishap in the Other Lands. The leaguemen explain that their trade has never exactly been with the Lothan Aklun. The Lothan Aklun are middlemen who cater to a larger population, the Auldek. Frustrated by years of knowing little about the Auldek, the league began "seeking intelligence" about them. Unfortunately—they claim—several league spies were found out. Fearing the blunder will interrupt the trade, the leaguemen request that Corinn sail to the Other Lands to renew the good faith of the trade agreements. She does not accept the offer, but she arranges for Dariel to go in her place. She sends Rialus Neptos along to keep an eye on things. The Numrek chieftain, Calrach, and several of his clan, including his son, Allek, are assigned to go, to serve as envoys to help convince the Auldek to continue the trade with the Acacians.

Several supporting characters introduce important narrative threads. Barad the Lesser, a battered laborer formerly of the Kidnaban mines, is now a social activist. He travels around the empire, making speeches, trying to build an organized resistance to the Akaran dynasty. He believes that the Known World can be governed with more equity. He comes to trust the Aushenian king, Grae, who wants to see Acacian power reduced. The dashing monarch agrees to visit the queen's court to woo her and gain intelligence on how best to topple her.

Kelis, the Talayan who was Aliver's close companion in his youth, leaves Mena's service to answer a call from his chieftain. He learns that Aliver had fathered a daughter, Shen, with one of his lovers, Benabe. The child has dream conversations with the Santoth. They have been calling her to them. Since Kelis had helped Aliver find the sorcerers, he is chosen to escort Shen and Benabe to the Santoth. A young man, Naamen, goes with them. They trek into southern Talay on foot, a journey that becomes more magical the closer they get to the Santoth. Eventually they meet Leeka Alain, the old soldier who had killed the first Numrek. He has been living with the Santoth all these years. He leads them to the sorcerers, who snatch Shen away and disappear.

Delivegu Lemardine, a seedy agent Corinn uses for her more unsavory assignments, brings the queen information about Barad the Lesser, telling her there is a conspiracy afoot. He also discovers that Dariel's lover, Wren, is pregnant with his child. Once Corinn finds out about this, she sends Wren to Calfa Ven, to keep her out of sight while she decides what to do about her.

Mena continues to hunt the foulthings, ranging all over Talay, thinking up ingenious ways to trap and kill the beasts. Eventually, she faces the last monster. It is supposed to be a dragon, but she finds that it is a fusion of reptile and bird, a strangely gentle, feathered beauty. Before she can stop them, Mena's hunting party attacks it. The princess is snatched into the air by the injured creature as it flies away. The animal crashes in a remote region. The two heal from their wounds together, and form an affectionate bond. Mena names the animal Elya.

Dariel sees many wonders on his journey across the Gray Slopes, including mountainous waves and schools of angry sea wolves. What he does not know is that his host, Sire Neen, secretly hates all Akarans. He holds Dariel responsible for the death of many leaguemen on the platforms. Incredibly ambitious, Neen has embarked on a scheme to eliminate the Lothan Aklun and to monopolize the mist and quota trade. Arriving at the barrier isles of the Other Lands—Ushen Brae in the native tongue—Neen imprisons Dariel and explains that the league has used the occasion of a Lothan Aklun ceremonial ritual to spread poison among them. The entire Lothan Aklun culture has been wiped out.

Neen arranges a meeting with the Auldek. He plans to hand Dariel over as a peace offering. But nothing about his meeting with the warlike Auldek goes as planned. The arrival of the Numrek throws the meeting into chaos. During it, Sire Neen is decapitated. Both Dariel and Rialus are captured, but by different factions. Dariel becomes a prisoner of the resistance movement of quota slaves, the Free People. He is treated harshly for a time, reviled for being a prince of the family that established the mist and slave trade. Despite this, he becomes fascinated by his captors: Mór, the beautiful, angry leader of the group; Skylene, her lover; and Tunnel, a hulk of a man made more impressive because his skin is tattooed gray and he sports golden tusks in his jaw. Many of the quota slaves have had extreme alterations made to their bodies—tattoos, piercings, implants—to make them look like the totem animal deities of their Auldek masters. Tunnel and Skylene gradually tell him more and more about life in Ushen Brae.

Rialus was captured by the Auldek. To his surprise, Calrach comes to his cell and explains that it was not just the league that had treacherous plots at work. The Numrek had their own reasons for coming to Ushen Brae. They are an individual clan of the Auldek people, one of several, but they had been exiled years before for violating Auldek taboos. It was this banishment that took them into the far north, from where they eventually found their way down over the pole and into the Known World. The years they spent in service to Hanish and, later, to Corinn, were a continuation of that punishment. Now Calrach has returned to his native land with news he believes will regain his clan's status among the Auldek.

Calrach explains to Rialus the same crucial information that Dariel learns from the Free People. The Lothan Aklun had a device called the soul catcher that could remove the souls of quota children and implant them inside Auldek hosts. They stored them in their bodies, making them effectively immortal but also infertile. They need quota slaves for their souls, for labor, and to be able to watch the natural cycle of life that they are no longer part of. The Numrek, however, found that on arriving in the Known World they regained their fertility, as Calrach's son, Allek, proves just by existing. Calrach returned to Ushen Brae to convince the Auldek to march to the Known World via the northern route and make war. They can have new lands, new children, and new lives in the Known World. The Auldek force Rialus to tell them everything about the Known World, and he becomes a personal source of information for the head chieftain of the Auldek, the ever-confident Devoth.

Dariel, convinced that he can do something to right the wrongs of the quota trade, offers to help the resistance. They eventually give him a mission. They have found a soul ship—one powered by trapped souls—that they do not want the league to get its hands on. They ask Dariel to pilot the ship to a remote place and destroy it. He jumps at the opportunity. He even lets Mór tattoo his face so that he looks like a quota slave. The vessel proves to be fast, maneuverable, and absolutely unlike anything Dariel has ever seen. As he races away in it, he discovers that the league has occupied the island of Lithram Len, on which the soul catcher is housed. If they find the device and learn how to use it, they could make themselves immortal. Dariel does not let this happen. Like the brigand he used to be, he steals explosive pitch from the docks and uses it to blow up the soul catcher. A little later, after destroying the soul vessel and freeing the spirits captive in it, Dariel meets up with Mór. She offers him leave to go as thanks for his deeds, or says that she could take him into the interior of Ushen Brae, to meet the elders of the Free People. Following Mór, he sets off into the wild expanse that is Ushen Brae.

Back on Acacia, Corinn narrowly escapes being charmed by King Grae. Delivegu captures Barad the Lesser and presents him to her. Delivegu has deduced that Grae is conspiring with Barad. The queen imprisons him and turns his eyes to stone. Corinn simply sends Grae home.

Corinn is relieved when Mena returns from Talay. The princess flies in on Elya. Corinn is wary of the creature, but Mena adores her. Soon Aaden is in love with Elya also. Mena reunites with her lover, Melio. The two of them discuss having children, something they have long put off. It is a pleasant reprieve, but it does not last long.

Sire Dagon gets word of what happened to Sire Neen in Ushen Brae. He learns of the Numrek's treachery and of the impending invasion. He runs to tell the queen a modified version of events—one that puts no blame on the league. The Numrek in the palace see Dagon's unease and know something has happened with their clansmen. They rise in rebellion. The queen is safely locked away with Dagon and Rhrenna when the slaughter begins, but Mena and Aaden are out in the Carmelia, with Numrek guards watching over them.

The Numrek attack the young prince. They stab both him and his friend before Mena can stop them. Mena kills the Numrek, grabs Aaden, and tosses him to Elya, who flies the injured boy away. Melio and other Marah soon join Mena. They fight the Numrek, killing them and all the other Numrek on the island.

Corinn uses the song to heal Aaden's injuries, but the boy remains unconscious. She dream travels all the way to Ushen

Brae. She cannot find her brother, but she does contact Rialus. Through him, she gets proof that the Auldek are marching to war. They have mustered a great host: Auldek; tens of thousands of slaves; and all manner of beasts, including antoks, batlike kwedeir, and fréketes—large, intelligent beasts with massive wings.

Wanting the nation on her side completely as they face the invasion, Corinn authorizes the distribution of the vintage, thereby addicting the people to artificial cheer once again. She gives Mena the King's Trust, Edifus's ancient sword, and sends her to be the first line of defense against the Auldek, to defeat or delay them while they are still in the far north. She sends Melio with an army to prepare an assault on the Numrek in Teh. The couple's plan to have children will have to wait.

Aliver's daughter, on the other hand, reappears. Kelis, Benabe, and Naamen had been left distraught by her disappearance. They searched the desert for her for weeks, but in the end Shen, Leeka, and the Santoth simply reappear. The girl tells Kelis that the Santoth are ready to return to the world now. As Aliver's descendant, she has freed them, and now she wants to go with them to Acacia. According to Shen, the Santoth believe Corinn is making grave mistakes with her use of *The Song of Elenet*. They claim to want to help her. Kelis reluctantly agrees. The group begins the long journey back to Acacia.

After the tumultuous part he played in igniting the Numrek uprising, Sire Dagon takes solace in communing with the League Council. They conclude that however the conflict plays out, they will be able to find a way to benefit from it. One of them, Sire El, seizes the opportunity to get approval for a project he has been working on—developing an army from the slaves raised on their plantations. Sires Faleen and Lethel head off to take over Ushen Brae.

In the final chapter of the book Corinn works several acts

of magic. She goes to Barad and injects sight into his stone eyes. She binds him with a spell so that he will appear to be free but will only say the things she wants him to. Having found out that Elya has laid eggs—information she got from her clever spy, Delivegu—she sings sorcery into the unborn creatures, charging them to grow into great monsters for her. And then she summons a spirit from the dead: her older brother.

Aliver Akaran is back in the story.

Book One

The Singer
and the Song

CHAPTER
ONE

Corinn Akaran stepped into the brilliant morning light. She walked across the deck of her transport ship, descended the plank to the Teh docks, and strode through the military officials awaiting her as if all of it were one continuous movement. The men—including Melio Sharratt and General Andeson, Marah and Elite officers—parted around her, stunned even though they had stood in preparation for greeting her since the dawn. For a moment the group did nothing but stare.

The queen wore armor that melded influences from the empire's provinces. Chain mail covered her arms; it was thin and light but made of fine links of steel, cuffed at the wrists with a hint of Senivalian style. A Meinish thalba wrapped her torso, snug against the contours of her hips and breasts. Her skirt, also of chain mail, was as short as any Talayan runner's. Leather straps wrapped over her legs, completely covering them in a second skin that was tight around the calf, loose around the knee, and tight again around the upper thighs. Over all this she wore a light Acacian cape that flapped around her as she moved.

Baddel, the Talayan who had jockeyed to be the first to address her on his homeland's soil, welcomed her with a barrage of enthusiastic praise. He poured forth condolences for the injury done to Prince Aaden. "Numrek treachery knows no bounds! I still can't . . ." For a moment he got no further. The queen's Elite guards swept down in her wake, jolting the advisers into motion. They scurried to keep up with her, all except Melio Sharratt, who seemed at ease and said as she passed, "Your Majesty, I've never seen you . . . dressed in armor."

"We're at war," Corinn said. "In this I'm the same as any in the Known World. General Andeson, tell me."

By which she meant update her on the most recent intelligence. The general did. The first wave of Marah had swept in upon the Numrek's seaside villas, catching them at least somewhat unawares. They'd fought among the rambling estates, across the beaches and piers and gardens in which the Numrek had lived in sun-drenched splendor. Soon they had the coastline blockaded. Corps of the Elite pushed inland as the Numrek retreated.

"We pressed them back into the hillside fortress the locals call the Thumb," the general said. "It's an ancient structure. We'd thought nothing of it, but the Numrek must have reinforced the walls and stocked it with supplies. They've had time to prepare their treachery. We've offered battle daily, but they no longer engage."

"They've suddenly gone coward," a younger officer said.

"No, they're toying with us," Melio said. "They send their children onto the battlements to float paper birds on the air. They're clever with such things."

Andeson's sideways glance at him was disapproving. Melio shrugged and mouthed, *What? It's true.*

"It's become something of a waiting game," Andeson said. "The fortress is built atop a butte. There is but a single track that wraps its way up around it, too narrow and unprotected to march an army up. We've lobbed stones and explosives at them, but they're well dug in. There are tunnels deep within the butte, accessed only from inside it. There's a water source in there somewhere as well. It may be a matter of starving them to death."

"An unheroic strategy," Corinn said.

"I would choose honorable battle every time, Your Majesty, but at times one's foes make that impossible. These Numrek are vile. They massacred their own servants, you know. Built a wall of their bodies at the base of the Thumb. If you had seen—"

"I'm sure our soldiers have performed well," Corinn interrupted, "and I have every faith in your leadership. I've arrived now. I'll finish this."

They progressed out of the docks, through a makeshift storage area in the dusty open space beyond. The Teh coast was somewhat wetter than most of Talay, but this late in the season the grasses that covered the hills to the north were bleached golden by the sun. Corinn was glad to have arranged for horses ahead of time. The mounts awaited them, held by Talayan youths who looked nervous about their unaccustomed work.

"Queen Corinn," Melio said. "Anything new from Mena?"

"Not since she sent a bird from Luana. I expect to hear from her again soon. Ride with me, Melio. When the Numrek have been dealt with I have an assignment for you. We'll discuss it as we ride."

Melio bowed his head, and they stood as the squire attending Corinn's horse tried to swing it around into position for her.

"There's a rumor among the soldiers," Melio said. "It came across on the last few transports. About . . . Aliver."

"A rumor? Have Andeson and the other generals heard this rumor?"

"I'm closer to the troops than they. That's where I heard it, but the rumor is trickling up. It can't possibly be true, though, right?"

"Between you and me, yes."

Melio's face lit up. All his disparate features aligned in a manner that was surprisingly handsome. "Truly? Where is he?"

Corinn stepped on the stool that had been set down for her. Preparing to swing onto the horse, she said, "He is safe in the palace. He needs seclusion just now. He remains fragile. Best not to fan the rumors yet."

※

The night ten days earlier that she had worked her spell had been long and beyond exhausting. She was drained already, what with the sorcery she had worked on Barad and the song she had sung to Elya's children. She could have dropped into slumber before she even began her third spell, but she needed someone to help her carry the burden of rule. She needed her brother.

As soon as his body became fully corporeal, he slumped forward. He would have fallen had she not sprung up and guided him onto her bed. For a time she stared at the wonder of him. He was really there! Solid, warm to the touch. Breathing. He was naked, but she thought nothing of that. His eyes moved beneath his lids in dream. What does a man dream after returning from death? What was death anyway? Was it not the conqueror of all? No, it wasn't, for she had just denied it at least one victim. She had so many questions, but even as they formed, her mind went sluggish. She knew that he would slumber long, and so she left Aliver and collapsed on a divan in an adjoining room.

Rhrenna and two maids woke her two days later. Rhrenna would not have disturbed her even then, she explained, save, "He is awake and asking for you."

With those words Corinn sprang up and rushed back to the other room. Aliver Akaran stood on the balcony, his knuckles

white, gripping the stone balustrade, his jaw loose with astonishment. He wore a morning robe, tied at the waist. Rhrenna
must have ordered it brought for him.

Corinn turned to figure out what fascinated her brother so.
The sky above was the color and texture of a blue eggshell. The
morning sun, just free of the horizon, was cut in half by one long
sliver of pink cloud. A flock of black neck divers folded their
wings one after another and plummeted like darts, exploding
into the water of the harbor in a feeding frenzy. Thin lines of
smoke rose like flower stems from the lower town. It could have
been any of these things.

Aliver set his gaze on her. His eyes were a darker brown than
she remembered. His skin was no longer as pale as it had been
the first night. It was a richer color, tanned to a light brown.
Now that she saw him clearly, she realized she had combined
his features with Hanish's when she had pictured him. He
was older than when she knew him last. Immeasurably older,
though he gave that impression not so much in the details of his
features as in the distance of the consciousness behind them.

He said, "I'd forgotten so much."

"I as well," Corinn answered.

"You were a girl," he said.

Corinn shook her head. "I never was."

Aliver tested an expression on his face. Disappointment. Or
confusion. Disapproval. Some combination of these that his features could not spell out yet. "I am sure you were."

Corinn brushed her hand down the curls of hair near his
temple, wrapped her palm around the back of his head. She
pulled him close and touched their foreheads together, something her father used to do with her. "I remember a smaller version of myself, but not a girl. No girl should be as afraid as I was."

"You still are."

Drawing back, she shook her head. "No. I have to explain many things to you."

In the few days before she left for the Teh coast, Corinn tried to convey as much as possible to him. The world had not paused outside the palace to grant her a respite. It felt necessary that she have him to herself, that she bind him to the truth as she knew it.

She ordered Rhrenna and the two maids to complete silence about Aliver's return. She had her quarters emptied of other staff and servants, stationed guards only outside her chambers. She wanted to be alone with her brother. She did not even try to find a reasoned approach to what she told him. She just spoke. She offered what information came to her, circling back to give context, jumping forward to the present and then realizing by the look of glazed distance on his features that she had lost him. His eyes sometimes went as stone-dead as Barad's, vacant, sightless, and yet staring. Each time she stopped and breathed and began again. She reminded him who he was. She assured him that it was urgent that he return to life and complete the work he had left unfinished. Not only that, there were new complications and threats, and she needed someone she could trust completely at her side.

Aliver moved about the rooms, restless, studying things, lifting objects and turning them in his hands. She walked, following his lead as he explored the gardens, touching plants and watching birds and stopping to marvel at things—the pressure of the wind when it blew, the heat of the sun on his skin, the colors in the terrace tiles. Corinn sometimes thought he had forgotten her, but if she stopped speaking he shifted his attention to her.

They ate together as often as Corinn could manage. Simple meals, at first, without the sweet and sour spices common to Acacian cuisine. Watching him dip flatbread into olive oil, Corinn almost thought herself a new mother again. He shoved the bread into his mouth and worked his jaw, so focused on it that he ignored the oil dripping down his chin. He ate as a child does: the food had his attention completely.

She could not stay hidden in her rooms all day. There was no end to the work of the empire. She had to meet with advisers and senators. Emissaries still sailed in from around the Known World, both to offer condolences for the Numrek betrayal and to ask if the news of a pending invasion should be credited. She told them it could. It was real. She allowed no doubt about it, even though in other meetings she drilled Sire Dagon as if she did not believe, trying to rip more information out of him.

The world was in turmoil, and she alone had the responsibility of calming it. Good, then, that she did not feel as overpowered by it as she had before bringing Aliver back. In some ways things had quieted. He had a long way to go before he could emerge as the symbol of her power that she hoped he would, but for the time being it was good just being with him. He made her think of her father. He even made her feel closer to Mena and Dariel. She wished they were here to see what she had done. How pleased Dariel would be! Mena, too. Aliver's return would make up for all the strife that had tainted their relationships. They would start anew.

✳

For two days the Numrek in the Thumb did not answer the messages Corinn sent them. It was only after she had stood in clear sight of the butte-top fortress and shouted up to them herself that they believed she had come to speak with them. With the chieftain Calrach gone to the Other Lands, and with

Greduc and Codeth slain on that bloody day in the Carmelia, Corinn had not been entirely sure with whom she would parlay. Gathered within the shade of a gently billowing linen tent, she learned that Crannag, a relation of Calrach's, now held power. He was older than the chieftain, more a warrior than a states-man. Good. That suited her.

Crannag sat alone. He set his hands on his knees, tossed his black hair, and grinned. This man had once stood at the door of her quarters, of Aaden's. Now she could barely recognize the guard he had been in the smug lines of his face.

"All right, Queen. I'm here." He held up his strong arms and made a show of searching his torso for weapons. He was shirt-less, the muscles of his chest sectioned and defined. He was some thirty paces away, so he had to project his voice. "What do you want of me?"

"I want you to die," Corinn said.

Crannag guffawed. "You could have that. Your Marah there . . . ah . . . together . . . me with no weapons, them fully armed . . . I think they might have me, if they wanted. Of course, I might just be able to get a hand around your neck first." He reached out, pretending to suffer body blows as he grasped for her. The pantomime was too much for him. He bent forward around his laughter.

"It's not just you that I want to die," Corinn said. "I want all Numrek to pay for your treachery."

Crannag's leather-brown face went grave. "You want me to go back in there and get my people to come out and be slaugh-tered. We have other things planned now. A long plan, Queen. You didn't know Numrek have patience, did you? You always thought us grumpy, grumpy Numreks. Ah . . ." He snapped his fingers, and his eyes rolled up as he searched for the right word, then found it. "Taciturn. You like that? You thought us ta-ci-turn.

You thought we had nothing better to do than stand by your door as you slept and ate and thought yourself the queen of the world. It's a tiny piece of turd island, but it's the center of the world!"

Crannag leaned back in his seat. It was but a campstool with a slim backrest, but he managed to lounge in it. "We were acting, Queen. Just acting. Waiting. You promised us that you would help us return to Ushen Brae. You never meant to keep that promise. You lied. Now you pay for it." He drew phlegm from his throat and spat toward Corinn. Considering the distance between them, the spittle landed surprisingly close to her feet. She felt her Marah tense. Someone drew his sword a few inches from its scabbard. "You came for nothing. We won't fight. We can wait there"—he pointed up toward the plug of stone that rose out of the rolling landscape behind him—"for as long as we need. When the Auldek come, we will greet them as cousins and brothers and we will show them the bounty we've found for them."

"You don't know that the Auldek will come. For all you know they still scorn you."

"You know nothing." Crannag rose, and his shoulder swiped at the air as he turned away, almost like a blow.

"I know this!" Corinn said. "You are a coward!"

Crannag trudged away. He waved one arm, dismissing her accusation as if it were an insect.

"The Numrek hiding in that fortress are quivering," Corinn continued. She stood and began to follow him. Her guards jumped to keep pace with her. "Your men are dogs, no braver than your children. Your women are whipped bitches. I will tell the world this is so. News of it will fly on every bird to every province. The Known World will scorn you, and if the Auldek ever arrive, they will learn of your cowardice. I would not wish to be you." She spat toward him. "Not after I tell the world that I came here and offered you battle on these terms: an equal number of my force to fight yours. Equal numbers, Crannag! One Acacian for every Numrek. No more."

The warrior paused but did not turn back to face her.

"How will you explain that?" She stood in the full sun now. The shade tent flapped behind her with a sudden gust of air. She waited a moment longer, then added more lightly, knowing that Crannag would turn to make sure he heard her correctly, "I will be one of them. I will take to the field myself."

※

A few days earlier, on the evening before she was to leave for Teh, Corinn had been occupied with affairs of state all day. She did not join Aliver until after her late meetings. She found him, to her surprise, standing inside the door that would have led him out into the upper courtyard, into the view of the guards and general palace staff.

"What are you doing?"

He blinked rapidly for a moment. "I want to see my quarters. My own rooms, with my things . . . I should see them. I should stay in them."

"You will." Corinn gently turned him and led him away from the door, back into her own chambers. "Don't rush, though. You have everything you need here. Stay here until I return from my trip."

"Your trip. Why are you going? What trip is it?"

Having gotten Aliver seated in a side parlor, Corinn lowered herself to the plush chair opposite. She relaxed into it, truly fatigued, knowing that she should rest in preparation for the morrow. A small fire burned in the hearth, and she commented on the warmth of the room and the early chill in the air tonight. Aliver watched the fire, but not with the curiosity he had shown during the first few days. He was changing already. The world did not amaze him as it had before. He was more at ease in his body, quicker with words. In the new clothes Rhrenna had brought for him he looked very much a prince. At times his eyes still glazed over, but just as often he snapped out of it with a shake of his head.

"There are things I don't understand," Aliver said.

Corinn bent her head forward as she unwrapped the lace shawl from around her neck. "You have to relearn the world. It can't happen overnight."

"I'm already forgetting death."

"Good, Aliver, good. Life is what matters. Even in death, spirits told you of the living. That's what you said to me the first night we talked."

"I thought that, but it doesn't seem the way it was anymore. When I was dead, I was not a self. I was not a single mind. I was spread thinly across the world. I was part of everything. Like a very fine dust that gets into everything." Aliver no longer had difficulty controlling his facial expressions. He frowned, and Corinn did not question whether he meant to or not. "When I was like that, the lives of humans did not register as of much import. I cared about the tree of Akaran about as much as a stone on the path in the gardens outside does."

"But you said you knew things that had happened after your death."

"I learned those things in the moments you were pulling me together. I did know things. I do, but they didn't have meaning until I was becoming Aliver again."

A piper announced the midnight hour then. Both siblings cocked their heads to listen as the tune passed from the palace down toward the lower town, a delicate cascade of sound.

It reminded Corinn of her fatigue. "I wish that we could stay locked away for days upon days. I would tell you everything.

Absolutely everything. I'd have you understand me completely, so that you saw the world with my eyes."

The rapidity with which his gaze snapped back to her caused her to pause. "I prefer my own eyes," Aliver said.

"I mean only that I will help you, until you can see fully on your own. The world has changed, Aliver, as I've been explaining."

He shook his head. "No, you haven't."

"What do you mean?"

"You told me you needed me. That I am here to help you."

"You are," Corinn said.

"But you're not telling the things that matter! You're going away tomorrow, but you haven't told me why."

For a moment Corinn was speechless. She stood up and moved behind her chair, running her hands over the backrest and then gripping it. "Of course I did."

Aliver's mouth puckered into a sour expression Corinn remembered from years ago. He said, "No, you didn't. You brought me back from the dead, but you haven't even explained how. You haven't spoken of Mena or Dariel. From your lips— nothing about them."

"That's not true." She must have! They spoke for hours. What else was more important?

"You talk and talk, but you tell me nothing. You haven't even told me of your son."

To that she had no response. It was an impossible statement. She thought of Aaden always; she visited him several times each day; she whispered to him all about Aliver's return; she had come back to Aliver and . . .

I told him nothing of my son, she thought. Why? It took all her concentration to nod and say, "Aliver, I have a son. His name is Aaden. He is your nephew. He is to be heir. He will be the greatest Akaran monarch yet." There! That's what I meant to tell him.

"I would like to meet him."

"You will. He is not well right now, though. When I return from Teh. Just rest here until then. When I return, you'll meet Aaden and see the rest of the palace. You'll see others and talk to them. We'll send a bird to Mena and we'll talk about Dariel, too."

Aliver eyed her. "You are going to confront the Numrek in Teh?"

"Yes."

"What are you going to do?"

"What I must," she said. "What they brought upon themselves."

"You can't kill them all."

"What do you know of it?" Corinn retorted. "You know so little of what's happened. Let me explain it to you, but give me time."

"As you have made such good use of the time we've had so far?"

Corinn rubbed the plush arms of her chair. She watched the way the passage of her hand changed the look of the velvet, from light to dark, dark to light. "I don't like this side of you."

"Which side is that? The one that thinks?"

"The one that blunders through the world with noble ideals based on nothing. Look at the fact that you died and I did not. That you failed and I did not."

"If that's what you believe, you should have left me with the dust. You've made a mistake."

Was that a note of threat? Corinn wondered. It was, wasn't it? Back among the living so briefly, and already we are at odds. If they fought here, now, what battles lay ahead? He would be a thorn in her side instead of an ally. She knew then that she had made a mistake. A small error. One that could be corrected.

The notes of the song swirled in her mind before she had even called for them. She would have him as that ally, a symbol and miracle to a world that needed symbols and miracles. She would also have his obedience. The song would make it so.

She spoke through the spell playing out in her mind. "When I return, Aliver, we will start to make plans for your coronation. Brother and sister, king and queen. No marriage, but a union unlike anything the world has ever known. Why not? Are we not unlike any that have come before? The old laws don't apply to us. We will be stronger, and wiser together. Our strengths will bring the empire closer together than ever before. Can you see that?"

Aliver looked away from her, unwilling to answer. The song whispered through Corinn's lips, quietly binding him. Binding him, so that when he did answer he gave her exactly the affirmation she wished for.

✳

Corinn walked at the head of a contingent of one thousand, three hundred, and seventeen soldiers. With her included, their numbers matched the remaining Numrek adults, men and women both, all those of fighting age and some beyond it but still proud. The Numrek children lined the walls of the Thumb, watching from high above.

The two forces met on the field to the west of the fortress. The land was arid and flat, perfect for battle. The sky a light, cloudless blue. Beneath it, the Numrek gathered. They were tall, seven feet the norm among the men, the women shorter perhaps but just as stoutly built. Their hair hung as it always had, thick and black, oily. Most wore light armor, but many went bare armed; and some left their chests exposed. They were warriors. Their curved swords and battle-axes and the jagged slivers of knives at their belts attested to it.

Corinn heard her officers conferring. She turned and drew General Andeson's eyes. "It remains as I told you last night," she said. "No weapons are to be drawn. Understood? I will do this myself."

She turned back to face the enemy. There was a sudden buzz of arguing behind her. She knew what they were saying. They thought her some fool version of Aliver, trying to re-create his mistake in fighting Maeander Mein on a field much like this one. If they had their way, she would be shunted to the rear of the army and encased within a wall of Marah, long-legged soldiers who would stand ready to lift her and sprint at the least sign of danger. That's what they had said last night, at least—that her safety was paramount.

In truth they feared fighting the Numrek without a much superior force. Why offer the terms she had? They argued it was madness. They might have balked at her order, but they feared shame even more—just like the Numrek. They feared her, though they likely half wished she would perish. Die and yet somehow leave them alive afterward to fight among themselves for power. All this was true. No matter. Let them watch and learn yet more of who she truly was. What had she told Aliver she was going to do? She had said . . .

For a moment she could not remember. And then it came to her. She had said, *Destroy them. I'll destroy them.*

With that thought behind her, she opened her mind to the song. At first she kept it within the curve of her skull, letting it build, searching for the rhythms within the dissonance. And what a cacophony it was! Had she not known better, she would have thought the noises in her head were the tumultuous ravings of a world exploding. Raw emotion and anger and beauty and longing and hunger screamed in a thousand ways at once, with the timbre of myriad voices and notes played on all man-ner of instruments at war with one another.

She could also hear order within the confusion. She could pinch with her mind's fingers the song fragments she wished, each of them a living, moving line of codes and runes and words all held in fluid motion along ribbons slithering through the tumult. She could hold much more of it now than when she had first begun her study. She found meaning more easily than even a few weeks ago, before Aaden nearly died and before she worked her spells upon Barad's eyes and Elya's children and before gathering back the spirit that had been Aliver. Yes, she had much more mastery now.

She walked forward. She parted her lips and let the first notes of the song escape her mouth, barely louder than exhaled breaths. The Numrek, accepting her commencement of the bat-tle, strode to meet her. As the distance between them closed, the song grew stronger and began to shift the substance of the air, creating currents around her that seethed and squirmed. She felt the heart of the spell gather in her chest, a stone of greater and greater density. Her mind seethed with hatred. That was what she would give them. She would hurl at them a roiling animus that could take no single shape but instead erupted in ever-changing forms. What she saw happen on the field before her reflected this. Had she not owned it so com-pletely she would have been just as shocked by the horror of it as the soldiers behind her were.

Suddenly the stone inside her surged up out of her chest, scorched through her throat, and rushed from her mouth in a great torrent. The Numrek paused in their tracks. Some back-stepped. Many fell as if shoved savagely. Corinn centered her gaze on Crannag. She knew as it happened that his face was going to blister with a heat from within, that his hair was going to burst into flame, and that a moment after his skull would burst.

The man beside him tried to flee, but his legs and arms moved stiffly. They folded and snapped. In seconds he was on the ground, writhing but incapable of action, his bones fracturing with each effort. Another Numrek stepped over him, coming forward, and Corinn knew the moment his skin would erupt with maggots that consumed his living flesh. His armor and weapons and even the sudden wig that was his hair fell to the earth along with the squirming mass that had been his body.

And so it was throughout the entire Numrek force. No two among them died the same way, but each one did die. A woman became a sack of flesh with nothing solid inside. A man thrust his hand into his breast and pulled out his own heart. Some panted and contorted with unknowable tortures. Some blistered with poxlike scars or went yellow or gangrenous. Things grew inside a few, protrusions and antlers that burst their skin as they screamed. Some danced as if they were being hacked by unseen weapons. One youth ran raging, his mouth red with blood. An old soldier lowered himself to the ground and—a single still point among the chaos—folded into himself, and turned to ash.

Through it all Corinn let her body be the song's instrument. It gave her what she wished and went further, making it more terrible than she could have imagined. At some point the stream of sound slowed, slackened. And then ceased altogether.

The silence was gorgeous, even if it was not a complete silence. She heard her soldiers retching. At least one of the officers behind her spilled his breakfast in a splatter on the ground. A few mumbled prayers or expressed disbelief. And yet in the wake of the song such sounds were dwarfed by the magic that had come before. Homage, really, to the language of creation. And destruction. The reverence did not just come from the Numrek dead. Not just from her trembling soldiers. This silence was sung to her by the entire world. All creation had been awed speechless.

So it seemed for the stretch of many breaths. The army came up behind her. Realizing that her officers stood hushed and waiting, Corinn said, "Send soldiers to the fortress for the children. They are to live, for now, as our hostages."

The queen turned around, the links of her chain mail clanking as she did so. General Andeson was staring at her, pale faced. Melio stood beside him, his eyes fixed on the carnage. They recoiled when the stench of burning flesh and offal hit them. The stink and gases of bodies turned inside out was almost too much to bear. Corinn breathed through her mouth. She took her strength from the awe and revulsion and fear in the men's faces.

"But these that I've eliminated here," she continued, "burn them all. Reduce what's left of their corpses to ashes and have them brought back to Acacia. We will mix them with mortar and repave the streets of the lower town with them. From now on, even the humblest peasant will walk atop the remains of the Numrek. Thus it will be for any who oppose me."

Andeson's throat caught. Instead of speaking, he nodded.

Corinn turned on her heel, satisfied.

She almost reached the horses before she wavered, stumbled, then fell.

CHAPTER
TWO

The Scav met Princess Mena Akaran on a desolate stretch of beach littered with whale bones and dotted with chunks of translucent sea ice. He stood shirtless despite a frigid wind, his scrawny chest exposed and his small, dense muscles pronounced beneath a thin membrane of white-blue skin. His flaxen hair hung limp and matted, plaited in several places with strips of hide. He did not look up as Mena leaped from the landing boat and kicked her way through the froth to the sand. He did not meet her eyes when Gandrel announced her or return the gazes of any of her party. He answered the questions Gandrel put to him in a rough dialect that Mena could not follow at all.

"He says this is where the Numrek came through," Gandrel translated. He pointed at the man with one thickly ringed hand, while his other hovered near Mena, as if to keep her from stepping too close to him. He was like that, protective, large as a bear and with a jagged scar across his nose as if he had fought on equal terms with clawed creatures. "Where the Mountains Cry the Sea, he calls it. A narrow pass that leads to a route through the mountains."

Mena glanced up at the sheer black rock that rose from the

sand, cracked and fissured, marbled with veins of silver flaring here and there. Clouds hung low enough that the tops disappeared into them. Cascades of frothing water poured through numerous crevices, looking like they were draining the sky itself.

"His people are poets, then," Mena said. "I wouldn't have guessed it."

"Hardly," Gandrel said. "They just can't say things right. He says a little south of here the mountains jut into the sea. Unpassable. The only way through is to go inland via this pass and eventually come down through the Ice Fields."

"Can we believe him?" Mena asked.

Gandrel spoke to the man again, listened to the answer. "He claims his father died here and that many of their clan were killed when they confronted the Numrek. Burned by pitch, butchered." Gandrel pointed at the man's chest. "The bones on that necklace are from his father's right hand. That's what he says, at least."

Mena did not look at the bones. An artery pulsed at the base of the man's neck. Having noticed it, she found it hard to look away.

"They fought them?" Mena's first officer, Perrin, asked. He stood beside the princess, tall and long limbed, nearly as rangy as a Numrek. He would have been imposing, save his face was so clean lined and pretty it seemed suited for an actor, not a soldier. His brown hair was perpetually tousled. This, too, managed to be endearing.

"So he claims. He comes here sometimes to listen for the ghosts of those who died here. That's part of how they hunt: they claim the dead guide them."

"And did he hear ghosts?" Mena asked.

After Gandrel translated the question, the Scav's gaze lifted and touched her face a moment. His blue eyes might have been attractive were they not embedded in such a pale, weathered visage. He dropped them and mumbled his answer.

"He always kills," Gandrel said, "because of the ghosts he captured there." Aside, he added, "That's why he's so plump, I guess."

"Can we believe him?" Mena asked again.

"No reason to do that. We can listen, though. And look. Judge for ourselves."

"What's his name?"

"His name is Kant. It doesn't mean what it sounds like. It's the name of a bird, one that dives into the swirls along rocky shores." He tried to demonstrate with the edge of his hand. Gave up halfway through the motion.

"All right," Mena said. "Tell Kant to show me the pass."

✳

For the past fortnight Mena had sailed north aboard the only Acacian warship stationed on the west coast of the Known World. *Hadin's Resolve* was paltry compared to the vast array of Ishtat crafts floated by the league, but she had three masts and was deep bellied and armor plated on the prow. She flew the flag of the empire: the black silhouette of an acacia tree across a brilliant yellow sunburst.

A hastily gathered fleet had flanked her, mostly made up of imperial soldiers stationed at bases along the Coastal Towns and of Candovian civilians conscripted for the empire's protection. The ships were a hodgepodge collection. Some were Acacian naval vessels, but the armada contained Candovian merchant ships, brimming with supplies. A few of the larger fishing boats from the Coastal Towns carried contingents of troops while simultaneously trawling the waters for fish to salt and dry.

North along the Candovian coast, they pushed off the empire's maps and into frigid waters. They threaded through mountains of ice that jutted from the water, slow-moving floating islands of white and blue and green, some carved into intricate shapes, ghostly to behold and ever changing with the slip of the sun across the sky. Never before had an Acacian army crossed seas like this. They did it on this occasion only because the league and Queen Corinn believed an Auldek army marched to invade them, following the land route the Numrek had stumbled upon during their years of exile.

Mena fought not to think too often of the two beings she loved most in the world. Melio had his own missions. It was better, she knew, that he not be here with her. This was war, not the hunting expedition that chasing the foulthings had been. She needed to make the right decisions. Many of those would send her soldiers to their deaths. Would she be able to do that to Melio? Or would she protect him unfairly? No, he wouldn't allow that, which might mean he ended up in greater danger. Far better that he serve the empire elsewhere. Far better that she make her decisions without thinking of his crooked smile, the smell of his hair, or the time he held her in their tent on the Teh plains the night after Aliver was killed, or her promise that she would, one day, take his child inside her. What good was thinking of such things—of longing for the past or hoping for the future—when she had a war to fight? Better not to think about him or about Elya.

She had left the bird-lizard in Corinn's care on Acacia, after a tearful parting that she had ended abruptly. Mena feared she had left Elya with the impression that she was angry with her. Nothing could have been further from the truth, but Mena had pushed her away, loving the kindness of her eyes too much. Mena tried not to think about Elya, lest the thoughts somehow reach her across the miles. This was no place for Elya. War was no task to set her.

Mena's mood blackened with the passing of sea miles. The

air became colder, the wind seemingly trying to shove them back from whence they came. But return was not an option. Queen Corinn had made that clear. Meet the Auldek horde, she had ordered, outside the Known World. Delay them, so that the empire had time to better prepare. Defeat them, if such a thing were possible. And in all this the implicit: be sacrificed for the good of the nation.

✵

Gandrel set his hands on his hips, listening as the Scav spoke and gestured. "This is where the Numrek first came through. The tracks from their carts are still deep in the ground, he says."

They stood about a half mile from the coast on a buttress of rock thrust close to the ceiling of clouds. Below them, the jagged ridgelines on two sides sloped down, leaving a gap that headed toward the heart of the Ice Fields, a swath remarkable for its flatness and for the promise of ease of passage, as it veered off to the east and out of sight.

"They must come this way?" Perrin pressed. "If we invest everything here and then they go elsewhere . . ."

"Aye," Gandrel translated Kant's response. "It's the only way. The mountains to the north stand like wolves' fangs. Those to the south he calls Bear Teeth. Only here, between the two ranges, is navigable. He calls it the Breath Between."

Perrin guffawed. "They've got a name like that for everything."

Mena's gaze drifted over the bleak landscape, from the sheer heights down to the flat tundra. No doubt about it. This was the place Corinn meant her to hold. This was where her sister wanted the invasion thwarted. Feeling cold to the core, Mena pulled her fur-lined robe tighter around her body.

"I want to go down and check these cart tracks he talks of," Perrin said. "I can't believe they're still there all these years later.

Should I send word for the ships to begin unloading camp supplies?"

"Not yet," Mena said. "Come. Let's all see these tracks. We should send a scouting party along the pass as well." She began walking before any of the men had responded.

See the tracks they did. They were there, obvious once Kant pointed them out. The ruts were each a carriage-length wide, cut by massive wheels that had churned up the soil. Even covered with spongy moss and tough grass the slashes were knee-deep. According to the dispatches that chased them with new information from Acacia, the Auldek would come with vehicles with massive wheels like the ones that had scarred the land.

She listened to Perrin's astonished rambling and Gandrel's translations of Kant's tales of how the Scavs had been the first in the Known World to face the monsters. She asked questions and made comments and ruminated on how they might use the terrain to their favor, speculated on where to place troops, set ambushes, where best to join battle. She acted as a royal war leader should, but in truth a question greater than all these details had settled in her mind.

That evening her officers dined with Mena on *Hadin's Resolve*. Though cramped and simple by Acacian standards, the dining hall was quite comfortable. The table was one large slab of stained wood, beautifully grained and worked so that the contours of the edge seemed to fit each particular person, with resting places for each forearm and a modest concavity to accommodate expanding waistlines. Spiced pork and grilled vegetables sat on white-gold trays, with small dishes of relishes, pickled whitefish, and bowls of sliced fruit. The dark red wine was the same consumed on Acacia itself. To soldiers new to positions of command it must all have seemed quite grand.

By and large these soldiers were new to her, a very different lot from the Talayans with whom she had hunted the foulthings. Paler men and fewer women than she was used to, blue- and gray-eyed Candovians, some Senivalians, and even a few who might have claimed Meinish identity had that clan not been so defeated and scattered throughout the empire. They all seemed so very young. Few of them had fought against Hanish Mein. All of them wished for glory. They seemed to both relish the danger marching toward them and disbelieve in it.

When they all finally left to return to their vessels, Mena found herself alone with Perrin. They sat opposite each other, reclining in soft chairs near the small stove that heated the room. They sipped a liqueur made from yellow plums. Despite the warmth caged within the metal stove, a chill crept around the edges of the chamber through chinks in the woodwork. The portholes had begun to rim with ice.

Perrin propped his shiny leather boots on a footstool and set a hand on his abdomen, patting his stomach. "I'm going to miss meals like that. No matter how well we think we've provisioned, such bounty won't last long. I had to laugh at how much the troops complained when we didn't accept the casks of wine the league offered us. They acted like we were spoiling their planned holiday."

"When the league comes bearing gifts, beware." Melio had said those exact words before. Saying it herself, she heard his voice.

"Too right, Your Highness. The stuff wouldn't have lasted long in any event. I know this from experience."

"You trained on the Mein Plateau."

Perrin nodded. His shoulder-length hair swayed with the motion. "Two years based in Cathgergen. Rather boring, really, considering that there weren't actually any Meins to be worrying about anymore."

"Did you see much of the plateau?"

"It's mostly much of the same. Snow and trees and ice. Snow

and trees and ice. Oh, there's a mountain!" He feigned surprise. "That sort of thing. I went west as far as Scatevith. Wintered for three months in Hardith. Saw Mein Tahalian in the height of summer."

"What was it like?"

"You've never been?"

Mena shook her head.

"In summer it was a misery of mosquitoes and biting flies. Place was deadly with them—we were bitten and the air was so thick with them, we could not help but breathe them in and choke. It wasn't the winters that made the Meins so cranky. It was the summer wildlife."

"Is what they say of Haleeven Mein true?"

"That he camps outside Mein Tahalian? Yes. That he is insane from grief and shame? That, too, perhaps. I think I saw him once, but he was so covered in furs that it was impossible to tell for sure. Not much of a life for a man who could have been chieftain of the Mein. I almost feel for him."

Perrin drew back his legs to let a nervous servant through to the stove. The boy fed the fire with the thin shavings of hardwood. Watching him, the young officer continued, "Tahalian itself I saw only from outside. It was sealed shut by then. It huddled against the ground, pretending to be dead, waiting for you to come too close. Don't laugh at me, but I used to dream that the Tahalian you could see—the wood beams and buttresses of it—was the headgear of a buried giant. I woke up sweating in my bedroll more than once to the image of the head rising, eyes opening, and the whole thing clawing up from the tundra. Am I embarrassing myself here?"

Just the opposite, Mena thought. He was diverting, pleasant to look at and to listen to. Rare to find a man so at home in his body, so easy with life and able to talk without self-importance or hidden meanings. Knowing well the conspiratorial world of court life on Acacia, Mena found this apparent naïveté refreshing.

"Did you ever see the route from Tahalian to Port Grace?" she asked.

"No. It's a well-established road, though. The ascent from the coast is gradual, wide. A fortnight's march, if the weather isn't troublesome."

Mena glanced at the portholes again, even more rimmed with delicate lacings of frost now. The wind had picked up, gusting and setting up a sporadic clanking from the rigging. "Let me ask you something. Do you think we'll survive a winter camped here?"

"Many will die, Princess Mena. Not even the Scav stay out here. Not exposed this way. We could travel inland a bit, find a sheltered spot along the pass, but still . . . it will be a long, hard winter. Ice will lock us in. In a month we'll be trapped here until the spring. And we'll need every day of that month to prepare. Each day will be shorter, colder; before long there'll be little daylight at all. We'll need to divide our labors quickly. Some building the shelters, some bringing the ships to shore, some hunting and fishing. Kant says there are seal beaches just to the north. We should send as many ships as we can, fill them full of the blubber. We'll need it."

"You make it sound like the war is with the winter."

Perrin looked at his wineglass again, studying it as if the act of doing so would be enough to refill it. "It will be. The other officers can think about slaying Auldek. I almost wish the Auldek would hurry up and get here so we could have this fight. Who knows? Maybe they will, but I'd wager we're in for a wait." He paused a moment, drained his glass, then rolled the stem between his fingers. "It's what's been ordered, though. The queen's command. So we'll do it."

"You don't think we should?"

"I won't say a word against the queen's wishes. I understand completely how the situation would look from Acacia. She's right, of course. If we could stop the Auldek here . . . Even if we just weaken them, delay them, the empire could be that much better prepared to meet them if they ever stumble out of the Ice Fields. No, I see the advantage of this move very well. It's just . . . we won't be the ones that reap that benefit."

Mena dropped her eyes when his met hers. "Good night, Perrin."

※

The next morning Mena met with her officers on the northern ridge along the pass and traversed its spine as it snaked inland. It afforded an even better view of the mountains stretching off to the north and the curve of the coastline as it vanished into the distant mist. Perrin and Edell, the Marah captain Bledas, and the Senivalian Perceven represented the military units at her command. Daley, the captain of *Hadin's Resolve,* and several others attended on the naval side. Gandrel was there for his knowledge of the Scav.

The princess waited as the men gathered around her, all of them taking in the view, desolate yet strangely beautiful to behold.

"Look," Perceven said, "a chase."

On a sloping stretch of rock-strewn tundra below them, two figures moved. They were tiny amid the vastness of the valleys and mountains, but their motion was easy to follow. A white hare leaped in a crazy, jolting, zagging line. Behind it a snow cat bounded.

Mena kept her eyes on the hunt but said loudly enough that all the men could hear, "We will die here." None disputed it. They looked at her, at one another, then back to the pursuit that held Mena's gaze. "The Auldek will arrive to find an army of ice sculptures waiting them."

Gandrel said, "True. Or they'll find us cut to pieces by the Scav. There are more of them around here, I tell you. Even if they're hard to spot. I wouldn't put anything past them. Not even jolly young Kant here." Kant watched the hunt and made no sign that he heard or understood.

"There are too many ways our deaths here might be for naught," Mena said. "If I knew what was coming—when and how—that would be one thing. But for all we know the Auldek might arrive six months from now. Or they may take a different route. Or they might never arrive. Considering all this, I cannot have us winter here."

The snow cat slapped at the hare's hind leg. For a moment the prey seemed frozen, its body tilted as it floated above the tundra. Then it landed hard. The cat fell upon it and the two rolled into one ball of motion. When they stopped, the cat had its jaws around the hare's neck, patient now as it suffocated its prey.

Mena looked away, as unsatisfied with the outcome as she had been watching the pursuit. "That's my decision," she said.

"But the queen . . ." Perrin began.

"We leave here immediately," Mena said. "Sail to Port Grace. From there we march inland to Tahalian. We'll winter in the fortress and adjust to whatever challenges the thaw brings with it. Go and see to it."

❉

The next afternoon Mena sent a ship south to alert the small settlement of Port Grace that they would soon be inundated with a passing army. On it she also sent a note to be flown by messenger bird, once they were far enough south to ensure the bird would know the landmarks. She had spent the previous night composing a long missive to explain the situation in all its complexity. In the morning, she ripped it to pieces. Instead the message she sent was terser.

Queen Corinn,

The plan to meet the enemy in the far north is untenable. I am moving the army to Mein Tahalian. We will winter there, training.

With your permission, I will lift Haleeven Mein's exile and ask for his aid. . . .

CHAPTER
THREE

When Dariel Akaran first looked upon the ruins he had to steady himself by grasping Birké's shoulder. "Scoop it up," the young Wrathic man said, grinning and lifting Dariel's drooping jaw with a finger. "You'll catch flies like that."

They stood at the summit of a hill on an old road that snaked down into the valley. A great ruin of an ancient metropolis stretched before them. The city reached up to the hills that held them in, wrapped completely by a defensive wall that rose and fell over the contours of the ridgelines. Dariel got lost in gazing at the maze of thoroughfares and alleys, buildings and spires of what must once have been a grand city. It matched Alecia in size, but the pale green of the building stones showed an intricacy of workmanship that would have left Acacian architects envious.

"What is this place?" the prince asked.

"Amratseer," Mór said. She came up and stood beside them. She said a sentence in Auldek.

"What?"

"*Seeren gith'và.*"

Birké translated. "A dead city."

"Dead? It's hardly dead."

Large beaked birds patrolled the skies in raucous groups; gray doves labored into the air; black starlings darted, seemingly for the joy it. Golden-haired monkeys similar to those on Acacia sprinted around the streets and lounged on rooftops, calling to each other in argumentative bursts. Behind that, there was another sound, the rustle of vegetation slowly engulfing the city, as quiet and relentless as a constricting snake winding tighter and tighter around its prey. There was life in abundance here, just not the sort the makers of the place had intended.

Since Dariel dropped down from those slabs of granite, following Mór eight days before, this new world had swallowed him whole. With Tam and Anira, the other two who had come with them, they spent the first day climbing over high fingers of stone, plunging into damp forests, and climbing up over more fingers of stone. That night they had camped in a cave mouth that opened toward the west. Dariel sat staring at the sun setting over an unending undulation of forest, as vast as the ocean.

The third afternoon they had followed the banks of a tributary of the Sheeven Lek. The river water was crystal clear, rippling liquid glass that displayed the blue stones of the riverbed and banks. When they stopped to eat, Dariel stripped off his shirt and prepared to leap in, ripe with the sweat and dirt of so much walking.

Birké caught him by the arm. "You don't want to do that."

A short time later Birké led him to the trunk of a fallen tree, atop which they could look at a deep pool at a bend in the river. Beneath them schools of crimson-finned fish swam in shifting ribbons of motion, stretching thin and then clumping together, one school joining another and then splitting. They could have been dancing some elaborate routine. Dariel asked if they were edible.

"Oh, yes. Very tasty."

That was when it happened. A section of stones on the bottom of the river slid forward slowly at first and then with a sudden upward rush. Dariel stared as a gaping slit opened. It yawned wider than a person was tall, and engulfed an entire swath of the unfortunate fish. Only when its maw shut again and the creature swam forward with leisurely, pleased swipes of its tail did Dariel understand that it was a massive salamander of some sort. Its back was patterned to replicate the blue stones of the river. It had only to stop moving to become invisible.

"Anything else I should be afraid of?" Dariel asked.

"Plenty of things."

The fourth day they snaked down through crevasses cut deep into the whitish stone of the earth by a labyrinthine network of narrow streams. It was a different world, with forests of amazingly thin trees that stood side by side at any bend in the river—anyplace that afforded a chance at sunlight—and stretched upward, branchless, until their crowns could explode in plumes of long, narrow leaves. Tiny birds darted through the trees. They made their nests well up in them, cast between several like hammocks.

In places the walls pressed in so close on either side that the group disrobed and swam with their clothes and supplies bundled on top of their heads. Dariel's heart thrummed in his chest, more from fear of hidden creatures than from the exertion. Despite this, his eyes still managed to linger on the patterning of tattoos on Mór's back, on the way her blond hair billowed in the water, and on the lovely motion of her legs. Mór herself rarely looked at him. She may have been his escort to meet the Elder Yoen at the Sky Isle, but the role had not made her any warmer toward him. She made it clear that she had left her heart with Skylene back in Avina.

I guess that makes her heartless, Dariel had thought.

✸

At the close of the fifth day they climbed back to the surface of the world and camped, sheltered by the thick roots at the base of some massive trees. The next morning the prince awoke lying on his back, with something gripping the sides of his head, pressing on his chest, and still another thing moving inside his mouth. He opened his eyes and stared into the metallic blue, bulbous face of some sort of enormous insect. Its eyes were each the size of a man's handprint, moist and as delicate looking as soap bubbles. A pulsing tube from the center of the face extended into Dariel's mouth, and the long stretch of its segmented body pressed him down.

Dariel tried to swat at it, but one of the creature's many limbs pinned his wrist down. He tried the other hand, but he got no further than wriggling his fingers. He kicked and thrashed and screamed. Or he tried to do those things. He could not actually kick because the creature had lowered its segmented torso onto his, and the cage of its legs trapped his own. So pinned at all his points, he created little actual motion. Whatever the creature had inserted in his mouth made it impossible to vocalize. That did not stop him from screaming inside his mind.

Tam's face came into view, looking down at him calmly, his eyes shadowed by the dark, circular tattoos of the Fru Nithexek's sky bear. A moment later Anira and Birké and finally Mór appeared as well. None of them shared his alarm. Anira reached out and stroked the creature's side gently. Dariel directed all his confusion into wrinkling his forehead. Birké laughed and made some remark. In answer, Anira brushed her palms over the creature's eyes and then leaned her forehead against it. The tube in Dariel's mouth withdrew, a feeling like many fingers that had been pressing his teeth and tongue to the roof of his mouth releasing all at once. The creature's bulbous head turned, its legs rippling into motion as it curled away from Dariel.

The prince wrenched himself to one side and scrambled to his feet, spitting and cursing, wiping his mouth. He cast about to locate the monster, and saw it slipping away on its numerous legs. The others laughed.

"They're harmless, Dariel," Mór said. "Dou worms, they're called. You should thank them." She said something in Auldek. The others grinned. She began to turn away, but could not stop from translating for him. "I said that it has just cleaned your teeth for you. It will improve your breath."

✳

That evening, looking out over Amratseer, Dariel felt the parameters of how he measured the world crumbling. In this place monsters hid in plain sight. One beast might appear to swallow you whole. Another might improve your hygiene. This land was cluttered with signs of a civilization older by ages than his own, and yet cities and culture and centuries of history had been defeated. It all made him feel like he knew nothing about the fullness of the world and all the people and creatures that lived in it. Instead of frightening him, the battering of realizations he had received in Ushen Brae blew air into his lungs. He wanted to see it all. . . .

Dariel strolled over to where the others huddled, though he did not take his eyes off the panorama. "Will the gates give us trouble?"

Mór looked up from the simple map Tam had drawn in the dust. "Why should they? We won't be troubling them. Amratseer *seeren gith'và.*"

"Are the gates locked?"

"The gates are open," Tam said, without looking up. "That's not the problem."

"Let's go through, then," Dariel said. "We could camp in one of the plazas. Oh, I'd love to explore. . . ."

"We don't enter *seeren gith'và*," Mór said.

"Afraid of ghosts?" Dariel asked.

"We are mindful of them," Anira said. She rose from her squatting position and crossed her arms. She was Balbara by birth, very dark skinned, with a sensuously muscular physique. Instead of tattoos, she showed her Anet clan affiliation in scale-like plates beneath her eyes and on the bridge of her nose, subtle enhancements that one had to peer closely to see. "They are Auldek ghosts. They mean us no good."

"You really don't intend to go through it? That's what you're telling me? Who told you tales of ghosts? Your Auldek masters? Maybe they told tales because they were afraid to go back, and they didn't want their slaves scouring their old cities for treasure."

"Which is what you want to do," Mór said. "Still an Akaran, I see. Still love to pillage and steal."

"Just look at the place! I don't want to steal, but aren't you curious? Don't you—"

Mór closed the distance between them with a rapidity that made Dariel step back. "No," she snapped. "Amratseer *seeren gith'và*. I care about the living. About the People. We sleep here, and begin to skirt Amratseer tomorrow. That's all. Birké, take the prince and fetch water for camp."

If Dariel appeared to accept the dismissal it was only because his mind was already beyond it. He climbed down to a nearby stream and filled waterskins with Birké. He ate a stew made from dried strips of meat and fresh roots with the rest of them, and he asked questions as if the answers to them were enough to satisfy him.

"In the north there is an even greater ruin than Amratseer," Tam said, in answer to one such query. He sat cross-legged, a small stringed instrument cradled in his hands. He played it in short bursts of plucked notes, as if he were writing, or remembering, a tune. He seemed to have forgotten the several blunders he had made during their operation to destroy the soul catcher. "It's called Lvinreth. It was once the home city of the Lvin. They abandoned it centuries ago. Even now they say that snow lions live among the fallen stones. They walk the empty corridors and roar at night, calling for the clan to return."

"Why did they abandon it?"

"The Auldek were once as numerous as the stars. This city proves it. But that was long ago. They killed one another off, suffered disease, even invasion from a race across the mountains that came, plundered, and then went home. Many things left them the weakened race the Lothan Aklun found huddling together by the coast. They never said so, but I think they were a scared people on the brink of extinction. The Lothan Aklun saved them from that. They gave them immortality."

"And us," Anira said. "They gave them the quota."

"The Auldek are the ones who really think their old cities are haunted. It's they who want a new land instead. A war has given them a new purpose in life."

"And given us Ushen Brae," Anira said. "It's a blessing that they've gone."

Mór said something in Auldek. The others received it in silence.

Dariel glanced at her. She sat with her back to the group, looking not at Amratseer but toward the east. Dariel did not ask her what she had said. He was convinced she only spoke Auldek to keep him out of conversations, to draw the line between them, and remind everyone of it. He had a mind to ask her why she chose her enslaver's tongue at all, but he left it.

Later that evening, Tam nudged him awake. The excitement that surged through Dariel was not anticipation of hours sitting quietly on watch, listening to the sleeping and alert for the sound of any creature that might make a meal of them. That was not what he had planned. Whatever was to become of him, being in this land was a part of it. He was here, in this foreign place so far from home. He needed to know it completely, to learn, if he could, why his life was entwined so deeply with the fate of Ushen Brae.

He sat cross-legged for a time, but once Tam's breathing slipped into its steady near snore, Dariel lifted his thin blanket from around his knees and stood. With his boots pinched between his fingers, he tiptoed across the stone, down toward the moonlit city.

The wall was massive. Draped with veins, fissured with cracks, cast in shadow and highlight by the moon's gray glow, it dwarfed even the great wall around Alecia. Dariel had to walk along it for a time, climbing over roots and debris, around stone blocks that had fallen from the crumbling barricade. The night was loud with insect and bird calls, with scuffling noises nearby, and several distant roars, sounds that Dariel had heard before but that troubled him more acutely now. One of these rent the air in a way that he felt physically, as if it flew at him along the long stretch of the wall. The beast they called a kwedeir? Dariel had yet to see one, but he had heard about them, enormous batlike creatures the Auldek had domesticated and used to hunt fugitive slaves. *They bite the head. Not hard enough to kill*, Birké said, *but just enough to get you screaming. They like that.* Dariel had not believed the description. Now he wondered.

He reached a two-doored gate. One door was closed. The other—an enormous thing of old-growth trunks bound together with intricately worked steel—had fallen from its hinges and slammed back against one side of the entranceway. If he had not known better, Dariel would have thought giants had built this place.

The roar came again. He could not tell if it was closer, but it was certainly outside the city's walls. He wondered if it would wake the others. Probably. Mór would rise, cursing him for a fool. He would not argue with her if she did, but when in his life would he ever stand before these gates again? What Akaran had ever been here to learn of the world as he was doing? None that he knew of. Of course he had to see what could be seen. Dariel crept into the shadow beneath the leaning door and entered the dead city of Amratseer.

The green stones of the place glowed with a low luminescence that Dariel could not figure out. As he moved through the cluttered lanes and alleys, he first thought the light was from the moon, but it was not only that. The glow seemed to fill even shadowed spaces, even the insides of houses viewed through the gapping mouths of doors and open crescents of windows. It was night, still dim and shadowy, but it was a different sort of night than Dariel had experienced.

He walked on the balls of his feet, careful not to trip on the vines or debris littering the stones. *Just don't get lost*, he told himself. He proceeded straight ahead as best he could, sighting on the position of the moon and studying the shape of hills behind him for landmarks. Soon the high walls of the multistoried buildings blocked his view. Realizing this, he spun around. His heart pounded in his chest and a film of sweat slicked his forehead. This is absurd, he thought. I've only come a hundred paces. The way back is just there.

He decided to look around the buildings near at hand. Stepping into the entrance of one, he let his eyes adjust until he could see his way by the dim glow of the walls and floor. Intricately carved wooden chairs and benches took shape before him. No spirits, though. Not yet. An overturned bowl on the floor, a clutter of long rods leaning in a corner, a cloth hung from a hook . . .

He entered the next apartment down, a living space, chairs oddly arrayed in a circle, but with no table at its center. He found bedrooms and storage chambers, tiled rooms that must have been for bathing, balconies that looked out onto back gardens that were no longer gardens. They were overgrown enough that trees surged out of them and monkeys—several of whom Dariel startled as much as they startled him—climbed right from them to nest in shelter. How strange it was to walk into homes devoid of their intended inhabitants and yet so full of the signs of what had been.

Stepping out into the night again, Dariel noticed an arched gateway a little farther in. Framed by tall buildings on either side, he could not see where it led. He walked toward it, under the shadow of the archway, and through into a massive courtyard.

What must once have been a marvelous tapestry of paving stones stretched before him. There was a patterning in the colors, he could tell, but it was stained and scarred and faded. The stones were heaved up here and there by tree roots that had escaped their plots, sending out shoots that burst through to become new trees and creating a ragged patchwork. The space was so immense that Dariel could barely make out the opposing archway through the screen of trees. Buildings on either side hemmed the courtyard, reminding him of the upper terraces of the palace on Acacia. Only much, much larger.

Some of the trees were massive, bizarrely so, trunks thicker around than any he had ever seen, branches like scaffolding devoid of foliage but cluttered with . . . No, Dariel realized. The largest of the trees were not trees at all. They were sculptures, with branches that served as perches for batlike, hulking figures. Some sat atop the limbs. Some hung below them. Kwedeir. Kwedeir carved in stone or cast from bronze or some other metal. Dariel walked toward the nearest of these sculptures, into the stencil of shadow beneath it. Were they life-size? It did not seem possible, but Birké had said they were large enough that an Auldek could ride on their backs. These were certainly that.

"This place . . . Corinn would hate this place for so many reasons."

One of the kwedeir turned its head toward Dariel. The prince froze midstep. It thrust its snout forward and sniffed the air. The creature's two black eyes pinned Dariel between them. It was not a statue at all, a fact which suddenly seemed absurdly obvious. It was furred and dark and so clearly alive, quite different from the stone family among which it perched.

Dariel let out a whispered curse.

The kwedeir leaped into the air. Its wings flared out, black against the night sky. It let out a cry that seemed to tear the skin from Dariel's face. He turned and ran. At full sprint he just barely reached the arch before the kwedeir. He bolted straight through as the creature flapped above it.

He was halfway to the row of buildings he had just explored when a moon shadow swept down on him. He jumped to one side as the kwedeir landed on the ground just beside him. It was all flapping membranous wings and awkward limbs and a snapping, inhaling, fetid snout full of yellow teeth. Dariel backed from it, tripped, and then he scrabbled away on all fours for a moment.

The beast grunted and leaped into the air again. It came down just behind Dariel as he hurtled through the nearest open door. The prince stumbled into a chair and sprawled over a table, slid off it, and crashed onto the floor. The kwedeir beat its wings. It kicked at the decaying stone around the doorframe, part of which collapsed at its first blow. It folded its wings and squirmed forward, bursting through the stone with the wriggling force of its body.

Dariel fled further into the apartment. He heard the creature break through and scrabble behind him. He ran through the apartment and into a small courtyard. He darted across it, leaped through a back window, down a flight of stairs, and into a dim passageway. He could not hear the beast anymore, but he kept moving. Through alleys, splashing through ankle-deep muck, under a bridge, and into a small cubicle of a room, in which he stood jammed into a corner.

When his panting had quieted enough that he realized he could hear a rodent squeaking somewhere in the room, Dariel let himself relax. He touched the tips of his fingers to his nose, clipping them together as if they were scissors. "By Tinhadin's nose," he said, an expression he had not used since boyhood, appropriate now, for his knees felt weak as a child's.

How quickly would a thing like that forget him? Short memories. They must have short memories, surely. It would be on to something else by now. And if it did appear again? Be ready for it. That's all. Fight it. He had not even thought to draw his dagger against the kwedeir. He tugged it free now and stepped into the doorway's frame.

He stood there for some time, his eyes scanning the sky and moving over the buildings rising around him. Nothing swept down from above. The sounds were all the same as before. He had just moved farther out into the lane, hoping to get his bearings, when something rounded a nearby corner and snapped to stillness, staring at him.

It was not the kwedeir, but when a growl started low in its throat and the hair along its ridgeline rose in an angry bristle, Dariel knew it might just as readily kill him. A hound. A lean, long-legged creature as tall as the hunting dogs at Calfa Ven. Its eyes shone the same color as its short tan hair. It crouched with its head stretched low to the ground, the muscles in its shoulders taut and bulging. It stepped forward. Once, and then again, muscles and joints smooth in action.

Dariel hunkered down, slashing the knife in warning.

The winged shadow swept in, blocking out the sky and freezing the hound with one paw upraised. The kwedeir hovered over it. The hound cocked its head, sensing it. Before it could react the kwedeir folded its wings and dropped. It slammed the hound to the ground and clamped its jaws around the canine's head and neck. The hound struggled, but the kwedeir raked its hind claw down its back, ripping deep gouges. It pressed down, driving its weight through its hind legs. The hound began to yelp in short, frantic bursts. And then the kwedeir bit hard. The cracking of bone was audible, as was the squelch of fluids spraying through the creature's jaws. It did not pause a moment, but flared its wings and surged upward. The dead hound swung sickeningly from its jaws as it labored up above the height of the buildings, over them, and out of sight.

Dariel did not move from where he stood framed in the doorway. He simply lowered himself to the stones and sat, panting just as heavily as if he had been running again. "Did that just happen?" He looked from side to side as if there might be a companion there to verify it for him. There was no one, of course, but that did not stop him from asking the question several more times as he gradually caught his breath.

As before, he realized he should move again because he heard squeaking somewhere in the room behind him. Or, not squeaking exactly . . . more like whimpering, snuffling. There was a pattern to it, as if rodents were making noise and then going silent. Calling and then listening. Come to think of it, the sounds were nothing like those of a mouse or other rodent.

Dariel rose and crept back into the room. There was a crate

there he had hardly noticed before, turned on its side, its opening facing the wall. He approached it and stood silent beside it long enough to hear the whimpering again. With his dagger thrust before him, he caught the crate with his toe and pushed it to one side until he saw what lay huddled within.

Two pups. Big-eyed and cautious, staring at him. Innocence in rounded features and floppy ears and slightly trembling jaws.

"Oh . . . look at you," Dariel said. He sheathed his knife and reached in cautiously. "Look at you." He stroked one of the pups on the head. It tried to back away. "Shhh. No, no, it's fine." His touch was gentle. His fingers sank into the soft fur, over the ears, and then down under the chin. The other pup inched forward. Its eyes were the same color as its fur, a slightly auburn tint now that he was up close. Just like the hound outside. Dariel offered his hand for it to scent. After doing so, the pup slapped its pink tongue wetly against his knuckles. Before Dariel could smile with the joy this gave him, a realization stopped him.

"That was your mother, wasn't it?" Dariel moved to the doorway and scanned the scene. It lay as it had before, dark and glowing at the same time, still and crackling with unseen motion, silent and filled with a cacophony of sounds. Exactly the same, yet different now.

Looking back at the pups, Dariel asked, "What am I going to do with you two?"

CHAPTER
· FOUR

Rialus Neptos went to bed each evening swearing to himself that he was not betraying his entire race. To really be doing what the Auldek asked of him would make him the greatest villain in the history of the Known World. He could think of nobody else who had sunk so low. Not even during the unfortunate years he served Hanish Mein had he been such a traitor. He had just been biding his time then, pretending to serve Hanish and the Numrek. He had proven as much by bringing the Numrek into Corinn's service and saving the empire! He would find a way to do so again. He would lie and fabricate, confuse and obfuscate, trick and deceive and somehow emerge from it a hero for the ages. He had to. He had a wife, Gurta. He had a child who might already be born and living in the world. Didn't that matter more than anything?

Going to sleep thus convinced made waking in the morn all the more peculiar. He found himself surrounded by the enemy. He watched himself go through motions that looked, smelled, and felt like the very treason he so despised. The situation was complicated enough to challenge his capacity for knotted excuses. The Numrek had never, in fact, been true to the Akarans. The "allies" he had brought Corinn had been planning the conquest of the entire Known World all along. The Auldek horde progressing around the curve of the world were every bit the threat they considered themselves to be, and they were daily educating themselves on all things Acacian—with Rialus as their instructor. At what point, exactly, would he transform himself into the agent of Acacian defense that he believed himself to be?

"Hey, Rialus leagueman!"

Rialus heard the shout from outside his room. He recognized the voice—Allek's. He sat cross-legged with a writing cushion before him, pen poised above it. Just leave me, Rialus thought. Go on. He had begun yet another journal attempt at outlining his actions, justifying and explaining how he was handling himself while with the Auldek. He thought such documents would prove useful should he ever be called before Queen Corinn. For some reason, he found it quite hard to organize his arguments coherently.

Fingel uncurled herself from the corner of the room and moved for the door. Rialus waved her to stillness. Don't play dumb, girl! he thought, as he had many times before. The Meinish young woman, his slave since Avina, showed a dogged unwillingness to ever anticipate his desires. It should be dead obvious that he would not want to be disturbed.

"There is someone at the door," she said, staring at him with her gray eyes.

As if on cue, the circular portal was yanked open, letting in a howling beast of a wind that surged through the chamber, making it instantly frigid. A furred figure stepped across the threshold. He was bundled from head to foot, hooded, and wore black goggles. He cast about a moment, no doubt letting his eyes adjust to the dim lamplight.

"Rialus," Allek said, "get dressed. Stop all that scribbling. Sabeer wants to massage your feet. Or . . . she wants you to massage her feet. I forget which. Either way, she asked for you. What charm have you put on her?" he asked.

"No charm but my wit and the pleasure of my company," Rialus said.

The hooded figure guffawed. "Right. Your charm. Come, Rialus! Show me your charm at work. She's in the steamship."

"Please tell her I'm busy. I'm—"

"I'll drag you by your locks if you don't start dressing now. I'll enjoy it, too. Just like last time."

Still an ogre, Rialus thought. "Fine," he muttered, setting his pen aside and tidying his supplies. "I'm coming. Keep your nose on."

Rialus carefully pulled on his fur-lined leggings and boots. He shrugged himself into his sealskin jacket. The garment draped bulkily about him. He had learned the hard way that if it hung loose, wicked fingers of cold found their way to his skin, so he cinched down the buckles. He even strapped on the visor to protect his eyes, and then tugged his hood in place. All this for a walk that would only take a few minutes. Damn this place. So thinking, he followed Allek out.

The wind smacked him as if it had clung just above the door, waiting to pounce on him. He stood on a platform running along one side of what the Auldek called stations, rocking, taking in a scene he still barely believed. His room was but one chamber of several in the large wooden and steel structure, a rolling tower that churned across the frozen earth with unrelenting steadiness. All around him other stations rolled, pulled by long lines of harnessed rhinoceroses, the same woolly breed that the Numrek had ridden down into the Known World. The structures creaked and groaned. The creatures bellowed and snorted. The blown snow obscured further stations, making it feel like they went on forever, out beyond the reach of his vision.

The vessels were relics of ancient Auldek travel, quickly outfitted for this journey. Indeed, much of the preparation was made easier because of the great stores of old equipment and devices the Auldek had but to dust off and haul into use. The stations. Cargo wagons. The sleds. Stores of arms and supplies, tons of grain and other foodstuffs in crates and barrels. All of it slid into motion more rapidly than Rialus would have thought possible. Slaves had tended herds of the beasts outside Avina. Rhinoceroses. Antoks. Kwedeir. Not to mention the fréketes. Rialus had not seen much of the monsters since the cold weather had set in, but he understood them to be housed in stations outfitted for them.

Beneath and between the structures figures moved, driving animals, hauling supplies, doing the million things needed to feed and care for an army in constant, rolling motion. Rialus had doubted it would be possible, but the Auldek—or their slaves—were more efficient than he thought. They unpacked food stores in an organized manner that meant they could abandon the vehicles that had carried them. They ate the animals freed up from this, or any that got injured or sick. Rialus even suspected that the slaves themselves became food for the animals or worse. He tried not to think about it.

A man rode by atop an antok, swaying with the beast's strides, as at ease as a horseman on a trusted mount. The swine blew plumes of white vapor from beneath the heavy patchwork of throws that covered it. Rialus felt the vapor billow around him, fogging his visor. He smelled the rank scent of the creature's breath. But that did not make sense. It was not that close. Rialus scrubbed at his visor a moment, smearing the scene before him. He pulled back his hood and yanked the visor from his head.

The antok had moved away, but still the steaming breath blew past him. A noise at his back turned Rialus around to meet the clear blue eyes of a snow lioness. The cat crouched just a little distance away on a ledge of the station, tensed as if it might pounce. It thrust its chin forward, and then cocked its head, then righted it. Rialus had no idea what that was meant to convey, but the female of the species worried him as much as the massive males. In the wild, he had been told, it was the females that did most of the hunting. The males just used their brawn to fight one another and win wives. Miserable beasts! Rialus thought. He fumbled for the ladder poles, dropped over the edge, and descended.

Dropping from the ladder onto the frozen earth, Rialus pitched over, as he always did when jumping from the ever-moving structure. He scrambled to his feet, wary of the vehicle's massive wheels, and had to shuffle run to catch up with Allek. They cut a zigzagging path through the rumbling, roaring, groaning flow of men and machines and furred and horned and tusked beasts, all the while buffeted by the wind.

They entered the steamstation through a trapdoor that lowered for them to leap up to. A moment later, after climbing a winding staircase, Rialus was shrugging out of his garments, the air warm around him. At least the steamship had that going for it. It was a specially constructed station, one that featured an elaborate heating system fueled by the flammable pitch the Auldek had brought with them in great quantities. A fire burning somewhere inside pumped in enough hot air that the Auldek lounged about half naked, slaves fanning them and serving them chilled drinks and giving them massages. It never failed to remind Rialus of the baths at Cathgergen, a memory which he ran from, remembering just how that had turned out.

"Ah, Allek, you've found my leagueman," Sabeer said. "You never disappoint."

"I try not to, dearest one," Allek said, bowing his head.

Dearest one? Rialus sneered inside. As if you have a chance with her.

"Come, Rialus, sit with us."

Sabeer lounged on a low divan, propped up on one elbow, sipping something from a tiny blue glass. She was tall and long limbed, with a tensile muscularity that hummed like a coiled spring, making even languid movements seem somehow dangerous. She wore a thin linen garment, perfectly designed to hug her contours and yet hang loose. Another woman, Jàfith, lay in a similar posture. A man named Howlk sat with her feet in his lap, an absurdly submissive posture for a warrior who, Rialus knew, enjoyed wrestling naked in death matches—or as close to such as an immortal could suffer.

Two humans stood just outside the group, one beating out a rhythm on a waist-high drum while the other smacked a rattle on his palm. If not for the sloshing liquid in the glasses one might have forgotten the entire station was rolling across an icescape.

Rialus sat on the cushion to which Sabeer directed him. He had been petrified when he learned she was Devoth's wife, but what that distinction meant Rialus could not figure out. He rarely saw them together, and when he did they treated each other more like siblings than anything else—deeply familiar, enough so that they were also deeply dismissive. They kept separate quarters, and Sabeer spent her time with whomever she chose. For some reason, Rialus was one of those.

"Howlk was reciting a song to Sumerled," Sabeer said, squeezing Rialus's thigh. "Continue, sir. Let Rialus hear the end."

The Auldek warrior cleared his throat. He closed his eyes, his fingers kneading the ball of Jàfith's foot and his upper body swaying with the effort, as if he were putting all of himself into the pressure of his fingers. He tilted his stern features up, long hair flowing over his shoulders, and told a tale of epic love and tragedy that would have brought the entire Acacian senate to tears. Two lovers suffered the wrath of the Lvin for some crime

Rialus could not quite pinpoint. Rialus had heard poems performed like this before, but Howlk had a particularly good voice
for it. Despite himself, he was transfixed.

Rialus had ceased being surprised by the complex collage
that was Auldek culture. At times they seemed as barbaric and
prone to violence as the Numrek. But those moments did not
define them entirely. Devoth with his dancing hummingbirds.
The time Rialus watched them draw garden tapestries with colored pebbles, complex works of art that would blur and disinte-
grate under the first rain. They achieved a balance in their lives,
but it was a balance of extremes. Here was a race who would
howl for blood in the morning, and then tend beetle farms on
their terraces in the afternoon. Here was a people who would
abandon their land to march to war, but then bring with them
strange artifacts of gentility.

He would never forget the makeshift banquet held on a
black stone beach, waves crashing in the distance. The Auldek
delicately plucked the violet leaves of some flowerlike vegetable.
They dunked each leathery leaf in fragrant oils and scraped off
the softer tissue with their upper teeth. The thing tasted fine,
when you got used to it, but it was the spectacle of such rough
creatures all silently attending leaf dipping that ranked as one
of the strangest sights he had ever witnessed.

When Howlk finished his song and had shaken off the praise
offered him, Rialus asked, "How old is that tale?"

"A couple hundred years," Howlk said. "It's a newer poem,
really."

"So as new as that? Then . . . did you know these ill-fated
lovers? Personally, I mean."

Howlk looked away without answering, opening an awkward silence.

Something over Rialus's shoulder caught Sabeer's attention.
Several Lvin women climbed the circular staircase. Though they

were human, Rialus knew them instantly. Their every movement shouted their status, not just with their clan affiliation but as simple sublime motion. Their bodies were lithe and sculpted, honed through torturous training that made them fighters almost on par with the Auldek themselves. They went about wearing only short skirts. They were bare breasted, with chiseled arms and long muscles taut in their legs as they climbed. Like their totem animal, they moved with feline grace, circling and climbing up toward the next level without pausing.

Behind the women came the white dreadlocks and the pale, leonine visage of Menteus Nemré. Like the women before him, he was nearly naked. The slave's muscles bulged absurdly on his chest and arms, cut fine divisions on his abdomen, and stood out in thick bands running down his legs. He paused halfway up the stairs, taking in the room. For a moment, he seemed to stare so intently at him that Rialus wanted to squirm. Actually, he did squirm. Nothing about the attention of Menteus's gaze changed, though.

As his torso narrowed, the color of his skin changed from powder white to rich, dark brown from his abdomen down—his natural color. A shade of Talay. He paused on the landing and studied the lounging Auldek group.

Strange to think of this man as a slave, for not an inch of him betrayed the slightest subservience. Rialus had never been this close to him before. He could not think of him without seeing images of the damage he had done during the games back in Avina. The speed of his attack. The way limbs and blood flew from his blade work. The death he inflicted for no other purpose than to determine the order in which the clans would march away on this campaign.

Realizing the man was staring at Sabeer, Rialus looked back at her. She smiled and dipped her head in greeting. Her gaze ascended as Menteus Nemré continued his climb. "You shouldn't ask such things," Sabeer said, returning to Rialus's question. She leaned a bit closer. "You embarrass us. You see, we've forgotten."

"Forgotten?"

She shrugged, waved him away with her hand, and then pointed at the musicians. "Sing."

Howlk asked, "So what do you believe, Rialus? I've heard the quota speak of few gods. There is one that gives, yes?"

"The god of presents," Allek quipped.

"Yes, that one. Can you get him to give me something? I want a great many things."

They all looked at Rialus with playfully serious faces, expressions that grew more amused as he tried to convey the essential details surrounding the Giver. Before he had gotten far at all, Jàfith said, "What nonsense! Did you just make that up, League-man?"

"No, I've heard others speak the same many times," Allek said. "Theirs is a feeble faith. Don't look offended, Rialus. What sense does it make that one god would create all? Why would he create . . . rabbits. Soft and cuddly, yes? And then create foxes that hunt them down and tear them to shreds? Why do that? That god is no god to the rabbits. He is a demon that favors their enemies. But nor does that god honor the fox, for he creates other animals bigger than it. Creates wolves. Creates you Acacians. Even you, Rialus, could kill a fox if you were lucky and had the right weapon."

"And if the creature was lame or old," Jàfith added.

"It simply makes no sense. It's an addled god who creates hunted and hunter both, killer and those to be killed. Health and disease at the same—"

"No, the Giver did not create disease," Rialus said. "Elenet did that!"

"Elenet?" Sabeer asked. "Who is Elenet?"

"One of the first humans. He followed the Giver and learned

his language and tried to use it, but when he did he released disease, illness, death. Things like . . ."

Rialus's voice faded as the triumphant expression on Howlk's face grew. "Listen to yourself. You're telling us that a human stole the words of creation from a god? All he had to do was talk like a god and he became a god?"

"That's like saying if you stole Devoth's armor and wore it you would become as he," Allek said. "Do you think that, Rialus?"

"No, I—"

"But that's what this Elenet did," Howlk said. Rialus tried to say more, but Howlk talked over him. "Foolishness from start to finish. You know how the world really works? Life is war. It's the struggle between forces that defines it. Hunger gnaws your belly until it is defeated by consumption. But then just when consumption lies down to sleep, hunger rises and grabs it around the neck and starves it. The night overcomes the day; the day burns away the night. Back and forth. Back and forth. War, Rialus, but not chaos. That's the difference between us. In conflict you and your people see confusion, see something to be lived through in waiting for peace. We, though, see conflict as what the gods intended."

"I think this is good news for us, yes?" Allek asked. The others agreed that it was.

Sabeer rose to her feet. "Rialus, pay these fools no mind. Come, let's entertain ourselves privately."

"Me?" Rialus said.

She smiled suggestively. "Yes, you, none of these others interest me tonight."

A howling protest answered this, mixed with invitations and suggestive encouragements for Rialus. The humorous remarks followed them to the edge of the chamber, where Sabeer slipped on boots of white fox fur and a coat of some other hide that she wrapped around herself loosely. Rialus, unsure what he was heading to but trying to be relieved to get away from the others, fumbled himself into his outer garments. He dreaded that Sabeer would expect him to perform in intimate ways. Dreaded it, and yet it was not only his stomach that tingled with anticipation.

※

Another drummer played in Sabeer's chamber. Still other servants hovered near, but Rialus forgot about them as Sabeer lay down with him. She pressed her strong body against his frail one. She spooned around him, breasts pressing against his back, her long legs entwined with his spindly ones.

So positioned, she stroked her finger up and down his arm. "Do you understand what the two lovers did wrong in Howlk's song? They were old. You know yourself that none of us Auldek are old in body. We all took our first soul at an age of vanity. You understand? If we were to be immortal, we wanted to be forever strong, young, good for fighting and lovemaking, no sign either of our beginnings or of our ends. That's why there are none of us in child bodies, no immortal children. That would be very disturbing, I think. That's why I chose to look forever as I do now. I made a good choice, yes?"

Rialus blushed. "You are . . . very well formed."

"Such a silver tongue you have." Sabeer chuckled, and then grew serious. "What those two lovers did wrong was that they disdained immortality. They gave up on it and died back into their true souls. And then those true souls let their bodies age. That itself made them . . . I don't know what to call them. Outcasts. Not exactly. A holy couple. Perhaps they would have been. But then, nearing death, they asked for life again. They wanted souls from the soul catcher then. You understand that they could not have this. Can you imagine? Them old forever? In love and old forever. No, we could not allow that. I do wish I remembered them, though. Truly remembered them."

"Do you not?"

Sabeer slid her leg over Rialus. Her skin was soft and hot, and he was glad he faced away from her, curved around the arousal in his groin.

"No, I haven't for many years. None of us do. I'm making a confession to you, Rialus. We know what's written. We know things because we keep the knowledge alive. In records. In songs. We can only hold the memories of eighty years or so. The length of a long normal life. As we grew past that age our childhoods disappeared, and then our youth, and even the day we ate our first soul and gained lasting life. Rialus, I once lived in the interior, in a palace in the Westlands. I loved a man named Merwyn. We lived seventy-five years together but could have no children. The sadness of this became too much for him and he let free his lives and died a final death. At least, that's what the written histories say of him. Myself, I remember none of it. We claim we abandoned the cities because of ancient wars and slaughter. Perhaps that's true, but that's not why we fear to return to them. I think what scares us is not remembering, not knowing our own lives, being strangers to ourselves."

"I—I understand," Rialus said. "That must be like—like when the old in my land lose their minds and memories. Not just like it, of course, because they forget yesterday and remember fifty years ago, but the same sort of thing. Sabeer, you are like us. Your immortality hasn't made you different at all. You're just like—"

"Don't be silly," she said. She propped herself up on her elbow and pressed her finger to his lips to silence him. "Rialus Silver Tongue. That's what we should call you. Always trying to save your people." She smiled and leaned close enough to kiss him.

"I like you, Rialus Silver Tongue, but when we reach your lands, I'll take to the field of battle with my kinsmen just as we've planned. You can't change that."

She pulled her finger away, but Rialus felt it still, as if it had left a brand on his lips, an old, bitter wound already scarred over. What was he doing in bed with this creature? Listening to her. Talking to her. Aroused by her and, for a moment, understanding her. Fool, Rialus! He tried to remember Gurta instead. She had wrapped around him like this also, but she had done it with true love for him. She had said so many times. Gurta, I won't let them have you.

"You know, Rialus, I can see the beauty in your race. I've had quota lovers, you know. There's no shame in it." She circled her finger on the soft skin of his inner elbow, smiling at some revelry this line of conversation brought back to her. "No shame at all. I even like you, Rialus, though that's strange. You're not . . . well, a specimen considered attractive by your race, are you? No one ever called you handsome, did they?"

She was a vile, barbarian woman. He could have found a hundred ways to insult her. Instead, he heard himself say, "No, no one ever called me handsome."

"Rialus," Sabeer said, "my poor leagueman. I don't think you're handsome either, but I like you. You'll always have a place with me. After all this is over and your world is ours, you should come stay with me in some palace somewhere. You can bring your woman, too. Where do you think I should take a palace?"

You never will, Rialus thought. You and all your kind will die first. I'll make sure of it.

"Tell me about the best of them," she prompted, nudging him. "Tell me things you've not told Devoth."

And, despite the thoughts that played inside his mind, he began, "You should see Calfa Ven, in the Senival Mountains. It's a hunting lodge. . . ."

"Oh, hunting. That sounds good."

If we go there together, I'll use you for target practice, he swore. Out loud he said, "Or the cliff palaces of Manil . . ."

"Palaces on cliffs? Wonderful."

I'll push you from them and watch you fall into the sea.

Sabeer squirmed against him. "Tell me more."

And he did. He could not help himself. "Of course," he said, "there's the isle of Acacia itself. . . ."

CHAPTER
FIVE

Aliver Akaran reached out and touched the statue's chin. He traced the Talayan's jawline. He brushed his fingertips over the full lips and caressed the clean-shaven crown of its head. All so very lifelike down to the finest details—the texture of the skin and eyelashes, the expression of focused engagement, the collarbones and lean runner's chest, and the muscled compartments of its legs. It stood frozen in a posture of motion, iron spear high in the fingers of one hand. The other arm was wrapped above the bicep by an arm ring. A tuvey band, Aliver recalled.

"I know you," the prince said. "We once ran together."

He said this and knew it to be true. It warmed him, but he also understood that this figure was only a work of wood and iron and fabric. The others spaced out along the lamplit hallway were as well. The Senivalian wore scaled armor and hefted a curved sword with a brawny arm. The Vumu warrior's eagle feathers flared from a band around his head. The various Acacians in different military garb, their faces like Aliver's—light brown, even featured, with a haughty lift to their chins and sagely dark eyes. There was even a Meinish soldier, blond and gray eyed, his nose and cheekbones sharp. A tuft of gold bristled on his chin.

"I know you," Aliver said. "We once fought each other." Again it was true and not true. So many things were true and not true.

Looking back down the corridor that led to his boyhood room, Aliver saw not just the scene before him, dimly lit and quiet with the dead of night, but also a thousand other views of this same place. He saw it in the morning light and by the afternoon glare from the skylights, muted by gray skies and crimson when the setting sun shone through the western windows. He saw it with the eyes of the child who ran down the corridor, light on his feet and full of play. He saw it as the youth he was on the day his father died, striding straight-backed and very foolish in his pride. He saw it filled with the people who had once moved through life with him.

"I know you all."

The same sensation surrounded him as he sat in his old room. He ran his hand over his silken bedspread. He picked up the statue of Telamathon—he who had defeated the god Reelos and his five disciples—and felt the man's face with his fingers. He studied the tapestries on the wall and the busts of the early kings, facing east to greet the morning sun. His room had remained furnished as he remembered, almost as if it had been preserved for his return. He knew it had not been. Nobody had expected his return, least of all him. But he was here, body and mind; and with each passing hour he became more and more himself. Less and less whatever he had been.

It felt almost like his flesh and skin were shrinking to fit his form, just now growing snug around him. Whatever Corinn had done to bring him back to life should not have been attempted. He knew that as surely as he had ever known anything. But it was done, and he could only live with it. Just *how* to live he was not sure. Wandering about the palace seemed to be helping, though. He rose and continued.

He could not have explained how he knew where to find the boy. He simply rose and looked. And looking, he knew. He entered the room as a servant came out of it. Surprised by his presence, she slammed herself against the doorjamb and stood straight as a board as he approached. Much the same reaction the other servants gave him when he encountered them. He studied her soft-featured face a moment, not recognizing it but finding it pleasant, and then he nodded as he passed by her into the bedroom.

Aaden, a child of eight, lay on his bedspread. Dressed in silken green bedclothes, he curled to one side, his knees pulled up and his hands clasped together. Something about the posture looked choreographed, too precise to be natural. Perhaps the servant had just repositioned him. Yes, that was it. They were caring for him as he slept.

Aliver sat beside him. He felt as if he already knew the boy, as if he could sit without fear that the boy would think it a trespass, as if he had spent time with him already. He had not. Corinn had always delayed their meeting, but she was gone for the time being. A good thing, too. He was coming to know himself and the present world faster without the tightly wound energy swirling about her to contend with.

"When will you wake?" he asked. "I should like us to talk, just us for a time. I was a boy like you once. A prince promised the world. No doubt you've been lied to . . . for your own good, they'll believe. But nothing good comes from lies, not even well-intentioned ones. One thing they don't tell you is that the world is not truly yours. You are but a part of it. You have been born not to be served by it but to serve it. At least, that's how it felt with me. Perhaps your birth into this family is no accident. You may be the greatest of us all."

Greatest of them all? Was that his idea? Strange to feel it anchored in him, though he knew nothing of this boy beyond his parentage. Corinn had said something about Aaden's greatness. She had said many things; and she had not said many things. Aliver was aware of both. Their conversations had created an unease that itched at the edge of his awareness. He could not find a way to draw it nearer or to pull it over himself and inhabit it as some part of him wanted to. Even when she had said things he did not agree with, he was powerless to truly object.

✳

A few days ago, before she left for Teh, she had told him that she believed the Santoth had reached out to her. She claimed that they had spoken to her through people in her dreams. "Once I wouldn't have thought that possible," she had said. She sat sharing the late evening with him. The fire had burned to glowing coals and grown warmer for it. He watched her fingers as they kneaded a lacy shawl, squeezing and letting go, squeezing and letting go. "But now anything is possible. Anything at all."

"What do they say?" Aliver asked.

"Promises. Entreaties." She did not look at Aliver. She seemed almost to be carrying on both sides of their conversation herself. "They ask and ask and promise. It's all quite jumbled really."

"What do they ask?"

"They ask me to rescind their banishment, bring them back to Acacia, and give them *The Song of Elenet*. They act like it's theirs! And what do they promise? They're vague on that. To be my army of sorcerers. To protect me from forces I don't understand. As if I need them for that."

"Perhaps you do. They cared for me. Corinn, I went in search—"

"Of them. A foolish thing to do. They helped us win the war, so I don't fault you too much for it, but it was the song itself we needed, not other singers of it."

Perhaps she knew best. His thoughts were still cloudy on his past life. And yet . . . "In the end I didn't find them; they found me." That was exactly right. He had thought they were stones. He would have died just a few feet from them, had they not risen and saved him. "They wanted only to be released from banishment and to study the Giver's tongue again."

"I know that much," Corinn said. "They're desperate for my book. Too desperate."

"Wouldn't you be desperate, too?" This brought her gaze up. "Imagine if—" He could get no further. With Corinn's eyes on him, intense and flashing warning, his words clipped off as if his throat had been squeezed shut. For a moment he did not breathe. Then he gasped and knew that he had breath. It was only words that could not pass his lips.

Corinn looked back to the shawl in her lap. "They've left me alone recently. I'm glad of it. My dreams are cluttered enough without them. We don't need them. Tinhadin didn't; I don't."

"But what if—"

"No, I am right," she said. "Leave it at that." Before the reverberation of her words had completely faded he believed she was right. It was a relief in a way. So much confused doubt replaced by her certainty. He was not even sure what he had been about to say.

"Oh, look at this!" Corinn plucked at something on the shawl. "A slipped stitch." She tugged on the yarn pinched between her fingers. It slipped free easily. She clicked her tongue on the roof of her mouth, a reprimand for whoever had knitted it. Then, after a studied pause, she continued ripping the stitches out.

᠅

Sitting beside Aaden now, Aliver sighed. Thinking of his sister fatigued him and exhilarated him at the same time. He could make no sense of it yet. He reached out and stroked strands of wavy hair back from the child's forehead. He was handsome. How could a child of Corinn's not be?

"I do wish you would wake and speak to me, but you can't. I should speak to you. How about a story? Would you like a story?" Aliver stretched out next to him. "Let's see. . . ."

And tell stories he did. Not just one. Several. He told of the girl Kira, who had one magical gift. She could fold bits of paper into winged shapes and toss them into the air, turning them into living birds. It was a simple talent that she thought largely useless until she learned better. He told of an adventure Bashar had while hunting his brother in Talay, how he fell into a deep pit and could escape only with the aid of a legless man who climbed on his back and described the way out for him. He told bits and pieces as he recalled them from his own childhood, and he told half the tale of Aliss, the Aushenian woman who killed the Madman of Caraven. Only half, though, for he realized at some point that the ending was a bloodier thing than he wished to describe to a sleeping boy.

He talked long enough that his voice grew hoarse and he fell into a long, ruminative silence, staring at the ceiling and listening to the boy's quiet breathing. Eventually, when the pipers played the passing of a third hour, Aliver swung his legs to the floor and rose. "Sleep peacefully, my nephew. Wake soon."

He had just started away when the boy's eyes fluttered open. He looked at Aliver. His irises were Meinish gray, a startling contrast with the fullness of their Acacian shape. He worked his mouth a moment, licked his lips. "I—I had dreams."

It did not occur to Aliver to be surprised by his awakening.

He chose delight instead. Settling back on the edge of the bed, he asked, "Of what?"

"That I walked outside and the clouds were stones. Big stones floating."

"Really? I don't think stones can float."

"These ones could. And I dreamed that the water floated out of the pools on the terraces and all the fish started swimming in the air. And I could swim, too, so long as I was touching drops of floating water. It was fun until I remembered about the hook-fish. When I remembered them, I knew they were coming and fell down to the ground."

"Your dreams have a lot of floating in them."

"Not always. Once I was very thin." Aaden lifted his arms and shook them slightly, demonstrating some aspect of his temporary thinness. "And one time I could eat anything. I mean anything. I could just bite the wall and chew it, and the bed-spread, and the lamp oil. Anything. Nothing tasted like much, but I could still eat it."

"That would be convenient in many ways."

"Yes, it would. When you're fighting a war. It would make it easier to supply the troops if they could just eat anything. Stones. Grass and stuff."

Aliver grinned. "That would be an advantage, but only if the enemy could not do the same."

"No, they couldn't," Aaden said, as if he had thought that through already. He looked up at the ceiling, clearly consider-ing something else and weighing whether or not to voice it. "I dreamed that my friend Devlyn got killed."

"Oh." Aliver squeezed the boy's wrist gently. "That was not a dream. Or . . . it was not only a dream."

"I know. I hoped you would say it was, though. I wish you had. I would have believed it if you said it. Who are you?"

Aliver leaned closer. "I am your uncle."

"You're not Dariel," Aaden said. "He's gone across the Gray Slopes."

"I don't claim to be Dariel. I'm Aliver."

Aaden let out an audible breath of affirmation. "Of course you are! Did Mother bring you back?"

Aliver nodded.

"Are you going to get them?"

"Who?"

"My guards. The ones who stabbed Devlyn. I saw them do it for no reason. They wanted to kill me, too. Is he really dead?"

"I believe so," Aliver said. "I . . . know that he is, yes. I'm not sure how I know, but I do. I know a lot of things, Aaden, but they're new to me. It's like . . . I just discovered a new library of books. I have them. They're mine, but I haven't read all the books yet. It may take me some time."

A gasp drew their attention. The maid stood inside the door, her mouth an oval around a question she could not manage to speak. She tried several times, then turned and darted out of the room.

"She'll be back soon, I think," Aliver said.

Aaden sighed. "Will she get Mother?"

"No, your mother has gone to Teh. She was angry at all the Numrek, not just the guards who hurt you and Devlyn. I believe she went to punish them."

"Good. There's no excuse for such behavior. What is she going to do to them?"

Aliver ran his hand over the boy's hair. "What would you have her do to them?"

"I don't know," Aaden said. "They killed Devlyn. He was my friend."

"That was wrong of them."

Aaden pressed his lips together, nodded. "Why did they do

that? He didn't do anything except be my friend." All of sudden, as if the grief of it had just exploded in him, Aaden crumpled forward, falling against Aliver. "He was my only friend."

Aliver held the boy to his chest as he cried, stroking his hair. So Aaden had not inherited his great-grandfather's gift of being loved by all his peers. Gridulan was the last Acacian monarch to have a band of brothers with him always, loyal and adoring if the stories of them were to be believed. Leodan had only his traitorous chancellor Thaddeus Clegg. Aliver himself might have had Melio as a close companion, but he had been too foolish to accept the youth's overtures with the sincerity with which they were offered. At least Aaden knew to call a friend a friend.

"Your mother will take care of them," he said. "She told me she would treat them fairly."

"Good," Aaden said, a bitter edge cutting through his grief. "She should kill them all."

This drew Aliver up. Kill them all? Was that the boy's idea of fairness? Or was it his mother's? He knew the answer immediately, and with it came a greater understanding of the ruler his sister must have become. And the sort of mother as well. He could not decide how to respond, so he held the boy until his sorrow spent itself. As he did, his horror at the boy's wish for vengeance lost its acute shape and blurred at the edges. He found it hard to grasp.

Eventually, Aaden pulled away from him, looking exhausted in addition to miserable. "I think I'm tired." The boy lay down, resting his head on his pillow in the indentation already pressed into it. "When I get up, we have to go find Elya."

"Elya?"

"You don't know Elya? She saved me. She is a dragon. Well . . . of sorts. A dragon. A lizard. A bird. All of them together. I'm not sure what to call her other than a dragon, though. What do you think?"

"I don't know," Aliver admitted. "I haven't thought much about dragons. I heard an Aushenian tale about dragons before. I think it was a scaly creature that Kralith, their white crane god, fought against for some reason. I never thought there really was a white crane god, so I never gave much thought to dragons either."

"You will. She's wonderful. She flies. Mena found her and brought her here. Where is Mena?"

Where was Mena? Just framing the question did something inside him. He did not have the answer immediately, but having put the query in words he felt it leave him and hook into the fabric of the world. He did not know, but he felt he *could* know. He could if he waited for it. Just as he had learned his way around the palace simply by remembering it. Just as he had known where Aaden slept simply because he had wondered it and felt the answer as accessible as the air around. He could not touch it. Not grasp it. But he could inhale it. The answers to things were there for him if he breathed them in.

"She is north of here," Aliver said, "in the cold. She's gone to make war. She's taken the King's Trust."

Aaden squinted at him. "You just said you didn't know where she was. A few moments ago you said that. Now you know?"

"I'm not as I was before."

"You were dead before."

"Exactly."

"And now you're not."

"Just so."

Aaden pursed his lips, considered, decided. "I like you better alive."

Aliver smiled.

"What else do you know?"

"I can hear the maid returning," Aliver said, "with reinforcements."

The next moment Rhrenna rushed into the room, followed by a jumble of others—servants and physicians and officials. The room fell instantly into chaos.

CHAPTER
SIX

Kelis of Umae feared that the Santoth would be so conspicuous that they would announce their presence to all Talay. As he, Shen, Benabe, Naamen, and Leeka marched up from the Far South, the silent, hooded figures trailed behind them. They blurred when they moved and had faces only at a distance. Near at hand they became less distinct, not more. Though he spent days near them, Kelis was never sure how many there were. He tried counting them, but he got lost, found them blending together, realized he could not remember if he had counted that individual or not. Their silence was more unnerving than anything. It was not simply the absence of noise; it was as if they absorbed the sound around them. Because of this his head often snapped up, seeking them, feeling as if something had been stolen from the fullness of the world in the area they occupied.

Was he wrong for not trusting them? He could not say. Shen treated them like an escort of loved uncles. Aliver had spent time among these same phantoms. They had welcomed him, loved him, mourned him, and even avenged his death. No matter how horrible their violence in battle against Hanish Mein's forces, they had fought for Aliver. For the Akarans. They had saved countless Talayan and Acacian lives. That counted for a great deal. Kelis just wished they didn't make his skin crawl.

When they crossed the shallow river that marked the boundary of the Far South, Kelis tried his best to weave through the loose netting of small villages and herding communities without making human contact. Shen looked at him skeptically at times; Benabe did the same at others. He directed them without explaining. When they could not help but thread a rocky band of hills via a valley that spilled down into the Halaly town of Bida, Kelis took Naamen off from the others and conferred with him.

"I don't know what will happen when we pass through the town. Be ready for anything."

The young man touched his sheathed dagger with his strong arm. "I am."

"Shen thinks nothing of meeting other people, but even the Halaly have eyes to see. I don't know what they will make of the Santoth, or what the Santoth will do in return. If the people fear them, they may allow us to pass. Or not."

"Should we speak to the old man about this?"

"Leeka Alain is of two worlds now. He doesn't understand this one fully anymore. I would not share too much with him. Just be prepared to meet whatever happens. We're guardians. We don't make Shen's decisions; we just protect her as best we can, yes?"

Naamen said, "I can't remember when I had any other purpose."

Surprisingly, neither could Kelis.

The townspeople of Bida built their houses out of volcanic stone, irregular shapes that they secured together with a concrete made from ash-white sand. From a distance, the town looked like a herd of spotted ruminants grazing among the acacia trees. As they descended toward it Kelis and Naamen led the way, with Shen, Benabe, and Leeka a little distance behind. The shifting wake that were the Santoth was behind them all.

The first villagers they passed were herdsmen driving long-horned bulls. They had full, round Halaly faces, dark in a way different from the Talayans. Their expressionless stares offered neither hospitality nor aggression. They let their eyes flick back to the mother and daughter. And then they looked beyond them. One said something to the other in what must have been a local dialect. They carried on, switching at the bulls to keep them on course. Kelis turned to watch, amazed to see the three men and their bulls walk straight through the gathered host of sorcerers. The Santoth flowed forward without pause, allowing a pathway among them to open so that the villagers passed without even noticing them.

A little farther on, near the entrance to the town proper, a man peeled away from the defensive wall and stepped into their path. He held a spear, a twin for Kelis's own with its finger-thin shaft and long, flat spearhead, all one piece of iron. "Do you know thirst?" he asked.

Kelis answered, "I do, but there is water in the sky." The man nodded his acceptance of this truth, and Kelis added, "We are passing through. Simply passing through."

The man would have been within his rights to ask a host of questions in response. What were Talayans doing walking out of the Far South with a woman and a child? Why were they on Halaly land? Who were all those hooded figures lurking behind them? Any of these, simple as they were, would have been knotted traps to answer, and Kelis felt the responses he had already composed like dry sand on his tongue.

The sensation was such that it took him a moment to understand what the man was saying as he described where the public well was, offering them water if they needed it. He said that the market would close soon, but that if they hurried they could purchase food for their journey. Kelis stared at him. Naamen actually had to tug his arm to get him to move.

"That's strange," Naamen said, once they were among the houses of the village.

"What is?" Benabe asked. "That we're being followed by a host of undead ancient sorcerers? Or that nobody seems to see them?"

"I told you nothing bad would happen," Shen piped.

They passed through the village drawing no more curiosity than a small group of strangers would normally merit. They took water from the deep well. It was clear and sweet. In the market stalls they purchased twists of dried antelope meat, powdered kive, leaves of bitter tea, and a long chain of purple peppers that Naamen wore around his neck like jewelry. Benabe chose beads to string into a bracelet for Shen.

All the while the Santoth trailed them. Unseen by the villagers, they crowded the streets, wove around and through stalls, brushed past people who gave them no more notice than they would the touch of a breeze.

Kelis tried not to look at them, but it was hard not to. The Santoth took more notice of the villagers than the villagers did of them. One Santoth stopped in the entranceway of a hut and stared in for a long, chilling moment before moving on. A few others seemed to fall out of the collective flow and linger among the shop stalls, running their shrouded hands across the food items. One stood just inches in front of a talking woman, the hooded figure so close that the woman's breath ruffled the sorcerer's hood. Kelis's heart beat faster than if he had been running.

One child suddenly spun around and ran into the wall of Santoth. He went right through them, and the Santoth walked forward with only a ripple of disturbance to mark the boy's impact. It was only after, when Kelis caught sight of him again, that the child stood, touching his chest with the fingers of one hand, looking around, puzzled. Kelis kept the group moving. His heartbeat did not slow until they were well away from the village, moving into the safety of the plains once again.

❋

The sight of Umae glowing gray under moonlight was the most tranquilly beautiful thing Kelis had seen in ages. His home. His base for so many years, where his family still resided, a place filled with memories—including many of Áliver. He approached it alone, having left the others a few days' journey away. Fearing Sinper Ou's interference, he did not want them anywhere near the town. If anything happened to him—if he did not return at a set time—the others were to carry on north at all haste.

He walked into the sleeping town like a thief, which is just what the village dogs would take him for if they heard, saw, or smelled him. He circled around so that the wind blew his scent away from the village. He knew the route to Sangae's enclosure and made his way to it, in and out of the shadows, around huts, and along storehouse walls, stealthily, stopping often to listen to the night sounds. He passed right by his mother's garden wall, running his hand over the sunbaked bricks and whispering a greeting to her. The dog that confronted him as he passed the mouth of Adi Vayeen's hut he had known from its birth. He chirruped and swept his hand out in the greeting he often used with canines. The dog found his hand and pressed against his leg. Kelis scratched it for a time.

Despite all the familiarity, Kelis's fingers trembled as he stood in the lane beside Sangae's sleeping structure. He plucked the thin curtain, a hanging wall swaying on the night's breath. He flicked it with a motion meant to mimic a gust of wind. In the time it took the curtain to fall back into place, he scanned the room. He crawled through the opening.

Sangae lay sleeping on his side on a woven mat. He was alone, as was his way in recent years, since his first wife had died and he had found most restful sleep in solitude. Kelis had only moved a step closer when the old man's eyes snapped open. They fixed on Kelis, who must have been a featureless silhouette against the star-touched fabric of the opening.

Kelis said, "Father, forgive the night its darkness."

The old man took a moment to respond. "I do, for the night air is cool. Kelis?"

"Me."

Sangae pushed himself up to sitting and received Kelis's embrace. He squeezed him tight for a moment and then pulled back. He ran his fingers over the younger man's features. "You are living?"

"I am. We all are. Shen as well."

"Light a lamp so we can see," Sangae whispered, motioning toward a tea lamp on the floor beside him. "Keep it low. There is danger here. No, let's move farther inside first."

A few minutes later, the two men sat facing each other on low stools in the compound's storage shed. The lamp cast a yellow glow that etched their features from below; around them were the large vases, shelves of household goods, and stacks of grain sacks. Sangae had called softly for his dogs and tethered them to guard the shed.

Kelis told of their strange journey to the Far South. Sangae listened, brewing a tiny pot of tea above the lamp as he did so. Kelis found words pouring out of him. He had not realized he had held so much in. Running from the laryx pack with Shen strapped to his back. Mountains that moved around them, as if the land were sliding under their feet instead of they moving over it. Flocks of birds that flew above them like thrown darts, only to crash down and die. The way the peaks just ended one morning, and the famous general, Leeka Alain, stood waiting for them, alone in a desert. Walking still farther south, until the Santoth appeared, stones whirling into sand and taking Shen with them for a time, then bringing her back and announcing that they would all march to confront the queen.

"That was wise," the old man said, when Kelis explained that he had left the rest of the party in hiding well away from the village. "Sinper Ou has spies everywhere. Even here, I fear. He never trusted you. Ioma even less so. Do you know he began sending spies across the plains just after you left? It ate at him that he had let the girl go. He only let me come home because he thought he would catch me at something."

Sangae poured a small saucer of bush tea and offered it to Kelis. The man took it and sipped. "Ou has many friends, Kelis. And many more wish to be his friend. Money such as his has bought many eyes."

"Shen has friends of her own. The Santoth, I mean. They have come with us. They want to stop Corinn from doing harm with her magic. They feel it, Shen told me, and know she is opening rips in the world or something."

Sangae worked his mouth, but found nothing to say.

"I doubt any could take Shen from them against their will. I don't know what the Santoth are. I don't know what they really want. I have been with them weeks now, but they don't reveal themselves. Shen trusts them, though, but—"

"Then you must, too."

"I don't," he heard himself say. "I've tried, but I can't trust them."

"Why?"

Kelis clicked his tongue off the roof of his mouth. "I don't know. They feel . . . wrong. They never speak a word."

"Because their tongues are dangerous. You know that. Perhaps the time has come for them to rejoin the world. If Corinn could teach them . . . she might become incredibly powerful. Another Tinhadin. That would have frightened me before, but, listen, there is something else." Sangae placed his old, coarse hand over Kelis's and squeezed. "Forgive me for not saying this first. I wanted to hear your words before clouding your mind with this. It may not be true, but many believe it. People are saying that Aliver lives. They say Corinn brought him back to life using the song. Word came just last week. Anywhere north of here has heard already. Pilgrims are rushing to Acacia."

So was a portion of Kelis's mind. His thoughts flew out of him in such a rush that his body was left momentarily empty.

"There is no better time to take Shen and the Santoth to Acacia. It may resolve everything. Sinper Ou is still a danger, but if you get Shen to her father, he will be no threat. You must take her, just as they asked you to. Stay in your small group. Keep the Santoth hidden. Join the pilgrims converging on Acacia and announce Shen directly to Aliver."

"And if he has not really returned?"

Sangae worked his fingers into the wrinkled skin of his forehead. "Pray to the Giver that he has. I feel that the fate of the world depends on him once more."

CHAPTER
SEVEN

Standing before a gathering of Bocoum's merchants, Barad the Lesser knew exactly what he wanted to say. He had rehearsed the words inside his head both waking and in his dreams. He would tell them this: "The Akaran dynasty was founded on acts of evil. Deep in the cushion of the royal chairs is the blood of two brothers slain by another brother's hand. It's a nation built on the split between old friends, one that sent the other into exile. It's the product of a man driven so mad by the power of his sorcery that he banished his companions from the land to punish them for raising him up. A people has but two choices when faced with such dreadful truth: deny it and live sucking at the tit of the lie like infants or face it with the open eyes of adults. And if you face it, what then? Only one possibility. You must dismantle the lie. You must tear down all the things built on it, for they are corrupted and will bring you down ere you look away."

The merchants listened, applauded him, praised the queen, and thanked him for his words.

Days later, speaking to the rich of Manil, he decided to say this: "You may ask me, 'Why must I change what has worked so well? Why must I cast my wealth and pride and history onto the ground?' I say to you that you have no wealth. You have no pride. You have no true understanding of history. These things you cling to are vapors in guise of truth. A man cannot eat vapor. A woman cannot wrap vapor around herself and find warmth. A child cannot wake in the night and rush to vapor for solace. And you may say to me, 'My mother lived and died like this. My grandfather lived and died like this. The world thinks my nation is supreme. What madness that you want me to turn from that.' How do I rebut those words? With a certainty. That certainty is that each and every crime and lie and falsehood will be returned to you with interest. You may say, 'Prove it.' I have only to point north to do so. That is what treads toward us across the ice. Not foreign invaders. Not the whim of fate. Not horrors set against us without reason. What treads toward us are the living forms of our years and years of folly and injustice."

The rich of Manil offered him toasts in his honor.

Before a meeting of the Acacian Senate in Alecia—called into session specifically to hear him—he intended to roar, and did: "There is but one thing to do! We must tear apart the lies. We must shred the swaddling clothes we were born into, pull back from the delusion, stand naked and afraid for just long enough to reorder the world as it rightly should be. It will be hard. It will be painful. It will be a trial like none we have faced. But we will emerge closer to the true beings we all wish to be. We will be Kindred."

Among the jubilant faces that applauded him as he exited the chamber, Barad saw Hunt, the Kindred representative from Aos. He was still, close-lipped, and grave. Barad wanted to rush to him, but instead he walked by, turning his face away as he neared. Why did I do that? he wondered, even as his feet moved him away.

When he was done with each of these speeches, when he had no more words and his bass voice went silent, when he dropped his animated gestures and looked through his stone eyes at the faces his words had worked miracles on . . . he knew that he had not said any of the things he had intended to. Instead, he had praised the queen. He had sung her praises and reinforced the empire's shackles. Somehow, she controlled each word spoken through his mouth. Each destination she had chosen. Each time he turned his strides in a specific direction it was following a path she had laid out.

At times the words he uttered were his own, but only for short moments. On occasion barbed comments and asides and even criticisms of the queen escaped his lips. In his first days he had thought he could build on these, string them together so that he might explain his true sentiments. But he managed only to weave a folksy, familiar humor in with the comments.

Nor could he express how much he loved the people to whom he preached, something he was reminded of at every turn. He recognized the faces of the farmers north of Danos. They were the same ones among whom he had shepherded King Grae of Aushenia. Now, as he spoke to them, he could see in their faces how they struggled to twin his former message with whatever it was he now espoused. In Bocoum an elderly woman fixed him with her bloodshot eyes, her face ridged with some great effort of comprehension. He so wanted to explain everything to her. Instead, he had pressed his lips together as he turned and walked away.

Watching as his boat sailed out of Alecia's harbor, he saw the rocks from which children swam with dolphins. He caught a splash of spray on his fingertips and touched them to his lips. This was a land to love, peopled by souls who had never yet been allowed to be fully themselves. Though he returned to Acacia full of dread, even the sight of the isle itself reminded him of this. To his eyes, the island and the sky, the moving sea and the leaping creatures in it were all gradations of stone, different textures of a granite world. Solid stone here. Liquid stone there. A stone as transparent as vapor there, and stone as glistening as a wet dolphin's back there. He saw with a clarity no different from before, but it was a clarity of sand and rock, of white and gray and black.

In his dreams the world was as it had been, sometimes so vibrantly colored that he gasped himself awake with the joy of seeing it. Awake into his gray curse of world. The way Acacia thrust up through the turquoise sea. Layer upon terraced layer climbing ever higher, so full of color, each spire a jewel trying to outshine its peers as it pierced the belly of the sky. How could the heart of a nation so corrupt be so terribly beautiful? How could a world he had lived in for so many years continue to astonish, confound, defeat him? How could he see one thing and remember another each and every minute of his imprisoned freedom?

It was maddening, but he should not have been surprised. The queen had told him it would be this way. Weeks ago, when she leaped at him and grasped his head in her hands, he had lifted his hand to smash her. He would have done it, except that she slipped her fingers into his eyes and pressed. On her lips and in those fingers hummed a power that took away the connection between his will and his ability to act on it. His anger did not die within him, but the fist raised to crush her recognized no kinship with it. It hung there a moment, until the fingers opened and the hand came to rest gently on her arm.

She whispered, "Your mind is mine."

In answer, he formed curses behind his lips, refutations, a litany of condemnation. When his lips moved they said, "Yes." He heard this and screamed "No!" but his lips said "Yes."

No longer a pariah, Barad could wander wherever he wished in the palace, even up to the higher terraces near the royal quarters. He was trapped, but to all the world he looked to be a free man. He could follow his feet wherever they cared to take him. Clearly, the queen had given instructions that he was to be indulged like some dignitary of high rank when he was on the island. But he could not form actions from any desires contrary to the queen's wishes. He might decide to leave the island and flee into hiding, but he would forget his mission after only a few steps. One time he even imagined his own death. Instead of using the knife he had chosen for the purpose on his own flesh, he peeled an apple.

Because of this curse, he was sitting on a bench in the center of the maze work of canals, listening to the gurgling fountain and watching the slow-moving piscine forms gliding through the water beneath him. He was exactly where the queen wished him to be. He knew it, and he could do nothing about it.

Rhrenna sat beside him, scribbling notes on a sheaf of parchment. "A successful trip, I would say. The queen will be pleased with you."

Barad pulled his gaze from the water and rolled his eyes toward her. The effort of moving the stone orbs was considerable. It fatigued him more than moving his large frame through the world, and if he moved them too much he developed headaches that lasted for days. There was an advantage to them, though. At times they saw with a clarity his old eyes never had. It was not a matter of visual acuity, really. It was more that they translated the truth more completely, as if he read emotions and thoughts as clearly as he saw the features that hid them.

He cleared his throat to avoid responding to her comment. He would have told her that he hated the queen, not cared that she be pleased. He would have spat at her and called her a servant of suppression, a deluded tool of an evil mistress. But none of it would come out as he intended.

"Did you meet any of your former conspirators? Any of the Kindred, as you called them?"

"In Manil, yes," he heard himself answer. "Hunt came down from Aos."

"And?"

"He thought me insane," Barad said.

Rhrenna smiled, an expression that pressed her pale blue eyes nearly closed. "Yes, but for an insane man you speak such wisdom. I'm sure that's what affronted him."

"What affronted him," Barad said, "is that the Kindred has crumbled. He blames me. Word of my support for the queen spreads beyond me like a disease."

"More like a cure, a contagious cure." Rhrenna folded her hands on her writing board and studied the sky. Thin strips of cloud scalloped the blue. The air had a touch of cold in it, the chill that passed for autumn on the island. "The queen will be pleased with you when she returns."

Barad noticed that one of the slivers of hard charcoal Rhrenna wrote with had fallen to the bench. While she still looked up, he placed his large hand over it. "When will she return?"

"A week or two at most. Her campaign was a complete success. I got a bird last night. She is recovering from her exertions and will soon be on her way back. She would have been back sooner had she not fallen ill after destroying the Numrek. It was quite taxing on her. You should hear the things people are saying about her now. She destroys whole armies. None can stand against her."

"Is that true? Can none stand against her?"

Rhrenna wrinkled her sharp, small nose before answering. "None that I know of."

She massacred your people, he thought. He knew better than to try and say it, so he just held on to the thought and stared his stone gaze. He tightened his hand around the charcoal until he held it in his fist.

"Don't look at me like that," Rhrenna said. "You're not the first person to have to bend to her will. We all do. You should find peace with it. I have. Barad, we live in truly wondrous times." Rhrenna set her parchments to the side and stood. "You may not love our queen, but if anyone is capable of leading us now, she is. Look, we have princely visitors."

Aliver and Aaden entered the gardens. Barad had not yet seen Aliver, but he knew him instantly. Uncle and nephew walked side by side, talking softly, with the winged creature a few steps behind them. The princes saw them, waved, and quickened their pace. The creature hung back, moving off along the edge of the canals, peering into the water as she stepped gently, like some benevolent hunter. Barad knew she was a wonder spoken of all around the empire, but it was the risen prince that truly fascinated him.

He looked just as Barad had imagined him. Young. Slim and leanly muscled, his posture upright and his motions casually regal. He wore the same face Barad had seen breaking through his mist dreams years ago, as the rebellion against Hanish Mein grew in power. He knew that when he spoke it would be with a voice he already knew, the same one that had encouraged him with the power of the truth. If any man had ever been his king, this one had.

Barad did what he did then without even knowing he was about to. Barad the Lesser, he who had spoken for years of the fallacy of monarchal rule, fell forward. He landed hard upon his knees and bent farther still, until he pressed his face against Aliver's thin boots. He heard the prince bid him rise.

"That's not necessary," he said. "Really, Barad, you have no need to bow to me."

"He should too bow," the young prince, Aaden, said. "He was my mother's enemy. We could have killed him!"

"*Was*," Rhrenna stressed. "He was our enemy but is not anymore."

"No," Aliver said. He touched Barad on the shoulder, worked his fingers under him, and pulled him to stand. "He was never an enemy. Not truly."

Barad looked up at the prince's face. He wanted to tell him that he had heard his voice in his dreams many times. Years ago, his voice had saved him, had given him purpose, had spurred him to rise to revolt in Kidnaban. He wanted to admit all these things. Instead, he said, "Praise to the queen, for she has brought back the dead."

This seemed to underwhelm Aliver. "Barad," he started, but then thought better of it, glancing at Aaden. "Yes, praise the queen. She brings much life, doesn't she?"

"You should see how she made water in the desert," Aaden piped.

Barad took his seat on the bench again and sat listening to the easy banter between Aliver and Aaden, with Rhrenna playing the third. Aaden reported that he had just shown his uncle Elya's eggs. They were near to hatching, he thought. He even saw them move inside the hard casing of their shells. "They're just waiting for Mother to return," he declared.

The thought of that return ran a shiver of dread through Barad, but he knew it did not show on the outside.

Aliver reminisced about when he was a boy and had swum the tunnels that connect one pool to the next. He had discovered that the pools were all part of one system. If he held his breath long enough, he could vanish in one area, swim through the darkness, and emerge in another canal, one that looked from above to be separate.

"I could do that," Aaden said. "My breath is good."

"Oh, I don't know," Aliver said, sizing him up. "I was older than you before I tried it."

"But I'm a better swimmer."

"How, exactly, do you know that?"

"I just do."

Aliver made a sour face. "Perhaps a wager is in order." Aaden jumped at the suggestion.

"It's too cold!" Rhrenna said. "He'll catch a chill. It's nearly winter, Your Highness."

Aliver blinked at her and whispered, "The pools hold the summer's heat a little longer than you'd expect. One last swim won't hurt anyone."

As the two princes talked through the details, Aliver pointing and gesturing, pacing a bit as he recalled the way the tunnels worked, Barad wondered why the queen had brought him back to life. Surely not just to play with her son. Was there some part of her that was truly willing to face Aliver's ideology of the world? He could not imagine that. Perhaps she had changed him already, made him into yet another mouthpiece to speak her words. He saw none of the hesitation with words that he himself felt, no hint of frustration. Barad peered at him, bringing the full pressure of his stone gaze on him.

There was something beneath the skin of his face. Something not physical and yet tangibly there, features that slipped beneath Aliver's façade like another face pressed against the thin barrier of his skin. Just for a moment, and then it was gone. Beneath the prince's face there was another face. Or another version of his face.

"All right, then, Aaden, let's settle this bet," Aliver said. He began unbuttoning his shirt. In nothing but his breeches a few moments later, Aliver dove into the water, much to Aaden's delight. The boy leaped in, so near the prince he would have landed on him, had the man not ducked under water.

Barad turned to Rhrenna. He tried to say out loud the words his mind would not let him form in his head. He knew what he had seen and should have been able to speak it. It was Corinn's doing. Another abomination. It was just there. If he could point it out to her, she would see it, too. He grasped her by the wrist and said, with all the gravity he could muster, "The queen's work is a blessing to us all."

No! That's not it! He tried to slam his hand down on the stone, but only managed to gesture vaguely toward the princes.

Rhrenna nodded. "Isn't it amazing? Life from death. Makes you wonder what else Corinn will do." She gently pulled free of his grasp, gathered her things, and walked away, crisp in her steps, looking official once more.

Alone on the bench, Barad remembered the charcoal. He was not a very skilled writer, having learned to read only later in life, but he knew enough to scratch a brief message. He began to write, *Prince Aliver, we are both enslaved!* He imagined letters forming on the stone. He saw them side by side, spelling out his true intent. When he finished, he could feel his heart beating in his chest. This could do it. He had only to wave Aliver over and have him read the message. That would break through. He knew it would. He tried to catch Aliver's eye, but the prince did not see him. He would have to stand. He did so, glancing back at his message as he rose.

He froze, only half standing. The words he had written were: *Prince Aliver, we are both saved!*

Barad lowered himself back to the stone. He smeared the words with the flat of his hand and let the charcoal fall from his fingers. His heart, which had been so profoundly happy a moment before, seemed to die within him. He watched the princes swim and splash each other, dive, and chase fish. Aaden shouted the impromptu instructions of a newly imagined tunnel game. Aliver added to them with enthusiasm, looking like a boy of exactly the same age.

Watching Aliver's face as he treaded water, Barad saw the vague motion beneath his skin again. Aaden could not see it. Nobody could. Only he with his accursed stone eyes. Not even Aliver knew. He doesn't know that he is trapped inside himself, and I can't tell him. I can't tell anybody.

CHAPTER
EIGHT

Melio Sharratt watched Clytus exit the tavern. The thatch hanging from the roof brushed his hair as he emerged, leaving him no more or less neatly coiffed for it. Clytus strode over and stood beside Melio. With his thick arms crossed and shoulders bunched with muscle and his weathered face one notch down from a full scowl, he seemed more like a figure to fear than like one who needed to be cautious. Once he had been one of Dariel's close friends, a brigand then and still now. He said, "He's here."

Melio asked, "Will he talk?"

Clytus cleared his throat and brushed the hard knuckles of one hand along his chin. "Yeah, he'll talk," he answered, sliding his gaze over to study a group of children playing a betting game with seashells.

Melio nearly said that nobody on the street was paying them the slightest bit of attention, but this was not his territory. He had been out of that since Corinn sent him south on the *Ballan*, all the way around the Far South and back up along the western coast of Talay in the company of some of Dariel's old brigand crew. Clytus captained the ship now, with old Nineas still as the chief pilot, and Geena in command of the crew. Strange the way the passing of time made enemies friends, folding one thing in upon another so that it was hard to imagine the old order of things. Dariel, going by the name Spratling, had once pirated the coast south of here, a criminal in the eyes of Hanish Mein's authority. Now he was a prince of the empire, and the brigands who had once been his lawless crew sailed in service to the crown. Although now he was an absent prince, missing in a faraway land, perhaps no longer among the living . . .

"All right, come in," Clytus said grudgingly, as if it were against his better judgment. "Let's get this over with."

As he slipped beneath the overhanging thatch, Melio reflexively grasped for the hilt of his sword, to rest his hand there and feel the tilt of the sheath trailing him like a tail. He had to settle for gripping his leather belt instead. His sword was back on the *Ballan* with the rest of his things. Prominent weapons were not allowed in the taverns of the Coastal Towns. He did, however, carry a smaller one, unseen by the eyes of the tavern guard who looked them over as they passed.

Melio followed Clytus back through the dim room, lit only by the candles at each table and torches along the rear wall, where young men poured ale. The air oozed with the scent of it, mixed with pipe smoke and the pungency of garlic.

The table they stopped at was no different from the others, a circle centered around a thick-wicked candle. The yellow glow lit two men in sharp highlights. One of them rose and moved away when they arrived, without so much as a glance up. Clytus turned and followed the man, only turning back when he had seated himself at another table. The second man had stayed put. Large bone earrings, shaped like primitive fishhooks, dangled from his ears. His beard covered only his chin and had been oiled to a curving tip, something he kept shaped with caressing fingers. His face, behind all that, was forgettable. If Melio had turned away and had to describe him, he would only be able to recall the earrings, beard, the oily fingers.

"This is Kartholomé Gilb. Formerly a small ship pilot for the league. Now . . . what are you now?"

"I'm between employers at the moment. Working for myself."

"A brigand, then."

Kartholomé dipped his head in acceptance of the title. "Clytus already told me who you are, Sharratt. If you want a drink you'll have to get it yourself. Ale only. We don't drink the league's wine here." When neither man moved, he leaned back on his stool and motioned with his hand that they should feel free to sit.

"So . . . Clytus says you've come all the way from the monkey's pucker itself. What brings you to Tivol? If it's whores you want, you've come to the right place. Though I'm disappointed. I take it the princess doesn't do the . . . interesting things. Royalty can be like that. With a little coin any girl in town will play the princess for you, though."

Melio threw an angry look at Clytus. "I thought you said he was ready to talk."

"He is. Kartholomé, stop shifting crap with your tongue and let's get on to what we discussed."

"But it's not every day one meets the mighty steed a princess rides. He doesn't look so—"

Melio lunged across the table so quickly that he had completed his attack and sat back in his seat before Kartholomé knew what had happened. Kartholomé touched his nose, the tip of which bloomed with a thin line of blood that quickly began to drip onto the table. He murmured a curse, but seemed more impressed than angry or pained. Melio's hand lay on the wood, resting over the hilt of the short knife he had just cut Kartholomé with.

Clytus glanced around the tavern, and then broke the short silence. "Calm heads. Calm heads. Look, Kartholomé, Melio Sharratt isn't only a Marah; he trains Marah. Understand that? He moves different, yeah? Walks upright and is . . . a little delicate with his hands." Melio cocked an eyebrow. "But don't think that just because he talks like a toff that he couldn't remove your liver, cut it up, and feed it to you before you knew what you were eating. He's not to be trifled with, and the princess is not a topic he's interested in discussing." Clytus leaned forward. Through gritted teeth, he said, "He's here in the service of the queen."

Kartholomé shrugged. "I was just making conversation." He pinched the tip of his nose between his thumb and forefinger and seemed, if anything, more curiously amiable than he had been before receiving the injury. "All right, assuming you let me keep my nose hairs, let's talk about what you want to."

"I want to know what happened to Prince Dariel in the Other Lands."

"You don't ask much." Kartholomé let go of his nose and dabbed it a few times, then put pressure back on it. "What I heard is that the prince was an offering. A deal sweetener. The Auldek just weren't in the mood for making nice. Grouchy buggers they are."

Melio stared at him. "What in the Giver's name are you talking about?"

Kartholomé rolled his eyes and began again. "Fine. Try to follow, though. Sire Neen didn't care a pear about Dariel, or about the Akarans. No leagueman does. He also didn't give a pear about the Lothan Aklun. Hates them, truth be told. Neen came up with a grand plan to get rid of both of them. Kill the Lothan Aklun with some poison or something, and then he would go direct to the Auldek. You see it? Figured he would control both sides of the trade—quota or mist or whatever it was going to be. But, like I said, the Auldek didn't like the look of him. Their chieftain chopped Neen limb from limb and took a bath in his blood. Wouldn't have minded seeing that. You?"

"You see any of this with your own eyes?"

"Nah. I never went across. I worked the Outer Isles, the Thousands, mostly. That doesn't mean I don't know what happened. Thing like that, people talk."

"And Dariel?"

Kartholomé, finally satisfied his nose was no longer bleeding, released it and sat back. "The prince. He was there when it happened. Neen was offering him to the Auldek, sort of a token of good faith. 'Here, have a prince. Do with him what you will.' He's probably dead. Though—mind, I don't really credit this—one of the Ishtat who survived claimed to have seen someone grab Dariel. Not Auldek. Not Ishtat. Just someone. Guy that looked like a boar. He was standing near the prince, he said, and the guy knocked into him as he passed."

"Do you believe this man?"

Kartholomé dipped his eyes toward the table for a second. "You going to cut me again?"

Melio realized he had tightened his grip around his knife's small handle. He released it, lifted his palm, and tented his fingers over the blue metal of the blade. "Can I speak to him?"

"Not a chance. He's Ishtat. He talked too much even talking to me, but they were all spooked. Pretty big to-do if you ask me. I wouldn't know where to find him even if I wanted to, and he wouldn't talk to you anyway. Not a chance."

"How do you come by this information? I thought the league never let anyone get out of their fold. You shouldn't even exist to be here talking to me."

"The league scrubs their own decks. No doubt about it. The

league used to use contractors for interisland stuff. Not any-more. They're keeping everything in the family now. I just got lucky, managed to get away before they permanently retired me. If they knew I was alive, I wouldn't be." He grinned. "They think I'm dead, and I'm happy with that. Look, Marah trainer, I've got more reason to doubt you than the other way around. I'm only talking because I know Clytus." After a moment, he added, "And because I knew Dariel."

In answer to Melio's questioning look, Clytus nodded.

Kartholomé smeared drops of semidried blood onto the tabletop with his finger. "Anyway, there are more than a few reasons to hate the league. I could show you a few if you're up for it. You all in the Inner Sea have no idea what goes on out here. At least, I hope you don't."

"You know I don't. That's why I'm here."

"All right, then. Let's go fishing tomorrow. You'll have to show me that knife trick, though. That was something. Didn't even see it coming."

"What trick?" Melio smiled his crooked smile. "I just mis-judged the distance."

***

Melio had been on his share of dubious vessels in the Inner Sea—and even rafted out as far as the Vumu Archipelago, where he had found Mena that wonderful day years ago. Still, when they rowed through the breakers off Tivol the next morning he had to swallow hard to keep his breakfast down. The boat was too small. He could jump from gunwale to gunwale. It took—what—eight strides to teeter from the stern to the bow? Pow-ered by a single square sail, the boat skimmed across the water at a good clip. Faster than he liked, considering the size of the Gray Slopes' swell.

Geena from the *Ballan* joined them, making for a crew of four, a crowd in the tiny fishing skiff but the right number to look like they were working the yellowgill that passed between the mainland and the Outer Isles. That, in fact, is what they did. They spent the afternoon fishing the current that flowed through the channel, tacking into the northerly wind the whole time.

League transports passed in the distance several times. Once a patrol clipper skimmed the horizon to the north. They were in a loose flotilla of fishing boats, though, and the clipper paid them no mind. Melio lost himself in the work that was their cover, baiting hooks, throwing out lines, keeping them from tangling, and then hauling them back in turn. The tiny eel-like fish he had crooked onto the hooks came back as lean slivers the length of a man's arm, sparkling silver. There was no sign of the trait that gave them their name until they were unhooked and gasping in the water-sloshed bottom of the vessel. Each flare of the gills revealed a bright burst of yellow, a vibrant hue that would have made a beautiful flower.

Without knowing where the thought came from, Melio remembered Mena. He had letters from her wrapped in oiled paper and buckled tight within a case in his satchel back on the *Ballan*. He had read through them many times before. For in the space of the reading he heard her voice and could imagine where she was and knew her to be safe. That illusion held only when the written words spoke in her voice inside his head. Now, on a small boat in the salt air of a vast ocean, he knew that she could not have imagined he would be here. So how could he have any true idea where she was, what she was doing, or who with? Alive or dead? He hated it that he did not know. He should just be able to feel her. She should be able to speak his name and he should be able to answer. What did miles matter between two people in love?

The league brig appeared as if it had emerged right out of the water's depths. To the north of them, heading southwest. It looked to be at a safe passing distance, but as it grew nearer its trajectory skimmed it closer. Figures appeared at the bow. The glint of glass catching the light betrayed their spyglass.

Kartholomé growled, "Bastards."

"What? They've noticed us? They're too big to—"

"Bastards!" The pilot leaped around the boat, adjusting the sails. Clytus leaned on the rudder, changing their tack so abruptly Melio nearly pitched overboard. Cursing, he spread himself low in the boat, half soaked by the warm water sloshing among the fish and tackle and salt-caked old ropes.

"A nervous bunch, brigands," Melio mumbled. Looking back at the galley, he noticed that a school of dolphins leaped and dove in the wave surge pushed out from the prow. Beautiful. Then the galley's bow veered toward them in earnest. Sails bowed as they caught a larger portion of the wind. The ship leaned with the turn, a sudden change by the big ship's standards. Nothing to account for it as far as Melio could see from peering over the gunwale, especially as it brought them churning directly toward the fishing vessel. "Ah . . ."

Geena appeared beside him. "Grab on to something," she said, worming her way under the seat slats.

"Grab . . ." He did not need to be told twice. He worked his hands under a beam, pressed against others with his feet. Like that, on his back, he could not see the water anymore, but he could see the frantic motions and darting eyes of the two seamen. The vast rise of the galley bore down on them. As tall as any building he had ever seen, it came yawning at a slow rhythm out of time with the speed it traveled.

"Furl the sail!" Clytus roared.

Whether or not Kartholomé managed this Melio did not get

to see. The hull of the ship pushed before it a curling fury of water. The swell lifted the small boat up. The wave curled over them, terrifyingly smooth, glass green and translucent, frothed across the crest with white. Three dolphins leaped out of the glass and over the boat. Beautiful. Then the wave struck. The vessel went over. The hull bucked and the world tilted and water rushed in like a monster made of liquid muscle. Melio closed his eyes, held his breath, and clung as the boat churned over and over, jolting and shuddering when it contacted the hull of the great ship. For a time all was black motion. His lungs began to burn. Water yanked and smacked him. It felt like actual hands and fists battered him, trying to get him to let go.

When the boat popped into the air again, it did so with the bow pointed toward the sky, twirling. As water drained toward the stern, Melio clung to one of the low benches. Just as he began to doubt he could hold on any longer, the bow smashed back down. Geena got jolted away from her hold. One side of the boat dipped, and a gush of water washed in. It swept her with it, dragging her along the gunwale. She fought it, clawing for purchase. She began to slide overboard, one arm upraised and flailing, while the tongue of the sea slurped her in. Melio caught her by the wrist. He braced his feet against the submerged gunwale and hauled back with everything he had. She smashed into him. Their limbs entwined as Melio scrabbled back toward the rear storage compartment, Geena in his grip. She understood and crammed in next to him. The two of them knotted together and stuck fast just as the boat passed into the swirling chaos rushing around the galley's rear end.

Again the small boat's stern submerged, making the bow pirouette in the air above them. Melio watched it against the sky. Among the falling debris, water glistened as it dropped.

The mast had snapped in half and the sail hung like a dead thing. A tide of hissing, bubbling air rose around them. Melio tried to breathe, but the air was foaming water in his mouth. He spit it out, but it rushed in again. He spit it out; it rushed in again. He gave up trying. He closed his eyes and clung to Geena.

CHAPTER
NINE

It could have been worse. Mór had been angry, fuming and spitting venom, on the verge of using those stubby nails of hers to rip new tracks across Dariel's face. She danced through an improvised tribute to her anger. One of her eyelids twitched out a rant of its own. By the time it all ended Dariel had admitted his fault and claimed to be chastened. He swore he would never do something as foolish as sneaking alone into Amratseer again. Eventually, Mór left her exasperation at Dariel's feet. She ordered the others into motion and she told the prince to leave the pups behind. He didn't. Chastened, yes, but not without some resolve.

It took them a full day to circumambulate Amratseer. By the second morning they cleared the semiorder of the agricultural region outside the city and plunged into Inàfeld Forest. It extended all the way north as far as anyone had been, hemmed in at the west by the mountains of Rath Batatt. Tam claimed that they were following a route of sorts, but it was one of many that the People had developed over the years. Not wanting to leave a traceable path to the Sky Isle, they used a variety of trails, each of them trodden on rarely enough that they betrayed few signs of actually being trails.

They wormed over and beneath tree roots, along fallen old-growth trunks, and through dank waterways, stepping carefully on the moss-heavy stones. The forest grew thick enough that the sky was only a distant idea. The pups did not make it any easier. Fully half the terrain was unmanageable for them. Before long Dariel had given up on encouraging them forward and instead carried them in a sack slung over his back. When he complained about the weight of them one afternoon, Birké took one and walked with it cradled like a baby in his arm. "You'll have to name them, you know?"

"Yes, I guess I will."

"You must geld them. Not yet, but before too long."

"Cut their balls off? No, I don't think that's—"

"Scoop it up, Dariel," Birké cut in. "They're cathounds. Male ones. The Anet used them to hunt lions. In six months they'll be almost as tall as you are. At least they'll be lighter without their balls."

"Be sane! I saw their mother. She was—"

"Young. They birth children young. And the females are smaller anyway. No, Dariel, believe me, you've got more on your hands than you know. Snip them. I could do it for you if you like." Birké made his fingers into shears and demonstrated the ease of the action. He smiled. What should have been fearsome—the thick hair that covered his entire face, the canine incisors that shone savagely through his grin—usually managed to cheer Dariel. Not so this time.

Dariel reached for the pup. "I don't mind carrying him after all."

He still carried them both an hour later when they stepped into a clearing in the woods created by an enormous fallen tree. A man stood atop it, arms crossed and still. Blinking in the unaccustomed bright light, it took Dariel a moment to believe that he was really there. Mór shouted something to him in Auldek; the man responded and pointed to a route up onto the tree. Without a word of explanation, Mór led them up.

The man was slight of build. His head was clean-shaven, with a splattering of tattoos across his scalp, patterning that Dariel had not seen before. "So this is him?" the man asked, switching to Acacian. "There is much talk of him in Avina. The destroyer of the soul catcher. The Rhuin Fá." He studied the prince with a trader's critical eye, as if he were considering a purchase. "Funny, he just looks like common Shivith clan, not even ranked. I hope he is what he promises."

"I never promised anything," Dariel said. The pups churned in the sack, trying to get a view of the stranger. Dariel tried to stand without flinching, but they really did have sharp claws. "And I'm standing right in front of you. You could address me directly."

The man gave no sign that he heard him. "Last word from Avina was that the clans are squabbling and that league ships are patrolling the coastline. More each week. If this Dariel Akaran wishes to prove himself, he'll have ample opportunity, and soon."

Before Dariel could respond, Mór asked, "Tell me, messenger, why have you come?"

"With a message, of course." He drew himself up and spoke more formally. "I carry an elder within, a voice meant for your ears."

Mór said, "May the vessel never crack."

As she and the messenger moved away together, Dariel unslung his sack. He poured the pups out onto the wide tree trunk, across which they surged with bumbling enthusiasm, greeting one person and then the next and then starting over again.

"What's this about?" Dariel asked Birké, once the others had settled down to wait.

Birké stroked a puppy's head. "The council sent him with a message."

"About what?"

"We'll see shortly," Tam said, laying out a spread of hard crackers and cucumbers on the tree bark. He set out a wooden bowl. Above it, he used his knife to cut off the bottom of a plee-berry, a nondescript fruit, brown, slightly hairy, and oblong. The liquid inside it gushed out as he squeezed the length of it. The juice looked like a collection of frog eggs, blue tinted, slimy. The first time Dariel had seen it he had gagged and stared in horror as the others drank it with relish.

"Some of your favorite drink, Dariel?"

After having made a show of being disgusted by the frog-egg look of the fruit pulp, Dariel had to admit he had grown to rather like it. It was like drinking liquid sugar, and the strange texture of the seeds had actually become his favorite aspect of it. He took a slurp from the offered bowl, rolling the slick orbs around on his tongue.

Tam pulled his tiny instrument from his pack and began plucking it. Dariel watched Mór and the messenger, but could gather little from their distant exchange. He thought he saw stiffening in Mór's spine, an indication of anger, but the next moment it melted into something softer as she gestured with her hands.

"What's he mean he has an elder within him?"

"It's quite a trick. Can't say I understand it, really." Birké pushed one of the pups into Dariel's arms. "Here, take your pup. I shouldn't handle them so much. I'll end up liking them. Have you named them yet?"

The pup climbed happily enough into Dariel's lap, churning in a circle around the geometry of his folded legs. Dariel stilled it with his hand, rubbed under its chin, and looked into its eyes. They were the same color as its fur, which was a reddish-brown, soft, short coat. Only the ridge along its back was different. There the hair bristled back against the grain, almost spiny. It was the only part of him not completely adorable. "I was thinking of this one as Scarlet."

"Scarlet?" Birké asked. "That's no name for a cathound!"

"No? What is, then?"

Birké did not hesitate. "Ripper. Killer. Punisher."

"Jaws of Death," Tam said.

"Devothrí-grazik," offered Anira. "It means 'Devoth's bane.'"

Tam said something in Auldek, pointing at the other pup, who had just tumbled over in an effort to lick his bottom. The others laughed. No one offered a translation.

A little later, they all stood as the two rejoined them. The messenger looked as pleased as ever, but Mór's lips pressed a new measure of annoyance between them. She barely opened them when she said, "The council has spoken. We have new instructions. From here we go to Rath Batatt. We seek the Watcher in the Sky Mount."

"Nâ Gâmen?" Birké asked, a measure of awe in his voice.

"Yes," Mór said. "Nâ Gâmen. Let's go. Time is more important now than ever."

Dariel came close to asking who Nâ Gâmen was, but the group was already in motion.

❋

The mountains that the People called Rath Batatt sprouted like bony crests along the backs of horrible, reptilian beasts. Rank upon rank of them, stretching off unending into the west.

"Beautiful, eh?" Birké asked.

"Not the description I had in mind."

"They say the Sky Mount is not far in. We won't hike more than a day or so in the mountains. Just along the edge of them."

"The edge?" Dariel asked. "How far do these mountains go?"

"I don't know. No one has been all the way through them. This was once Wrathic territory. My clan's home. They lived at the edge of Rath Batatt but ranged into it, hunting. I've always wanted to do that."

"You never have?"

"How could I?" the young man asked. "The time that the Wrathic hunted in Rath Batatt is but legend now. Tales they tell the children to bind them to the clan. Wonderful tales of packs of wolves and how they hunted mighty beasts together. I never even thought I'd live to see these mountains with my own eyes."

Dariel placed a hand atop his shoulder. "I imagine the hunting is good now. Shall we? We haven't had fresh meat in a while. Even Mór would like that."

That afternoon Dariel and Birké loped away before the others. They climbed a steep slope, navigated the pass at its peak, and dropped down into the alpine valley on the other side. They picked their way through massive boulders, some of which pressed together so that they had to squeeze through or beneath them. Beyond the boulders stretched a long descent to a crystal blue lake, rimmed by short grass, abloom with purple wildflowers. A herd of woolly-haired oxen grazed— stout creatures thickening to face the coming winter, with flat horns that spread across their foreheads like helmets welded to their scalps. At first they were unaware of the humans, and then unfazed, and then—when Birké sank an arrow into one's shoulder—furious.

The insulted beast charged them. After a brief moment of consideration, Dariel and Birké turned and fled. They reached the relative safety of the boulders with the ox's hooves pummeling the ground just behind them, grunting insults into air suddenly thick with its musk. The creature pursued them in. It rushed through the narrow crevices between the stones. Dariel, trapped in a dead-end corridor of granite, had to scramble up it.

"I don't think it was quite like this before!" Birké shouted, laughing as he hopped from boulder to boulder. The creature snorted outraged breaths below him, following them farther into the maze, looking rather murderous for a thing that fed on grass and flowers.

"Not a Wrathic technique, then?" Dariel called back.

It was not the most heroic hunt ever—they made the creature a pincushion with arrows shot from safely above it—but the result was satisfying. That night they fed on thick steaks roasted over a fire and told stories surrounded by an amphitheater of stone. Birké recounted the great Wrathic hunts of old, and of the ancient times when young men were sent alone into the wilderness, to return only if they wore the jawbones of a slaughtered kwedeir draped over their necks. Listening to him, Dariel almost forgot Birké was talking about members of the Auldek clan who had enslaved him, not about young men like himself. He almost forgot that this was not just the hunting trip it briefly seemed. He almost accepted it as an evening spent in the company of friends, with no purpose save enjoyment. Almost.

"So, tomorrow we'll see the Sky Mount. Why don't you tell me what that is, and who the Watcher is?"

In the silence after his question Dariel realized how different the night was here from what it had been just days before in Inàfeld Forest. Here, in the mountains, the main feature of the near silence was the scrape of wind over the jagged peaks. That and the sound of Mór honing the blade of her dagger on a stone propped on her knee.

"Well?" Dariel prompted.

Anira pulled another strip of meat from above the fire, set it on the small stone she was using as a table, and sliced it into bite-size pieces. When she had a few, she pinched them in her fingers and offered them to Dariel. "The Sky Mount is a palace built by a Lothan Aklun called Nâ Gâmen. He built it long ago, back in the early years after they arrived. We should see it tomorrow, perched atop the highest peak in this area."

"So what is it that Mór doesn't believe?"

"That the very same Nâ Gâmen who built it all those years ago still lives in it."

"A Lothan Aklun lives?"

Anira shrugged. "He may. The elders among the People say that long ago he exiled himself there for his own reasons. He once came down from the Sky Isle and gave them—"

"Promises." Mór looked up from her work. "He spoke promises and regrets hundreds of years ago, and has done nothing else since. But the elders, in their wisdom, believe that he still sits up there, waiting for something. For you, perhaps."

"You don't believe that?"

Mór bent forward and began the rhythmic drag of steel over stone again. "What I believe doesn't matter. I'm taking you."

✳

By noon of the next day Dariel had fixed his attention on a single peak in the distance, one that came in and out of view as they navigated the ridges preceding it. The high clouds that had obscured it in the morning cleared, revealing a ring of snow crusting its peak, the only mountain thus accoutred so far. Or so he thought.

Later in the afternoon, when they mounted a pass and began down the slope facing the great mountain, Dariel realized that the snow was not snow at all. It was cast around the heights in too peculiar a manner. It was actually a solid substance. Though the white draped across the stone like the cellophane nests of certain birds, there was an order to it, a geometric intention within the contours. He had seen such structures before. When he sailed through the barrier isle he had gaped at Lothan Aklun abodes similarly hung from stone. This one, however, was much larger, a fact that grew clearer as they climbed toward it through the lengthening shadows of the aging afternoon.

When they reached the gate, it did not seem they had reached much of anything except a dead end. The path had contoured along the steep precipice. It dropped off dizzyingly to one side. As they came around a corner, the path simply stopped, and a wall of smooth white stone faced them. Though it was obviously a man-made structure and a substance quite different from the rough granite of the mountain, it molded seamlessly into base stone. The mountain curved away out of sight to one side, while a buttress of rock hid any view upward. They could see nothing of the palace that had been so visible from a distance.

Tam asked, "Should we knock?"

Though the wall had no doorlike features, they did just that. Lightly at first, and then with fists and feet and harder objects. The material absorbed the beating, deadening the force of their blows. Anira tried to climb up over the buttress, but only fell crashing back down. Mór scraped the blade of a knife across the surface, searching for some crevice to pry open. Nothing. Not even a scratch left behind by her honed point.

Eventually, the group gave up. There they stood, Dariel with a sleeping pup in his pack and Birké with one in his arms. Tam massaged the knuckles of his hand and asked what they should do now. Anira stood with arms crossed, head cocked, her thoughts trapped in the pucker of her lips. The crimson light of the vanishing sun shone on Mór's delicate features, somehow bringing out the Shivith tattoos with more vicious contrast than usual. Dariel kept expecting her to say something. She looked like she wanted to, and he wished she would.

Entertaining such thoughts, he was the last to notice that the wall did, in fact, have a door in it. The last to notice that the door not only existed, but was open, and that a figure within had leaned through and was intently studying them.

Corinn started awake. She lashed out, sure that Hanish Mein was attached to her face and devouring her. It took a moment for the panic to fade and for the solidity of the world to materialize around her. A small, comfortable cabin. Windows open to salt-tinged air, seabirds calling. A flap of sail and a slow sensation of motion. She remembered. She was aboard her transport, heading back to Acacia. The terror had just been a dream. Just the nightmare she had suffered through since she destroyed the Numrek.

"You fool girl," she whispered. "You almost killed yourself."

She realized this first on waking in a villa along the Teh coast that had once belonged to Calrach. She had been unconscious for days. Feverish. Helpless. With no memory of being lifted and handled and transported. Touched by unknown hands. The acts of magic she unleashed upon the Numrek had nearly ended her. The same brutality that ripped them apart could either have left her so spent she just ceased to be, or it could have exploded inside her. In the future, she would have to be much more careful. She could only do so much at once. If she misjudged what and how to sing, she could lose everything in the space of a single mistaken note. Why was that so obvious after the fact, but so easy to forget during the moment—when all she felt was power?

She kicked off the blanket covering her. She stood and studied herself in the mirror on the back of the cabin door. For a horrible moment, she could have been looking at her mother in the throes of her illness. Gaunt in the face. Her eyes large and sad. Her body a decaying framework upon which her old beauty hung in tatters.

"Why so morbid, Corinn?" the image asked. "Afraid of your dreams? That's silly. You're not silly, Corinn. Don't act as if you are. Who is that man anyway?"

Corinn stepped closer to the mirror, touched the frame and slid her hand down it, across the glass lightly. She studied the wrinkled face looking back at her, loving it, comforted by it, no matter that it frightened her. "He is nobody. He is dead. He's the one who tried to kill me, Mother. I am not afraid of him when I'm awake, but in my dreams he has power over me."

Changing angle, moving to the other side of the mirror, the image said, "Only because you let him. Don't do that. Don't give in to weakness in your time of triumph. Remember what you did!"

Corinn did remember. She saw in her mind image after image of the horrors she had unleashed. She saw more in her imaginings than she had seen in the few moments the horrors actually took. It was as if each individual death had been stored within her, whether she had actually seen it with her eyes or not. She watched them all now. The stomach-churning revulsion of it matched the raw, teeth-grinding pleasure of it. That power! She could rip apart the fabric of life like nobody else walking the earth could. She had to be careful, yes, to plan better, to foresee even more. But she had the power of a new Tinhadin.

"And what of that worm beneath the sea?" her mother asked. "Do you still dream of it?"

Whatever that vague, writhing, wormlike enormity had been, it no longer troubled her. She had managed to push it out of her mind, to stop seeing those strange images of it. She had been so worried, in fear for Aaden's life. That worm must have been an internal manifestation of that, another creature of nightmare that she had allowed into her waking mind. Her actions recently had beaten the beast back. When it tried to push into her mind—waking or asleep—she had the power to push it back.

"It's gone. Gone, gone."

Not only that. So many things she had fit into their proper places recently. Aaden was back on Acacia, awake and waiting for her. She had received news of this a few nights back. Aliver walked and talked and made himself at home in the palace once again. Word of that was spreading, too. She knew her song danced over his skin, binding him to her, making him the combination of his mind and her will. What a partner he would make in the struggles to come. Elya's eggs were maturing. Even from a distance she felt them growing. They were hers already and would soon stun the world in her name. And Delivegu should have taken care of the small thing she asked of him by now. Another threat to Aaden removed.

There were many reasons to feel confident. For the time being, it did not even matter that Mena had deviated from her orders and gone to Mein Tahalian. It sounded crazy to Corinn, but she must have her reasons. Corinn would soon ask her directly.

"Are you proud of me?" Corinn asked the reflection in the mirror, and then answered, "Yes, of course. You are strong in ways others are not. You are the queen. You are—"

A noise from the other side of the door caused Corinn to start. She moved quickly away from it. She turned, drew herself up with a breath, straightened her posture, and lifted her chin.

There, she thought, seeing herself returned in the image in the mirror, no doubt at all who she was anymore, is the Corinn the world knows. Let it always be so.

The image slipped away as the door opened, a servant timid behind it, peeking in to announce the approach of a skiff carrying the head vintner of Prios. For a moment, Corinn could not remember who the head vintner of Prios was, or what he would wish to talk about. She could not ask anyone but Rhrenna such a question. Instead she called for documents pertinent to the meeting. From them, she refreshed her memory.

An hour later, Paddel entered the transport's conference room sweating, his gait a rolling waddle. He patted his forehead and scalp with a handkerchief. The action did little to clear away the moisture but much to highlight that his scalp had been tattooed in imitation of hair. It looked like he wore some tight rubber cap on his head. The man seemed entirely oblivious to this effect.

The queen sat at the far end of an oval table, the room's central feature. Wearing her light chain mail once again, she looked the picture of royal composure. There was a martial edge to the slant of her head and position of her arm, which was crooked to one side in a masculine manner. She modeled the posture after a remembered image of Maeander Mein, but she made it her own now.

"Surely it's not that hot outside, Paddel." She had no problem using his name. She remembered him quite well now, and his little project.

"No, no, not at all. It's just that sea travel doesn't agree with me. Turns my legs to jelly and my guts to . . . Oh, but you don't want to hear my troubles. Your Majesty, I'm overjoyed to see you well. These past few weeks we've been so worried about you."

"As you can see I'm fine," Corinn said.

"Yes, you are. May I just say that you are a wonder! The talk of the entire empire. News of your triumph in Teh competes with word that Aliver has risen from the dead."

As always with this man, Corinn decided on brevity. She cut off his babbling before he could work up momentum. "It's all true. We won't discuss it now, though. You brought a sample?"

The one virtue Paddel had was that he did not seem to mind being cut off. "I did," he said, and began a fumbling search of his silken robes. He produced a small blue vial, delicate like something used for perfume. "This, Your Majesty, is the vintage. Pure. A drop of it in a goblet of wine, and the drinker is never the same again."

Corinn gestured toward a carafe of wine on the table. Paddel, taking the suggestion, uncorked and poured a glass. Then, making sure the queen could see his actions, he let a single drop of the clear liquid land in the wine, lost instantly in its rich maroon. He swirled. "And that's it."

"And that's it." Corinn studied the liquid as it slipped around the glass. "Paddel, you have heard what I did to the Numrek. It was a demonstration of my power, and I know that word of it is flying about the empire as quick as a thousand wagging tongues. Now, that could be good, or that could be bad. In relation to power, people can choose to bow in adoration to it, or they can choose to fear it. I prefer one reaction instead of the other, understand?"

Paddel nodded, unsure.

When he said nothing, Corinn added, "I would have the people adore me."

The vintner's jowly face jumped with relief. "That's exactly what the masses do. The vintage is already going down throats across the empire. Everyone thinks your acts are wonders, works of beauty, magnificent! They'll rally behind you more than ever. They'll go to battle—if that's called for—with even more confidence. I promise you that."

"Good," Corinn said. She held up her hand for the glass. Paddel came around the table and handed it to her. Bringing it close to her nose, she inhaled the scent of it. Paddel looked like he had a word pinched between his lips, something dangerous that he wished to release. I'm not going to drink it, fool, Corinn thought. But I would know the smell of it. It wouldn't do for me to be poisoned with it, would it?

When she was confident that she knew the scent and could build her sensitivity to it with the help of *The Song*, she set the glass down. "You know that I want none of this consumed in the palace."

"Understood. Completely and utterly. Each cask and bottle carries a label marking it. I briefed your secretary on it. Gave her all the information. As I understand it, she will pass the knowledge on to those who will keep the palace free of it. You and family will remain quite untouched by it."

"What of the question I put to you when we last met? About the effects when one who is addicted is then deprived. I told you to bring me a report on that."

"Ah . . . yes, of course." Paddel's scalp bloomed with a new coating of sweat. "I hope that you'll forgive us. We've been so very busy with distribution, with getting it out fast behind the news that you've abolished the quota. In all the confusion the results have been inconclusive."

"Which means what?"

"We just don't know for sure."

Corinn stared at him. "Are you lying to me?"

"I would never, Your Majesty! I would die before a lie escaped my lips in your presence." He made the Mainland gesture for death, a quick motion of mimicking plucking out one of his eyes and tossing it over his shoulder. "But it's all a bit confused. The league tabulated the data, and they were not clear with us on wh-what they found."

Corinn's brow grew more and more creased as the vintner talked. "You should have told me this before."

"A thousand pardons, please, Your Majesty. If we'd had the time, we surely would have seen it all through. But even now I assure you this changes nothing. They assured me the vintage is fine, and I assure you the same!"

Corinn snatched up the vial and stood. "This displeases me, Paddel. I asked *you* to do something, and you handed the job to another. That is not an action of a loyal servant. I've come to doubt you." Pocketing the vial at her waist, she paused and smiled at the look of utter dismay on Paddel's face. "But since you are confident, I propose you drink in celebration." She pointed to the glass on the table. "Do so. Drink."

※

Once on Acacia, Corinn disembarked into the pleasantly cool air. Acacian winter at last, just chilly enough to require long sleeves and a lace scarf. She had just taken the reins and prepared to step up onto her mount, when a buzz of noise followed by a sudden hush drew her attention. She paused, stepped back, opened her fingers, and let the leather reins slip from them.

Aliver walked hand in hand with Aaden. They were talking, both to themselves and saying things to passersby. They waved and touched peoples' hands or the crowns of the heads of those who were kneeling. They quietly beamed. Corinn had never seen a finer sight. As she rushed toward them through a sudden blur of tears, nothing mattered more in the world. Aliver smiled and Aaden lit up at the sight of her. When the boy pressed himself against her belly, and when she remembered in that moment the first time his baby arms had hugged her, and when Aliver slipped his arm around them both . . . in those few moments she knew joy more completely than ever before. Here was life, and it was a fine thing, free of fear, radiant.

The mood held through to that evening. They dined on the back terraces of Corinn's gardens. Servants brought up standing torches that ringed the diners and fought back the evening's chill. They ate braised eel in a ginger sauce, served over sticky rice that Aaden insisted on forming into balls with his fingers. Corinn let him. They were not on display this evening, not even among the court. They were alone, all the family she could have near at hand. When Aliver pinged Aaden with a long bean, Corinn laughed as loudly as anyone. When Rhrenna toasted the queen's victory in Teh, Corinn sent a charm snaking up her arm and into all the glasses as they clinked together, just a further lightening of the mood, a feeling like bubbles floating in the air around them, popping in gentle kisses on their skin.

They talked of nothing pressing. Aaden peppered his uncle with questions about his youth. Aliver responded with tales of his boyhood, of his journey into Talay in exile, of growing to manhood there. After dinner, he acted out his laryx hunt with a spear fetched from one of the statues in his hallway. He made the whole thing seem deathly frightening and hilarious at the same time. By the time he finished, Corinn's stomach ached from laughing. That was a pleasant pain she had not felt for many years.

"Is it just me, or does the harbor seem busier than usual?" Aliver asked a little later, as they sat on the crescent balcony that offered a dizzying view out over the harbor.

Corinn thought of the ridged back of some beast that she had seen cutting through the water earlier, but that was not what he meant. Since nobody else had seen it, she knew it was an imagining for her alone. She was almost used to seeing things that were not real. It was a small price to pay for having the song coursing through her.

What Aliver referred to were the hundreds of very real ships that bobbed on the sea. They choked the harbor and spread out into the open water itself. Black shapes and white and red sails rode the swells, many of them torchlit like an aquatic constellation.

Rhrenna licked lime cream off a tiny dessert spoon. "It appears that we're being flooded by pilgrims."

"Pilgrims?"

"Most are from Talay, but not just there. They come to praise Corinn. To pray for Aaden. To spot Elya on the wing. But mostly because of you."

"Rumors of you have spread far and wide already," Corinn said to Aliver. "Considering that you strolled through the lower town this morning in broad daylight, we'll soon be flooded with many more than what you see here."

"I should go down to greet them," Aliver said, setting aside his porcelain bowl and spoon as if he would do so at that moment.

"You will," Corinn said, "but let them talk a bit longer. Let them all talk, from here to the Senate and the league great ships and beyond. Let them talk you into a god. Then we'll show you to the world for real, and they'll be all the more amazed. We'll soon announce your coronation. It will be abrupt, but we'll already have half the empire floating around us."

Just then a servant girl dashed into the courtyard. She drew up and stared at the group with frightened eyes. "Your Majesty, pardon me, the—the eggs, Your Majesty, they are cracking. Hatching, I mean."

Corinn would have chosen to witness this alone, but there was no keeping Aaden and the others from dashing through the hallways with her. Aliver made a show of racing Aaden. Rhrenna asked who would get to name the young. Aaden himself was too giddy with excitement to do anything other than run.

They rushed onto the terrace balcony that had served as Elya's private hatchery. The creature snapped around. For a moment there was something fierce in the glare of her eyes and the way her head slipped low on her subtle neck. It only lasted a moment, though, and then she was gentle again. When Aaden threw himself around her neck, burying his face in her plumage, Corinn's fine mood flooded back. She approached carefully, touching first her son's shoulder and then Elya's soft back. She leaned forward and gazed into the basin.

And there they were. Elya's babies. Two of them were completely free of their shells. They squirmed at the edge of the basin, clawing at the fabric that lined it as if they wanted to climb right out and face life. One still stretched and struggled with its shell, and the fourth was but a small snout protruding from a crack in its egg. They were tiny versions of Elya in many ways, plumed with a sleek coat, with serpentine necks and delicate claws. The feathers around their heads were a bristling confusion, though, and they were variously colored. One was crimson at the head and fading to black, while another displayed yellow stripes across a brown back. The one kicking free of shell was sky blue, and the last, from the look of his protruding snout, was all black.

Corinn said, "Look at them. Little beauties."

At the sound of her voice, all three of the exposed heads turned toward her. They blinked. One's nostrils flared. The red one cocked its head. The one in the shell thrust its head through in one great effort. It, too, set its gaze on Corinn. My smart babies, she thought. My little dragons. She extended a hand toward them. All four of them followed it with their yellow eyes. When she was near enough, the red one slammed the crown of her head into Corinn's fingers like an affectionate cat. The others clamored over one another to do the same.

Elya shifted sideways. She touched her shoulder to Corinn's

side and pressed her back. When Aaden tried to stroke the young as well, Elya slipped her own head in before him, pushing against his chest so that he had to step back. She exhaled an impatient breath.

"All right, Elya, care for your children," Corinn said, pulling back. "Raise them strong for me and for the empire."

CHAPTER
ELEVEN

"Are you sure?" Mena asked.

Perrin nodded. He was red-faced from the cold and from the brisk hike that had brought him out to meet Mena and the main column of the army. "That's Tahalian."

"It looks to be a ruin."

"It's seen better days." He studied the view a moment and then added, "It's a bit nicer inside."

"It would have to be." Mena glanced back at the ragged line of troops moving like a slow river through the valley behind her. Realizing that her eyes were scanning them in search of Melio, she lifted her hand and pressed her eyes closed for a moment.

"Is it habitable?"

"Yes. I might not have thought so a couple of days ago, but two days' work can fix a lot."

Perrin and a small corps had gone ahead on horseback to open the fortress and get the steam vents pumping hot air. Judging by the gaping mouth of the thing before them and the plumes of mist that billowed out of several outlets and hung above the place, he had achieved that. His efforts had done nothing for its forlorn appearance. Tahalian huddled close to the ground, more like a huge pile of debris than the grand structure that had once housed the entire Mein race. Its massive pine beams were bracketed together with iron rings. The wood had been silvered by weather. The whole mass was edged with ice and pocketed with early snowfall. The beams canted at angles that were hard to make sense of but that seemed no work of intentional design.

Pointing at a long, low mound a little distance away, Perrin said, "That's the Calathrock. We're having trouble opening the vents to it, but we'll get the place heated soon. It's impressive, Mena, most of it is dug down into earth. It'll serve us well."

I hope so, she thought. I truly hope so.

❈

That evening she arranged for Haleeven Mein to be brought to her in the Calathrock. She stood awaiting him in the massive chamber, inhaling the dank air. It was sulfurous from the partially functioning vent system. The beams that supported the roof fitted together in an intricate lacework that left an open space largely free of columns beneath it. Workers had lit several of the large lanterns. Though their mirrored backings cast considerable light, Mena could barely make out the darker edges of the space. She knelt and ran her fingers over the hardwood floor. Worn to a smooth polish, it was crisscrossed with scrapes and gashes, the telltale signs of the years of martial practice that had gone on in this room, hidden from the Known World. Right here was where Hanish Mein had fought his Maseret duels. Right here he had honed his army, devised his plans. From right here he had launched the assault that nearly ended the Akaran line and that had changed Mena's life in so many ways.

Perrin appeared in one of the large entranceways some distance away, behind him three others. Mena picked out the man she was here to meet, for his dress and demeanor were so different from that of her soldiers. The four of them began to come forward, but she motioned with her hand. Perrin paused, studied her a moment. He whispered something to the others. The soldiers halted and Perrin indicated that Haleeven should proceed alone.

She had seen the man several times in the aftermath of Aliver's War. He had escaped the slaughter that took his nephew's life on Acacia. He had tried to rally what forces he could on the Mainland, but only until he had heard the news of the Talay Plains. After that he gave up. A patrol captured him on a woodland road near the Methalian Rim. It seemed he was walking home, a handful of men around him. None of them put up a fight.

When he was brought bound for a trial in Alecia, Mena had watched him sit stone-faced as the crimes of his people were read out to the new Alecian Senate. He offered no rebuttal. No justification. Nor did he plead for mercy. Never had she seen a man look more defeated.

The Senate had called for his execution—a fate that several of the high-ranking Meinish survivors had suffered—but Corinn had commuted it. Instead, she had sent him in exile back to the Mein. He had been there ever since, living in a simple hut from which he hunted and chopped wood for the long Meinish winter. She had never been sure if Corinn's decision had been intended as a punishment or as an act of kindness. Watching Haleeven shuffle toward her now, she thought it more the former than the latter.

Grimy furs covered him, not so much like a coat and leggings as like a motley mass of different pelts, formless and foul smelling. The guards must have taken off his cap. His thin, straw-colored hair was yet pressed to his scalp. Quite a contrast to his beard, which cascaded from his face in unruly swirls and waves.

This, too, was soiled, dotted with debris and grease. For a second she doubted that this was the famous brother of Heberen, uncle to the brothers Hanish, Maeander, and Thasren. But only for a second. She recognized his gray eyes and strong nose.

Haleeven's gaze drifted around the chamber, mouth drooping and lower lip trembling. He seemed to have forgotten Mena before even reaching her, save that he walked in an orbit around her, as if she were a fire that he did not wish to move too far away from.

"Haleeven Mein," Mena said. "I am Mena Akaran. We have met before. We never spoke, but I . . . know your face well."

The old warrior kept circling her. He said something in his tongue, words that rolled out of his mouth like rough-edged stones.

"You have been too long locked out of Tahalian," Mena said. "It's time for you to call it home again. For you and—"

Haleeven broke out of his circle and strode away. Mena followed, indicating with a flick of her fingers that Perrin and the guards should stay where they were. Haleeven went to a section of the wall. He ran his hands over it, clearing away the dust. Whatever he saw spurred him on. He wiped in wide sweeps, reaching as high as he could. A cloud of dust gathered around him. He coughed and spoke Meinish and worked his way across the wall. Only when she touched a portion of the cleared area with her fingers did Mena notice the inscriptions in the wood. Names. They ran up and down it in columns. They must have risen to the ceiling, though most of this stretch was coated in dust thick enough to hide them.

Mena was startled to find the old man watching her. He walked back toward her slowly, his gray eyes steady on her. He stopped before her and said something in Meinish.

"I don't speak your language," Mena admitted.

"I wish I didn't speak yours." Haleeven's Acacian was accented but clear enough. "I wish I'd never had to learn it. If you are a phantom of my nightmares—"

"I am not a phantom," Mena said. "Feel my touch." She held out her hand. He made no move to reach for it. She stepped forward and, hesitating for a moment, grasped the fingers protruding from his furs. "See. We are both flesh."

"This is really true?"

Mena nodded.

"Why?" Somehow he made the word into more of an accusation than a question.

"Because we face war once more. The entire nation does. Things from the past need to be set aside. Forgotten. We have to—"

"Look at this wall!" Haleeven cut in, gesturing with a quick sweep of his hand. Mena felt the guards stiffen. "The Chieftains' Tree. These are chieftains' names. All of them. All of them from the Hauchmeinish's generation, from the first that your people sent into exile. See? They are all here. From Hauchmeinish to Hanish. With all those who died challenging each chieftain's given glory here in turn. Look at them."

Mena raised her chin and did so.

"You want me to forget this? I can't. Of all the things in the world, this I can't forget."

"I've . . . misspoken. That's not what I mean. I don't mean that you forget your past. No, it's important that we remember. Our pasts will forever be entwined, just as our role in creating the danger we face is shared between us even now. My officer explained some of what is happening, didn't he?"

"They told me of a nightmare that walks in daylight."

"It's our shared nightmare, Haleeven. Your people did, after all, first invite the Numrek across the Ice Fields. But we Akarans have done our share to bring them back in an even worse form.

Now we need you. We need Tahalian breathing again, warm at her belly. We need the Calathrock to once more ring with troops in training. The fate of the Known World depends on it. The only thing I want us to forget is the animus that caused us both so much grief. Let us remember the facts and learn from them, but let's start by forgetting hatred."

Haleeven guffawed. His eyes again slid up along the Chieftains' Tree. "Two things, then. Two things I can't ever do." He walked away, trailing a hand across the wall until he reached the beam that marked its edge. He carried on walking into the dimmer areas of the Calathrock, mumbling to himself again in his own tongue.

Perrin arrived at Mena's side a few moments later. "Anything accomplished?"

Mena called loudly, "Haleeven Mein! You want to remember your former glory? You can do more than that. You can rebuild it! This can belong to the Meinish race again."

The figure, deep in shadow now, paused.

"I would not ask things of you without offering things in return." She grabbed the torch that one of the guards held and walked into the shadows.

"Your sister destroyed the Meinish race," the shadow said. He had turned to face the princess, and his voice came clearer now. "We are no more."

As Mena approached, his features flickered into existence again. "My sister punished the Mein. She was harsh, yes, but don't ask me to forget what you did to us. Don't ask me to forget the Tunishnevre! What would they have done to my people? No, don't ask me to forget either. Let's forget the word *forget*. It's a useless word!"

The other smiled with a corner of his thin lips.

"Haleeven, I've known your name since I was a child, and you must have known mine from the day that I was born. We've spent all that time being enemies without even knowing each other. Our fight is over, though. Now we will both be destroyed if we don't find a way to prevail."

"I'm not sure that would be so bad," Haleeven said.

"I doubt very much that the Auldek deserve our world more than we do, or that they'll rule it more benignly. And you're wrong about one thing. Completely wrong. Corinn was in power when your people were defeated, but she did the exact opposite of destroying the race. She gave birth to Hanish's child. You know this. Your bloodline goes on."

The old man crossed his arms, a difficult act with all those layers on. He gave no sign of how being reminded of Hanish's child affected him, but Mena had his full attention now. "What do you want of me?"

"I want you, who know this place the best, to help us open it. I want you to train my army here in this chamber. I want it to ring with singing swords and battle cries. I want your help in preparing to face the Numrek. Who better than you?"

"What will you give me in return for making me your soldier?"

"Your life back. Tahalian. Acknowledgment of your race and your name."

"You can promise me that?"

"I promise you that."

Haleeven's eyes bored into hers. "I would have to call all Meins to me. From all around the empire, whether enslaved or in hiding or imprisoned. I would want them all here in Tahalian. I will not be the only one."

Perrin cleared his throat skeptically, but Mena said, "That will be done. Write a summons yourself so that your people will believe it. I will pen a sealed note to accompany it. We can send it tonight. There are birds fed, rested, and ready to fly."

"I have your word on it?" the man asked. "Truly?"

Mena met Perrin's eyes a moment, then slipped a hand down her collar. She fished out a chain, on it a silver pendant. Pinching it in her fingers, she held it up for Haleeven to see. "I found this at the base of a great tree. It is the reason I fought and killed the eagle goddess Maeben. It was not a present or a gift or payment, even. It's a burden. It was sent so that I would remember the children sacrificed in the name of the goddess I served, then abhorred, and then killed. I made a mistake. When I realized that, I did the best I could to correct it. That's the way I am, Haleeven." She pulled the chain taut, letting the curves of the serpentine figure on the pendant catch the light. "I swear on this, on the children I carry with me, on the wrongs I will yet see righted. Fight with us, Haleeven Mein, and if we live, your people will live as well. I swear it."

Haleeven drew his head back and then let his eyes drift up and around the great arched roof. Finally, he said, "I am not without ideas."

Mena nodded, curt. "I thought as much."

"The air is not flowing properly. It should not smell of sulfur. Someone has opened a ventilation tube improperly. Send me a few capable men. We'll survey the heat ducts. Before anything else, we must see to that."

"As you advise," Mena said, not quite smiling but close enough that he responded with a not quite smile of his own.

CHAPTER
TWELVE

On the night he arrived at Calfa Ven, Delivegu Lemardine lingered a while over the scene rolling out beneath his private balcony. The King's Preserve, a vast stretch of woodland deep in the mountains of Senival. Unending crowns of trees crowded the entire view, broken here and there by granite protrusions. Plumes of orange and brown, some bursts of yellow: the leaves still displayed their late autumn brilliance.

Why he stood so long watching the night creep over the landscape he could not say. Perhaps it was nostalgia for some aspect of his forgotten childhood. It was not that he remembered a view like this, or had any particular fondness for the notion of roaming the wilderness beneath that canopy, but he was Senivalian by birth. He had spent his first years in some village or another near here. Perhaps the memory was in his blood. Perhaps he should spend more time here. Not this trip, though. This trip had a particular purpose and would be brief.

That evening's banquet had a rustic charm. Delivegu went to it dressed in a manner he felt fit the occasion. He wore a shirt of thick Senivalian cloth, its collar a tall ring around his neck. He squeezed his private parts into tight black trousers. He was particularly fond of his crimson leather boots, strapped snug all the way up to the knee. One should always take care with one's appearance, Delivegu believed, even when far from court.

The lodge's guests gathered in the winter dining room, a crowded space centered around a single oval table. Wall lamps lit the place, but something about the dark wood walls, the pelts pinned there, and the heads of several stags and a boar jutting from them gave the room a somber air. Two fires roared in large fireplaces at either side of the room. That was another thing Delivegu had noticed about the lodge. Many corridors opened to the outside air. Windows often sat crooked with age in their frames, rattling in the wind and spilling warm air and letting in cold. Instead of correcting these things, the servants set blazing fires in every room. Inefficient. Wasteful, really, but there was a certain style in this rugged excess. Delivegu approved.

He did not, on the other hand, much approve of his dinner company. Nothing wrong with them per se, but not one seducible maiden among them: Gurta, so fat with Rialus Neptos's pup she would have been better off rolling than waddling around as she was; a senator from Aos, his middle-aged wife and several other relations; along with an old merchant and his two teenage sons, the latter flushed from the day's adventures. Adventures that featured Wren, Dariel's mistress. She was pregnant with the prince's child, though from the story the two sons told she was not much hindered by her condition.

"Mistress Wren warned us it would be a long ride in any event," one of the sons said. The guests stood in a loose circle, sipping the mint liqueur that was customary for early winter evenings at Calfa Ven. "We rode north through the valley and then up along a ridgeline she called Storneven. Wren knew the route well."

"Or the horses did," the other son, slightly younger, said.

"No, she knew it. She's ridden it several times during the weeks she's been caretaker here."

Caretaker? That was a clever way to describe her situation. Better than she who is banished until the queen decides what to do with her. "She rides so often?" Delivegu asked.

"Every day," Gurta said. "Keeps her from going insane with boredom."

"There was no chance of that today," the younger son piped. "We had a run-in with a wolverbear!"

"An old wolverbear," the other corrected. "Peter, the warden, said so. It picked up our trail about halfway around Storneven, spooked the horses. It followed us for a good hour, sometimes right out in the open. It loped along as if it were just biding its time until one of us fell off our horse or something."

"Peter said that's what it was doing. Said if any of the horses had gotten lamed—or if one of us had fallen—the thing would have been on us like a flash. He got it off us by tossing down two of the squirrels he had shot. When the wolverbear couldn't resist them, we took off as fast as Wren could ride."

"Dreadful," the senator's wife said. "Those creatures are beastly. They should hunt every last one of them."

"Oh, you don't mean that," Delivegu said, finding himself drawn to flirt. Force of habit. "There need to be wild things in the world. Things to give you chills at night thinking about them."

"My wife has far too many chills already," the senator said. "Goes to sleep wrapped in three layers of undergarments."

"That's a pity," Delivegu said. "A crime, I'd say. No woman should go to sleep so encumbered." He flashed her a smile and sipped his liqueur. Then he wondered why he had bothered. He had no interest in her. And then he realized that without knowing it his senses had picked up on a person of interest. The sudden rush of vigor he felt was not for the senator's wife at all. It was for one of the girls setting the table for dinner. Oh, yes, that was it. He watched her bend over the table, arranging cutlery.

What is it about youth? he wondered. Even though her body was half hidden beneath her simple frock, unadorned and meant to go unnoticed, Delivegu saw the contours beneath the fabric. No Acacian beauty, this one. She was of Senivalian stock, clear enough in her short stature, with hips that would go wide in a few years, breasts that stood at attention for the time being, and dark hair she wore clipped at the back. He decided he would see those locks flow free. Reconnecting with his ancestral roots. That's what it would be.

When he caught the flow of conversation again, the senator's wife was saying, "If you ask me, it's just reckless. Why put the child in danger like that? I enjoy a good brisk ride myself, but there's a time for all things."

Delivegu tried to imagine her enjoying a brisk ride. It was not a pleasant imagining, too full of jiggling flesh for his liking. He glanced at the serving girl again and caught her watching him. Oh, good. She's noticed.

"Mistress Wren!"

She walked in with a careless air, as if she had happened on the place by accident and was not entirely sure she would stay. She was pretty enough. Small and lithe, she had the body of an acrobat. "Ready to eat?" she asked. "I could eat an entire wolverbear."

Delivegu managed to secure a place across the table from her. Despite her reckless riding and adventures with wolverbears, she did seem fully aware of the child growing inside her. It was a small bump yet. She rubbed it often, making him wonder what it felt like. It was sensual in a way he had not considered before. As was the way she ate, heartily, without any courtly reticence. He was not sure why Dariel would invest so much in her, but such things were often hard to explain.

"To what do we owe the pleasure of your company, Delivegu?" the merchant asked.

"Yes," Wren asked, slicing through her roasted boar, "why are you here?"

"I conducted business for her majesty in Pelos," Delivegu said. "She asked that before I return I stop in and check on the preparations for winter. She'll not be able to make a last visit herself this season. I know very well that the staff here has everything in hand, so it's an easy assignment for me. A pleasing one. She asked me to look in on you as well"—he nodded at Wren—"to see how you were settling in here."

"I'm so disappointed," the senator's wife said, "that the queen couldn't make it! When we received the invitation, oh, months ago, I so hoped the queen would be here enjoying Calfa Ven as well. I love her so, you know? She's just magnificent. I'd devour her if she were here."

Somehow I think not, Delivegu thought, wondering if Corinn arranged to schedule certain visitors to the lodge when she planned not to be there. This woman might qualify. No doubt she complained mightily to her husband when they were alone. Hoping for a retreat with the queen, getting one with two pregnant discards instead.

"This horrid invasion!" she said. "I'm sick of hearing of it already. I hope the whole business is over by the spring."

Surely she was old enough to remember the last two wars that had ravished the empire. Some forget so quickly. Delivegu said, "That's my hope as well. By the queen's grace, so it shall be."

The attractive servant appeared at Wren's side. "Mistress?" She offered an orange glass bottle, half filled with a clear liquid. Judging by its consistency, it was not water. Wren nodded, and the girl set the glass down, along with a tiny snifter of the same glass.

"What's this?" Delivegu asked, once he had made eye contact with the servant and held it long enough to establish an intimacy.

"Wren's little poison," Gurta said.

"Palm wine," the younger teen said. "It's so tasty she won't let us have any. See if she'll let you have some, Delivegu."

He played along, tilting his head questioningly. Wren pushed the bottle toward him, the glass just after it. The liquid smelled of palm nut flesh and more strongly of straight alcohol. Compared to the liqueur from earlier, there was little tempting about this. The eyes of the group were on him, though. He smiled, saluted the room, and then tossed back the glass.

Instant regret. Searing heat. A gag reaction so torso convulsing that he shot away from the table. His chair slammed into the wall behind him and for a few horrible moments he was sure he was going to spill his dinner onto the floor. A string of curses, muttered all the louder because the room had erupted in laughter. It wasn't just the raw alcohol content. It was that—that . . . "Agh! That's foul!"

"It is. It is," they all agreed.

"Only Wren drinks it," the senator said. "She says it reminds her of what they used to brew on the Outer Isles. Reminds her of her brigand days, apparently."

Wren did not deny it. Grinning, she reached over and hooked the bottle back. She poured and, with a nod in imitation of Delivegu's salute, she drained the tiny glass. She did not so much as blink. In fact, she licked her lips with the tip of her tongue and looked as if she had drunk nothing stronger than sweet tea.

Delivegu regained his seat. "You don't drink much of that, do you? It's poison. I doubt very much the baby is well served by it."

"But a short glass a day," the older teen said. "That's all I've seen her take."

"Good. That's all right, then. I guess . . ." Leaning forward, he said to Wren, "I do insist that you stop riding. You're putting the child at risk."

"Is that an order from the queen?"

"No, just an expression of concern from myself. I'm confident she would say the same, though."

"You care about my baby?" Wren asked. Her Candovian features could have been classically beautiful had she been raised with any sense of courtly decorum. She had not, and her facial expressions—when she made any—were as blunt and straightforward as a tavern owner's.

"Of course. Why wouldn't I? A royal child is a royal child."

"A royal bastard, you mean."

"Surely you don't mean that. It's . . . just the pregnancy. It affects women's moods, I've heard. Mistress Wren, do you think me so crude?"

"Of course I think you crude. Look, neither of us was born to royalty. I never planned to be mistress to a prince, let alone mother of a royal bastard." She speared a morsel of meat and brought it near her mouth, waiting for a retort.

"You should be overjoyed," Delivegu said. And for the moment he said it, he lost sight of the irony of the statement. "You've been lucky. I know what that's like."

She jabbed the morsel in her mouth and chewed. "Am I lucky? Dariel is lost, probably dead. My child has no father. What it does have is—" Glancing around the table, she backed away from whatever she was about to say. "I live with uncertainty. That's all. I know you know what I mean."

She directed this pointedly at Delivegu, but the senator said, "We all do. Trying times test us all."

❀

The later hours of the night found Delivegu entertaining the serving girl Bralyn. It turned out she was the warden's daughter and therefore granddaughter to the first Peter, the one who had overseen the lodge since King Leodan's youth. He had died only recently, and the girl spoke fondly of him. It seemed to be the only thing she had ever liked about living at Calfa Ven.

"Will you take me back with you to Acacia?" she asked.

Delivegu lay on his back, with his head resting against her shoulder, enjoying the sweaty press of her breast against his cheek. "Oh, that's a tempting possibility."

"Take me with you, and you can have me whatever way you want. Whenever you want. Are there courtesans at court?"

"So many it's hard to miss them."

"They're all better than me, aren't they?"

Not the sort of question Delivegu would ever answer honestly. He sat up and studied her, to look as if he were giving the question due consideration. The girl pouted as she awaited his answer. In truth, most of her appeal was the raw stuff of youth. She kissed with a sloppy abandon that he had not been able to make sense of. He had liked her best when he got behind her and did not have to duel with her tongue. She was country, and would remain so for the few short years of beauty she had left. He said, "You're gorgeous by any standard. A lover of infinite talents."

She swatted at him, clearly pleased. Delivegu surged in on her, growling. The two of them wrestled a moment. He found a fleshy place to press his mouth and blow skin blubbers. A strange habit of his, he had to admit. But when he was not yet ready to perform sexually he often played in such childlike ways. Nobody had yet complained. Not really.

"Why do you want to leave?" he asked a little later. "Your life is good here. Better than most. You work is guaranteed for life. You get to serve the queen. Many would trade places with you."

"When the queen is here, it's grand," Bralyn said. "But she hardly ever is. It's boring most of the time."

"Somehow I doubt that. You have guests of some sort here constantly. Men to seduce . . ."

She swatted at him again.

"You must know the queen intimately."

"A bit," the girl admitted.

"Have you seen her work magic?"

Bralyn considered him but then dropped any reticence the moment she began answering. "We're not supposed to, but it's hard to miss. She sings all the time when she's up here. Prince Aaden is always on her to create things."

"Like what?"

"All sorts. Animals you've never seen before. She created these bird things and set them flying over the archery meadow. Those she didn't hide in the slightest. She and Aaden used them for target practice, and some of the staff ran about retrieving the fallen ones. They were strange things, birds with feathers, aye, but with three and four sets of wings, stiff ones like dragon-flies. Strange . . . but beautiful, too. I saw her once blow life back into a slain stag. My father had just come in from a hunt and had a wagon stacked with dead deer. The prince didn't like the sight and got upset, and the queen just went over and worked a spell and then kissed the stag on its nose. A moment later it got up and looked around, and then bolted from the wagon like it never had an arrow in its side. She did other stuff, too, things she really didn't let us see."

Delivegu considered that a moment. With all the things Corinn was letting the world see these days, what sort of sorcery might still merit secrecy?

"I'm hungry," the girl said, stretching back across the cot and sliding one leg over the other, as if this were what one did to combat hunger.

"Of course you are. How about I get you something?"

"Are you serving me?"

Delivegu leaped to his feet and looked around for his robe.

"Exactly. What would you like? Bread and cheese? Some of that roasted venison?"

She puffed out her cheeks. "Cheese gives me nightmares. And venison? I'm sick of the stuff. I could never eat another deer in my life."

"Ah, what then?"

"You'll get me in trouble."

"Nobody in this place can say a word against me, or against you, if that's my pleasure. What will you eat? Be quick. I feel a stiffness coming on."

"Custard. Bring me custard. Do you know how to find it? I should show you."

"What would be the use of my serving you? Just lie there looking ravishing."

The notion did not seem nearly so romantic as he scurried down the exposed passageway toward the kitchens. The wind batted his robe around, thoroughly shriveling his sex in the process. He paused at the kitchen door, first to check that he was alone, and then a moment longer to listen to a wolf's lonely call floating up from the valley. "Hello, brother," he whispered, and then opened the door and entered.

A single oil lamp burned in the center of the preparation table, and by its light Delivegu began his search. He was not looking for custard. It did not take him long, for the servants had left the bottle in easy reach. It stood aligned with the condiments and relishes that had earlier been cleared from the table. He picked up Wren's bottle of palm wine, uncorked it, and sniffed. Just as foul as before. Strange girl, Wren. Something about the fact that she drank this stuff without flinching brought the blood back to his groin. In different circumstances, he would have loved to have a drinking contest with her. Another life, maybe.

He stood still a moment, listening, letting his eyes roam the dark corners of the room. Satisfied that he was alone, he slipped a vial from his robe's inside chest pocket. He plucked out the vial's little cork and measured a few drops into the mouth of the palm wine bottle. Wren's little poison indeed.

A few minutes later, bottle set back in place, Delivegu slipped into the chill air of the corridor again. He carried a large bowl of custard, enough for two. He would enjoy the night and be on his way in the morning. The queen would want a report.

Bralyn would, alas, not be going with him.

CHAPTER
THIRTEEN

The view over the rooftops of Avina had always transfixed Skylene, never more so than now. From where she stood on the balcony of the offices that had once belonged to the Lvin Herith, the city looked endless. It thrust up to the south in a jumbled bulk that went on for miles, farther than she could see: all the towers with their sun-bright colors, flags of the clans hung now just as they always had, lines of smoke rising to a certain height, at which point the wind bent each column and sent it off to the west. Seabirds and starlings and pigeons cut arcs through the sky and filled the morning air with their calls.

"The only city I've ever truly known," Skylene said to herself. A child of the Eilavan Woodlands, she had only ever seen Aos from a distance, on the march that took her to the league transport that began her life in bondage. Her memory of that city was that it was vast, but she suspected that was not true. A child's perception of things. This city, Avina, truly was vast. It had been too large to occupy entirely even when the Auldek lived in it. Now, with them and their chosen servants and the divine children gone, the dead haunted the city as much as the living. It did not have to be that way, but the glory that could have been a free Avina had already started to fracture.

Out of the corner of her eye, she saw a person emerge through the archway that led onto the rooftop. Tunnel strode toward her, moving his bulk with a heavy, muscular grace. Standing beside her, he touched the metal tusks curving up from his face. "We should go now."

Skylene nodded. She let her gaze linger over the city a little longer and then she turned and walked back toward the arch, down the slope, and onward. Beside Tunnel, she was as slim as a reed, a figure drawn with the smooth lines of a thin brush. Her skin powder white, nose the elongated point customary of selected Kern slaves, hair tufted in a manner that made her otherwise peaceful visage look potentially savage, touched with avian anger. She might need some of that for the meeting they headed to, the first summit of leaders of the clans of the quota slaves of Ushen Brae.

Randale of the Wrathic had called for a full gathering of the people; Dukish of the Anet and Maren of the Kulish Kra had balked, saying they should decide some matters at the level of the chieftains before airing their differences in public. Skylene did not welcome talk of chieftains. Nor did she like that they already defined themselves by the clan groupings of their enslavement. She agreed to attend only to buy time until Mór returned—and the elders, too, if that was possible.

Since Mór had left her in charge of the Free People of Avina, Skylene lived a troubled life. Part of it was being without her lover. They had slept entwined together for several years. Trying to find slumber by herself proved difficult, and her dreams rushed unpleasantly at her when she did sleep. She woke most mornings knotted in her sheets, more desolate for realizing it was only linen that bound her, not Mór's shapely limbs.

The Avina she found on kicking off those sheets challenged her in new ways each day. In the first days of freedom the city's occupants huddled nervous, unsure that what appeared to have happened really had. The Auldek gone? All of them? The divine children with them and many of the other slaves as well? They had all watched it happen, but they stayed in the same rooms, in the same buildings, finding it hard to believe that the Auldek would not appear again suddenly, ready to punish them for even daring to think themselves free.

Some youths rode out of the city on an antok. They returned a week later with verification that the Auldek carried on to the north, making haste, none of them looking back. At Skylene's suggestion, the People agreed to set up watches to the north of the city to provide a warning should the thing they feared return to them. With that in place, they rejoiced. People ran through the streets, reveling in their new freedom. They were as giddy as the children they had not been allowed to be, laughing and dancing, feasting and making love and dreaming of what they would do with a city—an entire continent—all their own. It was too much for them, vast and filled with another race's history—such a challenge, but a challenge all their own now. The very thought of it made them drunk with joy.

Skylene made speeches often during these early days. She reminded the revelers that the Free People had always planned for this day. The Council of Elders had lived far from them, but they had never ceased laboring for them, taking in the abandoned, hiding those who had run from abuse, keeping alive a dream of unity once they were as free in reality as they were in moral truth. Soon, she told them, Mór and Yoen and the others would join them. Together they would build their nation. It sounded wonderful. It was all true and all possible. But barely had the tail of the Auldek migration slipped over the northern horizon before the problems started.

By the end of the second week one man had killed another in a dispute over who had rights to an estate. The slain man was of the Kulish Kra; his murderer, an Anet. Skylene was at the trial called to decide the matter. She was one of the many who agreed to the punishment of a tattoo identifying the Anet as a murderer to be stenciled across his shaved scalp. Before the sentence was carried out, a group of Anet mobbed the chamber in which the man was imprisoned. They bashed their way in, freed him, and fought a battle in the streets to escape. They claimed the trial had been unjust. It was biased against Anets. Only other Anets had the right to try their kind, they claimed. How could they know justice was done otherwise?

The one who led them was a short man named Dukish, an Anet who had once been a golden eye, one of the quota slaves who handled financial affairs for the Auldek. He had been a man of some station, but he had not been chosen to go with them. Declaring himself the clan's chieftain, he called on other Anet slaves to join him in putting clan interests first, saying none should govern them but themselves. Many flocked to him. He armed them, seizing a weapons cache he knew of from his former work. Before anyone could organize to stop them, they took control of a portion of the city, including a warehouse stocked with grain and beans and salt, great vats of vinegar and wine.

It got worse after that. Former household slaves laid claim to their master's palaces, while field workers were kept at a distance. Golden eyes and others who had held higher offices for the Auldek claimed that those privileges should be transferred to positions of a similar rank in the new order. A gang of young Kulish Kra men harassed Kern women. It began as a joke played on one avian clan by another. But it grew violent, sexual. Before long the rumors were that the Kulish Kra youths had taken to raping and molesting Kern women. The Kern formed armed groups against this, to which the Kulish Kra responded in kind; and still other armed groups formed in response to the increasingly violent tension in the city, further fueling it. The league returned. They plied the water in their ships and in the Lothan

Aklun's soul vessels. It became clear that they were establishing themselves on the barrier isles, and everyone wondered how long it would be before they landed on the mainland.

Skylene tried to speak reason to them all. For a time she found ears listening, but as the weeks passed she was surprised at how often her perfect reason fell only on the backs of people's heads. She forgot, perhaps, that as Mór's lover and as an active member of the Free People she had learned to look past the clan markings more than most. To many, their clan members were their kin, not just the arbitrarily selected other slaves. It was in households and fields with others of their clan that they had labored. It was to the Auldek masters of those clans that they had looked with fear, with eyes first of children, then of clan members.

Skylene knew this. It had been her life, too. Still, she had expected to manage the peace for a few weeks. Instead, she scrambled to prevent a riot that would ignite the entire city. To hear her, the people had to truly listen, to understand, to be brave. To heed men like Dukish, one only had to feel fear.

"We must be careful," Tunnel said as they walked the last corridor that would take them to the meeting. "I don't like this one."

"I don't like Dukish either, but that's part of the reason we have to speak with him."

The chieftains and their seconds met at a ring of chairs in the center of the same massive chamber in which the Auldek had slaughtered Sire Neen's group. The circle of chairs looked tiny beneath the high ceiling, dwarfed by the pillars and the shafts of light that fell diagonally from openings in the ceiling. The men and women milling around hardly seemed capable of making decisions for the mass of people that could have filled the entire chamber.

"We shouldn't be meeting like this," Skylene muttered as

she moved to take her seat. "We should all be here together. All of us."

Tunnel grunted his agreement from where he stood behind her chair. He crossed his bulging arms over his chest and reached up with one hand to pull contemplatively on a tusk.

"Who is going to begin?" Dukish asked before everyone was fully settled.

"You just have," Plez, a thin woman with the same Kern features as Skylene, said.

When Dukish smiled the scales on his face shifted in a manner that Skylene always imagined must feel uncomfortable. "But I am not the one with complaints. I am happy. Let the complainers complain."

Than, the leader of the Lvin, scowled at him. He had only light clan marks: pale white shading around his nose and eyes, steel whiskers, the ends of which he pressed often with his fingertips. Still, he had a fierce demeanor akin to his snow lion totem. "I am no complainer," he said through gritted teeth, "but I have much to say against you."

"Do you? Say it, then."

He did. Than related a long list of grievances, most of which Skylene shared. At times, he could have been speaking for her. Randale, a Wrathic, added to the mountain of complaints against Dukish. The representative of the Kulish Kra, Maren, topped that mountain with a cold, snowy peak. She accused him of wanting to use Lothan Aklun relics. "He would use their ships. Ships driven by *souls*. Look at him. He would find a way to steal souls and become immortal if he could. He wants to live like an Auldek."

No, not that. No souls should ever be taken again.

Dukish listened to it all, unimpressed.

All that is true, Skylene thought, but it's not the heart of the matter. She readied her words and cleared her throat to speak.

Plez beat her to it. "Don't look so smug," she said to Dukish. "You and your people are alone. You think you can hold half the city by yourself? You think you can make a life without the rest of us?"

"He doesn't have to," the Antok spokesman, Haavin, said, speaking for the first time. "We Antok have no grievance with him. He is not so alone as you think."

"And there are always new friends to make." Dukish shared a knowing look with Haavin. And then, as if he had been pressed, "I might as well tell you all. I've been in contact with the league-men." The others cried out, but he spoke over them. "Yes, I have! Why not? Somebody had to. You want them just lurking out there? I will meet with them, and they have said they wish to meet with me." Smiling, he added, "Afterward, I'll tell you what came of it."

Than was out of his seat and across to Dukish in an instant. The Anet second nearly toppled his chieftain, so hurriedly did he rush to defend Dukish. Others rose and moved forward as well. The circle of chairs became a ring, hemming in a pushing, shoving contingent of the new leaders.

"You people are driving me mad!" Skylene shouted. Her voice, high-pitched and sharp, cut through the mêlée. She looked all the more striking because she had not risen with the others. Her hands clutched the seat on which she sat as if she were holding herself from shooting up from it. "Stop it. Stop it! This is all so—so unnecessary. Don't you see that? We're arguing about things we don't need to be arguing about, and we're losing sight of our dream."

"*Your* dream," Dukish said. He plopped back into his chair, crossing one leg over the other. "Your dream, Skylene. We've heard enough of it. From you, from Mór, from those who came before you. It was fine to dream when we were slaves. Now we're not, and real things need to be done. That's what I am doing. You all act like I'm a criminal, but I have not killed any-one. I have not stolen from any of you. I have just acted more quickly. Don't blame me if you did not do the same."

"What you've done is divide us. We should be the Free People. All of us. We need to leave behind all this talk of clans. It's part of our history, but it needs to be held within its place. It's our past, not our future. We can make more—"

"You are still dreaming," Dukish said. "How will you change all this? It already is and cannot be undone. The tales you Free People told—of prophecy and saviors, your Rhuin Fá—what has come of it? Nothing at all. There was no Rhuin Fá. The world changed, and it was not your dreams that changed it."

"That's not . . ." Skylene felt Tunnel grip her shoulder and knew what he was cautioning against. She and the others had already debated revealing Dariel's presence among them. When he was in the city, they had kept his survival a careful secret, only letting the most trusted of the Free People know. Now that he had destroyed the soul catcher and was safely away into the interior, some argued it was time to announce him. The Rhuin Fá had come, finally. The old prophecies could come true. What better thing to unite the People?

Mór, before leaving for the Sky Isle, had been against reveal-ing his presence, but Skylene thought that her opinion was tainted by her anger. She did not yet trust Dariel, and did not want to offer false hope. A reasonable concern, really. Tunnel was also against it. In his case, he had no doubt that Dariel was the leader they had been waiting for. Because of that, he wanted him protected until the right moment, until he could be announced in such a public way that nobody could deny him.

Skylene swallowed down the words she so wanted to say. Instead, she began, "Can we simply agree not to do anything further until Mór returns? And the elders as well. They should all have a say in this."

"I have said what I needed to," Dukish said. He stood and scanned the group, dismissive even as his eyes touched on them. "You do what you wish. I will do what I wish." With that, he turned and strode away. The others stirred, then rose, grumbling. The meeting, clearly, had broken up.

Tunnel leaned close to Skylene and said, "See, I don't like that one."

CHAPTER
FOURTEEN

Dariel lost track of time the moment he stepped through that doorway. He answered the slim man's beckoning. He went first, and the others followed. He could not now remember the words they had spoken, or how introductions were made, or any of the things customary to a meeting. None of that mattered, for nothing inside the Sky Mount was the same as outside. It did not so much cling to the mountains as belong to them, a part of them, smooth and organic, as if the rock had once been living tissue. It was sparse, clean, with none of the everyday items of life: no tables or chairs, no beds or hearths or cupboards. Dariel had the feeling that all these things had once been here, but now there was nothing but a long sweep of corridors that led to empty rooms.

The whole time he was there, he knew that the others were also somewhere within the dizzying sprawl of the place. He could feel them. He could even hear faint indications of their thoughts, like voices heard at a distance. His hound pups were inside as well, somewhere in the maze of rooms and passages. All cared for. All safe. This was not about them, though. From what felt like the first moments his time in the Sky Mount was spent with only one person. Nâ Gâmen.

That was why he seemed to pass all his time—immeasurable as it was—by the Lothan Aklun's side. They walked from room to room, sharing thoughts, conversing without opening their mouths. This, too, was a thing Dariel did not remember beginning, but it soon seemed natural enough. Shape a thought. Send it. Hear the answer within his head. Never a sound except the wind that whipped through the passages and the scuffing of his feet across the smooth gray stone. Aliver had said he spoke to the Santoth in a similar manner. Now Dariel understood.

Nâ Gâmen was slender in the extreme, famine faced, with copper skin that lay thinly across the bones of his bald skull. He stood a little distance away, gazing through an opening in the wall of his sky-top sanctuary, looking at the dizzying drop to the valleys far below. He looked so lost in thought that Dariel feared he was about to fall forward through the opening and plummet from the heights. Why Dariel should care what happened to this man he could not have said yet. But he did care. He already believed that Nâ Gâmen, the Watcher of the Sky Mount, was entwined with his destiny.

You are an Akaran, Nâ Gâmen said. *I can smell it in the oils on your skin. It's in your breath when you exhale. I hear it when your heart beats. I see it in the vibrations of the air around you. Do you know, Dariel Akaran, that you trail your ancestors behind you on a silver string? I see them waving in the air. All the living trail behind them those who came before. A portion of each soul grasps the string and stays with you always. I didn't always see them, but I have for a long, long time. Do you know how I know this?*

How? Dariel asked.

Because the same is true of me. I trail many strings. Thousands. Tens of thousands. And each of these touches a million souls. Sometimes I feel very heavy, pulling them behind me. Sometimes lifting my arm is like moving a mountain. As it should be for one like me. An accursed one like me.

The notion of weight was hard to equate with the tall, slight man who placed the words in Dariel's head.

How do you know me? Dariel asked. *The smell of my skin. My breath. How?*

Because you are of Tinhadin's line. I see him in you.

You knew Tinhadin? You are truly from my lands?

Nâ Gâmen turned and set his green eyes on him. They were larger than normal, jewels in his gaunt face. His earlobes spread out in large curves shaped like butterfly wings. They moved when he did. When he stilled, they swayed as if rocked by a gentle tide. *We are children of the same land, yes. And I did know Tinhadin. I know him still. One does not forget the man who tried to murder him. That man who helped, in his way, to make this accursed life.*

You have said that before. How are you accursed?

You would know it all?

Yes.

It will come at a price, Dariel. A gift, but a dear one. One that will be hard to live with. Do you want it?

Whether I want it or not, I'm here, he thought. Sharing, he answered, *Yes.*

Nâ Gâmen gestured that they should continue walking. Dariel fell in step beside him. Again, the sound of his feet stood out strangely compared to the silence with which the Watcher moved. If the man's feet—hidden beneath long gray robes—touched the stone at all, they gave no indication of it. Not even the fabric of his robes swished audibly. Beside him, Dariel felt awkward and loud. Every motion he made was too large and cumbersome when compared to the silent grace with which Nâ Gâmen floated beside him.

Listen. See. I will feed it to you.

Dariel did not get a chance to ask what that meant. Before the words had faded from his head, images began to scroll across his vision, scenes through which he could barely see the real world behind. Mixed with this, thoughts and emotions came to him, delivered not with words, not explained, just given to him. He felt them as if they were his emotions. His thoughts. And through that Nâ Gâmen's voice came and went, moving him forward, answering questions as he thought them.

The name Lothan Aklun, he claimed, was the Auldek translation of their name, given to them in this land. Before that they were called the Dwellers in Song. They were a religious sect in the Known World. It was they who had preserved the Giver's tongue through the eons. They long lived in cloistered seclusion, respected by all the tribal powers. They kept *The Song of Elenet* safe, the actual book itself, written in that thief's crimped hand.

Back then, they still believed the Giver would return. They believed they could make amends for Elenet's arrogance, for his crime of stealing the language of a god and using it in folly. They did not use the god's song for themselves—as Elenet had—but sang it for the pure beauty of it. They did not create things. Instead they formed the song into a hymn in praise of creation. They sang it so that the Giver, wherever he was, would hear it ring with purity and would know they were worthy of his attention. That was all they wished to do. Make amends for Elenet's crime and bring the god back into the world.

Also, they worked to purify the song. There were, even in Elenet's own hand, errors and impurities in the song, evil or hateful flourishes. The Dwellers worked to find them and remove them, so that the book would be pure. It was an ongoing task that gave their lives meaning.

When new devotees were ready, they journeyed across the land, in small groups or singly. Dariel saw all this as much as heard it through Nâ Gâmen's words. Cloaked figures greeted the dawn with their heads raised and voices flowing out over the hilly Talayan landscape. A single man walked a mountain pass, keeping time with the tapping of his walking stick on the stones. Women knee-deep in the tranquil waters of a blue ocean praised the sun as it burned its way into the rim of the world. A circle of singers around a campfire, wrapped in cloaks against the frigid wind, eyes gazing at the millions of stars as their lips moved, asking the Giver to come back and bring harmony to the world again.

As he listened, Dariel understood the word-notes that were that strange language, so filled with longing, so true and perfect. Somehow, they carried the solidity of the substance of the world rendered in living sound.

For hundreds of years we lived and died and worked at this mission, Nâ Gâmen said. He held Dariel by the wrist now. They walked along a narrow shelf of rock that dropped off down a steep slope on one side. Before them, a stone staircase curved up toward the peak of the mountain. They carried on toward it. *The world was in chaos through all that time. See it.*

And Dariel did. Warring factions. Uprisings. Tribal betrayals. Atrocities. The Known World as it had once been flashed before Dariel's eyes in a torrent of images. He saw things real and surreal, things that made sense and things that did not. An army of mail-clad warriors smashed against howling tribesmen in furs and leather. Creatures with the lower bodies of horses and with human torsos above pounded across dry plains. Black skinned as Balbarans, they screamed war. A queen bearing a narrow, simple crown spoke before a gathered host of snarling monsters, crammed together inside a huge chamber. She showed no fear of them. She just spoke on, her freckled face serene before the madness.

Nâ Gâmen explained that Edifus left the Dwellers alone as his conquest took shape. He even visited them on occasion, learning the song himself and adding his voice to theirs. Perhaps he still respected the god. Perhaps he believed as they did. For a time it seemed so. He convinced them that the world they were building—once the warfare was over—would have a beauty in the god's eyes. In that way, he would aid in luring the Giver back to the Known World.

We came to trust him. We freely gave him The Song of Elenet. Who better than a king to protect it? His sons, Thalaran, Tinhadin, and Praythos, wanted to become students of The Song, but we would not teach them. Even Edifus would not teach them. He did not trust them. He wanted them to wait, to grow older, to find wisdom through warfare first. He hid The Song in a place he thought nobody could find it. When Edifus died, one of the sons showed himself to be everything Edifus had feared. Tinhadin, the middle son, was a man apart from his siblings. He fell into warring with them. Even as their Wars of Distribution spread the empire farther than Edifus had ever dreamed, he found ways to kill both his brothers. Still he wanted more.

A man with Akaran eyes and a twice-crooked nose raged into a temple, pushing through chairs and desks, his sword slashing at any of the robed pupils near enough for him to cut down. Many fled from him, but one man did not. He stood, leaning against a lectern, his hands clasping it behind him, holding it, his face defiant. The warrior swung his sword, sloppy with rage. It sliced through one of the priest's arms and most of his torso. He let loose the weapon and climbed over the gore slipping from the dying body to reach the text that the priest had been protecting. The look of rapture on his face was like nothing Dariel had ever witnessed.

We should have been prepared. We should have seen it coming. We did not. He stole a text that should never have been read and made himself a sorcerer. He used it to teach his chosen warriors. Together, no army could stand against them.

Warriors in orange cloaks waded into a great host, an army like the entire world. The sorcerer warriors hewed forward with great sweeps of their long swords. They whispered words that Dariel heard as if their lips were pressed against his ears. He knew the meaning of the words for the space of time it took to hear them. Horrible words. Sounds that were the unmaking of the world. Notes that tore and destroyed. Phrases that twisted in Dariel's ears like living cancer. And then he saw the man with the twice-crooked nose on a field of carnage. The man ripped off his helmet and stood, the only upright figure in a graveyard that stretched to the horizon on all sides, bodies countless. The silence terrible.

The Santoth, Dariel said. *You are like the Santoth. You use the same magic.*

No, came the reply. *No, we do not speak the same magic. No, we were not like them. No more so than a scholar of warfare is a warrior. We were scholars. We kept The Song. We preserved it. For centuries we stayed outside the world's power struggles. We kept The Song alive and refined the Giver's tongue for the good of all. You must understand that. We made it even purer, so that if ever the Giver returned we could speak with him and show him that we were not all like Elenet. That's what we were.*

The Santoth . . . What they stole was not The Song of Elenet. It was the texts we had removed from it, the parts of it that were most foul and twisted. If they had been true scholars, they would have known this, but they were warriors. They only ever wanted the things that warriors want. Conquest. Power. To be feared. These evil texts were aid enough. And Tinhadin only wanted their rage, so he inflicted them with pain to plague them all the moments of their lives that were not spent fighting for him. That was why they fought so mercilessly. By inflicting pain, they escaped it briefly themselves.

It was not until later that Tinhadin discovered where his father had hidden The Song of Elenet. He retrieved it, and once he had it, none could stand against him. Not the Dwellers, not his Santoth. He sent his own sorcerers into exile without sharing the true Song with them. They were raging evil, hateful, but they were powerless against him. He had only to speak to destroy them, so they accepted their exile.

Dariel shook his head. *But I saw them on the Teh Plains. When they thought my brother dead, they marched north to search for him. Aliver had promised to release them once he found The Song of Elenet. He died before he could. When they confirmed that he was dead, they unleashed a nightmare on the Meins. It was a horror, but they did it for us. They did not seem vengeful. They won that war for us.*

No, not for you, Nâ Gâmen corrected. *For themselves. If what you say is true, they fought and destroyed—as is dear to their hearts. Don't believe they did it for you, though. If they destroyed your enemy, it was because that was the only place they could direct their anger and disappointment. Dariel, be thankful your brother died before he released the Santoth. Be thankful he never gave them The Song of Elenet. If he had, they would have destroyed him and taken the world as payment for their suffering. That's what they want. Time does nothing to change men like them.*

So that is the truth as I know it, the Watcher said. *Tinhadin stole from us and created the Santoth. We should have fought him before that, but we had no gift for prophecy. We did not know what was coming. How could we? I ask you, how could we?*

❊

A week away from the question, out of Rath Batatt and back into Inàfeld Forest, Dariel sat away from the others, on night watch. He pressed his back against the base of a large tree. The group slept—or lay quiet with their thoughts, like him—in the small clearing just below him. He still pondered Nâ Gâmen's question. He had not answered it when asked, but now he thought he knew. They could have known what was coming if they had paid attention to the world. If they had kept their eyes open to the struggles of nations and the ambitions and fears of man, instead of believing they could ignore such things for their higher calling. Of course a thing that *could* be made into a weapon *would* be a made into a weapon. It did not matter if it was a thing of beauty. It did not matter if their mission was holy and benevolent. It only mattered that *The Song* could be twisted to serve human greed. If that was so, it was only a measure of time until someone grasped for it.

A man like Tinhadin, whose blood—Nâ Gâmen reminded him—flowed in his veins. He did not let himself think also of a woman like his sister. That thought lurked at the margins of his consciousness. He knew it was there and that it would not likely go away, but he could not face it yet. There was too much else to face, too many things more pressing on him. As he had thought before, he needed to solve the problems of this land. It was here in Ushen Brae that he found himself, and here that he had to carve a path forward. The fact that Nâ Gâmen looped it all back to the Known World did not change that. It just made everything more urgent.

"Dariel?" Anira climbed the small rise up toward him. He had not seen her until she spoke. "May I sit with you?"

Dariel indicated the space beside him, with a crescent of root that would make a comfortable seat. "I'm no good as a watchman tonight."

"When were you ever? Are you still thinking of him?"

"Of course. You?"

Anira sat back against the trunk, her arm pressed against his. "I never had trouble sleeping before. Now . . ."

"Was your time with him . . . bad? I mean . . ." He hesitated. "I don't know what I mean. It's still hard to talk about."

"No, my time with him wasn't bad. Was yours?"

"I don't know how to answer that," he said.

An eruption of monkey calls peppered the air just then. For a few moments, the creatures leaped and swung through the trees above them, passing like a great herd along a road of branches and limbs. When they were gone into the distance, both of them let the silence be. Anira did not seem to mind that he had not answered the question. Dariel was glad, as he was grateful for the press of her dark skin against his.

Anira said something in Auldek.

"Why do you all sometimes speak Auldek? I would think you would hate it."

"The tongue of our enslavement?"

"Something like that."

"All the tongues offered us were the tongues of our enslavement. Would you have us speak Acacian?"

"You do speak Acacian," Dariel said.

"Out of necessity. It's still the language that sold us to slavery. It's the language of the league. We all came here with a first language, not always Acacian, but we also spoke some Acacian. We had to. It's the language of your empire. If we could have sorted ourselves we might have kept Balbara alive in us or Candovian or Senivalian. But we were thrown into a world where two languages were the only true currency. Auldek among the Auldek, Acacian among ourselves. At least we speak two languages. What about you?"

"I speak a bit of lots of things."

"A bit?"

"I had to. I traveled all over. I worked among the people in Aushenia. Right in with them, rebuilding after the war with Hanish Mein."

"My noble prince," Anira teased. She leaned her knees up over his and rested her head on his shoulder. "And how much of their talk can you speak? You can say, 'Hello.' You can say, 'My name is Dariel. What is yours?' You can ask where is the toilet and comment on the weather, so long as it's something you know the words for, like raining. Am I right?"

"I never *had* to speak anything other than Acacian. I did it because I . . . wanted to show that I cared."

"Do you know what Mór would call that? Insulting."

Dariel looked away. "I can't be accountable for what someone finds insulting."

"No, but you should try. Trying counts for a lot."

"That's what I just said!"

Anira laughed. "You want me to teach you Auldek? Real Auldek, not just polite phrases?"

"Yes," he said. "I do. If it's your language I'm learning—not the Auldek's."

"There are no Auldek here anymore. They are your people's problem. I'll teach you if you will try to learn."

"I'll try," Dariel said.

※

Back on the Sky Mount, Dariel and Nâ Gâmen had stood atop a pinnacle of stone, a high protrusion at the very tip of the mountain. Clouds flew past them at incredible speed, wet against Dariel's skin. It was terrifying each time they cleared and the entirety of the mountain heights fell away beneath them. A span of time had passed since last they spoke, he knew. He had reached this place by walking up the stone staircase. He knew that. But he had not walked up it in a continuous journey from when this conversation began. Time, or his awareness of it, did not progress with such reasoned steadiness.

What did you do? he asked. *How did you respond to Tinhadin's crimes?*

Look there and see, Nâ Gâmen answered.

Following the Watcher's gaze, Dariel looked down and saw, overlaid on the mountains, a vast ocean. At the edge of it a tiny fleet hugged an arctic shoreline colder and more forlorn than any Dariel had seen. They were specks on an infinity of water and waves, stone and ice. He swept down closer. Figures huddled on the decks, wrapped in blankets. None of them worked the sails, and yet the ship moved forward. Among them, on the deck of the last vessel, a man stared directly at Dariel, his green eyes desolate, hopeless. He opened his mouth and spoke with the Watcher's voice.

Cowards, we fled. We did not even manage to get The Song of Elenet *back from Tinhadin. We tried, but he attacked us with a savagery that combined the true song with the evil texts. He threw a curse at our backs, one that forever banished us from the Known World. It burned, and we fled before it. We were not warriors, Dariel Akaran. We were the faithful, and our faith had been raped and violated. The Giver had truly forsaken us. He was gone and would never return. His abandonment of the world was complete. No prayers or devotion or singing his praises would ever bring him back. Instead, he gave the world to men like Tinhadin. We thought the world had ended.*

They were years in the Far North, progressing slowly or not at all. At times they were stuck fast in the pack ice for months on end, often floating back toward the Known World. They survived by murmuring the words of *The Song*. They kept it going constantly, passing it from ship to ship like a lantern to warm and light them. They did not have the actual text of *The Song of Elenet* to guide them anymore, but they had studied it hard before fleeing. They knew enough, and they had seen that the Giver's words could be twisted to serve man. So they sang. Not to call back the Giver, though. They sang to live. To stay alive. And as they did, floating in a lifeless land, they learned hatred.

When they finally sailed south along the new coastline that was Ushen Brae, they saw the possibility of life returning to them. A new nation, a new people.

I stood on the beach the first day we made contact with them. They bunched before us, all threat and armor and weapons. No language between us, but they made themselves clear. They would kill us, destroy us. *Throw our corpses back into the sea if we offended them. That's all they offered us, though we arrived with no heart for war. We looked past them, over them, to the land beyond. Ushen Brae was rich and fertile, bursting with plant and animal life. The Auldek were fools to have turned their backs on it and to have spent themselves at war instead of peace. They were, we thought, no better than Acacians.*

Dariel saw all this. He felt what they had felt. They could live on in the new land, but not among the Auldek. They would live separate from them. They would scrape by, living on the barrier isles, where the Auldek feared to go. So they did, building at first a crude settlement. It was not life as it had been. They could not rekindle the love of the world they had once felt, but they would survive in defiance of Tinhadin. They would spurn him. They would be revenged on him by that very act. Once awakened, revenge is a hunger as great any other.

There was a problem, Nâ Gâmen said. *Already our mastery of the song had begun to lose its purity. Our voices warped from true, like instruments losing their tuning. Soon, it seemed, we would have to abandon it entirely. That was too much to bear. So we learned to preserve some of the Giver's tongue outside ourselves. Knowing it would decay in our minds until it was nothing but curses, we worked to put the song into things. We trapped our intent inside stone, wood, metal. We built with material and sorcery bound together. For, yes, the song was sorcery to us now. We became like Elenet, seeking to use it for our own means.*

The soul vessels, Dariel said.

Nâ Gâmen stared out toward the horizon. His large eyes open against the buffeting wind. *And other devices, yes. These made our lives easier, gave us power, made it possible to trade with the Auldek. We thought for a time that would be all. We would trade with them what we could. We would survive. But then a ship reached us from the Known World.*

Dariel saw it. A floating wreck. A ship with a shredded mainsail and the smaller ones in tatters. The men upon it skeletal. The dead and living mixed together, hard to tell apart. They had not sailed to Ushen Brae intentionally. They had floated with the currents after being battered by a savage storm and blown far from their normal waters. They were suffering from illness and delusion. Some spoke to the sorcerers they saw as if they believed them to be keepers of the afterdeath.

The sorcerers nursed the sailors back to life, a few of them, at least. It was not easy. They were far gone, insane from their ordeal. To save them Nâ Gâmen and the others fed the sailors a diet of mist threads, keeping them in a chamber rank with the smoke of the stuff and using the threads to sew their festering wounds and made poultices of it to soothe their sores. They bound their heads and squeezed the madness out of them, bringing them back in a form that suited them.

Then the Dwellers in Song developed a scheme to use them. They would send them back to the Known World in a new, better ship, one that could sail directly across the Gray Slopes without fear of succumbing to sea beasts. They could not do this themselves, for Tinhadin's curse would forever hold, but these sailors could. They would offer trade with a vast new nation.

We called ourselves what the Auldek called us: Lothan Aklun, the Dwellers in Song. We said nothing about our origins. Through these sailors, we offered a deal with Tinhadin, though he would never know with whom he partnered, or why we offered it. This, Dariel, was the birth of those you call the league.

Of course it was, Dariel thought.

We saved them, created them. They have thought themselves apart from other men ever since. And we made this trade into a punishment. Revenge on the Acacians. Punishment for the Auldek for being so like them in their love of war and destruction. The Auldek needed to repopulate their nation after years of war. We took that ability from them, made them barren with the song. Tinhadin, the sailors told us, was fighting with his own sorcerers. They had turned against him, or he against them. He was trying to hold together an empire that denied it even was an empire. He was at the verge of losing everything. We had only to find a thing that each side could provide the other. We did. Children for Auldek. Sedated peace for the Acacians. So it was arranged.

We did not understand at the beginning how long it could last, how we would prosper. We harvested souls from the quota children and kept them within our own bodies. We became immortal by sucking lives from Acacia. We gave them to the Auldek so that they would live and live and live, always needing more. We made the quota children infertile, so that the Auldek would always need more of them. So it has been ever since.

How was that a punishment? Dariel asked. You made us prosper. We ruled unbroken for twenty-two generations.

What greater punishment, Nâ Gâmen asked, is there than sacrificing your morality for a delusion? What's worse than living with lies woven into the fabric of your every interaction? We are nothing but the lives we lead, Dariel Akaran. Even poor children sold into slavery may live honest lives. No Akaran has done that since Tinhadin became the despot he was. Your people have escaped death these many generations, but they have lived failed lives in the process. Yours, prince, is as yet a failed life.

CHAPTER
FIFTEEN

The League Council had been clear: Sire Dagon needed to find out everything he could about Aliver Akaran's being alive. Such a thing was unthinkable, and yet here they were, forced not only to think about it but to weigh just what it meant for them and decide how to respond. If it was true, Corinn had reached into dimensions she should not have interfered with. Either she was more powerful than they knew, or she was more foolish.

Or both, Dagon had thought at the time. Or both.

Finally summoned to the palace for a meeting of the Queen's Council, Dagon sat impatiently through Rhrenna's opening remarks. As always, she called on the spirits of the first five Akaran kings to instill the council members with wisdom. What rubbish! The only Akaran kings to demonstrate wisdom had been covertly removed or manipulated by the league. Well, Dagon thought, considering it that way, yes. By all means follow their examples.

He kept his face expressionless as Rhrenna went over routine matters. Sigh Saden sat, feigning composure as well, looking down his aristocratic nose, vaguely bored. He was neither composed nor bored, though. The tremulous way the index finger on his left hand tapped on the edge of the table said as much. Old Julian was more honestly at ease. Dagon knew that he had actually spoken with whoever it was they all believed to be Aliver. Obviously, Julian had been convinced. He had been close to Leodan. Perhaps he was one Agnate who honestly wished the Akarans well. Balneaves Sharratt just looked hungry, Talinbeck full of questions, and General Andeson subdued. Baddel, the Talayan, bubbled with energy. He looked as giddy as a ten-year-old girl on her name day.

Dagon would have continued his examination of the councilors, but happily Rhrenna concluded her opening routine. The queen began without further delay.

"I know what you all want," Corinn said. "You want to see Aliver. We've to discuss what happened in Teh and the coming war and the vintage and all manner of other things. But what you want to know is if what you've heard and seen can possibly be true. Well, judge for yourselves."

Corinn pointed toward the far end of the table. Only then did Dagon realize the seat facing Corinn had been left vacant. He must have been truly distracted not to have noticed that earlier. Sigh Saden had been accustomed to sitting there. Perhaps that explained his agitation.

On cue, Rhrenna intoned something about welcoming his royal majesty, brought from the dark lands to light again and so forth. Dagon was not listening, for a man had stepped through the open door. He walked toward the end of the table, popping in and out of view as he passed behind the far row of seated councilors. Dagon did not get a clear view of him until he reached the vacant seat and turned, smiling on the council.

Aliver Akaran. He was older than when Dagon had last seen him, but Aliver had only been a boy then. This was a man, slim and well formed. His cheekbones and jawline cut stronger angles than before. He held himself with a trace of his old stiff posture. He was a little darker than Dagon remembered, with wavy hair pressed neatly to his head by the jeweled leather band that circled his forehead.

"Hello, councilors," he said.

They answered with a frayed chorus of "Your Majesty." Dagon bowed his head, though less from deference than from a desire to hide his face. It was really true. Not just rumor. Not a clever illusion. Not an impostor. He knew all these things with certainty already. Part of him wanted to fly from the chamber and seek communion with his fellows, to tell and show them everything with his mind. That would have to wait, though.

He did his part in the clamor. Praising the queen. Wondering at Aliver. Baddel even rose and ran around the table, clapping his hands as he went, and embraced Aliver. "Will you become king, Your Highness? Oh, there will be so much rejoicing! All Talay will celebrate! This is just the thing to bring the tribes together again. Just as we were when you rallied us to war against Hanish Mein!"

Nedona, a new councilor from the Ou trading family of Bocoum, shoved Baddel away. Then he pulled Aliver close and whispered in his ear. That could not go unmet. Soon the entire council was afoot and jostling to make contact. These jackals are quick to start nibbling, Dagon thought, staying seated and decorous.

It was some time before the council returned to order. "How . . ." Saden had a question but did not seem to know how to phrase it. "How . . . are you to govern now? I mean . . ." He gestured to the queen, then across to Aliver, and then he wriggled his fingers. Not at all a clear illustration of his question, but they all understood it. "There's no precedent. The Senate will have to—"

"The Senate will do what it does," Corinn said. "They have no role in this. Aliver and I will rule together."

"But we can't have two monarchs!" Talinbeck exclaimed. The idea seemed to horrify him. He looked to Jason, the most scholarly among them. "Has that ever happened in all the generations of the empire?"

The scholar took his time in answering, but not because he needed to search for it. He just seemed stunned. "No," he said, "there is no precedent. But I don't recall any record of the dead being returned to life. It's all . . ."

"Unprecedented," Corinn said. "Yes, that much is confirmed. So we will rule together."

"There will be a coronation, then?" Baddel asked.

Corinn deferred to Aliver with a nod. He answered, "Yes. At the winter solstice. I know—that's not when it's usually done, but it's what we have to do. We'll be at war this spring. No time for the ceremony then."

"Your first order of business," Corinn said, "will be to help Rhrenna put together the guest lists. Quickly. We've but a month."

"Send birds today," Aliver added. "Shout it to the world!"

"It will be a week of festivities like none the empire has seen for years," Corinn continued. "My coronation was a bit muted. So much mourning and death, the aftermath of the war and all that that entailed. None of us had been in a mood for a grand display. This time it will be different! We'll assure the people of the greatness of the Acacian Empire. We'll show them strong leadership, power beyond their imaginings, and—"

"Food!" Aliver said. "We'll feed them food!"

Before the astonished eyes of the council, both siblings doubled over in laughter. The two of them, Dagon thought, are like children suddenly out from under the heel of their parents, gleeful at the idea of discarding the old rules. He said, "That is truly gracious of you, Your Majesty." He looked to the queen. "Your mastery of the song astounds us all. What you did on the fields of Teh I scarcely believed when I heard it. Now I don't doubt it. Aliver is evidence that you are truly heir to Tinhadin himself. Is there a limit to your powers?"

"None that I have yet discovered."

But you cannot read minds, can you, bitch? Dagon thought. He said, "Wonderful. May I ask you to detail how you come to these powers?"

"No," Corinn said. "I'm sure you have theories, notions. You may even have the truth. But don't ask me to show my hand entirely. The league would never do that, correct?"

"Ah," Dagon said, leaving the expulsion of breath as a neutral response. "May I ask if Aliver will take up the study of sorcery as well? He went in search of the Santoth before. Even brought them into the battle with Hanish Mein, yes?"

Corinn did not defer to her brother this time. "Aliver has other skills. He works magic with the populace. All Talay worships him. That's what he will focus on, preparing the Known World's forces to fight the Auldek—assuming Mena does not rob him of that glory."

"Good that you mention the war," Dagon said. "A great part of my joy in seeing the prince returned is knowing that he'll be with us during the coming war. Perhaps we should consider that issue and its many faces. I would very much like to hear the prince's thoughts. I'm sure we all would." He tented his fingers. In truth he did not care that much about discussing the war, but he needed to see how Aliver addressed such matters.

The long conversation he sat through convinced him of two things. First—and he tested this several times—Aliver Akaran said nothing that differed from his sister's opinion. The vintage? Not a protest. He saw no problem with the common people of the empire being drugged into faithful reverence once again. Mena's choosing Mein Tahalian as a base to train her army through the winter? What a fine idea! Corinn's hope that she could sing Elya's children into accelerated growth and make them winged mounts by the spring? A pleasing possibility. Strange that nobody had thought of it earlier.

Corinn said, "We were thinking, Jason, about the charge I gave you earlier—about creating a horse lore."

The scholar jumped at the mention of his name. "Yes, I've been working on that. There are many ancient references to be expanded upon. Did you know that Talayans once had a horse culture? I didn't know until I dug deep into the archives. You'll be fascinated. I've collected documents for you to consider." He turned to hand the folder to a servant, who would bring it around the table to Corinn.

"Um . . . I don't think so," the queen said. She indicated with a curl of her lip that the servant need not bother. "We're going to scrap that idea."

Jason stared at her, at a loss for words for a moment. "Your Majesty," he eventually said, " 'scrap' it?"

"An idea for yesterday," Aliver said, picking up for his sister. "The notion of another life entirely. No, instead, work on a lore of winged riders."

"Winged riders . . ."

"Are exactly the thing to excite the masses."

"But . . . there have never been winged riders. Not until Mena and—"

"There will be more than just Elya," Corinn said. "There will be."

In the face of such dual certainty, Jason withered. He took back his documents and mumbled that he would begin researching that very afternoon.

Winged riders? Dagon wanted to laugh, but the knot that formed in his stomach told him there was something to this. When was the last time his agents had seen Elya's young? He had a sudden realization that the maid who funneled information from the palace had been silent on the subject lately. He would have to check. Could the queen be doing something with them? She must be. She was confident enough in her actions to flaunt it here, among her councilor enemies.

In everything as they talked on, the royal siblings shared the same mind. How bothersome. Even when Aliver set his light brown eyes on the leagueman himself it might as well have been Corinn doing so. "Sire Dagon, what of the search for my brother? I read the last dispatch, but you must give us more than vague hopes and possibilities."

"I'm afraid I cannot, Your Highness. Our search continues, of course, but there has been no word of your brother at all." Aliver stared at him. "It's our top priority in the Other Lands, I assure you."

The prince made a sour face. It was startling, until he followed it with a gesture of his fingers, as if he were opening his hand to drop seeds. Dagon recognized it for what it was—a Talayan expression of grudging acknowledgment. "I'm sure that's so, but Dariel is lost in a foreign land! What can be more important than finding him?"

More likely he's dead in a foreign land, Dagon came very near to saying. "Dare I say it, but we may never do that, Your Highness."

Aliver leaned forward, set both elbows on the table. "Then the league will have me to answer to. Let me be clear. This will happen. You will find Dariel. Everything about the empire's relationship with the league depends on it. Do you understand that, Sire Dagon? Need I detail exactly what I mean?"

The whelp is threatening me! Dagon thought. *He's threatening the league and making sure everyone here knows it.* Corinn looked as pleased as a proud mother.

The other thing it convinced him of was that Queen Corinn had evolved into a greater danger than the league had anticipated. It was not just that every rumor about what she had achieved through sorcery appeared to be true. Nor was it that her demeanor was more self-satisfied than he had ever seen. It was none of the things Dagon detailed about the weapons she had at her disposal. It was, instead, that for brief moments he was sure her eyes sparked with madness. He was sure nobody else noticed. It was there, though, a quiver at their corners on occasion. Once it looked as if she saw something in the room that was not actually there.

By the late hour that the meeting concluded, Dagon knew he would have to send his brothers a troubling report. The situation was not as chaotically tranquil as they had anticipated. More was at work than they had known. The league could not simply float above the bloodshed, watch the shuffling of pieces, and accept any outcome as beneficial. Not when Corinn raised the dead and destroyed small armies and planned to fly men on dragons. With all that, she might actually triumph! What a terrifying thought.

In his quarters in the league area of Acacia, Dagon moved swiftly. There were enough leaguemen in Alecia to convene a partial council. He would sail for the Mainland and commune with them there. He wrote a quick missive and had it sent ahead of him via the swiftest of his messenger birds. He penned it in the league's archaic script so that he could speak directly. No fear of anyone decoding the message.

Brothers,

Aliver lives. I have seen and touched him. The queen's power expands to danger.

We must meet.

He signed it by pressing a fingertip smeared with his own blood on the parchment.

CHAPTER
SIXTEEN

Rialus did his best to explain that he need not be brought along. Calrach was going. He could surely provide all the pertinent information. He knew more than Rialus did about the Ice Fields and all that. Rialus would just be deadweight. An extra burden. Besides—and this was no small thing—Rialus was not good with heights.

He need not have tired his tongue. Devoth's mind was made up. Rialus's objections influenced him no more than a buzzing gnat would have—if there had been any buzzing gnats in this arctic hell. Devoth only acknowledged his protests as if Rialus were being self-denigrating. A willful misinterpretation if Rialus had ever seen one. It did not help matters that Sabeer offered to ride with Rialus between her legs, for extra warmth, she said.

Devoth pointedly ignored her. "Come, Rialus, it's no bother. You're my guest."

Rialus found himself standing in the blistering cold, so weighted with furs that just staying upright was a mighty effort. Before him, like stone statues brought to life, moving with their strange, regally bestial mannerisms, stood the fréketes. Rialus had learned that there were only twelve of them. Though furless and naked, they took no notice of the cold. They shifted every so often, but did so as if posing before an audience, flexing their muscles and stretching their wings, which shone blue-black against the gray wall of the sky. Quota minders moved around them. Some climbed about on the leather harnesses strapped to the creatures' backs, making adjustments. A few seemed to be massaging oils into their skin.

The massive size of the fréketes was bad enough. The fact that their bodies had humanoid musculature—masculine yet somehow sexless—was even worse. But their pale faces truly made Rialus want to slither away. Large, round eyes set in ape-like features, proud and cocky and malicious at the same time. They did not look like dumb beasts at all. Rather, they gave the impression of intelligent creatures bored and unimpressed by life, doubtfully hoping that this whole mad invasion might prove diverting.

"That one is my mount." Devoth smacked Rialus on the shoulder and pointed at one of the nearer fréketes. He named it something that Rialus did not catch in the slightest. It sounded like a sputtering grunt cut short by a sneeze, then snapped away on the wind at that. "But you can call him Bitten. You will like him, Rialus."

Not likely.

"Listen, though." Devoth pulled him near and whispered, almost as if he feared the creatures would overhear. "Don't look them in the eyes."

"What?"

"I'm telling you. Don't look them in the eyes. They don't like it. Not from any but their riders. They're particular, Rialus. Take no offense at it." Devoth smacked him on the back, an impact that nearly sent Rialus sprawling.

Other Auldek arrived, jolly and shouting at one another, blowing plumes of mist. Calrach had never looked more pleased with himself. Herith and Millwa actually sang verses of some ghastly song. Menteus Nemré was among them also. He stood with the Auldek, not with any of the quota slaves. Even with his body wrapped in furs the sculpted musculature showed through. His hood was thrown back. Perhaps it had to be, considering the way his mass of white dreadlocks jutted out from his scalp like an unruly mane of thick snakes.

For a while they milled around as if just enjoying the morning, but at some point the Auldek announced that it was time to depart. The quota handlers jumped from the beasts as the Auldek clambered up them. With Devoth climbing up after him and several slaves directing him, Rialus scaled their frékete's back. Slaves pushed him into position, shoving his limbs through straps, buckling him down. Before he knew it he was spread-eagled against the creature's back, immobile. Devoth took up a position just behind him, pressing against him in a more intimate position than Rialus had ever experienced with a man. Rialus set his cheek against the frékete's warm skin, closed his eyes, and tried to think of . . .

The frékete bellowed. Rialus felt the vibrations through his cheek and chest and thighs, a sound so complete it became everything for a few moments. As it faded, the creature shifted from leg to leg. The muscles in its back quivered, and then it leaped. Rialus's internal organs tried to slip out of him and stay earthbound. They caught down around his groin and went hurtling into the air with the rest of him.

For a few seconds it seemed they would just rise indefinitely with the power of that first leap, but then the momentum slowed. They reached a zenith and the mighty wings flared. They flew, slanting away with a speed that this time shoved Rialus's insides up against one side of his rib cage. Devoth howled in pleasure; the frékete answered; Rialus clung, eyes still shut, miserable.

For a time the frékete pounded its wings vigorously. The beasts called to one another, and the riders on them shouted as if to top them. Soon they developed a slow rhythm, one wing-beat followed by a long pause before the next. Judging by the way wind ripped at him and howled in his ears, they must have been moving at great speed. Rialus could not know for sure, though. He kept his hood fastened tight and endured the passing hours and constant motion as best he could.

The expedition took nearly a week. They flew east along the ragged, ice-choked coast, camping on the boulder-strewn beach with a wall of stone pressing them toward the sea. Massive rivers of ice choked the few gaps in the mountains. Fissured. Groaning and cracking as if alive. Impenetrable. Beautiful in a way that confounded Rialus. The ice glistened blue, clear as glass in some places, touched with swirls of red in others. Certain formations he would have thought sculpted by artists, save the scale was too massive. It was a work out of proportion for human contemplation, as was his view of it on the occasions he looked down from thousands of feet in the air.

For a few days Rialus felt a bubbling of hope and fear in his chest. He knew that farther south the mountains jutted right out into the sea. No rolling army could pass there. Perhaps there was no route. Perhaps they would have to turn back and Calrach would lose his head and Rialus would . . . well, he would spend the rest of his days in Ushen Brae.

It was a short-lived notion. Flying on south, they found the gap in the stone barricade, the very one that Calrach insisted existed. No river of ice flowed in this one. Perhaps it once had, but now it just lay before them, the long tongue of a peaceful valley. They turned inland, scouting a route through the mountains and eventually out onto the Ice Fields. The Auldek became more and more pleased with everything they observed. The route through the mountains was navigable. The ice of the fields was solid enough for all their structures and beasts to roll over. Everything was as Calrach had said. Because of it, his stature among the small group grew in direct proportion to the degree to which Rialus's hopes shriveled.

Their destination before returning to the war column was Tavirith, the northernmost trading outpost along the Candovian coast. Rialus himself had named the place a few days before they flew out. He had been there only once while governor of the Mein satrapy. He had never thought he would return.

When Bitten touched down, Rialus did not really believe they had made it that far. They had been flying long enough that he had lost track of time and distance, but at some level he could not believe these arctic wastes would ever end. He did not so much feel as if they were hiking toward one world as he felt they were marching out of the world entirely, into endless nothing.

Devoth dismounted before him, and was off conferring with the other Auldek by the time Rialus touched his feet to the ice-crusted stones of the windswept beach. He moved away from Bitten, not trusting the beast without Devoth beside him. He found himself too close to one of the other hulking fréketes, so he moved forward and a little to the side of where the Auldek stood conferring. He tried to make sense of the low, dull light, but he could not even say what time of day it was. They could be anyplace. Anyplace at all in this forsaken barrenness.

He had just begun to turn and look toward the north when something caught his eye. Shapes huddled in the shadow of the dunes to the south. A cluster of geometry just ordered enough to stand out. As he stared, the details became clearer and clearer. A village. There a second cluster of houses. What looked like large stones on the shore were the hulls of beached boats, and that clutter of sticks was actually an old pier. Smoke rose from several chimneys. The moment he spotted the plumes he smelled them as well. Embedded in the side of one building was a square of glowing yellow light. He had been inside that building. He had looked out of that very window.

"Is this it?" Howlk asked. "Tavirith?"

The Auldek had gathered to either side of him, studying the same view he was studying. Rialus yanked his eyes away, as if he could deny that he had seen anything. He did not want to answer. And yet, there it was, a piece of the Known World again.

"Rialus, tell us," Sabeer said. "Is that Tavirith?"

He only meant to acknowledge it to himself, but the word escaped him. "Yes."

"Yeesss!" Howlk hissed. "Yeesss! I knew it. I can smell Acacians."

The people of Tavirith were hardly Acacians—more a mix of ancestral Candovians, combined with some of the Scav who were their own race, perhaps a few of Meinish stock and a motley collection of others, misfits who had fled the real world and washed up here.

The Auldek shouted something at the fréketes, and then pointed toward the village. The creatures followed the gestures. They glanced at one another as if coming to their own agreement on the order, and then rose one by one into the air. They flew for the village. Devoth had never looked happier. His eyes followed them with childish amazement, as if he somehow were not the architect of all this but just a witness. Then he marched after them without a word of direction to Rialus. As he strode, he reached around and yanked free the long sword strapped to his back. The other Auldek also freed their various weapons.

Rialus almost stayed where he was, an act of protest against whatever was about to happen. But as the Auldek got farther away, the howling emptiness at his back shifted closer. His feet moved of their own accord. He stumbled forward. The fréketes circled above the village. A few of them touched down. Several alighted on the structures' roofs. The Auldek lumbered forward, getting faster. Rialus himself began to run. On the one hand he hated being pulled forward. On the other he wanted to shout an alarm, to somehow alert the villagers to the enemy upon them and to explain that he was not one of them. He did not get to do any of this. Instead, he was in place to watch what followed.

One of the fréketes on a roof leaped into the air and, holding its wings angled up vertically, slammed down on the structure. The houses, Rialus knew, were built around a framework of pinewood and whalebone, layered with a latticework of beams and skins and covered with turf. The house being attacked was solid enough that the frékete needed to leap several times before it punched through. It half disappeared inside. Only its wings protruded as the rest of its body twisted and slashed around inside.

The others went wild. One shattered another roof. Another punched in a door and shoved an arm in. The first to break through climbed out of the wreckage, a flailing body clenched in its jaws. When its upper body was clear of the rooftop, it grabbed the person in one hand and hurled him out toward the onrushing Auldek. The man screamed as he tumbled through the air and crashed down. Howlk slammed his spear into the man's abdomen, pinning him to the ground for the moment it took before he strode over him, yanking the weapon out as he did so.

The Auldek reached the village as the inhabitants began to emerge. A man burst through a door and ran roaring into the open. He carried an ax in one hand, raised above his head not so much in an attack as in a gesture of warning. Rialus could tell it was not a war ax. It was one for chipping away ice. Devoth, who was standing directly in the man's path, spun to one side.

As the man passed him, he swung his sword around, angled it up, and severed the man's arm at the elbow. It and the ax looped away. The man ran forward a few strides, waving his stump as if it still held the ax. Devoth let him turn, spraying blood in a circle around him. He let him understand a portion of what was happening, then he sliced his legs out from under him.

Other men followed, to variations of the same fate. Women and children died the same way. The villagers fought as best they could, or they begged for mercy. The Auldek were like cats playing with baby mice. When the villagers stood still, the Auldek smiled and laughed and said incomprehensible things to them. When they dropped to their knees or ran or lashed out, the Auldek slashed them to pieces. Sabeer was just as gleeful as Devoth or Howlk. Menteus Nemré worked his own bloody havoc. He dove into houses and chased out the inhabitants. He shoved them savagely toward waiting Auldek, slicing to pieces any who ran in a whirling dance of butchery, his face expressionless, his white locks wild and living as he moved, whipping about like snakes searching for victims to bite.

It did not last long. Yet it went on forever. All in the settlement—men and women, old and young, even a few children— were hunted out and slaughtered. All of them. This could happen to Gurta, he thought. This could be what happens to my— He did not let himself finish the thought. It lingered, incomplete, within him.

The last few died within a howling circle of monsters dancing around them, gleefully cutting them down one after another. Until they were all gone. All dead. The Auldek held to that circle, drawing in closer over the bodies, their weapons finally lowered. The fréketes already looked bored. They rummaged through the debris of the houses. One began stoking a fire that had spread from a chimney. The others took up the task, caving in whole walls to watch them ignite.

Rialus hovered at the margin of the carnage. It was like he was standing too close to the fires. The blaze of shame scorched his face even as the raging winter froze his back. The people of Tavirith were not warriors. They had been whalers, hunters, traders, women and children, as poor and simple as any in the Known World. Why kill them? For what purpose? What sense did it make? Didn't they see what they had done? He wanted to find Devoth and ask him, show him how vile this all was. The work of cowards. An act to be ashamed of for the rest of his eternal life.

That was why he stepped forward across the blood-splattered stones. That was why he approached the circle of Auldek backs. That was why he moved around them, searching for Devoth. That was why he was right in among them when he understood what they were doing. In a crack between the huddled bodies, Devoth worked over a slain villager. The furs and clothing had been cut from his body. Devoth slid the point of his short dagger up along the man's thigh, slicing away a strip of flesh that he then held dangling from his fingers. He stared at it, the other Auldek silent around him. Their blood joy was gone. This was something else.

"Do it," Calrach urged. "Believe me, and do it. This is not as in Ushen Brae. This is a new world for us. I tell you, do this thing. Your soul will rejoice."

Devoth's eyes moved from face to face. He had never looked so circumspect, so unsure of himself. But when he acted he did so decisively. He held up the strip of bloody flesh and bit it. He had to rip off a morsel gripped in his teeth, with a slice of the knife and a sideways jerk of his head. Immediately, he thrust the rest of the flesh up for someone else to take. Howlk was first. The others followed.

For a few minutes there was no sound but their chewing. That and the crackling of the fires and the screech of gulls that had suddenly materialized; the crash of the waves over the stones and the wind buffeting about Rialus's head; and the strange calls the fréketes exchanged, like some language of cackling grunts. And the roar of something that was not quite sound but that felt like a storm building inside his skull. Somehow, a sort of silence contained all these things, broken only when Devoth began to laugh.

"Yes," the Auldek said. "I think this is yes. Something is here."

Howlk cupped his groin. "I can feel it here. I can feeeellllll it!" He stretched the word out and lifted it into a shout. The other Auldek responded in kind. One after another confirming that they felt it, too, whatever it was.

Calrach danced from one blood-splattered diner to another, clapping and patting them on the back. "I told you so! I know what you're feeling now. I felt it, too. I didn't know what was happening. I didn't believe it. I thought, 'What's this I'm feeling? What's come to life down there?' But I learned. I learned and I brought you here to give you life back. Tell me you feel it!"

They did.

Rialus turned and ran. He got only a few steps before he lurched over and vomited. As he crouched there on all fours, his insides escaping him, he was more miserable than ever he had been in a life filled with misery. He would not have thought it before, but oh how he loved the people of the Known World. They were his people. His! Even these villagers were his people. He wanted to rise and run from body to body, kissing their faces and pouring his grief over them. But he couldn't. He had failed them. It was his fault. These monsters were eating human flesh! They were vile, vile, vile. He was vile for even the brief moments he had taken pleasure in their company. Sabeer. She was eating this flesh, too. He had not seen her, but he knew she would. She would eat him if the desire took her.

And what now? After watching this slaughter was he to climb back on that winged beast, with Devoth again pressed against his back? Was he to sit with them as they told the tale to the others, stirred their blood, promised them more was coming for them all? Would he be beside them still when the bulk of the invasion arrived to destroy everything about the world that he had ever known?

No. Better to die. Right now. Here. All he had to do was attack them. He never had! In all his days with them he had never fought! The truth of it stunned and sickened him. All he had to do was grab one of their daggers and stab. They would kill him, but maybe he would even take one of them with him. Or just take one more life out of them. That would be something.

He straightened, got his balance on his bent knees, turned, and looked back toward the group.

Menteus Nemré watched him. The Lvin warrior sat outside the carnivore's circle, not participating in the banquet but not perturbed by it. He stared at Rialus. No expression that Rialus could read on his thick, tattooed-white features. He stared, but he communicated nothing at all through the stare. And then he lifted his gaze over Rialus's shoulder.

"I see you, leagueman," a voice beside his head whispered. Rialus tried to spin, but a body pressed against his back and an arm clenched him immobile. "You think us wretched," Devoth said, speaking close to his ear. "You think us animals. We make you sick. Isn't that so, Rialus leagueman?" Devoth squeezed him, but did not wait for an answer. "This is no custom of ours. It was an abomination. A violation of our long laws. You understand? Numrek were banished for eating quota. We took away their totem and sent them into exile. We thought them just as wretched as you think us now. But that was before they came to your lands and returned to us with Allek, a child to prove they were fertile again. Everything is different now. This is why."

Devoth's other hand swung into view, a piece of human

flesh squeezed in his fist. Blood seeped around his fingers and dripped to the ground. "Coming here, killing your people, eating this meat: these things will give us full lives again. You cannot blame us for wanting that. Are you any different? Don't you want things, leagueman? Of course you do. If I said to you, 'Here, eat this. Just one bite and you will have what you most want to have.'" He held the flesh close to Rialus's face, near enough that he could smell the wet rawness of it. "Take a bite, and you can go home. Take a bite and you can have your woman beside you. You can fly in the air to your queen and tell her the secrets of how to defeat us. Take a bite, and I will drop dead just here. I'll soil myself and shake with fear and collapse in pain and die, right here. And you would be a hero. What would you do if a bite of this meat offered you that?"

Rialus said, "You don't . . . you don't know that this will cure you."

"It's what the Numrek did. True, they were starving when they did so, but who is to say that the flesh of the fertile didn't help them? Who is to say? Can you say? No. So if this deed will bring us what we most want . . . Well, what would you do? You would eat, that's what. Tell me if I lie."

Rialus said nothing.

"That's right, my leagueman. That's right. You would eat. I know you would."

CHAPTER
SEVENTEEN

Aliver has returned. Aliver has returned. Aliver has . . .
Since leaving Bocoum, Kelis kept forming the sentence
in his mind, making it a chant. The three words made him light-
headed with joy. If it was true, it was wonderful beyond anything he had ever dreamed possible. Aliver could pick up where
he left off. He could take the crown from Corinn and shape
the world back toward what he had always dreamed. Kelis
could love him again in life, not just mourn him as a memory.
He would deliver Shen, and Aliver would know that Kelis had
cared for her from the moment he knew she lived. Even the Santoth would bow to him, a king who has walked the afterdeath
and returned to the living.

But as he drew near the hiding place at which he had left
the others, a knot of doubt like an enormous knuckle root took
shape low in his abdomen. He paused atop a hillock not far from
the ravine in which the others camped. Before him, the plains
stretched under the dark of the night. Behind him, a copse of
trees in whose star shadows he hesitated, trying to shape his
thoughts and decide what to say or not when questioned. Some
small creature moved in the trees, a ground bird, perhaps, stirring the leaves. He ignored it. He had been all euphoria at first,

yet now he could not help but wonder why Corinn brought her brother back. She might love him in her crooked way, but she would never let go of power. What did she . . .

When he realized what the sound in the trees had become, it was too late. The man hit him at a run, smashing into his side with his shoulder. The attacker was fast. As they fell, he jabbed his fist repeatedly into Kelis's abdomen. By the time Kelis hit the ground, scraping across the dirt with the other man's weight on him, the man had Kelis knotted within the hard limbs of his body. They came to rest, panting, with the attacker's chin pressed like a weapon against Kelis's temple, pinning his head to the ground. All this in a few seconds.

"Fool!" another man said. He appeared suddenly, out of breath. "We could have followed him to her!"

"Shut up!" the first hissed. His chin ground Kelis's skin as he spoke. "Gag him."

The other punched Kelis in the jaw several times and then jammed a wad of cloth in. He secured it with a leather strap that tied behind Kelis's head. The first man changed position. He squirmed across Kelis's back, as intimate as a lover, except that his movements were all sharp pressure and corded muscle. For a moment Kelis felt one of his wrists slip free of the man's pincer grip. He slipped his hand around and tried to get purchase on the ground with it.

The man pressed the flat of a knife to Kelis's throat. The back-curved point cut into the skin to touch his lower jawbone. "No," the man whispered. "Don't do that." The man pulled Kelis up to his knees, the knife at his neck the whole time. "Bind him."

The second man did so. Once Kelis's hands were tied, the two attackers changed positions. The second man slipped his own dagger into place, clamping his other hand on Kelis's shoulder and driving one bony knee down on his calf. Kelis fought not to wince at the pain.

"Kelis of Umae, I'm assuming," the first man said. He stood tall in the starlight, his black skin silvered in sharp highlights. His teeth flashed when he smiled. Kelis wanted to make out his features, but his vision blurred, his eyes clogged with dirt and tears. "I am not impressed. Was such an important one really put in your hands? Oh, but you can't answer, can you?"

"We should have followed him," the second said.

"They're near. I could see it in the way he was moving—a daydreamer wasting time. That's why I took him down. We won't have to deal with him when we grab her. One less."

"No!" Kelis screamed into his stuffed mouth. He raised his bound hands before him, a begging gesture.

"What?" the first man said. "Are you not Kelis of Umae? Do you not protect a girl called Shen? This may all be a mistake, yes? Just tell us so if it is."

There was a trick in the question, Kelis knew. He tried to figure it out, but the possibilities of it seemed as knotted as the wrestling moves that had trapped him.

"Tell us that the girl is not hidden down in the ravine just there."

Kelis writhed as much as he dared, gesturing with his eyes, touching his fingertips to the gag. *Let me talk*, he tried to say. *Let me talk!* He did not know what he would say, but he needed to try.

The man spat in his face. "Ioma said I was not to kill you, but I piss on that. You've kept me waiting here too long. This story is yours no longer. Bleed him for the jackals." The man grinned.

He was still doing so the moment his teeth exploded from his mouth. They flew to the side in a wet spray, propelled by a black shaft that shot through his cheek and out of sight in an instant. The man dropped in a howl of pain, falling away down the slope of the hillock.

Kelis planted his two hands on the dirt and bucked up against the man who held him down. Getting his feet under him, he used the bunched strength of his bent legs and smashed his backside into the man's torso. He collapsed his upper body into a roll as he did so. The man's feet went flailing into the air, and he fell headfirst over Kelis to the ground. Kelis rolled, got onto his two hands, and popped up again. He came back on the man before he could rise. He shot out a low, thrusting kick. It caught the man's head against his heel and snapped it to the side. Solid contact, but the man scrambled up, slashing the air between them with his knife. Kelis circled away, trying hard not to trip. His hands were still bound. Going down again could be the end of him.

The second man kept the blade between them. The whites of his eyes glowed in the moonlight. He looked frantically between Kelis and the first man, who was on the ground, scraping at the dirt as if he would crawl away but did not remember how to do so. "Jos?" the man yelled. "Jos, what is it?" The high pitch that cracked his voice gave away that he knew clearly enough what it was, as did the fact that he snapped around and ran. Two steps and a low branch of an acacia tree scratched his face. He stumbled back from the thorns, cursing.

Kelis reached him. He slammed his bound hands over the man's head and then hauled back with the full weight of his body. He yanked the man from his feet, swung him around, and then twisted as the vertebrae in the man's neck snapped apart. He fell in a tangle with the dead man's body. He had to struggle to get free of the man's sickening, lolling neck and scrabble to his feet. This took longer than the act of killing him had.

Upright, Kelis stood panting, his eyes darting between the

two men. He whirled at a sound, his fists clenched. Ready to kill again.

"Kelis, brother, it's me." Naamen moved out of the shadow of a tree. He held a knife low in his strong hand, pinned in place with his thumb so that his fingers stretched open in a gesture that conveyed that he would drop the weapon instead of use it if attacked. Those fingers stilled Kelis, brought him back from the murderous rage coursing through him. "Are you all right?"

Kelis looked between the two attackers, one still living. After Naamen removed his gag, he said, "I heard only a bird." The words just came out, without thought.

Naamen studied him a moment, and then he used his knife to cut the cords on Kelis's wrists. "Two birds. Assassin birds, I think. They fly no more. We should, though. We should fly fast."

"Did you do that?" Kelis pointed at the man still writhing on the ground.

Naamen shook his head. He did not need to explain further. Leeka stepped out of the shadows. He walked around the fallen man, picked up the spear that had shattered his jaw. With one swift movement, he slammed the point into the man's back, aimed at his heart. He held it there a moment. The prone man did not move anymore. Leeka's fingers loosened around the shaft, his fingertips light in their touch, as if he were measuring the effect of his strike through it. Then his hand clamped again. He yanked the weapon free and walked toward the two watching men. He held out a spear that Kelis realized belonged to Naamen.

"Let's go," the old man said.

Kelis and Naamen did so. It was only later that it occurred to Kelis that those two words were the most normal sounding he had heard from Leeka since the day he had vanished, years before, running in pursuit of the Santoth.

They roused Benabe and Shen just minutes after their encounter with Ou's men. Their bodies would still have been warm as Kelis strapped Shen to his back and loped away into the last dark hours of the night, iron spear gripped in his fist this time. Benabe, after a few questions, was kind enough to leave the explanation of what had happened alone. She ran with them. She was stronger now, Kelis realized, than she had been at the beginning of their journey together. Or perhaps, like Kelis himself, she just wanted to see all this to a conclusion. Running took them there faster than walking. So they ran.

They pushed on into the morning, climbing into the rocky uplands. They passed through the afternoon, into a land of sheep and goats. They rested only when they stopped for water at the wells the herders marked. Twice they drank from ponds frequented by the grazing animals themselves. Exhausted by the late afternoon, they shared Shen's weight between them, first one and then the other carrying her. On like this into the merciful cool of the following evening, through which they ran until Naamen stumbled, spilling Shen into the dry grass beside him. After that they cut the pace. They waited through the next day inside a vault of granite boulders, and then took to moving only at night as much as possible.

Throughout all this the Santoth hung there behind them. Sometimes Kelis pushed their pace, unconsciously trying to outrun them. But nothing ever changed. The sorcerers never seemed to fall behind, even though their gait—an ambling rocking motion—stayed steady. They could not be outrun. That did not stop Kelis from trying.

Aliver, I know these are your chosen sorcerers, but lend me your faith in them. Lend it to me, for I have need of it.

CHAPTER
EIGHTEEN

Melio held his mouthful of water so long that at some point he lost the world. Probably only for a moment, for when his eyes opened again, his mouth was still filled with water. Geena's body still touched his. Wet ribbons of her short auburn hair striped her round face. "That was fun," she said. She planted a quick, salty kiss on his lips. "Great to be alive, isn't it? Thanks for the grab."

Melio realized his cheeks were ballooned out, his mouth still full of seawater. He spat, which unleashed a fit of coughing and retching. He crawled out of the compartment. The fish that had crowded the hull were all gone, as was anything that had not been secured. The boat pitched about at the mercy of the chop.

Geena was already checking the sail for damage. "All well?" she asked, looking unaccountably chipper. "Everyone have all their fingers and toes and wiggly bits?"

Clytus held the broken mast for support. His shirt had been stripped off, and he stood, sending a string of curses after the league ship. Kartholomé did not waste his breath on them. He sat panting near the bow, his beard canted off to the side. One of his bone earrings was missing. Judging by the dribble of blood down his neck and the stain on his thin white shirt, it had been yanked free.

"They do that on purpose," Clytus said. "They have a betting pool. The captain that runs over the most fishing vessels each moon cycle wins it."

The galley lumbered away, looking slow and dull now, hardly the mischievous creature that had nearly sunk them. "The league," Kartholomé muttered. "Nothing else like them in the world. Wait until you see, Melio. Wait until you see what I have to show you."

Since the mainmast had snapped, they took up oars and bent their backs to pull on them. They headed west, sailing lightless under a sliver of moon. They kept the islands north of them, bulky shadows that they ran alongside of, until sunrise. They pulled into a small cove, managed to hide the boat in the overgrown foliage, and slept under the dappled light, to the ever-present sound of crabs creeping across the fallen leaves.

The next night they turned in to the Thousands. They inched forward slowly, sharing the post of lookout on the bow, at the tiller, or on the oars. The place took its name from the numberless islands that jutted up everywhere. Some just reefs barely parting the surface of the ocean, others large outcroppings bursting with vegetation, loud with birdlife, and crowded with small monkeys that Kartholomé claimed swam between the islands regularly, hunting snakes.

"Snakes?"

"Yeah, there are a lot of them on the small islands. On the bigger ones the league has mostly killed them off."

They reached one of those large islands that afternoon. They pulled the boat aground on a small beach, hemmed on one side by a sheer rock face and on the other by a tangle of vegetation. The beach dropped quickly so that only a few feet out the water fell away into deep blue. This was why Kartholomé knew the place. Midsized frigates and transports could pull up to the beach. Leaving Geena to watch the boat, Kartholomé led the other two up a fissure in the stone that became a steep path. The beach was lost from view almost immediately.

The climb was short, and soon they walked through a forest of palm trees. The fallen fronds crunched under their feet. A few minutes later, Kartholomé brought them to the edge of a slope above a large valley. He indicated with a wave that this was the view he had brought Melio to see.

Melio stepped beside him, wrapped a hand around a palm trunk, and looked out over a compound of buildings and clearings, water tanks and training fields. Military units marched through maneuvers in one area. In another, soldiers sparred with wooden swords. In still another archers shot at distant targets. Men and women filed in and out of the buildings. A line of wagons pulled in and people began to unload them, passing the crates into the gaping mouth of an enormous storehouse. For the second time in recent days, the sigil of the league blazed out at him, this time burned into the slanting roof of the warehouse. The leaguemen, it seemed, wanted even the heavens to see their prosperity.

"What is all this?"

"This is what the league gets up to in private. This is where they train their army."

"The Ishtat?"

"No, no. That's on Lavren. This is Sire El's little project." Kartholomé propped his foot up on a root and leaned on his thigh, continuing to survey the scene below them. "The league started a breeding program years ago. The idea was that they could make quota slaves themselves instead of having to collect them from around the empire. The Fanged Rose let them take over the Outer Isles to do whatever they wanted. Sort of compensation for Dariel blowing the platforms to bits. The last eight years they've been hard at it, but they were breeding even before that. Ever wondered why the Ishtat are so loyal to a bunch of cone-headed freaks? The Ishtat are loyal because they're part of the family. Each and every one of them, Melio Sharratt, was fathered by a leagueman and a concubine herself bred for the purpose."

Melio's gaze snapped over to him.

"You heard me," Kartholomé said. He ran his fingers down his beard and then gave it a tug. "It's quite a regime they have set up. I don't know much about it—just what some of the Ishtat let slip when drunk and disgruntled with Papa. Seems that all the leaguemen are descended from just a handful of founding members. They breed children, and select some of them to have their heads bound. Those become leaguemen. Others they make Ishtat. Others become workers and all that. Some get discarded. Heard about worse things, but you don't even want to know the details."

Melio did not want to know the details, the logistics, the methods of such mass impregnation. Yet he could not help thinking about it. He saw storehouses of beds, leaguemen moving from one to another, a woman in each, babies crying beside them. He hated the thought. Leaguemen raising children like livestock, while he and Mena had not made their real love into a child. He still wanted nothing more than that. By the Giver, if she had only allowed it when they had the chance!

"I see you're thinking about it," Kartholomé said. "Don't. Like I said, the Ishtat are raised on another island. These guys are a newer thing, not the same bloodline. Sire El's army. They're from quota stock, born and raised for it. If they don't show an aptitude for fighting, they're sent away as regular quota. Or they used to be sent as quota. That's all changed now."

Melio asked, "So what are they training for?"

"Good question. Answer: any eventuality. To the league it

doesn't really matter who wins or loses, because they know that either way they're the real winners. If that's all that matters to you—if you don't have a sliver of morality in your body—well . . . it's easier to adapt. No qualms and questions to wake you at night, you know? These soldiers may help take over the Other Lands. They may be given something to do in the Known World. I think it all depends on what happens with the Auldek invasion."

"Any chance they're being trained to help protect the empire?"

Kartholomé turned a withering look on Melio. "I think the league has decided that the empire's days are numbered. Maybe the Auldek will finish it. If they don't manage it, Sire El's boys will finish whatever's left. Either way . . ." He slid his fingers down his beard again and let the fate he pulled from it loose on the air.

All three men heard the running feet at the same time. Geena bounded into view. She slid to a halt and wiped her ginger hair back from her forehead before saying, "We have a problem. An Ishtat patrol found our boat."

Clytus cursed.

"Gets worse. They saw me."

The plan they came up with was simple. Geena smirked disapprovingly at it, but she took up her post without a word. Using the point of Kartholomé's fishing knife, she made a small cut in the flesh just above her knee. She smeared blood up and down her leg, and then she sprawled across the path as if she had fallen. Melio and Kartholomé hid behind trees off to one side. Clytus sank down behind a root network on the other, draping a few palm fronds over him for good measure.

It's mad to do this, Melio thought. We're not at war with the league. I could approach them and explain . . . what? That the queen had sent him to spy on them? Would he convince them that he had not seen or would not report what was clearly in view? If he named himself he would die just the same as if he did not. He had not fully understood it before, but he was so pressed up against the league's private parts that nothing he could say to them would explain it away. What the league was doing was deeply wrong. Witnessing it put him at war with them, whether he declared it or not.

The men arrived at a jog. Melio heard their feet grinding the coarse sand, pressing fronds flat. One of them demanded that Geena stand and face them. She answered that she could not stand. She had hurt her ankle. Twisted it running away from them. The soldiers moved again, assuring her that she was in for more hurting if she tried anything.

Melio slid one eye out from behind the tree trunk. Two Ishtat soldiers stood near Geena. They had their swords out. Another had stopped a little way down the path, looking nervous. Geena clutched at her ankle in pain, her face a mask of fear. The expression looked absurd to Melio. She would never quiver that way. She would never let her jaw drop like that or lean forward in that manner, surely offering a view of her breasts. The Ishtat did not know her, though. Melio pulled his head back behind the tree.

The soldiers demanded to know who she was, if she was alone, how she got here, what she was up to. Geena answered their questions in a pitiful, trembling voice that Melio could barely recognize. He was not sure if she was a terribly good actress or a terribly bad one. He guessed it depended on what things one expected to come out of the mouth of a distraught young woman. She was sputtering and circuitous and even sounded a little insane. Piecing together what she was saying was as confounding for Melio as it must have been for the soldiers. But it gradually took shape.

She had been on a fishing boat, she explained. She and her

father and brother. They were working the channel when a league galley ran them over. So stupid of them! Of her brother, she meant. Stupid, stupid to be in the way of the big ships. She told him they shouldn't taunt the big ships, but he did.

Nice use of the truth, Melio thought. Exaggerated, adjusted, but with a twisted kernel of fact in it. She had them listening, which was strange in itself. Ishtat did not usually let people talk much. They should have pinned her to the ground beneath a savage knee and fanned out in the woods. Ask questions later. But they didn't. These soldiers weren't the sharpest.

"Melio was so stupid!" Geena wailed. "I hate him! I'm glad he fell in."

Melio glanced at Kartholomé, hoping to share a wry smile at the use of his name. The pilot did not seem to be listening. He stood with his back plastered against a palm trunk. One of his arms was a flat paddle at his side; his other had unbuttoned his shirt and was fumbling on his abdomen as if he already feared an injury. His gaze fixed on something in the distance, and his lips silently mouthed something. He had gone gaping, as Hephron—a boy Melio had trained with—used to say of younger boys who showed their fear. Melio cursed himself for getting so far into danger with nothing but a dagger on him and without even men he knew he could trust. Stupid indeed.

"Did he drown?" the soldier asked. Melio could feel the man's gaze scanning the palm forest.

"Yes," Geena said. "He and my father both died. They left me. They . . ." Emotion, apparently, overcame her.

One guard said something to the other that Melio did not catch. The one down the trail must not have heard it either. He called, "What are we doing? All those tracks on the beach. Don't forget that."

Melio wanted to smack him. Or to smack himself on the forehead.

To his surprise, the two nearest Geena seemed to buy her explanation that she had been running back and forth when she got to the beach. She had been delirious. Only her alive in the boat for three days, drifting on the ocean waves, seeing islands but not able to get to them. She tried to make the sail work, but she had never been good at it and it was broken. "I couldn't fix it."

"Of course you couldn't," one of the soldiers said.

"She got here, though," the farthest soldier pointed out. "I don't like this. Just grab her and let's take her back with us. Let Finn decide."

"No, no, don't let Finn decide," Geena pleaded. "He'll decide wrong. What does Finn have to do with it? He didn't find me. You did." Her voice changed slightly—grew less pleading and more certain—when she repeated, "You did."

Am I hearing this? Melio glanced at Kartholomé again, but he hadn't moved.

"I'll do anything. Let's do anything you want. Let's do that first. Can we?"

After a pause one of the soldiers said, "Anything we want?" So much lechery in three words, so much pleasure at another's distress. So little true sympathy when he said, "Let's take a look at that lovely leg, then. It's a nice leg. I think we'll all like it."

"I'm getting Finn," the far soldier said. "I'm not going to answer for this later."

And there it was. Melio had not come up with a plan as he stood behind a tree, but plan or not, he had to act. He came from around the tree just as one of the soldiers slid his sword into its sheath and knelt near Geena. Melio had walked forward several steps before they noticed him. It was the farthest soldier who called, "Hey, there's one! I told you! Stop! Sta—"

He cut off his cries when Clytus rose in a shower of palm fronds. The soldier turned and ran, Clytus in pursuit.

The soldiers by Geena reached to draw their swords. The one closest to her should have used the moment to back away from her. He did not, though, and because of this oversight he was perfectly positioned to receive the full force of a kick from her lovely, muscular leg. He doubled over, clutching his groin. Geena snapped another kick into his face, grabbed him around the neck, and yanked him down. That was all Melio saw of them.

Melio neared the third soldier himself. Though he walked with confidence and military precision, he had no idea how he was going to get past that Ishtat sword. The dagger held out to his side had never seemed smaller, like a wasp's stinger. The confident way the soldier moved his weapon into ready position showed that he felt the same about it. His sword had a gentle curve to it, similar to a Marah sword. It was thinner, but Melio knew the steel of it was unusually heavy. In all likelihood, I'm about to lose limbs, he thought. All these years I've kept my limbs. For this. For this . . .

He thought that as he closed the distance. He thought it as he saw the soldier draw the blade back, tense through his arms and shoulders and torso and legs. Thought it as the man began the step that would initiate the swinging arc the blade would cut. In the face of that, he knew that what his body began—a spin during which he would drop low and try to kick the man's forward leg—would not work. He knew he would never get to use his dagger, but he held the weapon white fisted and wanted nothing more than to carve it through this stranger's abdomen with a fury that came upon him sudden and raw and filled with longing for the woman he was about to lose. Though he cried her name in his head and saw her as she had been that first day on the docks in Vumu—lean and bare breasted, suntanned and salt caked, a priestess of Maeben—he knew their story was over. He knew she had never really been his. Knew it and hated it.

What happened next took only an instant. As he began his

spinning kick, something small zipped over his shoulder. He heard it whirring in the air, though it shot straight and fast as an arrow. He carried through with his kick, turning his back on the swordsman as he did so. In the blur when he faced away from him, he saw a shape moving toward them, and then he was around. His tensed foot impacted the man's weighted leg with all the force he could have wished. He felt one of the lower leg bones break instantly.

His eyes flicked up. The soldier's face was fixed in an absurd expression: his mouth loose, cheeks flaccid, eyes crossed and staring at the jagged crescent of metal protruding from his forehead. Melio spun with the force of his kick, and then used the motion to twirl away from the sword, which carried around for a moment before falling from the man's limp hands as he crumpled. Melio sprang up and stood, gaping at the soldier.

Kartholomé strode past him. He bent over the man and thrust a fish knife into his chest. The soldier gasped, a slow grotesque elongation of his mouth. Kartholomé put his hands on the protruding metal disk and began tugging it. It took some effort to get it free. When he had it out, he turned, holding the bloody, sharply pronged disk in front of him. It was small enough to rest on the palm of a hand. The prongs looked as sharp as knifepoints, backs curved treacherously. He met Melio's gaze. "As a child," he said, "I was good at darts. Later, I got good with these throwing stars." With his knife hand he indicated the pouch of the disks strapped around his torso, inside his shirt. "I am not the bravest man, but I have good aim."

Melio, breathing hard, said, "I believe you."

He picked up the fallen soldier's sword. Geena had done the same. Both of them began to move in the direction Clytus had chased the third soldier. A few steps on, they saw him returning, also newly armed, with the man's helmet sitting tiny on the crown of his head. When he reached them, he spat off to the side and then grinned a bloody, fat-lipped grin. "Who's got a plan, then?"

✳

Bait again," Geena grumbled. "It's somebody else's turn next time."

She went in the lead as they descended through the crevice to the narrow beach at the cove. Melio, just behind her, wore the black tunic stripped from the soldier she had killed, helmet tight on his head. He carried the Ishtat sword unsheathed. He smacked Geena with the flat of it as they scrabbled through the stones. Clytus and Kartholomé followed, likewise dressed in stolen garments.

The white-hulled clipper had been driven right up the beach. It dwarfed their battered fishing boat in its shadow, all sharp lines and glossy coating, masts absurdly tall and wide. A rope ladder from the bow descended to the sand. Three sailors sat or stood a little distance down the beach, along with a single figure in Ishtat black. Melio saw one man on the bow and another walking forward from the stern. If there were more, he could not see them.

The trick would not survive more than passing scrutiny, so Melio did what he could to give them a few more seconds. "Hey, Finn," he called, infusing his voice with mirth, "look what we found." He shoved Geena, sending her tumbling out the mouth of the crevasse. She landed on the sand, crawled forward, then ran toward the group of sailors on the beach until she saw them, and tried to circle them as if she would dive in the water and swim for it. The men rose to the bait. They spread out to intercept her, trying to hem her in, their hands out as if they were herding a chicken.

Only the Ishtat soldier, Finn most likely, stood where he was. He fixed Melio with his gaze, a question on his lips. And then he noticed Clytus and Kartholomé, both of them on the beach now and closing behind Melio. "Who are you?" he snapped. His hand shot to his sword hilt and he began to draw. "Stop right—"

Melio ran the last few steps, sword out at his side. He swung, cutting off the man's words as his blade sliced through his abdomen. Clytus and Kartholomé drew their weapons. Geena dropped flat on the sand just before Kartholomé's throwing stars hissed through the air above her. One scorched by without hitting anyone. The next slammed into one man's chest. Another hit the base of a second's neck. A third man caught the twirling steel in a warding palm. He twisted around with the pain and force of it. Melio hit him with his shoulder and carved him as he tripped on his own feet. Clytus arrived, screaming like ten men and hacking with brute force. The sailors were soft sacks for the hewing.

Kneeling a few moments later, hand resting on the hilt of the sword he had sunk into the sand, Melio panted out the fear and exultation. He was not a squeamish killer. He had seen too much violence for that luxury. Nor was he haunted by it afterward, as he knew Mena was. He knew it was necessary. He just didn't enjoy it much. And, most important, if he had died here, Mena would not have known how he died. He would not have been able to explain it to her, to talk it through, to assess what his death meant to her. That, as much as the actual combat, was the possibility he breathed out onto the beach.

Clytus and Geena took care of the two men on the boat. Still another Clytus found at the stern, trying to climb down into their skiff. This one begged for his life and offered his services as pilot. Clytus seemed willing to consider it, but once aboard Kartholomé would not hear of it. He stabbed the man as he had done the first soldier, turned his hunched over body around, grabbed his legs, and hefted him into the sea. Melio watched this as he hung on the ladder, about to climb aboard. He would have to study this Kartholomé closely. So far, he hadn't figured out what to think of him.

I'll have to study them all closely, he thought.

Once they had checked the ship, named the *Slipfin*, and confirmed there was no one else aboard, they gathered at the stern. They watched the sea for other vessels as they decided what to do next. Melio assumed they would take a few supplies and flee in the fishing boat. They would sail for home with the news they had gathered, perhaps bring Kartholomé along to be further questioned. He had assumed this, but not because he had actually thought it through.

"What if we took this ship?" Geena asked. She stood on the railing, balanced on the balls of her bare feet. "Took it right now and sailed for the Other Lands. We could find Dariel. You said he might be alive, Kartholomé. Let's go get him!"

"How would we do it?" Clytus asked.

"Straight across," Geena piped.

"This boat is fast," Kartholomé said, "and I'd expect some very decent winds on the Slopes."

"Faster than the *Ballan*," Clytus admitted. "Fast enough to outrun sea wolves?"

Kartholomé shrugged. "Could try it. I think some league captain has probably done it. They do treat their clippers with the skin." He slid his hand over the white coating on the railing, the same that covered the hull and portions of the deck near the bow.

Melio expelled a breath. The others gave him a moment to follow up on it, but he just lifted a palm to the sky and motioned vaguely.

"Melio's right," Clytus said. "There's more than one way. What about going up and over, along the ice?" He cocked his head, lips pursed to warn against hasty judgments. "Might be safer, but it could take months. Longer if we get caught in the ice. It might even drift us backward, or out to sea. Could be a slow death. That's never been the way I planned to go to the afterdeath."

"Straight across," Geena repeated. "It's faster to our fate no matter what."

"We'd need supplies," Kartholomé said. "There's a whaling outpost north of here." He pulled his beard in thought. "Yes, on a small island. It's called Bleem. The league used it as a landmark between here and the old platforms. There should be supplies. They outfit ships for long trips. Might even be men on it looking for work."

"Looking for work?" Melio asked. "You want to gather up a boatful of whalers and head across the Gray Slopes on Queen Corinn Akaran's business, a rescue mission searching for a prince?"

The other three shared an expression. "Does he always state the obvious like that?" Kartholomé asked Clytus.

Clytus did not answer. "We could use another body to crew this thing. Help with the watches. Not to mention some strong arms to throw harpoons, and then again to fight if we ever get there. We could send a message from Bleem. You could write one, yes?" Melio nodded, just an answer, not a commitment. "We send a message to Nineas on the *Ballan*, and he could send a bird to the queen. They'd know what we were up to, at least."

"Perilous journey to foreign lands," Geena said. She was not quite grinning, but there was a mischievous tension twitching her cheeks. "No guarantee of return. Death possible. In case of success, riches beyond imagining!"

"It would work for me," Kartholomé said.

Geena grinned. "Me, too. It's making me tingle just thinking of it."

"You're all mad," Melio said. "It's a crazy idea. It's sailing off the map. Who knows what we'd be sailing into?"

Clytus stood on his toes and scanned the sea a moment. "We could leave it and try to limp back to Tivol in the fishing boat. Might not make that either, though. If we leave the clipper, it'll be found by tomorrow, and we'd be captured a little after. No good options, as I see it."

"Look," Melio said, "I know you all are chancers. You'd have to be to be brigands. You like risk, fair enough. But think for a minute: we sail west . . . and die. Name the method. There's a thousand to choose from. If that's what waits for you over there, would you still say go? Tell me truthfully."

"I would," Geena said.

"Aye," Clytus agreed.

Kartholomé shrugged. "Why not? Riches beyond imagining . . ."

Geena jumped off the railing. She stepped close to Melio, took hold of his arm at the elbow. "I want to do this because Dariel would do it. Don't you think he would? He'd do it for you. For Clytus. I'd like to think he'd do it for me. Let's do it for Dariel. If we die . . . what's it matter? We'd die in style."

She was so close and so attractive in a boyish, playful way that he remembered her kiss on the boat after they had both almost drowned, tangled together as close as lovers. And that reminded him of the pledge he had made to Mena. If he lived, he had sworn he would do anything for her. Everything for her. If he had the chance, nothing would stop him. That was what he had thought in his last moments of consciousness.

"All right," Melio said, "but only because Dariel would do the same for us."

"We'll need harpoons," Kartholomé said. "Lots of them."

"Harpoons?"

Geena said, "A whaling outpost has plenty of those. Come,

Melio Sharratt, let's get to know our new ship. Welcome to the order of brigands."

Melio pulled back. "No, no. Welcome, you three, to the proper service of the crown."

"Call it what you will," Geena said. "Let's go. No use waiting for a patrol to stop by. I'm done being bait."

CHAPTER
NINETEEN

The first day she arrived with baskets of fruit for Elya's children, Corinn stepped through the corridor opening onto Elya's terrace to the sight of the redheaded dragon flapping its silken wings, maintaining a jolting, unsteady hover a few feet above the patterned tiles. Po, she called him. He grew inches every day. How much of that was natural and how much was accelerated by the Giver's tongue she had used on them while still in the eggs she could not measure. She knew some of it was her doing, but the young ones already had traits distinctly their own. In hatching, in reaching out to touch her, in flight—in everything so far—Po had always been first. He would be the first to take a rider also. She was sure of it.

Elya stood, watching him, her eyes wide and her mouth opening and snapping shut, as if she were on the verge of shouting encouragement but was too nervous. Two of the other young ones flanked her. These also had names—in Corinn's mind at least. With Mena away, who else would give them names? The brown one with the yellow stripes down her back was Thaïs. The sky-blue male, hopping from foot to foot at the moment, was Tij. The completely black one lounged atop the balcony railing, a drape of long, sinewy curves. She opened an eye and watched Corinn. Kohl, Corinn called her.

It took her a while to figure out how she had identified their sexes. None of them had any visible genitalia. Neither did Elya, for that matter. But Corinn had no doubt about her guesses. They did look a little different. The males were more vibrantly colored and thicker in the jaws and neck, with crest feathers that bunched behind their heads and erupted out to either side down their necks. The two females were more modestly hued, a little longer in their limbs, and more serpentine. Their crest feathers flared straight up when they lifted them, thin and high. The females had the same citrus scent in the oil on their feathers as Elya did. The touch of it always left Corinn's fingers tingling. The males—Po in particular—had a musky, burned fragrance. When touched, their oils did not so much tingle the flesh as heat it. Still, it was not unpleasant. Just potent in a different way.

"Hello, beauties," Corinn called. "I have fruit for you."

She stepped forward with a jaunty enthusiasm she would never have let human eyes witness. She held the basket out before her as if it contained treasures, which is just how the young dragons reacted. Po froze midflap and fell to the stone tiles. Thaïs and Tij snapped their heads around, recognized her, and scrabbled forward, going down to all fours and slither-crawling. Kohl was slower to rise. When she jumped from the wall, her wings spread out and slowed her descent. She landed gracefully, retracted her wings, and scurried forward to join the others.

They crowded around Corinn's legs, making it hard for her to walk. They dipped and bobbed and circled her. They climbed over one another, nipping and hissing on occasion. Tij clawed at her velvet skirt, as if he would climb right up her. Corinn reprimanded him playfully, and made a mental note to wear sturdier garb in the future.

She sank down among them, setting the basket of fruit in front of her. For a few moments, she held herself still, the center of a squirming ball of raucous, attention-hungry children. They fought for her touch. They pressed their crowns against her outstretched palms, rubbed her legs and back, and leaned into her chest. Corinn knew this could not last. She had wanted to make them love her, and she had. Soon she would have to break them out of childhood. She would need to harden them for the struggles to come.

Soon, she thought. Soon, but not today.

Thinking this, Corinn looked up at Elya, who had moved away a little distance, to a corner of the terrace. She paced several quick circuits of the space before settling her backside against the stone, lowering herself with a comically avian motion, a bird settling onto a nest. Only when she was situated did she deign to look back at Corinn. Was that annoyance in the squint of her left eye?

You don't trust me, Corinn thought, but you don't exactly think I'm a threat either. But I am, Mother Elya. I am. I want your children for my own.

She repeated that: *I want your children for my own.* She watched for any sign that Elya heard her, but the creature sat, watching. Nothing in her demeanor changed. Corinn often tested Elya this way. She explained her desires in taunting interior language that she held within her head, all the time looking for signs that Elya could read her thoughts. Mena believed so, but Corinn, after weeks of uncertainty, had concluded that Elya could not. For all the ways she dilated her pupils or blinked her eyes or bobbed her head, it was only the human eyes watching her that construed intelligence in her actions. The gifts Mena endowed Elya with were Mena's own creations. It was a relief, really. Elya would be easier to deal with, harshly if necessary.

They can't be both of ours, Corinn went on as she stroked

the fine feathers along Po's neck. If they were yours, they would eat fruit and be playthings for children. They would fly circles above the palace and make people gasp with pleasure. No harm in that, but those are such small goods. If they are mine . . . well, then they can be warriors for the empire. They can be creatures for the ages, new symbols of Acacian power. Don't think me evil, Elya. I want only the best things for my family, for the empire, and for the people of it. That's why I want your children to be my warriors. It's already begun, anyway. They started being mine when I sang to them in their eggs. I've only to sing to them again to seal them to me, to help them grow into the weapons I need them to be.

Corinn stood and looked around, feeling as if somebody were watching her. She turned a slow circle but saw nobody. She caught a scent in the air and recognized it at some level that she was not interested in reaching down to. With a few whispered notes of the song, a breeze brushed past, freshening the air and clearing her mind. No need to give in to the illusions her use of the song stirred into the world.

The fruit consumed and their greeting enthusiasm spent, the young dragons moved off one by one to find other distractions. Kohl unfurled her wings and leaped up onto the terrace wall and stretched them wide, absorbing the mild winter sun. Thaïs stood on her hind legs, head craned, studying the nubs that housed her wings. She had not, as far as Corinn knew, spread them yet. Tij lifted his snout, half opened as he watched condors circle high above the island.

Only Po stayed beside Corinn a little longer. He rested one arm against Corinn's thigh, and pushed her other hand—as delicate and expressively fingered as his mother's—through the peels and the few remaining orbs of fruit.

"You want something more than fruit, don't you?" Corinn whispered to him.

The dragon slid his head toward her, mouth open as if await-ing an offering. The yellow of his eyes shone with a wavering intensity, as if his irises were a thin foil of gold and a fire burned just behind it. Corinn stroked his crest feathers. They rose at her touch.

"Soon I'll get you something more. Something to make you grow strong."

She began to pull her hand away and rise. Po's head dipped, his eyes on Corinn, and then his serpentine neck snapped up. His jaws opened, and when the blur of motion ended, he had Corinn's wrist pinched in his mouth. He did bite down, but his teeth only dimpled her flesh. The movement had been so swift that Corinn jerked her arm, causing the sharp, tiny teeth to scratch her skin. She and Po both froze.

Staring down at him, unsure whether to be frightened or angry or amused, Corinn spoke with a sharp-edged calm. "Not me, Po. Not me." She reached around with her other hand and tugged his upper jaw. She slid her wrist free. Just a few scratches, thin white lines like the tracks of kitten claws. She pinched Po's jaws shut with her fingers and tilted his face toward hers. "Never put those teeth on me. Never. If you do, I won't love you."

With that, she snapped her fingers and strode for the cor-ridor. Just before she stepped into the shadows, she glanced toward Elya and met eyes already watching her. Really, she thought, I have to do something about her.

✳

With that in mind, she spent the next several days trying to convince Elya to fly north to retrieve Mena. She stood before the creature and spoke simple directions to her. Elya puffed through her reptilian nostrils. She pulled her eyelids back and then squinted. She answered with a variety of bodily motions and quirks, quick bouts of preening, her gaze often darting away toward one of her children. None of it showed any sign she comprehended Corinn in the slightest, or cared to.

Recalling how Mena had explained it, Corinn formed her directions in her mind and offered them. When that did not work, she stood on the balcony, pointing and waving, shooing Elya away. Once, she pressed her palm against the gray plumage and shoved. This got her a hissed rebuke. Through it all, Elya watched her with narrowed, skeptical eyes. When she did finally decide to leave, the event did not seem to have anything to do with Corinn's orders.

✺

A morning several days into her efforts, Corinn found Elya waiting for her on the terrace that had become the avian nursery. Her young huddled close to her. For a second Corinn thought they looked like children gathered around a storytelling nurserymaid, but then she saw the dangerous slant of Elya's head. She pushed through her children, jostling them behind her as she moved on Corinn. She lowered her head and dropped to all fours. She covered the short distance in a burst of speed, her shoulder joints pumping. Her head rose so close to Corinn that the air blown from her nostrils stirred the queen's hair. Standing tall, she hissed down at Corinn, her neck feathers jutting out in an instant bristle.

Corinn breathed through her mouth. She moved only her fingers, which she flexed out of a need to move something, to steady herself somehow. Resolutely submissive, she just stood. Inside, however, she had a spell dancing, ready to be released should Elya strike. It would rip her apart and leave them all splattered in feathered gore. She would do it if she had to.

She didn't. The mock attack was Elya's version of a parting discourse, perhaps for her young's benefit as much as a warning to Corinn. She curled away and returned to her agitated children. A few moments spent soothing them, touching them each with the soft spot below her jaw, and then Elya stood back from them. They tried to stay with her, but she huffed them back. Her wings unfurled from the knobby protrusions on her back. They snapped into place with a rapid clacking sound, the flowing motion of it almost liquid until it was complete. Then the finger-thin bone framework went rigid, only the silky membrane hung throughout rippling before the touch of the air. Elya leaped backward onto the terrace railing. She glanced from her young to Corinn once again, then twisted around and dropped out of sight.

Corinn raced the young dragons to the wall. They reached the railing together. Tij leaped up first. Kohl scaled it like a lizard. Thaïs scurried to a section with flowers carved in the stone. She stuck her head through a leaf. Po released his wings and flew up, almost overshooting the wall and having to flap back for a moment.

Elya's wide-winged shape soared beneath them. She skimmed down toward the lower town wonderfully fast, then shot out low across the green waters of the harbor. Her shadow danced on the waves below her, like an aquatic companion. Then she turned to the north and beat her wings to rise higher. Her audience stayed transfixed until her shape faded into the northern horizon.

Only then did Corinn acknowledge the bubbling excitement inside her. Her abdomen tingled with it. She had her babies all to herself. She spoke to them softly at first. "You'll be my greatest warriors."

Kohl nipped the fabric of her sleeve in agreement.

"You'll be the weapons your mother wasn't cut out to be."

Tij slammed the crown of his head against her left shoulder.

"You won't be beautiful like her. You'll be exquisite terrors instead."

Thaïs brushed against her side.

"You want that, don't you? To fight for me?"

Po chirruped, flapping his wings and lifting himself up off the stone.

Of course they did. Corinn read it in their eyes. "You were only waiting for it, weren't you? Let's begin."

Corinn undid all the venom of the spell she had woven and held loaded against Elya. She lured her babies down from the railing and began a new song for them. She moved through them, touching them, lifting their chins and meeting their golden eyes. She whispered out the words and notes and sounds that lay behind the fabric of the world. She felt them slither in the air around her, and she let the young dragons hear them, too. No need to hide the serpentine scaly friction the ribbons of the song sliced through air.

Once the spell she wanted was strong, she began to release it into them. She stroked them as she sang, one after the other as they jostled and vied for her attention. Each of them vibrated with a sort of pleased purring. With each touch she felt the power of the song passing from her into them. Beneath her fingers and palms she felt the bulging pressure as they changed, as they truly became her babies, as they grew beneath her touch.

End of Book One

Book Two

All the
Evil Seeds

CHAPTER
TWENTY

Mena awoke, knowing that something was in her room, standing at the foot of her bed. Her thoughts flew to ghosts, to angry spirits, to the Tunishnevre. She was lying on a floor bed that had once belonged to Meinish royalty, in a room that may have been Maeander Mein's. She had gone to sleep, thinking of the last time she had seen him, as his prisoner on a ship bound for an Acacia ruled by Hanish Mein. The knotted irony of it all had slithered around her all day. That was why she was sure it was the anger of the Meins that stood breathing just beyond her feet. She sat up, faced it, and gasped at what she saw.

"Perrin?" She knew his tall physique even in the partial light. She stretched for the lantern in a stand beside the bed and opened the vent to increase the flame. Yes, it was Perrin. Clothed only in his underlayers. His hair, as ever, kicked about in a small chaos atop his head. "What are you doing?"

Something was wrong with him. His eyes were open. He was awake, standing, but his face wore the limp flaccidity of sleep. He swayed. His arms hung straight down at his sides. He was asleep on his feet.

"Do you think me here to warm your bed, Mena?" Perrin's mouth said. The voice was his but not only his. "What would Melio think?"

"Are you mad?" Mena asked. "Perrin, I am true to Melio. We are—"

"I won't tell him, of course. Who you bed is your business, Sister."

Then she knew the second voice, the one that created the words that Perrin's mouth spoke. "Corinn?"

"You cannot avoid me, Mena. You should not try."

"I haven't," Mena said. She put a hand to her chest, a gesture that looked like modesty, but that she made to quiet her heart and rate of breathing. "I never would. You have . . . taken Perrin's body?"

"You are closed to me, Sister. Don't you find that strange? Of all the people in the world to whom I can dream-travel, the two closest to me will not answer my call. When I search, I can never find you or Dariel. I could find fine-looking Perrin, though. He has brought me to you. A pleasing form, is he?"

Mena could think of no response. His was a pleasing form, but not like this. He might as well have been a reanimated corpse.

"Why did you abandon my orders? Mena, stop gaping like that! It's me, Corinn, talking through this man's mouth. Now, answer me. Why did you abandon our plan?"

"Our plan did not include sacrificing the entire army before ever seeing an enemy," Mena said. "That's what would have happened."

"You exaggerate."

"No, I don't. If you had been there, you would have seen. To wait up there would have been a slow death. We would have been weakened by cold and in no shape for when the Auldek come. I had to make a decision in the field. I did. Military matters are my area, Corinn. If you don't trust me, take away my command."

"I trust you, but . . . Tahalian? Do you do that to taunt me?"

Suddenly feeling uncomfortable sitting up in the bed, Mena yanked her covers off and folded her legs under her, back straight. "Tahalian is the perfect place to settle," she said. "We can train in frigid conditions, hike the Black Mountains, work on navigation and communication in the worst of conditions. But we can also return to a warm base. We can run maneuvers in the Calathrock. We can learn from men like Haleeven, who know war in the north better than anyone. Instead of huddling in frozen hovels, struggling to survive, we'll be fit and prepared. I was sure that you would agree if you knew all the facts, so I acted on that."

Perrin's eyes stared at her a moment before answering. "You have done well," Corinn said. "I myself could not have made that choice. I could not have set foot in that place. It's good that you could." Despite the strangeness of hearing this from Perrin's lips, it warmed Mena to hear the vulnerability in her sister's voice. "You should know something else. Our brother has returned."

"Dariel? Did the league—"

"No, not Dariel. He is still unaccounted for. I mean Aliver. I sang him back to life. He is here in the palace even now. He played this afternoon with Aaden. Mena, you should have seen them!"

Mena asked for Corinn to say again what she meant. Corinn did so. Mena asked her to speak it one more time. Perrin's lips curved into a smile. "I am not insane, Sister. I worked a spell and brought him back. I can do such things. You have the blade; I have the song."

"I don't understand. How can . . ."

"How can something dead and spread as ashes on the wind live again? I can't answer that, but it's true. You'll see him yourself." Perrin's eyes closed for a long moment, and then opened with a start. "Call Elya. Call her to you and fly back on her for the coronation. I have already sent her toward you, but call her to make sure she comes to you."

"The coronation?"

"Aliver will be king. I will be queen. We will rule together. Come, Mena, be here to share the moment with us. Summon Elya. Summon . . ."

Corinn's words faded. Perrin sighed, his body loosening, swaying. Corinn was gone. Just like that the force that had animated him vanished. Mena began to ask if he was all right, but stopped as he climbed onto her bed and fell, facefirst, onto her sheets. "Perrin, you can't . . ." He grasped her sheets and curled into them, coming to rest on his side, facing her. Fast asleep.

Mena watched his sleeping face for a time. She lay down next to him, close enough to take warmth from his body as she tried to sort through what she had just heard.

❋

The mock battle the next day was Haleeven's idea. After three days of steady snowfall—a strangely windless storm that allowed the snow to blanket the world around Mein Tahalian evenly—he proposed, "Let's stage a battle along the slope of the mountains. We did so in the old days. Even with Hanish we trained that way on occasion."

When Mena protested the heavy snow, Haleeven said that was the point.

"This is the Mein, Princess."

The old warrior's face was a creviced mask. He had trimmed his wild beard, but it was still bushy and longer than anything seen in the empire's warmer climes. Leather cords wove color into several braids of his thinning gray-blond hair. Mena was not yet used to looking at him. At times she marveled that the world could be so varied as to produce these hairy, blond, fair-skinned northerners in one case and the richly dark, smooth-skinned people of the south on the other. With her kind in between, like a blending of the world's extremes.

"This is the Mein," Haleeven repeated, "and north of here it's been known to snow as well."

Not sure what to make of his statement—ill-tempered humor or more kindly jest—she nonetheless agreed. Haleeven was a hard man to read. Since their first conversation, he had shown little emotion. He had revealed nothing more of himself and seemed to regret having ever shown himself a victim of the world's turning. Instead, he threw himself into work. He, more than any single person, brought Mein Tahalian back to life again. That he did it for her benefit Mena doubted, but she was grateful for it.

As they marched out to do mock battle, the sun shone blindingly bright. The clouds that had pressed down upon them for weeks had vanished, revealing a dome of sky impossible to look at. They all squinted as they gave and received commands, trying to form up on opposing sides of the slope. The snow was fluffy and soft. A few soldiers scooped it up in their naked fingers and ate it.

"You'd do well to keep those fingers covered," Perrin said. He walked at Mena's elbow. It relieved her that he occupied the role as he had before. The morning after Corinn had used his body to speak through, it had taken Mena some time to explain how he came to wake in her bed. He had no memory of it, and Mena convinced him that he had simply walked in his sleep. She had found him in a daze in the corridor, she explained. She directed him to the first spot to lie down that she could find—her bed. She had not been discomforted. She just slept on the couch in the adjacent room. Nothing inappropriate happened. Nothing they needed to discuss with others. Such things occurred during the stress of approaching war. Better he believe that than know the truth, including that she lay, taking heat from his body, for some time before crawling away. Some things were better kept to oneself.

Gentling as it was on the contours of the land, the snow was a misery to walk through. The soldiers kicked curses into it, struggled to keep their balance. They paused after only a few steps, breathing hard. Several lost their boots in the stuff and had to dig around in it with their hands, one socked foot exposed to the cold.

They spent several hours tugging and shoving several catapults and ballistae into place. By the time they were ready and the two sides faced each other across a stretch of trodden and slashed snow, they were exhausted, panting plumes of vapor into the air.

Though they would not have wanted to know she heard them, more than one soldier on her side grumbled at the incongruity that his face could be plastered with sweat while vapor froze into ice nuggets in his beard, or that his torso could be drenched while his toes had gone beyond cold to numb, or that his mouth was parched for liquid while his bladder made him stop to pee every few moments.

When a soldier noticed her within hearing of such a complaint, his face flushed red with embarrassment. She let him see the sternness of her face. In truth she felt all the same things herself, the problem of wanting to pee being chief among them. She also noted his Candovian accent. He did not belong in the frozen north any more than she did.

Not a good start, she thought.

It got no better when the battle began. The two sides roused themselves sluggishly at the horns' call. They slogged forward. They tripped and had trouble rising. Their wooden swords and axes encumbered them as they toppled over one another, cursing. The two sides did not so much hit each other as collide, stumble, and fall back, swinging their weapons either as an afterthought or in search of balance. Archers lofted blunted arrows into this mêlée. A pathetic effort. The catapults' gears got stuffed with snow, frozen in place. Only one managed to lob a weighted ball. It flew over the opposing side. The ballistae did not shoot at all; the padded bolts had been lost somewhere.

Mena trod the sidelines, growing more dismayed the longer she watched. She was on the verge of calling a halt to the whole exercise. Haleeven commanded the day, but she had seen enough. Judging by the words she heard the old soldier shouting, so had he.

"What's wrong with you?" Haleeven bellowed. "You look like drunken boys playing in the snow! Is this the best of Acacia's army? Woe to the empire if it is. Now fight, you fools!" He dodged in among the troops, sword in one hand, mallet of a fist in the other. He smacked soldiers of either side on the head, jabbed with his sword, knocked them off their feet with his punch. He seemed to move on a different surface than the others, so loud and such a fury of motion that many stopped to gape at him.

"This is not going well," Perrin muttered.

Haleeven kept up his harangue. The soldiers lowered their weapons, stood dejected. Even those face-to-face with the opposing side gave up the fight and watched the old Mein dance among them. He shouted about the pity of it, about how Meins used to drink ice instead of tea and pee crystals. "It never bothered us! A little snow?" He scooped a handful up in his free hand and lofted it at a soldier near him. "It's like sugar to us. We flavored our cakes with it!"

"Go eat cake, then," a soldier grumbled.

Haleeven stopped dead. His head turned back, his gaze locking on the offending soldier's. He studied him as if he had never seen a creature so bizarre. He sheathed his sword, and then stooped and drove his gloved hands into the snow. "You say that to me? You, soldier, tell Haleeven Mein to eat cake?"

I should stop this, Mena thought. The old man is . . .

Haleeven roared, ran toward the man, and then hurled a ball of hand-packed snow at him. The snowball exploded on his shoulder, dusting his face white. Haleeven shouted something in Meinish. Pointing at the soldier, he said, "Did you understand that? I told him to eat sugar! You hear? Eat"—he ducked down again and hurled another clod of snow at a different soldier—"Meinish"—and still another—"sugar!"

One of the soldiers tossed snow back at Haleeven. With that, chaos erupted. A chaos of flying snow, shoving, kicking, insults, curses. Laughter. Both sides converged with an energy they had not possessed moments before. The tense atmosphere shifted, replaced by boisterous mirth.

"This will not help us against the Auldek," Mena said. The next moment, she got pelted across the chest with a snowball. Who dared?

Haleeven himself. He kicked his way through the snow toward her. He looked like a madman. Stopping just before Mena, unsteady on his feet a moment, hair and beard splattered with snow, he said, "I say it will help us, Princess. I say it will. Next, I'll teach you to make snow caves. Warmer than your tents. There's so much to teach you, and I will do it!" He bounded off, scooping up fresh handfuls of snow and tossing them as he did.

Mena understood it then. The mock battle. The snow. The apparent futility of it. Yes, there was a lesson in all that, and she had learned it. But also there was a joy in life to be had, even in the face of absurd obstacles. Haleeven Mein had chosen to remind them of that.

Perrin said, "I'll still be packing my tents when we march. Should I call for them to—"

Mena did not so much throw the handful of snow at him as

spoon it onto his clean-shaven face. Stunned, he lost his balance and pinwheeled backward, feet stuck fast in the snow. Seeing the look first of surprise and then of mirth on his face, Mena burst into fits of laughter.

She was still laughing when the shouts reached her. The sound had an edge to it different from anything they had done that day. Casting about, she saw soldiers running with real alarm. Others stared at the sky, shading their eyes and pointing. The archers fumbled in their supplies. They were looking, she realized, for real arrows.

A shadow passed over her, and she knew just what had alarmed them all. She felt the presence rush into her mind so suddenly that it overwhelmed everything else. Elya! Spotting her lean, wide wingspan through eyes squinted against the glare, she shouted, "No! Don't shoot at her! It's Elya!"

Perrin picked up Mena's order and spread it. When she was sure that the men were calm enough, Mena sent a welcome up to Elya. She envisioned her descending to the snowy battlefield, landing in a space cleared just in front of Mena. She saw her wings spread wide and beautiful, translucent with the sun's light shining through them as she touched down as softly as a songbird landing on a branch, though infinitely more magnificent. She sent her the message that she could roll tight her wings and rest them from her long journey, and she showed her in images that Mena would rush to embrace her the moment she could.

That was exactly what happened. Met with a collective inhalation of breath from soldiers that had never seen her, Elya touched down. Mena buried her face in the creature's soft plumage, inhaling the sweet scent of her. The citrus smell flooded her with memories of their first days together in Talay. Golden, warm days spent walking the wind-touched grassy hills, just the two of them falling in love with each other.

"You shouldn't be here," Mena whispered. "You shouldn't be here."

In answer, Elya's breast hummed, a soft vibration that felt like nothing else in the world. Warmth and energy and life and love all captured in the thrum of the whole of her body. Mena gave herself over to it. She tried not to hear Perrin say that he had no idea Elya was so impressive a creature. She pressed her face deeper when Edell said that with this mount, the princess could own the sky and know exactly what the Auldek were doing without them ever being the wiser. She tightened her grip when Bledas mentioned that the Auldek may also have mounted riders, and squeezed with her fingers when Perrin came back with, "Yes, they *might*. But they won't be like Elya. Did you see her wings?"

No, Mena thought, this is not for her. War is not for her.

CHAPTER
TWENTY-ONE

I think I have names for the hounds," Dariel said.

"What?" Birké lay beside him, the two of them staring at the stars, absurdly bright and numerous above them. "More colors? Flowers?"

Dariel nudged him with an elbow. He held a few of the odd, slimy plee-berries in his mouth, rolling them around on his tongue. He swallowed them and said, "When I was young, my father used to tell us stories. There was one about Bashar and Cashen."

"The two cousins?"

"No, brothers. They were brothers."

Birké made a skeptical noise low in his throat. "Bashar and Cashen were cousins. Bashar could throw lightning bolts, and Cashen was jealous of it. He roared every time Bashar showed off. He pounded on the earth and grumbled."

Dariel said, "That's not the way we tell it."

"How does your way start?"

"Bashar and Cashen were two brothers. They had a great fight over power."

"That would make more sense."

"I always remembered that story. It scared me. I didn't

want to think of brothers fighting—not with the way I loved my brother. Anyway, later Aliver told me that the Santoth had explained that tale differently. He said Bashar and Cashen were not brothers. They were tribes, whole races of people. The friction between them was that of a world turning on itself. Once, though, they had been close. And they could be again. That's what Aliver told me."

Birké cleared his throat. "So Bashar and Cashen. Brothers or tribes or cousins . . . and now hounds?"

"That's what I was thinking."

"Better than Scarlet and Blue, or whatever colors you were thinking of naming them." Dariel reached over and jabbed him in the ribs with a finger. The motion brought one pup's attention. Cashen, the reddish one, scurried between them, plopped his butt down, and sat waiting for something interesting to happen.

"Tell me your tale," Birké said.

"Which version?"

"Both. Tell me both. I'll judge them for myself."

Dariel did so as best he could, hearing his father's voice and taking on the cadence of it. He told both stories, and did not mind losing sleep that night. Tomorrow they would reach the Sky Isle. He would finally meet Yoen and the elders. For some reason, he felt he needed to be awake for as long as he could. He needed to sort through all the things Nâ Gâmen had told him.

❄

Dariel, I've been waiting for you, the Watcher said. At first I thought it might be a short wait. I thought our sins could not go long without punishment. And then, later, I began to doubt that you would come. There was no Giver, after all. Why should there be justice? There isn't, but all things do come to pass. Just never in the ways that we imagine.

Yes, Dariel thought. They sat side by side in a dark, rectangular room now. The wall in front of them was blank. The floor bare, smooth stone. A river of air rushed from one side of the room to the other. Had Dariel to name the purpose of the room, he would have failed. Had they needed to speak words, they would have had to yell. Because they spoke directly to each other's minds they conversed despite the roar of the air and the flapping of their garments. Nâ Gâmen sat as if he did not notice it all. Dariel did the same, and it was almost true.

I want you to know how I came to be here. Why I waited for you. Look.

A magnificent palace appeared on the wall before them. Dariel saw it from high above, dizzying, as if he were somehow a bird on the wing. It lay like a lace scarf draped in serpentine curves across the high reaches of one of the barrier islands. So it looked from a distance. Closer, it was a flowing, molten structure similar to the Sky Mount, only sumptuous and alive in a way the mount was not. Gardens of trees sculpted by the wind into fantastic, eerie shapes. Fishponds and waterfalls and dining terraces cut into improbable promontories, with views of the sea and the other barrier isles, many with similar estates.

See this? This was my home for several hundred years. I adored it. I built it from nothing, first by my own labor, soon by the labor of others. I made something of a rock that had never known human habitation. I was proud. And I was angry. I hated Tinhadin as fiercely as any among us. I jumped at the opportunity to punish his people. For many years it was I who sorted the spirits that eat death. Do you know what that means?

No.

I chose which children would go into the soul catcher. Not all souls are strong enough for it. Some have a greater force within them than others. I learned to sense it. That became my work. I decided which children would give their lives in labor, and which would give their lives through the gift of the soul energy. I was good at this work, and I did horrible things because of it.

The things he did Dariel saw and felt, though for a time he did not hear the Watcher's voice in his head. It was not just that the children were scared seven- and eight-year-olds, who had been stolen from their homes and families and taken across a vast ocean to a foreign land. It was not just that he sorted through them and decided which ones would receive a fate worse than death. Wasn't being fed to the soul catcher worse than death? They lost their bodies. Their identity. They became the life fuel of strangers. They died, yet were reborn more completely as slaves to others than any that labored in the thread fields or as builders or farmers or served as fodder for military slaughter.

Not just the fact that he was responsible for this. He went further. For a time, he chose the children he would reserve for himself. Not all Lothan Aklun took souls into themselves, but he did. In his youth this was because he hungered for years and years of life in which to punish Tinhadin's people. He did not care that one who accepts a soul inside himself loses the ability to father children. That did not matter, not when he could go on forever. He set his hands on the shoulders of child after child. He smiled in their faces and looked through their eyes and into them. If he truly liked what he saw, he had only to nod, or gesture with his fingers, and the child was his.

There is more.

With the passing of decades he aged. Physically, no, but still, he aged inside. His body stayed young, but as he passed the normal span of a long mortal life he began to forget his own childhood. The lack of it became a yawning chasm chasing him. His work grew harder. He felt different when he set his hands on children's shoulders and looked into them. More and more often, his gaze lingered on their faces, on the small curves of their muscles and the lines of their collarbones. More and more, he found a beauty in their small, growing life.

One day, performing his duties as selector, he met a boy. Perhaps it would have happened with another boy or a girl. The next day or the week after or in a year's time. It would have happened at some point, he now believed, but fate had it that it was this boy. Ebrahem, a Halaly boy from one of the tiny villages along the western coast of Talay. The boy gazed up at Nâ Gâmen's face with timorous, hungry, desperate hope. He had seen this expression a thousand times. All the boy's hopes were there on his face. All his dreams written in the lines of his lips and the bushy flares of his eyebrows and in the uneven circlets of his nostrils. All the things he had left behind, all that would not be for him—the loved ones lost, the home he would never see again.

Nâ Gâmen knew all these were there, things that he had always thought small, just punishments. Childish things that he recognized because in them he recognized himself. He had always understood them, and, understanding, he had found the strength to be cruel. But this time, written there . . . was nothing. Features like he had seen before, and yet this time he saw nothing but the boy himself.

❋

Later that night, after telling both his stories, Dariel could not find sleep. Birké lay flat on his back, snoring. Bashar sat beside him, studying the night. Cashen walked the patrol he had set up from their boulder down to the hollow where the others were and back again.

Nothing but the boy himself, Dariel thought. He remembered the boy's face as if he had seen it with his own eyes. That face began to change Nâ Gâmen from what he was into what he became. Dariel wondered if Val had seen the same thing on the night he found Dariel shivering and hopeless in a mountain shack in Senival. He had never considered the changes he created in his adopted father's life. He had shied away from thoughts of himself. Perhaps he had changed Val. Maybe that was what he was telling him when he stayed behind to set the platforms ablaze.

"I've never forgiven you for that," he whispered.

"For what?" Anira's voice startled him. She had walked up behind Cashen and stood with her face shadowed. Her body, in silhouette, was muscularly feminine, strong as a man's but contoured like the woman she was.

"You like seeking me out in the night?"

"Yes, I do. I hope you're more vigilant when you're on watch."

"Sorry. My mind is elsewhere."

"Elsewhere can be a good place to be," she said. After studying him for a moment, she added, "Or not. Sometimes it's better to be right here. Are you worried about tomorrow?"

"Should I be?"

"I used to be afraid of Yoen . . . when I was a child. When I grew up, I learned to love him. He's gentle, wise. Deliberate. He'll see through you if you lie to him. So don't do that."

"I hadn't planned on it."

"Then you've nothing to fear. Now, tonight, come swim with me. There's a pool just down the ravine a little."

"It's too cold," Dariel said.

"We can warm each other. Come." She stretched a hand toward him.

✳

Children are how we return to youth, Nâ Gâmen had said. *There is no other way. A span of years does not make one immortal. Children do.*

That was why he selected that boy whose face told him nothing. He did not take the boy to the soul catcher. It took him some time to understand what was happening to him, but he knew it was not the boy's soul he wanted. He did not want to steal his life. Instead, he watched him. The boy lived in his fabulous palace. Nâ Gâmen let him explore it, fed him, had him cared for. He watched as the child lost his timidity and began to play. He marveled at the sound of his laughter, at the way he made stories in his head. He brought another boy to him. And then a girl.

There, in secret, I became the father that I couldn't be. I raised child after child. For years upon years I thought nothing of it. It was simply my way, a kindness I did to my slaves, treating them as my children. That's how I thought of it. In truth, it was more than that. I had forgotten my own childhood. Do you understand? I had forgotten part of what it means to be human. Without them, I would have lost my humanity entirely.

Nâ Gâmen told of how much he loved to have them near. The vibrancy within them. The innocence. The capacity to heal and thrive no matter what the world threw at them. He gave those children the happiest lives he could. He gave to them—for increasingly it felt like he owed them and the other quota children a great debt—but they also gave to him. He watched them grow into men and women over and over again, and then grow old and die. In all of it he learned and relearned the natural order of life.

They made me human again, Nâ Gâmen said. *After all the wrongs I did to them, they made me human again.*

Why did you walk away from that? Dariel asked. *How did you end up here?*

The Watcher's ears flexed and rippled in the air currents. It took him some time to find the words to go on with. Eventually, his voice resumed inside Dariel's head.

I had a network of swimming pools on the upper level of my palace. I didn't swim in them myself. Hadn't for hundreds of years. But the children did. One day I was lounging near the pools, at a short distance. There was a barrier. He divided the air in front of his face with the edge of his hand, squinting one eye closed. *I could see the edge of the pool, but not the area just next to it. Two boys . . . I remember their names, but I'll hold them inside me, if you don't mind. Two boys would both run to the edge as if to jump in, but pull back at the last minute. I would just see them appear, sprinting suddenly at the edge, in motion and then skidding, arms wheeling around to stop them. One would tease the other. Plead to jump the next time. Again and again they did this. I wanted to call out to them to stop it. They might slip and crack their heads. The words were in my throat, but I couldn't speak. They were so joyful—and I so afraid—that I couldn't speak.*

For a moment Nâ Gâmen's face was warm with the memory. Then the expression faded. *And that was it.*

What do you mean? What was it?

Watching them, I realized for the first time that I would die so that either of them could live. That's what I thought: I would trade my life for either of theirs in an instant. And if that were so, what sense did it make for me to steal the lives of other children? What a crime. It all came to me at once. Not understanding our crimes. I had always done that. But the knowing. That was new. The horrible knowing. It was love, Dariel. I loved those children. I had loved all of them, from Ebrahem onward. I loved them as if they were part of me. Knowing that, I could no longer sort souls. I feared what became of the stolen souls once they died. Would they know peace? Would they understand who they were, or would they be trapped in between? I knew the answers, and I hated them.

Images poured into Dariel's mind again. He watched Nâ Gâmen speaking before an audience of the Lothan Aklun. They watched him with faces of sublime indifference as he implored them to stop the trade. He asked them to search in their hearts. They knew how wrong it was. They knew that the punishment of Tinhadin was hurting innocents and also making them into greater villains than the one they hated. He railed at them, but he could not change their course. He could not stop them. Their hatred was too deep. If they had looked into so many children's souls—as he had—they might have understood, but they had not. They did not wish to listen. Nor could he fight them. They were his brethren. He loved them, more so, perhaps, because of the sadness of their error.

I did not sort souls after that. Instead, I learned to shepherd them.

He traveled to Rath Batatt with the quota slaves he had learned to call his family. He chose the peak atop which to build the Sky Mount, and he set to work. He used the song trapped in simple tools to work the stone. He made it malleable and shaped it to suit him. There he lived through the lives of those mortal children, doing the best he could to give them joyous childhoods, meaningful lives, ease in the elder years, and pain- less deaths to true release. One by one, he shepherded them through lives worthy of them and then let them go.

I have not done enough. I took apart an evil castle built of stone one small block at a time. Much of it remains, and ever will. I did what I could, though. Now, I hope you will as well. Dariel, seeing what I have done, can you forgive me? Do you forgive me?

Of course, Dariel said.

Nâ Gâmen closed his eyes for a time. Opened them. *Thank you. Forgiveness is a circle, Dariel. A band that joins us. Thank you. If you will accept it from me, I will give you a blessing. It's the last thing I have to offer you. Will you accept?*

Of course.

※

The pool was beautiful. Boulders hemmed it in on all sides, with a large shelf of rock blocking most of the downstream end. It was deep enough to dive into, lit from below by some of the rocks—which glowed the same pale green as the stones of Amratseer.

"Is this safe?" Dariel asked.

"It's not the Sheeven Lek, if that's what you mean," Anira said. "Don't just stand, gaping. Off with your clothes!"

A few moments later, naked herself, Anira dove. Her body speared the glassy water, sending the clear image of the riverbed stones into sudden confusion. She kicked toward the depths. At the bottom she turned and stared up at Dariel, as if taunting him. He finished stepping out of his trousers and jumped.

The shock of the cold water froze the air he had just pulled into his lungs. He had planned to slice toward the bottom gracefully, but instead his arms and legs set hooks in the water. He pivoted toward the surface and broke into the air, gasping. Had it been possible, he would have clawed his way right out of the water. Instead, he paddled in circles, looking for a place to get ashore, teeth chattering.

Anira rose from underneath him. She ran her hand up his abdomen, her body sliding up after it. Her breasts slipped over his chest. Surfacing with her face inches from his, she parted her lips. Dariel thought she was going to kiss him. She seemed close to it, but instead she exhaled her long-held breath. Her legs kicked rhythmically to keep her up, close enough that he felt her thigh brush his. No accident, for she did not draw away.

"Dariel, I want you to dance with me," she said. The green, liquid shifting light was lovely on her skin. Droplets of water slicked the scaled plates beneath her eyes and over the bridge of her nose. They highlighted her eyes. "I need you to. Do you know what I mean by dance?"

It would have been hard not to know, considering the way her hands caressed his torso. They were so warm, as were her legs, smooth against his. He felt himself stiffening despite the chill water. "It wouldn't be right," he said. "I have someone back on Acacia."

"I would be surprised if you didn't have someone. Can I take the love you feel for her from you?"

The image of Wren that popped into his head was an unlikely one. He saw her as she had been the night they blew up Sire

Fen's warship. Just after they dropped the pill that ignited fires inside it, she had climbed over the tall ship's railing and leaped into the air. He remembered the way her hair rose, waving at him. He remembered exactly what her face had looked like and how much he had wanted her.

"No," he said, "you can't take my feelings for her from me."

"Good. I don't want to. Are you sure that you will live to see her again?"

"You know the answer to that."

"I hope you do see her again. If you do, it's up to you to tell her of the evening you spent making love to a black-skinned snake woman. Or not." Anira smiled. Her teeth shone wonderfully white in the moonlight, like little jewels. They looked so smooth and clean and cheerful. "You are part of my destiny, Dariel Akaran. Making love with you is part of that. Anyway, you made your decision when you took my hand to come down here. Can we stop talking now?"

He felt her hand take hold of his sex. That did it. He could well imagine that Wren would box him bare knuckled when she found out, but what Anira said was true. He had already consented. Being with her already felt necessary in a way he could not explain. He pulled her closer. He touched the tip of his tongue to the enamel of her teeth. It was as he had thought. They were smooth and clean and cheerful. When her lips pressed full against his, he responded with more hunger than he knew he had felt.

CHAPTER

TWENTY-TWO

Delivegu folded himself into the chair. He managed to do nothing overtly indecorous, and yet he pushed up close to the line with every gesture: the manner in which he leaned back against the plush backrest, the way his fingers brushed the open collar of his white shirt, the cast of his long legs, parted just enough to invite eyes toward his virility.

Corinn watched him from the far side of her desk. With his trace of a smile and the way he seemed to shift his focus from one eye to the other and back again and the way his lips stayed parted, moistened by his tongue before he spoke, Delivegu acted as if there were no space between them at all. They might have been plastered together after lovemaking. Such was the sensual excess that dripped from him like sweat.

"Did you do it?"

"I saw to it, Your Majesty. I timed it to cast no blame upon myself. Or upon you. It's done. Soon you'll hear wailing coming all the way from Calfa Ven."

Corinn let nothing show on her face, but inside, her heart caught for a moment on the thought of Dariel—wherever he was—hearing that wailing. Perhaps he would not hear it. Perhaps he was dead and gone, and would never know what she had done. Am I such a monster, she asked herself, that I would kill my brother's lover and his child—and then look to my brother's death with relief?

Worse things had been done by her ancestors, and for less reason. Reading through the Akaran royal archives had shown her that. By comparison to the secret crimes of her ancestors, Corinn's acts were small wrongs done for larger goals. Who but other monarchs could understand the decisions rulers must make? Not even Aliver had carried such a burden. Not Mena. Not Dariel.

"None but my ancestors could judge me," she said.

Delivegu dipped his head. "It was a small thing, Your Majesty."

You're right about that, Corinn thought. It had not seemed like a small thing when she gave him the mission, but so much had changed. The palace hummed now with energy for the coming coronation. She had been hosting the flood of dignitaries arriving from all over the empire for several days. Banquets and dances, speeches and parades and performances in the Carmelia. It was all hastily prepared. A good portion of the empire also mustered for war, but there was a giddy vibrancy to everything. She felt like a child, as if she believed again that the world could be as she wished. She was not sure that she had truly felt that as a child, but she knew a princess was supposed to feel that way. Now, because of her own hard work, she did.

Rhrenna appeared in the doorway. Standing framed within it, she reminded Corinn that Aliver would be along soon to escort her to the meeting. Corinn watched Delivegu appraise the secretary as she turned on her heel and moved out of sight. She was lovely in a thin-featured, Meinish way. Under Corinn's critical eye, Rhrenna had developed a fine fashion sense, wearing clothes that flattered her slim figure.

Corinn wondered if Delivegu had slept with her. Rhrenna

was discreet in her romantic life, but she had recently admitted to Corinn that she could not have children. She had never
yet gotten pregnant. By her own estimation, she should have
by now, if it was possible for her. Corinn made a mental note
to advise her not to be seen with Delivegu, not if she wanted
a chance at being an Acacian queen. And why shouldn't she
become queen? Rhrenna had been a more faithful servant to
her than anybody. Hers was a disgraced people, but allowing
such a marriage would be seen as an act of benevolence, forgiveness. Considering that she could not bear children . . . well,
there would not be that complication to Aaden's inheritance to
deal with. It would not be so hard to weave an attraction to her
into the binding spells around Aliver. She decided to begin to
do that, slowly, at a pace that would bloom right around the
coronation.

Delivegu found Corinn's eyes still on him when he swiveled
back to her. "With this behind us, what more would you have me
do? You know I wish to serve you in any manner you require."

The queen lifted her chin. "Enjoy it while it lasts."

Delivegu bowed. "As you order. All I wish is to fulfill whatever you desire."

*Delivegu, you musky animal. As if it's my desires you con-
cern yourself with,* Corinn thought after he departed. *You will
never have me. Nobody will.*

"Nobody after me, you mean?"

The voice entered Corinn's ear as if the speaker's lips were
just beside it. At first it was just a voice. She recognized it,
though. She could not have mistaken the superior tenor of it, so
smooth and confident, the speaker as pleased with himself as a
pampered cat. By the Giver, she knew that voice!

"Because I certainly had you. Body completely. Soul . . .
almost."

She had heard it in so many variations. Giving speeches, rallying crowds, barking orders. She had heard it jesting over a banquet table, telling tales, poking fun at her. She had heard it panting her name in passion, and had lain entwined as it spoke softly, breaths against the nape of her bare neck.

"Don't tell me you've forgotten."

Then she felt the physical presence that came with the voice. He was there in the corner. She did not turn to look directly at him, but she saw him at the border of her vision. Just barely physical, so near the edge that with a step he could have slipped back around the corner of her mind, out of sight. He leaned against the wall, watching her with his gray eyes. She knew they were gray. Beautiful and gray, more at home in the face that displayed them than any eyes she had ever seen. She knew when he swept a hand up over his blond hair, combing it with his fingers. She did not look. For some reason it felt very important that she not look directly at him.

"Look at me, lover. You haven't forgotten me. How could you when I left you proof? A proof that you love more than any-thing else in the world. Which, in a way, means I still possess you, Corinn. That's why you'll never take another man."

"No, that's not why."

"No?" He shifted. She imagined the curious purse of his thin lips, the way he would lift his eyebrows and fix her with all his charismatic attention. "Then why have you never been with another man?"

"Because none are worthy."

Hanish laughed. "So after me, no other man is worthy of you? I have ruined you. The pity for the world of men!"

"No, that's not what I mean." She still did not wish to talk, but the words came anyway. "You were not worthy either. You were all weak, treacherous. Every man I . . . Every man who loved me failed me. My father died. He said he would protect me. Instead he died. There, that's one. Igguldan—"

"Oh, that's right. He died, too."

"He spouted love and promises, and then went off and died, yes."

"Who else?" Hanish taunted. "Your brother, don't forget him."

"Aliver died. Dariel disappeared—"

"You can't hold that against him! He may still be alive."

"And you . . ."

"So you've been shaped by the failures of men?"

"No, you don't understand me! None of you shaped me, but all of you taught me to trust only myself. Only myself. You most of all taught me that."

"I know." Hanish's tone changed. Just two words, but they instantly filled with regret, with a sincerity it was hard to doubt. "About me you're right. I knew what I was doing was vile. I hated it, and yet I went forward. But, Corinn, don't pretend you don't understand the pressures of leadership. Didn't you just have your beloved younger brother's lover killed? Forgive me if I misunderstood the exchange, but that's what it sounded like. I know why you did it. I'm not sure you had to, but I understand that you were protecting our son. I can't fault you for that. I want him safe, too."

It was so hard not to look at him. It took all her control to keep her eyes pinned to a spot on the wall opposite. "You tried to kill us."

"If you had a chain of undead ancestors demanding blood, you'd kill for them, too! Besides, I didn't know you were pregnant. That would have been . . . complicating. Corinn, if I had known, I would never have tried to go through with it. You know that, don't you? You must believe me on that. If you had only told me, I'd have turned on the Tunishnevre instead. You and I would still be together. Still in love."

"No."

"Let me prove it."

"No," she said again. It was hard to make the word, and she got no further.

"You know it's true. Look at me. I'm here, aren't I?"

"No, you're not."

"Well, not completely," the apparition conceded. "You almost brought me back. It could have been me instead of Aliver. I was that close. You wanted someone to trust. Someone to help you. Despite everything, Corinn, it was nearly I you brought back to life. Think of that."

The pipers began to play the hour. Their crisp notes cut short the moment. Corinn stood. "I have another meeting," she said. She felt the figure move as she did. He reached for her. She quickened her step, out into the hallway and then down it toward Rhrenna, who had risen from her own desk as Aliver arrived. She did not need to look back to know that the figure that had been Hanish Mein fell into vapor as she moved away.

CHAPTER
TWENTY-THREE

The summoned group awaited Aliver and Corinn in the assembly kitchen that the servants used to keep food warm and drinks chilled on banquet nights. Corinn chose it, she had explained, because its exterior door opened onto the Terrace of First Light, a semienclosed space near Edifus's original hold. With the door to it closed, none of those milling around in the room likely even knew of it. Aliver knew little more about what awaited them on the terrace than any of the others, but Corinn had thought it best that he see her work revealed at the same time as the others.

The members of the Queen's Council jockeyed for position just inside the room. Balneaves Sharratt greeted her first, with Baddel beside him. Talinbeck and General Andeson bowed their heads, and Sigh Saden received them with a thin smile meant to demonstrate the patience he was showing for her benefit. No doubt they all wanted to know why she had gathered them.

The two Akarans acknowledged the other senators and nobles in attendance. They kept their exchanges clipped until they reached the cluster of men standing with Jason. Aliver had met them for the first time only a couple of nights before: Ilabo, a slim Bethuni man wearing the long, intricately stitched robe of his people, and a Candovian called Dram, who looked more Meinish with his pale skin and high cheekbones and gray eyes than he did like the sloe-eyed people he claimed.

Corinn faced the crowd. "You may have guessed that you were not summoned here just to enjoy my company."

Baddel piped that that was enough of an enticement by itself. Polite murmurs of assent.

"There's more to it than that," Aliver said, remembering the lines Corinn had given him. He grinned and lifted his slim glass of wine. "These two are the best horsemen to be found in the empire, or so we've been told. Is it true?" Neither of them boasted, but Dram's involuntary chin lift could have spoken for both of them. "Dram of Candovia is so skilled he rides without reins! He talks to his horse through his legs, while above he launches arrows with a master's speed and accuracy. And we have Ilabo of the Bethuni." Aliver released the imaginary bow he had used to demonstrate Dram's prowess. He set a hand on the young man's shoulder. "I'm sure everyone here knows that the Bethuni have kept up a horseback riding tradition that faded in most of Talay. Ilabo has, since his early teens, been his nation's champion at the games. Those games, mind you, can be deadly."

Having named them both, Aliver stood smiling. Corinn brushed past a servant offering her a drink from a silver tray heavy with wineglasses. She asked the two men, "Do you know why you're here?"

"To ride," Dram said.

"You're correct," Corinn said. "You will ride. I'm offering a way for you to carve a place in history for yourselves. I want for you to be the arms and legs and wings of the empire, as Aliver is the heart and I the head. Do you wish to know what I'm inviting you to ride?"

She walked briskly out the door. A servant opened it just

in time. The others followed, looking at one another, and then squinting as they emerged into the bright afternoon light. They came through singly or in pairs, so it took some time for the entire party to emerge, especially as some paused in the door-way, stunned by what they saw. They had to be pushed forward by the weight of curiosity behind them.

Aliver felt it as much as any of them.

There they stood, Elya's children, preening within the high walls that hemmed in most of the terrace. The young were not as they had been only days ago. All four of them lifted heads big-ger than river crocodiles', with snouts as long as those reptiles', frightening in their length. Their eyes were each the size of a man's fist. Po's golden orbs studied the group with cold indif-ference. What had once been soft-feathered plumage now looked more like spiny plates. They still held the shape of feathers, but when Tij's crests flared, they rose like blue sword blades. Thaïs stretched her head up high and chirruped a greeting to Corinn. It was no longer the high, light sound it had been. Now it thrummed out with bass notes that Aliver felt as vibrations tossed through the air.

He nearly rushed forward to pull his sister away and shout the beasts back, but he knew that Corinn would not want that. His mouth only opened enough to inhale. His legs only moved forward a few steps.

"Behold my winged children," Corinn said. She descended the stone stairway that brought her down to their level. "Mine. Not Elya's. Not Mena's. These children belong to me and to the empire. Mena may have been the first to ride a flying mount, but these are not feathered lizards, as you can see."

She reached Tij. The dragon lowered her head toward Corinn, causing gasps from watchers. Po growled in response, his crest plumes spread. Corinn rubbed Tij under her snout. "They are war mounts, fit for the bravest men the empire has to offer. They will be your mounts, if you are men enough to strap yourselves on them and fly. Doesn't that sound enticing?"

"Your Majesty," Dram said. "They have no . . . wings."

"Of course they do," Corinn said. "Po, show them your wings!"

As if knowing that he was to make the most impressive show he could, the dragon stretched its neck toward the sky and roared. He shook his black, scaled torso furiously. His shoulders gyrated for a few awful seconds, until the protrusions on his back audibly cracked open. Wings erupted out of either side. Each section snapped into place with concussions of sound like tree trunks breaking. Kohl followed Po's lead, with Tij and Thaïs just behind her. In jolting, sinuous waves of motion, each dragon bellowed wings into existence. Where there had been nothing moments before, mighty frameworks of bone suddenly blocked out the sky. They hung, glistening, moist from their creation, with flaps of skin the same various hues as their bristly plumage.

"Now, you may have noticed that there are two of you and four mounts," Corinn shouted above the dragon cries and the peoples' gasps and confused babbling. "Two of these mounts—Tij and Thaïs—are for you. The other two are for Aliver and me, so that we may join Mena in the skies. Perhaps one day Dariel will fly with us as well. I pray that will be so. But now, if you are ready to be legends, I offer you the reins to ride into them."

She grasped for the leather cord attached to Tij's harness. The slim length of hide hung from her fingers, swaying, waiting for someone to step forward and take it.

Aliver felt tremors ripple across his cheeks, the precursors to an expression that could not manage to form itself. He was not sure what the expression would be. He could not make up his mind. This was *wrong*. For a moment he knew it. Whatever Corinn had done to Elya's children was a mistake. A crime. Whatever goodness there had been in them—and there had been much—had been twisted. That could not be good. Just like Elenet, Corinn was creating things that should not be created. He knew this with a burning intensity that he almost pushed past his lips into words.

But when Corinn turned to him and smiled and dipped her eyes toward Kohl, Aliver felt his chest swell. Yes, he thought, why not fly above the world? It seemed a wonderful idea.

CHAPTER
TWENTY-FOUR

Midmorning of the day on which he would first see the Sky Isle, Dariel dropped behind the others and stood ankle-deep in a narrow little brook, one of many that flowed toward the Sky Lake. He welcomed the cool touch of it on his feet. He was here. Those were stones beneath his feet. The water brought an icy chill, cleansing. Bashar and Cashen both crashed through the underbrush nearby, filled with exuberant energy. He was here, and in just a few minutes he would see the man he had come all this way to meet. Would their interaction be as profound as the days he spent with Nâ Gâmen? That hardly seemed possible.

"Dariel?" Anira came toward him. "Are you ready? You can see it over the next rise. The others are waiting. Come. The Sky Isle awaits. Take my hand."

She stretched out her hand. He grasped it without a second thought, content to feel the strength and gentleness of her grip. Here was another thing. They had not spoken of their intimacy beside the pool, but it was there between them. He was sure it would happen again, and he wanted it to. It felt right. He did not think too often of Wren, as he feared he might. He promised himself he would later, but really he felt no shame in what he had done with Anira. That had to mean something.

They joined the others on the grassy slope of a hill that tumbled down toward a horizon-wide lake. They all watched as he and Anira approached. They must know, Dariel thought. He could not tell if it mattered. By Birké's smile and Tam's indifferent expression and Mór's impatience he surmised that it did not. Something about this disappointed him. Mór, at least, should have shown some emotion. Jealousy was too much to hope for. He would have settled for derision. It would only have been fair, considering the effort it took for him to turn his thoughts from her. And that made no sense either. He had done nothing with her. Never would. Why did his thoughts about Mór feel like betrayal of Wren while his actual intimacy with Anira did not? He would never understand matters of his heart. Best to stop trying.

Looking at the vista beyond them, he said, "I can see where the name came from."

The Sky Isle appeared to hover above the earth. Its peak was the smooth, pointed cone of a volcano. Partway down, its slopes disappeared into a narrow circlet of clouds. Beneath them ran a hazy band, colorless and vague above the sparkling green waters of the lake. It looked as if they would be able to sail across the waters and pass beneath the mountain, gazing up into the clouds upon which it floated.

The hike down took an hour. As they dropped out of the heights Dariel lost sight of the lake. They picked up a path and wound through a forest of slim, silver-skinned trees. Their bark came away in delicate peels that crunched underfoot. The leaves of the trees formed triangular points, tiny kites that quivered when the breeze brushed their boughs. They had a touch of red mixed with the green. Dariel could not tell if this was their regular coloring, or if it was a sign of the winter season. It should be winter, but this land gave so little sign of it.

Behind them came a commotion of limbs snapping. Dariel spun to see the tree crowns near one side of the path behind them swaying and trembling. Something large pushed through them and stepped out onto the path with a sickening, lumbering grace. A kwedeir. A man stood attached to its back, high behind its wolfish head.

Bashar and Cashen bristled and growled. Dariel clawed for the dagger strapped to his leg, but before he got it loosened Mór had raised an arm in greeting. She called something to the rider in Auldek and snapped at Birké. Birké squatted between Bashar and Cashen, pulling them to his side and soothing them. The mount came forward. It walked on its wing limbs, all angles and joints, flaps of skin like oil-black leather. The rider answered, and then found Dariel with his eyes. Stared.

No more was said. Birké nudged Dariel back into motion by handing him Cashen to carry. He hefted Bashar himself. The kwedeir and rider followed them the rest of the way. Dariel would have looked back more if the hounds had not done so for him. Between them they passed their growling displeasure back and forth.

A little farther on they passed guards posted on either side of the path. Before long they had an escort flanking them: two older men with short swords sheathed at the thigh; a youth who walked with a limp; a tall, rangy woman with a bow and arrow pinched between the fingers of one hand.

A group of a dozen old men and women awaited them on the shore. Behind them a pier crooked out into the lake, a barge secured to it, motionless on the clear, mirrorlike water. In the distance the volcanic peak of the Sky Isle thrust up into view again, still growing from an island of cloud. The air was moist with the smell of the lake. It was strangely saltless. It's not the sea, Dariel thought.

He glanced at Mór. She looked breathless with relief and joy. For a moment, her guise of control and detachment fell from her face. By following her gaze, Dariel picked out Yoen. That was who the look was for, the look of a daughter seeing a father. Yoen stood at the center of the elders. A short, frail-looking man, he favored one leg over the other, leaning on a cane of carved wood. His hair was disheveled, unruly like a child's that had been tousled. His skin was Acacian brown, a complexion just like Dariel's. He smiled, briefly, at Mór.

They stopped in front of the waiting elders. For a moment no one spoke. Dariel remembered the squirming burden in his arms. He set Cashen down. The pup stood, unsure of the moment's protocol.

The woman to one side of Yoen wore a circlet woven of leaves. It looked like it could be dismantled by a light breeze. Her features had more solidity, and her voice was Talayan. Dariel could tell from the timbre of it, even though she first spoke Auldek. Mór answered her, bowing her head as she did so. The two spoke for a moment, and then the woman turned toward him.

"Are you the one they call Dariel Akaran?" she asked, speaking Acacian.

"I am."

"Did you speak with Nâ Gâmen, the Watcher of the Sky Mount?"

"Yes."

The man whom Dariel already thought of as Yoen asked, "Did he tell you to come here?"

"Yes." Dariel looked at him, realizing that he wore no signs of belonging, no tattoo or piercing or any other enhancement.

"What did he tell you of the circle?"

"That it could be closed," Dariel said.

"It can be, though the way is hard." The man lifted his left arm, crooked in an invitation to an embrace. "I am Yoen. Come to me."

Dariel stepped forward. He raised his arms, thinking that he would set them lightly on the man's thin shoulders so as not to harm him. He was completely unprepared for what happened next.

It was not that the old man was fast, but just that the action did not make sense until it was completed. Yoen's lowered hand snatched the hilt of Dariel's dagger. He slipped the blade free from the sheath and thrust it upward into Dariel's gut with a force that should not have been possible from such a frail-looking arm. The impact doubled Dariel over on top of Yoen. The pain did not stop. It stayed, the moment of impact sustained and unrelenting. It was so great that the burning sensation on his forehead barely registered.

When Yoen pulled back, Dariel looked down at the shaft of the dagger, the blade deep in his abdomen. "I am sorry," the old man said. "This had to be done. You had to be killed, so that . . ."

That was all Dariel heard before he toppled to the ground.

Chapter
Twenty-five

Have a drink, brother," Sire Grau said, motioning toward the servant entering with a tray of tall, thin glasses. Another servant set down a display of cheese parcels wrapped in edible leaves. A third hovered nearby, an intricate mist pipe in his hands. "Or a pipe, if you wish it."

"No, thank you." Dagon waved the servant away. He lowered himself to the floor cushions in Grau's plush quarters. Why a man as elderly as Grau would choose to sit on the floor baffled Dagon, but he sighed and patted the pillow beside him as if he liked nothing more than to lie about in the middle of the day.

"You really should have a drink," Grau said. He selected a glass from the tray and handed it to Dagon.

"If you insist," Dagon said.

"I do," the older man said. His glossed lips smiled, though the expression was limited to the mouth. His cheeks and eyes and forehead did nothing in support. He waved the servant away, having not taken anything for himself.

Dagon held his frown hidden deep below the surface of his face. He sipped, smiled, and made an audible indication of pleasure. He was certain that Grau knew he did not like liqueurs, especially pungent ones redolent of fennel, as this one was. At least, he thought he knew. Perhaps there was nothing sinister in it. Grau was past his hundredth year. He could be forgiven for misplacing specific likes and dislikes of the myriad leaguemen he communed with.

Though the room was deeply shadowed, one wall featured a long balcony. From his reclined position, Dagon could see only a featureless swath of sky. If he stood on the balcony, he knew, he would take in one of the grander views of the teeming city of Alecia. To the right the Akaran palace sprouted from a hill-ock. A rambling estate with large gardens, it went unused by the royal family. To the left he would have seen the white stone estates of the richer nobles, with those of Agnate families flying their lineage's crest. Just beyond them the green dome of the senate building itself. Straight out from the balcony the view stretched over the city proper. Business and trading districts, markets, residential quarters, areas rich and poor, all thronging with their own heartbeats.

Dagon had sometimes imagined stripping himself of his league regalia and wandering into the city's alleys and lanes. What world would he discover there? How different from the existence he had always known and worked so hard to main-tain? He even wondered, on occasion, if he might lose himself within the anonymity of the urban vastness and take on a new identity. The thought never lasted long. With the distinctive cone shape of his head everyone would know him for what he was. He was Sire Dagon of the league; why would he ever wish to be anyone else?

"I wanted to discuss a few things with you," the senior leagueman said. "Did you find our council meeting as unsatis-factory as I did?"

Having no idea just how unsatisfactory Grau had found it,

Dagon dipped his head, something that was balanced between a nod and a shake. Better not to offer anything more committing just yet.

"Most frustrating," Grau went on. "We're too spread apart. With Faleen and Lethel in the Other Lands and half the council on the Outer Isles . . . Seems that some of us believe the center of the world has shifted west. No longer Alecia. It's those islands now. You and I, Dagon, are on the margins, it seems. Our so-called official council. Most unsatisfactory. Hardly a trust of mighty thinkers. Not enough of us to truly meld. Didn't you find it so?"

He had very much found it so. The emergency council had been called at his urging. After witnessing the queen's growing power he had needed to meld his mind with his fellow leaguemen. In so many ways that was the basis of their success over the generations. One of the first things they were taught as children was to blend their minds, to take solace in one another, to share fears and doubts and ambitions and lusts and everything else that ordinary people had to handle while locked inside the solitude of their skulls. As a child, Dagon had found the melding more soothing than anything else in life. The fact that it had always been augmented by copious quantities of high-grade mist helped, but there was something comforting about sharing with others.

That had not happened during this last council. They had gathered in the chamber in Alecia. It was the largest of their council halls, rank upon rank of reclining chairs rising from the center. It could hold a couple hundred leaguemen, but this time only twenty-six attended. Most of these were not even senior enough to sit within the first three circles. Their thoughts reached Dagon muffled by the distance between them. Never before had he noticed how often others held opposing thoughts on the same issue, and never before had he noticed the noise of minds trying to hide the very things they were there to share.

Perhaps it was the particular individuals involved. He did not think so, though.

He had never noticed it before precisely because a chamber filled with minds made it easier to hide. To join. To share. To remain a single fish within a shoal of similar fish. Without the great collective motion and comfort it brought, Dagon had felt more dissonance than he wished to coming from his brothers. They were more separate individuals than he had acknowledged. The disquiet of the experience lingered with him. As, apparently, it lingered with Grau.

"As you say," Dagon said, "there were not enough of us in attendance."

"We grew no clearer on how to proceed. It's the issues we face as well. Mustn't forget that. Let us discuss it now, just you and me."

Grau picked up a cheese parcel pinched between the curved talons that were his long, painted fingernails. "When last we met in a proper council, it had seemed likely the Auldek would inflict great damage on the Akarans. Either side might win; both would suffer. At this last attempt at a council you expressed doubts about this."

"A few weeks ago I would have said the outcome was a toss of the bones, going either way as chance blesses. Now . . . I fear Corinn has made herself a new Tinhadin."

"*That* old bastard," Grau said. "The worst of the lot."

"And she is not alone," Dagon continued. "Aliver is beside her. I do not think his mind is entirely his own, but if Corinn has shaped it—"

"He may be worse than the old idealist he had been."

Dagon pressed the sour truth of this between his lips. "She's powerful. Raising the dead and making dragons. Don't forget that she did destroy the Numrek at . . . What was that place called in Teh? The Thumb. I find it unsettling that there are almost no rumors of discontent among the populace. What with Barad the Lesser singing her praises and the vintage putting a shiny new gleam on the entire world, there are no voices fomenting against her. None that I've heard of recently, at least."

"That vintage was our own fault."

Shrugging, Dagon said, "It seemed like a good idea at the time. She even gets credit for ending the quota trade, as if she had any choice in the matter."

"You think she could defeat the Auldek."

"I fear that's a possibility."

Grau seemed to have something else to say on this matter, but instead he swallowed it along with a cheese parcel. "Think about our situation. Without the Lothan Aklun for us to trade with . . . without an enemy they fear like the Auldek . . . how long before the queen aims her ire at us? Sire El may think his army will be a match for her, but do we really want to become just another petty power, settling matters with the sword and spear? I find that distasteful and far too uncertain. Our success has never come from martial prowess; it never truly will. I once thought we could float through any change. I am no longer sure of that."

"Nor am I."

"We could try to remove Corinn. We've done such things in the past. I myself helped shorten Gridulan's life. That old bastard. I've come to feel we must kill her. And her brother as well." Grau made an expression as if he had burped and found the taste unpleasant. For the first time since they had begun, Grau's eyes fixed on Dagon's. "We are in agreement on that?"

There was something about the directness of Grau's eyes that unnerved Dagon. "Yes," he said, "we are in agreement."

Grau held him pinned to his yellowish eyes for a little longer, then relaxed again. He puckered his lips and made a kissing sound. Dagon might have been unnerved yet again, had not the pipe-holding servant peeled away from the wall in answer.

He brought the delicate instrument to his master. He lit it by snapping the flame strips glued to his thumb and forefinger. It took him several tries to get the resulting tiny burst of flame to catch the threads in the bowl. Once they did, the young man darted away. He returned a moment later and lit a second pipe for Dagon, who did not refuse this time.

Grau held the tubing of the mouthpiece and smelled the pungent scent a moment. The threads were potent, pure, as the rich aroma of them attested to. "Dagon, I wish to send you back to Acacia with a charge, one outside the unsatisfactory proceedings of the last council. Council Speaker Sire Faleen should be here, but he isn't. Sire El should be here, but he isn't. Many others should be here, but they aren't. It falls to us to take action when the council cannot. Are you prepared to do that?" Before Dagon could answer, Grau added, "Soon I will step down from all council matters. I am ready for Rapture."

Of course you are, Dagon thought. It made perfect sense, and it perplexed him that he had not anticipated it. Grau was old. His body no longer took the physical pleasure in living that it once had. Why wouldn't he be ready to join his predecessors in perpetual bliss? That was what awaited every leagueman who lived long enough—and who earned enough for the league over that long life. Rapture. It was the Tunishnevre in reverse. Instead of undead, ageless suffering, Rapture offered continuous life, unending bliss through a process that drained one's body of blood, replacing it, very gradually, with the purest distillation of mist. It was a process that took the better part of a long life to prepare, and then several years of slow transition. Dagon had been tithing toward his own Rapture for decades, but it was still a faraway goal. Such a gift was incredibly expensive. Grau must have finally paid his dues.

"You have served many years," Dagon said, realizing he had not responded yet.

"When I am gone, I would like to believe Sire Faleen won't hold the reins of power. He may be council speaker, but I'd be remiss if I left it up to him to appoint his successor. I want a bold man in the position, one who will keep the league powerful forever. What use is going to Rapture if it all comes crashing down in a few years?"

Dagon nodded.

"I see several prospects for this role. I'm sure you know those I mean."

Of course he did. Bold—or at least ambitious—leaguemen were as numerous as pimples, and as hard to scrub away. Sire Nathos with his vintage. Sire El creating his Ishtat army. Even the upstart Sire Lethel had the scent of blood in his nose. Dagon had damned them all more than once in moments of ill temper, but he said, "There are none like you, but many worthy men who aspire to be."

"Well . . . there are one or two individuals that I would rather not see ascend. Lethel, if you must know."

Dagon almost spilled his drink. Had Grau just—just . . . spoken ill of another leagueman?

"I am going to take you into my confidence. The next council speaker could well be you, Dagon. Why not? You've served us right from within the wolves' den all these years. You've done a great deal more than you've received credit for, haven't you?"

Answering that in the affirmative felt like a trap. Dagon tried his diagonal head-shake/nod combination again.

"Now comes the time when you can truly earn it." The old leagueman studied him a moment, lips squinched together in a contemplative pucker. "I have in mind a coronation of death." He pointed with his jaw. "Take the pipe. Ease yourself and we will discuss it."

CHAPTER
TWENTY-SIX

On the morning she was to depart for the coronation, Mena left Elya in the care of gentle handlers and went to say good-bye to her troops. She paused in the hallway just outside an open doorway in the Calathrock. The chamber was still musty, damp, stained with mold and decay. It would take more than a few weeks to undo the years of neglect. But it had been a corpse before. Now, soldiers' feet pounded its floor. The air clanged with the clash of weapons and shouts of orders, and it smelled of men and women training. Volleys of arrows flew like single-minded birds. Once a dead ruin of a defeated people, now the building lived and breathed.

She had worked as hard as anyone to bring about the transformation. She had lifted new timbers with her own hands, pulled on the rusty-toothed saw to cut them, and leaned her weight to push them up into place, shoulder to shoulder with her soldiers. She had filled buckets with snow and brought them inside to melt, and then scrubbed the floor clean like a servant. She had held the safety ropes as climbers scrabbled into the chamber's higher reaches, shoring up the ancient beams and repairing broken panes of glass. And she was among the first on the scene when a blockage in the vents caused an explosion that killed three and steamed the skin half off several more.

It was hasty work, done mostly so the chamber could function once more for its most basic purpose: to train an army sheltered from the winter that raged above it. This, too, she did in among her troops. She walked the Calathrock as Perrin shouted the soldiers through drills. None of them had fought more recently against the Numrek than she. So she taught what she knew. She lectured as she sparred with the strongest, tallest, and most skilled of her warriors, hoping that things learned from fighting Numrek would apply to the Auldek as well.

She was there to correct missteps, adjust weapons. Her eyes on the young men and women pushed them harder than they would have worked otherwise. She knew she had this effect on them. She used it not for herself but so they would become stronger, faster, more skillful than they thought themselves capable of. Perhaps one or two of them would learn just the extra bit he or she would need to survive the Auldek.

"Much has changed, hasn't it?" Perrin's shoulder brushed hers as he came to stand beside her. "Just a few weeks, but you'd barely recognize the place. It's you who did that."

"They did it," Mena corrected. "One person can do little. Only together—"

"I know. Only together is great work accomplished. But I don't know where we'd be without you. You, Mena, kept us marching and working and training. I've never known anyone more suited to lead others. You're . . ."

She glanced at him.

The easy confidence on his face fell away. He went suddenly shy, as if the touch of her eyes was a rebuke. "I was going to say that you're an inspiration, but that doesn't sound like something a soldier should say to the princess he serves."

"No, it doesn't."

"I should probably quit while I'm ahead."

"I think so, Captain." Looking back into the Calathrock, Mena smiled. Despite the interest she had always seen in Perrin's eyes, she thought Melio would like him. I'd love to see them spar together. Melio would win, but this young man would give him a good contest. She stepped through the portal and into the massive chamber.

A visiting dignitary or senator from Alecia would not have recognized her, dressed as she was in simple garments meant for function, mobility, and warmth. Her soldiers recognized her; they were what mattered. Their survival in the face of the coming onslaught mattered. That was the main thing she hated about command—that the one thing she wanted to spare them from was the exact thing she was sending them toward. Aliver had warned her that leadership was like this.

She rejoiced when new arrivals swelled their numbers, knowing at the same time that many of them would likely die. A unit of new troops arrived from Candovia, as well as a team of laborers and young recruits from the Eilavan Woodlands. The former had acted on Corinn's orders; the latter on their own initiative. Barely enough to make up for those taken by the hazards of trekking and working in a Meinish winter. As yet they did not fill even half the chamber, but it heartened them all to know that some were willing to join their cause. The trickle of arriving Meins had especially lifted Mena's spirits and had done wonders for Haleeven's.

She could see as much when she passed where Haleeven was talking with several of his clansmen. The Meinish men wore rags. Their hair hung in matted, golden knots that were, somehow, attractive on them, despite the bits and pieces of debris that clung to them. They were fresh faced and sharp featured, and each of them was sprinkled with peeling curls of pink skin on his or her nose and cheeks. It still amazed Mena that they had answered Haleeven's call. They had appeared out of the frigid nothingness surrounding Mein Tahalian as if they had been camped just over the horizon. She stopped among them long enough to learn their names and to welcome them.

Just the previous morning they had rolled out wagons meant to imitate the wheeled structures the Numrek had arrived with. "Too bad I won't be here to see you get squashed by these things," she said, patting a young woman on the back. She wanted to work through the problems posed by antoks and to see the other beasts the Auldek might arrive with and form strategies against them. "I'm sorry to miss you all fighting that as well." She pointed to where someone had mounted the head of a woolly rhinoceros on a wheelbarrow. The efficacy of training against such a comical imitation was questionable at best. She welcomed the laughter it was already invoking, though. "I'll miss the lot of you."

Gandrel's booming voice called for quiet in the chamber.

"You began this campaign with me a few months ago," Mena began. "Most of you did not know me. I did not know you. We know one another now. We were called upon by the nation as the first line of defense against invaders none of us have even seen. My sister, Queen Corinn, asked for bravery. You arrived wearing it on your chests. Didn't you?"

Apparently so, judging by the shouts of affirmation.

"I thank the Giver for it every day. I cannot tell you how proud I am of the army we've become. I know none of you would have expected to be training here, in Mein Tahalian, but I thank you for accepting the task of rebuilding this ancient chamber with me. Our time grows near. I won't keep you from your training but a minute. I know you want to get to it."

She grinned at the groans they responded with. Her eyes touched on Perrin, who was watching her with undisguised admiration. All right, so she did have a way with her troops. She wondered if he understood how much they all gave her, how much she needed them to need her. Her soldiers. A different sort of family from the one she was about to fly to, but one she loved just as much.

"I leave you only briefly. I'll fly on my dragon. You've heard of her, right? The great dragon Elya? I fly on her to be at the coronation of Aliver reborn. You see? My sister raises the dead. She slays Numrek with the words out of her mouth. You think I'm scary with a blade—you should hear her sing!"

A great noise greeted this, mock horror and praise mixed together.

"When I return, we'll march north and defend our nation. When I return, I will hold out my hand for you all to touch. I will bring a blessing from Aliver reborn to you."

Walking through the crowd as she exited, nodding and shaking hands and continuing her flow of humorous remarks, Mena wondered why she was so capable of appearing certain about things that she was not at all certain about.

She had just stepped into the hallway when the man threw open the reinforced doors at the end of it. "Princess Mena, come . . . please. A Scav come from Tavirith . . . Something has happened."

The jog back to Tahalian was short and brisk, but it exposed her enough that winter's fury ripped and snarled at her for a few ferocious moments. It always did that, but this time it felt much more sentient, intentional, personal. It poured out of the gap in the mountains that led toward Tavirith with a physical violence made no less by the fact that it was only air and tiny ice crystals. She had no idea what message awaited her, but it already felt like a punishment for the certainty she had feigned before her soldiers.

In an anteroom just inside the inner doors of the fortress, Mena found Edell, her military secretary, standing beside a seated man. She recognized the Scav as soon as his blue eyes lifted and met hers. Kant, the same man who had shown them the route the Numrek had taken. Since Gandrel had to be fetched to translate, she stood looking at the man, unable to communicate with him for several minutes more.

"Get it from him," Mena said as soon as Gandrel and Perrin stepped inside, flushed from the rabid cold.

For a few moments the two men talked the guttural confusion that was the Scav tongue, and then Gandrel stopped the man midsentence. He touched the scar on his nose as if it were a talisman against what he was about to say. "A massacre . . . in Tavirith."

The rest came out in the maddening stutter stop of translation. Kant's words were unhurried. He stared at one object after another, as if talking to the chair and the wall and the door, not the people in the room. He had returned to Tavirith to winter, he said. He did not usually do so, but with the bounty Mena had paid him for his earlier information, he had much to trade and gamble. He arrived to find the place sacked. Houses had been smashed and gutted. Ash blackened the snow. Frozen bodies littered the ground. Hacked, defiled bodies. Limbs chopped off. A few had lost their heads. Some had been half eaten.

"He says it was not animals that did it. Not all of it, at least. Flesh was cut away by knives."

"Do the Scav make war this way?" Mena asked.

Gandrel passed her question on. The look Kant turned toward her was so full of derision she felt suddenly ashamed. "No Scav would do this. It was the Auldek."

"That's madness!" Perrin said. "How could they? It's too soon! They couldn't have marched this far already. By his own testimony they couldn't."

Edell asked, "Is he after more booty? We gave him too much before. Now he thinks we'll pay for any fool story."

This got no translation, but the Scav must have read his tone.

"He says if you don't wish to believe him, you don't have to," Gandrel translated. "He saw what he saw, and he heard what the dead had to say. With his own eyes, he saw there were no tracks of marchers. A small party, perhaps a dozen of the invaders, touched down a little distance from the village and walked toward it. No tracks brought them to that point. They just dropped from the sky. They flew."

"Flew?"

"Atop beasts with large footprints. Like a man's print, but massive."

"This is foolishness," Edell said. "How much does he want to go away? I'll pay him myself."

The Marah captain Bledas and the Senivalian Perceven had just arrived, but they paused inside the door. Haleeven shouldered between them. He spoke to the Scav.

"Haleeven is greeting him with respect," Gandrel narrated. "They seem to know each other. Kant's . . . telling him what he has told us. . . . Now Kant says that he did not come for himself. He did not come for the Acacians. He came for the dead. They want vengeance. They howl for it." Gandrel paused a moment, before finishing. "There is another thing we should know, he says. The invaders have made the turn inland. The bulk of the main force, that is."

"He saw this?"

"No, but his ancestors did," Gandrel said. "He speaks to their ghosts, remember?" He smirked, but the expression quickly faded. "The Auldek are making good time. He says they move despite the weather, day and night, slowly and steadily. That means fast in the north."

"And that was over irregular terrain," Perrin said. "They may be able to move faster when they reach the Ice Fields."

Gandrel said something to Kant, heard his answer, and nodded. "He thinks the invaders will be out of the Ice Fields before the spring."

Edell began, "But do we believe him? What proof—"

"He needs none," Haleeven said. "I know this man. I know his people. They saw the Numrek come through. Back when you knew nothing of them, we did. The Scav did. He had relatives in the town of Vedus, the first to be slaughtered and left flaming with that vile pitch the Numrek brought with them. If he says this about Tavirith, it's true. About the war column—it's true."

"How do we know that?" Edell asked. "It was you who invited the Numrek down in the first place. You lit the torch on the pitch that burned Vedus."

Haleeven looked at the young soldier secretary with a measure of the disdain Kant had shown earlier. "We never meant for that to happen. I have reckoned with Kant on the past already. That's between us. Do you doubt my word?"

"When your word is based on stories of ghosts, yes, I'd say so."

"The dead don't lie. And they don't speak without having something to say. That's a trait of the living."

Edell's mouth twisted into a snarl, but his voice kept an official precision. "The Acacian military cannot move on the word of a Scav who claims he's been talking to the dead. You may have sucked from the same mother's teat as this Scav, but I didn't. I think we need confirmation before we do anything."

Mena cut in before Haleeven could respond. "Peace, Haleeven. Peace, Edell. I want no arguing between you."

"Especially not now," Perrin said. "Mena leaves this afternoon. Let's give her no cause to doubt our leadership when she's gone."

"Will you still go?" Bledas asked. "This changes everything."

"It doesn't change anything," Perrin said. "We'll be here doing the things Mena would want us to. We'll start for the Ice Fields earlier. If the enemy can travel in winter, we'll find a way to travel in winter, too. No matter what, we'll still meet them on the fields and defeat them."

Edell touched his temple, wincing. He was prone to head-aches. "We should send a party to Tavirith to check the Scav's story."

"In these conditions?" Haleeven asked, swinging an arm as if asking them to take in the view. "The howling wind from Tavirith is well known to my people. It may not stop for weeks. Marching into it would eat men alive."

"You both speak wisdom," Mena said. "We should step away from this, regroup in a moment. Let's go to the conference room. It's warmer there, and there are the old Meinish maps to con-sult. We'll plan while we can."

Bledas pushed his unanswered question. "Your highness, the royal coronation—will you leave to attend it?"

The room hushed as Mena considered her answer. "Yes, I'll go. I meant what I said—I have faith in you all. We'll plan what we can before I fly, but I will fly."

She looked at Kant, who sat motionless, a bland look on his face as if he had already forgotten the confusion he had just brought with him. "Haleeven, stay with us a moment. Translate for me. I would speak with Kant about some things, just the three of us."

※

With the Scav's promises still in her ears a few hours later, Mena climbed atop Elya. Her head cleared as they rose into the frigid, angry skies. Mena leaned into Elya, her cheek on the scented feathers, breathing them in. She smelled and felt so good that Mena almost could not ask of her the thing she had decided to ask. What part did Elya own in all this anyway? None of it, perhaps. In a perfect world she would be home with her babies, raising them, but this was not a perfect world. Mena was not perfection herself, so she had to rely on someone. Fair or not, it was to be her winged companion.

They slid down along the eastern edge of the Black Mountains. The raging torrent of air funneled through the pass from Tavirith shoved them forward. They could not have fought it if they tried. Mena let Elya ride it instead, over Scatevith and the woodlands rimming the Sinks. They scattered herds of woolly oxen beneath them. From there they traced the meandering line that was the frozen River Ask. Ironic, Mena knew, that she was flying the same route Hanish Mein had attacked by, first on sleds and then on boats. She wondered what the landscape had looked like to him. To her, despite the cold, despite the coming war and the many things that roiled in her stomach . . . To her the frozen land beneath her was beautiful. All Acacia, all the Known World was filled with wonders worth fighting for. She had long ago decided she would die for it. Before this was all over, she would die. It seemed the only possibility, the only way through it for the people and the nation and the land she loved. The certainty of this belief made what she did next easier.

Back when Bledas asked if she would go, her answer had not been as certain as it sounded. Now, on the wing and with the world cold beneath her, she decided upon another course. She turned Elya toward Candovia. From there she would keep flying, all the way to Tavirith and then beyond. She and Elya would see these Auldek with their own eyes.

CHAPTER
TWENTY-SEVEN

Kelis jogged up from the town at a steady pace. He told himself to be calm, to move efficiently but not in a hurry. He had just enough time. It wouldn't do to attract attention with too much haste, or to trip and twist an ankle or something foolish like that. He had come too far—and brought Shen and Benabe too far—to spoil it with a careless mistake.

Since the night Kelis was attacked, they had traveled with all the stealth they could manage. It never felt like stealth, though, considering the crowd of Santoth that trailed them every step of the way. He had still not gotten used to them. He could still not quite believe that nobody outside their group saw them, but as he had no choice in the matter, he did the best he could. And the best he could do, he decided, was to ignore them.

It seemed to work.

They crossed through Balbara territory heading toward the trading city of Falik. It was exposed country, flat as a plate and spread like a clear night sky with a constellation of settlements, villages, and farms. The entire time, Kelis felt like any eye within twenty miles could see them. Gone was the solitude of the south. Daylong, from whatever scant shelter they found under acacia trees or beneath a geometry of cloth propped by

Kelis's iron spear, they watched movement on the horizon. Near or far, there was always somebody: herd boys switching droop-eared goats, tenì root farmers piercing the ground with their pronged spears, groups of women attending to some work Kelis could not imagine, who seemed to communicate mainly in bursts of laughter.

Once an entire caravan of merchants trudged by not thirty feet from the cluster of rocks they huddled beside. Person after person waved at them in passing, singing a story in song that they passed from one person to another. Kelis did not catch all their Balbara words, but he knew enough of their traditions to know that their travel songs tended to incorporate whatever things they saw along the way. Likely, the group huddled beside the rocks had been documented in the song. So much for stealth.

They kept to their night travel, but it was harder here, with village or camp dogs always ready to wake the world to announce their passing. He had never seen such moisture on the plains. In the late hours of the night a knee-high layer of mist flowed across the ground like slow liquid, leaving their lower legs dripping wet. It was as if the land were dreaming itself into an ocean, making water phantoms.

In among the stew of races and cultures of Falik their progress changed. No running through these choked streets. The only hiding they could do was to walk in plain sight, to be invisible by being visible. Kelis had known many Balbara. He had fought with them during Aliver's war and had hunted foulthings with a few of them under Mena's command. Now, though, he made eye contact with no one. He knew that faces, marked with the dotted lines and swirls that the Balbara found beautiful, turned and followed his progress, but he did not look. That would invite interaction, make a certainty out of what might only be a question. He just kept moving, busy, distracted, like so many others.

They made a point of never walking together as a group of five. When they divided, the Santoth always stayed near Shen. Kelis tried to take comfort in this. They were there to protect her as well, right? They knew Aliver. Loved him. Kelis said the words. He knew them by heart. He took a measure of comfort in them, but only a tiny sliver. A moment later, he returned to fearing them more than Sinper Ou's spies, more even than Corinn, whose reaction to the girl he could not predict, no matter how many times he tried to run through the moment in his mind.

Once, while walking with Leeka through a market at the edge of the city, Kelis lost the old warrior. He cast about for a moment and spotted him at a stall a ways back, bent over a table, studying something. He turned the other way and watched the Santoth's backs as they followed the others out along the road that would take them away from the city. He retraced his steps.

Drawing up beside Leeka, he started to urge him on. The warrior said, "An Acacian blade. Look, Kelis, this was my weapon once."

The Balbara stall keeper standing just on the other side of the narrow table said, "Nah, nah. This one was fair trade. Not yours." He was a short man, with eyes that were set at irregular angles. It was hard to know what he was looking at, though he did not seem troubled by it.

"How much is it?" Leeka asked.

The stall keeper appeared to size him up before answering. With one eye or the other, he took in Leeka's tattered robe, the leather cord at his waist, and the small satchel of supplies draped over his shoulder, then studied his weathered face. "Too much for you, old tortoise. Too much coin; too much blade. What, would you join Aliver's war?"

"Aliver's war?"

"Aliver's war?" The stall keeper imitated Leeka's Mainland accent. He looked to Kelis to share the absurdity of the question with him. Kelis returned nothing. "The coming war! The war with the invaders. The Snow King's new war!"

Leeka blinked his green eyes. "The Snow King . . ."

"I know what you want. You want to dress fancy for the coronation. Is that so? You want to impress the king, make him think you're an old warrior?"

"Coronation?"

"Do you know nothing? Or is it age? Too much wine in your young days?"

The Balbara found Leeka's confusion hilarious. In what must have been a local dialect, he called something over his shoulder to a group of men playing stones a little distance away. They looked up, and one of them said something back. All of them laughed. Turning back to Leeka, the man grew suddenly friendly. "See if you remember this tomorrow. Aliver Akaran is reborn. He is to become king. Finally, he will be king! He'll fight a war and we'll get on with it. It's good for Talay. Good for Balbara." The man reached out and squeezed Leeka's shoulder with one hand, even as he made a show of guarding the sword from him with the other. "But, no, old tortoise, I can't sell you this steel at any price. This sword needs a warrior, not a grandfather. Walk on."

Tension trembled on Leeka's forehead. His eyes moved away from the man's face and focused on the hand resting on his shoulder. For an awful moment, Kelis was sure the old warrior was going to break the man's arm. The Balbara smiled, undeterred, but Kelis knew things about Leeka. The Leeka who had greeted them alone in a vast plain had been unreadable and strange. This Leeka was different, though Kelis had not noticed the change until now.

"Come, brother," he said to Leeka. "You do not need this sword." He slipped the wedge of his hand under the Balbara's wrist and lifted it.

From there, at least, their journey north up the coast and then along the trade roads that ran along the western edge of the Teheen Hills proved easier. Without knowing they were doing so, they had joined a river of pilgrims flowing north, toward the shore, toward the isle of Acacia and the wonders it now purported to offer. All who could drop what they were doing to make the journey, it seemed, had done just that. Among them, the five travelers with their escort of sorcerers were just some of the many.

※

I found a boat," Kelis said on meeting Benabe out a little way from their camp.

"Did you?"

"Yes." Kelis moved to pass her, but Benabe stopped him.

She looked into his eyes for a long moment. "Perhaps we should go without them."

He knew what she meant instantly. He had chewed on the same thought himself many times. "I did not book passage for them, but . . . I don't imagine that will stop them from coming."

"We could go ourselves," Benabe said, bending urgency into her words, "leave them here."

Could we? Kelis wondered. Had they power to? Had they the right? It wasn't to Benabe or Naamen or Kelis that the Santoth spoke. It was to Aliver's daughter. And it had been Aliver himself who first sought out the Santoth, found them, and came back even stronger and more driven for his time with them. Wiser. "Benabe, Aliver wanted nothing more than to bring the Santoth back into the world. *He* would have done what we are doing now, if he had lived and found the way. How can you ask me not to do a thing he thought was so important?"

Benabe did not have an answer. "We should have discussed this more."

"We have discussed it plenty," Kelis said. "All of us, in our heads."

Naamen jogged over to them. "What?"

"I found a boat," Kelis said again.

"An Acacian ship?" Naamen asked. "Do they know who you are?"

"No, nobody knows. And it's not an Acacian ship." He glanced at Shen. She lay sleeping on a narrow blanket cast on the hard ground. "You all will probably not like it much, but it's the best I could do. Come. Wake Shen. We must go now."

Naamen approached him as he gathered up their scant supplies. "And them?" the young man asked.

Kelis did not need to look up to know what he meant. He slipped their bowls and foodstuffs into his sack, then stood, slinging it onto his back as he did so. "Just the five of us," he said. "That's all I can account for. We will do what we do. They will do what they will do."

What the Santoth did was shadow them as they came down from the toes of the Teheen Hills in which they had spent the last few nights. Before them ran the thin line of white sand that marked the northern shore of Talay. The Inner Sea stretched north toward the isle of Acacia, unseen but there, surely, just a little over the horizon. Though not a city or town, the entire area crawled with life. Flat transports crowded the long stretch of beach. Pilgrims like themselves converged from all landward directions. A network of wooden pens described ragged geometries from the beach up through the sea grass. Inside them, herds of creatures grazed. They were fat things, hairless and pink—and not just from the early sun.

"Pigs? You're joking," Benabe said, in a tone that indicated she knew he was not. "Those . . . are pig barges. Where is our ship?" She did not look directly at Kelis, choosing instead to scan the scene as if she had somehow overlooked a nice stout galley with their names emblazoned on its side.

Kelis slowed because she had, but he tried to keep them moving forward. "It's the best way I've found. They're taking pigs to sell on the raft of boats floating around Acacia. They asked no questions and they're not Sinper Ou's people. We'll be safe on them. They will get us as far as the flotilla surrounding the island. Then we'll have to make our way as best we can. We . . ." He cleared his throat, hesitated a moment, and then decided he might as well get it all out at once. "We will have disguises."

"What disguises?"

"As pig keepers."

The look of derision Benabe set on him made him feel like a naughty child facing a grandmother's disapproval. She must have practiced the look, for she was too young to be so skilled at it. "I am no pig keeper."

"Today you are," Kelis said, "if you want to reach Acacia."

"I thought you knew people. I thought you were connected to the royal family! I thought—"

"Pigs!" Shen said. She and Naamen had just caught up with them. "Look, Mother, pigs. Are there piglets?" She grabbed her mother's hand and tugged her back into motion, fighting her reluctance with pure childish enthusiasm. As Kelis watched them, relieved, Shen glanced back and winked.

The hundreds of human feet and the thousands of hoofed ones had torn and slashed and gouged the white sand. The smell pushed straight for the backs of their throats. It fought against the fresh breeze blowing in from the water and seemed to be winning the battle. As was the sound warring with the peaceful lapping of the waves: oinks and grunts, squeals and shouts, voices raised in entreaty, booming with directions, announcing bargains on foodstuffs and fresh water for the journey.

Kelis, in the lead once more, kept them moving until he had retraced his route to the livestock merchant who controlled a small fleet of barges—only one of several such along the beach. He had agreed to carry them across, but it was no act of charity. He required both the coins Kelis had left in the sack and their labor. Divided up and set to different tasks, they worked the frantic loading of the barges: opening and closing pens, prodding animals to get them moving, luring them forward or kicking them onward, making human barriers to block one herd from mingling with another, loading slops into troughs that were then tugged onto the barges. A few minutes into the squealing chaos of it, and all of them were splattered with filth.

Leeka went to work with awkward solemnity. Naamen, Kelis noticed, kept his weak arm hidden beneath the shoulder wrap of his robe. He eschewed the shoveling duty a boy half his age directed him toward. He was adept at appearing both deaf and stricken with blind spots in his vision, much to the younger boy's annoyance. Benabe wore an evil expression, one corner of her lip curling whenever she caught Kelis's eye.

For Shen, however, the work looked more akin to play. She ran around with her arms outstretched, darting and shooing as if she were herding chickens instead of barrel-shaped swine several times her own weight. The pigs rushed from her with a wide-eyed intensity that stayed just this side of panic. It would have been comical, except for the animals' agitation. Behind the girl the Santoth fanned out in wings. They changed nothing of their demeanor or silence. They simply shadowed her; and the pigs—whether seeing or sensing them—looked for escape that they found by rushing up the gangplanks onto the barges.

"I've never seen the like of that," the merchant said, coming up and nudging Kelis with an elbow. He wore a perplexed grimace as his eyes followed Shen, taking no notice of the Santoth at all. "You ever want rid of her I have work that girl could do.

Replace the whole lot of my boys. Be happy to see the back of them."

Kelis did not answer.

A few chaotic hours later the pigs were loaded. Kelis stood ankle-deep in the water, watching as the others, having finished their tasks, joined him. The incoming tide had begun to lift the barges free of the bottom. They moved now with the undulation of the waves, much to the consternation of the passengers. Pigs crowded each barge so tightly that they stood shoulder to shoulder, haunch to haunch, sliding against one another with grunts of protest. Boys climbed into the rigging. Dangling above the animal's backs, they worked on the sails that would catch the evening breeze and pull them from the shore.

"Is this safe?" Naamen asked. "I know we need to go, but . . ."

Kelis was not at all sure, but he said, "You saw the merchant. Does he look like a man who lets his pigs sink to the bottom of the sea? Acacia is close. Come."

"Just a walk across a sea of swine," Naamen said. He hoisted his sack up over his head and motioned for Shen to walk beside him. She began to, but then spun around.

The Santoth stood as if rooted to the shore, away from the waterline in the dry sand.

"Aren't you coming?" Shen asked.

One of the Santoth said, "May we?"

Before Kelis could consider the question and the possible answers he would offer, Shen gave hers. "Of course, Nualo. You've come all this way. This is the easy part."

"We may come with you?"

"I just said so."

The Santoth lifted his foot and set it down a few inches farther, on the smooth wet sand. Another of them spoke, his voice tremulous, more solidly of this world than Kelis had imagined possible of them. "We may go to Acacia? You allow us?"

"That's where we've been heading all this time. Yes, come on."

A tremble passed through them that was different from the usual ripples and disturbances around them. They are afraid, Kelis thought.

"Shen," still another Santoth said, "do you lift the banishment upon us?"

"Will you come if I do?"

"Yes," they all answered.

Kelis splashed forward toward the girl. He reached for her arm. He suddenly wanted to stop her easy answer. "Shen, wait—"

"I lift it, then." Shen waved her hand in the air to indicate something vanishing just like that. "There's no banishment. Now, come. Ouch! Kelis, you're hurting me."

Kelis let go of her arm. He had not even realized he had grabbed it.

Shen massaged the arm with her other hand. "You are odd sometimes."

She turned and walked up the gangplank onto the barge. The Santoth followed her. They dispersed across the raft, causing no more disturbance to the pigs than would a breeze touching them.

As he splashed through the ankle-deep water and stepped onto the gangplank, Kelis thought, Aliver, I pray this be right.

CHAPTER
TWENTY-EIGHT

The man had hairy nostrils. Sire Lethel could not help but imagine tweezing the hairs out one by one. Quite distracting. More so than the scaly plates on his forehead and cheeks. More so than the fact that the tip of his tongue was split, presumably in imitation of the hooded snake that was his clan's totem. Lethel did not look away as the man spoke his rough, choppy Acacian. Lethel ridged his forehead and pursed his lips, appearing to respect this Dukish, the self-proclaimed headman of the Anet slaves of Avina.

The two men sat across from each other in the center of a marble courtyard, open to the clear sky. A wedge of advisers flanked the leagueman, with Ishtat soldiers among them. Archers lined the last row and fanned out to either side. The slaves were not the threat the Auldek had been, but it paid to come prepared for trouble. Behind Dukish stood a crowd of quota slaves. They were well dressed and looked healthy enough, but Lethel could not help but think of them as a motley horde. They were slaves, after all. Had been raised as servants, victims to whatever whims the Auldek—beasts themselves— could conceive. Their very bodies were testament to that. He did not know or want to know what their lives had been like.

Dukish did not know this, of course, hence his long diatribe on just this subject.

As he sat pretending empathy, Sire Lethel's mind journeyed elsewhere. There were a million more important things to consider than the woes of slaves. He had arrived in Ushen Brae only five days ago. He sailed in along with Sire Faleen, both of them with full blessing of the League Council, with authority between them to handle affairs in Ushen Brae on the league's behalf. He had spent most of that time on the barrier isles, where he had fed ravenously on all the information he could gather about this place, about the details of the quota trade, about the Auldek tribes and, most crucially, about the Lothan Aklun.

The few nights he had stayed in the Lothan Aklun's estates, those strange dwellings hung from cliffs and almost otherworldly, had left him dizzy, most pleasantly so. Most of the things he saw were indecipherable. But the small things that he could see function—tabletops that floated in midair, glass that darkened or lightened beneath the touch of his fingers, grooves in the hallways that, when stepped into, propelled one forward as if sliding slowly downhill, the soul vessels that surged over the water without any obvious power source, propelled by the will of whoever held its wheel—tantalizingly hinted at further possibilities. They certainly had other vessels. Sire Faleen had mentioned finding enormous transports capable of carrying thousands of troops, as well as numerous smaller vessels, some tiny enough that they held only a single person. What other wonders might be uncovered? Weapons? Other soul catchers? Had it been possible, he would have stayed out there or sailed to Lithram Len to see the ruins of the soul catcher for himself—as Faleen was doing at this very moment.

It was not within his purview to pursue such things yet. That went to Sire Faleen, he being of higher rank within the league. Lethel had volunteered to handle matters on the mainland. This mostly entailed sorting things out with the emancipated slaves. Later, he would explore inland, seeing what use could be made of the abandoned Auldek cities. There might be benefits from that as well, but Lethel hoped to find some way to take over Faleen's duties. Perhaps he would fall off a boat, stumble after having inhaled a bit too much of the sweet red mist he so enjoyed. Uncharitable thought, yes, but Faleen had always been a windbag, politely incompetent in the manner that assured his political rise among the League Council. Lethel was sure he would find the real world more challenging.

Dukish droned on.

Lethel would have raised his eyebrows, except that the tweezed slashes that were his eyebrows had been shaped to mimic a fine-lined version of that expression already. It amazed him that foolish men so often took silence and a concerned expression as an invitation to blather. Small price to pay, for this Dukish had just made his life considerably easier. Just three days in Ushen Brae, Lethel had received word that Dukish wanted to meet and come to peaceful terms. He should not have been surprised, though. These people had been slaves. They were freed by the actions of others. Of course freedom would scare them. Of course they would seek a new master. The league would oblige. Not as holders of whips and chains, of course. They did not need such things to enslave.

Dukish offered Sire Neen's ashes as a special gift. The unfortunate man's parts had been gathered up and put through some cremation ritual, and this Dukish had come into possession of them. A strange offering, but Lethel accepted the urn with a rather specific idea of what he would do with its contents.

"I hear all and am saddened," Lethel said, once he could bear sitting through no more. "These things you say are grave. They twist my heart. They fill me with shame. You must know that the league was an innocent accomplice in all this. For all these years, we served the will of the Akarans. We sailed the Gray Slopes at their bidding. And here in Ushen Brae we were mistreated ourselves by the Lothan Aklun, the haughty, arrogant, vicious Lothan Aklun. In our own way we have also been duped by both of them."

Someone in the slave crowd grumbled and a few others responded. Lethel wished he could have the grumbler killed, but that would not do. He looked past Dukish and brought his entreaties to the entire party.

"I hear that this is a surprising revelation to you," he said. "But ask yourselves, how could we know what became of you? As far as we knew, we delivered orphaned children into the hands of a nation that welcomed them. We were but the middlemen. Search your mind. Look back. Was it a man like me—a true leagueman—that took you from your homes? No, the— What did you call them? The Red Shirts! They did that on Akaran orders. Did any leagueman set foot on Ushen Brae in your memory? Did we stand in that chamber as some of you were robbed of your very souls? No. Consider everything from this perspective and you will hear the truth of it ringing in your ears. I am certain."

Dukish turned his head to one side and drew back his long hair to reveal mangled tissue where his ear should have been. "A leagueman did this to me, for no reason other than that it amused him."

Ah, Lethel thought, likely that's Sire Fen's work. He was rumored to take pleasure from such things in his day, before Dariel Akaran slit his belly. Too bad. Lethel had always rather liked the old codger.

"If that is true, you have my deepest apologies. Even within the league there are . . . reprobates. We do our best to weed them out." Changing tack, he said, "Let us look to the future. The game board that is the world has been overturned. Now that it's righted, what came before is gone. What you see are new players, new rules, new possibilities. The league is willing to deal with you as equals. Look, I'm here before you, speaking to you as an equal. You and your people are the new masters of Ushen Brae. Likewise, the league will, in the future, not be pawns for the Akarans. We have broken with them because of what we learned here. If we trade with them again, it will be on your behalf. I do say 'if,' though, for as you know the Auldek will destroy them. I very much hope they succeed."

Grumbles again. Lethel realized he was speaking too quickly. "What I mean is that I hope they succeed in reaching the Known World. I hope they do battle with the Akarans. Friends, what better punishment for them than that they spill their own blood in a massive slaughter?"

This did not get quite the enthusiastic response he had expected.

"Where are they?" a gray-faced woman behind Dukish asked.

"Where are who?"

"The Auldek."

"Oh, I don't know. Far, far away." Lethel indicated vaguely with his fingers.

"Are you not tracking their progress?"

What we're doing or not is hardly your concern, Lethel thought, but he said, "The Ishtat had birds following them for a time. Quite easy to, really, as they're an entire nation on the move. A fortnight back an early storm blew the birds off course. And so began winter in earnest. It happens that way in the north."

"You've lost them? Your man before said the league was tracking them. Said you rule the seas. See everything. Now you say you've lost them already."

"I wouldn't say that." Lethel ran a finger over the jagged line of one of his eyebrows. He felt the first twinge of a headache coming on. He got them all too regularly. He thought it a result of some mistake with his head binding when he was a child. "We know where they are—in a hell of ice and snow. No need to journey there with them. The Auldek are Queen Corinn's concern, anyway. They are a problem for the Akarans, not for you or me."

Dukish stood abruptly and turned into the group behind him. A tad erratic, Lethel thought. They spoke in a fast murmur, Auldek by the sound of it. Lethel crossed his legs and bobbed his foot up and down. Noticing a spot of dirt on the red satin of his boots, he pursed his lips. A punishment was in order for his body servant. He might have had nothing to do with the stain, but still, how else would he wash the filth from his memory but to make someone pay for it?

When Dukish resumed his seat, he said they were ready to talk about a treaty.

Lethel tented his fingers sagely. "I am here to extend a hand of friendship to"—he almost said *you slaves*, but recalled the name he had been instructed to use with them—"the Anet people, and to all the People of Ushen Brae. But I must know something before we can proceed any further. As I'm sure you know, somebody destroyed a facility on Lithram Len. I cannot say what foolishness drove them, but I can say that our displeasure over this is beyond measure. That's no way to begin a new partnership. Were you responsible?"

By Dukish's emphatic response it was clear that he was not.

"Who was?"

"I know not."

Dukish glanced around behind him, seeking confirmation of his ignorance from his peers. They gave it.

"Have you heard anything about survivors from the group that Sire Neen brought to meet the Auldek? Any Acacians?"

"One leagueman," Dukish said. "That's all."

"That's not possible. We accounted for all our leaguemen. Do you mean a soldier?"

Dukish laughed. "Not this one. He was no soldier. This one was a weakling. Devoth imprisoned him. Took him away."

"And there were no others?"

"No."

Lethel eased the tension of this line of questioning out of his fingers. It was silly, really, but he could not help thinking of Dariel Akaran. If the prince had somehow survived and managed to get up to his old tricks . . . Unlikely, though. Highly unlikely. "One, you will find the criminal and deliver him—or them—to me," Lethel said. "That you must do. And, two, there can be no more destruction of Lothan Aklun artifacts. They are all henceforth league possessions. Any act against them is an act against us."

"That thing was evil," a voice from Dukish's entourage said.

"Perhaps it was. Or perhaps it was a device that the Lothan Aklun turned to evil. Is a knife evil because it can kill a man? No, it can also do a thousand useful things. We of the league have scholars among us, physicians and men of learning. It may be that for every way the Lothan Aklun used their tools to make your lives misery we could use them for good. This is not negotiable. You will leave such artifacts to us. Indeed, you will alert us to any that we have yet to discover."

"The Anet do not seek these Lothan Aklun things," Dukish said. "We have no interest in them. I cannot speak for the other clans, but you have my faith on this. Now, let me have your faith. Your man, the one who spoke to us before you, said you could provide us with settlers, with women who are fertile and can breed. Is that so?"

That's easily enough done, Lethel thought. We have whole breeding islands for just that purpose. "That is within our capacity."

"Have I your faith, then?"

Lethel did not correct the man's usage of the word. "In all things, sir. It will take some time, but it can be done. In addition to the barrier isles, we would need to base some operations here in Avina. If we are truly to—"

"He lies!"

The shout was loud, sharp enough to cause Sire Lethel to start. He craned around, looking for the source, for it was not among the two groups in the courtyard.

"Leagueman, he is lying!"

"Who speaks?" the gray-faced woman said. "Show yourself."

The voice said, "Dukish does not speak for the Free People."

"Who does, then?" Lethel asked.

"Promise me that your soldiers will not shoot us."

"Give us no reason and we won't."

"I have your faith, then?"

Lethel rolled his eyes. "Certainly."

A woman rose to standing on the bridge Lethel's party had passed under to enter the courtyard. Several others to either side and a few more on roofs nearby also rose or stepped from behind the stones that had hidden them. They did not appear to be armed, except for knives that were as yet sheathed. Dukish barked something at the woman in Auldek, gesturing profanely as he did so. The woman gave it back. Other Anet added their voices, and for a moment it seemed the entire meeting would erupt into chaos.

The Ishtat reacted. They enveloped Lethel within a bristling wedge of bodies. They pressed so tight against him that as they pulled him back he was not sure if his feet touched the ground, or if they lifted him bodily. The bowmen readied their weapons—aiming both at the Anet and at the newcomers—and the captain shouted the clanspeople to stillness.

Lethel sighed. The difficulties of dealing with primitives. One never knew where the power resided. Always upstarts and bickering to contend with. Though in this case, he doubted it truly rested with this woman. Her face was pale blue, and she wore a headdress that sprang up from her hairline. Did she hope to pass that off as a crown? She was slim, though, limber looking, just Lethel's type, actually, except for the . . . feathers. That's what they were. Not a headdress exactly, but plumes of feathers instead of hair. These people!

The woman said, "We don't come to fight you—just to tell you the truth before you err. Dukish does not speak for us, for those who were once quota and are now free citizens of a new nation."

The Anet raged at this, and it took the Ishtat a moment to quiet them.

"Do you, then, speak for these people?"

Dukish tried to say something, but the Ishtat captain punched him in the jaw. It was a quick jab, just a warning, as was the way he drew his short sword from its scabbard for Dukish to see. A tense moment, but it went no further. Lethel repeated his question.

"For the moment I do," the woman answered.

"And what's your name, then?"

"Skylene."

"Ah," Lethel said, fully in control of his composure once more, "well, Skylene, this news surprises me. I found Dukish to be quite convincing. You can't say that he does not control a considerable portion of the city. That he does not speak for many. I've seen the evidence of it with my own eyes. Don't ask me to disbelieve them. Perhaps you should come down from there and talk with me here."

"I will speak from here."

"That's hardly the way to hold council. Really, you—"

"Leagueman. I cannot hold council with you. I simply want you to know that Dukish does not speak for the People."

"Who does, then?"

"Our Council of Elders. Yoen. Mór. There are many who speak faith. They are away, gathering the People in the Westlands to return here. They will come soon. The Anet have just grabbed for power in their absence. Careful, leagueman, some among the Kulish Kra and the Lvin scheme to do the same. Do not make any pacts with them. They will not be valid. The council speaks for all the People, not just for one clan or another. Dukish is a fool who would make chaos out of what could be peace. Don't listen to him!"

Lethel wished he could express on his face the full measure of his displeasure at being given commands. He did not. He showed nothing but troubled interest. "Most disturbing to hear this. Come down and let's—"

"Ushen Brae is for the People. You have no place here. Nor can you divide us. We are stronger together and we will hold."

"Ah," Lethel said. He made a face as if he had burped up an unpleasant taste. Holding up the palm of his hand, he asked for a moment to consider a response. On the one hand, a council of elders who speak for all the people, high ideals, a loathing for the league, grandiose notions of this as a free land. On the other hand, several fool clans who would fracture Ushen Brae into small powers squabbling among themselves, all wanting nothing more than to buy league wares. It was an easy decision to make.

Glancing at his Ishtat captain, Lethel said, "Shoot the bird."

CHAPTER
TWENTY-NINE

Shirtless and sweating, Melio faced the massive warrior. His Marah sword sliced the air. He backed and parried. The warrior stepped toward him on legs like tree trunks, his blade hissing in the air with each massive swing. Several times Melio dodged to the right or left as his foe's sword struck the frozen ground, sending up splinters of ice. He felt the giant's anger growing, possessing him, driving him to more and more furious attacks. He bellowed and swung his blade around. Melio ducked and spun and leaped with a swirling aerial attack of his own. It would have been a wonderful move. He would have soon followed it with a head-hewing attack.

Except that the timing of his landing was off. The ground moved beneath him in such a way that he landed on the edge of his foot. His ankle twisted and he yanked it into the air, hopping on the other leg, cursing. His sword hung limp, and his foe, for that matter, went forgotten. Forgetting the slickness of the surface on which he stood, Melio's good foot suddenly took off in a horizontal direction, bringing the rest of his body crashing down a moment later.

"What, exactly, was all that about?"

The voice was Geena's. She sat suspended from the rigging of the league clipper, the *Slipfin*. She had one leg wrapped around the rope ladder. That was all she needed to feel secure, even though the vessel rose and fell at a rapid, wind-whipped clip. As Melio had fought his battle, she had munched dates and spit the pits out over the water. Sometimes upright, sometimes hanging upside down, she had watched the entire scene with barely contained mirth. It had taken Melio an extra measure of focus to block her out.

He lay prone for a moment, as if he had decided to make a close inspection of the deck planks. Like everything else on the outside of the vessel, the deck was coated in white skin, slicker for it. It was not the first time Melio had found himself studying it. Things had gotten a bit better since Kartholomé had found a supply of gripping deck socks, but even these only seemed to work when he remembered that he was wearing them.

"A revised version of the Eighth Form," he said, pushing up. "The Eighth Form is the combat routine that reenacts Gerimus's battle with the guards of Tulluck's Hold, when he fought the giants that guarded the—"

"Who's Gerimus?"

"You don't know who Gerimus was?"

"Not everyone sucks at the tit of Acacian lore!" Kartholomé called, though from where was not immediately obvious.

"A king from the Second Candovian Kingdom." When this did not seem to register with her, Melio wiped the sweat from his brow with his shirt, which he had taken off before he began. It was actually quite chilly, but he liked the feel of air on his skin when he trained. They were eighteen days out of Bleem, heading west with a slight edge toward the south. Clytus made that small adjustment for his own reasons, which he did not share. Around them stretched the Gray Slopes. As far as the eye could see, waves, sky. It was bleak, the sky a lighter version of the water it hung over. He took a swig from his waterskin, feeling her eyes on him all the while.

Geena flipped upside down again. Her shirt began to fall with gravity, but she pinned it to her abdomen. "Where's Tulluck's Hold?"

"It's . . ." Melio set the waterskin's spout in his mouth again, but pulled it away without drinking. "I don't know, really. Candovia, I believe."

Geena unwrapped her leg and climbed down the ladder, managing to do so without actually putting her hands or feet on the rungs very often. He had seen her do that before, but could not for the life of him figure out the technique. She landed on one of the horizontal stacks of harpoons they had bought at Bleem. Balanced at the topmost of them, Geena walked along it. "You're guessing? You were there, weren't you?"

"It was a long time ago," Melio said. "There's not a Tulluck's Hold anymore." She just looked at him, eyes expectant. "I mean a really long time ago. Before my time."

"And yet you remember every move this Gerimus made?"

"Anyway, that's only part of it. What I was doing was the revision created by Leeka Alain, an officer of the Northern Guard. It's partly the traditional Form and partly the way he modified it when he killed the first Numrek." Geena began to speak, but Melio carried on. "And this Leeka I actually knew. He detailed the battle, and I even worked some of it through with him. So . . ." He toasted her with the skin and took a drink, not sure he had won the point but keeping up appearances.

Clytus climbed down from the bridge. "Sharratt, enough playing with your sword," he said. "On to your evening round of duties. Might as well start."

Melio grabbed for his shirt.

"Oh, don't do that!" Geena tossed a date pit at him.

"Geena," Clytus said, a warning in it.

"What? I just like to watch. Melio Sharratt, my private performer."

"Performance over," Clytus said. "Up to the nest, girl, or I'll get the strap out."

"Don't you wish?" She scaled the swaying ladder effortlessly.

Clytus stood beside Melio. The two of them watched her ascend and then tip herself into the tiny basket of the crow's nest. "How old is she?" Melio asked, once he was confident Geena was well out of talking earshot.

"Acts just like a girl, doesn't she? You'd think she was sixteen and had never seen an obstacle she couldn't leap. She's always been like that, all thirtysome years I've known her. Giver bless her." The brigand set somber eyes on Melio. "It's not true, though. She's seen hard times, especially when she was a girl. She likes you, but don't get the wrong idea. She'd not roll with you. It's the dance she likes; not the wrestling."

"I . . . I never thought—"

"You know why? In your case, it's because of Mena. For a certain type of woman, the princess is . . . well, a person to aspire to. Like a hero if she were a man. You understand me?"

Melio thought a moment and then said, "Yes, I do. I know the feeling. About Geena, though, I wouldn't have tried anything."

"Good," Clytus said. "She'd go off you in a minute if she thought you would. You're a fine lad, but if you slighted Mena she'd likely introduce your stiffy to a blood eel's teeth. She's done it before." Before Melio could configure his face in response to this, Clytus slapped his shoulder. "Now, to chores. This ship runs clean in many ways I've not figured out yet, but there's still work to do."

As he always did, Melio went to his chores without complaint. Since leaving Tivol he had learned more than he had ever wished to about nautical matters. Four was not nearly enough to crew a vessel like the *Slipfin*, but Clytus and Geena had enough brigand tricks up their sleeves to make hard things easier, to finesse the impossible into only improbable. He had to respect them for it, and do his part.

If these were to be his last days, Melio could not complain that they were being spent poorly. He had seen wonders at sea before. In the time before he found Mena on the docks of Ruinat, he had worked for a feeble living among the Floating Merchants. The Inner Sea was beautiful, but its teeming life had not prepared him for the things he saw riding the Gray Slopes.

❇

One afternoon, a week from land, Geena had shouted from high in the rigging. He did not catch what she said, except that it was an alarm. Melio turned. He saw the movement low on the horizon. He could not make sense of it at first. Low clouds? A storm brewing? Neither. It came on fast, with a speed and swarming quality that set it apart from some phenomenon of the weather. But it did not ride the water like a fleet of boats, nor was it in the water, as aquatic life should be. It was above the surface, skimming the crests of the waves.

Geena slid down the rope at a speed akin to just plain falling. She hit the deck and sprang up with purpose.

"What is that?" Melio shouted.

"Dinner or death," she said as she passed him. She flipped open one of the wooden deck crates and hit him in the chest with a wad of netting. She bolted away, climbed the stairs to the bridge, and disappeared inside.

"Or make it both." Kartholomé slid up to them with an uncanny grace on the skin, looking like a performer skating on ice. "Dinner *and* death." He grabbed one of the nets and careened away.

Standing where Geena instructed him to, netting loose in his fingers, Melio stared at the rocking view of a seething sea atop which a great mass of something approached. Thousands of them. Hundreds of thousands. They were innumerable. Large enough to see at a distance. They flew, but something told him they were not birds. There were no birds out here. Not so far from land. Not low-flying birds like that.

Geena, back again, grabbed him by the elbow. "Don't get skewered, love. Stay near the cabin door."

It was not until they were upon them that Melio understood what they were: a massive flock of flying fish, with flipper wings so wide and nimble that individuals wheeled like starlings within a vast, unstoppable torrent of momentum. The front wall of them broke over the ship. Motion engulfed them: that of the sailing ship and of the fish flying across it. Sound that textured the air with scales. A sea-deep stench of salt and life and moisture splattered Melio's face. The air became liquid enough to swim in.

Of course! Melio thought. That's how they fly. They swim the air!

The fish careened over the deck. They slipped between the sails. Most flew with amazing precision, even snapping their wings against their sides to cut through narrow gaps. Their bodies were slim splinters, thick around as a man's leg and, fins included, a little longer. They were as dangerous in flight as javelins, striped down the side with one slash of violet. One sliced Kartholomé's shoulder through his shirt, several smashed so hard against structures on the boat that they skidded across the deck, broken. A hundred, it seemed, tried to cut strands of Melio's curly hair as they passed.

Melio would never forget the mad way he and Kartholomé and Geena dashed around on deck, fishing. They tossed nets up over their heads, and then fell to the deck, clutching the ropes as the fish's force pulled them. He would never forget that, try as he might, he could not say he saw even one of them jump from the water or fall into it. They just flew. Nor would he forget the taste of them afterward, when the crew gathered snug in the cabin, getting stupid on ale. Roasted over an open flame, the fish needed nothing but salt to flavor them. "Like tuna," he declared, and Geena had added, "If tunas could fly and were a white fish that tasted like sea air after a storm on an island of lemon trees."

She had it right, he had to admit.

※

And then there was the morning two weeks from land, nothing around them but endless ocean, when the sails suddenly appeared. Twenty or thirty of them, diaphanous white triangles blown by the same steady wind the *Slipfin* hitched. They came over the horizon behind them midmorning, and by the midafternoon they cruised right by the league clipper. But the sails were nothing human made. They trailed beneath them long tendrils of aquatic life, ribbons of yellow and blue, splattered with sparkles along the entire long length of them. Melio could not shake the feeling that each shimmer was an individual creature attached to the tendrils, passengers that watched him as they flapped in the current, as casual as so many Agnates passing them in their pleasure crafts.

There was the doubled sky at night. Above, the constellations he knew. Below, beneath the undulations of the waves, another universe of glowing orbs. They were not reflections from the sky, as he thought at first, but shone with their light from somewhere far below. He knew that the stars below were living creatures, which made him wonder if the stars in the sky might be likewise. Creatures of some vast ocean he could not comprehend.

And there were the deep whales. He had heard tales of them, but seeing them was another thing. They appeared in a pod off a way to starboard. They looked, from the middle distance, like a series of rounded granite boulders, save that they bobbed with the seas. One broke off from the rest, dipped below the surface a moment, and then rose and came toward them. The enormous wedge of its head pushed a billow of water before it. Just before its nose would have hit the *Slipfin*, the whale dove. Its tailfins stretched wider than the *Slipfin* was long. When it submerged, the surge of water it pulled down tilted the boat with it. The upsurge of water from the fin sent a wave over the boat, drenching all on board. Melio clutched a safety rope, laughing uncontrollably at the bizarre beauty of it. He was starting to understand the way Geena lived.

The way Dariel must have lived when he grew to adulthood among these people.

The trials to come should have daunted him, but for some reason they did not. It was not that he thought they would pass through the Range, survive a run-in with the sea wolves, or possibly find one young prince in a foreign land that he knew nothing of. Just the opposite. It was the fact these things seemed so out of the reach for four small people in a relatively small boat that heartened him. They should fail. They would fail. There was no way they could *not* fail. With that established, he could go forward without struggling with expectations.

✳

Dead calm. The third week in. Just as far from land as was possible. Near where the Range might well have begun. Instead of that roaring tumult—stillness. It just came upon them while nobody was paying attention. Melio did not feel the boat's constant rocking stop; he just realized that it had when he awoke that morning. It was not even the lack of movement that woke him. It was the silence. No creaking of boards, no murmuring off somewhere in the ship's innards, no whistle of wind or slop of water against the hull, no tinkling from the bells high up on the mainmast.

They all gathered on deck and stared at the breezeless sky and the mirror-flat surface of the water and the ghosts of limp cloths where the sails should have been. The *Slipfin* sat as if stuck in a sea of glass.

"When did this happen?" Clytus asked.

"Didn't you notice?" Geena responded.

"Nah. I was deciphering what I could from league manuals in the bridge back room. I set the course and stepped away from the wheel, stuck my nose in the books. Don't know how long for, but when I looked up this calm was on us. Couldn't have been more than a few minutes," he said, but none of the confidence of the statement was in the voice making it.

Geena jumped up onto the port railing. She stood there, balanced above the water. For a moment, she looked like she was going to leap down onto the hard surface of the once-was-water and go running across it, playing. A few seconds standing there, however, took the jauntiness out of her posture. "Passing strange," she whispered as she climbed back down to the deck.

Kartholomé had heard of a league fleet becalmed for nearly a month during an early crossing, but that had happened so long ago the tale had the feel of legend. He seemed more disbelieving than any of them. "I've never seen a stillness like this," he said. "It isn't possible. We're supposed to be in the Range now. The Range of the Gray Slopes, for the love of light. This isn't possible!"

"Shhhh," Geena said, and Melio was glad she did. A voice should not, he felt, speak loudly into such stillness.

For two days the impossible continued. No wind stirred. No ripples moved on the surface. No fish darted in the water, or flew above it, or sailed across it. No motions or sounds in all the world other than the ones they themselves made. The silence in particular grew in intensity. Melio had never experienced a silence like this one before. The lack of noise made them all shy of making any sounds. Each scuffing of a foot on the deck or the thrumming of fingers on the railing, a cough at night or a clearing of a throat: they all seemed like an affront to the emptiness that was the world. A sign that would betray their existence to something that should not know of their existence. They spoke only when they had to, and then only in whispers. Melio always felt ill at ease afterward.

On the third morning a fin broke the surface—the dorsal of a gap-mouthed shark. It moved with an eerie slowness, as if it worked at a different pace from the rest of the world. It seemed to carve not through water but through the thick syrup the water had congealed into. Watching the shark for the better part of an afternoon, Melio felt the *Slipfin* to be akin to whatever tiny creatures that behemoth sucked into its gaping maw. Just as vulnerable. Just as still in the water, waiting for the mouth that would engulf them, boat and all.

By the third night they had had enough of it. Gathered together in the captain's cabin, they ate their fill from the rich stores. More to the point, they got drunk. They filled the small room with more noise than they had heard in days. Awkward, forced humor. Boisterousness with a slightly mad edge. Kartholomé drank his warm ale from a languid stretch of glass that no doubt was intended for finer things. Geena raided the league's stores. She shared around a flask of something with an aniseed tang. None of them could name the liquor in it, but it went down.

"If it keeps on like this," Clytus said, "we're not going to get to die fighting sea wolves."

"It'll be boredom that takes us," Kartholomé quipped.

Geena drank from the flask, closed her eyes as she processed the taste and potency of it. Still doing so, she said, "I'll not abide that. I made a pact a long time ago with the afterdeath. I'm not going to it quietly. A howling death I'll have. None other." She slapped a hand on the polished wood of the table.

Kartholomé rose abruptly and went outside. They could hear him shouting out across the water, damning the calm and insulting the wind for cowardice, calling the waves craven. He returned and commenced to drink more.

Melio's gaze drifted up from the ring of familiar faces and moved across the walls. Leagueman walls, decorated with their sparse sense of nautical gentility. He could not see it well from where he sat, but there was a mural at the far end of the room, painted right onto the smooth wood panels. He had studied it before. A league brig plied a sea filled with carnage, the bodies of leviathans thick in water stained crimson. Sea wolves, Kartholomé had confirmed. The painting brimmed with details. Individual leaguemen and Ishtat on the deck of the brig. Harpoons caught in midair. A sea wolf pierced through a grasping tentacle, just one of many. Seabirds circling in the air above. Melio knew that detail to be true. The biggest brigs had their own contingents of birds that made the ocean crossing with them.

Despite the details, Melio could not quite believe the scene. The sea wolves themselves had no shape that he could credit. They looked like whales and squids and sharks all cut into pieces and floating in a wave-heavy stew together.

"What do they want anyway?" Melio asked. "The sea wolves, I mean. Why attack ships? Nothing else does that. Not even deep whales."

"Nah, they just come and take a look, near to sinking in the process," Clytus said. "You know how much we'd have made if we were whalers? If we'd taken that big bastard and dragged him back to Tivol?"

"The four of us? Not possible."

Clytus guffawed. There was a comment to go with it, Melio could see, but Clytus kept it in. "So, do they have a taste for man flesh or what?" Melio asked.

Kartholomé warmed to the question. "Leagueman flesh, I'd say. The league and they are enemies. Always have been. Just like in the painting you've been eyeing. Before they had the skin, the league lost a lot of ships to them. Even a brig went down once. Disappeared. None lived, but everyone believes it was sea wolves that took her. Long time ago, this is, but the leaguemen know how to hold a grudge. Once they came up with the skin they—"

"What is the skin? Do you know how it's made?" Melio accepted the flask from Geena. He drank with the help of her finger, which tilted the flask up to lengthen his measure.

"If I knew, I'd not be here," Kartholomé said. "I'd be sipping lemon liqueur from a cliffside estate in Manil, with two redheaded whores named Benda and Fenda."

"He's partial to redheaded whores," Geena explained. "An experience he had as a lad, see. Give him enough drink and you'll hear more about it than you want to know."

"Anyway," Kartholomé continued, "what I'm saying is that I'd be rich, is what. Nobody knows how they make it. Could be a process the Lothan Aklun clued them to. Wouldn't surprise me. It's the only thing that made the mist trade possible."

The mist trade? Melio mused. He never calls it the quota trade.

"So," Melio asked, "should we ever get moving again and come up against these sea wolves, will the skin protect us or won't it?"

"That's right," Kartholomé said.

"Which?"

"It will *and* won't. You were there when we bought and loaded the harpoons. You didn't think we were going whaling, did you?" He held up a hand to stop Melio's response. "Let me finish. You asked a question. Let me answer it. Once the league had the skin, their big ships were safe. Little ones not so much, but the big ones could sail as they pleased. The sea wolves just can't grasp the stuff. They slip off it. Tentacles and beak and teeth and everything. So the brigs just slid on by. That's all right if you're two hundred feet above the water. But when you're down low like we are . . . that's a different story. They'll jump clear out of the water and smash down on the deck. They've got these tentacles with grippers all up and down them. They get one of those around your leg and you're heading for their mouth. Beaklike, the mouth is. Ugly thing so sharp it serrates the flesh like two curved knives angled just so. You maybe should have asked more about them before you signed on for this trip."

Melio, remembering that he did not always like this man, met his gaze without humor. "You knew all that and you still came."

"There's more," he said, after a long draft of ale. "The league wasn't satisfied with just being able to get across untroubled. Spiteful bunch, they are. They took to slaughtering the beasts whenever they could. Harpoons. Those big crossbow bolts of theirs. They even threw out barrels of pitch and set seas full of the wolves alight."

"They still do that?"

"On occasion, I suppose. Did it for generations. Never did any good, though."

Kartholomé dabbed at the moisture at the edges of his lips. For some reason this prompted him to flash a sly smile at Geena. She responded with a finger gesture threatening his manhood with an unfortunate break. They did that every now and then. A game, Melio assumed.

"I haven't made a scientific study of it," the pilot continued, "but I don't think so. What I heard is, it never changed things in the slightest. The league got tired of the effort. Now they just sail through them."

"As we'll do as well," Clytus said. "Might have to tack a bit, but—"

"'Tack a bit'?"

The brigand, thickly muscled, masculine-featured in a blocky, weathered way, tried to shape his large hands into a demonstration of the maneuvering he had planned. He looked like a bear trying to explain the use of a pottery wheel.

Kartholomé chuckled. He started to say something but found it too amusing to put into words. Geena flicked a spoon at him. He found that hilarious as well. He got up, coughing out an overflow of humor as he headed back on deck.

Geena reached across the table and patted Clytus's hand with a solemnity that—on her—could only be in jest. "I'm sure the wolves have never seen the likes of how an Outer Isle brigand tacks. They'll wet themselves."

This sat a moment in the room before the dubious humor of it got Melio wagging his head. Geena slid her chair toward his and leaned into his shoulder. Clytus began to explain that it was not just tacking he had in mind. There was . . . He stopped midsentence. Melio turned, ready to nudge him back into it and feeling it best he get Geena's head off his shoulder. He caught sight of Kartholomé.

The man stood framed in the door. The blood in his face had drained out of him right along with the good humor he had stepped out choking over. His eyes searched the room without actually focusing on anyone.

Geena started to say something. Stopped. It was Clytus who asked, "What?"

Kartholomé said, very softly, "Come outside."

Stepping from the dim passageway onto the deck, Melio thought a full moon must have risen, so bone-blue was the light. A pungent scent invaded his nose. It flared his nostrils as it pushed inside, a sea stink so heavy he could barely breathe it. As he stepped on the slick deck, he heard the sound. Not silence anymore but a hushed slithering, a moist friction of something all around the boat, a wet sound like an enormous tongue licking his ear: all of these at once. Then he saw what made the noise, and the light and the smell. The sea was in motion around them again. Only, it was not the water that was moving.

CHAPTER
THIRTY

When he learned what the task would entail, Tunnel chose his tools accordingly: two mallets, each of them rectangular blocks of solid steel, with thick hardwood shafts wrapped with black leather. Leaving Avina, he carried one of them in each hand, a feat that few could have managed and that strained even his brawny arms and shoulders. He did not care. He was in a bad mood and did not mind if it showed. He did not like being sent away from Skylene, sick as she was. Nor did he plan to be away from the worsening turmoil of the city any longer than he had to. But the Lothan Aklun relics were part of the dance of power at play in Ushen Brae now. The league wanted them; Dukish wanted them. They all wanted to use them to gain Lothan Aklun powers, all except the Free People, who knew better. If the messenger had found what he claimed to have found, it needed to be dealt with fast, before it fell into the wrong hands.

Outside the gates of the southern end of the city, a small party waited for him: the vessel messenger himself, three youths true to the Free People, and a man who had recently left the Antok clan's service. This latter was the only one of questionable loyalty, but he brought with him a prize that could not be ignored—one of this clan's totem animals.

The antok was young, half the size of an adult, but it still stood a hulking bulk of muscle and hide and tusks. The harness on its back was not the standard issue—as usually younger antoks were not ridden—but was a crosshatch of thick leather cords and even thicker lengths of rope. Tunnel was not at all sure just how to mount it. The antok's tender, Potemp, convinced Tunnel to secure his mallets along the beast's side. "So they don't brain anybody," he said. Then he had each of them climb into the weight arrangement he thought best. This put Tunnel right atop the beast's shoulders.

If he had not been in such ill humor, he might almost have enjoyed the vantage point it provided him as they set out at a canter. Tunnel—who was still a member of the Antok clan, even though he had broadened his allegiance to include all the Free People—had never ridden one of the beasts upon whose form his own gray skin and prominent tusks were fashioned. He rather liked the feel of it. Looking forward over the mount's coarse hide, he watched the creature's tusk jut into and out of view as his head swayed back and forth with his strides.

He is strong like me, he thought, but young. Just a young one.

They made good time the first day, seeing nobody on the road. What a land this is, Tunnel observed, so much of it empty of people. We should change that.

It was not, however, empty of reminders of the civilization that had once thrived there. The second day, they traveled a section of old track called the Bleeding Road. On each side, erected at regular intervals, stood the decrepit remains of the stakes the Fumel clan had been impaled upon. All of them: every Auldek of that clan for the crime of altering their quota slaves to look like them. To be children instead of slaves. The crime was a hard one for Tunnel to wrap his mind around, and the sight of stout spikes and the small piles of bones still at the bases of some of them, half hidden among the weeds, did not help. Auldek bones lasted a very long time. Strong as iron.

None of the small company chose to comment on the sights or the history behind them.

They reached the bank of the Sheeven Lek on the third morning. A little farther downstream the river broke into the main channels of the delta, but here it stretched wide before them, at the full breadth of its single channel. They turned upstream, and reached the site by the middle of the day.

It was a Lothan Aklun structure, all right. That much was clear from the strangely organic shape of it, the melding of the recognizable and the bizarre. The building stood near the bank of the river, shaded by trees but with a clear stretch of beach and a series of ramps leading from the water up to its riverfront side. The beams of the frame looked to be thick tree trunks, irregularly shaped and even knobbed at the base of chopped-off limbs. All this was clear on the framework, atop which the walls and roof of the place draped like a loose skin. Or so it looked from a distance, as they stood warily contemplating it.

From up close, the skinlike material was as solid as stone, as smooth as glass. And inside . . . inside brought back memories that Tunnel had not turned over in his mind for some time. The white walls, the slick floors, the strange, unnatural scent in the air. The instrument panels, levers, and all manner of devices, many-limbed things that stood like spiders. Dead spiders, but ones that could spring to life at the touch of a Lothan Aklun hand. Tunnel tried to see only what was here, unused and abandoned and powerless. This was not a place he had ever been to. It was larger, with different instruments, but the memories came anyway, visions of that other place and of the things done to him with tools somehow kin to the ones here. Young Tunnel, having his tusks fused right into his skull, the pain of it, the utter calm in the face of the Lothan Aklun woman who worked over him . . . Nothing had ever frightened him more than that calm.

Fortunately, he was not a child anymore. He slammed his two mallets down on their heads, their shafts standing upright. "This is it, then? Not so much to see."

The vessel messenger had wide-spaced eyes and the tattoos of the Fru Nithexek, the sky bear. He seemed nervous inside the building, looking around as if he feared the old inhabitants might return at any moment. "It wasn't that I'd never heard of this place before. I had. You can see it from the river. Once I floated by in a shell from the Sky Isle, but that was at night and the Lothan Aklun still worked the place. With them around it was a place to avoid. When I saw it this time, though, I knew things were different. Can't just leave it here for anybody to find."

"Anybody other than us, you mean," Tunnel said. He studied the panels and levers closely, without touching them. "What does this place do?"

As simple a question as it was, none had a ready answer.

"You don't know what it does?"

The messenger walked in a nervous circle. "If you mean exactly what does it do, I can't say, but over there"—he pointed toward the riverfront side of the structure—"are bays that open onto ramps that lead into the water, a deep cove. I think they built the soul vessels here. Or built them elsewhere and brought them here for servicing of some sort."

"Maybe they put the souls inside them here," one of the youths said.

> The rest let that sit untouched. One of the other youths rubbed his nose. Potemp cleared his throat and looked at his feet.

"Yeah," Tunnel said, sniffing the air, "this place doesn't smell good. Back up." He bent his legs slightly, gripped the shafts of the upright mallets. His gray arms bulged as he raised them, the striations of his forearms twitching with the effort. "Back, back." The others retreated, and he went to work.

He swung the mallets in wild arcs, smashing the panels, snapping levers clean off. Bits of the stonelike material flew in all directions, twirling in the air and skittering across the floor like shards of glass. The two-armed attack was not easy, but he kept at it for a time, knowing the others were watching him in awe. Tunnel liked being strong. Might as well show it.

When the strain started to pain his shoulders, he flung one of the mallets away. He took the remaining one up in a two-handed grip. Just as impressive, really, as each blow now carried double the force, the whole of his arms and massive back and stout legs combining to drive the steel where his mind willed it.

Sometime later, he paused. He balanced the mallet upright and stood with his hand propped on the end of the shaft. Glistening with sweat, heaving in great breaths, he surveyed the damage he had done. Pretty good damage, he thought. To the watchers, he said, "Let's have a fire."

❋

Late the next day, a league vessel made its appearance. It slid silently atop the water, cutting the current with its sleek lines, effortless. Unnatural. Potemp had warning enough to move the antok well back into the woods, out of hearing and sight and smell. Tunnel and the others watched the ship from the woods behind the burned-out shell of the demolished structure. The ruins still smoked, hot with glowing coals.

Ishtat soldiers came ashore, too many for them to confront. Staying hidden, Tunnel watched them kick through the ashes. Later, a leagueman—cone headed, robed, and unarmed—came across on a skiff and inspected the site. It was not the same one who had ordered Skylene shot. If it had been, nothing would have stopped Tunnel from rushing him, mallets swinging until he bashed the man to pulp. He almost did so anyway, but Skylene had not sent him out to die.

He's a lucky one today, that one, Tunnel thought.

"We were just in time," the messenger whispered. "Just in time."

They stayed in hiding throughout the day, watching. By the time the last skiff had returned to the anchored vessel, it was clear the leagueman had gained nothing. After sunset, Tunnel and the others came down into the ruins carrying armfuls of branches. They collected driftwood from the shore. Using a coal from the ruins they got a new fire going on the beach. They fed it until it blazed and then proceeded to dance around it. They shouted out toward the vessel, seeing its deck brimming with onlookers. They yelled taunts across the water at them, declaring that this ruin was the work of the Free People of Ushen Brae, saying that this was their land and would be forever more. The league would gain no footing here. The People would not allow it.

And then, with a flash of inspiration, Tunnel turned around, shoved his thumbs inside the waist of his trousers and pulled them to his knees. He waggled his bare bottom in the torchlight, shouting over his shoulder instructions for what the leagueman could do with his ass. The others did the same, all of them offering their buttocks with rebellious glee.

"Leagueman," Tunnel yelled, "here's my ass! Here's Tunnel's ass. I pinch it for you." So saying, he did so.

The others added their own takes on the theme. They all

howled with laughter, so caught up in the moment that they retreated from the shore grudgingly and only after the rain of Ishtat arrows shot from the boat became too heavy to chance further.

※

Tunnel arrived back at the Free People's compound in the middle of the night. Without pausing to rest or even to wash the grime of his work and travel from his face, he went to Skylene. Her caretakers greeted him grimly at the door, then stepped aside to let him visit her in solitude.

She lay as he had left her, propped up on pillows, with a blanket pulled up to her shoulders. Lowering himself softly to the edge of the bed, he could smell the sickness on her. It was there in the tang of her sweat, in the spoiled scent of her sheets, and in the fetid stench of the festering wound in her chest. The crossbow bolt that Sire Lethel had so casually set in motion had punched right through her left breast, ripping apart tissue, fracturing a rib, and leaving a dirty, oil-smeared puncture wound that quickly turned bad. He had looked upon it before he left; he did not want to do so again.

Skylene opened her eyes. She smiled at him, warmly enough that Tunnel wondered if she was getting better. But when her lips released the curve, her face looked even more drawn, lined, and thin than before. She asked, "Did you destroy it?"

Her voice sounded dry. Tunnel poured from a pitcher of mint water on the bedside table. He moved the glass toward her, saying, "Nah, nah," when she tried to take hold of it. Big armed and shouldered as he was, with large-knuckled hands that made the glass seem a child's toy, he touched the rim to her lips with delicacy. He did not answer her question until after she had taken a few sips.

"We did. Smashed it up good. Built a fire. It was a fine show." He detailed what they thought the relic was and told of their encounter with the league ship. By the end he was on his feet, his bottom pointed toward her as he repeated the taunts he had shouted over his shoulder.

It hurt Skylene to laugh, but she did so anyway.

"Are you getting better?" Tunnel asked, sitting beside her again.

Skylene set a hand on top of his. Her touch was hot, dry. She meant it to be comforting, but it felt wrong. He felt the fever burning in her. He almost pulled his hand away. "The others are looking after me. They brought a healer from the Kern clan. She was very kind, but her poultice had fennel seeds in them. You know I can't stand the smell of it. I wore it for a day, but then . . ." She lifted her hand and gestured, a vague motion that erased the very thing she was describing.

"We should send a messenger to the elders," he said. "To Mór. She would want . . ."

"To rush here to my side." Skylene shook her head. "No, Tunnel, send no message. None of them can help me either way. Why add to their distress? Mór left me—and you—to hold the city until she returned . . ."

"With the Rhuin Fá," Tunnel said, nodding in acknowledgment of the fact that he had finished her sentence, just as she had finished his a moment earlier.

"But we have not done that here, have we?"

"Not our fault."

"I know, but—"

"Dukish, he is just a fool! Going to mess with everything that could be so simple and good. How we going to know that before he show us it? Stupid man. Should have squashed him the first time."

Skylene did not dispute it. "If you get another chance, do squash him. Do it for me. But otherwise . . . stay alive for Dariel. Be here when he arrives. That should be within a fortnight."

"What? You know this?"

Nodding, Skylene said, "The vessel messenger who took you to the relic, he came here with a message for me, a message from Yoen."

"You didn't tell Tunnel," Tunnel said, managing to convey a depth of hurt in the short sentence.

"No." Skylene smiled. "If I had, you might not have taken those mallets to the relic. You might not have shown the good sire your backside. I needed you to act without distraction, without waiting for your Rhuin Fá. I was right, wasn't I? Even a day's delay would have—"

"What's the message, then?"

"Mór and the others are returning via the Sheeven Lek. Dariel is with them."

Tunnel smiled. "This is news."

"There's more. The journey has been a success in many ways. They all still live, for one. For another, they visited the Sky Watcher. Nâ Gâmen blessed them all, especially Dariel."

"That's right."

"Yoen said to expect Dariel to look different. He wears a sign on his forehead, a spirit mark that combines his name with Nâ Gâmen's."

"He is the Rhuin Fá." Tunnel leaned in close and whispered, with passion, "He is. I always told it, didn't I?"

Skylene started to laugh, but it pained her. She choked it down. "Of course you did, Tunnel. You are the smartest of all of us, the truest."

"Should we tell everyone?"

"No, not yet." Skylene closed her eyes a moment, her breathing shallow. "Not yet. He is not the Rhuin Fá until the People name him so. We have all to do it, understand? Not just Nâ Gâmen, the elders. Not just you and me. Everyone must do it. And none who don't want to believe him are going to want to change, not without seeing him for themselves. We need to hold this news as long as we can, until they are nearly here, understand? We use it to call a gathering, but only at the last moment. We don't want Dukish or any of the others to have time to work against him. All right?"

"Yeah, that's all right."

"Tunnel"—she softened her voice, rounded it and weighted it with import—"I've told nobody else about this. If I . . ."

"That won't happen."

"But if it does, you . . ."

Shaking his head, Tunnel stood up. "Nah, won't happen. You love Mór too much to die. You'll still be lying here, waiting for a kiss, when she comes. Tunnel knows." He glanced around. "You hungry?"

He asked it casually, tugging on a tusk as if he had nothing more on his mind than his stomach. It was not true, but he kept it up until he heard Skylene breathe out the rest of the things she thought she needed to say to him. Once she did, he pretended to wander away, foraging. In truth he stood at the far end of the room, leaning against the wall and watching, thinking, You'll still be here. Tunnel knows, of course he does.

CHAPTER
THIRTY-ONE

When asked to describe it, Dariel said he did not remember anything. In truth, he remembered his return from death with a clarity not of an experience passed but of one yet to come. It went something like this. For a time, he was not a man at all. He was a single bubble—one of infinite millions that pressed softly against him—dislodged from the depths of an abyssal floor and rising through the black fathoms in which nothing at all lived. He knew the entire time that he might pop at any moment, might cease to be or be swallowed by some unliving mouth driven by unliving hunger, suddenly roaring out of the black. He would not have been able to explain that he became more and more terrified the closer he got to life. Nor would he ever try to describe that passing into life did not feel like surfacing or birth or waking. It felt like smashing against a ceiling of black obsidian and vanishing.

And then he was a man. He moaned the air out of his lungs, lay empty for a moment, and remembered to suck air back inside himself.

"Dariel," a voice said.

He had a name.

He opened his eyes. Anira's brown visage looked down on him. She ran her hands over his face and neck and chest. "Dariel, by Anet and her young . . . I thought you were dead. They said you would come back, but I feared . . ." She leaned over him and kissed him, and then, as if sensing that her relief may have been premature, she grasped him by the shoulders. "Can you hear me? Are you all right?"

He was not ready to commit just yet. His eyes darted about the small, tidy room. They were alone. He lay on a cot; Anira sat on a stool beside it. An intricate openwork band ran around the wall at eye level. Through it came the sounds of the village: people talking, a dog barking, chickens clucking their singsong rumination on the world. He could have stepped to the screen and looked through, but the sound made him hesitate. It was too mundane to be trusted.

"What happened?"

"You don't remember?"

"No." But saying it, he did. He had come to meet the elders. He had gone to embrace Yoen and . . .

He propped himself on one elbow and clawed his tunic up with his other hand. He ran a palm over his abdomen, searching for the wound he knew should be there. His skin was smooth, ridged with his muscles and curled with light hairs.

"There was a knife," he said, but there was no knife. Not anymore. Not sticking out of his belly, nor leaving any trace that one ever had. "He tried to kill me. You saw it."

"No, he didn't," Anira said.

"He stabbed me." He clutched his abdomen for proof, but again his body denied him. "I mean . . . he tried to. What happened?"

"He'll explain." Anira stood and stepped back from him, looking him up and down. "First, get ahold of yourself. We're on the Sky Isle, in Elder Yoen's village. You're not dead. Not even hurt. Tell me you don't feel stronger than ever before. You look it. And you have this."

She reached for his forehead. Her touch felt strange. He felt the pressure of her fingers but not the sensation of her skin against his. Pulling back, she indicated that he should feel for himself. Reluctantly, he did so. A section of his flesh was rough beneath his fingertips, raised and hard like a scab.

"Is there a mirror?"

Anira looked around a moment, twisted away, and came back, rubbing the curve of a metal saucer. The image Dariel saw reflected in it was distorted and blurry. He squinted one eye and studied what he saw there for a long time. A rune of some sort. A character in a language he could not read, drawn in short, assured swipes as if by an ink brush, black against his beige skin, a black so solid that the Shivith spots underneath the symbol did not show through it.

"What in the Giver's Name is that?" he demanded, feeling curiosity more than rage, but letting anger drive his words anyway.

"Your destiny. Your name. Come, meet Yoen again. He'll explain everything to you. Yoen said to—"

"Not him!" Dariel sat up. He swung his legs over the cot and drove his feet down against the floor. Standing upright so quickly made his head swim. "Not . . ." Though his eyes did not close, the world went black.

※

The second time Dariel awoke, he took care to sit up slowly. This time, there was more than one face to take in. Anira perched on the edge of the cot down near his knees, her hands clasped around one of his. Tam and Birké stood against the wall. The latter flashed his canine smile when Dariel's eyes passed over him. Mór was saying something to a white-haired matron with Shivith clan spots on her face, like Mór's. Like his, he remembered. Even as his gaze moved he knew that they had yet to settle on the person they must. He felt the presence beside him, sitting where Anira had sat before. He wished for anger as he shifted his gaze to the old man. Wished for anger and prepared for fear and . . . felt neither.

Yoen's expression of sad joy was etched in every crevice of his features. His eyelids drooped at the outer edges, giving his face an almost puppylike softness. He said something, his voice kind as he leaned forward. Dariel did not understand it, and the old man realized as much. "Forgive me," he said. "When I forget myself I speak Auldek. Mór teases me for it. Don't you, dearest? What she doesn't know is that it embarrasses me that the language of my enslavers comes faster to my mouth than the one of my native land. But we're not here to speak about me. I should explain to you what happened. Do you want to hear it now, or should we wait until you feel stronger?"

Lying there, feeling weak and yet refreshed at the same time, with the memory of death so near him still, Dariel knew there were a variety of things he could say in response. Angry things. Defiant and accusatory and indignant ones. He just could not remember what they might be. Instead, he said, "I want to know now."

"Of course you do." Yoen smiled, a quick grin full of large teeth so healthy that they seemed mismatched with his elderly face. "All right. I'll tell you a brief version of it. We can talk more later, but you should understand this much. You died." He did not smile again, though the pronouncement had the ring of a joke's revelation. "And then again you didn't."

Dariel just stared at him.

"The Sky Watcher Nâ Gâmen did something to you, didn't he? He told you things and showed you things, and he did something else. What was it?"

"You mean . . . the blessing?"

"Is that how you think of it?" The old man said something else, which at first Dariel did not catch. And then he did. *Yes, tell me of the blessing*, Yoen had said.

"He . . ." Dariel stopped, realizing that he wanted to know where the sentence was going before he began it. What was the blessing? A small thing compared to the wonders that Nâ Gâmen had showed him: yet it was this that came to mind. He could think of nothing else in answer to the question. "He . . ." And he had to pause again. The thing on his forehead. The rune raised out of his skin. He felt like he should understand before he spoke, but it was not working that way. It was hard to get his tongue around the words. "He . . . wrote upon my forehead with a stylus of sorts. A Lothan Aklun thing."

"Yes, he did," Yoen said.

Dariel reached as if to touch it again, but let his fingers just hover near it. "It wasn't like this. He wrote but there was nothing. No ink, or . . ."

"He was not writing with ink, Dariel Akaran. He was writing with his life soul. He wrote with the energy that was his true being, his first, the soul he was born with. He put that into you through that stylus. He asked something very precious of you, Dariel. He asked that you carry him here to be killed, so that in dying he might join with you. That's what he did. It was something different from what they did with the soul catcher. This time, it wasn't really you who died. And it wasn't really Nâ Gâmen. It was a little bit of both of you. You are now both yourself and him. He gave you the knowledge that you will need to fulfill the destiny written in this character. I imagine his soul is very strong, older and larger than a normal person's. You have more than a normal measure of life within you." The old man reached out and touched the raised symbol. "This will be hard to understand, so don't try to. There is more to it, I believe, but that's for you to figure out in time. Right now . . . Well, you already know more than you realize. Listen to the words I am speaking. Do you hear them? You do, yes?"

Dariel nodded.

Without breaking eye contact with him, Yoen asked, "Mór, what language have I been speaking since I began explaining the 'blessing'?"

"Auldek."

"And what language did he speak in response?"

"Auldek."

Dariel looked at her. She stood straight and beautiful, her face as astonished as he had ever seen it. The others' as well. They all stared at him with gravity enough that he almost believed them. "But I don't know Auldek," he said.

"Considering that you are speaking it," Yoen said, "I think you do. I think you will come to realize you know many things that you did not before. Now"—he looked around, squint-eyed as if he had forgotten his spectacles someplace and was looking for them—"I should show you the village, and show the village you. Come, walk with me."

As improbable as it seemed, even as it happened, Dariel rose. He set his feet more carefully this time, and stood with Anira's aid. She led him past the others and out into a humid, overcast morning.

It looked just as it had sounded from inside the small room: a village among the trees, with the peak of the volcano rising to the west. Small cabins, simply made from the slim, purple-skinned trees of the area. Hard-packed dirt lanes running through them. As they stepped into the light, a gaggle of hens scattered from the cluster they had formed at the door. Eavesdroppers.

The people in the street stopped what they were doing, as if their labors had been but an excuse to position themselves to see Dariel step out among them. They wore peasant clothes, brighter hued than what he would have expected in the Known World, but similar in their simple, functional construction. Two old men, a woman with gray hair tied back, another who wore Lvin whiskers tattooed on her cheeks, several others of middle age, with varying clan markings. A boy of twelve or so stood entrapped within the wooden framework of some tool. He had been carrying it, but he froze and just stood gaping. Just like the rest. Just like Dariel himself.

Cashen came bounding into view, his nose held high and his tail whirling in circles. He caught sight of Dariel, dropped the stick he was carrying, and sprinted toward him. Bashar was not far behind.

※

That was, what? Four, five days ago? Dariel was not sure. He was not yet free of the vision of death he had awoken with, so that each time he burst back into consciousness he was unsure for a time whether he was truly alive. He knew he had slept and woken several times, but the waking hours of each day were something of a blur. A strange blur, quiet instead of noisy. A blur of faces seeking out his face, touching his forehead, and speaking their names to him. A blur of conversations, questions asked and answered, which led to new questions to be asked and answered. The days passed as if disconnected from normal time. Dariel knew that was not really so. It was wishful thinking. He was not with Nâ Gâmen anymore. Behind the peaceful workings of his days in the village he knew the world went on. This reprieve was to be brief.

So, on whatever day this was—the fourth or fifth among the Free People hidden on the Sky Isle deep within Ushen Brae—

Dariel stood, sharing a long silence with Yoen. They had climbed out of the village and were taking in the settlement from a bend on the path that led up to the pear and apple orchards.

"Do you see that tree there, in the center of that clearing?" Yoen asked.

Dariel saw it. Not as tall as the trees that grew around the base of the volcano's rich slopes, it had a gnarled, aged quality to its twisting limbs, which stretched wider than it was tall. "It looks like an acacia tree, except that they don't grow that large."

"Here they do," Yoen said. "It's a very ancient tree. It's sacred to us. Nâ Gâmen himself planted it there from a cutting taken from the original. It is, as you say, an acacia tree. Another transplant to this land, yes?" He lifted his cane. He speared the ground ahead of him and began his slow ascent again.

Dariel knew him well enough to know that was all he had to say on the subject of the tree. He walked, taking in the view. The village was such a small part of it, dwarfed by the trees that hung over it and the volcano and the rolling landscape that hulked off to the west. The peaks of Rath Batatt were hazy shapes in the distance.

"I'd expected there to be more of you," Dariel said. He spoke Auldek. He believed it now. He could switch between it and Acacian with complete fluency. The word structures and grammatical rules were vastly different, but both languages were equally clear to him, neither one more or less foreign than the other. "Mór made it seem like . . . like I'd find a paradise of Free People thriving out here."

"Is that not what you see?"

"In a manner of speaking, I guess."

"Mór sees not just what is but what she hopes will be. The two live in her at once. Give her purpose. You must consider this when you speak with her; but, no, we are not numerous, Dariel. If we were, the Auldek might have had cause to destroy us. That was why we split into smaller villages, spread out along the rim of the mountains."

"Did they attack you often?"

"Years ago they hunted us for sport, but they grew tired of that over the centuries. Many of us were unwanted anyway. To beings enslaved by their immortality, the aged are no welcome sight. We make them uneasy. We remind them of themselves. You saw all the gray hairs in the company and fewer teeth than our numbers might suggest." In contradiction to this, Yoen smiled. "What immortally young person would want us around?"

"You're not all old."

"Oh, not all. No, no. Some of the young ones the Auldek deemed defective for some reason. Not many, but occasionally the Aklun missed a frailty of mind or body. And some suffered injuries not easily healed. Ones like that the Auldek did not concern themselves with if they disappeared. I've lived these many years not sure what the Auldek think of us."

"Look at these here!" the elder exclaimed. He careened off the path at what seemed a dangerous burst of speed, into an orchard of manicured trees that hung heavy with fruit. "The size of these! Aren't they beauties?"

Dariel admitted to never having seen pears so large. He had to cup one in a two-handed grip to tug it free. Yoen was more selective. Dariel watched him sort through the branches, testing different fruit beneath the pressure of his thumb. "The season is perfect for them. Mór will like these, I think."

"She could have walked with us," Dariel said, "except that she can't stand to be around me. I thought she had softened after I helped destroy the soul catcher. She seems to have forgotten all about that."

Yoen looked at him for a long moment. "It's not a matter of hatred. She fears you. She wants desperately to believe you are the Rhuin Fá. She wants you to help us make this nation of ours, and she hates it that she wants that so much. She has waited all her life for this, never knowing if change would come in her lifetime. Now it has, and part of it arrives bearing the name Akaran, a prince of the very family that enslaved us. You can see her point, I trust. It would have been easier for many of us to recognize the Rhuin Fá if he arrived with Akaran blood on his hands."

Finding a pear that suited him, Yoen grasped it in his palms and gave a quick tug. The fruit held on stubbornly, but the shaking of the branch dropped another one softly into the grass. Yoen smiled down at it. "This one doesn't want me; that one does. I can take a hint." Dariel moved as he began to bend, retrieving the fallen fruit for him. "Thank you," Yoen said, taking it.

A little farther up the hill, the two men moved off the trail and sat down on simple stools, with a tree-stump table between them. Yoen sliced the fruit with agile motions of a slim knife. The skin of the fruit was brilliant yellow, smooth to the touch; and the flesh inside had a pinkish hue.

"Dariel, it's a miracle that any of the People remain whole. They were taken as children. You know that, of course, but can you imagine what it means for an entire nation to share a common trauma? All of us. Whether we are now young or old, all of us were made orphans. All of us were taught we were slaves to the whims of the world. It may be that all people are that, but most don't learn it at seven, eight years old."

Birké and Anira came up the trail. Dariel nodded to them. They saw him but did not return the gesture. They stayed near the path.

Yoen went on. "So, what would happen to a nation of people deprived of the love of their parents? If nobody taught them morality, what sort of adults would they become? What if their captors told them time and again that they deserved their slavery—that they caused it somehow, or that their parents sold them or simply gave them away? A child can believe great lies, especially the ones that hurt him. You see the problem."

"Yes," Dariel conceded. He felt sick to his stomach, unable to eat the fruit Yocn had sectioned for him. "Yes."

Tam and several of the elders also came into view. Behind them, Mór walked by herself, her head averted as if she did not want to make eye contact with anyone. Dariel almost said something, but from the determined way Yoen managed not to acknowledge them, he knew he should not. As the elder talked on, several more of the villagers and a few elders just arrived from farther-flung settlements joined the procession.

"Each of us had to reckon with the fate the Giver abandoned us to. So I—and many generations before me—did what we could to remain whole. We had to invent a semblance of a nurturing culture by trial and error. We treat one another with compassion. We teach the young that they are loved, that the world has done them a great wrong, but they own no fault for it. We tell them stories, dream with them of a better world. We ask them to believe in the possibility of a hero, a champion. Mór and the others think that the elders have organized resistance and prepared them for the fight facing us. We have helped with that, yes, but the young own that more than we. No, our true work for many generations has been in teaching the young how to grow into human beings. It hasn't been easy. We haven't always succeeded. We can only do so much from here, but we've done our best. I want you to understand that. Do you?"

Dariel nodded. Following Yoen's example, he did not watch as the others moved from the path and proceeded toward them. "I think so. I . . . in my own way, I was an orphan, too. I had to learn how to be a man from people other than my family or siblings. I understand the gift that is."

"I'm glad to hear you say so. I'm afraid I don't have any more time to explain it, even if I needed to. The other elders think

I've taken too long with you already. Has anyone spoken to you about the news from Avina? The last messenger brought much news, none of it good. Confusion. The People breaking into factions. The league crawling over Lothan Aklun sites like scavengers. The unity that kept us tight around a single cause broke apart when the Auldek left. We out here are not powerful enough to control the People in Avina. We need them united with us, not as enemies. But you knew that already, didn't you? We are walking on the sand when the tide has drawn out. The moment won't last. The wave will come crashing in soon. Don't you agree?"

He did. Even though he had not spent as much time thinking of Avina as he should, he did agree. He had seen enough of war and of power struggles to know that the paradise Mór so wanted would not come easily. He could not help glancing at her. She stood a little distance away, one of the loose circle that surrounded Yoen and him. Her gaze was on him, frank and at the same time unreadable. "Yes," he said, answering Yoen's question.

"Good," Yoen said. "Then you will understand that we must move swiftly now. Dariel, had I my way, you and I would spend many more days talking and walking in these orchards. Seeing as how I killed you, I feel some obligation to explain more about what you've become after that death. I cannot have my way on that. I can't explain more because I don't know any more. What you are to be to yourself—and to us—you must figure out yourself. And, as time is short, I must put all other things aside to ask you a question. More than just a question, really."

Ask it, Dariel thought. Ask it. He had his answer ready.

Yoen straightened and looked around at the gathered company, finally taking them all in. "I don't just ask for me, of course. It's for all of us."

"Yes," Dariel said.

"But I have not asked it yet."

"My answer is yes." Dariel looked from face to face around the circle, at friends he felt he knew well and others he had only just met. It didn't matter that he had not known any of them a few months ago, or that he didn't know exactly what Yoen was going to ask. It didn't even matter that Yoen had thrust a knife into his belly. If anything, that act had just brought Dariel closer to them. He had already decided. For each of them he had the same answer. "Yes."

And then a question of his own. "When do we start?"

CHAPTER
THIRTY-TWO

High, high above, looking down at the patchy view allowed through the layers of clouds, Mena and Elya flew the length of the invading army. The Auldek force crawled across the frozen world, a slow-moving stain on the white landscape, with wheeled structures the size of large buildings; dots that were people; and numerous animals of varying sizes, beasts she feared would be entirely new to the Known World. The trail of trodden snow and debris that marked their progress stretched behind them in a wavering line that had no end. She and Elya turned and circled back.

"I didn't want to believe it," Mena said, more to herself than to Elya, who sailed on, her wingbeats a steady rhythm. "All the time and training, the work of opening Tahalian, hearing the Scav's story . . . beneath it all I still hoped it was for nothing."

That possibility had just ended. The tiny figures below her, which were as small as ants from her height, confirmed this. She felt uneasy above them. It was unlikely that any would see her, hidden as she was among the banks of cloud, the gray sky dull above her. Still, she felt watched each time she passed through a clear patch. She remembered to keep her eyes scanning the air around her. If the Auldek really did have flying creatures, she saw no sign of them.

She tried to estimate their numbers. She could not do so with precision. Thousands. Tens of thousands, enough to fill the Calathrock with more to spare. Enough to fill all Mein Tahalian. She wondered how many of them were Auldek and if it was true, as the league had claimed, that they carried extra lives within them, making them almost impossible to kill. She circled a third time, aware that she was delaying but also using the extra moments to plan her next move.

And what might that be? What if she flew down and landed in the middle of the war column, announcing herself with one of Maeben's screams? Or she could touch down before the army and brew a pot of tea as she waited for them to draw up to her. She rather liked that idea. Let them see she had a sense of humor. Let them know that Acacia was not afraid of them. Only that would not be true, and she was not confident she could pull the deception off.

No, she would do no more than spy on them, and then turn south bearing news of them. "Let's make this quick," she said, patting Elya on the shoulder. "Let's go lower. We might as well get a good look. Corinn will complain if we don't."

Elya adjusted the tilt of her wings. They dropped through the bank of cloud. Mena was still not used to the sensation. The material of the clouds looked so tangible, thick and almost solid, as if they should be able to land atop it. Instead, it turned to wet vapor before their touch. Mena licked it from her lips and tried to ignore the chill bite. It was so near to freezing that for a few moments she leaned her face against Elya's neck, feeling her warmth, coating her cheeks with the lemony scent of Elya's oils.

Mena had just straightened to check their position when, without warning, Elya corkscrewed in the air. It was so fast that Mena's head snapped to the side. "Elya!" she called from upside down, her hands grasping for purchase as she slipped partway out of the harness. "Elya, what—"

The thing hit them with incredible force. It impacted from above, driving Elya downward. She and Elya twirled as they plummeted, the air a roar around them. Each cloud hit them with physical force, as if they were smashing again and again through a body of water. Mena thought, I knew it. The clouds are firm. They have substance. But it was the briefest of thoughts, gone in an instant.

Something fell with them, some sort of beast that Mena only caught glimpses of. It bellowed and grunted. Elya hissed in response. The two of them struggled, clasped together and fighting. It was larger than Elya, hairless and thickly muscled, with enormous wings. It had a flat face that looked vaguely like an ape's and a mouth of incisors that once came close enough to snap at the princess. It was all bulk and weight compared to Elya's sinewy length. It wore a chain about its neck, thick and decorative, with a large amulet dangling from it. Elya kicked the beast away. It came back a moment later, lashing with a closed fist that smashed the side of Elya's head. All three of them somersaulted wildly.

Mena caught a glimpse of the invading army below them, so near. Then she lost all sense of direction, dizzied by the spinning, confused by the flapping of wings and the roars of the attacking creature. She knew the ground rushed up to them. She tried to connect with Elya, but her fight was too frantic. All Mena could do was hang on. Then the monster released them. It broke free at the last moment, using the force of their tumbling to send Mena and Elya hurtling for the icy ground.

Elya flared her wings enough to slow them a little, but still they landed hard, just missing the rear of one rolling structure and crashing down on the trodden tundra. The impact snapped one of the buckles on Elya's harness. Mena twisted off to one side, one leg loose in the straps and the other pinched painfully by them. The flying monster roared in just behind them, touching the ground for a second and then leaping up. It thrashed its massive arms in threat; gnashed the air with its teeth; grinned at them, bug-eyed and crazed.

Mena tried to keep an eye on it as she scrabbled to get her seat back, but she was so tangled and Elya was moving and hissing so fiercely that she could not keep track of the creature. Beyond it, another of the rolling structures moved toward them, coming on like a fortress on wheels. Mena clamped down as best she could, half in her harness, a clump of Elya's skin and feathers gripped savagely in one hand. *Fly!* she thought.

Just then another beast announced itself. It slashed at Elya before crashing to the ground. It danced away a few steps, then skirted them, drawing up opposite the other of its kind. It came back toward them snarling, crouched on its hind legs. Like the first, it was naked except for a thick chain and medallion on its neck, snug against the muscled flesh.

Fly! Mena commanded.

Another skimmed Elya's head as it landed. And another. Each time Elya's muscles tensed to leap, a beast dropped from above. Others now beat the air above them. In among the bestial cries came a human voice. It spoke guttural words that Mena could not understand. Then she picked him out. An Auldek rode strapped to the back of one of the hovering monsters. He was directing the others. Perhaps his commands were the only thing stopping the beasts from ripping into them. His mount landed among the others, shouldering its way savagely to clear a space for itself. A moment later the rider sprang to the ground. He shouted something and gestured. As he walked toward Mena and Elya, the monsters rose, bellowed and stomped, and then leaped one after another into the air.

As the creatures lifted, the view they had hidden snapped

into place. Mena saw soldiers coming in from all directions. The war column slowed fitfully to a halt. Armed, fur-covered shapes poured out of hastily thrown-open hatches, steam billowing as they emerged. Still others flowed between the structures. Mena half thought the fly command, but the winged monsters circled above. She stroked Elya's neck and soothed her. The mount did not settle. Her crest feathers made a jagged crown, her serpentine neck coiled and vicious.

Mena kept whispering to Elya as she pulled free of her buckles and slid down to the ground. Her left leg throbbed, but she did not betray it. She took a few steps forward, stood straight with her shoulders back. She tugged the mitten from her sword hand and took hold of the hilt of the King's Trust. She waited like that as the enemy army crowded around her.

"Steady, Elya," she said. To the invaders she called, "I am Princess Mena Akaran of Acacia. I speak for the queen. Who speaks for you?"

They barely acknowledged that she had said anything. They inched closer, pushed in as more arrived. They spoke among themselves in their own guttural tongue. The sounds were like threats and accusations, animal and wild, spoken from furred, tall beings, most hooded against the cold, their faces hidden from the dull winter light. They were not all Auldek. Mena could see humans among them—many, in fact—but they spoke and gestured with a fierceness akin to their masters'. Elya spread her wings. The crowd only swayed back a moment, and the flying beasts nipped from above, forcing her to fold in.

The uproar died down when several new arrivals pushed to the edge of the circle. A man stepped out in front of the others, followed by a woman nearly his height. He was tall, like most Numrek, but when he pushed back his hood Mena saw that his hair was auburn, thick, and long. He ran his fingers through it to loosen it, and then set his intense gaze on Mena.

He carried a sheathed long sword in one big-knuckled hand, but he showed not the slightest intention of drawing it. The woman wore no headgear. Her dark hair was pulled back in a ponytail, her cheekbones high and distinctive. Their features were not so physically dissimilar from that of the Numrek Mena had known, but the demeanor behind them was different, calmly intelligent, at ease in a manner no Numrek's had ever been.

Auldek, Mena thought. Not Numrek.

As if to verify this, Calrach appeared behind the man. The Numrek's face was a blunt twist of angry surprise. "Akaran," he said, his accent thick with disgust. "You stupid bitch!"

Mena shifted her posture, ready to draw her sword.

"Princess Mena?" another voice said, in clear Acacian this time. A man squirmed between the two warriors and stood beside the Auldek's shoulder. Despite the fantastic strangeness of it, Mena recognized him immediately. Rialus Neptos. "Is it really you? By the Giver—"

The Auldek snapped at him in his language.

"Yes, yes," Rialus sputtered. He switched to the foreign tongue. Mena understood none of it, save when he said her name. The Auldek's eyes widened at it, his interest gaining substance. The woman's, in contrast, narrowed.

"Princess," Rialus said, "what are you doing here?"

Elya hissed and snapped at one of the flying creatures.

Looking up, Mena said, "Tell them to call those things off. I can't talk with them above us."

"Oh, yes, the fréketes," Rialus said. "They are vile. I'll ask Howlk to call them back." He spoke Auldek to the man who had been riding one of the creatures. The Auldek man looked up, bemused, as if he had not noticed the circling monsters. It was the woman who barked a command. Several others picked it up. Noisy moments passed, but eventually the fréketes flew

away. Most came to rest at vantage points on the now still carriage buildings.

Attention back on her, Mena cleared her throat. She released
her sword hilt. Considering how outnumbered she was, gripping it could show weakness instead of strength. She tried to
find a different place for her hand to settle. She kept the focus
of her eyes deliberate: her gaze on Rialus, on the Auldek directly
in front of her.

"Rialus Neptos," she said, "we must do this correctly. Introduce me to them, and them to me—if these be their monarchs."

"Oh, they don't have monarchs," Rialus said. "Clan chieftains,
yes, but that's not the same as—"

The Auldek man nudged him. If Mena had not been so tense,
she might have been amused. Even if he could not understand
Acacian, the Auldek knew a Neptos ramble gaining speed when
he heard one.

Rialus spoke Numrek—Auldek, Mena corrected—again. A
few moments later, he turned back to Mena. "They understand
who you are. This man is Devoth of the clan Lvin. This woman
is Sabeer, his wife. They are . . . like monarchs, in a way. There
are chieftains from other clans as well, though. It's complicated.
You see, there are—" Devoth clicked his tongue. Rialus spoke
rapidly. "Yes, yes, you can speak to them. There are no higher
among them."

"What of you?" Mena asked. "Can I trust you to speak my
words as I say them? You have betrayed your country, after all."

Rialus looked stricken. "No! Never. I am a prisoner among
them!" He said this last with his voice slightly lowered. A
strange action, for it was still easy enough for the others to hear.
"I am faithful. The queen can be assured of it. Tell her that if
you get back to her. I—I always work to . . . deter them. It's not
easy, though."

"No, I don't imagine so." Mena pursed her lips. What choice

did she have but to use this man as her translator? "Tell him I speak for the Empire of Acacia and for all the Known World. By Queen Corinn's charge, I demand to know their purpose here."

"Isn't it obvious?" Calrach said, gesturing around him. "See with your eyes."

"Rialus," Mena asked, jutting her chin at the Numrek chieftain, "has this one any status here?"

Rialus considered. Shrugged. "Not much."

"Good. Then tell him to shut his mouth. He has no status in Acacia either. No status. No kin. They are all dead."

"You lie."

Mena crossed her arms as he spoke. "I killed the assassins sent to slay Prince Aaden myself. We butchered Greduc and Codeth in the Carmelia. My Marah and I cut them to pieces. I wish you had been there to see."

"Do not believe her, Devoth," Calrach said. "My clan is in a fortress that cannot be taken. They await word of us to begin a new slaughter." He seemed to catch late that he was speaking Acacian. He switched to his own tongue.

"That plug of stone in Teh? That was no protection. Corinn called Crannag to the field and used her sorcery against them. They all died, Calrach. Your clan is no more."

"You lie!" Calrach spat. He stepped toward her.

Mena backed up, her hand on her sword.

Devoth slammed an arm against the Numrek's chest, stopping him. He demanded a translation from Rialus. After it, he responded through Rialus, "If what you say is true, I am filled with happiness."

"He misunderstands me," Mena said. "Queen Corinn's powers are unmatched. She killed all the Numrek, and she will do the same to you if you continue into our lands. She sent me to tell you to turn around. She sent me so you know her conviction. Tell him so that he understands."

Before Rialus could begin, Devoth said, this time speaking heavily accented Acacian, "I understand."

Rialus turned and gazed at him, stunned.

"I know your tongue. I once had thoughts to . . . know your country. I learned your talking from the divine children. I asked them about your people. They could tell little, though. They were children only. Always children. I grew bored and forgot much. Years long back." He grinned. "As you can see, I have found interest again."

For the first time, the crowd was hushed to real silence.

"I understand what you say," Devoth said. "It's good what you say."

Calrach tried to speak.

Devoth ignored him. "The Numrek are the Numrek." He gestured with his fingers, trying to find the words to explain himself. His fingers opened as if they were dropping something inconsequential, dust that could be blown away on the breeze. "It is good to hear that your queen defeats them. A better foe for us, then."

Mena was speechless, unsure how to respond. It was not just what he said that unnerved her. It was the undisguised confidence with which he said it. Not bravado. Not arrogance. Not foolery. Just . . .

"What else do you want to say to us? Rialus, translate so that all can hear."

"I . . ." She hesitated, and then had an idea. She spoke so that her voice would carry. "I see you have humans among you. The queen wants them to know that we have no quarrel with them. We would welcome them back to Acacia, free citizens of wherever they choose to live. They need not fight for their enslavers anymore."

Devoth listened, both to Mena and to the conclusion of Rialus's translation. He looked around, content to let the offer sink in to all who heard it. "That is a clever idea, but you have it wrong. Your queen may have no quarrel with them, but they have a quarrel with her. You sold them as children. We raised them."

"As slaves!"

"What do you know about it? We raised them. We gave them clans to belong to. We taught them a way to belong."

"You made them slaves."

"No, *you* made them slaves! We made them our children!" As fast as Devoth's temper flared, he reined it in. With a calm, assured voice he said, "We have already made a pledge to them. After they help us defeat you, they will all be free to do as they wish. They will be slaves no longer, and we—not you—will be the ones who freed them. If what I have said is not true, anyone may say so now."

The silence that followed was interrupted only by the grunts and chatter from the fréketes. No one spoke.

Eventually, Mena said, "I have said what I came to say. You will find no Numrek waiting for you. If you fight us, we will destroy you just as we did them, and we will not make these offers again. If you turn now, we will not pursue you. Turn now. Let us forget each other."

Devoth shrugged. "If you are done . . . Would you stay long enough to eat with us?"

"What?"

"To eat." The Auldek scooped imaginary food into his mouth. "You are safe with us. Come eat. Have a drink. Rest before you go home."

Mena realized that sometime in the last few minutes fear had drained out of her. Confidence with it. And purpose. She tried to pull it back into her voice. "I will not offer you peace like this again."

"Good," Devoth answered. "Your peace is nothing to talk about. Vapor. It's talking about the wind. You can hear it. You can see that it shakes the trees. But you can never grasp hold of it. Better to leave it. You will not stay with us?"

Mena shook her head. Dine with them? No, that seemed a horrible idea, worse than fighting them all. She could not have said why the prospect chilled her so completely. "That's not what I came for."

"You came to spy," Devoth said, cocking an eyebrow at her. "Isn't that so? You didn't come to threaten us. If you did, you did not come well prepared."

The Auldek woman, Sabeer, muttered something in her tongue. A few grunted agreement. Some laughed.

"What did she say?" Mena asked.

Rialus sputtered a moment before saying, "I had told her of your life previously—that you were a great warrior. She—she finds that hard to believe now that she sees you."

"If she wishes a test, she may have it," Mena said.

Rialus frowned. "I won't tell her that."

"Why not? Tell her."

"Princess, you've not seen how they fight."

"I've killed Numrek. Tell her that."

"These are not Numrek. Sabeer is—"

"Enough," Devoth said. "Do not be women. Don't die on Sabeer's point." He paused, a hand raised in mock concession to Mena's snarl. "Or don't kill my dear wife. No use in that. Be a messenger for us, Princess Mena Akaran. You will, yes? Take this message: the Auldek come for your lands. We come for slaughter." He broke out of Acacian and shouted something in his own tongue. By the way the throng yelled in response Mena knew he was translating his words. He turned back to her. "This has been amusing, but if you will not eat and drink with us, go. Go now, fly home. Tell your queen our nations are at war!" Again he turned and barked his translation. Again the crowd exploded in enthusiasm.

Mena felt Elya at her back. For the first time she realized how much the creature had surrounded her, her wings tented in a protective manner. "I would speak to Rialus Neptos in private." She was not sure what she had to say to him, but thought she should try. Perhaps he would have something to offer.

The chieftain weighed this. "You can, but I would have to cut his tongue out first." He gestured toward the dagger on his belt and waggled his tongue, and then grew serious. "He would be of little use, empty of words. If you wish, though . . ." He pulled the blade free and made to grab Rialus with his other hand.

"No," Mena said. "I will take your message back. Do I have safe leave from here?" She indicated the flying beasts perched on the wagons.

Devoth grinned, shoving the dagger home and nudging Rialus playfully. "You do." Calrach growled something close to the chieftain's ear. Devoth flicked him away with his fingers. He said something softly in Auldek.

Rialus translated it as: "Fly safe, Princess. Fly true. Make your world ready for us."

Turning from him, Mena slipped under the canopy of Elya's upraised wing. She climbed into the saddle, slipped her legs into the harness, and fastened it. The Auldek waited in near silence. The fréketes cried out, holding some fragmented conversation among themselves, eyes on Elya.

Sabeer said something to her, pointing a long finger at her as she did so.

"She says she will see you in battle," Devoth said, acting as translator.

"Tell her I will kill her then."

They spoke a moment, and then Devoth guffawed. "She says which of her souls will you kill? She has many within her."

As Elya rose on her bunched hind legs, Mena said, "All of them. I'll take all of them." Elya leaped. Her wings flared and they were in flight, beating hard to rise above the raucous fréketes, who trailed, snarling behind them for a time.

CHAPTER

THIRTY-THREE

The morning of his coronation, Aliver was up before the dawn. He watched the coming day lighten into a dull, drizzly morning. Not an auspicious start. A little later, the day remembered color. The rain slowed, stopped, and patches of sky broke up the cloud cover. For a midwinter day it was quite mild. Corinn, no doubt, would call the weather perfect. What better way to welcome a new monarch than with a world glistening wet beneath shafts of eager sunlight? Without even talking to her—without needing to hear her say it—he would think of it that way, too. That was how it was between them. Two minds; one mind. He knew he had not always felt that way about her, but he could not remember what it was he had felt instead. This must be a good thing, though. It certainly seemed like it.

They were doing right, acting bravely, making decisions for the empire. There were coming trials to face, yes. A foul invasion that they would have to meet with force. But how could any ragtag group of brutes stumble out of the Ice Fields and expect to defeat Corinn's magic? Mena's sword? Aliver's joyful masses? There was the fact that Dariel had been lost in a distant land. But he might be found! Corinn would remind him of that. Nothing was certain yet. Until it was, live with hope.

Remember, Corinn had told him, that only he had walked through death and returned. Only he. She and he had done that together, and now they would rule together. The nation was on the cusp of a mighty change. They were creating it, and it was good.

Though he could not remember the exact details, he knew that in his earlier life leadership had sat much more heavily on him. No longer. Now he had only to think of a fear to have it swept away by confidence, reason, purpose.

When a servant opened his door and slipped inside to wake him, Aliver stood from the window seat and waved at the young man. "You wouldn't expect me to sleep late on my coronation day, would you?"

"Your Highness," the servant said by way of answering, a quick bow as he did so. Eyes pinned to the floor, he asked, "Are you ready for your bath? It's all prepared, with all the special oils and fragrances for the day."

Aliver watched him, a hint of frustration rising at the sight of his deferential posture. He almost instructed the man to raise his head and stand straight. What had this man ever seen him do that had instilled such subservience in him? Nothing, and in that case the respect was not true. It was an act, a delusion. In Talay, when he was a young man, he had no servants. Men and women and children, old and young alike, could talk to him as an equal and yet somehow honor him by doing so. In Talay, he had slain a laryx and earned his tuvey band. He could run from sunrise to sunrise without pause. He had been a warrior, and an entire army had watched him slip beneath the belly of a raging antok and slice it end to end. Many had real reasons to honor him. What reason did this man have?

Before the question was completed, he already heard Corinn's inevitable answer rising in him. All those things were still true, she would say. For all those deeds and many more he had earned the reverence of the entire empire. This man need not have stood beside him in battle to believe him a warrior, or have witnessed any of the things for which he was famed. That would be impossible, and it would deny this man the prize of serving a king. For him that was a great boon. His bowed head said as much. A good king lets a servant be a servant.

As quickly as she spoke—or as he spoke to himself with her confident voice—he was reassured. "Yes, I'll bathe now," he said, to the obvious relief of the waiting servant.

So he set off for his first official duty that morning with the servant trailing him through the hallways. He stripped naked before attendants, who acted as if he were not naked, or as if his nakedness were nothing to take notice of. He submerged himself up to the neck in hot water and sat there as sachets of oil-soaked herbs bobbed around him. His toenails and finger-nails were snipped. The soles of his feet scrubbed. His entire body massaged with warm oil that was kneaded into his skin by skilled fingers. He stood swaying as several towels dried him, and stayed standing as another contingent of servants swept in with his apparel for the first half of the day. Thus, the king to be acted like the king to be.

When he emerged in the central courtyard of the royal resi-dential grounds, Aaden ran to meet him. "Aliver! Look at all the boats! It's unbelievable how many there are. More than yester-day. Come look."

Aliver let himself be tugged toward the terrace railing, smil-ing at a contingent of Agnates fresh in from Alecia. They would want to greet him, he knew, but he had made so much small talk with so many vacuous aristocrats the last week that he wel-comed any excuse to put them off.

He grasped the weathered stone, Aaden beside him, point-ing. The boy need not have, for the sight could not be missed. The sea around the isle of Acacia did not sparkle glassy blue or green under the shafts of sunlight. Instead, an enormous, undulating blanket had been cast over the water. A quilt sewn of boats all sizes and shapes, flying flags from every portion of the Known World. It was amazing. Beautiful not just in appearance but in terms of what it meant.

"Have they all come for you?" Aaden asked. "I didn't know there were that many boats in the whole world."

"There are more than this even," Aliver said, "as you'll see on your coronation."

"If they keep coming, one will be able to walk from here right across the sea to the mainland, hopping from boat to boat. That would be fun."

Aliver agreed that it would be.

"Today will be good, won't it?"

"Aaden," he said, turning his full smile on the boy, "today is the beginning of a new age."

"That's what Mother says!"

"She's right."

As if to demonstrate this, a shadow passed over them, with it a whoosh of air that ripped exclamations from everyone on the terraces. Thaïs flew by. The creature's wings beat once, and then she glided in a curve out over the bay. Her rider, Dram, sat small on her back. A few moments later, Kohl—flying riderless—sailed into view from the other direction. Cries echoed up from the lower town, climbing the terraced levels as others joined in. Aliver could not make out words in the chanting, but he knew the tenor of it. Euphoria. Joy. Awe. When Po's black form surged up from below the railing, having skimmed so close to the cliffside that he only appeared at the last moment, Aliver turned his gasp into a shout as well. They were mighty, Elya's children. They were mighty.

But when he turned to Aaden, he drew back, unsure how to read the boy's face. There was a tremor of excitement in it, yes, but it edged more toward fear than joy. "Aaden, are you all right?"

The boy looked sheepish. "Do you think they are . . . good?"

"Good?"

"That they are good things? Before, I knew they were, when they were Elya's children . . ." He glanced behind him. He leaned toward his uncle and whispered. "I don't like them as I did before. Mother made them . . . dragons. But they weren't dragons before. They were something else. Something wonderful. I haven't told Mother, but I don't like them now. Don't tell her. Please don't. She is so proud of them."

While the boy spoke, Aliver agreed with him completely. He was saying things that Aliver himself had thought but had forgotten. Hearing them brought it all back. Hadn't he said the same before? Hadn't he cautioned Corinn about squeezing the gentleness out of them? No, he realized he hadn't. He would have to take the matter up with Corinn.

These thoughts were clear in his head only for as long as his nephew spoke. After that, they vanished. When Aliver went to respond he said, "Aaden, people will remember this day for ages." That was true, wasn't it? They would, and that was wonderful. "For ages, Aaden, and you were here to see it!"

"But—" the boy began.

"Dragons over Acacia!" As he swept his arm through the air, he caught sight of Rhrenna and several of her assistants, who had just mounted the main staircase. She stood looking around for a moment, until she saw him. She gave some direction to her assistants and then, to his delight, left them and started toward him.

She looked luminescent. Her dress was slim-fitting yellow velvet, cuffed high on the arms and cut low in the front. It had very few frills, and yet it managed to look elegantly formal. Her golden hair flowed in wavy locks below her shoulders. He had not seen her wear it down before. He'd had no idea it was so long and thick. Really, he was not sure he had ever truly studied her before.

"Here you are," she said, grasping him by the arm as if he might dash away. "You're not to be out of my sight a minute more. The queen's orders."

"Rhrenna, you look lovely. Has anyone told you that today?"

Color instantly flushed her cheeks, drawing two curves that traced from her cheeks to her jawline. That was fetching, too. And why had he not noticed how delicately drawn the lines of her lips were? They sparkled with some cosmetic, but, like her dress, this only highlighted what was already there.

"Not yet today," she answered. "You're the first. Thank you, Aliver."

She told Aaden his mother would be arriving in just a moment. She asked him to give Aliver and her a minute alone in the meantime. The boy hardly noticed, transfixed by the sight of the dragons skimming above the masts of the largest ships.

A few steps down the terrace, Rhrenna said, "I have foul tidings, and I would like to say them quickly. It's word from Calfa Ven, about Wren. She's taken ill."

Aliver pulled out of her grasp, but Rhrenna moved with him, as quick as a dance partner. He felt the press of her small breasts against his upper arm. He tried not to be distracted by them. "Is it serious?"

"I'm afraid so. The physician doesn't know what's wrong for sure, but it may be the return of a contagion she caught in her youth. Something tropical, you see, from when she was a brigand. That's not unheard of. I'm afraid it puts the baby in jeopardy as well."

"Who is caring for her? We should send physicians from here."

"The queen has seen to it that Wren has the best care possible. Have no fear on that count. And don't, for yourself, let it spoil this day. That's why Corinn asked me to tell you quickly and assure you that if she can be saved, she will be. We, however, have to proceed with the day. It's all tightly scheduled, as you know. Oh, there's Corinn now."

His sister strode before a buzzing swarm of attendants, senators, and guests. Surprisingly, Barad the Lesser walked at her elbow, his large head tilted to hear whatever the queen was saying.

Aliver parted his lips as they drew near, intending to ask Corinn about Wren, but she spoke first. "Doesn't Rhrenna look charming, Aliver?"

Aliver could not help but turn and study the woman again. "Very much so."

Rhrenna said something about being a stray dog beside a fox in Corinn's company, but Aliver could see no reason for her modesty and said so. One of the Agnates behind Corinn piped up in agreement. "Just a different sort of canine, if you don't mind me saying so. An arctic fox! That's it. Though not so fluffy."

"No need to compare us," the queen said. "Rhrenna is a beauty in her own right. Aliver sees it, don't you?"

"Yes," Aliver said, " I do."

Corinn beckoned Aaden to her side. She touched Barad on the shoulder, dragging her fingers down his arm languidly, as if stroking a cat. "Barad just gave the most rousing speech in the lower town. Didn't you?"

Barad smiled. "I am most pleased by the reception."

"You're an asset to us," Aliver said, meaning it. Convinced of it. "Nobody understands the people as you do."

"Thank you, Your Majesty." Barad closed his stone eyes for a moment.

Those eyes, Aliver thought. Those horrid eyes. He liked the man who saw through them, but he found it hard to meet that stone gaze. Expressionless. That was what they were. Lifeless, though they moved and saw. Aliver shifted his gaze from him as something else occurred to him. "Is Mena still not here?"

"No, it seems she's been delayed."

"How so?"

"I wish I knew," Corinn said, reaching out to touch Aaden on the neck.

Rhrenna answered. "Something must have kept her. She is on the Mein Plateau in midwinter. The weather may be foul. I know it well, arctic fox that I am."

"It's sure to be foul," Corinn said. A wrinkle of frustration creased her brow, but only for a moment. She touched her index finger to Aaden's nose, then intoned, "The wind over the Mein is always keen. The snow likes to blow, and the frost will toss. If you like to freeze . . ."

"You'll be terribly pleased," Aaden finished, "because the wind over the Mein is always keen."

Aliver acknowledged the childish verses with a nod. "That's fine, but perhaps we should—"

"What?" Corinn asked. "Wait? Postpone the coronation? Don't suggest that. The ceremony is set for today. Everything is arranged. Aliver, do understand that we've pushed as much as we can on the coronation date. We may be monarchs, but I still had to court the high priestess of the Vadayan like a silly lover." She tutted and glanced back at the sycophantic choir gathered behind him. They jumped at the inclusion, affirming how correct she was, laughing as if she had told a joke private to them all. "Mena will come when she comes. I've all but given up on expecting her to follow my instructions."

Aliver frowned. He did not want to let it go, but forming words of protest felt like trying to swim against a strong current. "But . . . what if something has—"

"Happened to her? This is Mena Akaran we're talking about! Maeben on earth. Vanquisher of the foulthings. Tamer of dragons." The choir loved that. "She's fine. She'll probably fly in and make a show of herself. She'll be here in her sweet time."

"Time," Rhrenna said, "is not a luxury we have today. The nobles are already gathering in the Carmelia."

"And so should we."

For a moment, Aliver burned with annoyance. He could barely finish a thought without—

"Are you ready to become king?" Corinn asked. She stepped closer to him, her tone intimate in a way that made the onlookers dip their eyes.

Aliver's annoyance fell away, replaced by the pleasant glow Corinn's question created. Yes, he was ready to become king. Of course he was! It had been so long, so much longer than it should have taken. He should have been king years ago. Now, finally, he was just hours away from it.

"Yes," he said, "I am ready."

CHAPTER

THIRTY-FOUR

The journey north from Teh was uneventful, slow for most of that first day, but faster that night, as the salt-heavy breeze picked up in the early morning hours. The second day they rode the current in its swirl toward the west. That evening, the barges rowed out of it near enough to Acacia to see the glow of lights throughout the night.

Around them the sea bobbed with life. Crafts of all sorts hitched to the breeze or scooped the surface with oars or even dipped paddles to propel themselves. People called to one another, unusually festive. Some tossed foodstuffs across the water. Bottles and skins of wine. When they fell into the waves, young men dove for them, coming up dripping wet, their teeth shining white. It seemed that to everyone but Kelis and his party this passage was the beginning of a grand celebration.

If anyone noticed that immobile figures stood in among the close-packed swine, they did not voice it in Kelis's hearing. The Santoth took up posts throughout the barges. Once positioned, they went as still as standing stones. The other passengers and crew avoided them, but they did so without being sensible of it. A boy, picking his way toward a Santoth on some errand, would choose a route that took him around the sorcerers. Once, two men cast their bedrolls in a clear spot at a Santoth's feet. Instead of lying down, they stood shuffling, talking, ill at ease. They fell to arguing. Both of them moved away in a huff. One slept awkwardly wedged between two pink-skinned swine. The other sat forlorn near the area used as the latrine, staring into the night. As far as Kelis could tell, the man slept very little.

For his own part, Kelis did not sleep at all. Swollen sacks drooped from his eyes, and when he blinked, his eyelids hesitated before rising again. He had never been so tired in his life, but sleep was not a comfort he could visit. Since boyhood, when his ability to find visions of the future in his dreams had emerged, sleep had been a troublesome thing for him. Back then, he had dreamed the future. He had walked in other worlds and conversed with animals and commanded tongues that he had never learned during his waking hours. A gift to the boy but not to his father. His father beat sleep out of him. He wanted his son to be a warrior, like him, not a dreamer. A man of spear and sword, a lion and laryx slayer. Not a man of visions and words, no dealer in things he could not see with his own eyes.

His father had succeeded in molding him, but Kelis never forgot the visions he had seen and the way they made him feel. It was not power that he felt, but a sense of rightness. He thought of it sometimes when he watched fish in water. That was where they belonged. They breathed what men could not and thrived. He had once, briefly, been a fish in the ocean of dreams.

For the first time in many years, Kelis wished he could regain the gift he had abandoned as a child. Would that he could sleep now and see what the future held for them. He could not. When he closed his eyes, he just saw more clearly the scene around him. Some gifts, once neglected, can never be reclaimed.

The next morning—that of the actual coronation—found them one of hundreds in a logjam of vessels that surrounded the isle of Acacia. The crafts bumped and jostled one another. Whether a barge or a sloop or a fishing rig or a rowboat, tall or short, long or narrow or wide—none could move any farther. Those that had small enough skiffs inched them through what gaps they could find, but as the numbers of ships joining the raft grew, such pathways were squeezed out.

"Look at this mess." Benabe stood atop a crate and squinted against the glare of the sun, which had just cut its way through clouds that had left them sodden with rain during the night. "We'll never get anywhere near the island!"

Kelis climbed up onto the crates. Acacia was there to be seen. He could make out the higher reaches of the palace, the spires adorned with long, silken ribbons that wafted on the breeze. To the south, the promontory of Haven's Rock was also visible. He knew the contours of the place, but it looked different. Squinting, he realized it was as crowded with tents and people as were the seas below it. Shen must have noticed them, too.

"Will it sink?" Shen asked. "Because of all those people, I mean. I saw a raft sink once when too many climbed on."

"No." Benabe mussed her curly hair. "An island can't sink. Not unless the pillar that holds it in place breaks, and the Giver made those to last forever."

Shen considered this with one eye narrowed. Instead of responding, she asked, "What are those?"

The adults studied the view again. "What?" Naamen asked.

"I saw something flying. A giant bird."

"One of the queen's dragons, no doubt." Benabe pursed her

lips sourly. "Some boys last night were talking of them. They bear riders, they say. I'll believe that when I see it."

"I saw one, just for a moment, and then it dipped out of sight. I want to see it closer."

"One day," Benabe said, "if we ever get through this mess."

Naamen rubbed the elbow of his stunted arm. "They have to clear a way for us. We're with the pigs. They'll want pigs. There must be a way through. A lane kept clear for—"

"For pigs?" Benabe huffed. "You're seeing what I am, yes? Look at that. We're stuck! And there's the island right there!"

"But the pigs—"

Benabe cut him off. "People who want pigs will come here, not the other way around! No, we're stuck."

She had it right, Kelis knew. He had just come from unsuccessfully trying to speak with the captain. He overheard him making arrangements with an empty whaling ship stuck just as fast nearby. They had ovens on it that could be used to roast pork, a smokehouse to cure bacon, large decks for slaughter, storage in the hull for the offal. The captain had decided he need go no nearer to sell his product. Indeed, he thought he could double his money.

"We could leave the barge," Naamen proposed, "and move from boat to boat. Others are doing so."

Kelis had noticed that, too. Men and women and children moved from vessel to vessel, clambering up the sides, sometimes with the help of ropes thrown down to them. Some swam between the ships, flopping wet onto the decks. A few captains balked at strangers climbing across their vessels, but most were oddly cheerful about it. With the shouted greetings and bursts of laughter and occasional impromptu songs, the festive atmosphere grew. Kelis wished he could feel some of that himself, but he had only to catch sight of a Santoth to feel his insides knot with worry. He could not imagine them passing from boat to jovial boat. Nor was that what they intended.

The sound, at first, was like the start of some holy man's prayer to the Giver. Kelis heard it but did not turn his head immediately. It was not until a second and then third and then more voices merged with the first that he snapped around. He was stunned twice by what he saw.

The Santoth were singing. They had gathered in one group, standing as still as a choir, and each of them intoned the same song, if song it could be called. It was a mixture of foreign words and sounds that were like notes. These had an almost physical presence. The air around them rippled with it. It was transfixing, but there was no beauty in it. There was a garbled undertune, something that gurgled and squirmed within the music. An evil thing like a snake slithering quicksilver fast through and around and over the notes.

The Santoth looked different. Their robes were not the colorless garments they had been. Now they bloomed with a rich orange, like dye seeping into the fabric even as he watched. For the first time Kelis could see their faces. The roiling emptiness that had obscured their features was all but gone. Instead, he saw them for the men they were, with cavernous cheeks and eyes that seemed absurdly bulbous. Ancient and weathered, their skin had been burned by the Talayan sun, brutally creviced and parched as desert soil, stretched over the bones beneath. They looked every bit their great age. Like dead things standing and walking . . . and singing.

Kelis jumped from the crates and waded through a pen full of pigs to where Leeka stood staring openmouthed at the sorcerers. "Leeka, what are they saying?"

The old warrior was still for a long moment, staring at one of the figures in particular. Instead of answering, he approached the sorcerer. "Nualo? Aged one, what work is this? What do you—"

The Santoth swept his hand in the man's direction, his fingers flicking whiplike. Leeka staggered. Nualo's mouth still contoured around the song, but anger burned in the sorcerer's eyes. He flicked his fingers again, and Leeka flew back, lifting into the air so that only his toes dragged on the deck. A pen railing clipped his ankles and he spilled over on the backs of several startled pigs. He was up from beneath the squealing swine a moment later, his face a carved exaggeration of fear.

Then the barge began to move. It jerked forward once, throwing people off balance and sending panic through the pigs. And then it began a more steady progress. In seconds the linked barges collided with the nearest vessels. A skiff overturned, tossing the youths onboard into the water, and was promptly run over by the barge itself. The barge pressed the shell down and smashed into the side of a larger ship beyond it. This one leaned toward them as though the masts would crash down atop the Santoth, but it only came so far before stopping abruptly, as if colliding with an invisible barrier. The ship slid to one side and around the barge, which carried on with increasing speed.

Kelis heard Naamen exclaim, half hopefully, that the Santoth were clearing a way for them. It was true. They were heading toward Acacia. But this was all wrong. Kelis knew it without doubt. Whatever the Santoth intended had evil slithering within it. They were wrong, and Kelis could not let them continue. He had made an enormous mistake in letting them come this far. Any doubt he had about it was gone now. He struggled toward them, his eyes on the one Leeka had named Nualo.

"Stop!" he said. "You must stop!"

Nualo did not answer. Closer to him now, Kelis could see that his skin still crawled with tremors and crevasses, but the face they distorted was emerging. The jagged peaks of his hair-line, the strong hook of his nose, eyes the color of an overcast winter sky: his features were that of one man, flesh and bone, born of a woman. For the first time to Kelis's eyes one of the San-toth looked like a human, not a phantom in the guise of a man.

"Stop!" Kelis roared. He realized he had his spear in hand. Though he did not remember snatching it up, he held it now in his right hand, gripped to throw.

Nualo's gray eyes found him. His mouth kept at the song, in chaotic time with the others, but he spoke directly into Kelis's mind. Soundlessly, he said, *You are nothing. You know nothing. You will learn.*

"I will not let you pass."

The girl released us, Nualo thought-spoke. *You already have let us pass.*

Kelis raised his spear, balanced it on his strong dark fingers. The Santoth were flesh now. He could pierce them. They always had been, but now he knew it.

We are again. We are again, and the world is ours again!

The sorcerer extended one arm toward Kelis and squeezed his hand into a fist, saying something different from the others for just a moment. The spear in Kelis's hand went suddenly molten. Not hot, but as soft as melting wax. The shaft and point drooped as if they would drip to the deck, then instead they curved back in time with the twisting motion of Nualo's fist. Kelis cried out and tried to release the spear, but it would not come loose. The shaft wrapped around and around his hand until it and his wrist were encased in ribbons of soft metal. Then it went hard, forming a cage of iron.

Trouble me no more, Nualo told him. With that, his attention moved away. He rejoined the others fully, Kelis forgotten.

Kelis stared at his hand, expecting pain but feeling none. It felt different, trapped, immobile, but not in any way he had experienced before. He knew that the song continued. He had not stopped anything. He felt the impact of the barge against other vessels, grinding through or over them. People cried out, some in anger and some in fear and many in confusion. Ben-abe and Naamen reached him. Naamen pulled him back while Benabe tried to get her fingers under the metal gauntlet. She couldn't. There was no separation between it and his flesh. As she tugged and scratched, Kelis could feel her fingernails through the metal. Not on it, but through it. It was part of him now. In that instant he knew that it forever would be.

Shen started toward the Santoth, who had carried on with their song as if nothing else mattered to them. Kelis grabbed her with his unchanged hand. He was surprised at how steady his voice was. "No, don't. They are not your friends anymore. You can see that, can't you?"

He expected the girl to protest, but she did not. She stayed silent. Her face, for the first time, was stricken with doubt. Kelis knew from it that she had heard what Nualo thought to him. It was written there in the skin around her eyes and in the slight tremble of her lower lip. His heart rushed out to her. He searched for the words to convince her that whatever was happening was not her fault.

The barge smashed against the bow of the whaling ship. The jolt sent them all reeling. The bow of the whaler rose above them as the ship's stern jammed against something else. It crashed off to one side of the barge, just beside the Santoth, crushing a pen of pigs and grinding them across the deck in squealing confusion.

Kelis yelled for them to move. They rushed toward the rear of the barge. It picked up speed as they stumbled over the railings and shoved through the increasingly frantic swine. Kelis managed to swing Shen onto his back. She clung there as he kicked savagely at pigs, fearing they would bite. One tried to, and he smashed it across the snout with his metal-clad hand. Kelis clustered with several others at the rear. They hunkered down and watched as the barge crashed its way forward, propelled by sounds mightier than any wind.

The chaos of the smashed and overturned boats and the screaming people was so overwhelming that Kelis did not see Acacia until they were upon it. Their barge splintered through the last few vessels, tightly packed and firmly secured to the docks of the main harbor. When they could go no farther because of the sheer bulk of compressed debris and wood and iron, the Santoth ended the song. It dropped into nothingness instantly. The next moment Kelis realized he had already forgotten what it sounded like. He would never be able to describe it. It had been horrible, but he would not be able to explain how in any detail.

"Look," Naamen said. "They're going."

Kelis shot to his feet. "Come with me," he said to Naamen. To Benabe and Shen he added, "Stay here. Right here. Do not move until one of us comes back. Agreed?"

Benabe nodded. Shen, for her part, stayed curled in a ball trapped within her mother's arms.

Leeka was already at the barge's railing when Kelis and Naamen joined him. For a moment they all watched the backs of the receding sorcerers. The Santoth had already cleared most of the packed ships and debris. They climbed over the ships. In some places they scrabbled over obstructions like excited children. In others they leaped gaps as if finding purchase on the air itself. Kelis still had no idea what their intention was, but there was no doubting the eager fervor with which they pursued it.

The sorcerers leaped onto the dock and began shoving their way furiously into the crowd. The people were too closely packed to flee, but they drew back before the figures as best they could. The impact of their progress pushed through the multitude in waves. Those who saw them pressed back to avoid them, causing still more confusion.

Naamen said, "Kelis, they're madmen. I see them now. Really see them! What should we . . ."

Kelis did not hear the rest of his sentence, his mind stuttering over the realization. Those who saw them . . . For people did see them! It was clear in the way they cringed in surprise, the way confusion melted into fear as soon as their eyes touched on them. The Santoth were visible now, and horrible! Revealed here right in the heart of the empire. They now looked taller than normal men. Seven, eight feet, perhaps—towering over the gathered crowd. Their long arms swung in great arcs, like scythes attacking wheat. They headed for the gates of the lower town, the entry point for everything else on the island.

"Brother, go back to Benabe and Shen," Kelis said to Naamen. He turned away from the sorcerers long enough to draw his gaze. "That's what you should do. If anything happens"—he paused, snapping his head around to watch the disappearing Santoth, then met Naamen's eyes fiercely—"protect them with your life. If this goes badly, hide them. Don't hesitate. Hide in the lower town. Do what you must, but protect them. Do not try to go to the palace. Stay in the lower town. If things are calm, come at sunrise to the inner gate—the lion gate that opens to the second ring. I will come for you there."

That was all he had time for. He peeled himself away from Naamen's entreating eyes and looked at Leeka instead. He called the man by name, and when he had his attention said, "Are you with me? Or with them?"

Leeka answered, "I've been deceived."

"We've all been deceived," Kelis said. He raised his ironclad hand, as much for himself to note as for Leeka.

"Yes, but I for many years now." He stared after them, thoughts clearly racing behind his eyes. "They used me. When

I thought they were teaching things, they were really pulling knowledge from my mind, learning about the world. Without even knowing it, I helped them find Shen. I can't explain it, but I feel it. They worked to win her trust from a distance. When they felt Shen was within their reach, they sent me out to bring her in. They couldn't do it themselves, so they used me. Now my eyes are open. I know things about them as well."

To Kelis's surprise, Leeka jumped the gap to the pier and began shoving his way through the roiling, agitated crowd behind the sorcerers. He moved not with their speed but as if he were grabbing hold of the energy in their wake and heaving himself forward.

Kelis made the same jump and ran in pursuit.

CHAPTER
THIRTY-FIVE

Though aspects of Acacian royal culture had always been strictly formalized, one thing had remained variable. Akaran monarchs had never been required to wear a specific insignia of their rank. They had to wear something for official state functions, but just how they chose to mark their status was left to their personal inclination. Edifus had stayed a warrior, choosing to display his status purely through the deference strong men showed him. Tinhadin was often pictured with a narrow crown; but others over the years had necklaces fashioned for their coronations, earrings, even brooches like the one Corinn's mother wore—a turquoise acacia tree set against a silver background.

Corinn had worn that piece at many a state function. She did not wear it today. She had a choice from her ancestors' jewelry, but when her servants had offered to bring her the family's heirlooms, she had said that it was not necessary that she examine them. She knew what she wanted. "I'll wear Tinhadin's crown."

That was what she wore as she entered the Carmelia via the same tunnel through which she had run in panic just a few months earlier. She walked along the causeway at the slow, ceremonial pace the priestess of Vada inflicted upon them from the front of the processional. Corinn's eyes flew around joyfully, taking everything in. How different this entry was from last time. Back then, she stumbled in with her garments shredded. She had been stained with her own blood, her lungs heaving, and every fiber of her body twisted in fear. A scene of carnage greeted her. Dead Marah on the field. Numrek swinging their massive swords. Mena fighting the monsters with a sword so large she looked like a child holding it. Aaden nowhere to be seen. Oh yes, things were different now.

Joyous onlookers filled the massive stadium. Thousands upon thousands of them. Agnates and other Acacian aristocrats; senators from Alecia who sported that city's latest fashions; Aushenian royalty and chieftains from all the Talayan tribes; all the generals and officers near enough to attend; merchants from all the provinces in their respective garb, colorful, bejeweled, grinning: they all stood up and applauded the royal party's entry. Corinn adored the colors of people's garments and the various hues of their skins and idiosyncrasies of their cultures. Think of the breadth of rule they symbolized.

The floor of the stadium thronged with Marah officers, each of them stationed before units of troops adorned in all their finery. They were but a fragment of the army she could call on, and everyone admiring them knew as much. In the sky above, Elya's children circled. Their wings stretched wide and glorious, beating with strength the world had never seen. Savagely beautiful. Awe-inspiring. The queen controlled the skies and the land. It would not be long before the seas were hers as well. She imagined that the leaguemen in their plush viewing boxes sensed as much.

She loved it all, even the way the sky had cleared to a marvelous blue, a mild winter day with enough of a breeze that the long banners attached at high points all around the stadium rippled with serpentine grace. She had filled the Acacian air with a mild euphoria for several days now, and she knew that the Prios vintage flowed freely. Still, the bliss that she felt came from satisfaction with what she had achieved. There was an irritation somewhere beyond the euphoria, some other song out in the world beyond the Carmelia, but she ignored at, as she ignored the visions she had of things that nobody else saw. It would not ruin this day.

The tunnel gates slammed shut heavily. They would stay that way for the duration of the ceremony.

The procession turned and began to ascend a series of five flights of stone steps toward the ceremonial dais. Corinn studied her brother. He would be king in just a few short hours. He looked marvelous. It was impossible to imagine that he had ever been removed from life. The energy in him shone from his tan face as if a sun heated him from the inside. His smile was a gift he gave out freely as he walked. He greeted people by name, nodded at others. Occasionally taking a hand offered to him, he blessed them with his touch. His flowing blue robe hung perfectly on his slim frame, the rich hue of the satin fabric radiating kingly calm, depth, and even an air of wisdom.

Corinn had been skeptical of the emblem he chose to wear as the embodiment of his royal rank, but she had to concede that there was a bit of flair in the simplicity of the gold tuvey band he wore around his right biceps. All Talay would love him for that—and fight to the death for him.

Perhaps as the years passed she would loosen the grip she held on him. No, not perhaps. She would. Absolutely, she would. She would restrain only the parts of him driven to dreaming ideals the people were not ready for. That rash side of his nature, which had cost him his life, needed to be starved out of him. At her side all his strengths would shine; his weaknesses would atrophy and fall away. He would learn the rightness of her rule and take it into his heart. Then they really would do fine things together.

They would fight off the attacking horde. The Auldek could not stand against her command of the song any more than the Numrek could. After that, who knew the extent of what she and Aliver could do? Wash the sin of the quota away from reality and from memory? Put the league in its place, humbled and obedient? Extend the empire right across the Gray Slopes to Ushen Brae? Of course! That was why a double monarchy was so perfect. Aliver would eventually rule in the west as she would rule in Acacia. The possibilities were endless.

After them, Aaden would be there to inherit it all. He walked just behind her, beaming, bubbling with excitement. Already, she found herself concocting the wonders that would mark his coronation. By then she would speak the Giver's tongue as if it were her first language. And he will, too. Aaden will, too.

The queen sat with all this humming within her as the priestess opened the ceremony. She watched as Elya's children dropped out of sight, to rest until after the coronation. She listened without listening as the sect's purple-robed scholars read through the entire chronology of monarchs since Edifus. She greeted the procession of representatives offering gifts from around the empire: a pair of mating cranes from the Aushenian marshes, dining bowls of blue glass from the Ou family of Bocoum, a silver and turquoise necklace from Teh, a clutch of large crimson ostrich eggs, some delicacy of the Bethuni that the chieftain claimed made them more valuable by weight than gold.

The league's offering was elegant and understated. Sire Grau himself presented it to them, both he and Dagon with their heads bowed. It looked like a marble bowl, wide based, with a gold-framed glass dome over it. Closer inspection revealed a specially constructed version of one of their navigational instruments. Inside the dome a carved metal serpent floated in a clear liquid. Beneath it, a map of the Known World. At Dagon's urging, Corinn cupped the bowl and moved it. The serpent rotated.

"It always," Dagon said, "stays faithful to the one direction it loves above all others." Aliver, too, tested it, grew pleased, joked that he would have the royal scholars make a study of it. The engraving across the gold rim read: *Whether My World Be Large, I Always Know My Place in It.* Corinn smiled her acceptance of it.

The gifts went on: a suit of armor in the Senivalian style, a heavily bejeweled diadem from the Creggs of Manil . . .

After the gift giving, a poet from Aushenia recited long, grandiose verses from one of the Aushenians' rhyming epics, modified at key points to make it all a tribute to Acacia. It took hours to get to the actual moment of coronation, but Corinn did not mind. She was not the girl who had hated sitting through state functions anymore. No, she thought, I'm not that girl at all.

The priestess of Vada was not the old crone that Corinn remembered from her own coronation. Youthful, she was almost attractive, even with the sides of her head shaved to the skull and the hair on her crown bound into a large knot. She took far too much satisfaction in her brief role of importance, intoning with the same ostentation as her predecessor, cutting others with her dark eyes as they brought her the ritual items she washed and blessed. She submerged an old tunic—said to have belonged to Credulas, the fourth king—in soapy water, squeezed it, and then hung it on a frame to dry. There was a story in that, Corinn knew, but she had never learned what it was. Nor was she entirely sure what the Vadayan sect's function was, other than as scholars of Akaran lineage. They had once had a more defined religious practice, although it was dead now.

When all is settled again, Corinn thought, I'll make a study of them. And of other things. There is so much to know.

And then, finally, it was time. The priestess called Aliver before her. Corinn did not really register the words she was saying or the replies that Aliver was giving. She knew them by heart and had been through the same oath herself. What she focused on was the way Aliver's handsome face managed the perfect balance of deference to the priestess's duties and ultimate authority. He already was a monarch. That was what his visage and upright bearing said. He knew his authority, but he had the patience and confidence to see through the customs into which he had been born.

"You've trained him well," Hanish's voice said.

Corinn stopped the inhalation of breath that the voice caused before the air had passed her tongue. She fought the instinct to turn toward it.

"Look at him. He's playing his role perfectly and doesn't even know it. You may have chosen correctly," Hanish said, "in bringing him back instead of me. You could have your way with me in bed, but I wouldn't have been so easy to control in other matters."

He stood beside her, in the small space in front of a Marah guard and beside Sigh Saden. She could feel the brush of him against her shoulder, the touch of his skin when he nudged her. She did not glance at him or acknowledge him in any way. None around her did either. He was a figment of her powers over life and death, that was all. Nothing more. She blew the breath out again.

"How can you be sure, though? Perhaps he's playing you for a fool." Hanish laughed and stepped toward Aliver. "He is about to become king. He did come back from the dead. One wonders. . . ."

Corinn's gaze darted around, trying to see if anybody else noticed him. No one seemed to. The priestess slid the tuvey band down Aliver's biceps, around his elbow, and off. Hanish had to draw his head back as she swung around with the band, lifting it high so that the audience could see it. He stood at Aliver's shoulder now.

"Looked at from another perspective," he said, "our dear Aliver has pulled off an amazing correction of his misfortune. You think it all a gift you gave him, but what if he's outmaneuvered you? Just consider it a moment. That's all you have left, anyway."

The fact that only she could see or hear Hanish should have been a relief of sorts, but it was more an aggravation. She had a thousand retorts for each of his comments but could offer none of them. He seemed to know this, and to take pleasure from it. She tried to find a spell within the song, something with which she could erase him. It was not easy, for she had first to explain to the magic just what he was. Only then could she find the necessary spell. As she was not sure what he was, her mind drew circles in the song, the head of the spell chasing a tail it could not catch.

"What if he learns what you've done to him?" Hanish asked. "Do you imagine he would still love you then?" He rested a hand on Aliver's shoulder, thrummed his fingers. Aliver extended his arm as the priestess slid onto it the tuvey band—adorned with a blessing in the form of a short length of crimson ribbon. Hanish acted as an aide would, touching the band when it was in place and then smoothing the fabric of the monarch's upper sleeve. The ceremony was almost complete. All that was left was the recital of the final sanction. Corinn had a part in this, which the touch of the priestess's eyes reminded her.

Hanish made a show of stepping out of her way when she took her place beside Aliver. At a signal given by touching Aliver's hand, the two siblings began. "Hear us, Acacia, empire of the four horizons, of the tree of Akaran, of the six provinces . . ."

They spoke loudly, but as the Carmelia was far too large for everyone to hear, designated speakers took up their words and repeated them. The speech cascaded down from the dais and around the high ranks of benches like a song in the round.

"Edifus was the founder," both Akarans said, repeating words that had first been drummed into them as children working with their tutor. "You know this to be true. He was born into suffering and darkness in the Lakes, but he prevailed in a bloody war that engulfed the whole world. He met the Untrue King Tathe at Galaral and crushed his forces with the aid of Santoth Speakers. Edifus was the first in an unbroken line of twenty-one Akaran kings. . . ."

Hanish said, "Unbroken until I came around. Don't forget that. You haven't written me out of the histories already, have you?"

Corinn fumbled the words of the sanction. She tripped over them for a moment, trying to remember them and to match her timing to Aliver's. She felt him glance at her. A bead of sweat broke loose from her forehead and ran down her left temple and cheek. "Are the living con . . . We are the continuation of those who came before, Akaran all . . ."

"You probably have," Hanish said. "You're capable of anything. Two monarchs! What a strange idea, Corinn. I hope you are half as crafty as you think yourself. I really do. For the sake of our son I do."

He is nothing but a distraction, Corinn told herself. Control yourself! Divide your thoughts. Make them whole but doubled.

She did. Her lips found the words of the sanction. Her face maintained its calm. Her mind danced with the spell that would wipe this phantom Hanish from the world forever. She thought she had the substance of it. She bunched up her malice toward him into one seething ball of song. She held it in the back of her mouth, needing only a break in the sanction to release it.

Because of all these things, Corinn was as jolted as any of the others by the sound. Perhaps more so, though at first she kept on as if she had not noticed. A bang echoed across the stadium, a sound like a battering ram against a mighty door. Another.

"Oh, something is knocking," Hanish said.

Aliver stopped speaking. He turned toward the tunnel through which they had entered.

Corinn kept on speaking for a moment, but with Aliver's gaze went the turning heads of the crowd. A third boom rocked the place with a force that shook the foundations of the stadium. Something broke. She realized what the sound was. The iron gates through which she had entered had been bashed open. The rush of air was palpable from where she stood. It tore at the hats and garments of those near it. That's impossible, she thought. The gates could not be flung open. They were always locked for the ceremony. No one in her service would even think of it, and if they did it would not be possible, not as heavy and secure as they were.

The words finally fell from Corinn's lips—and the song dissolved in her mouth—as figures strode through the tunnel and into the stadium. "Take the prince away," she said. "Rhrenna, do it now."

"Not just knocking," Hanish whispered, suddenly at her ear again. "They've let themselves in."

B arad had thought that the presence of a ghost made physi-cal was to be the most disturbing thing he would witness that day. From his box below the dais he watched the figure appear at Corinn's shoulder. He nearly called out, but the fact that nobody else did stopped him. Or, not just that. Whatever sorcery Corinn had bound him with stopped him. He feared the man was an assassin, and then wondered why he feared that. Let the queen die. That would be a fine thing. Let his inabil-ity to warn her be the death of her. As ever in his life since the queen had captured him, his mind rocked like a boat atop choppy waters, first leaning one way and then the next, all the time making him sick to the stomach.

Because he could only watch, he did. Through watching, he saw. The queen could hear the words the dead man whispered in her ears. She fought not to show any sign that she acknowl-edged the phantom's sudden appearance, but to Barad's eyes it was obvious. Her jaw clenched when the man's lips moved. She shifted away from the touch he gave her elbow. Her eyes darted around, checking to see if others saw the man at whom she would not herself look. Not an assassin, then. Barad stared harder.

The man's hair was long and golden, with a few thin strips of colored leather woven into its braids. Meinish. His face looked odd beside Corinn's. His features did not show the contrast of light and dark that hers did. No touch of the sun on them. He seemed to stand in the dull light of another place entirely. He did stand in another place, Barad realized. He was dead. As soon as he had the thought, he knew it to be true. A ghost was whispering in the queen's ear. Why could he see the dead man when nobody else seemed to? His stone eyes, surely. They were works of sorcery, after all, and they were Corinn's doing. Through them, he watched as the man moved around the dais unseen, talking much of the time. More than that, Barad knew every word the man spoke. Intimate. Playful. Teasing. Even his whispers reached him. He did not follow the intricacies of the ceremony at all, just watched the queen and the ghost, hearing his one-sided conversation, wondering what was going to happen.

He had no better understanding of it when the gates to the Carmelia crashed open. He rolled his stone eyes away from the dais and watched the figures march through the tunnel and into the crowded stadium. They were not ghosts, these ones. For a moment Barad thought them monsters with elongated heads like eaters of ants, but that image faded as the light touched them. They were men, larger than normal, but men. They cast shadows and had about them a solidity that was even more tangible than the crowd who drew back in horror from them. They must have been heavier than normal men, for their feet split the stones across which they trod. Even the tattered robes they wore swung with a martial weight, as if the fabric were woven of metal and as likely to cut as a blade. They drove a wedge through the people standing on the entry causeway. The crowd cringed away from them, some pressing back so hard that those along the inner railing went toppling over onto the lower benches.

The intruders took no notice of the people at all until the guards remembered their duty. With a lieutenant shouting them into motion, they snapped into ranks and began marching toward the intruders. The front rank thrust before them a treacherous bristle of halberds. The foremost of the intruders raised their arms in unison and roared out something. The soldiers' flesh went liquid. Their clothes and armor dropped to the stones, sodden with blood. Their weapons clattered down among the filth, all of which was trodden over by the intruders' feet a second later.

Sorcerers, Barad named them. They are sorcerers.

The sorcerers turned and ascended the stairs toward the dais. General Andeson barked a command. Archers—Barad had not even known there were archers—on the ledge up beyond the dais let loose a volley of arrows. They should have fallen a hundred or so right on top of the intruders, but the sorcerers tilted their heads and blew at them. The motion was like shooing away a bothersome fly. The arrows skidded away from them. They careened through the stadium, looking suddenly like sleek, black birds, erratic fliers that impacted randomly among the crowd, puncturing chests and throats and embedding in skulls. People sprang away from the injured, sending waves of panic through the tightly packed audience.

Andeson did not repeat the order to shoot. He stood with his mouth hanging open. Aliver asked something and in answer the Marah shifted around the dais. They bunched tightly together on the stairs below the royal party, swords drawn.

The intruders climbed one flight of stairs before slowing. They paused and looked around, taking in the view from the landing. The action was so casual that the Marah held their positions. No new orders came for them. The sorcerers' gazes roamed over the assembled crowd, both the ranks above and below them, both the motion of those trying to flee and the awed stillness of most of the crowd.

Just like that, by stopping their raging forward progress, the men looked almost normal. Their faces, though mature and weatherworn, were not animal or massive or even particularly fierce. They contained two expressions at war with each other. On the surface they conveyed disdain, as if they owned all the people they surveyed and found them lacking. Beneath their condescension a terrible eagerness squirmed. That was the main thing Barad saw. Behind their features, and in their eyes, were passions at odds with the aged façades they occupied. There were twenty-two of them. Barad did the math on his lips. Twenty-two, the same number of generations as the prophecies had predicted would pass before a time of great change.

One by one they completed their survey, began slowly up the next set of stairs, and set their gazes on Corinn and Aliver.

Barad did the same. He had forgotten about her for those few moments of chaos. Corinn was there at the same spot on the dais. Prince Aaden was nowhere to be seen, but Marah were all around the queen and Aliver like living armor. Even the priestess had been bustled away as the guards closed in. She was pressed uncomfortably between a soldier and the stone pedestal behind her.

The ghost was still at Corinn's elbow, even then whispering in her ear. "Friends of your brother's or friends of yours? Late arrivals. I'm hoping it's one or the other. . . ."

Hanish. Of course it was Hanish Mein! Barad had never met him, but what other Meinish ghost would haunt the queen? Who else would say the things he was saying? Seeing that, knowing it, Barad knew as well that the number twenty-two was not random. They were still living within the same generation. Hanish had not been the change at all. This was. Whatever these had come for. That was what he was whispering in the queen's ear. By the pallor of her face, she believed him.

The priestess of Vada, aghast at the interruption, began a babbling reprimand. Several officers and a senator added their ire. Sigh Saden's wife screeched something about the ghastliness of it. Compared to them, the intruders seemed tranquil.

"Where is *The Song of Elenet*?" The voice that said this was almost too genteel to be believed. It carried to every corner of the Carmelia with a soft-spoken lilt, tinged with an accent Barad could not place. The crowd near and far fell silent. "Tell us where it is. Our time to have it is now."

"More courtly than the Tunishnevre, that's clear," Hanish said. His eyes just happened to touch Barad's. He paused, surprised to see the man staring at him. He nodded and, looking straight at him, he said, "Still, I don't like their tone."

Barad did not return his greeting, but even that was a form of communication between them. It was all he had time for.

"How does one speak to madmen?" Corinn asked. No one hearing it would have known she had just watched these men slaughter soldiers with a gesture of their arms or had turned falling arrows to flying dart birds. "I wish I knew, for surely you are madmen. You seem not to know that you are speaking to the queen of the Acacian Empire. You seem to not know that you've interrupted—"

"We know," another of the sorcerers said. He stood at the second landing now, again having paused there. His voice dripped sickly sweetness, as if he were answering the question of a toddling child. "Give us *The Song* and we will bless your reign with wizardry you have not yet even imagined."

Corinn's mouth hardened. "Madman, what name do you claim?"

"I am Nualo," the first man said. He gestured to the others.

"We are the Santoth. We are Tinhadin's chosen warriors. We are the exiled returned. We who have been imprisoned are free." And then, proudly, "You both know us. We called to you, but you would not listen."

"You can't be. The Santoth are exiled." Corinn snapped a quick glance at Aliver. "Do you know these intruders?"

The prince mouthed something—the name the man had given, Barad thought—but did not say it out loud. Turning to her, he said, "If—if this is them, they have changed."

"Are they the Santoth?" Corinn pressed.

Aliver hesitated. Was what he wanted to say at odds with what Corinn wished him to say? Or was the hesitation something else? Barad could not tell. "They were not like this before. They were . . . wise men. Peaceful men."

"We still are," another Santoth said.

"Why did you kill?" Aliver asked. "Nobody here deserved death. The Santoth abhorred killing. They wouldn't—"

"We defended ourselves," Nualo said. "That is all. It is not our fault that the Giver's tongue has curdled within us. We abhorred corruption in the song. We want it cleansed and sweet in us again." As he spoke, he unfastened the clasp that secured his cloak. He shrugged it from his shoulders and let it drop in a heap on the stones. Beneath it, he wore a breastplate, snug trousers, and thick warrior's boots. "We are just men, like you. But we have been in torment for so long. In exile. With corruption roiling in our heads. You cannot understand this."

Another of them turned as he spoke, letting his words sweep across the crowd. "When the song is corrupt, there is no joy in it. Let us have it true again, and we will serve you."

Shaking his head, Aliver said, "You are not the men I knew."

"I don't care what they were," Corinn said. "Say it simply: Are these the Santoth?"

Though she looked focused on the exchange, Barad could

sense something happening around her. He could partially see it—a blurring disturbance in the air around her. He could partially hear it—something like music almost too far in the distance for him to hear.

Staring at the one who had last spoken, Aliver said, "Yes. I see you, Dural. You are not the quiet one I met in Talay, but I can see you." He glanced at another. "And you, Abernis. Tenith. All of you. I can see you all. Nualo, I see you most of all."

"You have living eyes, then," Nualo said. "It is good that we have come, if you see us true."

Corinn gathered her answer around her like comfortable armor. She spoke impatiently, as if she would spare them only a few more words before returning to the interrupted ceremony. "No, it is not good. As Santoth you breathe by our leave. You should not be here without our permission. You were exiled. This is no place for you unless we ask for you. We do not. Go back to exile."

At the same time as she said these Acacian words, something else came out with them, woven through them. The Giver's tongue. That was what he could almost see and hear. A spell. Barad heard it writhing through the words. So, too, did the Santoth. For a moment the order seemed to have power over them. As a group, they were pushed back on their heels, off balance as if hit by a gust of wind that no one else felt. But they came back to flat on their feet fast enough.

Abernis smiled and said, "We are free from the curse. The girl released us. We will not go back."

"What girl?"

"This one's daughter." He pointed at Aliver. "Shen. An Akaran. She released us."

Barad heard Hanish make a sound low in his throat.

"Lies," Corinn said. She might have been refuting either Abernis or Hanish. "He has no daughter. You wish to trick us into truly letting you free. I don't acknowledge it. Go back to exile!"

This time, both the spoken words and the spell imbedded in them flew, propelled by anger. Barad watched it leap, not from Corinn's mouth but from her shoulders, a coiled thing that struck like a snake secured around her neck.

The Santoth flicked it away, just as they had the arrows. The spell skimmed across the air above them, transformed from something nearly invisible into writhing, wormlike shadows that splattered across portions of the crowd. Where it touched, people died. The liquid shadow cut through them like molten steel thrown against bare flesh. Barad was not sure if the others saw it as he did, but they certainly saw the ghastly result.

Panic rose again. People near the shattered doors started pushing and shoving, rushing out even as they craned their heads back to see what other horrors might come. Some in the upper tiers climbed over the back wall, even though there was nothing there but cliffs and rocks and the sea below.

"Your song is pure, Corinn, but you are not powerful," Nualo said, ignoring the confusion below him. "We are powerful, but our song is not pure. Where is *The Song of Elenet*? Tell us. Give it to us."

"If you do, we will make the world beautiful for you. All of it, for you," Tenith said.

Nualo nodded as if he had just been about to broach that topic. He hooked his thumbs through the cord at his waist. "That is so. We owe you much, Corinn. The girl released us, but you taught us much of the Giver's tongue again."

"I did not," Corinn said. This time her words were tentative. A trace of doubt trailed them.

"You sang it, did you not?" Abernis asked.

"That is my right as Tinhadin's heir."

Nualo brushed that away. "By singing it, you released it into

the world again. We had only to listen to hear. And we did listen. You are foolish, Queen Corinn. Foolish for reaching into
death. Foolish for spinning trinkets for your child. Foolish for
taking creatures already warped by unpure magic and making
them all the greater. Foolish for taking from one place and giving to another, with no understanding of balance. You have no
control over any of the things you've done. You see? Your world
needs us to correct your errors. Give us *The Song* and we will
help you."

"No."

"Give us *The Song*," another Santoth said. Several others said
the same. Then they all spoke at once. A bombardment of
entreating voices, all asking for *The Song*, all promising to serve
her. Swearing to do only her bidding, trying to explain the torment they lived in. It was too much all at once.

Corinn stopped it by asking, "What would you do with it if
you had it?"

"Whatever you wish."

Hanish said, "I don't trust that answer. Make them be more
specific. Will they destroy the world in flaming retribution?
Enslave us as punishment for—"

"Shut up!" Corinn snapped, turning to spit in the man's face.
"Be gone you fool! Let me think."

Hanish blinked his dreamy gray eyes closed. "As you wish,
my love." He bent his head and disappeared.

Those around Corinn looked at her with troubled eyes.
The charlatan, Delivegu, wrinkled his face in a manner that
made him look momentarily absurd. It was so hard for Barad to
remember that only he saw and heard Hanish.

To the Santoth, Corinn said, "Would you destroy the Auldek
in our name?"

"Of course," the sorcerers answered. "In your name, we
would."

No, don't believe them, Barad thought.

"Would you defend Tinhadin's line and protect me and accept my heir?"

"Yes," came back all twenty-two voices.

"I don't have it," Corinn said.

"You have it!" Nualo's voice boomed. Nothing about his gestures or expression changed, but in the moments he spoke it was as if there were no other sound in the world. His voice was everything. Inside Barad's ears. Inside his head. When Nualo spoke, it felt as if the beat of his heart hitched itself to the rhythm of his words. "We know it. We can feel it singing around you. We knew when you read it. We know!"

"It is not here," Corinn said, "but if you return to the south I will retrieve it."

"Do not anger me," Nualo said.

"Aliver and I will consider your request. As king and queen we will. Not with you here in violation of exile. Not with you demanding what you have no right to demand. We will treat with you fairly, but not like this."

"You lie."

"I am the queen of Acacia. If I say a thing, it's the truth. You see? I cannot lie. Now go back to exile!"

Again, the words flew tethered to magical commands.

This time, Nualo raked them out of the air with his hands, screaming as he did so. He took the stuff that was her spell and blew foulness into it and sent it ripping across the crowd. A swath of people went down, beginning not far from the queen herself. Jason, the scholar Barad had often seen tutoring Aaden, was among them. The curse splashed out in a crimson curve. The color splattered over the crowd, starting wide and thinning as it went, whipping all the way around and snapping out high on the bleachers above the royal dais. The people touched by it writhed. They clutched at themselves and reached out for others, most of whom pulled back in horror. It took Barad a moment for his eyes to understand what had happened. They had not been covered in something. The color had been revealed because they had been stripped of their skin. Flayed alive. Hundreds of them.

Nualo glared at the royal siblings with narrowed eyes. "You did that. Not I. You did that! You make us defend ourselves. You see that, don't you? We will defend ourselves. Every time. Give us *The Song* and stop this!"

Queen Corinn stared at the raw corpse that was Jason, and let her eyes follow the bloody path away from him, her face pale, her expression bleak and naked. She and those directly around her were the only ones standing still. The rest of the crowd became a shrieking, maddened mob, clawing to escape, ripping and tearing at one another.

The other Santoth moved to form a ring around Nualo. They began to sing. They built their garbled version of the song and let it loose in the air around them. Barad could not understand a word of it, but it was horrible. He hated it, and he pushed into it with his eyes. It was pain and suffering. It was hunger and rage and spite. It was venom and fire, the breath of monsters and the claws of demons, disease and rot. And there was something else. Something he could almost taste with his eyes. Something he could almost grasp. It was something in the disparity between what they claimed and what was in their sorcery. Their song was corrupted, yes. Even Barad could tell that. He did not need to understand the language to know how wrong it was, how warped and cancerous.

"If you send the song against us, we will throw it like seeds atop your people. Corrupted seeds. Are you such fools? We would give you the entire world, but you scorn us! You want us to return to exile? Why should we do that?" Nualo's voice slowed. His words gnawed their way through the spell-thick air. "We only ever did what Tinhadin asked of us."

No, Barad thought. He was certain the answer should be no. He wanted to shout it, but he had no language. . . .

"We were only ever faithful. For that we were exiled? Not again! I say it one last time. After this we will not ask again."

And then Barad had it. Language. That was what was different between Corinn's song and the Santoth's. They were not speaking the same language. Their sorcery was the night to Corinn's day. It was not a corrupted version of the same. It was fundamentally different. They spoke a different sorcerers' language, one that was by its very nature warped and horrible. They had power, yes, but nothing like what they would have if they studied the true *Song*.

"Will you give us *The Song of Elenet*?"

Another one of them said, "If you will not, we will ask the same question of your son. We will ask it of Aliver. Of Shen. We will ask until we get our answer."

She is defeated, Barad thought.

"I can't give it to you," she whispered. "It's not here."

"Where is it?"

Don't tell them! Barad shouted, but only inside himself. He could not move his tongue. Not open his mouth or push forward toward her. He desperately tried to make his body do this, but he could not.

"In Senival," she answered.

Noooo! Barad wailed. Silently. Motionless.

"At Calfa Ven."

Chapter
Thirty-seven

Delivegu had never been a soldier. He considered himself a dangerous individual, good in a brawl, quick with a knife, capable of staring down the most belligerent of drunken louts, with a sharp enough mind to outwit even an Alecian senatorial whore. He was his own man, and he rather liked things that way. What use was the discipline of the military? Taking orders; chain of command; subservience to officers; blind, meaningless courage in the face of danger? None of that suited him.

But standing near the Santoth sorcerers throughout their exchange with Corinn, jostled by the nobles around him who were bolting for the exit, he would happily have folded himself under the wing of a commanding officer. He would have run away himself, but his scrotum packed up and climbed inside him when Nualo swept Corinn's spell out across the crowd, ripping people's skin from them. And when they stood in that terrible circle, Nualo at the center demanding that Corinn give them some book, Delivegu had wanted to shout at the queen to hand it over. Whatever it was, give them the damn thing! He knew there must be some reason not to, but he just wanted them gone.

Relief, then, when she named the place. Calfa Ven. Having

been there so recently, he remembered it well. He thought for a moment of Bralyn, but only for a moment.

Nualo stared hard at the queen. "Calfa Ven?"

"You know the place, surely," Corinn responded, derision twisting around her words.

"We do."

"Then go! Leave my sight!"

Delivegu had to acknowledge it. If she had looked at him with such complete scorn, he would have withered and skulked away.

The sorcerers did not even notice. Instead, they flashed glances at one another. Nualo scowled and others scowled back, more like animals that communicated through growls and bared teeth than like men. Whatever they had said with those grimaces, they reached consensus quickly.

"No!" The voice boomed up from the entry causeway. The place was in turmoil, people still trying to flee, trampling one another, but few of them actually getting anywhere.

The one who spoke worked against this. For a moment Delivegu thought he was another Santoth. He dressed similarly, and he moved with inhuman speed. He seemed to run on top of people's shoulders and heads, light and nimble, his robes flapping behind him. "Noooo! Nualo, hear me! I can get you what you want."

Nualo just barely held in whatever foulness he was prepared to scream down on the man, letting him come, until the man stood on one of the torch pillars, near enough to be seen clearly. His features were normal, battered and aged, those of a man who had seen most of his living days already.

And who, exactly, are you, old man? Delivegu wondered.

"What, Leeka?" Nualo asked. "What knowledge have you? Speak quickly!"

"Leeka?" It was Aliver, looking more stunned than ever.

"Yes, Your Majesty," he said, bowing low. "I have been with these ones all these years. I know them well, even if they hid the truth from me. They did do that. They hid—"

"What?" Nualo roared. "Speak only to me!"

Leeka held out a moment longer. He did not speak, but he kept his eyes on the two monarchs, looking grave and mournful and strong all at once. Then he turned to the sorcerers. "My knowledge is this: you cannot kill any of Tinhadin's line. They have only to know that they are safe from death at your hands for it to be true. And now they know." He looked back at Aliver. "And they cannot—"

Whatever he was going to add he did not get to finish. The sorcerers spat fury at him. When the spell hit, it tore his body to pieces and sprayed him in chunks and splatters across a great swath of people.

"You people!" Nualo yelled. "You see what you make us do!"

Nualo swung back toward Corinn. His hand rose behind him and hurtled over his head, as if he were a hunter wielding a throwing stick. He roared as he did so, a sound that was simultaneously earsplitting and indistinct. Sharp but muffled by the echoes of time and space. Delivegu was certain that the rapidity of Nualo's throw altered as he released whatever he snapped from the ends of his fingers. Blinding speed one moment; a blurred, slow, tortured syrup of a long moment just after. Corinn's head reared back, her mouth open and speaking. And then something happened around her mouth. She turned away and fell back into her soldiers too quickly for Delivegu to see. He knew that something had been done to her. He just could not say what.

"Stupid woman," Nualo said, his features jagged and cruel and—for the first time—mirthful. "It's true that I can't kill you now that you know it, but I have not killed you, have I? I've done something better."

The next instant, Delivegu watched the Santoth bound up the staircase, driven with sudden purpose. They passed near the royal dais, bunched as it was with warriors with weapons drawn. The sorcerers took four and five steps at a time, leaped over railings, and scaled one section of wall that blocked their way. They shoved through any people trapped or fool enough not to get out of their way. Right up into the highest ranks, they went. They mounted the Carmelia's barrier wall. One by one, their cloaks flapping behind them in a manner that for some reason made Delivegu think of rats' tails, they leaped out of sight.

Delivegu did not rush to the edge to stare after them. He did not need to see them. What he imagined was vivid enough. In his mind he saw them careening down the cliffs toward the rocky beach. From there they roared through the revelers on the sand and jumped first onto skiffs pulled up on the beach, and then from them to other ships, across barges and transports and onward, using the collection of ships as one enormous bridge, hurrying them toward the mainland. Toward Calfa Ven and whatever prize awaited them there. They were gone. A brief wave of relief washed over him. He turned to catch sight of the queen, but the shove and tumult all around him was too confusing. He could not find her.

The exodus through the one open gate was a full flood now. The entire stadium drained toward it. They were mad, frenzied, and clawing over one another. Delivegu jumped away just in time as a man rolled head over heels down the stairs past him. "What, you fools? They're gone! Find your senses!" No one around him seemed willing to do that. He shouted that the sorcerers were gone and that, with calm, they could open the other exits as well. Nobody listened. Instead they shoved and cursed and scratched him as they rushed past. He got a hand on his dagger and kept it there, ready to slash out with it. He began pushing back toward the royal dais.

He reached it, but the royal party was gone. The priestess and her entourage took flight as he arrived, carrying what they could of the ceremony's accoutrements. Corinn and Aliver were down in the mass of people, although heading for a different passageway from the mob. Marah were tight around them, forming a protective human rectangle that moved with a mind of its own, following some evacuation plan, no doubt. Some plan devised just in case. Just in case what? In case some ancient sorcerers stepped out of the centuries in time to disrupt the coronation of a new king?

"They say the Marah consider all possibilities," Delivegu muttered. "Did you ever imagine this one? I think not, friends. I think not."

He watched the wedge of soldiers disappear through the exit opened for them, then slammed closed behind them. Well, he had to admit the exit was efficiently done. He wished he was with them. If he could rush there now, he might just get inside before the palace slammed shut. Within minutes the place would be locked down, bristling and stupid with fear. He stood on the deserted platform, considering diving in with the mob. But just look at them! People were being trampled and suffocated, needlessly. The thought of joining them rankled his sense of scoundrel's dignity. No, he would not be one of them, resolving himself to a long delay before he could gain his quarters again.

His eyes drew themselves to a person moving against the mob's crazed men. He was only one person in the mass of bodies. He did run above them, as Leeka had, but still stood out because he was moving against the outflow. The black man's arms lashed forward, as if he were trying to swim through the torrent of fleeing people. As frantically as he struggled, he made no progress. Indeed, as the exodus gained momentum he began to be dragged back by the surge of them.

Delivegu muttered about their sanity, but then caught himself. Insanity was driving people out of the stadium. That man was fighting against the madness. The Talayan, he thought, looked more and more familiar. Whatever the man was thinking, he had purpose the others did not.

Grabbing a passing soldier by the shoulder, Delivegu yanked him close. The young man wore a glazed expression. "Soldier? Soldier!" Delivegu smacked him and stared in his face, waiting for eye contact from him, as he used to do with his dogs as a boy. Only when he had his full attention did he continue. "Recognize me? I'm Delivegu Lemardine. I'm the queen's man. Listen to me."

The soldier could hardly have done otherwise. Delivegu was roaring in his face.

"That man. See him? The Talayan there." He stabbed the air with his finger, trying to shoot a straight line between the guard's eyes and the man's chest. "Get him. Bring him to me. He knows something. Get him, and bring him to me alive."

The soldier began sputtering excuses, but Delivegu sent him on his way with a kick to his backside. The young man went wobbly legged down the steps for a while, then carried on like a good soldier. They like their orders, don't they? Delivegu smiled and sat down to wait right there on the dais, letting his legs dangle over the edge. All right. He was feeling a bit better. Sorcerers made him queasy. Regular folk he could handle just fine. Chaotic situations . . . he preferred to think of them as opportunities.

One of the dragons, Kohl, he thought it was, flapped up over the far stadium wall, black as tar and just as glistening under the now bright sun. Another one slid along the rim for a moment before catching an updraft and lifting into full view.

Thaïs, the brown one with yellow stripes. She was rather plain looking, but Delivegu always got a thrill saying her name. Thaïs. It would be forever a sexy name to him, recalling the face of a young woman in Alecia who simply would not succumb to him throughout a long night of cunning and chivalrous advances. Why was it always the ones who eluded him that he remembered the most vividly? For that matter, why was he capable of thinking of a brown-eyed beauty from a decade ago right after meeting mad wizards who were likely going to plunge the world into chaos and darkness?

He shrugged. Anyway . . .

Two other dragons hove into view as well, long necked and angry looking.

"A bit late," Delivegu said. He jabbed a thumb over his shoulder. "They went that way, if you care." They could not, of course, hear him.

By the time the soldier returned to him, with the Talayan man in tow, the confusion had mostly passed. Soldiers were establishing some rough semblance of order. A few people, good-hearted or desperate for their loved ones, had even begun to trickle back into the Carmelia to help the injured and deal with the dead. The soldier handed the man off awkwardly, looking around at his fellows and only then seeming to question why he had taken orders from someone so obviously not an officer. Delivegu dismissed him with a shooing motion of his fingers. He turned his attention to the man.

He had seen less bedraggled men laboring as life prisoners in the Kidnaban mines. The Talayan's tunic was a thin, tattered garment hung across a wiry frame, muscles lean and taut beneath his skin. His thigh-length skirt looked to have been dragged across the ground all the way from central Talay, leaving a tattered fringe. He was coated in a layer of dust lighter in tone than his skin, with a crackly film of salt around his hairline. Most bizarrely, his right hand and wrist were completely encased in a metal cage. Delivegu considered the possibility that he had escaped imprisonment, but he had never seen anything like that gauntlet. Besides that, he knew who the man was. No criminal, he.

"You've seen some miles, Kelis of Umae," Delivegu said. "The hard way, by the looks of it."

The man looked surprised, but whether the surprise was at Delivegu knowing his name or at the fact that he was that person, Delivegu was not sure.

Kelis said, "I must see the queen."

"You'll not get near her looking as you do."

Kelis, agitated, scanned the stadium. "The queen. I thought she was here."

Delivegu caught him by the elbow as he tried to move away. "Listen! I've got sense enough to recognize you, but I doubt any Marah would see anything but a cushion to pin an arrow in." Realizing he had grabbed the arm with the steel fist of a hand, he let it go. "What happened to your hand?"

"The queen," Kelis repeated. "And Aliver, if he truly lives. And where is Leeka? He came this way before me."

"Ah, he was with you, huh?" Delivegu asked. "He's . . . around here. All over the place, really." He gestured vaguely. "Anyway, what's your message for the monarchs?"

"I'll tell the queen," the Talayan snapped.

"You'll tell me first," Delivegu said. "And then, maybe, if I say so, you'll tell the queen. You'll not get near her without me, and you'll not find anyone else to help you. You're lucky to have found me." He stopped and studied him again. "I shouldn't even waste my time with you, but I'm thinking you've had a part in all this?"

Kelis looked down.

"And that you have things to tell the queen. Things she really ought to hear?"

The Talayan nodded.

"I can probably arrange that. You'll have to start by telling me, though. Have a seat. Let's do this like reasonable men. I, by the way, am Delivegu Lemardine. The best friend you have at this moment."

Chapter
Thirty-eight

By the time Sire Dagon reached his compound in the league quarters, his clothes were so disheveled he could barely walk without tripping over portions of his flowing garments. The sole of one of his shoes flapped maddeningly, and he had lost his ceremonial skullcap. His lip was fat from having been punched by a commoner, and dark liquid soiled his front. His own vomit. Several layers of it had been squeezed out of him by more than one sight, but mostly by the glimpse he caught of the things that had writhed in and around and over Queen Corinn's face. What were they? He asked, but he did not want to know. There could be nothing good in knowing the name of such things.

He plowed through the servants waiting to greet him and went straight to his office, ignoring their exclamations of concern. He could think of nothing save the horror of what he had seen and the dread at what he had done. Never before had his timing been so disastrous. Absurdly, fantastically disastrous.

"What have we done?" he asked himself, once seated and panting in his office chair. He really was not sure. He knew *what* he had done. Yes, but not what the effects of it would be now. Nor what the Santoth had done to Corinn. Nor what they would do to the world. He could not get his mind around it, but the terror squeezing every fiber of his body told him he had to, and quickly.

"Sire?" His secretary peeked in the open door. "You're upset, I see. Should I send for Teeneth? She would want to—"

"No! This is no time for concubines, you—you . . ." No insult came readily enough, so Dagon let the sentence hang, unfinished.

"Of course, sire," the man began again, his voice simpering from the first word. "Do you need—"

Anger rose in Dagon like alcohol tossed onto a fire. He suddenly hated that this man was talking to him, distracting him, making it harder to get a grasp of his thoughts. What's more, the room was full of people! They were *his* people, but he loathed them. "Get out!" he shouted. "All of you. Spies and leeches. Out!" He tossed a paperweight at the secretary. It missed him but grazed a servant across the temple. In a flutter of motion, the servants abandoned their posts and dashed for the door. One knocked over an end table. Another caught it before it hit the floor.

"Wait! Come back."

They all hesitated, secretary and servants, unsure whom he meant.

"Send for Grau and the others," Dagon said to the secretary. "All of them. Bring them here."

Seeing the man scurry away at the task gave Dagon a moment's comfort. Yes, he needed his brothers! That was why he had no control of his emotions. He should not be without his brothers at a time like this. In the chaos of exiting the Carmelia, everyone in such a mad frenzy, Dagon had lost sight of the other leaguemen. One minute he was among them; the next some ruffian yanked the silver chain from his neck as he pushed him down to be trampled. By the time he gained his feet again—

much abused in the process—he found himself alone within a mob. He tried to put the dreadfulness of that out of his mind.

Like him, the other sires would just now be arriving back at their guest quarters. They had to meet that very night. They had to decide what to do and how to do it. Dagon knew that the arrival of the Santoth changed everything. He did not know *how* it changed everything, but that it had was a certainty. He was sure the others would see it the same way. None of them had planned for this. What he had planned for—and just executed—was something very different. And that was what made things worse!

"You fool, Grau! Your stupid plan. Your bloody compass!"

The compass. The very gift that the queen had lifted with her bare hands just a few hours ago. He found something almost sexual in the positioning of her palms as they cupped the polished gold. And Aliver. He had run his fingers over it, tracing the words of the inscription as he read them out. Dagon could barely grasp that such a beautiful piece of science and artistry had become a tool of death, but he knew it had. Those brief touches, Grau had assured him, were all it would take.

※

It had all seemed so perfect when Sire Grau first shared his scheme with him. The queen and the new king eliminated in one untraceable action. No bloodstained knife. No arrow in the breast. No assassins to employ and then, in turn, have assassinated. No. It was as simple as league chemistry was complex.

"We have a poison," Grau had said through the mist-filled air in his quarters that afternoon in Alecia.

"We have always had poisons," Dagon replied.

"Yes, but this one our chemist can paint onto whatever object we request." The old man demonstrated this with an imaginary brush. "It goes on as an invisible film. It dries there, leaving no trace to the eye or to touch. No smell at all. When they first showed me, they pointed at an apple that had been coated in the stuff. I almost picked it up despite myself, such was the illusion that nothing was there at all. If I had touched it, though, you and I would not be speaking now."

All those who handled an object thus treated died. Not immediately. Their deaths were delayed. The poison needed to work its way into their systems. From the tests the league had done—and they were nothing if not thorough with testing—those who were so poisoned died within a cycle of the moon, sometimes a little longer or shorter. The end, when it came, was swift. They would drop to sleep and not wake. They would be found glassy-eyed, their tongues green, their fingers mottled with spots. In short . . .

"They will look to have overmeasured a concoction of the mist," Sire Dagon had finished.

Grau showed his pleasure by exposing the filed points of his teeth. "Oh, the vices of royalty. We all know Leodan was an addict. Why not his children as well? The crown sits heavy, doesn't it, on a brow as delicate as Corinn's. What's most charming about this poison is that it doesn't overstay its welcome. All traces of it fade away from the treated object after the first few days. The poison—I don't know—it evaporates or something." The long-nailed fingers of his hand drew the process vaguely in the smoky air. "Anyone trying to find traces of it *after* the unfortunate death will find nothing whatsoever."

"So no fingers can be pointed at us."

"Fingers can point," Grau said, shrugging, "but that's all they'll be able to do."

"And how would we guarantee that the Akarans will touch a particular object? With all their servants and—"

"The coronation," Grau had cut in. "We will put it in their hands ourselves at the coronation."

❋

So they had. And now it was done. The siblings—and a good number of servants and any guests unfortunate enough to have handled the compass—would be dead within a month. They were walking corpses.

Dagon had been so pleased. Sitting in his box as the ceremony continued, he even began wording his condolences to young Prince Aaden. Dear Noble Lad, he had mouthed in his head, I can scarcely fathom the cruel hand fate has stricken you with. . . .

He had to stop himself remembering it. It no longer amused him that he had planned to claim to the boy that he would gladly exchange his own life if it would spare Corinn's, or that he imagined sitting with the boy as they studied the compass together, both he and the young prince touching the then harmless instrument.

No, he need not think back on that. What mattered was thinking forward.

"How have things changed?" Dagon asked himself. He did not notice that he spoke his thoughts out loud, or that most of his servants had crept back into the room and resumed the regular posts. He did not even flinch when a servant handed him a lit pipe. He just took it. He sucked on the mouthpiece, the gurgle of the water loud in the room. He held it for a long time and exhaled the greenish vapors along with his words. "We have sorcerers living in the world, that's how things have changed. The Santoth."

He inhaled again. It felt good to do so. The mist was in him now. With it came the possibility of calm. The tension that had crawled across his skin grew coy, flirtatious. He thought briefly of Teenith, his concubine, but this was no time for seeking solace in her arms. After a few more inhalations, he said, "Now, what do I know of these Santoth?"

With the mist's aid his mind picked up the question. He knew what he had seen just an hour ago. They lived. They commanded some foul magic. They killed without remorse. They had redirected Corinn's attacks to horrible effect. And they wanted something. *The Song of Elenet*. He repeated the name as he rose and, pipe in hand, shuffled to his library. His loose sole smacked the floor the entire way.

Setting his pipe on a reading table, Dagon flipped through volumes so rare that the Vadayan scholars, had they known of them, would have put down their parchment and quills and trained as assassins to get their hands on them. One by one, he tossed them on the floor behind him.

At first he was not even sure what he was looking for, but he remembered having read about the Santoth before. Just after they came out of exile and destroyed Hanish Mein's army on the Teh plains, Dagon had searched for information about them. A short-lived course of study, it was. The sorcerers had gone back into exile, seemingly just as trapped there as they ever had been. Other matters had pulled his attention away.

"Sire?" The secretary's voice was barely audible.

Dagon yanked around. How much time had passed? Measuring by the clutter on the floor it could have been hours. "Are they here? All gathered?"

"No," the man said. He stood with one foot out of the room, seeming to slide farther out as he spoke. "They are all gone. Sire Grau and Sire Peneth. Sire Flann. All their attendants."

"Gone?" Dagon let his arms droop. "Gone how?"

"They sail even as we speak, through the channel the Ishtat

kept open. I'm sorry, Sire, but I could not reach them. The Ishtat withdrew. The channel closed."

A folder slipped from Dagon's hand. "All of them are gone?"

"All of them," the secretary said. And then, stepping a little closer, "We're alone. Trapped."

Normally Dagon would have slapped the man for being over-dramatic. Instead, he cast around, found his simmering pipe, and sucked on it like a pup on his mother's tit.

❋

The dark hours of the middle of the night found Dagon still in the library, having picked himself up from the floor, and again rummaging through what volumes had not already been strewn across the stones. When he found the book it was obvious he could have done so all along, had his mind been calm enough to organize a more orderly search. It stood on a shelf among some of the oldest books. Jeflen the Red's account of the Wars of Distribution. That was what he had been looking for, even if he had not been clearheaded enough to know it.

Dagon tipped it down. He placed it in the stand on a round table, the one best situated beneath the reading lamps, and he stared at the cover. Jeflen had been Tinhadin's official chronicler. As such, his account of things was suspect, but it was the most complete single volume of the times that Dagon knew of. And it was also vivid. Dagon remembered that now. He felt it in the pit of his stomach and in his fingers, which trembled despite the mist's sedative effects. He got up, flapped across to the other table, and worshipped at the pipe until he killed it.

Opening well into Jeflen's account and flipping forward, Dagon skimmed the pages that documented the wars them-selves. His eyes stuck on descriptions of battle, on numerical equations that measured the massive death tolls of the time. It described scenes of incredible carnage, in numbers that made the Santoth's destruction of the Meins seem a minor skirmish in comparison. It was horrible, made more stunning because Dagon had images of his own to compare them to. That ribbon of red, torn flesh. It had taken him a long time to understand what he had seen. And when he had, he had vomited all down his front. This book, though, told of such things on a massive scale. Entire wars fought that way, between all-powerful sorcerers and armies that could do nothing but march forward to their ghastly deaths. The Santoth had never been defeated by any army of men. Never even close. So there was that.

Moving forward, he read of the growing friction between the king and his sorcerer knights. They each of them were ambitious, greedy men, ravenous for greater portions of the world. Were they not gods walking the earth? Did not the very words from their mouths destroy or create? According to Jeflen, Tinhadin came to believe the Santoth would soon turn against him. Against each other as well, but first against him, as he sat as king over them all. It was in reading his father's journals for guidance on how to handle them that he discovered something his father had not intended him to discover. It was there in the journal, hinted at, suggested, promised. He came to believe that he and the Santoth had learned only a portion of the Giver's tongue. The first text he acquired from the Dwellers was incomplete. It was only much later, after his father died and he began to piece together clues from his journal, that he realized there was an even more complete volume.

The Song of Elenet.

It was not, as Dagon had dimly remembered, an old epic poem. It was not a lament or a dirge or a eulogy. It was the first thief-sorcerer's manual for speaking the language of a god. Dagon had known that, come to think of it. He just had not credited it. It had never mattered. He doubted it ever existed. Doubted such a language ever existed, or Elenet to overhear it. He had doubted, really, that there had ever been a Giver.

"You believe now, don't you?" he asked himself.

Even when the Santoth proved themselves real on the Teh plains he had not truly had to face the ramifications of their existence. And when Corinn had begun to work sorcery, Dagon had thought it a nuisance peculiar to her alone. If she was removed, the nuisance would be as well. How foolish that seemed now.

He read on.

Tinhadin had gone in search of *The Song of Elenet*. Jelfen wrote at length about the epic journey Tinhadin had undergone to find it, but Dagon skipped that. What mattered was that Tinhadin had found it, studied it, and returned as a more powerful sorcerer than all the Santoth combined. The song lived in him. It coursed through him. He breathed it and sweated it. He dreamed in the language of creation and sometimes woke to find the world changed.

When Tinhadin returned to Acacia—for his search had taken him far away—his sorcerers came against him. He threw them back. He would have destroyed them, but a moment of compassion stayed him. They had been his companions from youth. Like brothers to him. Soldiers beside him for so many years. He hated their betrayal, but he did not want to sing them out of existence, as he could have. Instead, he banished them to the Far South.

The Santoth went, for they could not disobey their master. They could not stand against him, not when he was so much more a god than they. The sorcerers vented their rage on the land and up into the skies and upon any who got in their way as they moved south.

Only one nation massed to stand against them. A race of centaurs from the far south of Talay, the Anniben Dur Anniben.

These horsemen had for eons roamed rich southern grasslands that teemed with life. They were among the Giver's first creations, and they had always scorned humans, the spawn of the Betrayer, as they named Edifus. They had stayed outside the affairs of the Known World, and Tinhadin had not risked battle with them before. In his act of banishment, though, he sent his sorcerers against them.

Behind Burith-ben they ranked to face the raging sorcerers. They stood side by side in one great herd and said the Santoth could not pass into their lands. The Santoth destroyed them with fire, with worms that dropped from the sky and rolled across the plains, flattening the grasses and leaving them charred, with diseases that blistered their skin and split their hooves and ignited their hides and—

Dagon stopped reading. The words burned his eyes. It was all as horrible as he had feared. Before, if he had read descriptions like this, he would have thought them the fancies of imaginative, if twisted, minds. Now, he read them as truths that might as well have been written in the paving cement the queen had recently had spread across the streets of the lower town. The Santoth were loose in the world again, soon to have the book that would grant them even greater power. They would each of them be as strong as Tinhadin ever was, and much more twisted. How would they punish the world then? How long before they turned one against the other?

"They'll destroy us all," Dagon said. Only Corinn could possibly fight their sorcery, but she . . . Regardless of what had happened to her in the Carmelia, the clock of her life was winding down, and she didn't know it. If she didn't act quickly . . . "They'll destroy us all," he said again. Dagon heard Grau's voice: What use is going to Rapture if it all comes crashing down in a few years? He tried to laugh, but he only managed to blow air through his nose. "It is the end of Rapture."

He called for his secretary. The man stepped into the room before the sound of his voice had faded. He glanced around for a moment, looking as aghast at the state of the place, and then found Dagon with his eyes. "Sire?"

"I will visit the palace," he said. "Send a messenger to alert them. Prepare an escort. Ishtat to go as far as the royal grounds. Do it just now. I must see . . . no, not the queen. I shouldn't want to see her. Or tell her what I have to. Make it the . . . king. Aliver, I mean. I'll tell him. Arrange it."

The secretary nodded but did not set to it. He worked his nervousness with fingers, curling them over each other like spider legs. "You will have to change, Sire. Your clothing . . ."

Dagon looked down. "Yes, I'm filthy. This is not my blood. I don't know if it is blood. It's filth. It's . . ."

"We'll run a bath," the man said. "I'll get fresh clothes. We'll burn those. Do not concern yourself with them." He darted away.

Into the silence after his departure, Dagon said, "He thinks you're mad, you fool."

He ran his fingers over the crackly, yellowed pages of Jeflen's account. He flipped the pages absently, lost not in thought but in the absence of it. So much to think through, and yet he felt empty. His gaze drifted down to the pages of their own account. His eyes began to move across the words there with an interest not really matched by the mind seeing through them. Monsters. The words described monsters. Wolves, leviathans, a great worm at the black bottom of the ocean . . .

He tore his eyes away.

What am I thinking? I can't go to the queen and tell her she's dead on her feet. That would be madness. Don't make yourself a fool, Dagon.

He called his secretary back and retracted the message to the palace. Fortunately, it had not yet been sent. "Bring me parchment and a pen. Oh, and the fading ink. I'll write a note. Much better idea. And then alert all the staff—everyone essential—that we are leaving."

"Leaving, Sire?"

"Yes. We will take everything we can and . . . go."

"For how long, Sire?"

"Assume that we will not be returning at all."

End of Book Two

Book Three

The
Silent Queen

CHAPTER
THIRTY-NINE

Mena arrived back at Mein Tahalian partially snow-blind, with the tips of her fingers and toes frozen twigs, yellow patches on her nose and cheeks. Despite the protests of Perrin and the other officers, she did not go to the physician. She slept right there in the relative warmth of the stables, curled against Elya's exhausted body. Mena let attendants pull off her boots and gloves, and then ordered them to step back. When her hands and feet were free, she pressed them up against her mount's plumage. She slept like that, the two of them dead to the world and nearly dead outright. It was the best thing she could have done.

When she awoke hours later, she lay for a time without moving, knowing that any motion would stir the interest of the people watching over her. She could tell that life had tingled back into her limbs and facial skin, stimulated by that amazing healing power that Elya's feathers had. She was whole again. She would still be able to grip a sword, to run into battle. Though she very much wished that she could roll over and return to sleep, she knew she could not. Images of mornings she had lain wrapped in her sheets in the palace rose up to haunt her, as a girl, as a woman, with the heat of Melio's body just a finger's breadth away. Days spent stretched naked on her pallet in Vumu, or times she had watched the morning chase the stars from a bedroll in Talay. She hated that those moments were forever in the past. They taunted. They teased her. They would not let her go, but she could not have them back, either. They were moments of peace that seemed impossible luxuries now. Had life ever been so carefree? She did not trust that those moments had ever been as she imagined, but she wanted them so badly for those first few waking moments that she bled tears as her body healed.

And then she rose and called her officers for a briefing in which she explained what she had seen and done instead of flying to the coronation. After that, she sent several letters via messenger bird to Acacia, detailing everything she had learned from her meeting with the Auldek and everything she now planned. She wrote things, in fact, that she had not disclosed to her own captains. She asked—more openly than she ever had, more like a younger sister than ever before—for any guidance Corinn could offer.

That done, she kept moving. She did all the things she had to as she waited for a response, all the tasks and problems and duties that kept her from being too much with herself. She mustered the troops. She sent horsemen riding for all the remote, northern settlements they could safely reach, warning that war was upon them. They should evacuate for the south, if possible, or come to see out the winter in Tahalian, if they could not. With her officers, she went over battle plans and studied charts and calculated the probable toll in human lives. It was not an arithmetic she could live with, though she betrayed no sign of it. Secretly, she met alone with Haleeven and the Scav Kant, talking late into the night.

The work of each day kept her busy. Every minute she hoped to hear back from Corinn. From Aliver, for that matter! Though she could not yet really believe he lived. Part of her clung to a hope that Corinn would find some way to fix it all, a solution only her cunning mind could manage, something that would save the troops Mena had grown to love. She slept little, and when she did she often woke in the pitch-black of the Meinish night, her mind a cacophony of concerns, problems, calculations, doubts. On occasion, she started awake in the hope that Corinn was there in the room with her, or a dream-travel version of her moving in Perrin's body. But that did not happen. Nothing came back from the south. Nothing at all.

Behind it all, she chastised herself for not having done better when she spoke to the Auldek. She should have found a way to make peace with them. Instead, she had let anxious bravado snap her tongue, puff out her chest like some adolescent boy's. Because of it, they would have war. Because of it, many would die. That had always been the purpose of her mission—not so much to defeat the Auldek but to blunt their attack so that a second army led by the queen could finish them. What sort of plan was that? A desperate one. A cruel one. One with a cold, calculating efficiency that she did her best to sharpen, even while she did not, secretly, accept it as the only way.

At the last meeting she was to have with her officers before some of them went into the field, she asked them to attend her after all the other business had been concluded. The troops were again gathering inside the Calathrock, to hear their orders as a group one last time within that chamber.

"Before you go to them," she said, "I have two things to ask of you. I'm sure you have all thought much about why we were sent here. We've had even more time since coming here to Tahalian, but things will unfold quickly from now on. I think it best that we are honest about it. We are not marching to defeat the Auldek. I've seen them. We can't do that, not with the troops we have. They control the air, so we cannot surprise them or flank them or any such thing. When we fight them, it will be in the open, our cunning against their might."

Bledas, the Marah captain, began to tout the training they had put in recently.

Mena quieted him just by touching him with her eyes. "All that aside, Bledas, we don't march to defeat them. I need us all to acknowledge this. Our task is to die fighting them. To *die*. To kill as many of them as possible, and to hurt and delay them as much as we can, to fall so that our bodies trip their feet and slow them. That way, they will enter the Known World battered and frozen, weakened. It will then fall upon the next army to destroy them. If we do our work, they'll be able to, but none of us should think that we will see that victory. I want to ask two things of you. First, I ask you to decide today that you are going to die in this fight. I need each of you to do that. If you cannot, you may leave my service."

Letting this sit with them, she glanced around the room at each man's face, offering him the opportunity to respond. Talkative Edell said nothing. Bledas worked his finger into a crack in the old wooden table. Perceven's Senivalian mouth, narrow and full, pursed, accentuating the two mountain peaks of his upper lip. Mena read thought behind the gesture. Kissing life good-bye. That's what he was doing. Haleeven was a comfort to look upon. His face was solid, untroubled, as if he welcomed this conversation and thought it right. Perrin watched her with his lover's eyes. Despite herself, she had often wondered if Melio would mind if she sought solace in the soldier's arms. She would not do it, but at times she wished to.

"All right," Mena said. "Now the second thing. I want you to go before me to your troops. Tell them what I have just told you. Make them the same offer."

"Princess Mena!" Edell started. "We can't offer them—"

"I have to," Mena said. "I won't order soldiers to die. I'll lead them to it, but not command them. I've thought about this a long time, Edell. You will not change my mind. I will command an army only of willing soldiers. That's what I want for Acacia after this war. If we are to win it, we must start now. So, that's all. If you wish to leave my service, do so now. If not, go and speak to your soldiers."

She said this with all the calm resolution she could muster, and then she stood as the men filed out. She wondered that she could manage to show so little emotion on her face, and then she realized it was because she felt so little emotion. She was just saying what was true. What she believed, and had to say and to do.

❋

And yet an hour later she could not pretend, as she approached the doors behind which the entire army was gathered in the Calathrock, that her insides weren't knotted and her palms sweaty and her jaw muscles sore from being locked in a clench she was not even aware of. She was supposed to be returning with a blessing from Aliver reborn. Instead she had returned with a choice of life or death. What would she do if each and every one of them took her up on her offer to leave? She had no plan for that. No speech to change their minds. No heart to keep them against their will.

If it comes to that, she thought, the Auldek will truly witness a sight to laugh at, a lone princess with a sword, come to vanquish the lot of them all by herself.

A soldier pulled the door open for her. She stepped into the underground chamber and knew that she never had anything to fear. Not with soldiers like hers. Not with free hearts like theirs. Men who knew why they fought and did so out of their own convictions. That, she thought, is what Acacia should be. It was what it could be, and it was the reason she would not be standing all by herself before the Auldek. Not by a long shot.

※

The next day the first contingents of scouts and supply trains began the march that would prepare the way northeast along the perimeter of the Black Mountains, around them, and north into the Ice Fields, where she intended to meet the invading Auldek. Not one of her soldiers had abandoned her. They playfully shamed her for even thinking any of them might. They joked, Perrin told her, that she had been mistaken if she thought she commanded them against their will. Perhaps in the first few weeks, yes, but after that they were with her because they wanted to be. She was one of them and they would be proud to die with her. Soldier after soldier told her this, each speaking it low like a secret. Like a declaration of love. Morbid as it was, it was good, very good, to hear.

The body of the army left the steaming warmth of Mein Tahalian in a long, narrow column. They traveled mostly on foot, draped in layers of furs and woolens and oil-treated outer skins, hoods pulled tight around their faces, with glass shields to protect their eyes. They carried packs on their backs, necessary, for they did not have enough sleds or dogs to pull all their supplies. It would be slow, tortuous progress, but they had all known that.

The day never fully lightened. Instead, the sun skimmed the rim of the world, sending slanting rays of light over the land for several hours before disappearing. They traveled on in the dark, sighting on fires the scouts had prepared for them.

Mena would have marched right along beside them, but Haleeven convinced her that was a self-indulgent gesture. "The troops know you would suffer beside them, and that means you don't have to prove it. You mean more to us in the sky, Princess. That's what the men need to see."

So she had taken to the sky. On Elya, Mena soared above them, riding down the long column from end to end, marveling both at how small it was on the landscape and at how much it filled her with pride. The first week out, she flew back from the marching column to Tahalian as often as she could, knowing that any correspondence from Acacia would not easily get beyond the fortress. No bird could be trained to seek out a moving army in a hostile landscape, and any messenger sent after them from Tahalian would have to travel slowly, in pursuit of a target that was moving away from them.

Eventually, she had to give up hope of receiving any correspondence. She did not even have a bird left to send with a final message. She did write two missives, though, and left them with the villagers gathered to shelter in the fortress. When a bird did reach them from the south, they would forward her letters for her. One addressed to her sister and brother. One to her husband.

And then she left. She circled above Tahalian for a time, looking down at the scruffy, snow-covered wildness of it for what she thought was likely her last time. Strange how a place that she had once thought of as an enemy's lair had come to feel so quickly like a second home. Is all the world like that? she wondered. Perhaps, if we take the time and give our enemies a chance.

❄

One morning a week later, Gandrel requested Mena join him on a glacier-scoured hillside. As Perrin was briefing her for the day, he went as well. The hillside afforded a view of the passing army and well out toward the terrain ahead of them. The Black Mountains gnawed at the sky off to the west, but they were no obstacle to them. It was the jumble of frozen debris out on the northern horizon that was. Mena had seen it from above yesterday, but had planned on getting a better look today. The low light made the shapes mysterious, hard to make sense of. All shadow and highlight, the stuff seemed to change shape and color even as she stared at it.

"Those are slabs of sea ice," Gandrel said. He handed her his spyglass. "Beautiful stuff to look at, like green and blue glass when the light hits it right. But it's treacherous. It's been getting pushed up against the shore since Elenet threw the Giver's world into chaos. Crossing it will be miserable. Rife with fissures, crevices, and weak spots. It's always moving, see, breathing as the season changes—believe it or not. It'll be a few days of all-out scrambling, I'd say. Feet and hands, ropes, hauling and praying to the Giver. It'll be hard to camp in there. Might need to divide up at night to find decent spots. We'll lose some men. Animals, too. Only good news is that beyond it, once we're well out away from where the ice buckles against the shore, it goes smooth. Good place to have a battle, I'd say."

"There's no other way?" Perrin asked. "I never came this far north, so I don't know, but are you sure there isn't some alternative?"

"No, there's no other way. From what the Scav told me and from where Mena met them, the Auldek will come this way. Take Elya out and scout just in case, Princess, but I'm as sure as I can be."

"I don't doubt you," Mena said, lowering the spyglass.

"We could wait for them here," Perrin said. "Let them do the work of crossing the stuff."

Gandrel pursed his thick lips. Released them. "Won't be the obstacle for them that it is for us, not if they've come this far already."

Mena thought for a while. "No, we can't sit here waiting for them. We'd lose more than we'd gain. The Auldek wouldn't do it. If we do, they'll see it as a sign of cowardice. Plus they have many flying creatures to our one. Those alone could make life miserable for us." And, she thought, our men might start to think they can flee south if things go bad. I don't want them thinking that. Not yet, at least. It was an uncharitable thought, out of keeping with the brave mood of the men. She could not help having it, but she did not choose to voice it. "I'd rather we meet them boldly, all at once."

Both men seemed to accept this. Gandrel moved on. "I called you because I wanted to show you something else. Here." He motioned for her to lift the spyglass again, waited for her to squint an eye and pressed the open one against it. He adjusted its direction. "A little way before the ice begins. Just west of due north. Do you see them?"

She would not have unless he had directed her to them. And still it took a moment to see the moving figures, antlike even within the warped view of the glass. A line of people worked their way toward the ice slabs. They were not numerous.

"Who are they?" Perrin asked. "Those aren't Auldek soldiers. And they're not ours."

"No," Gandrel agreed. "They're Scav."

"What are they doing here? They want to join us? If so, somebody should tell them to wait."

"Not join us, no. That's not the Scav way." He squinted out toward them, though Mena could not imagine he could see them with his naked eye. "They've got something planned, though."

Perrin motioned for the spyglass. Looking through it, he asked, "How do we know it's not treachery against us?"

"To aid the Auldek?" Gandrel scoffed. "No chance. They hate them with every stringy muscle in their bodies. And they're not hiding. Even at this distance, they'll know exactly where we are. The Scav want us to know they're with us, but I don't imagine they'll want any official welcome. When they want to become invisible, they do. If I know them, we'll not see much of them. However, if they're going to help us, they'll follow no one's orders but their own."

Smiling, Mena said, "They sound like trouble."

"For the Auldek, let's hope. Wave to them, and wish them well, I say."

Mena happily did so.

*

They crossed the edge of the ice fields as soon as the light allowed the next morning. From ground level it was hard to measure what faced them. From above Mena could see the width of the jumble, but it was still hard to make sense of the shifting colors and shadows, the glasslike shadings and hidden crevices. It was not a territory meant for humans, a landscape that in no way acknowledged the possibility of people traversing it. Elya despised the place. She did not even like landing among it. When Mena forced her to touch down, her feet slid, skittish and unwilling to settle, her wings flapping. Mena had to resign herself to shouting her encouragement from the air.

Throughout her flights, Mena saw no sign of the Scav group at all, but on one flight north she spotted the coming army, rolling and marching, torches burning against the coming night. Their flying beasts saw her as well. Several of the winged creatures flew toward her. In response she and Elya rose high, circled away in a manner just leisurely enough to show no fear.

Of course, Mena did feel fear. For the first time in weeks she realized she had not thought of protecting Elya from all this. Hadn't she always said Elya would never see war? What happened to the resolve with which she had spoken to Corinn? She had meant it, but instead of staying true to it, she had taken

Elya into danger, far from Acacia, a world away from the Talayan grassland on which Mena had found her. What right did she have to do that?

The worst of it was that she had taken Elya away from her children. She did not even know what Elya thought of that. If she thought anything of them, she kept it hidden, no trace of what emotion she might feel in her mind. That, more than anything, made Mena believe that Elya was hiding her thoughts from her selfish mistress, she who was too afraid to face death alone. Mena thought all these things, but she did nothing to change it. This is how we are with the ones we love, she thought. Too afraid to set them free.

She hovered at the edge of the flat ice, waiting for her army to join her, watching the enemy emerge into reality. They rose out of the ice on feet and hooves and wheels, leaping into the air, winged. She whispered a prayer to the Giver, hoping that the plan she had come up with might work, might even save some of her soldiers' lives.

That evening, once the army was through the ice maze and settling in to camp, Mena called her officers to council. Inside a tent flapping and loud from the wind that had kicked up, she said this: "I thought it necessary that each soldier come here of his own free will, and that each of them face death as a foregone conclusion. I will never be able to explain how proud I am of every one of our soldiers."

"You don't have to explain it," Perrin said. "We feel it, too."

"Then you won't be surprised that I am not willing to send them all to their deaths." She let that sink in. Her eyes drifted from one face to the next. The candlelight they huddled around made them look like somber participants at some arcane ritual. It will not, she thought, be a blood sacrifice. "I've been trying hard to find a way that some of them might live while also doing what we can to hurt the Auldek. I think I have such a plan. It will require treachery, deceit. It will not be entirely honorable, certainly not in keeping with the Old Codes."

"I'm liking the sound of this," Gandrel said. His creviced face was one of the most frightening in the light, no less because he was smiling. "Never had much use for the Codes anyway, and treachery and deceit are underrated." The others laughed.

"It will also require you to trust the Scav," Mena said. This was not met with quite the same joviality. "Haleeven, explain to them what we've worked out with Kant and his people."

As the old warrior began to speak, Mena withdrew to watch the unsteady light play across the men's faces. It was a lot to ask of them, she knew. To hear the scheme from the mouth of one of the empire's recent enemies and to learn that it involved depending on a ragged people that scrounged a living out of frozen waste so far to the edge of the world that they lived on unmapped terrain. Strange, indeed, but it felt right, necessary. If they were to win this war, they would have to remake how their society worked in the process.

That might as well begin here, she thought, with us.

CHAPTER

FORTY

As they came down from the mountainous wave peaks of the Range, when they caught their first glimpse of the barrier islands of the Other Lands, and when shore birds darted out to greet them, Melio decided that he might not die on this voyage after all. It would not make sense to die now, not after getting this far, not after seeing so much, and especially not after what happened that night on the *Slipfin*. One doesn't have such moments without reason.

The night that Kartholomé called them out of the cabin into the glowing, slithering motion was the strangest Melio had ever experienced. All around them—where there had been calm water for days—shapes rose and fell and rolled, like enormous chunks of luminous, writhing, and somehow living ice. The ocean *was* these creatures. They pressed so thick around them that the boat shimmied and rocked with the pressure of their bodies brushing against the ship's hull. They were silent save the wet sounds of their motions and an occasional expulsion of salt-rich vapor from slits along their bodies.

For all the terrified beating of his heart, Melio could not move. None of them could.

"We shouldn't have spoken of them," Clytus whispered. "These are sea wolves. Be calm, lads. Calm for the moment."

"They're nothing like wolves," Melio said. They did not look as they were depicted on the mural inside, but, then again, in all the slurping, seething of their bodies, Melio could make no sense of their forms. Whitish hulks, yes. Tentacles and rippling ridges and flat, circular eyes, yes. But he had no feeling for the whole of any one of them. It just felt that the sea had been revealed for what it really was—a mass tangle of slippery, sentient life.

Geena brushed his shoulder. "I don't think you're the first to notice that."

"Stop joking," Kartholomé said. "They'll swarm us in a moment." He moved over to a pile of spears. He began untying the ropes that held them in place. Clytus, seeing what he was about, joined him. They moved on tiptoe, with stealth that Melio thought absurd considering the massive, round eyes that watched every move as they rose and fell and slid along above the railing.

Melio still did not move. It was not fear that held him immobile, though fear did pump through him with every pulse of his heart. Something else froze him and kept him staring. He could not help but notice that the creatures seemed to be caressing the *Slipfin*, searching it, learning its contours. He could not shake the feeling that the eyes paid even more attention to him than they did the men lifting weapons to hurl into them. A tentacle slipped over the railing, slid across the deck, and then withdrew. He knew what he should think. That was a probe, searching for victims. There would be another, and then another. And then they would tear the ship apart and consume them in a savage swarm. Of course they would.

Kartholomé said something and jerked at his arm. Melio looked down to find a harpoon in his hands. It was old, worn, a discard bought cheaply in Bleem. Kartholomé had spent days sharpening the blade. The iron barb of its point was deadly enough.

When Melio raised his head, he was eye to eye with one of the creatures. Its orb rose above the railing as the leviathan slipped along the ship's side, plastered by the pressure of the wolves behind it. The lid closed, a strange circular motion to it, nothing like the workings of a human eyelid.

Melio lifted the harpoon into throwing position. There was a target, if ever he saw one. He watched the vague outline of himself and his companions reflected in the eye, warped by its shape and the moisture dripping down it. Instead of sinking the harpoon into it—as he knew the others were preparing to do—he wondered just what the creature saw looking at him. He had never questioned such things when looking into the eyes of the foulthings. He had felt only their abhorrence, the awful war with life that raged within them. This eye contained none of that. This eye saw him. It knew him, and it . . .

He found his tongue just when Kartholomé pulled back his arm, harpoon high in it. "No!" he whispered. He wanted to scream it, but feared raising his voice. "No!"

Kartholomé heard him. Weapon still raised, he snapped his head toward him. His face savage with questions, impatient.

"Don't," was all Melio could say in answer. How could he begin to explain what he himself could not believe? That the creatures meant them no harm, and that they would do harm only if they were attacked? "Don't."

If he had not shared the experience that followed with the others, he would have thought it a dream, a vision conjured up from the eerie stillness. He bent over and set his harpoon on the deck. Stepping forward, he raised a hand and held it near the creature's slick skin. Its eye watched him, completely still now. He touched just beside it. The eyelid opened and shut with its bizarre circular motion, but that was all.

A moment later Melio turned as Geena let out a gasp. A tentacle had stretched across the deck and touched her leg. It drew back and rose, mobile and lithe and completely inhuman. It touched Geena's hand. She responded by raising it, and the tentacle moved with her.

"By the Giver," Clytus said, "what is this?"

Melio did not know, but he knew not to fight it. He knew he had discovered something, and that it was huge, that it was important. In this was something that nobody living knew. If he did not make a misstep, he might someday find out what.

And then it ended. The creatures pulled back their tentacles and slipped away from the ship. They became seething motion again. The *Slipfin* rocked as they released their grip on it. The bell high on the mainmast tinkled, first with the swaying, and then to announce the wind that filled the sails a moment later. Melio glanced up, just for a moment. When he turned his eyes to the sea, it was water once more, not a creature to be seen. What's more, it was water in waving, rippling motion, waves building right before his eyes.

"Come on, then," Clytus said, his captain's eyes already scanning the swells the wind pushed them toward. "There's a range of waves between us and Spratling. Let's ride it."

They were blown right into them and spent the next two days rising and falling over peaks incredible to behold. Clytus and Kartholomé took turns at the wheel. Together they steered them through. Coming out on the other side was a relief only shortly. For there on the horizon were new peaks, of stone this time. Also, they caught glimpses of ship's sails. No time to rest or be pleased with themselves. They were in as much danger now as ever.

Kartholomé's systematic rummaging through the captain's library paid off, at least in bits and pieces of knowledge that they put to use. Their vessel had clearly not been assigned to the

Other Lands, but there was still information about the place to be found. They studied a chart detailing the barrier islands, at length, determining the best route to the mainland, which the map called Ushen Brae. Melio had never heard the name before, but he liked the feel of it on his tongue. Of course, he thought, the lands would have their own name. They weren't "the other" to themselves, were they?

To avoid the Angerwall—which Kartholomé was not sure how to navigate—they decided to sail north around the islands, then come down along the coast. The islands up that way appeared to be less developed than the ones to the south. They would put ashore north of Avina and travel toward the city on foot. The plan was simple, if incomplete. While avoiding the league and Ishtat patrols, they would search for the quota slaves. With their help they would learn what they could about Dariel's fate.

Before they had seen any trace of the quota slaves, however, they came upon a bounty of league vessels. The galleys appeared behind them as they cut between a large island that the map named Eigg and the small skerries that trickled away to the north. First three ships, and then two more in the distance. They stretched many stories tall but had a sleek appearance different from the bulky brigs, with more sails than Melio could count. From their viewpoint on the *Slipfin*, the league ships looked carnivorous sawing through the waves behind them.

"What are they up to?" Kartholomé said. There was a tenor of dread in his voice similar to when he called them out to see the sea wolves. "I know those ships. Never set eyes on them, but I'd heard talk they were building them. Five war galleys. That's them, all right. They can each carry eight hundred soldiers, not counting the ship's crew. There's tons of storage capacity in them, but they're fast, with keels that barracudas would envy. Steel reinforced, with turrets, baskets for crossbowmen." He looked at Melio. "If the league sent these here, it's because they mean to take over the place."

Clytus kept the *Slipfin* moving north at a steady clip, and the others did their best to stay visible on deck and up in the rigging. If anyone on the galleys studied them through a spyglass, it would be obvious the boat was undercrewed. Kartholomé ran up a flag that he said was a greeting to the other boats, acknowledging them but also indicating that they were on a mission they could not interrupt.

The ruse may not even have been necessary. Once the first galleys rounded a long isthmus at the tip of Eigg, they looped around and lowered some sails. They were, apparently, going to anchor there. "Yeah, they're all pulling in," Kartholomé confirmed some time later, one eye stuck to a spyglass as the *Slipfin* sailed away from them. "Should we—I don't know—spy on them? Circle back after dark and get a better look?"

"No," Clytus said. "We didn't come to get caught by the league. Let's get out of here."

They caught sight of Avina at dusk. The city's stone walls pressed right up against the sea, the sky behind them scalloped with crimson-highlighted clouds. They sailed northwest along the coast, not daring to get too close to the city in the *Slipfin*. The land changed to stretches of agricultural fields. By dark they were past those, skimming cautiously along a maze of wooded coves and inlets. Pulling in to one of these, they spent the night at anchor. The next morning they left the *Slipfin* in as secluded a cove as they could, disembarked, and set out toward Avina on foot.

❋

It was Kartholomé who first realized what the plants were. They had walked through them from late in the afternoon through the better part of the night. Rows and rows of low shrubs, with long green leaves that silvered in the moonlight. They stretched on for miles. Though the fields were deserted as far as they could tell, it had not been long since they had been tended. They were uniform in height, recently pruned, and the ground between them weeded. The plants bore no fruit, but they did have fuzzy clusters of flowers that gathered around a long, somewhat phallic protuberance. Melio acknowledged that it might have been his imagination, but they seemed to grow longer after nightfall, as if they were growing aroused at the sight of the moon's round glow.

Kartholomé, walking at the front of their line, paused when Geena called for a break to relieve herself. As she went off, he stood, fingering one of the plant's erections. Melio felt inclined to make a joke, but he could not think of one fast enough.

"These are thread fields," Kartholomé said. He pulled his hand away, stared at it a moment, and then wiped his palm on his trouser legs. He looked at the others. "Mist. This is where they grow the mist. Can't you smell it?"

The moment he said it, Melio knew he was right. He *could* smell it. A pungent scent, musky and almost animal. It had been there when they entered the fields, but it grew thicker in the air as he breathed. The realization somehow made the ranks upon ranks of shrubs look suddenly ominous. He could almost see the scent, the flowers' pollen released to their lover the night, wafting on the air, searching for victims.

Clytus called, "Geena! Let's get out of these fields before we all see visions."

She did not answer. They all cast around. She was nowhere to be seen. There was nothing around them but miles of the plants.

"Geena? You squatting in the bushes? Mind you don't touch them too much."

The silence was solid around them.

"Geena, what are you up to, girl?"

When the first figure rose, there was no possibility that it was Geena. He appeared a few feet past Kartholomé. A tall, tusked being lit by the moon, wide shouldered and, for a horrible second, not even human. He looked gray skinned, but that may have been a trick of the light. Before the shout of alarm was all the way out of Melio's mouth, the thing dashed toward Kartholomé. It struck him hard on the head with some sort of club, shoved his limp body into the bushes, and came on toward Melio.

Out of the corners of his eyes, he saw other figures emerging from the plants, converging on them in a sudden, savage attack. Clytus cried out in pain. Melio did not get to turn around to see. The tusked thing was before him, his bent arm raised to strike again. Melio dodged under it. He brushed past the man, under his arm, slamming a fist into a rock-hard abdomen as he did. He spun fast, drawing his dagger. He hoped to kick his attacker's knee from the back and send him sprawling, but the man was already facing him. Melio went for him, knife flashing as he struck. The man slipped beneath his attack, kicked one of his legs from under him, and swept back around on him. He accomplished exactly the move Melio had intended. Melio had just enough time to acknowledge that the horned man was fast for someone so bulky and to appreciate that he had misjudged him. Then the man's weight fell on him. Hard. The impact blew all the air out of him. Melio dropped his knife as his face smashed into the dirt. He might even have lost consciousness for a second. The next thing he knew, a fist yanked his head back by the hair and his own blade pricked his throat.

CHAPTER
FORTY-ONE

Not for the first time, Aliver broke away from the council's ongoing session—with its various arms and offshoots, crowded with dignitaries and senators and military personnel. All of them baffled and accusatory, fearful and more angry for their fear, self-righteous because of it, speaking in sureties because they were unsure of anything. And mourning. Some of them were in mourning. So much noise. Reports had come in about the Santoth raging their way across Prios, across to Danos on the mainland, and inland toward Calfa Ven. Panic spread throughout the empire faster than messenger birds could fly. Aliver needed to get away, just for a while, to clear his head and, of course, to check on his sister.

He stopped before he reached her quarters. He stood in the open air, in the courtyard between Corinn's wing and Aaden's. He knew what he would find if he entered. Her inner doors would still be shut, her guards and maids still huddled nervously outside. She had pushed them all out herself, locked herself in. She even beat back her own guards, with a masked fury, they said, that blackened one Marah's eye and scratched channels in another's chin. As much as Aliver wanted to believe she would be there, welcoming him, he knew nothing would have changed. Not yet. If it had, he would have known already.

The night was noisy with muted life, with whispers and coughs and the hushed conversations of servants without work to turn to and nobles without the promised festivities. No one slept. Every torch and lamp burned. The very stones of the palace seemed uneasy, confused, shifting. These were meant to be days of rejoicing, of pipes and drums and fiddles through to the dawn, of food and wine, hope and pride. There was none of that.

Aliver stood, his head tilted and his eyes drifting over a mud-brown sky. There was not a star to be seen behind the oppressive murk. That seemed as clear a sign as any that what he remembered of the day had really happened. No stars. Mud in the sky. Misery in a stadium filled for rejoicing. And Corinn . . .

Aliver had a vision of what he had seen as Corinn's head snapped back, but he could not credit it. It was a mistake of his eyes in a blurred moment of confusion. Something had happened to her, but surely not what he thought he had seen. Corinn had hidden her face. She fell down among her guards and twisted away, clawing at her mouth. Aliver had seen her from the back. It looked, in one instant, as if she had pulled her hands away from her face and screamed. Her neck and shoulders shuddered with the effort, but there was no sound. Such a scream as her body appeared to be issuing would have been vast, rending. But there was nothing, so it could not have been a scream.

He had been jostled away from her as the Marah pressed them to flee. Next time he saw Corinn she was on her feet, with the shawl that had been over her shoulders wrapped tightly around her face, clamped in place with a white-knuckled hand. Her eyes caught his a moment. In them he saw the scream he could not hear. It was more terrible for the utter silence of it.

All this because the Santoth had appeared from nowhere.

They had stepped out of a void, out of memories that he had within him but that he had not explored since his return to life. Why had he not asked about them? He had never said a word about them. For that matter, he had not questioned Corinn's use of sorcery. Again, he knew that he had always known—really known—that so much was wrong about what she was doing. Yet he had never said a word against her. Because of it, these sorcerers were free in the world, bent on things he could not yet imagine.

"Why didn't I know?" Aliver asked himself. "Why didn't I know it before?"

A passing maid started at his voice. She stood stock-still with bed linens pinned to her chest. Aliver turned away, waving that he had not meant to address her. He walked down the shallow stairs to the upper courtyard, across it to one of the railings. It was the same one at which he had stood beside Aaden the previous morning. To the east the indication of the coming sun just barely lightened the horizon, faint, only nibbling at the dark, slug-thick sky. The sea of boats still surrounded the island, alight with torches and small fires. It looked like a living thing, something breathing but pocked with flaming fumaroles. Would it have looked any different if the events of the day had not turned so foul? Or was it just the eyes of the watcher that gave character to the world?

Aliver realized he had not asked a question like that in some time. It felt familiar, though. The melancholia of it. The leaning toward doubt. Yes, his mind felt more his own than it had since he had awoken to life again. There was a burden in this, but truth as well. For the first time a thought rose in him. He could not grasp it yet. He just knew it was there. He could smell it. Could hunt it.

His thoughts turned to the Santoth again. The others had wanted to know why he had never warned them of their evil.

He had lived with them, hadn't he? Didn't he know them better than anyone living? There was accusation in the questions, an edge that grew as the night's hours curled toward dawn. He could not answer them. What they said was true. Deep in the desert south, he had shared a strange half-stone existence with them. Thoughts had flown silently between them, messages floated on a spectral tide that ebbed and flowed with a rhythm outside the world's turning time. He had been so sure that the Santoth were what they said they were. That they held themselves in exile for the good of the world. They had helped so much, in so many ways, during his war with Hanish Mein. They had destroyed Maeander's forces in one afternoon. Could that all really have been in service to a goal of greater evil?

Of course it was. He understood it now. The thinness of the lies they had told were so transparent now. He had always felt it but just not known he felt it. He had wanted to believe them, so he had. Their language may have been corrupted by time, but that was not what made it foul. It had always been foul. Time had just eaten away at it further.

He grew up believing Tinhadin was a noble man. Tinhadin, he who built a mighty empire and then banished the sorcerers who would, in their greed, have destroyed it. He who gave up sorcery himself, because he knew it was too chaotic a tool for humans to wield. That, in Aliver's youth, had been the truth of the past.

And then it wasn't. The Santoth said the truth was something else. Tinhadin had banished them not as an act of good for the world, but because he wanted the world all to himself. He was like an eagle chick, the strongest of the brood, that kicked his siblings out of the nest so that only he could live and thrive and grow. The Santoth, faithful servants, had been betrayed. That's what they told him, speaking right into his mind, making the thought his. If brought back into the world, they would again be his faithful servants. How badly Aliver had wanted to believe that.

How clever of them to discover that he wanted to believe it. For that's what they had done. In his communion with them they had explored every memory of his life, every desire and ambition and fear. He knew that at the time but thought it a good thing. He wanted them to know him. How good it felt to be completely understood, without judgment, he had thought. Now, he was certain that they had used what they learned to shape the lies they told him.

Something else troubled him, though as yet he only nibbled the edges of it. In defeating Maeander on the plains of Teh, the Santoth had saved the Acacian Empire. They had kept the Akaran line in power. What if the true reason they did that was so that they might have still other chances of a future generation of Akarans freeing them? That's what they had said: a child of his freed them, and freed them into a world still ruled by Akarans, a world in which *The Song of Elenet* had not been entirely forgotten. A child of his? A child of his . . . Somehow, he knew that to be right. There was a child of his, but where in the world was this child?

"Your Majesty?" A Marah guard approached nervously. He snapped to attention as soon as Aliver turned to look at him.

"What is it?"

"We received a message from Sire Dagon. His messenger said a Marah should bring it to you and that you had to read it without delay."

"Is that what he said?" It was more a statement than a question. Aliver raised a hand and the soldier slipped the folded square of paper into it. He unfolded the paper beneath the light of one of the oil torches set atop a pillar. The note was written in brown ink, the letters a little tremulous, like those shaped by the hand of an elderly person.

Prince Aliver,

This is quite awkward to write. I hope you'll forgive my lack of grace. I have to inform you that you and the people of the empire have been killed.

He stopped, exhaled through his nose, and then read over the lines again to make sure he had not misread.

I have to inform you that you and the people of the empire have been killed. Poisoned. I need not explain to you how I know this, but it is a certainty. I am, in part, responsible for it. Both you and the queen are quite dead. It's only a matter of weeks until your bodies realize it.

As for the people of empire, they have been addicted once again to a distillation of the mist that will kill them when they are denied it. It's in the wine, you see. The very vintage they have been toasting you with. This was the queen's doing, though she did not know the deadliness of it. If ever you hated and despised the league and thought us treacherous villains, well, then let that ire rise in you again now. Accept that what I say is the truth.

Why do I tell you this? I thought it important that you know, and I've come to believe that your death is unfortunately timed. I believe that you are a decent man, and that you and the queen want, in your peculiar way, what is best for the empire. I acknowledge that it may only be the queen who can save the Known World from destruction. That is why I've made this admission.

Aliver, please encourage Corinn to be quick in finding a way to defeat the Santoth. Neither of you have much time. If you love your nation, be quick. If you are, it's possible the league will continue to supply the vintage, thereby keeping the empire alive.

Yours fondly,
Sire Dagon of the League of Vessels

✳

Aliver still sat there on the balcony some time later. The coming day was clearly visible in the east now. The oil in the torch beside him had burned low. The flame wavered now, sending up more black smoke than before. He had been watching the changing appearance of the ships in the harbor. As the light increased, the patchwork of vessels looked more and more like a ragged scab on the skin of the ocean. It was smaller than it had been the day before, fraying around the edges.

People are leaving, he thought. I cannot blame them for that.

He opened the note again. Thinking he had it backward, he flipped the page over. There was nothing there. He held it to the uncertain light of the torch. He could just make out the tracing of the words that had once been there. Even as he watched, they faded further. Right before his eyes, they vanished completely.

For a long moment Aliver entertained the possibility that the paper had always been blank. He had imagined the words he read. Wouldn't that make more sense than that they were true? As soon as he raised his eyes and saw the sun had just broken from the horizon, he let that idea go. Fading ink. That's all it was. The words may have disappeared, but they had been chiseled in his consciousness and remained with him.

"Uncle?"

Turning, he saw Aaden. The boy had stopped some distance away, near a torch that lit him in rippling orange waves. Shadows—his maids, guards—hung behind him. "Is it all destroyed?" His voice edged away from its usual calm. He captured the pitch of it, but it was tremulous, ready to turn.

"No, Aaden," Aliver began, but he could not find the words to continue.

The boy moved forward, slowly. "I had a dream once. I told Mother. I said, 'I had a dream that the world ended.' She said that was silly. That it could never happen. But I knew it could. Do you know why? Because in the dream she died. She died, and the moment she did, the world did as well. I was left, but the world had ended. That's what I meant, but she didn't ask me.

She never asked me about it. Maybe she never will now. Is that the truth?"

Aliver closed the space between them. He gripped Aaden to his chest, thankful that the boy had not witnessed most of what happened in the Carmelia, and relieved that he would never be able to read the words of Dagon's note. Those were things to be grateful for. Corinn had whispered a spell that spirited him away at the first sign of trouble. One moment he was there; the next he was gone. "She loves you," he said. "She loves you. She took care of you first. That's the truth."

Aaden shifted against him, trying to break the embrace. Aliver kept his arms knotted, wanting to hold him like that forever, to keep him a child forever, to protect him from a world that constantly made a mockery of those who struggled to live in it. If somebody had just held him forever when he was a child. Just held him and never let life twist on . . .

"Where's Mother?" the boy asked, his words muffled. "What happened to her? Nobody will tell me. It's something bad. I know that already. I know what happened with the Santoth. I know they killed people and want *The Song of Elenet*. I heard that already, but nobody will tell me anything about my mother."

"You'll see her soon."

"I want to see her now!" Aaden writhed. He shoved his uncle back, slapping his arms and chest in sudden fury. Aliver took the blows without flinching, trying to soothe him by being there to be scratched and hit. He spoke nonsense, just sounds, just meaningless words. He tried to bring Aaden back into his embrace.

Tearing away, Aaden glared at his uncle. He had never looked more savage. His features twisted with anger, wrung through with the fatigue of fear. "She's dead!" he shouted, spittle flying from his mouth. "She's dead and you won't tell me!"

"No. No, she's not. I swear it."

"Why won't you let me see her, then?"

"You will, Aaden. Give her time. I'm not stopping you. She just needs a little time to herself." Ah, but that sounded daft! Insulting. Simple. It sounded just as stupid as the things adults had said to him after his father had been stabbed by Thasren Mein. Just as vapid and untrue. "Something happened," he said quickly. "I don't know what, Aaden. She fought with the Santoth and something happened. She is here, though, in the palace. She walked here on her own two feet. She went to her quarters. That's all I know, Aaden. Please, let's wait together. Let's find out more together."

The boy kept the glare on his features, turning it down just slightly. "Stop squeezing me like I'm a baby. Treat me like an adult. Like a prince."

Aliver let his arms drop. Like a prince . . .

"Will you stop?"

"Yes."

Aaden studied him a moment, skeptical, and then said, his tone growing surer, "If she's not dead, stop acting like she is. Whatever has happened, she'll fix it."

He did not say it, but Aliver thought certainty such as that marked the boy as yet a child. He had never found certainty to be a hallmark of wisdom. Let him have certainty, though. For as long as he can carry it. "If anyone can," he said, "your mother can."

Rhrenna emerged out of the shadows. Though she wore the same garment as at the coronation, the sparkle that had danced around her was gone. She looked tense, frail, as if her sharp features might shatter if there was too loud a noise. Aliver remembered the infatuation he felt for her before the ceremony. Where had that gone?

"I'm sorry," she said. "I'm sorry to disturb you."

"Does Corinn want us?"

"No, she still hasn't spoken to anyone. She won't answer my knocking. I don't know what she's doing in there." She glanced at Aaden. Hesitated. "I'm sure, though, that she's fine. She was strong enough to push out her guards."

"Don't comfort me like a child," Aaden said. "I am a prince!"

Rhrenna wilted a little but kept her chin high and spoke. "I know that, Your Highness."

"I know that bad things happen," Aaden said. He looked sulky for a moment, and then added, "I know that much is expected of me. Mother told me so. I know it already. Stop, both of you, acting like I'm weak. Make me strong, instead."

"I will," Aliver said, "if you help me. Rhrenna, what have you come for, then?"

"The priestess of Vada sent a messenger. They consider the ceremony to be complete. You are the king."

"I don't feel like one," was Aliver's flat response. "Anything else?"

"The council wants you back. More senators have joined them. They say there is still more to discuss."

"I've talked with them enough. They're just going in circles. Let them talk to themselves if they want to keep at it. I'll wait for Corinn. We go no further without her. Tell them that."

Rhrenna nodded. "They're asking after her. What would you have me tell them?"

"To wait. Tell them I'm working with her. Tell them to look toward tomorrow and plan what they can. We still have the Auldek to consider. Remind them not to forget that."

Aaden cleared his throat. "You can't put everything off until tomorrow. Whatever is wrong with Mother, we must do what we have to."

"Aaden, I won't sleep for a moment until I know just what's happened and just what we're to do about it. I'm not putting anything off. Talking in circles with the likes of Sigh Saden will not help anything."

"What will? Let's figure that out and let's do it."

Aliver wanted to hug the boy again. "All right, Aaden. I think we should find out more about who the Santoth really are. If we're going to fight them, we must know them. I thought I did, but I was wrong."

"And we should have friends with us," Aaden said. "Ones we trust. Ones we can listen to, and who will listen to us. Don't you think that's important?"

"Yes."

"Mother didn't. She didn't trust people." He paused, challenging him to disagree. "She didn't even trust you. Do you know that? She brought you back to life, but . . . not all the way. I could tell from the first day I saw you. It's because I know her magic. She's always shown me things. She brought you partly but not all the way. Do you know what I mean?"

The thought that had been shapeless inside Aliver took a step closer. "I'm beginning to," he said. Just having the boy name the thing he had always suspected helped him. Yes, his mind had been his own but constrained, molded in ways he had not recognized. It still was, he knew. "Let's go to the library. I want books around me. It will be our sanctuary."

"Do you promise me that you will be truthful to me? About everything?"

Looking at the boy's determined face, he heard the words come out of his mouth. "Of course. I'll tell you everything." He realized that they escaped him so easily because the spells that bound his thoughts did not recognize them as truth. Such lies are so easy because they are so completely the fabric of life. Yet now, though he said the same words that a liar would, he meant them. He said, "Everything I think I will do, Aaden. Everything that is true I will say, because nothing matters now but the truth." And if my lips hesitate, I will trick them. I will say such truths as can only be mistaken for lies. "How about that?"

"That's how it should always have been," Aaden said.

CHAPTER
FORTY-TWO

The day of his departure arrived so quickly that Dariel felt he had barely rested at all. He had not gotten to visit any but the nearest other village, though over the week he was in residence—on display, really—at the elder's village, a steady stream of pilgrims from the lose network of settlements stopped by to gawk at him. He had not learned a fraction of the things he had hoped to, but he did not imagine that another week or two or a month or more would be enough. The People's history was too tied with Auldek history, with the Lothan Aklun, and with aspects of his own kind that he was yet coming to grips with.

"I don't like leaving you unprotected here," Dariel said to Yoen as they strolled toward the edge of the village and the path that the others had already taken down to the river, a tributary of the Sheeven Lek and the fastest method for returning to the coast. "I know the Auldek are gone, but I wouldn't put it past the league to cause you grief."

"I don't think so. The league is going to cause *you* grief. That I believe." Yoen touched him on the shoulder. With a gentle pressure, he turned him toward the path to the river. "We will be fine, Dariel. Nobody will attack us here. We have nothing to fear but the cathounds and fréketes and . . . dou worms." He clicked his tongue. "Truly, Dariel, do not think us weak. Just do what you have to for the People. That's what matters. Go now. You have many miles to travel, and you must be quick if you're going to be there for the gathering the clans have called. It is your only chance to address them all at once. Don't be late!"

"Are you coming down to see us off?"

"Of course. Now go." He caught sight of something that drew his gaze. "Anira is there, waiting for you. Go to her."

She was. She appeared from around a wall, her sack slung over her shoulder. Dariel acknowledged her with a wave and started toward her. A few steps on, he turned to say something to Yoen, a non-parting that promised a proper one down by the water.

The old man had turned away already. He did not hurry. His back was not unkind. Yet Dariel felt emotion pour into him, a sadness like he had not felt since he was a boy.

The crafts they were to travel in were oval boats about twenty feet long, deep in the hull, with good storage space within. A frame of the white-bark trees crosshatched their centers, strapped in place by cords that wrapped down around the hull. The lines of the hulls had an ornate elegance. The keel was a gentle ridge from which smooth, organic contours flowed upward. Something about them reminded him of something, though Dariel had never seen a craft even remotely like them. It was only when he saw one overturned on the rocky beach that it occurred to him what they reminded him of.

"They look like turtle shells."

"Very observant," Anira quipped. She hefted a bundle and moved to load it into one of the boats.

Dariel did the same, double-time to keep up with her. "You don't mean . . . that they are turtle shells, do you?"

Anira tossed the bundle in and turned to face him, showing

him the full measure of her amusement. "What did Birké tell you about the Sheeven Lek?"

"Not to swim in it."

"Why did he do that?"

"Because other things swim in it. Bigger things."

"Exactly. Things like turtles."

"There are turtles this size in the river?"

"No." She tossed a leg over the gunwale and began to shove and wiggle the new bundle into place. "They're no more. Died out a long time ago." Before Dariel could expel the relieved breath he had at the ready, she added, "The scale leeches killed them off."

Scale leeches? Dariel thought it sounded like something she had made up on the spot. He said so, much to her amusement.

❈

They floated free of the riverbank by midmorning. Yoen did not come down to see them off, but it seemed as if the rest of the village did. They crowded on the beach, down onto rock outcroppings. Some of the children tossed flowers to them from a tree house high on a branch overhanging the water. He barely knew these people, but watching and waving to them, touching the rune on his forehead, he felt a weight of responsibility to them. He had agreed to help them, to try to secure this land for them to prosper peacefully in. He had agreed to try to become the hero they all hoped for. It felt right that he did so, but as he floated toward it, he feared he faced an enormous task that he still did not understand the shape of.

The seven shells were to carry the party of five back toward the coast from which they had so recently come and to take with them the young and hardy from the nearby villages, any who could help in the fight they all knew awaited them. Each boat went captained by a rower skilled at handling it. Perched on the thwart, the rowers moved the crafts with a quiet efficiency of effort. In the quiet pools of still water—of which there were many the first day—they drove the vessels forward by leaning their backs into timed pulls on the oars. When the current picked up, when pressed through rocks or down steeper sections, they turned the boats with a touch of an oar on the green water or spun them like tops with a cross-cross pull. There was an elegance to it that Dariel admired from where he lay among the bundles of supplies.

In the afternoon he took a turn at the oars. He had rowed skiffs on enough occasions to be confident, and he figured the study he had made of it from a few hours' watching had taught him what he needed to know. Wrong. He spent all his efforts on just moving the absurdly long oars. Just landing the blades in the water the right way proved difficult, and the right way never stayed right for long because the vessel was always in motion. When he lifted one oar to reposition it, he invariably pulled against the other, swinging the boat one direction or another. When he tried to correct on the other side, he found the water as immovable as setting concrete. If he managed to press down on an oar—thereby lifting its other end out of the water—the freed end flailed in the air with a life of its own.

"Anticipate, Dariel," Birké called. "Anticipate. Feel the momentum starting to—"

"Would you shut up?" Dariel shouted, jerking his oars in frustration.

Listening to the jibes the others tossed around him, Dariel wondered if he needed to harden his demeanor. He imagined returning the taunts with fierce expressions of disapproval. Or sharp reprimands. Invocations of his name. No, not his name. Of his status as the Rhuin Fá! That's what mattered here. Just look at his forehead! Of course, he got that status because of who he was in the Known World, not in this one. He had not done much worthy of a title yet. He still had no idea just how he would lead the People.

Other than that he could speak languages he had never learned, he could not say he felt any different having part of Nâ Gâmen's true soul in him. He knew that he was heading toward a clan gathering in which he would be presented to all the people of Avina, but nobody asked him what he would say or told him what he should say. Perhaps because of that, he had dreams each night in which he held long conversations with different people. In them, he listened to them, learned about their fears and worries. In them, he argued against the league's vision for Ushen Brae. He encouraged the People to unite, to find strength together, and to reject the league's enticements. Maybe, if he dreamed about it long enough, he would find the right words.

By the time he gave up on rowing, his face was wet with sweat and his shirt plastered to his chest. The other shells were far ahead, a few out of sight around a distant river bend. He nearly voiced a suspicion that the basic dynamics covering rowing were somehow reversed in Ushen Brae, but he knew a lame excuse when he heard one. He kept it to himself. He handed the oars back to Harlen, the captain of his shell, who had watched the entire show while chewing on a twig of sweet branch. He took the oars without comment and made up the time Dariel had lost in a few minutes, humming as he rowed.

When this brought new bursts of taunts from the distant shells, Dariel flipped his frustration over and gave in to it himself. Why not? He could not change who he was to them, even if he was mostly a walking invitation for mirth. He did not even want to, when it came down to it. If he was to be the hero these people needed, it could not be shaped by pretense. It had to flow from who he was, who they were, and what they could do together. As odd as it was to feel himself a constant source of humor, there was something he actually liked about it. A playfulness. A camaraderie that felt close to what he had experienced as an Outer Isle brigand.

"That can't be a bad thing," he said. He decided to build on it, to let it grow.

The rowing. The dou worms and tales of frékete nightmares, gagging on plee-berry juice, tripping in the whirling chaos that was Bashar and Cashen at play on the riverbank each evening: these were not the only things that kept the group laughing at the Rhuin Fá's expense during the trip downstream.

*

On the first day they confronted whitewater, he fell out of the boat at the very top of a long rapid. He had stood to take in the view, and a sudden rocking of the vessel threw him off balance. The minute he hit the water, he knew he was going to swim the entire long tumult of the rapid. He did. Had there not been a calm pool at the end of it, he might have drowned. Instead, he was able to crawl up on a rock in the slack current, panting, exhausted, fearful to the last moment that some creature was going to clamp its jaws down on his ankle and pull him back in.

He was the butt of jokes for the rest of that day. Did he really dislike the shells that much? Would he swim all the rapids, or was it only the largest ones that tempted him? Just what was it that he had dropped that made him so keen to go river diving? By the time he reached camp that evening, he was sure he had heard every variation of the earnest, perplexed questions his companions could possibly think of. He hadn't. They were still at it the next morning. Was it true that the little people with gills lived in tiny houses along the river bottom . . . ?

One section of the canyon was so narrow and the gradient so steep that the shells ran a gauntlet of whitewater rapids. Dariel sprawled atop the supplies and clung to the web of ropes that secured them as Harlen made the shell do things that defied reason.

Near the end of the torrent, a flume of water collided with a solid stone wall at a sudden turn in the river. It created a raging maw of a whirlpool that Dariel was certain would gnaw them to death and then spit them out in pieces. He screamed the madness of it when Harlen steered the shell right down the flume, catching the water feeding into the upstream edge of the whirlpool. The shell rode upon the pillow of water, plastered vertically along the stone. Instead of dropping down into the whitewater just below them and being devoured, the craft rode the pillow of frothing water. It skimmed along above the growling mouth of the whirlpool, to be deposited on the other side of it, downstream. The maneuver seemed so improbable that Dariel turned to share his amazement with Harlen. But the other man just smiled and stuffed a mint leaf in his mouth, as if there had been nothing remotely dramatic about the moment.

At least he could say he had not squealed at any point during the rapids. The same could not be said of the first time he saw the slick side of a scale-leech. He did not actually notice when it happened, for the writhing in the water all around the shells drew all his attention. Long, thick eel-like things slithered beneath them, bumping against the shell and almost tipping Dariel in. Their heads, when he saw one gnawing along the rim of the shell, were entirely mouth, teeth, and sucking lips that were instantly the most horrible sight Dariel ever recalled having seen.

The others jumped into motion. The rowers took up oars and went to work. Passengers stayed low. Harlen shouted for Dariel to draw the river knife sheathed on the wooden rowing frame. Dariel twisted one wrist painfully in the rigging ropes. He had no intention of falling into the water now. Clutching the weapon with his free hand, the prince snapped his head from side to side each time one of the creatures appeared. Awkwardly off balance because of the rhythmic surging of the rowing, he fought to see past Bashar and Cashen, who darted around him, barking madly. He stabbed several of the leeches. They squirmed away all the faster when cut.

"That's . . . the only problem . . . with the shells," Harlen said, panting hard as he pulled. "The scale leeches . . . remember how tasty . . . their old owners . . . were."

When the creatures finally left off their thrashing, Harlen explained that they lived in territorial groups. They had only to row through their territory to gain a reprieve before they passed into another group's region, and then the same again. Despite the real danger of them, after that first encounter it was his squeal that the group most focused on, not the creatures themselves. He was not at all sure he had made any alarmed sound at all, and would not accept Birké's effeminate imitation as accurate, but it was no use protesting.

Nor could he get any traction out of pointing out that Tam and Anira both took unintentional underwater excursions. Nor that two shells flipped over during the voyage. Nor that one of the young men passed too close to a flowering plant that made him break out in hives that, with his wolfish shivith spots, made him look truly bizarre. Nor that a couple, unfortunate in the spot they chose for their clandestine lovemaking, sprouted full-body rashes caused by the weeds they had bedded down in. None of that carried the humor of the frightened squeal Dariel doubted had ever escaped him.

Through it all Dariel came to laugh more easily at himself, with others, at the bizarreness of the world, and with a joy of discovery that shoved aside the burden of responsibility every now and then. He knew even as the days passed that the things he saw along the river would be lasting memories in his mind ever after. And he knew that the time spent with that small company would, someday, be just as precious to him as his days at Palishdock and sailing the Outer Isles.

So he laughed his way down the Sheeven Lek to the coast. He kept it up right until the river split into myriad channels of its delta. They floated through water growing brackish, patrolled by armored crabs, and leaping with prawns. They landed at a point not far from where he had watched the soul vessel go up in flames. They pulled the shells well up the bank, and stripped down their supplies for overland travel, and flipped them over. They hiked into the undulating ridgeline of sand dunes that hid the ocean. Reaching one of the heights, Birké, who was in the lead, stopped and crouched down. He motioned that there was something to see. Dariel sprinted with the others. He dropped flat on the sand as the wind coming over the peak mussed his hair and smacked blood into his cheeks. He saw then what Birké had seen.

Out there past the breakers, which curled in long, massive waves, stretched a rough sea dotted with vessels. League brigs, fast clippers, several of the sleek soul vessels. There went his enemy. Against them, his war was about to resume.

CHAPTER
FORTY-THREE

Corinn stared.

Eaters, she thought. That's what they were. Flesh eaters. Little monsters with teeth ringed around a circular mouth. They had flown as fast as angry hornets when they attacked her, propelled on an inundation of song. A malignant spell cast from Nualo's mouth to hers. They ate through Corinn's flesh for as long as the curse that gave them life rang in the air. Several frantic moments in which they swarmed her lower face. Their chewing and writhing had been such a loud garble, frantic and horrible, that for those moments they were her entire world.

By the time she wrapped her face in her shawl to hide it from others in the Carmelia, the eaters had already completed their work. They died inside her flesh. There they remained. She could feel them. She ran her fingers over the segmented ridges of their bodies. They were part of her, dead husks that she could feel half submerged in her tissue, their corpses hued the same chestnut brown as her skin.

Staring at her reflection in her dressing table mirror, she could see them. She sat there, straight-backed on the stool, looking into the glass as she had a hundred thousand times before. The room was still. True silence. Empty. She had made everyone leave, even the servants who would normally have plastered themselves invisible and forgotten against the walls and behind drapes. She was alone. The long, thin sliver of a knife rested within arm's reach on the dresser, but she only had eyes for the mirror.

What looked back at her this time was impossible to look at. And yet she did. If she could have screamed she would have. She would have given in to panic and ripped her fear into the world with shrieks. But she couldn't. One thing she would never again be able to do was scream. The fact of it was more horrible still, enough so that she could only stare, stunned to a place on the other side of terror.

The eaters had not consumed her flesh. They had processed it. They had curdled its substance. They swallowed it in from one end and expelled it out the other, turning her flesh into a thick paste that congealed in such a manner that where her mouth had been there was no mouth. Tough, doughy-looking flesh covered her lips, making her lower face a stretch of mottled skin. All this in a few frantic seconds. And there it was.

She would never be able to eat or drink again. She knew this, but she also knew that it did not matter. She would not die from hunger or thirst. She could feel it. Hunger was something she would not face again. She would waste away, yes, but it would happen very slowly. The Santoth wanted her alive until they got what they wanted. It would be an unbearable wait.

She ran her fingers over her damaged flesh. There. That was it. She could not speak. She could not say a word of explanation to anyone. She could not even hide behind a veil and issue orders. She could not use the song. It was in her head, just as before. It hummed and thrummed and banged against the sides of consciousness, but she could do nothing about it. Without a mouth to speak it, all her knowledge was useless. It raged like a cyclone confined to the dimensions of her skull. Just like that, with one malignant spell, Nualo had trapped all her weapons inside her.

You are hideous, she thought. There was something freeing in acknowledging it. It was a proclamation she could almost wrap around herself and be encased within, her funereal shawl. It was a tempting notion. Silent death. Leaving all this. You are hideous, best to turn inward and cease to be. How could you have been so stupid? You stupid bitch. Stupid, ugly, fool of a—

"Don't say those things." Hanish appeared behind her. He stood at her shoulder, studying her reflection. Corinn's eyes snapped to him. He was so close. Solid. Just there behind her, looking too much like a living man. "They're not true."

She felt the weight of his hand on her shoulder. This ghost version of him had never touched her. She had thought he could not, but she felt the weight of his four fingers, his thumb moving in a circle. For a moment she was glad of him, didn't hate him, didn't want him gone. The moment did not last. What could he offer her that was more soothing than death?

Leave me, she ordered.

"No, I won't," Hanish said.

Leave me.

Hanish shook his head. "I can't. Banish me if you can, but I don't think you can do that. You are stuck with me. And I with you."

Leave me.

After a time, Hanish said, "Corinn, have you forgotten that you imagined this before? In your dreams you did. You knew this would happen. You just didn't understand your own vision. Do you remember?"

She had not until he asked, and then she did. It came back as a set of images leering at her through a haze of forgotten dreams. For a time she had lived through the same nightmare over and over again. It began with Aliver returning to life. Just as she wanted. Just as she later sang him into reality. With joy at all the fine things this meant, she had dashed through the halls of the palace. That was how she came to find him, the figure with his back turned to her. All the joy vanished. The man turned . . .

"And it was I," Hanish said.

Yes, it had been he. The same beautiful man, lean and golden haired, with his dreamer's eyes. He had worn a black thalba, snug around the torso that she had so loved to wrap herself around. He wore the same now. But then, in the dream, his mouth had been sewn shut on her orders. Needle and dark thread through the lips she had kissed, pinching the soft tissue. She had placed a mass of jagged fishhooks in his mouth before sewing it shut, so that he would swallow them and be shredded from the inside.

"You wanted me to suffer. I remember it now. It's your dream, but I remember it. And the worst part . . ." He stopped, pulling back from it.

The worst part, Corinn acknowledged, *was that I changed my mind. I tried to run to you to undo it, but then you were not you. You were our son.*

"I became Aaden." He smiled. "Dreams are frustrating devils, aren't they?"

How could she have forgotten that? It was not even so long ago that this dream had tormented her. Just a few months back. Did she forget because she had set in motion the things that would make this version of that dream a reality? She had woken Aliver. And Aaden, he had slept and been awoken as well. And before all that, she had killed her lover's Tunishnevre ancestors with blood from her palm, and then she had ordered him killed as well.

Corinn placed her hand over the dagger.

"No, not that," Hanish said, reaching forward and pinning her hand down on top of the weapon. "You don't get off as easily as that. You killed me, and I'm still here with you. Death is not the balm it seems right now. I swear it."

What do you want? Are you here to gloat?

"No."

To relish this?

"No."

You want to humiliate me. Look at me, then! Stare. Get your eyes full of me and then leave!

"I'm here because I love you," Hanish said. "No one has ever been more beautiful. This thing that was done to you does not change that. It just makes it even more obvious."

Corinn yanked her hand from his grip. She spun around on him, blade out before her in threat, hating him, wanting to cut him down again, for real this time.

"You can't cut me, Corinn," Hanish said, so sadly it looked like he wished she could.

No, she thought, but I can do this . . . She lifted the knife and raked the blade across the mutated flesh that had been her mouth, screaming as she did so. Silently, inside her mind, she screamed. And cut.

※

Later. Some hour in the deep dark of the night, Corinn lay on the floor with her head in Hanish's lap, her hand touching her mouth, hiding it. The knife was on the floor a little distance away, under the edge of her bed, where it had fallen when she did. Despite the force with which she cut, the blade had done nothing but slide across her skin. For a moment she thought she felt the dead worms writhe, but that was all. No searing pain. No bloody slit to yell through. No death. Nothing changed.

When she could not carve herself a new mouth, she had tried to turn the knife elsewhere, to cut her wrists or to find the artery in her neck or to sink the blade to the hilt in her abdomen. Hanish prevented each attempt. She fought against him, but he was stronger, faster. He toyed with her, even turning their whirling struggle into a playful Maseret, humming a tune that he kept time to, as if that dance of death had ever been performed to music. "What would a servant think if she saw Corinn at this crazy dance?" he asked. They would see only her, knife in hand, swirling in choreography they could not fathom.

That was before she gave up. She let the knife drop, and herself, and came to rest partially on the smooth, cool stones of her room, partially on the lap of her dead lover. Crying.

She wanted to move her head. The wetness from her tears pressed against her face, but so did the warmth of his skin. True, living warmth. She was sure of it, even though she doubted it each time she felt the pulse beat against her temple. Was that Hanish or herself? His life, or hers?

His voice measured the passing of time for her. He talked. She did not listen to everything he said. She faded in and out as other thoughts tried to carry her away. He kept on, and at some point she realized she had been listening to him talk his way through his life. That was good, to hear about him instead of her. He claimed to have loved his boyhood. It had been a time of such promise. His father and brothers alive, so much to do, what dreams they had. The future gleamed with righteous promise, everyone he loved intact around him. Back then, he had yet to come under the service of the Tunishnevre. "I was innocent, and hungry for war. I was a boy, like Aaden. That changed, though."

He told of the time just before his manhood rites when he had danced a Maseret with Maeander. He was eleven, his brother just a little younger. It was the last time Hanish would ever perform the duel without it being to the death. They fought before the veterans in the Calathrock, a great honor accorded both of them, but mostly for him as his father's firstborn and chosen. What he remembered about it was that he realized during the dance that Maeander was better than he—faster and stronger and more focused. He pressed Hanish to the edge of his ability and stopped there. He nicked Hanish's nostril, yes, leaving a small scar for all the rest of his days, but he did not embarrass him, as he could have.

"I don't think anyone knew," Hanish said, "not even my father. I left there wondering why I had been born first. Maeander was more a Meinish warrior than I ever was. Thasren knew it. That's why he did what he did, to secure his name in another way."

He paused a moment and they both listened as someone moved about one of the adjoining rooms, making noise enough, Corinn knew, to remind her that the living world went on outside her room. She did not need to be reminded.

"Do you know what I did? That night I stole into his room and woke him from sleep with a knife to his back. I made him swear to never betray me. I made him swear on pain of death. He did swear, and he never betrayed me. In the years we had together, he was my strongest ally. Part of me always expected a knife in the back from him, but he stayed true. I wish I had thanked him for that. I couldn't say it to him, though. I could not say, 'Brother, I know that you consider killing me every day and taking over in my place. Thank you for not doing it.' I wish I could have. Now, in death, honesty like that seems such an obvious good. In life it's not as clear, but that's only because in life you always think you have more time. You always believe that things that don't matter do matter."

He stroked Corinn's hair, drew it back from her face with his fingers. "Another thing I wish is that I hadn't put that blade to his back that night. What if I didn't need to? What if he would never have betrayed me of his own accord? I can't know, not after I'd told him I would rather kill him than have him best me. There," Hanish said, raising his voice a little, "you've had my confession. More than one. I could go on, but my tales are of the dead. It's the living that matter. Are you ready to discuss the living?"

Corinn thought of Jason. She had killed Jason. The spell that ripped the flesh from his body began in her mouth. Jason, who had never been anything but loyal. Jason, who had taught her to read, to know the map of the world. Jason, who had made her recite the names of Acacia's monarchs from Edifus onward. Jason, whom she had set on the fool's errand of creating a horse lore for a people who had never truly had such a lore. Jason, who was going to write the mythology of her winged riders . . . He was dead, as were so many others. All from a spell that began at her lips.

No, Corinn thought, *tell me more things about the dead.*

And so he did. He talked on.

❊

The light had changed enough to foretell the coming dawn when Hanish said, "It's time."

Corinn sat at her dressing table again, staring at herself.

Hanish stood behind her, both his hands resting on her shoulders now. "I know it's not enough time, but it's all we have. There are people waiting for you. People you love."

Aaden, Corinn thought.

"Yes. He needs you to go to him."

I can't.

"Of course you can. You must. He's your son. Think of it as if you were he. Would you rather see your mother alive—no matter the curse set upon her—than be kept from her?"

The knock on the door was gentle, as it had been every hour of the long night. As she had done on each previous occasion, Corinn ignored it. She did not even turn her head. Hanish did, though. "They want you," he whispered.

She shook her head.

Whoever it was moved away after a moment.

"Aaden wants you."

Look at what he'll see. She drew her fingers across her not-mouth, elegant, gracefully for a few seconds, before she snapped her hand closed. *I'm repellent.*

"If this had happened to your mother, would you find her repellent? You saw your mother in death. You saw the bones of her dying hands and knew that they were yours. Remember that? Can you imagine not having that memory and not knowing that about yourself? What if she had forbidden you from sitting with her in her final days?"

That silenced her excuses. How did he know about that? Her mother's hands; her hands. The same. The memory of that had always haunted her. No, she could not imagine having lived without that knowledge. As sad a memory as it was, nothing else had made it as clear to her who she was. Her mother's daughter.

It's not the same, Corinn thought. *My mother fell ill. A sickness took her. She had no part in creating it. This, though . . . I brought on.*

She paused there, waiting. For what? For Hanish to refute that statement. For him to say it was not her fault, that she was blameless. A victim. She wanted all those things, but Hanish did not offer them. She knew he would not, and that if he had, he would be lying. The curse that was her face and the horror that was the Santoth free in the world were part of the song she had been singing. The moment she felt Nualo's spell burrow into her flesh she knew it. The spell itself. She recognized it. It was a part of the music that swirled inside her head. It was as akin to her as her hand had been to her mother's.

I brought The Song *back, and with it came evil.*

Hanish leaned down, his gray eyes meeting her reflection's gaze. "Tell him that. It is a bitter lesson, but it's the one you have to tell. He will need to hear it, and only you can explain it.

There is a way to speak to him. Corinn, there is. And not just to him. You have to speak to everyone, to Aliver and Mena, to the world."

I can't.

"You can. Listen, believe me on this. You have to be stronger now than you ever were before. And you were strong before, love. You were. I know that better than anyone." He tried a smile, but it slipped away almost before it had started. "I would not have loved you so much if you hadn't been. Nor would I have died as I did. Remember who you became when I betrayed you. You didn't fold in on yourself. You fought. You struck. You out-maneuvered a world of ambitious men who wanted things from you. You can do that again. And even more. In the days that we have left, you must become the queen you were destined to be. Not the queen you envisioned, but the queen you are fated to become. The two things are never the same. Trust me on that as well. You won't get another chance. That's all there is to it."

Her eyes brimmed with moisture. She twisted away and rose. Hanish moved with her toward the center of the room, where she stopped, unsure where she meant to go. *I thought . . . I thought that I would meet the Auldek. Before my gathered army I would fly out to face them. My people would watch as I flew on Po, singing, hurl-ing down spells that would destroy them all. I was going to save Acacia. It was to be legend. It would have been . . . magnificent.*

"Yes, it would've been that," Hanish said.

Now I've failed them.

"You'll have to find some other way to be magnificent. You have a choice to make. You can take this curse that you've received and you can give it life. You can let it eat at you until it destroys you, and all you love and hate with you at the same time. That outcome is within your power. I hope you turn from it. There is another way, the way that acknowledges that you have a boy to be a mother to. You have siblings to be a sister to.

You have a nation that needs leadership, and you have a band of sorcerers to deal with."

Why are you doing this?

This time the smile formed and held. "I told you already," Hanish said. "It's the same as I said on the day you had me killed. I love you too much to ever leave you. I am a ghost, but I don't haunt a place. I haunt a person. You, Corinn. You see, I also have a different destiny than I imagined. It wasn't an accident that I came back. I didn't just slip in randomly on the spell you brought Aliver back with. I had never left you, Corinn. I'd been haunting you, watching you, loving you. You didn't know it, but from the day I died I've been with you."

CHAPTER
FORTY-FOUR

It's finally come to it, Rialus thought. He stood atop an Auldek station in a buffeting wind, taking in the view south toward Mena's army. In the dwindling light the Acacians were visible as a stain, a dark slash across the pale expanse of snow. War. Another war. For the second time in my life I'm helping an enemy invade my own country.

He hated the words but could not shake them out of his head. He believed more fervently than ever that he was not a traitor. None of it was as it seemed. He loved the Known World and all its people! In his dreams he replayed his recent exchange with Princess Mena again and again. In his dreaming version he leaped across the few strides that had separated them. He joined her and rebelled against the Auldek. He flew up into the heavens on her dragon's back, snug behind the princess, so elated that he crashed into consciousness on the swell of it.

If he could dream that, there had to be the possibility of truth in it. His dream self did not know it was only a dream self. Was not the point of such imaginings to prove that he was, somewhere inside himself, the man who could act like that? He could feel the pride and euphoria of decisive, righteous action for once in his life. Of course he could. It was not too late. He still believed that the Giver rewarded his worthies. The fact that his waking hours contradicted that truth frustrated him more than he could bear. It was not a new feeling, but he was getting very, very tired of it.

He climbed down from the station after only a few minutes, already feeling his fingers and toes stiffening. As ever, he was absurdly bundled in layers of fur. No warmer for it, though. Howlk had joked that furs only kept a living body warm because of the heat within it. "Perhaps you are dead already," he had said, poking him, "just a shell of a man who doesn't know it yet."

Though Rialus climbed down with all the slow caution he could, his feet slipped off the rungs several times. On the lower landing he fell flat on his backside. At least the station was not moving. It had stopped the evening before at the first sighting of the Acacian force. Rialus knew that the Auldek had wanted to reach solid ground before meeting the Acacians, but they did not seem too troubled to be out in frozen arctic sea. The ice was so thick and constant it might as well have been stone. It did not creak beneath the weight of the stations.

The Acacian force had pushed their camp forward early the next day, staking out ground a couple miles from the jumbled shoreline. The battle would commence the next day. Because of it, Rialus scurried across the frozen ground between the steaming stations and spent several hours sitting beside Devoth during his war council with the other chieftains. Rialus was there to answer any last-minute questions about Acacian tactics. He had long since given up explaining that he did not really know anything about military matters. When pressed on details, he sat dumbly. He refused to answer, despite the chuffs about the ears and the threats directed at him.

It did not matter anymore. The chieftains were more intent on figuring out their positions in the line of battle than anything else. The Lvin took the center front, of course—the honor of the spearpoint, which Menteus Nemré had won for them in such bloody fashion back in Avina. The Kulish Kra got the left flank for some ancestral reason that Rialus could not fathom. The Antok, it seemed, won the right flank based on the toss of a handful of colorful bone dice. Millwa, the Antok chieftain, grinned his pleasure. The rest squabbled for positions behind them.

Rialus sat through it all, miserable, his head pounding. He might as well have been surrounded by a mob of jostling children. Did none of them understand that they were arguing over which of them was lucky enough to get them and their slaves killed first? It was almost like they did not know what the morrow really held for them. Yes, they would overrun Mena's forces. How could they not, when each of the Auldek had lives to spare imbedded in him or her? But it would still be a horror of pain and slaughter, and the divine children had only their one life to risk.

Just when Rialus thought the meeting might be drawing to a close, Skahill, the head of the Anet clan, offered to trade positions with the Antoks, arguing that the dice toss was not strong enough to override their seniority. He made some argument about their performance in a footrace they had held on a stony beach earlier in the invasion. Rialus wanted to smack him. Instead, Rialus took off his inner gloves and pinched a mist pellet in his fingers. Nobody took any notice. He stuffed it up his nostril with his thumb and inhaled. The first time he had seen Howlk do this he had been horrified. Now he was quite used to it. The ball disintegrated almost immediately, and the euphoria of the mist came fast afterward. Rialus closed his eyes and tried to relax.

Remembering what Sabeer had confessed to him, he realized that the Auldek did not personally remember the wars they had fought in more than a hundred years ago. They may have done battle themselves, but their knowledge of the events would be no more real to them than things they read in books. The actions they attributed to themselves would be like those of characters in the old tales.

How do they even know their own records are accurate? he wondered. Acacian histories were full of rubbish. He opened one eye and scanned the faces gathered around the table. You sad people. You don't even know who you are anymore.

When the meeting ended, Howlk steered Rialus into the frigid dark with an arm clamped over his shoulder, following Sabeer. Rialus did not protest. Within a few minutes he was stripping off again inside the station that the Lvin used for martial exercises. It was as hot as a steam room. Despite the cold outside, Rialus was sweaty from the moment he entered. He tried to cling to the mist's sedative effects, but doing so just pushed him further away from the mild bliss he had managed during the meeting.

"Rialus, I'm going to show you our secrets," Sabeer said. "Let me hear your opinion. Come."

She stood in the center of a sparring ring marked out on the floor, a small gathering of Auldek and sublime motion around her. She held one of the curving Auldek swords and stepped deliberately through a choreographed routine of strikes, parries, and footwork. At first Rialus thought she was wearing a black training suit of some sort. It clung as snug as leather shrunk to fit her contours, with a patterning to it something like fish scales. As ever, Sabeer wore it with a deadly sensual grace.

"Devoth doesn't like it that you've decided to shut your mouth to us," she said. "I don't either. Perhaps you are having pangs of doubt now. Perhaps you're dreaming that your princess will defeat us. For your own sake, you should forget such hopes. She has no chance against us."

When Howlk took up a sword and slashed at the back of her leg, Rialus thought he had finally gone mad from his lust for her. The strike was hard and fast. Rialus expected it to take her leg off at the thigh and send her sprawling, blood spurting horribly. He went instantly light-headed. A cry of "No!" escaped his lips.

Instead, Sabeer spun on Howlk and came back at him in a playful attack. The sword had done no damage at all. They carried on for a time, Sabeer obviously letting Howlk strike her. She even tossed her sword to Menteus Nemré, who stood watching, and went at Howlk with a sudden barrage of kicks and punches. She blocked his sword strikes with her forearms, and she kicked his blade free with a sudden roundhouse kick. The move was lightning fast, the first that Howlk responded to with true surprise.

The two of them were all grins as they turned to Rialus. "Our battle skin, Rialus," Sabeer said, raising her arms and twisting to display her suit. "You see, in this I will be very hard to kill. They won't be able to chop off an arm or a leg. Believe me, that's something we worry about. The souls inside us can do nothing about a missing limb." She paused a moment, looking as if she were wistfully disappointed in the souls for not being more diligent in their service to her. "But I won't lose any. The amusing thing is that the princess and her soldiers won't even know we're wearing it. It's against the skin, as you see. I'll have all my clothing on over it. For this battle, at least. Down in Acacia in the warmth of spring I'll fight just like this. It'll be a sight, won't it?"

"It's . . . armor?" Rialus asked, unable to twin the concept with the way the fabric showed the curve of Sabeer's hips and the contours of her muscles.

"Of a sort. It's flexible, but it can't be cut. It even absorbs the impact of a blow. You may come away bruised, but that's better than limbless. The records say that Lothan Aklun bestowed it on us so that we would have a harder time killing each other off. It worked." She lit up with an idea. "Do you want to try to cut me?"

He didn't, but she would not leave off the idea until he had tried several times with an Auldek dagger. It was as she described. He could not cut her. When he tried to stab her square in the sculpted abdomen, he did no more than twist his wrist. She went back on her heels, but that might have been in amusement as much as from the force of his thrust.

"Has Princess Mena anything like this?"

Rialus shook his head. The mist's effects were long gone. Fatigue and depression seeped up inside him again. "No, nothing like it."

"Did she really fight an eagle god? What was its name?"

"Maeben," Rialus murmured, hoping she did not ask him to retell the tale yet again.

She folded her arms and stood beside him, close enough to touch him with her hip. They watched Howlk work through some technique with Menteus Nemré. "All the things you have told me about her," she mused, "I almost don't want to kill her. Perhaps I won't. Not straightaway, at least. I'll cut her legs out from under her. We'll stop the bleeding somehow and then she and I can talk."

"If you're going to cut anything off, you should start with her sword arm," Rialus said. He regretted saying it immediately.

Sabeer grinned and ran a finger up his arm. "There, Rialus, you're talking again. Good. It's proof that you love me. You *think* you want me dead and buried. I see it in your eyes. But you're not only eyes, are you? Other parts of you like me very much."

She pretended to reach for his groin. She let him squirm away. "Have you decided where you want to live yet?"

This was one of Sabeer's favorite topics. Through the many long nights of the trip she had made Rialus detail every locale in the Known World that he could remember. When he grew bored, she had always pressed him to think about where *he* would want to live once the war was over and he was allowed to live a life of leisure. He had placed himself in a cliffside villa in Manil. He had walked the estates of Bocoum, or lived in a stacked tower surrounded by the teeming life of Alecia. He had taken in the view from Calfa Ven. He had imagined a rustic lodge somewhere in Talay, from which he could watch the sun set into the grasslands and sip cool beverages with his feet up, served for all the rest of his days by a staff composed entirely of brown-skinned women.

He had even, to his surprise, found himself thinking of Cathgergen. He could not understand why he had been so unhappy there. The idea of being cocooned from the cold, locked inside an immobile fortress of stone far away from the world's machinations seemed a sort of bliss. Back then, he had compromised nothing. He was just himself, Rialus, a governor with very little actual work to do. He had not yet become a traitor to the realm two times over, a pawn for Maeander Mein, a joke in Hanish's eyes, slave to the Numrek, now a guide for the Auldek. What a journey his life had been. So full of improbable twists and turns. Would that he wasn't knotted in the center of it all now, trapped and being dragged forward to a resolution that, no matter what Sabeer claimed, could only be another type of disgrace for him.

He answered Sabeer's question. "No, I haven't decided where to live yet." He thought, I haven't decided *if* I want to live yet.

This tendency toward morbidity was new to Rialus. He

had always valued his life highly. Increasingly, he mused on just giving up. That thought brought him back to Gurta. It seemed important that she and the child he had never met mourn him, but he was no longer sure they would. Gurta could know nothing of his fate at this point. When she found out, it seemed to him, she would reject him out of hand. A traitor. How could he ever have thought she would take him back after he arrived as the mascot of an invading army? Her temperament would never allow her to see beyond appearances. He could describe his heroic dreams all he wanted. *But what did you do?* she would ask. *But what did you do?* To have her back, he would have to do something to deserve her.

Rialus had just decided that he had stood around long enough to be able to depart when the first explosion shook the station. He thought for a moment that the vehicle was starting to move again, but that was not it. It did not move forward at all, just boomed and then trembled. It reminded him of an earthquake he had once experienced in Aos. Everyone stopped.

As the stillness stretched, Rialus could almost believe that they had all imagined the sensation. Then another boom came, more distinct this time, followed by shouts and the bellowing of some animals and the long, low groan that was a warning horn sounding.

The room erupted with motion. The Auldek and the sublime motion grabbed garments, tossed one another weapons, and then careened down the stairs and out into the night.

Sabeer pulled up just before descending. "Rialus, come!"

The night smacked him as he stumbled into it, still tugging his outer coat on. The scene that greeted him was utter confusion. Shapes darted around him, nearly knocking him from his feet. An antok roared by, the thick chain that was supposed to bind it skittering across the ice. The sky glowed a strange yellow. When the top of a station a little distance away exploded into flames, Rialus wondered why. There were several such fires blazing up into the night. How such an accident could occur in not one, but two, three—boom!—four different places. It couldn't, could it?

"We're being attacked," he concluded.

Sabeer yanked him into motion. They ran between two stations and along a line of frantic oxen, all the creatures pulling at the ropes that bound them, kicking and biting one another. Rialus thought he heard the clash of steel off in one direction, but he could not be sure. They came around a sledge piled high with supplies and stepped into the heat and glare of one station. The entire structure was aflame. It crackled and combusted, seemed to breathe air in and then roar it back out like the embodiment of some fire god. Figures ran around, lit by the blaze, trying to organize some way to fight it.

Devoth shouted orders, pointing and gesturing, half giving directions and half dancing through fits of rage. "My amulet! Bring it to me!" he shouted.

His frékete mount, Bitten, seemed just as angry as he was. He clawed the ice, shooting weary glances at the fire. His wings cast evil shadows, the veins in them glowing red when they caught the firelight.

Right through all this, a snow lioness trotted, a corpse dangling from her jaws. The cat seemed at ease amid the chaos, strolling almost. Sabeer pulled Rialus after it. The body's hands and feet dragged on the ice. He was not Auldek. That was obvious, but it was not until the lion dropped the body at Devoth's stomping feet that Rialus got close enough to see more. Devoth gripped him by the shoulder and pressed him closer, kicking others back so that light from the fire illuminated him. "Who is this? Who is this!" he snarled, beastlike himself in his rage.

On his hands and knees—with the lioness and her bloody jaws just inches away—Rialus peered at the man. He was a

stranger. His face was pale, with lean features scarred by frostbite.

"Who is he?" Devoth asked. "Answer me!"

"I do-don't . . ." Rialus pulled off a mitten, reached out with
trembling fingers and drew the man's stringy golden hair back
behind his ear. There was a tattoo on his cheek, a crescent
slashed like a tear escaping the corner of his eye. He had seen it
once before. "A Scav. He's a Scav."

"You know him then!"

"No, no, no. I knew some of his people before." Rialus started
to explain that he had only met a few prisoners brought to him
at Cathgergen for petty crimes and poaching.

Devoth was not listening. A slave ran up with the amulet
and thick chain he had been shouting for. Devoth wrenched it
from him. Rounding on Rialus, he seized him by the collar of his
coat with his free hand. "You didn't tell me she would do this!"

"How could I?" Rialus asked. "I didn't know."

"Your princess is a coward who sneaks in the night. She has
just made it worse for your people." The Auldek flung Rialus
away, and then strode toward Bitten. The creature bent to
accept the chain and amulet that Devoth slung around his neck
and fastened. A moment later, Bitten surged upward, one dead-
start jump that took him and Devoth up above the height of the
flames, where his wings fanned out and lifted them higher.

Rialus stood there a moment, forgotten even by Sabeer, who
had joined the fight against the fire. He knew he should check
on his station to make sure his room and all his documents
were safe, but he was frozen in place. He had just discovered
something. He was sure of it, but he could not quite place what
it was. Another station exploded with a concussion of sound
and flame, Rialus almost did not notice, so transfixed was he.
The Auldek shouted curse-laden orders. Divine children rushed

toward the new fires, as if they had anything prepared to fight them.

And then he had it. Rialus knew he had it because the thought began like a centipede at the base of his spine and ran up his back with a hundred legs. And having the revelation, he knew what he had to do with it.

CHAPTER
FORTY-FIVE

Barad was not familiar with this wing of the palace. He followed the slim shoulders of the young woman who showed him the way, feeling awkwardly massive behind her. How was it that he could live in his body for so many years and still feel an impostor within it? Perhaps Corinn had recognized that in him when she set her curse on him. She made his feeling into a real thing. Turned him into a puppet. Even now she controlled his heart. She must. Why else would he be so driven to learn of her welfare? Why else would he be so hard on the heels of this woman, like a dog running to answer his master's summons?

The servant did not look him in the face when she indicated that he should wait in the alcove outside the library door. She pointed at the two couches, the chairs, and even at the tree that grew from a circlet cut in the stone. She left before he could thank her. Barad stood, arms drooping, unsure what to do. He reached for one of the tree's long, silver-green leaves. Running his finger down it, he wondered how deep the soil in the circlet was. Did the roots run deep, or were they balled in a tiny knot, as he had seen before in potted plants?

Someone approached from down the hall. Just one person,

quick strides of some hard-soled boots. The charlatan Delivegu Lemardine clipped his way into view. Ah, Barad thought, what is with my luck today? One of my least favorite people in the world, and I'm waiting here to speak to my enslaver.

Delivegu took in Barad without a hitch in his step. He did not even seem troubled by Barad's eyes, as almost everyone was. Nodding, he slid right past him to the door, which he promptly rapped on with his knuckles.

The door opened. Aliver leaned out. His gaze touched on Barad, acknowledging him and then settling finally on Delivegu. The man leaned in and whispered something to him. Aliver's face went slack as he absorbed whatever he had said. Without a word, he beckoned Delivegu inside. The door closed.

Barad took his seat again.

The door to the room opened again a few minutes later. Delivegu strode through. He strode away. Aliver stepped into view. He watched Delivegu recede, lost in thought. "Everyone, it seems, has messages for me." Aliver only noticed the seated man long after the charlatan's footfalls had faded. "I hope some of them prove true. Barad, do you have a message for me as well?"

"No, Your—Your Highness, the queen summoned me."

He looked surprised. "Did she? And you were brought *here*?" When Barad nodded, Aliver expelled a surprised breath of air. He stepped back and motioned for him to enter.

The library smelled strongly of its primary inhabitants: old books, ancient papers, stained sandalwood shelves. Tall windows cast elongated rectangles of red-gold sunrise light, but the room's candles still burned, thick ones that jutted through the tables like tree trunks and burned with flames the size of spearheads. Prince Aaden sat at one of the long tables in the sunken center of the space, a large book opened before him. The prince looked tiny in comparison. What must he be going through? Barad descended the steps toward him. On reaching his level,

Barad hovered near, knowing that despite his kind wishes there was little he could do to comfort him, not with his stone gaze and his bulk and his mouth that he was never sure would speak his mind. He tried just to be near, to fill the space around him with compassion, protection.

"Is the queen not here?"

"No, not here. I have not spoken to my sister since the coronation. Not many people know that, but I guess I can tell you. You can't, after all, say anything the queen would not want you to, can you?"

Barad felt his pulse quicken. Why that should alarm him he could not say. It was not his doing, after all. He tested his lips. They seemed to obey him. "No, I cannot."

Aliver stood over Aaden. He looked down at the open pages of the book as he said, "I didn't think so. Aaden here was sure of it. It must have been hard for you these past months. I can only imagine that your heart has not been behind the words your mouth has spoken."

"Was yours?" Barad asked.

By the way that Aliver twisted his mouth before answering Barad knew he was not yet free to speak his mind. As if to prove this, he said, "My name is Aliver Akaran. My sister is the queen. The greatest queen the nation has ever known."

Barad blinked, unsure what to say. Could they manage to speak in coded messages? How convoluted that would be. How easy to misunderstand each other. He was glad that the prince's mind seemed intent on other things.

"We're trying to understand the Santoth," Aliver said. "That's why we're here, studying these old books. They are not proving helpful, though."

"I wish that I could help," Barad said. "I know nothing of these things."

Rhrenna arrived. She stepped inside the door but did not descend toward them.

"Your Highness," she said, brittle voiced, "Corinn has sent word. She's on her way here."

"You've spoken with her?" Aliver asked. "She told you she was coming?"

"No, she wrote a note."

"A note?" Aliver looked like he had never heard of such a thing. "And it said that she is coming?"

"Yes. Right now, I believe."

Barad watched the mix of emotions move across Aliver's face in waves: relief and then worry, happiness and then trepidation and then hope. When he turned to his nephew, it was that emotion that he clung to. "Good," he said, testing the word and then getting more forceful with it. "This is good. Aaden, your mother . . ."

"Is coming here," the boy finished. "I'm sitting right here, Aliver. I can hear, too."

A person appeared in the open door. Corinn. She walked in with a formal posture, with her hands clasped together at her waist. She wore a dress of light blue; she was shapely as ever, distinctive as ever. A knit cowl wrapped around her neck and up over the lower portion of her face, just touching her nose. The ensemble was elegant. She might almost have been dressed to step outside on a breezy winter day, but Barad knew that cowl was not there as a defense against the weather.

Hanish Mein stepped into view. He slid up beside the queen. He took her by the arm and, whispering in her ear, drew her forward into the room.

For a long moment the gathered company stared at the queen, not at the ghost that stood with her. It was only when Corinn turned her back to them and withdrew toward the farthest alcove among the stacks that Aaden ran toward her. He dashed through tables, bounded up the steps to the higher landing, and cried for her with his arms outstretched. Corinn spun around. One hand kept the cowl in place and the other palm slammed out toward the others, freezing any movement in the room other than her son's. Aaden impacted with her at full speed, knocking her back a few steps. His arms slammed around her and cinched tight. She bent over him, whether with pain or emotion Barad could not tell. Both, most likely.

Hanish stood with a hand on Corinn's back. With his other, he wrapped both mother and son into a protective embrace. Father, mother, and son. A triumvirate that only Barad could see. Hanish looked up and sought out Barad's gaze. "You can hear me, can't you?"

Barad moved his stone eyes around the room. Everyone stared at Corinn and Aaden. None of them, he could tell, had any inkling of Hanish being there. They were all silent.

"You can hear me, yes?"

Barad nodded.

"Good. We need your mouth, Barad the Lesser. The queen needs it. She cannot speak to anyone but me. And I cannot speak to anyone but you. That's why you were summoned, to be the voice that speaks for we who cannot. First, you must know that you are freed. The queen releases you. Right now, as I speak, she is wishing for the ties that bind you to fall away. This is an easy spell for you to break. Simply understand that you are free and you will be. You can feel it, can't you?"

It was true. Barad did feel it. It might have just been because of the way Hanish described it, but invisible cords did loosen around his neck and jaw and the crown of his head. They had been there so long, unseen and unfelt, that his skin prickled as it remembered the true touch of the air.

"I can see that you can feel it. Now, please . . . in your own words tell them that you can hear the queen's voice, and that she will speak through you. You need not say anything about me. Please, speak now, Barad."

"But . . ." He gestured toward the others.

"Just speak the truth. They'll hear it in your voice."

Though he did know his mouth was his own again, it was very hard to make it shape sounds. He moved his lips and jaws, as if unsure of how to use them. "Ah . . ." No one even turned. It had been but an incomplete whisper. "Aliver." Still a whisper. "Prince Aliver, I have something to tell you," he said. "The queen wishes to speak through me. She asks me to be her voice, for . . . she cannot be her own."

Hanish said, "Tell them that the Santoth took her voice, but that she is still herself."

Barad did. The others were looking between him and the queen now, confused. They all noticed when she raised a hand and drew circles in the air with her fingers. The gesture conveyed agreement with Barad's words. They all saw that, except Aaden, who was still clinging to her.

"What are you saying, Barad?" Aliver asked. "Are you deceiving us?"

Barad had no idea what to say. "No," he tried, but it was not enough. He looked to Hanish, pleading through his stone eyes.

Hanish turned his head slightly to the side, seemed to listen to something. He nodded. "Say this to Aliver. Tell him that you can hear his sister's thoughts. That she is speaking through you. Ask him to remember the time that she and he and Mena and Dariel rode horseback with their father down to the beach, where he threw seashells into the waves and Mena walked holding Leodan's hand and Dariel chased crabs and Corinn . . . Say that she stood on the trunk of a tree and imagined that she was a queen of an ocean empire. Say those things to him."

Barad did.

"Tell him that he is free from any of Corinn's control, just as you are."

Barad explained this and watched as the truth of it dawned on Aliver. He saw him become free beneath his skin. It was as if a ghost skin had covered him until that moment. As it vanished, the man beneath came into sharper view.

"Now, come to us," Hanish said.

Moving through the others, Barad climbed up toward the threesome. When he reached them, Hanish said, "Speak quietly to the prince. After this we will speak of other things, but for now, tell Aaden what I tell you. Tell him his mother loves him more than anything else in the world. . . ."

The old mine worker, the large man with a voice that had often boomed before throngs to whom he had preached both for and against the monarchy, was some time whispering closely into the young prince's ear. The words he repeated were Hanish's only for a few sentences. After that, he knew them to be the queen's, intimate things that he spoke with reverence. These things were between a mother and a son. He let them slide from his memory, a vessel that, for once, served the queen with all his heart.

CHAPTER
FORTY-SIX

"Where is he?" Naamen asked. "He said he would be back by now. How long must we wait?"

Kelis did not answer. He had heard the query enough times already. He knew it was not a real question. It was a nervous tic, an expression of agitation. His answer—"I don't know"—was the same. He saw no use in giving it again. He knew no more than Naamen himself did.

Kelis stood pressed against a wall behind a tavern, his weight hard on the rough stones and his eyes heavy lidded with fatigue. Behind him, Naamen and Benabe and Shen sat against the wall, hidden behind debris and shadowed from the structures all around them. Rats moved through the rubbish, growing bolder the longer the humans remained in their territory. It was a foul place, but in the chaos that the lower town had become it was at least a safe one.

When was the last time he had slept? Weeks, it seemed. He was functioning without sleep. He was, more than ever before, afraid of sleep. He did not want to take his eyes off the waking world for even a moment. Nor did he wish to dream, for he felt certain that his dreams would be horrible. Prophetic and horrible.

❋

It was days ago that he had left the Carmelia with Delivegu Lemardine, the man who had clamped his hand to Kelis's elbow, half an escort, half a jailer. Moving through the opulent upper terraces of the city had been difficult. People rushed about, scared and confused and unkind because of it. Some wished to lock themselves away in their homes. Others were intent on fleeing the island. Marah and regular soldiers and private guards ran rough through the streets, calling for order and stirring turmoil in the process. It was hard to know what had happened. Kelis saw and heard enough to know that all his vague fears had just been shown to be real and worse than he had imagined.

None of it fazed Delivegu. He walked with deliberate strides, cutting through the crowds as if he barely noticed them. In the quiet of his sitting room a little later, he made Kelis tell his tale. A servant brought them a pot of strong tea. Kelis did not touch it, but Delivegu sat sipping from a cup as he listened. The truth came out, the story as Kelis knew it, each step of just how he had brought destruction right to Acacia's shores. If he was going to have to tell it to the queen, he had better practice first. That was part of his thinking. Another, which never got near the front of his mind, was that maybe he would never have to tell it. Maybe this man would somehow do that for him. If he died before he had to stand before her, it would be no bad thing.

He blinked his eyes open without ever knowing he had shut them. Had he been sleeping? No, for the room was as before. He had only a second before he stopped talking. That was all. A second of time lost, no more.

"Look at you," Delivegu said with a sigh, "played like a puppet dancing a jig. Because of you we have a great problem on our hands. How great I don't know, but I'm thinking we may all be leaned over a barrel and magically shafted before this is all through. It gives me no joy to be the bird that conveys this to the queen, but to me it falls."

Kelis could not help thinking Delivegu did not look nearly as joyless as he claimed.

"Now, this girl you say is with you, is she really Aliver's daughter? You have no doubt about this?"

"No. There is no doubt."

"Well, that's something, then. We can use that."

Kelis looked askance at him.

"I'll have food brought for you. Sleep here on the floor. I trust you won't rob me. At sunrise, let's go find them. I hope they come to where you told them to."

Delivegu did not trust quite so much as that, though. As Kelis lay flat on the woven rug in the center of the floor, he could hear the scuffling sounds of the servant left outside the door to guard him. The servant fell asleep before long but did so pressed up against the door. His snores slid under it and crawled across the floor to where Kelis lay. He wondered if he should leave, but he could not see a better way in to the queen. He sat up, thinking how strange it was that a man who had fought so much for the empire and been so close to the Akarans could feel so powerless before the palace's gates. He thought about this all through the long night, unsleeping despite his exhaustion.

✳

In the faint light of the dawning day they found Naamen at the inner gate. He stood half hidden behind one of the lion statues, staring out like a frightened child. It only took a few minutes more walking to reach Benabe and Shen. They were hidden, tucked around a corner and in an alley that saw no light even in the day.

Delivegu had to beg them to come forward into the weak

light. "This is the girl? This is Aliver Akaran's daughter?" He squatted closer as Benabe said that she was. Kelis hated the way he touched Shen on the chin and moved her face from side to side. He almost smacked his hand away. He saw that Benabe was on the verge of doing the same thing, so he did not. His inspection of Benabe was no less insulting. Delivegu studied her lascivious eyes, weighing whether she was or had been enough of a beauty to seduce an Akaran prince.

He did not share his verdict with them, but he did say he would go and try to arrange a meeting with the monarchs. He told them to wait right there in the alley amid the debris. "Just stay hidden," he said. "I'll be back."

✳

And then days passed.

Kelis, blinking more and more often, fought to stay awake. His body was so tired, but his mind still reeled. He was starting to hope that Delivegu would not come back. If he did not, they could flee. They could join the outflow of people escaping the island. Why not do that? Whatever the Santoth were doing was beyond them. They could do nothing to help. Worse, they would be blamed for releasing them. Why step up and show themselves to have been the evil sorcerers' guides? It had all gone horribly wrong, but nobody would believe that they had acted innocently, not when they had walked beside the sorcerers every step of the way from the Far South. They were either traitors or fools, and neither freed him of responsibility. If it were only him, he would have cast himself on the stones of the Carmelia yesterday and called for the Marah to arrest him. He did not care about himself.

He sought out Shen with his eyes and willed her into focus. She sat wrapped in her mother's arms, face hidden against her breast. Shen was what mattered. This seemed no way for her to enter her father's life. Not that he yet believed Aliver was truly alive and truly Aliver. More likely it was some sorcery of the queen's, a walking and talking mirage of a man. This was one of the things he feared seeing in his dreams. He did not want to have it confirmed, or to have that confirmation make it true.

More than likely, the queen still held power as firmly as ever. She would punish them for releasing the Santoth. And Shen she might punish for simply being who she was. A sudden intensity of fear gripped him. What if bringing Shen here was as enormous a mistake as bringing the Santoth?

The desire to flee was so strong in him that Delivegu's sudden return hit him like a kick in the abdomen. The man smiled as if he had just come from an amorous conquest and said, "Okay, my friends. True to my word, I've gotten you an audience with the king. Sorry for the delay. Follow me. And stay close. The streets are still wild."

Kelis did not remember the walk to the palace at all. Suddenly, they were there inside the grounds, soldiers escorting them. And then they were walking through a long hallway, and then they stood before a wooden door. When it opened, the scent of aged knowledge wafted out over them. Books, old papers.

Delivegu ushered them inside. Rhrenna, Corinn's secretary, stood on the other side of the door.

For Kelis, the scene he watched for the next few minutes was as warped and unreal as a dream. He rubbed his eyes to clear his vision, but it did no good. He saw the people in the room as if through a gold-hued liquid that blurred their features and muffled their words. His eyes met Aliver's. It was he. A single look was enough to prove that. He saw the queen with a cowl around her neck and Aaden at her side and a man with stone eyes. And the others. He saw their mouths move and he heard the sounds, but the words seemed to pass through him and vanish before he could get ahold of them. Though he did not like Delivegu, he saw that the man was speaking for him and he was glad. He did not know what he was saying, but whatever it was, Aliver listened to him, looking often to Kelis.

For a long moment the scene went dark. And then the golden, muted room came back. He had closed and opened his eyes. He was so tired. He wanted this to be over. He wanted to remember the things he knew he needed to but could not anymore. He wanted to sleep. Benabe spoke for a time. Aliver embraced her and went on one knee before Shen. He asked her something and she answered.

Darkness pressed down upon Kelis again. He realized that if he stayed in this dark place he would not dream after all. It was tempting to stay in the dark, enough so that he was not sure why he opened his eyes, despite himself.

Aliver had turned from Benabe and was moving toward him. Kelis had no idea how to read the determination in his strides, nor the urgency that moved him so fast he upset a chair as he came forward. He thought the twisted expression on the prince's face was anger. Anger for releasing the end of the world and for being too late in finding Shen. All the years of her life, and he had never once looked for her. Never knew she was alive. Never searched his dreams for her. Kelis began to close his eyes.

Aliver grabbed him. He pulled him into an embrace, crushing Kelis's head into his chest and wrapping his arms around him. Kelis stood, his arms limp at his sides. Aliver spoke to him. At first Kelis could not hear him. The world was too deadened and the blackness that was his fatigue wanted so badly to drop on him.

Aliver seemed to understand this. He held Kelis's face in his hands and mouthed his words. Still it took some time for Kelis to understand that Aliver was calling him by his name. He was naming him his brother and thanking him. He put his lips to his ears and said, "Listen to me, Kelis. Can you?" He could. "Do you understand what you have done? You've brought me the future. Thank you. Thank you for knowing it all along. Stand with me as I tell them what you've done."

With those words, the film before Kelis's eyes vanished. The muffled sounds became sharp and the black wall withdrew. The prince propped him up and turned to face the queen with a formality that seemed at odds with the surroundings and the privacy of the chamber.

"Sister," Aliver said, "forget the other things for a moment and listen to me. This man has brought us a wonder, a ray of light to break through all this darkness. You see. Inside this misery are the seeds of the future. Aaden is one. This girl is one."

Corinn had watched it all from the higher landing. She said nothing, just stood there, straight-backed, with the cowl covering her neck and lower face. Kelis thought it must be there to hide her emotions, but then he decided that was not all there was to it.

"The wonder is my daughter," Aliver went on. "She was given the name Larashen before her birth, but she prefers just Shen. This is too bad, because it was Kelis who gave her this name."

Kelis started, turned to look in his face.

"Yes, it's true," Aliver said to him, and then continued speaking to his sister. "Kelis, he who taught me to run in Talay. He who was at my side when we killed the laryx, when I became a man. He who is a brother to me. He may not even know this, but I remember something now. One time, when he and I were alone in Talay, searching for the Santoth, I awoke to hear him speaking in his sleep. I listened and I heard him say a name. The name he said was Larashen. I did not know what it meant then. I do now. I know because he is a dreamer with the gift of prophecy. He tried to deny it, but it came up through him. And I know it because you are my sister, with a gift to restore life. Only with both of you is this possible. Do you hear me?"

The queen nodded.

"Then, Sister, come and meet your niece. Love her, as I already do. As I always have." Aliver's voice wavered, choked with emotion that he fought to contain. It escaped him, though, in sobs that made him hesitate before finishing. "Will you do that? Will you love her?"

The queen's head turned slightly.

The man with the stone eyes said, "I don't deserve to love her. If you knew all the things I've done, you would not ask for my love. I did not rule like you. I . . . am not the same as you."

Aliver kept his eyes on the queen. "I do know you. I ask you to love her now. . . . Love her now and earn that love with what you do from here. You can do that, Sister. I know you. You are the princess who dreamed of ruling an undersea kingdom. I've always known you."

After a moment, Barad said for her, "When I tell you the things you need to know, will you turn against me then?"

"Never."

Corinn's face went ugly for a moment, distorted with a sudden misery.

Barad said, "You don't know. You can't say that."

Aliver inhaled a long breath. He lifted an arm and Shen moved under it. He looked back at the queen and said, "But I *do* say it. I have no anger in me, Corinn. There's not room for it. I'm too filled with other emotions. Come meet my daughter. Aaden, come meet Shen. We have lost too much time already, and we have only a short time here. Let's not waste it."

CHAPTER

FORTY-SEVEN

The nighttime attack was Kant's idea. The Scav did most of the work themselves. It went better than Mena could have imagined. It amazed her that they had snuck into the Auldek camp, found the vehicles that housed the pitch, and then set charges delayed to explode as they retreated. They destroyed four of the rolling stations, cost the Auldek some lives in slaves, and came away with several vats of the flammable pitch hitched to a sled and pulled by dogs that were uncannily silent. The Scav lost only two of their number in the process, and they had not asked anything of the Acacians. Mena, her captains, and her troops watched from a distance as the night sky bloomed with beautiful bursts of flame, a strange show of light in the arctic night.

No one could blame them for the causalities suffered when one unfortunate group of soldiers was pounced upon by a crazed frékete. The creature dropped right into their camp, a rider shouting from its back. The animal ripped ten soldiers apart before being forced to withdraw. Those creatures were going to be deadly troublesome. Mena might have wings because of Elya, but her beauty could not prevail against such brawn.

Thinking this, Mena went to her tent, more troubled about

tomorrow than elated about the night's successes. She closed her eyes in the dark and opened them in the dark, knowing that hours had passed and that she had not slipped into sleep during any of them. How many will die today? she wondered. How many will I kill? Though she might have, she did not mean kill with her own blade or with her soldiers' blades. It was her own people's lives that she felt responsible for. She hated that even the more recent plans she had come up with were not sufficient for what faced them.

Mena found her first officer waiting in the anteroom of her tent, a small space just enclosed enough to be a shelter. "Perrin? How long have you been here?"

"Not long."

"Why didn't you call for me?" she grumbled, pulling her outer layers on in front of him, her breath clouding the air.

"You deserved sleep."

"And you don't?" she asked.

"I got some yesterday," he said. "I have someone you'll want to talk to. A patrol picked him up at first light this morning. He was stumbling around like a drunken man. He says he was looking for us, though he was off to the north. If the patrol hadn't spotted him, he'd likely have wandered off to freeze. Unless he was up to something more cunning. If I hear him right, he says his name is Rialus Neptos."

Mena and Perrin arrived at the command tent a few minutes later. The room was just a little above freezing, the air clouded with steam and heavy with smoke from the oil lamps. The light was imperfect, flickering, but it revealed a pitiful version of the traitor. He stood trembling in the center of a circle of glaring officers.

"What are you doing here?" Mena asked, slipping into the ring to face him.

Rialus's body jerked as if she had smacked him. His arms

were crossed across his chest, clutching a book within the clumsy embrace of all his layers. Instead of answering, he tightened his embrace.

"Speak fast," Mena said.

A moment later, she knew that was too much to ask of the man. He had a hard time getting his words out through his chattering teeth. "I—I've . . . ca-ca-come to he-help . . . Acacia. My nation."

"Too late for that, don't you think?" Bledas asked.

"Not . . . too late. Just late."

Mena watched the man tremble for a time. "Rialus Neptos, you've walked from our enemy's camp after having guided them here from the other side of the world. If you have something to say, say it. And then go back to die along with them."

Rialus's eyes widened in terror. "No! I can't go back. They'd kill me. They'll know by now."

"They know already," Edell said, "because they sent you. What lie did they send you to tell?"

"No lies." He fumbled to get the book in his hands and then thrust it toward her. "Here. Read my journal. Read. It's me in there."

Edell shoved the book back at him. "You expect us to believe you? You?"

"No lies," Rialus said, once he was steady on his feet again. "I came to you . . . to tell you th-th-things."

Edell seemed ready to shove Rialus again, but Mena stayed him. "If you have something to say, do so."

"The beasts . . . they ca-cannot fly on their own. They need the amulets. They have amulets. Chains that lift them—"

"What is he on about?" Bledas said. "Speak sense, man!"

"The fréketes need magic to fly," Rialus said, getting out the first complete sentence that captured the company's attention. The effort seemed to exhaust him.

"The fréketes need magic to fly." Mena chewed that a moment, and then said, "Let's get him food and hot water. Give him a hot water bottle and bring him a chair. I want him talking without chattering. And take that book from him."

❋

As the troops assembled for battle a couple of hours later, Mena stood, exhaling the irony of what she was about to do in perplexed plumes of mist, watching the enemy amass on the ice in front of them. Was she really reordering the day's battle plans based on testimony she had just received from a babbling mouse of a man who had betrayed her nation twice? Apparently so.

Because of the rest of the information she had pulled from between Rialus's chattering teeth, she had altered the arrangement of their battle lines. Perrin's company would hold the center, along with Haleeven and his Mein. But Mena spaced them loosely, and behind their core troops she stationed the newest arrivals to the army, praying that they never saw an Auldek face that day. Bledas and Edell would take the left flank, Perceven and Gandrel the right. Archers would stay to the rear of both flanks, able to shoot over their companions and into the enemy ranks. Nothing would look remarkable about the formation to the enemy facing it, but there was a reasoning behind it that was entirely different from what she had planned just hours before.

For herself, the battle would begin from the air. She stood, stroking Elya's feathers as her attendant finished tightening her rigging. Perrin trudged over to her. He carried a helmet stuffed under one arm and wore a breastplate emblazoned with his family's insignia—the profile of a wolf, black against a backdrop of gold. He asked after any last orders, and she said there were none.

"Rialus got away all right?" Mena asked.

"I think so. Kant's people helped him get back. He should be fine. The hard part was living through the shock of your sending him back to the Auldek."

"He won't buy forgiveness cheaply. I need more than what he gave us." The officer nodded his agreement, but looked uncomfortable doing so. "Perrin, I know we've changed this around at the last moment. It's decided now. We have to trust it."

"I trust you, Princess. I just wish we didn't have to rely on that rat. Maybe the Auldek had enough of him and kicked him out for the ice to finish."

"Possibly. I wouldn't blame them." She took in the scene a moment, mostly just the soldiers marching into formation. She could not actually see the enemy from there. "But, Perrin, this plan feels right. It's awful and unjust, perhaps, but . . ."

"If it saves our soldiers' lives, it's worth it," he finished. "I'm with you. Don't think I'm not."

"Are the others?"

"They don't like how the information came to us, but they're not foolish enough not to see the logic in it." He pulled his helmet down around his head, a snug fit with the fur padding that lined it. "If I die today," he said, "I'd regret not telling you that I'm in love with you. I hope you don't mind my saying so."

Tugging on her gloves and pulling the wrist straps tight, Mena asked, "And if you live?"

"I'll die of shame."

Mena nudged him away. She climbed up into position on Elya. *So I'm loved, Elya. I don't think Melio would approve, but it's good to know. You are, too, girl. You are, too. Let's stay alive, all right? Fly now.*

The ice fell away beneath them. The frigid air bit at her cheeks; a little way up, the wind buffeted them. They flew higher and found calmer air. From there she flew forward to take in what they faced.

The Auldek forces were arrayed across the ice in a patchwork, a martial geometry laid out in a manner she had never seen before, not from on high. Squares and rectangles of troops, divided by clan affiliations, status, and all manner of distinctions Mena had little grasp of. She knew the strongest clans were in the center front, with others to either side. At each flank went contingents of animals: antoks with harnesses brimming with archers; kwedeir with their awkward gait, wings tented around them; woolly rhinoceroses with riders carrying lances atop them. She saw white lions slinking through the lines, spotted cats like those from Talay, wolves the size of horses. A few bears, tethered to chains, roared as if they had not been fed in a week and smelled the banquet awaiting them. As she watched, a black swell of birds flowed up into the air. Crows.

"They've brought their own crows," Mena said. "Is this a war or a traveling circus?"

At the edge of each flank went the other troops, the slaves. They stretched all along either side and well back, eventually wrapping around to make up the mass that brought up the rear of the host. There were so many of them that the front of the line looked wider than the rear. It wasn't, though. It was just that the ranks went back so far that they faded toward their distant camp in dwindling perspective. Mena tried to do the math she had not managed before, but got lost when estimates went beyond fifty thousand.

Elya dipped a wing and swung them around, bringing Mena's army into view as she did so. The sight of them was not a surprise, but her heart sank, her stomach knotted. There were not enough of them. Four thousand at the most. They were spread too thin. They were simply humans, no beasts of war to bellow for them. Their defeat was not even in question. It was as inevitable as the fate of a hill of ants with a booted foot about to crush it.

Mena flew low over them, shouting encouragement. She touched down on the ice before them and told them not to fear the numbers coming against them. This was not about numbers, she said. It was about heart and right and cunning and freedom. She and Elya flew up and danced before the line, spreading the message as best she could. Without fail, they roared back their affirmation. Perrin blew the horn that signaled them forward, and the two armies marched toward each other.

Though the message was simple, and she doubted that many of the men and women in the ranks fully believed it, Mena was not lying. The vastness of the Auldek force actually gave her hope. Rialus had said the Auldek—though hundreds of years old—could only remember eighty years or so's worth of memories. They had not fought battles this size in hundreds of years. They knew of them only what they had read in books. They may be tremendous individual warriors, but that did not mean they would know how to fight a large-scale engagement.

This army now marching toward her troops was frightening, but it was also absurd. It was a little boy's fantasy of an army. It was brawn and numbers and bellowing creatures and an anvil of might . . . and it made no sense at all. If Mena had these resources she would never have arrayed them all against an army as paltry as the one she presented. With such vast numbers, most of them would never come anywhere near the soldiers they were meant to fight. They would be useless, standing with weapons at hand among a throng of themselves. It would only make communication impossible, orders unmanageable, strategy lost to the dull mind of the mob. It had taken them hours of precious daylight just to assemble, meaning Mena had had time to speak with Rialus. Nor would she have chopped the ranks up by a hierarchy that had nothing to do with an actual battle plan. It was vanity. It was foolish. If Mena had Devoth's army, she would have left the bulk of them back in camp, eating a hearty breakfast and preparing the evening's victory celebration.

"But I'm not fighting myself," Mena said, once they were aloft again. "I'm fighting them."

The fréketes rose then, one after another, from the Auldek camp. As they flew over the invading army, the troops erupted in cries, booming shouts as loud as the explosions of the night before. The beasts flew in dips and rises, slipping side to side among one another. Their wings were massive. The heavy weight of their bodies swayed beneath them almost like a separate load being carried by the span. The riders on their backs clung to them like young bats to their mothers. Mena had not thought it through before, but now she knew she had never accepted these creatures as they appeared. They were too dense, too thick with muscle, too large and bulky for even those great stretches of wings to lift them. Thanks to Rialus, she understood why now.

It was not that he could confirm it with certainty, but he had bet his life on bringing her the intelligence that the amulets that the fréketes wore around their necks helped them fly. He had seen them without them only a few times, only when they were on the ground, at leisure, being tended and fed. When aloft they always had them on. The night of the Scav attack, Devoth had waited for Bitten's amulet to be brought to him and placed on the beast before he flew. What if this was not vanity, not just a custom or an idiosyncrasy? What if the fréketes needed the amulets to fly?

The moment he asked the question, he knew the answer to it. "Devoth once mentioned a handful of relics the Lothan Aklun had given them," Rialus had said. "The amulets are some of these relics. They were things to trap Lothan Aklun spells and keep their power."

Mena had to end the meeting before she could question him

any further. Now, aloft above her marching soldiers, she hoped he had spoken the truth. She had not told the others this part of her plan. The first clash of the day should be hers. It had to be hers. She felt the eyes of her troops watching her, and she tried to forget them so that she could do what she needed to for them. She drew the King's Trust and urged Elya forward to meet them.

Which one? Which one?

Mena could not tell the riders or the beasts apart. They came on in a swarm. The fréketes grunted and bellowed to one another, carrying on some bestial conversation. They all wore chains around their necks, amulets heavy on them, just as Rialus had said. All their eyes stayed fixed on her.

At least I've got their attention.

She pulled up and hovered, Elya's wings feathering the air. Pointing with the King's Trust, she picked out a frékete and rider. "You!" she shouted. "Your name! What is your name?"

This set the swarm of them into confusion for a moment. They were in the air above and below and before her, out on either side now, too. But they did not attack. Eventually, the rider atop the mount she had pointed at turned it sideways and yelled back, "Howlk." He slapped his mount hard on the shoulder. "Nawth. Nawth!"

Mena shouted, "Howlk and Nawth, I challenge you." To make sure he understood, she scowled and pumped her sword hand in the air, then pointed to them and to herself.

Howlk understood. They all did, and for a few raucous moments they argued about it. As she and Elya hovered, the fréketes and their riders converged on one another like squabbling youths. Mena sheathed her sword, reached down, and checked her crossbow, memorizing just where the stock of it lay behind her hip.

The debate did not last long. Despite whatever protocol

Mena had usurped with her challenge, the others drew back. Howlk and his mount came forward, looking very pleased.

It's you and me now, Elya. First, we test them.

They surged toward them, darting to the side at the last minute. The fréketes howled as Nawth pumped his wings in pursuit. Elya flew higher, cut side to side, folded her wings in, and dove. Nawth followed her. After the first few moves Mena reined her back. Elya was faster, much more maneuverable. No need to flaunt it, though. She needed to use it instead.

On her mental order, Elya twisted her wings. She spun them around. Flaring out to either side, the membranes of her wings filled with the air she grabbed, stopping them dead in the air. Mena pulled out her crossbow. She stood in her stirrups and brought the weapon to sight over Elya's shoulder. She held it one-handed, something she could only do for a moment, as the weapon was one of the heavy, powerful ones her soldiers had used against the foulthings.

Nawth came toward them with wings flapping. His body convulsed and clawed at the air, as if he were swimming, as desperate to get to them as a drowning man is for the surface. Mena pulled the trigger and shot for the center of that writhing mass. The bolt thwacked away, scorching the line between them faster than her eye could see. Nawth caught it in his forearm. It was not an intentional block, just the result of his thrashing. It went in at an angle and hit bone, punched through, and then pinned his forearm into his chest. He howled and dropped.

Elya hovered, the two of them watching the frékete fall. The other fréketes did the same, all of them hovering nearby, stunned to silence for once.

The descent did not last long. Nawth flexed his wings. He rose beating them steadily. Looking up at Mena and Elya, teeth gritted and eyes simmering with new depths of hatred, he tore the prongs of the bolt head from his chest and then tugged at it until he had it free of his shattered arm. He tossed the bolt to the side. It fell toward the ground, spinning over and over.

Howlk ripped free the sword he had sheathed diagonally across his back. As Nawth reached their height, Mena drew the King's Trust. She adjusted herself in the saddle, blended her mind with Elya's, readying her.

Nawth moved first. He surged forward, turning at the last moment and dropping his shoulder so that Howlk could swing his sword. Elya slipped down and to the side. Howlk cut only air. Nawth turned and rose; Elya danced away. She spun. Darted. Mena kept her close to the frékete but used her speed to dodge Nawth's lunges, avoiding his kicks and Howlk's sword attacks. The two grew more frustrated. Both of them shouted at her, Howlk in Auldek and Nawth in some bestial bellowing akin to words but not quite.

Mena let their anger grow, fed further by the derision cast at her from the surrounding fréketes and riders, all of whom circled them. They drew closer, making it harder for Elya to move. One of the other fréketes slashed the membrane of Elya's wing.

Let's do it now, Mena thought. She let Elya choose the moment, felt it just before she was going to, and agreed. Nawth got closer than ever before, and Elya reared back, spinning to avoid his grasping, big-knuckled hand. The move put Mena in striking position above Howlk for the first time. She swung but not for him. She aimed for the metal chain on the frékete's neck. The combined motion of their bodies was too much. She missed. Caught Nawth's shoulder instead. She thought the strike—even though awkwardly landed—would cut through the coarse muscle all the way to the bone. It didn't. Instead the blade dented his flesh, barely drawing blood. It was as if she had hit him with a fighting stick, not a honed edge at all.

Nawth grabbed for Elya. She just managed to corkscrew away, diving toward the ice in the process. Mena would have lost her sword if she had not had the leather straps from its hilt wrapped around her wrist. She fought to get control of it, to keep it from cutting her or Elya. She lost all sense of the world for a few seconds, and then it snapped back into place. Elya spread her wings and went into a more controlled fall. Nawth was right behind her. He raked the air with his good arm, trying desperately to grab her tail, which snaked around just out of his reach. He was acting on his own, frenzied. He paid no attention to whatever Howlk was shouting at him. He ignored the way the Auldek tugged the steering harness. Howlk even reached forward and yanked on the chain that held Nawth's amulet to get control of him back.

The thought passed from Mena to Elya so fast it felt simultaneous. Elya flipped over, angled her wings to break her speed, lifting slightly. Upside down, sword in hand, Mena kicked free of her stirrups. She yanked loose the thigh buckle that secured her to the harness. She fell free and dropped onto Howlk's back.

She landed hard and almost glanced off to the side. She wrapped around the startled Auldek and caught hold of a handful of his long hair. Gripping it, she lunged forward, over his shoulder, and struck the chain on Nawth's neck with all her might. It snapped free and dropped away.

In the moment that Howlk stared wide-eyed at Nawth's bare neck, Mena yanked back his head, slipped the cutting edge of her sword right along the rim of his neck guard. She let go of his hair, grabbed the back edge of the blade with her free hand, and yanked the blade into his neck with all the might she had. The man's eyes—startlingly blue—looked up at her, a childlike disappointment in them. His hands came up as if he wanted to explain something to her, but they got no farther before his body started to convulse.

Mena shoved him, which pushed her body back away from them. The three of them fell, drifting slowly apart. She watched the distance between them grow, and then looked past them to the ice field far below, the armies just eating into each other. For a few moments none of it seemed to have anything to do with her. The fact that she plummeted toward the earth with the air raging at her ears and her arms and legs kicked about by the force of her fall did not matter.

And then Elya appeared beside her. She touched Mena with the bottom of her muzzle. That brought Mena back. She grabbed Elya's neck, loving her like mad, and slipped around and back into the saddle. Elya slowed their descent enough for them to watch from on high as Nawth and Howlk crashed down in the center of the Auldek formation. The soldiers beneath them were squashed on the ice, and those around them sprang back, sending a shock wave out around them. There was too much fighting for all the soldiers to understand what had just happened, but the fréketes swarmed down, landing one after the other around their fallen comrades, making the circle of confusion wider. Mena did not need to watch them.

She checked what was happening elsewhere. There was not much daylight left. She caught sight of the sun biting into the horizon and knew the battle had just minutes more before both sides realized they had to withdraw. It was hard to make sense of the scene from above, but she knew what she was looking for and saw it. The Auldek in the foremost square of troops—near where the two had fallen—had pressed forward against Perrin's troops. She knew they would because she had instructed them not to truly engage. To fight a slow backward retreat, cautious and defensive, just staying alive. The second thing Rialus had told her was about their hidden armor. No use wasting lives trying to injure soldiers who could not readily be injured.

Instead, it was the units facing the quota slave ranks that truly pressed the attack. From above, she could see that it was working, more so on the left than on the right flank.

What she did then she explained to Elya in images so that she would see it all and fear none of it. Passing over the crash of the two front lines, they swooped low over the right flank of quota warriors. Seeing the spot she wanted, she had Elya dip nearly to the ground above a patch of clear ice. At what she gauged to be the right moment, Mena pulled free of her harness for the second time that afternoon. She went over backward. Her legs kicked free of the stirrups and passed through the sky above her, all the way over until she was chest down and skimming off Elya's back. She hit ice knowing she had to roll. She did. Rolled and slid.

She came out of it with the King's Trust in her hand. She took out the nearest man by severing his leg at the knee. He went down screaming, splashing crimson across the ice. The next nearest she slashed across the chest. Another she hit awkwardly with the side of her blade, breaking his wrist instead of severing it.

As the soldiers pulled back to take her in, she got her footing. She gripped the sword in two hands and steadied herself. The fury that she recognized as Maeben came into her. It had been a while, but the screeching wrath of the goddess scorched through her veins now. She knew she would remember what she was about to do later with horror at herself, but in that moment it did not matter. She had a purpose in the world, and the blade in her grip was the instrument with which she wrote it. She blocked a spear thrown at her, cowardly, and charged the fool who had thrown it.

It got bloody after that.

When Elya returned, only a few minutes later, Mena was the center of a swirl of red desolation. Her blade was warm with the work, dripping. The ring of soldiers facing her tripped and stumbled on the bodies she had cut down. Elya swept in emitting a hiss so fierce the enemy soldiers dropped to the ice on hearing it. Mena sheathed the King's Trust and caught Elya at a run. She leaped just in time to grab her stirrup loop. She held on, though her arms wanted to pop free of their sockets as Elya lifted her into the air. A frékete pursued them. Elya grabbed Mena and darted away as nimble as a skylark, dodging thrown spears and arrows with a grace that made Mena grin.

Pressed into the creature's citrus-smelling plumage, arms aching and feet running in the air above two armies clashing, Mena laughed like a madwoman. Battle joy. A short-lived euphoria, but in the moment there was nothing else like it in the world. The princess laughed so hard it became crying. The two blended so that she could not separate one from the other, or tell apart the emotions that wracked her.

Battle joy. Battle shame. She owned them both. She always would.

CHAPTER
FORTY-EIGHT

Dariel's second arrival in Avina was markedly different from his first. This time he walked down the city's wide thoroughfares near a vanguard of escorts. Mór strode in front of him, Birké and Anira at either shoulder. Others from the Sheeven Lek river party made a wedge around them, and still more of the People who had met them outside the city increased their numbers. Dariel gripped leashes securing Bashar and Cashen to him, both of them excited by the commotion, stomping about, large pawed and awkward in their growing size.

For this entrance Dariel wore no bonds. He was not the prisoner that Sire Neen brought as a token for the Auldek, nor the one stuffed under Tunnel's massive arm. No bit clogged his mouth. Instead of bruises and an inflamed lip he wore a face tattooed with the spots of the Shivith clan. A rune rose from the center of his forehead, a declaration for all to see. And there were many who wished to see it.

The throng they cut through grew as they progressed. More and more people crowded the streets, pushing in to get a look at him. They were quiet, eerily so. The signs of belonging stood out even more than usual because many gathered in clan groups. Whereas Dariel was used to seeing the People as a collage of individuals, some tusked and others tattooed, some with metal whiskers and others with pale flesh, here most seemed to have segregated themselves, making blocs of individuals sharing skin tone or altered features.

They strode past groups of wolflike Wrathics, all of them looking like Birké's kin. A small clump of Fru Nithexek stared, their eyes somehow rounder than normal, seemingly unblinking. For a time several Shivith youths ran alongside them. They called to one another in amazed voices, shouting that the Rhuin Fá was one of their clan. The Rhuin Fá was Shivith! Their voices were harsh in the relative silence, and before long others cuffed them into silence and held them back to fade into the distance. On one section of street, Dariel and his group had to physically plow through a sea of light blue birdlike faces, all of them staring at Dariel. He could not read whether their expressions were kindly curious or hostile or something in between. He was glad that Mór kept the pace brisk.

When they passed down a thoroughfare lined with massive statues of strange creatures, Dariel knew they had arrived. They went through a colonnade of painted pillars, up a stone staircase, and stepped into the gaping mouth that cast them in darkness for a time. Just as before, Dariel thought. This is just as before. Except that it was not, and could not be as it had been. Before, he had no control over his fate. He had no voice. This time he had both, and he had the responsibility of using them for the good of everyone in this chamber, both those who supported him already and those who believed they hated him.

Though he still was not sure how he would manage it, he had never felt a clearer sense of purpose. He made sure that when he strode into the high-ceilinged chamber there was nothing but quiet confidence on his face. They came to rest at the edge of a large rectangle of light that fell from a skylight. Throngs of the People crowded the shadows, more than he could see or number. He did know that they were sectioned by clan affiliation. That had been a requirement of Dukish of the Anet clan. It was he who controlled this portion of the city, he who permitted this gathering and built his strength on keeping the People divided.

Dariel was trying to sort out who was who when a shape hulked up in front of him. A giant of a man converged on him, grinning madly, his tusks exaggerating his joy. "Rhuin Fá! There he is!" Tunnel crushed Dariel in an embrace, lifting him off the ground. He spun with him, making sure everyone heard and saw that the Rhuin Fá had arrived.

"Hello . . . Tunnel," Dariel managed to gasp. "Good to see you, too."

"Good that you are alive," Tunnel said, once he had set Dariel down. "I like this. It's good." He touched a thick finger to Dariel's forehead. "Yes, that's good. But what are these? Cathounds!"

If Bashar and Cashen found anything odd about Tunnel's appearance, they did not show it. They jumped into his arms, paws on his chest and knees, as he bent to greet them. He laughed as they slopped his face with their tongues.

"Hounds like me," Tunnel explained. "They should fear me, but . . ." Back on his feet again, he wiped his face dry with a handkerchief before greeting the others. He hugged Anira at length and Mór briefly, seeming to know that she would not return the gesture as fully as he offered it. Birké took the hounds' leashes and promised to keep them safe in the back of the chamber. Dariel let them go reluctantly.

Throughout all this exchange, Mór scanned the crowd. She nodded greetings to some, stared icily at others. "Where's Skylene?"

Tunnel grew somber. "She was injured, Mór. Shot with an arrow in the chest."

"No," Dariel said. "Is she all right?"

"She is not well."

"Where is she?" Mór asked.

"Safe for now. We'll take you both to her, after this. She wants that, but she did not want you to know before. She did not want it to change anything, to rush you or . . . You know how she is. As stubborn as you, Mór, but quieter about it."

Mór looked toward the contingent of Anets and Antoks that grouped beside them. She kept her emotions hidden, but Dariel saw the tightness in the way she moved her neck. "Who shot her?"

"Not them," Tunnel said. "The league did it. They—"

The deep sound of a bell resonated through the chamber, cutting Tunnel off. The long tones called the meeting to order. Each of the clans sent a handful of representatives into the center of the lighted space. As they moved, Anira whispered a few names in Dariel's ear. He knew who they were as she said them, and wondered how that was possible. Plez of the Kern. Randale of the Wrathic. Than, with his savage demeanor, of the Lvin . . . Each name he knew just before she uttered it. How could that be? He may have heard some of the names before, but he could place their faces now. He even knew things about them that he was sure he had never been told.

He did not have time to ponder it. Representing the Free People, Mór stepped forward, with Tunnel as a towering, muscled protector beside her. Anira brushed past Dariel. She reached back, took him by the wrist, and pulled him forward. More so than ever, he felt the touch of hundreds of eyes on him.

An Anet spoke first. He took a loop of metal that looked like a goat horn from the small table it rested on. Holding it high, he called the meeting to order. He was not Dukish, Dariel knew, but one of his secretaries. Dukish himself had a seat brought out for him. He sat while the others stood, legs crossed, head tilted, and his gaze on something in the chamber's shadowy distance.

He had not, as far as Dariel knew, even looked at him, and he did not seem to intend to. But looking at Dukish, Dariel realized he knew things about him. He knew too much about him.

Dukish's man said that they were all gathered here due to the Anet clan's generosity. He reminded them that weapons were not allowed. If any had weapons hidden on them, they should leave now or face disgrace and exile for violating that cardinal rule of the gathering. Someone from deep in the shadows shouted a curse at him, but he thrust the horn above his head, clenched tight in his fist. "The horn is the voice!" he shouted. "Only the holder of the horn speaks!"

Many grumbled, but nobody disputed the tradition. At least, not until the Anet had held on to it too long, doing nothing more than justifying the bloody actions they had taken to "secure" the city. Eventually, the man did let the horn be tugged from his hand, and another speaker stepped up to make his or her case.

The Free People, being removed from any particular clan, were to be the last to receive the horn. Dariel would have found the wait interminable if he was not experiencing so much each moment. His belief that he knew many of these people grew stronger all the time. He did not just read them based on the things they said and their demeanor as they said them. Dariel remembered other things about them. When Than spoke, he called Dukish a tyrant who should be put on trial for every murder he had incited. He roared his words with passion and a lion's strength of bearing. But . . . he said nothing about his shame over not being asked to go with his Auldek masters on their war march. Dariel remembered the man making that confession to him, admitting how much that shamed him. He saw that emotion behind every gesture, but knew that nobody else did.

Randale of the Wrathic reminded them that Ushen Brae was vast and should be settled, that the clans could divide and live separately. They should first share out the resources and wealth of Avina equally. Dariel, watching one version of him, recalled another speaking quietly about how he wanted only to go to Rath Batatt himself and range across the mountains there like the wolf his long teeth were modeled after. Plez of the Kern did not say the thing that troubled her most: that with the Lothan Aklun dead they no longer had any way to make the belonging changes to any new people who arrived. What would happen, she wondered, when the next generation of Kern did not have blue skin or a beaked appendage that lengthened their noses? Would there even be another generation of Kern? Nor did Maren, speaking for the Kulish Kra, admit that her mind was mostly on her lover, an Antok man who had been forced by his clan affiliation to leave her.

There was so much behind each speaker's words, so many hidden fears and objectives, thoughts noble and sometimes wicked. It was almost too much for Dariel to sort through. A bombardment beyond anything he had experienced before. He held it all within himself behind a calm façade. With so many eyes on him he could not show uncertainty. Whatever was happening mattered. It was important. It was part of what he was here to do.

During their discourses, each of the clan leaders mentioned Dariel in some way or other. Some praised him. Randale wanted very much to hear what he had to say. Some expressed doubts about him. Than questioned why he wore Shivith markings if he was truly of the old lands. Some attacked him as a fraud. How convenient, the Antok contingent said, that the Rhuin Fá had been found just after the Auldek fled! If he was truly the Rhuin Fá, why had he not come in all the years that the Auldek had enslaved them?

A good question, Dariel acknowledged. Not sure how to answer that.

And what sense did it make that the Rhuin Fá should be the heir of the bloodline who had sold them for generations? the Anet speaker had asked. Why should any of them believe that he was not just lying to them, trying to use their own legend against them? And why, he asked, should they turn their backs on the league? It was the league, after all, that set in motion the chain of events that destroyed the Lothan Aklun and set the Auldek on the warpath.

None of that is a lie, Dariel thought, and yet neither does it equal the truth.

When the horn finally passed into Mór's hand, the Anet who handed it to her made it clear it was an indulgence to even do so. How many did she truly represent? Who were the Free People now that everything had changed? The old and infirm, rejects living in the wilds of the country? "You have no voice here," he said.

Mór wrenched the horn away. "Don't I? What am I speaking with, then? This is my voice, and the Free People speak for all of you, whether you are wise enough to know it or not. Who but we kept the dream of freedom and unity alive all these years? You do us wrong to abandon us now. Yoen and elders—"

Than strode up to her. He grabbed the horn, ignoring the way Tunnel glared at him. He did not pull it away from her; he just held it with her for a moment. "We know what you think," he said. "We have all heard your speeches enough times to spit them back at you. I want to hear what *he* says." He thrust his index finger of his free hand at Dariel. Judging by the roar of voices that seconded him, the entire chamber awaited the same.

"Before you do," Mór said, "you should know that"—Mór turned and met Dariel's eyes—"that I did not want to trust him. I hated him when I first set eyes on him. I wanted him to fail and to be revealed as just another devious Akaran. But I was wrong. Dariel has fought for us. Without him, we would never have destroyed the soul catcher. The league would have it instead of the Lothan Aklun. The Sky Watcher, Nâ Gâmen, knew him, took him in, and gave his soul into him. Listen to what I say and think what it means. I have come to believe that Dariel Akaran can help save us, from ourselves, from the league. Listen to him carefully."

Mór tugged the horn from Than and extended it toward Dariel. He stepped forward and took it, staring into her eyes as he did so. By the Giver, she was beautiful! He had come to accept that she loved another woman and could never return his desire, but he would always find her features lovely. He had not known how much warmth would flood into him at hearing that she believed in him, but flood him it did, enough so that he looked away from her and took in the crowd. They stared at him, waiting.

The horn in his hand was heavy, solid metal, warm from the touch of the hands that had been holding it for the past few hours. All those hands, all the things they had argued for and secretly thought. He knew better than anyone that so far the meeting had been a vast confusion. They would never be able to vote on anything or to walk away from here with an agreement that would serve all.

Unless . . .

"You know my name," he began, his voice not nearly loud enough. He raised it. "I should declare it with my own lips, though. I am Dariel Akaran, third child of Leodan Akaran, who was the twenty-first ruler of Acacia. I wear this mark that says Rhuin Fá, but I will answer to that name only if you decide it belongs to me. I want to explain—"

The Antok speaker interrupted him. "How do you speak Auldek? If you are from Akaran lands, you would not speak it as you do, like it was your first tongue."

"I speak this way because I was meant to speak this way.

Because I was destined to stand before you and say the things I'm saying. I spoke barely a word of this tongue when I arrived here, but I am not the same man as when I arrived here. I wear this face now. This mark. I speak this language, and the heart behind all these things has found the purpose it did not have before."

Dukish whispered something under his breath to his secretary. The man came forward with a hand stretched out to take the horn back.

Dariel twisted away from him, holding the horn high and out of his reach. "You want to hear me speak? Then let me speak. Listen!"

When he was sure they all were listening, he began again. He admitted that he had been born in the palace of Acacia. He was raised in privilege, with maids about him, nannies and servants and guards, with a father he loved and siblings beside him. "Most of you had similar things, didn't you? At least parents and siblings you loved," he said, "and a place you knew as home. I know now that each one of you had those things taken from you. I know now that it was my family that sold you, and I know now how horrible a crime that was. I did not know it then. As you were children, so was I; as you learned what life held for you here, so did I learn hardship. I won't say it's equal to yours, but hear me."

He knew he was already talking too much, losing some of them, but he wanted them to know him. What else did he have but words? The more they heard his voice, the more they would recognize it. He described the first invasion of his childhood, Hanish Mein coming out of the north, his Numrek allies with him. He explained the betrayal of his guardian and how a giant of a man named Val became a second father to him. He spoke of his life as a raider and his war with the league, and of later reuniting with his siblings and of seeing his brother

killed and of feeling himself uncomfortable in the skin of royalty regained. He talked about the years he had tried to find a
way to live meaningfully, and said he had never felt he had until
the strange events that brought him to Ushen Brae and shoved
him under Tunnel's arm and earned him the scratches Mór's
Shivith claws made on his cheek, and which led, eventually, to
the Sky Watcher Nâ Gâmen showing him centuries of history
and writing the rune he now wore on his forehead.

"That is who I am," he said. "That's the journey that brought
me here, but none of it matters at all if I cannot help you build
the best nation you can here in Ushen Brae. That is the calling
I was looking for but did not know how to find. I had always
wondered what sense it made to be born in luxury and to lose
it. To have a family and to lose it. To have a nation but to be
taken from it. Now I know. Those are the steps in the life that
brought me here to you. Because of that, I know not one of them
was mistaken. Not one of them would I change, not since they
led me here to you."

He let his gaze move around in silence. He looked not just
at the clan representatives but at the crowds behind them. He
touched on face after face, remembering things about them all
as his eyes met theirs. That was when he understood why he
knew them. He had dreamed them. Those dreams in which he
had spoken to the people of Ushen Brae were not just dreams.
They had really happened. He knew it, and he tried to make
them know it as he gazed at them. Perhaps they already did, for
they held their silence, waiting for him to go on.

"Now that I'm here, I have to do something or my life will
not be worth anything. So here is what I argue for: unity among
you. Now is no time to forget the dream you've shared of being
Free People. It's no time to see differences. It's madness to think
that the souls and hearts of the Kern are any different from the
souls and hearts of the Wrathic. Do you know now just how

mad it is? In my country—I mean in the Known World. In our country back there." He pointed toward the sea. "Back there, we are divided. You know that, don't you? We are not one nation that acts together, that sent you to this land in some mutual agreement. Back there, we fight among ourselves. We have for centuries. We see difference everywhere. We see excuses to exclude, to suppress, to exploit. We always have.

"I remember when I arrived in Falik for the first time. It wasn't as if I had never seen the people of Balbara before, but being in among them hit me in the gut, in the eyes, in the ears. Everywhere. Black, black skin. Do you know it? Skin so dark that it looks, up close, like the only color skin could be. Compared to it, the weak brown that I am was embarrassing. And what, then, of the thin paper that is Meinish skin? What of the short stature of Vumu? The red hair and freckles of Aushenians? In the Known World we see all those differences. Seeing them, we're afraid. When I was a child, I was told my people were the center of the world, and that all around, from white to black, were races who had not the right to rule that my people did. If I was not to be afraid of others, I had to rule them, suppress them. That was our mistake. Look now at yours."

He pushed out of the representatives' circle and walked along before the front rows of the spectators. Standing before the gray skin and tusks of the Antoks, he said, "Look at you. You've all forgotten the racial differences that mean so much in my country. Here, if I look hard enough, I see beneath the gray coloration of your skin. I see Balbara features in you, Nem." He indicated an Antok man. The man looked stunned. Dariel stared at him and then looked around at those near him, seemingly verifying from their expressions that they heard him call him by name.

"And in you, Maris, I see Meinish blood. It's there in the shape of your nose, in those light-colored eyes of yours." Dariel moved on. He pointed out others, named them, and asked them to remember where they came from. They had been born in specific regions of the Known World, and yet here none of that mattered. The Auldek had not cared, and so the Lothan Aklun had ignored those differences as they sorted them into clan groups. The Lothan Aklun gave them different characteristics, ones shaped by Auldek fantasies.

"And now," Dariel said, "you've forgotten what you learned. The race you were born into doesn't matter. To you it doesn't matter if you're Bethuni or Candovian, Meinish or Talayan or Senivalian. It doesn't matter if your skin is black or brown or pale as milk. You've left those things behind, because you all came here united in bondage. Why should the clan you've been sorted into matter? It doesn't. Dukish wants you to think it does. He wants to teach you to fear one another. He doesn't say those words. He doesn't even know it himself. He says Anets are strong. That they should rule. Antoks can share Ushen Brae with them, take control, and have status. But why does any of that convince you? Because of fear. The moment you begin to consider having more than someone else, you begin to fear you might end up with less than someone else. That's the trick of the mind that Dukish has worked on you."

"Lies," a voice mumbled. Dariel knew whose it was. He had heard that voice in his dreams. "All lies."

"Dukish, I wish you no ill." Dariel had to wait as several people stepped out of the line of sight between him and the Anet leader. "I wish you no ill, but you have put Ushen Brae in danger. The war you have waged against the other clans and the deals you have worked out with the league are crimes that will keep the people in bondage. If you do not stop—"

"Who are you to talk?" Dukish said. He did not rise, but his voice was strong and his gaze, fixed finally on Dariel, shot hatred at him. "A prince!" He spit the words. "Do you know what a prince is? The child of a man. One who has done nothing and yet enslaves the world and is too much a coward to admit it. A prince!"

Dariel fingered the horn in his grasp. He held it still, but did not raise it. "Dukish, the league does not wish you well. They want us all weak. They want to elevate one of us above another only because it's easier to then exploit us all. That's what they have always done. They will use Ushen Brae now as much as they ever have. More, perhaps, because you'll be victims no longer. You'll be part of it with them. The league promises you fertile slaves. They want to sell them to you. They want you to become slavers. I can offer you something better. When we have sent the league from Ushen Brae I will call upon my country to bring you settlers. Think of that. Husbands and wives who will come here of their own accord, who want to make a place for themselves in this land. Why wouldn't they? I've seen Ushen Brae. It's beautiful. It's a continent that cries out for souls to live in it again, to fill its ancient cities, and to work the—"

"Lies!" Dukish shouted. He pushed up so fast his chair tipped over and crashed behind him. He was a short man, stout around the chest, menacing as he pushed closer. "Only the league knows how to make us fertile again. Sire Lethel can undo what the Lothan Aklun did to us. You cannot; can you?"

Before Dariel could respond, Anira did. "Yes. He has done it already."

Dariel stared at her.

She walked toward him and took the horn before she continued speaking. "I . . . Dariel, I didn't plan to tell you like this. I told you once that the Sky Watcher showed me a vision of the future and of the role I could play in it. He did not claim it was the future that would be, but just that it could be."

A small flock of raucous birds swept through the chamber, skimming the roof and squawking the whole time. Anira watched them until they slipped into the shadows and disappeared.

When she stayed silent, Dariel prompted, "And?"

She looked around, speaking to everyone. "In all the years that there have been quota children in Ushen Brae not one has ever grown into a mother or a father. This was the curse for us."

"We know this!" Dukish said.

"We wanted the trade to end, but if it did, we knew we would end," Anira continued. "The Free People, I mean. Our ways. The things we made despite our captivity. Eventually, we would age and die. Our freedom, if we ever won it, would be the beginning of our end. That was what I always believed. I think that we all did. Now"—she turned and looked at Dariel—"I know differently. Because of you, Dariel Akaran. Because of you and me, and because of what we are creating."

Dariel knew, at some level, that she was not talking about the pact between the clans and the fight against the league, but it was not until she slid one of her hands across her abdomen that the clouds blew completely away and the realization of what she was saying stood there clear as day. Clear as a palm pressed lovingly against a woman's abdomen.

"It's early days," Anira said, "but there is life within me. I know it. I can feel it. The Sky Watcher Nâ Gâmen told me it could be so, and it is. I'm sorry for not telling you, Dariel, but Nâ Gâmen told me this could be my destiny. I have your child in me."

The entire chamber erupted. Dukish cursed it all as a fraud. It was all planned, he said. A lie. He knew it to be a lie. He had proof. It was hard to know if anyone heard him, for people from all the clans pushed in close to Anira. Some of them touched her belly. Others looked her in the face and searched for the truth.

Others shouted the joy of it, and still others called foul. Tunnel, trying to protect her, got into a shoving match with several Antoks. Had they weapons, there would have been slaughter.

And if Mór had not clasped her hand over Anira's and raised the horn high, the place might have descended into chaos. "Calm! Show calm!" Mór shouted. "Do you really want to learn of life and respond with chaos? Free People, step away! Back!"

It took her some time, but the crowd did draw slowly back. Mór's voice grew calmer as she gained more control of them. "See? The leaguemen want to sell us something that can be freely given. There is nothing more to it than joining with Dariel's people. We have a future! A free future. All we need do is embrace it."

Hearing the buzz of enthusiasm this met with, Dukish shouted to be heard. "No! No, no, no! He is the one who sold us. His people. Now the league has freed us, and he wants us to be slaves again. I can prove it." He lifted his chin and projected his voice over the crowd. "Bring the prisoners!"

For a moment there was confusion, shouted words and questions, a murmuring throughout the entire chamber. Mór demanded to know what was happening, but Dukish, looking smug, ignored her and repeated his order.

People turned as a group of Antoks strode down one of the open corridors. They shoved and cursed as they did, making room. There in the center of them, four figures, weighted by chains. In all the commotion Dariel could not make out their faces until their escorts deposited them in the center of the lighted square. The brawny guards drained away, leaving the four prisoners standing, dejected, frightened, in the center of the gathering.

Dariel recognized them. He blinked, unsure if he could trust his eyes, still stunned by Anira's revelation. "Melio. Clytus. Geena . . ."

As he said their names, their eyes found him. They stared, each of them looking at him and none of them recognizing him. How different he must look! One of the quota slaves among others like him. He tried to move toward them, but Dukish's men blocked him.

"These prisoners were caught trying to enter Avina," Dukish said. "My brothers the Antoks captured them, and together we got the truth from them. They came looking for Dariel Akaran. They came as spies planning to take over this land."

"No," Dariel said.

"They want to make us slaves again. They don't like that the league is willing to partner with us. That's why this man is here trying to trick you. I don't know how he does it. Some trick of the Lothan Aklun. All to keep us passive as they tighten their chains around us again."

"No," Dariel said.

"No?" Dukish asked. "I have their written confessions—signed by them!"

Dariel tried to shove his way toward the prisoners, but Dukish's men beat him back. "They would never confess to that because it isn't true. Clytus, tell them the truth."

The man stared all the harder at the mention of his name, but he did not respond. Dariel realized he had been speaking Auldek. He switched to Acacian. "Clytus, it's me, Dariel."

"Spratling?"

"Yes, it's me! Don't worry. You'll be free in a moment. I promise it."

Dukish ignored him. He droned on, building his case on a foundation of lies. Dariel grasped for the horn. Mór released it and Dariel held it high. He jumped with it, shouting until people acknowledged him and Dukish began to lose their attention.

"These people are my friends," Dariel admitted. "But if they came here, it was to find me, not to harm you in any way. Don't let Dukish speak for them. He cannot be trusted. Nothing he has said here today has been true."

Dukish cursed him.

"You know in your heart that's not true. You told me so. You told me the truth of yourself."

"Never."

"You told me of the way you coveted your master's wealth."

Dukish moved nearer. People cleared away from in front of him. "I never did!"

"I don't want to have to say this, but I need you to speak truthfully. I spoke with Dukish as I spoke with all of you. You all know that's true. As you told me secrets, so did he. I know your hearts, and I do not judge you by what's in them."

"Liar!"

Dariel said, "Dukish has secrets from you all."

"No!"

"Of course he does. There were things done to him that—"

"No!"

Dariel punched the air with the hand that held the curl of iron. "I hold the horn," he snapped at Dukish. "Be quiet while I speak! Things were done to him that should not have been. You know of what I speak, don't you?"

Dukish started to say something, but Tunnel moved on him as if he would hit him if he spoke. Other Anets shouldered closer. They jostled Dukish and in the confusion he almost lost his footing.

Dariel continued. "Think, Dukish, about the things you confessed to me." He looked the Anet leader in the eyes. He really did not want to say what he was about to. It was cruel. It would hurt. It did not seem fair to break the man's confidence so publicly.

He could say that Dukish's master had raped him since his earliest days in Avina. He used him on a balcony overlooking the skyline of Avina. He set his head and shoulders out over the railing, and took pleasure in Dukish's fear that he might thrust him over the edge to his death at any moment. He could say just what Dukish had—that it was there, looking out over the city as his master used him that he learned fear and hate and that he first dreamed of the things he would do to others if only he had the power. *He was not born an evil man*, Dariel could say. *He was born weak, petty, scared. That is why he's done the things he has here. Not because he is strong, but because he is weak. I'm sorry, Dukish, to say that about you. I take no joy in it.*

He could say all those things and everyone would know that they were true. But he could not be that cruel. Instead, he said, "Admit to me that you know I hold your truth within me. Just do that and I will say no more about it, now or ever."

"You can say whatever you want," Dukish said. He pushed closer to Dariel. He stood just before him now. "Nobody will remember. I'll make sure of it."

His hand suddenly clenched a knife. He was so close and people packed so tightly around them that Dukish had only to thrust the knife forward. It sank into Dariel's gut before he could say or do anything. He could only manage a gasp, so overwhelming was the pain. Dukish held him on his knife blade, his face a rictus of hatred that Dariel stared into for a moment. Then the world turned black.

❋

This time, Dariel barely dropped out of life before he was thrust back up into it. When he could see again, he saw a chamber in chaos. Hands held him up, dragging him back from the center of the confusion. The pain at his center was incredible. The knife was still inside him. The hilt of it jutted out, the point jolting him with continued shocks of misery. He wanted nothing more than to curl over it, to wrap himself around it completely, and ignore everything else. Instead he looked up at what was happening.

No . . . Dariel thought. No.

Dukish and his Anets fought like mad with Tunnel and Mór and many others. They pounded one another with fists and elbows, punching and clawing. Tunnel bashed his way toward the Anet leader, using his forehead to smash the faces of any who opposed him. Dukish fought like a trapped animal, his face crazed, shouting something again and again. The Lvin converged on them. Than raked an Anet's eyes with the claws at his fingertips. Mór managed to sink hers into Dukish's cheek before getting pushed back on a surge. She seemed as desperate to tear him apart as he was to survive.

With all his strength, Dariel threw both his arms up. It hurt so much his vision blurred and rippled. He held his arms high, stiff and trembling, palms flat for all to see. "Don't!"

It was not a loud scream, but some heard it. First just those holding him. Anira's face came into view beside his. And then those around him turned to look, and then others as word began to pass. More and more faces turned toward him. The knot of fighting went on a little longer, but even Dukish sensed the growing hush. He froze, his arm cocked back to punch Tunnel, who had finally reached him. He followed the others' gazes and found Dariel. He stared openmouthed.

All of them did. All of them watched as Dariel shook off the hands holding him and stood on his own. I'm all right, he thought. He was not really. Part of him had just died. Part of his and Nâ Gâmen's soul was oozing out of him even as he stood there. He reached down and took the hilt of the knife with both hands. He held for a few breaths, and then pulled on it. It felt like he was ripping out a link in his spine, like it was part of him and would not come. And then it did. He screamed it out of him with a surge of blood. The knife clattered to the floor. He let his hands drop and stood there, swaying on his feet, trembling.

I'm all right, he thought. Then he remembered he needed to say it out loud.

"I'm all right."

To prove it, he stripped off his blood-soaked shirt. He wadded it and wiped at his torso, turning as he did so. He did not get all the blood off, but it was clear that the gash that should have killed him was already just a welt of inflamed skin.

Everyone stared at him. The silence hummed and vibrated in the air for a long time, until Tunnel called out his name. Not Dariel Akaran, though. His new name. The one only they could truly bestow on him. Tunnel's voice said it and then another repeated it. And then many more took it up.

Dariel stood, shirtless and bloody at the center of the chamber filled with the freed slaves of Ushen Brae, as they named him the Rhuin Fá.

CHAPTER
FORTY-NINE

O ne day, after Aliver told his sister about what Sire Dagon had written, they both agreed that they would permit themselves one day. For Corinn the news of what she had done with the vintage had a breadth of atrocity that she could fathom no more than learning of her own pending death, or Aliver's. It was all too huge. She wanted to collapse beneath the weight of it in utter misery. She wanted to take up that knife again and end herself.

It was only at Aliver's urging and Hanish's quiet whisper that she agreed to put the enormity of the world aside for just one day, the last they would spend with the ones they loved. From the middle hours of one morning, through an afternoon and evening, still further through the dark hours of the night and into the next sunrise. That was the span of time that Corinn and Aliver let the world wait for them. They spent it together with their children. For Corinn, it was a lifetime.

In the short span of time she had left to live, Corinn would cherish many moments from that single day. When she lowered the cowl from her chin was one such moment. She hated doing so and acquiesced only after Aaden had asked her to quite firmly. She searched his face for any sign of disgust. There was a tenseness in his jaw and a quiver on his left cheek and a sudden moistness that brimmed his eyes. But there was no disgust. He said, "Mother, look at that. Now why did they do that?" He sounded like an old woman, full of empathy. His fingers extended toward her, asking permission. She gave it with a nod and he touched her damaged face. To her surprise, she felt the warmth of the life within him, his skin soft, gentle. For a few seconds, she almost thought his touch had healed her. Then she raised the cowl into place.

A few days ago she would not have been content to sit with Benabe across the table from her. She would not have been able to look at Shen and acknowledge the loveliness of her round, brown face without fearing that it threatened her son's legacy. She would not even have allowed her brother to be fully himself. As she sat with them, listening to the tale they had to tell, the things that had once seemed logical reactions to a predatory world now seemed like rules composed in a foreign language. She did not understand herself anymore. The woman she had been stood unmasked. She felt that she, in her own way, had been a puppet to base parts of her nature that should never have been allowed to rule her.

"Leave that for now," Hanish said. She tried to.

They climbed up to the Terrace of First Light later in the morning. Elya's children were there, almost too large now to all crowd into the space. They seemed to sense that something was wrong from the moment Corinn entered. They greeted her half-covered face with suspicion, sniffing her and scenting the air with their slim tongues. Corinn calmed them by sending soothing, yet somber thoughts to them.

"I don't like them as much as Elya," Aaden said. He turned apologetically to her. "I'm sorry to say that. They are incredible, Mother, but Elya is special. I don't think that any of these would have saved me the same way she did. Do you?"

Corinn ran her palm over his head, all the answer she wished to give.

Still, when Aliver and Shen shot up into the air on Kohl's back, Aaden clawed at her, begging to follow. Po, competitive as always, was eager to oblige. The four of them swept down from the palace, over the terraced layers of the city. They swept over the lower town and then beat their way higher. Corinn thought of the day when all four Akaran children had ridden horseback with their father. They had galloped out from the town and along the winding road over the island's hills, down to that beach, the one she saw hundreds of feet below her now. That had been a memorable day. Perhaps, for these children, this was another such day. She hoped so.

They flew out to Haven's Rock, where they stood in the wind and listened to Aliver eulogize his former tutor, Jason, and Leeka Alain of the Northern Guard, the first to slay a Numrek and the only one to ever run down fleeing sorcerers. He thanked the tutor for being the first to draw the map of the world in Aliver's mind, for being such a lover of knowledge and a keeper of history. "It was he who first challenged my princely arrogance. I should have thanked him more for that before this." About Leeka, he said, "And here, after years of service, his last deed. He returned to us and said the words that saved us for the now." Looking at Corinn, he added, "In the end, he did what mattered. For that, he will not be forgotten."

After that, they returned to joy. They dove down from heights like seabirds. They skimmed out over the water, the waves growing more and more pronounced as the sea grew deeper. Aaden shouted above the rushing air, "It's wonderful, Mother. Let's go faster. This is like Mena said!" Corinn did not know quite what he meant and she could not ask. She could go faster, though. She urged Po to do so.

❋

And then all too quickly it was night. How tired they all were, or should be but were not really. The notion of sleeping hours away seemed so wasteful. When Aaden proposed that they stay together throughout the entire night, Corinn was amazed at how easily that problem was solved. Of course. Why sleep? There were not enough hours left to sleep! Listening to the two children's cheers, Corinn could not help but think of that day long ago when her father promised them a late-night snowball fight. That night never came to be. This one would.

They had the servants stoke the fire in the center of a small amphitheater on Aliver's terrace. Night sky clear and chilly above them, they curled up among the blankets and cushions and furs. So many things to remember: the shape of Shen's teeth when her head was thrown back in laughter. The way Benabe could make any sentence into a song just by putting music in her voice. The stories Barad told, the tree trunk of a man, stone eyed, holding the children rapt with his deep voice.

Corinn would always remember the comfort she took when she slipped Aaden's head from her lap, thinking he was asleep. She tried to move away, but he said, "Mother, it's not over, is it?" She could not speak and his eyes were closed, but he did not need to hear or see her answer. "You'll fix it. I know you will."

A little later, after sleep finally overpowered both children beside the fire pit, the two monarchs sat beside each other on the stone bench that looked out over the harbor. They had both read yet another message, this one from Mena, describing what she intended to do. Corinn tried to reach out to her across the distance. She was tired enough that it almost worked. She did shoot up out of her body and above the palace. She flew, wingless, toward the north. But as with that time she had searched in vain for Dariel, she eventually came to a halt, hanging in the air, no feeling for where to go or how to reach her.

"Mena is a warrior. If anyone can hold back the Auldek, she can," Aliver said. Then he asked her more about dream travel, about what it felt like to separate a soul from a body, and about what she knew of how the Auldek could hold spare life forces inside themselves. She had Rhrenna bring her documents the league had provided, and together the siblings talked through the fantastical horror of it. "What greater form of slavery could there be?" Aliver asked. "Enslaving not bodies but souls."

Corinn did not answer, for she could think of none.

As Corinn had wanted to speak with her brother without other men's voices, she had asked Barad and Hanish to stay among the others. Instead, she spoke with a quill and parchment. It made her choose her words carefully. She wrote, *I know. I just wish I could have seen her again, and Dariel. I sent them both so far away. Now I can't understand why I didn't want them near me and Aaden. Don't make Mena wait long. Go as fast as you can. Reach her. Fight beside her. If I could, I would go with you.*

"I'll get to her. I'll do everything I can to end this before I end myself."

I'll do the same.

Aliver slid a hand over hers, held it there a moment. She did not like the quiet hopelessness of the gesture. She pulled her hand away, wrote, and turned the page so he could see.

I know what to do. I have the book.

It took a moment for this to fully sink in. When it did, his eyes came back to hers, not so hopeless anymore. "You have it?"

Corinn nodded, and then playfully nudged him on the shoulder.

He understood. "Of course, you have it," he said. "You didn't send the Santoth to it. You sent them away from it. My clever sister."

The way lines formed at the edge of her eyes was the only way she could indicate that she was smiling. She saw that Aliver saw it, and was glad.

"What will you do with the book? Can you destroy it?"

She shook her head and wrote, *It's not mine to destroy.*

Aliver thought about that for a time. "All right, it's not yours to destroy. It was here before us and it might be wrong to take it from the world completely. That could be another mistake. I understand that. What, then?"

Return it.

"Return it to whom?"

To the worm.

"I don't understand."

Corinn looked at him, and then at where Barad slept. She seemed to consider waking him, but then shook the thought away. Pulling the tablet onto her lap, she leaned to write her response. With her posture, she told Aliver not to begin reading until she was done. She wrote for a long time, and then slid the tablet back into his hands. She moved away to the railing as he bent to read.

She had written: *From the day I began to study* The Song, *I felt a living force protest. In my mind it was a great worm. I sometimes imagined it rising from the floor of the sea, its jaws so large they could close around all of the isle of Acacia. I knew it to be angry with me, and I thought it a foulthing.*

I know now that's not right. That creature was always telling me to return the book to it. That creature is its protector. It was of the world before Elenet. Edifus called on it to devour the book, to eat it and hold it inside its body. That's what it did. Tinhadin should have left it there.

"How do you know all this?"

She pressed her fingers to her chest, indicating that she felt it in her heart. *I know it,* she wrote.

"How do you take the book to this worm?"

I find it. I don't think it will be hard. It is somewhere beneath the Gray Slopes. Po will fly me there.

The two siblings sat in stillness for a while. She thought of Leeka Alain in the moment just before his death. *What do you think Leeka was trying to tell us?*

Aliver shook his head. That was all the answer he had. Eventually, Corinn asked the question Aaden would have wanted her to. She wrote, *Might it be untrue?*

Aliver did not have to ask what she was referring to. "I know I should wonder that myself, but I don't. I feel the truth of it. I feel nearer to returning to where I should be. I feel no fear of it. Sadness, yes, but . . . I don't doubt that Dagon wrote the truth."

She wrote, *Nor do I. I wish the first time he was truthful wasn't this. So much conspiring. He and I—we've conspired our lives away. That's the only part of this that feels right. I couldn't live with this guilt. The Santoth. The vintage. Jason and Kelis and Barad. The things I did to everyone. I couldn't live with it, but knowing of my approaching death helps. We have little time and much to do.*

Seek Paddel, the vintner on Prios. Make him tell you everything about the vintage. It's mist by another name, Aliver, another of my crimes. Make him tell you.

Aliver nodded. "I will. What of Elya's children? They're monsters, Corinn. I know you didn't intend that, but—"

She stopped him by beginning to write. *I did intend it. They are monsters, but they are our monsters. Use them. As long as I live they will be true to us. I sang that into them before they were even born.*

"After that?"

I cannot say. After I die it will be different, but trust them until that. She paused a moment, and then wrote, *I don't deserve this day. The fullness of it. The time to talk with you, even like this. I don't deserve it.*

"Of course you do."

Corinn exhaled through her nose. *I've planted nothing but evil seeds. Now they have sprung to life, none of them as I imagined.*

Aliver's hand stopped hers. He had been reading as she wrote. "Don't. That's the past. I look at you and I see so much to admire. It means a great deal to me that you treat my daughter with love, and that you are kind to Benabe. I barely knew her, yet . . . still, it matters. And I know that the sister I had but a few days ago would have seen only challenge in them. Only foes and dangers to be clipped and controlled. You don't have to explain that to me. That's what it means to be siblings. I do know the worst of you, whether you like it or not." He smiled. "But I also know that you would not be here as you are today, with them sleeping over there after such a wonderful day, if the love that you are showing wasn't in you always. That's why I cannot be angry with you. Anger would be a waste of the moments we have, and it would make us weak in the face of the things we have yet to do."

It sounded so good when he said it. She sat with that a while, hoping it was true.

After a while, she wrote, *Did you love her?* She pointed her chin toward Benabe, who slept with her arm over Shen.

"I might have. I was too young to know." He thought a moment. "She was very beautiful. Still is, really."

If we had more time.

"Yes, if we had more time."

Still later in the night Corinn sat at a table not far from the others, quills, paper, and ink at hand. She had a note to compose.

Hanish stood with a hand on her shoulder. "You didn't tell him about the hard part," Hanish said. "About the fact that you're planning to lure the Santoth into the worm's mouth as well. That will not be 'easy.'"

She thought, *No need to worry him. That's for me to deal with. Now, be quiet. I have only a few hours to write everything I can for Aaden. You can watch over my shoulder but don't say anything.*

When she had confirmation that he would not, she lifted the quill and considered what she wished most to say. She knew how she would begin and how she would end it. The same phrase. The truth. It was all the things in between that would take some sorting.

She wrote his name, and then, *I love you. In all the long life that you have before you, I hope that you find love in all its complicated variations. And each time it confounds you and surprises you, hurts you and heals you—remember me, for the love I mean includes all those things.*

Pausing, she wondered how much she should say, what she should withhold. It pained her to think of some of the lessons she had given the boy, things she did not believe now and doubted she ever had, not completely. Hopefully, some of that would fall away from him. Hopefully, he would be better than she had taught him, less afraid, more trusting. It was dangerous to be all those things, but it was even more dangerous to be as she had been. One cannot be whole unto themselves. She knew that now. She would tell him as much. She would tell him everything she could, so that this letter spoke to him in the years to come.

She dipped the quill, and continued writing.

❈

The next morning she and Aliver met as the sun rose. They laid out the future as they agreed it should be, had it put in writing, sealed and official, and then locked away. The business of it took every moment up until the expiration of the single day.

Corinn kept her parting brief. Private. It was not vanity that stopped her from addressing the populace. She would proudly enough have stood before them. She was still herself in Aaden's eyes, so no one else could hurt or embarrass her. Nor did she mind asking Barad to be her voice to the world. He had a good voice. She had always liked it, and the fact that he gave it to her of his own free will did much to comfort her.

The reason she said good-bye to her family in private was that she wanted no pomp on her departure. She did not wish to speak grandiose words, to instill either hope or worry. Aliver would stay after her to speak with the people in ways that brought the best out of them. What she needed to do, she had to do alone, so that's how she set out.

Or . . . almost alone.

"You're finally going to let me ride on your blessed mount?" Hanish asked. He stood beside her as she made last-minute checks to her straps, harness, and supply satchels.

I never stopped you. You were just nervous. You don't like it that he can see you.

It was true. Po's eyes did follow Hanish. He was not a particularly curious creature, but he seemed to recognize something unusual in Hanish's presence. He squinted one eye and then the other when looking at him, as if testing something about his vision. There was no aggression in it, though. Corinn sensed that the dragon recognized that Hanish was somehow a part of her, that they were related to him through the magic that had shaped them.

She hugged everyone. She held Shen's face in her palms and stared at it a long time, and she had Hanish and Barad explain to her that there was absolutely no blame on her for bringing the Santoth to Acacia. That was Corinn's responsibility. Shen should never feel another moment of guilt for it.

In parting with Aaden, she slipped the folded and sealed note into his hands. She told him not to rush to open it. Read when he was ready. Wait as long as he wished.

She pressed Aliver's hand in hers and asked him to speak

the truth of her to Mena when he reached her. Let her know that in the end, at least, she tried to be somebody Maeben on earth would be proud of. And then, before emotion could get the better of her, she mounted Po and they leaped into the air. She did not look back until she was some distance away.

"So what do we do first?" Hanish asked.

First, we find the Santoth. Who knows what they've gotten up to, or how cross they'll be now that they know Calfa Ven does not contain what they seek.

"And then?"

And then we destroy them. If it's possible, we destroy them. We make things right again.

Hanish, with his arms around her waist and lips close to her ear, said, "All right. Let's do that."

CHAPTER
FIFTY

Rialus worried to no end about the frostbite that damaged the tip of his nose and the skin of his cheeks. It did not go deep, but he feared that Devoth or Sabeer or Allek—annoying Allek—would notice it and question him. To him, the dead flesh, which went red and painful and peeling as it warmed in his room, wrote his whole escapade right there on his face. He would cave at the first query. Where had he been that first day of battle? Why had somebody seen him trekking across the snow? Was that where he got that frost damage to his skin? Had he really thought he could desert them, and that his people would want him back?

It all felt like such a great folly. Shuffling away from the enormous torches that were the burning towers; stumbling into the dark; fearful every moment of discovery; and then, eventually, alone in the howling arctic night. How foolish. And then he had been found, bundled into the Acacian camp, surrounded, interrogated. As cold and as miserable as he had been, joy had sputtered to life, a single candle flame of heat and light within him. How foolish. He had spoken to Princess Mena in the flesh, offering his pathetic bits of information, thinking he was saved. He was with Acacians again. He was with his people! How foolish. Scarcely an hour of hope, and then back to the ice again, sent away by people who loved him not, back into the jaws of his enemy.

He would have liked to believe it was a nightmare, except that the proof of its reality was right there in the bits of flesh that Fingel trimmed away from his face, right there in the wounds she treated with an alcohol ointment that kicked his eyes back into his head with the scorching pain of touch. He could not tell if she enjoyed hurting him. She worked, actually, as if the pain did not occur to her at all.

"Fool Rialus!" he said. "Why even have your face tended? Let it fester and go green and kill you. Death, you know, is your only way out of this misery."

Fingel said nothing. She hardly ever said anything. Finished with her work, she turned away with the warm water, bloody towels, and shears. She put them down and then checked the small pot of broth she had brewing over a shallow pitch fire.

"They wouldn't have me, Fingel," Rialus said. He could not tell if she listened to him at all, so unresponsive was she to his words. He spoke anyway, a habit he took some comfort in, which soothed his occasional stutter right out of his voice. "I tried, but they wouldn't have me. They sent me back. Told me to bring them more. To them I'm nothing but a traitor." He watched the shape of her back as she worked. Even bundled under several layers of clothing, he could still make out her figure. He had studied it often enough, and thought of it many a time in erotic fantasies. Why had he never forced her? Because I'm afraid of what that would mean about me. It would mark the end of anything worthwhile in me.

"I wonder if you would kill me if I asked you to. It would be your last act as my slave. I could write a note explaining that I had ordered you to do it, so that you wouldn't get punished. I wonder if you would."

And yet he did not make the simple changes to his phrasing that would have made the question the young woman had to answer. Instead he looked at his damaged face in his hand mirror. He slurped the meat broth Fingel had made for him. He waited for the summons he dreaded and anticipated.

❋

It did not come. Not that day, at least. Not during the following evening, nor in the dark of that night. His station remained immobile, steaming away like a behemoth at rest. He heard movement outside, all the normal sounds. Men shouting, laborers at work. Beasts bellowing. A few times he heard the distinctive chattering of fréketes in flight. They seemed louder than usual, more agitated. And yet hour after hour passed without the expected knock on his door or the shout that would call him to explain himself.

On the morning of the second day since the battle, Rialus could not help asking Fingel what was happening outside. She had just returned from some errand. Stripping off layers, she said, "Nothing."

"Nothing? Where's Devoth? Why haven't they called for me?"

He knew she would not answer these questions. He followed them with others that she did not answer either. Eventually, he could not take her silence anymore. He pulled on his furs, yanked tight his hood, and shoved his hands into his mittens. He went out to find the people he most feared finding.

Devoth and the other clan leaders sat at council in the large station outfitted for the purpose. The human guards at the entrance barely noticed as Rialus walked past them. They seemed preoccupied. They talked among themselves. Argued actually. Rialus slipped inside.

The council was in full swing, crowded and contentious.

Several Auldek were talking at once, each of them vying to be the center of discussion and none of them managing it.

"I told you we were too many," Calrach said. When nobody listened, he slammed his palm on the table. "You forget that we Numrek did this journey before, fought these Acacians before. I told you it was foolish to display the whole army in front of them. Now you see why. We can do nothing with so many against so few! We should be more selective."

To this, Skahill offered the slight that the Numrek had made this crossing before, but they did so like thieves in the night, with no one to oppose them until they were welcomed as guests, given a fortress and a steaming chamber to feast in. Considering that, what did Calrach know about how to fight the war they were fighting, up here, on the ice? "You want to be more selective. Perhaps we should send the Numrek to do battle by yourselves, all eleven of you. Will that shut your mouth?"

"I would do it with joy," Calrach ground through his teeth, no sign in his visage of the joy he spoke of. "Not everyone is so afraid to die as you."

"Afraid! Anets were in the front lines. We pleaded for the cowards to fight us."

"So you say. Perhaps you pleaded them to bend you over and—"

Skahill shot to his feet, slamming a fist on the table as he did so and roaring in wordless rage. Calrach shoved the man next to him as he began coming around the table. Skahill did the same, upsetting chairs and the people in them, clawing with one hand for his dagger.

Faster than Rialus could follow with his eyes, Sabeer went from sitting to crouching on top of the table, with an arm thrust toward either man. Each fist clenched a curved crescent of steel. She stayed that way a moment, lean and gorgeous. Utterly terrifying. "Stop it! Keep bickering and I'll take you to death myself. Say another word in anger. Either of you. Just one more word . . ."

Neither man took her up on that. They continued to glare at each other, but they held their tongues and crashed back into their seats. If they had not been warriors they could have been chastened, angry children.

What in Hadin's name is going on here? Rialus wondered. He had never seen the Auldek so ill-tempered. Herith glared at Sabeer's back as she climbed down from the table. Or so melancholy. Millwa leaned forward on the table, his head cradled in his hands. Or so distressed. Jàfith . . . Well, if Rialus had not found the idea impossible, he would have said that Jàfith had been crying recently. And Devoth wore a look of profound perplexity written on the lines of his forehead and with the vague, unfocused way his gaze floated without fixing on anything.

What in Hadin's name? Rialus avoided the empty seat at Devoth's side. His seat. He slunk around the edge of the chamber and found a stool that hid him behind the bulky shoulders of several of the chieftain's assistants. There he listened. As the chieftains paid those behind them no mind, he even scooted up beside the assistants and whispered questions to them. In the hours that followed, he pieced together a mental mosaic of what had transpired.

The battle had not gone well for the Auldek at all. Instead of a day of glorious slaughter, they had experienced one of confusion, frustration, humiliation, and even an Auldek death. This latter thing it took him some time to understand. He could not picture how it came about, but somehow Mena had cut through most of Howlk's neck in midair, both of them riding on Nawth's back. The impact from his fall finished the job, sending his head twirling across the ice, through the feet of the high-stepping, horrified Auldek. His body spasmed through death after death, all his lives tearing themselves out of him in one long agony. The Auldek who saw this from up close—including Jàfith—were shaken to their cores.

Nawth did not die from the fall, but he was so crippled that the clan chieftains had decided he would have to be abandoned. Fréketes could not be killed for some sacred reason that Rialus could not fathom, but neither could injured ones be kept alive. Their bones do not heal, apparently. Nawth would never be anything more than broken. Better he be dead, then, by Auldek logic.

Incredible. And there was more.

The things he heard stoked the fires of rebellion inside him. The Auldek could make no sense of the tactics Mena had employed, but he could. He saw the results of the things he had told Mena in all of it. She had cut the amulet off Nawth's neck because *he* had told her she should. Right? Of course. Yes. She had avoided fighting the Auldek because *he* had told her about their impenetrable body armor. And she had sent volleys of arrows into the slave flanks because *he* had said they would be vulnerable. It all seemed so obvious to him. His culpability swam in his head, making him dizzy.

I did this, he thought. I helped this . . .

"Rialus leagueman!" Devoth's voice snatched him up from his paroxysms of self-congratulation. He had quite forgotten himself, and was stunned to find all the chieftains gazing at him. "Come to my side," Devoth said.

When Rialus managed to reach him, after stumbling over stools and having to squeeze among bodies that stubbornly did not move to let him pass, Devoth said, "Where have you been?"

Exactly the question Rialus had feared. His short-lived euphoria evaporated, replaced by the dread he had become so used to. "I—I've been trying to understand."

"You and all of us. Why do they not fight us, Rialus?"

Feeling his pulse quicken, Rialus picked up the stylus on the table before him as if he had just remembered something he needed to make a note of.

"Tell me. You know them. Why will they not fight us as they should? Are they cowards? Have we come across the roof of the world to fight cowards?"

No, you've come across to die, Rialus thought. He said, "Yes, they are cowards. Look no f-f-further than that. They're cowards."

Devoth did not seem to have heard. "It's like they are wolves and we the prey. They attack our weak points, the lame, the young. They avoid the strong. I did not expect this."

"Don't compare them to wolves," Herith said. "The Wrathic are not cowards."

"Perhaps the Acacians are not either," Sabeer said. She spoke to Herith, but her eyes were on Rialus.

He looked down and stayed that way as the conversation circled around the idea of Acacian cowardice.

Some time later, Sabeer remained the only one who saw something other than cowardice in the events of the day. "The princess did not avoid Howlk and Nawth," she said. "You cannot say she is a coward."

"Exactly," Rialus said. He regretted it the moment the word was out of his mouth. She had just said something so obviously true the affirmation slipped out of him.

The other chieftains fell silent. Devoth turned and looked directly at Rialus. "No, she showed bravery in that, at least. How did she know to cut loose the amulet?"

"She knew more than that," Sabeer said. "She knew our strengths and avoided them. She did not strike at us—at the Auldek—or engage the mounted warriors. Arrows may be cowardly, but they felled thousands of divine children. She hurt us more than we hurt her. Clever, in a way."

Having not taken his eyes off Rialus, Devoth pressed, "Rialus, how did she know these things?"

Rialus kept his head bent, his attention on the page. He did not want to speak. Words bubbled in him too ferociously. He did not want to let them out, and yet he did not even shrug. He did not motion with his fingers or purse his lips or give any answer to Devoth at all. He knew he should, but he did not. He wrote, *How did she know? How did she know?*

"Stop scribbling."

How did she . . .

"Stop scribbling and answer me!"

"I have no answer to give!" Rialus snapped. He slashed the stylus across the words he had written and tossed it down. He looked around at the Auldek faces staring at him. "What do you want me to say? That I snuck out of camp in the night, ran across the ice to them, told them all your secrets, ran back across the ice, and crept into my quarters unseen? Would you believe that? Even know I'm a spy? If you were wise, you would kill me, kill me now before I bring your entire race to ruin!"

Rialus finished shouting. His face flushed red and his hands trembled. The Auldek around the table stared at him with mild revulsion, as if he had just demonstrated his insanity in some depraved manner. Devoth asked quietly, "Is that true?"

"Yes, that's exactly what I did," Rialus said. His voice dropped to match Devoth's and lost its edge, but he looked at the chieftain as he said it. "I met a lioness on the way and I broke her neck."

The room was silent for a moment. The chieftains stared. The officers and assistants behind them craned forward. "Broke her neck?" Devoth asked.

"With my bare hands."

A grin tugged at one corner of Devoth's lips, and then won over the other as well. "All right, Rialus leagueman. All right." He slapped Rialus on the back and shared his sudden humor with the others. "He is a lion killer," he said. "Our Rialus. Who would have thought it?"

"Lioness killer," Sabeer corrected. The others guffawed, enjoying yet another joke at Rialus leagueman's expense.

Rialus sat looking at the scribbled words on the parchment before him, hating them.

***

By the time he left the meeting, well into the night, he knew of the other significant development in the war. The night after the battle, Mena and the Acacian army had packed up their camp and departed. That was why there had been no continuation of the battle the next day. Mena had the tail end of her forces into the ice slabs before outriders on woolly rhinos could reach them. This was another thing the chieftains debated at length. Whether it was cowardice on Mena's part or some design they could not fathom, there seemed only one course of action: to pursue. The Acacians ran toward the Auldek's goal anyway, so why not chase them out onto the Mein Plateau, then on toward the heart of Acacia?

***

The next morning the jarring sensation of his station grinding into motion awoke Rialus. Whips cracked like ice serpents, brutal, punishing sounds met by bellows of protest from the beasts.

Flakes of dust rained down on him from the beams above. The engines of the station gurgled and groaned. All the familiar sounds and sensations. They were in motion again.

"We're going home," he said out loud, knowing that Fingel would be sitting on her mat, engaged in some small work already. "We're going home."

It proved to be a difficult homecoming. The clear weather of the recent days ran away, pursued by a blizzard of snow and ice crystals. Rialus stayed huddled in his station as much as he could. Though he was secure inside, Rialus could not escape Nawth's anguished jabbering at being left behind. How could his voice travel so far, grate on the ears with such intensity? Nawth's entreaties were so close to language. He sounded like he was fumbling with speech to make a case for himself. It was made worse by the cacophony of cries and moans and bellows of the other fréketes swooping in the air above. And his circling brothers . . . they heard him. They left him anyway. Rialus could not be certain, but he thought that even days later the wind brought snatches of Nawth's ongoing misery to him, across miles of ice. Haunting. He would never forget the sound.

Allek brought him news of the troubles they were having. Rialus could not have said why, but the Numrek youth seemed to like spending time with him, belittling him, teasing him. Allek could not do so to anybody else, so Rialus served the purpose.

The weather was a frozen chaos. "You would get blown by the wind," he said to himself. "The cats would chase you as you bounced and screamed." Even without the storms, the ice fields would have been harder to navigate than anything they had faced so far. The enormous slabs of sea ice thrust up at chaotic angles. Dropped off into crevices they could not see the bottom of. Ice that looked thick shattered beneath the slightest touch. Animals slipped on the slopes and fell, wedged down below. They broke legs or bit each other or kicked their human handlers—to death in several cases.

The stations that had rolled over so much now could barely progress at all. The ground was too irregular. "It's not even ground at all!" It had none of the natural shape of mountains or hills or river channels. One of the stations was damaged beyond repair when the ice under one side collapsed, canting it sideways in a manner that broke its spine and sent pitch sloshing about, aflame, inside it.

And came the time an entire station—one of the dining halls that fed the divine children in efficient shifts—fell through the ice and disappeared into a cauldron of glass-blue water. Everyone in or on the station went into the water. People and animals near it slipped screaming on the tilted slabs. Nearly everyone involved died. The divine children who managed to claw back to the surface and get pulled out were as pale as death by the time they did so.

One Auldek was inside the station. Of him nothing was heard. Another had been on a kwedeir just beside it. Mount and rider went into the water. Neither came up. Allek had not been there, but you would think he had been by the glassy-eyed way he described the Auldek's plunge. He imagined him stoic in the moment of realization, still instead of thrashing, looking up with stern acceptance of his fate as his iron-boned weight plunged him downward.

More likely he was screaming like a girl and jabbering water words as he died. Again and again, Rialus thought.

"If that had been one of the chieftains' stations, or the temple of records . . . I can't even imagine it. The Acacians did it," Allek said.

Rialus looked up. He noticed that Fingel did as well. "What?" he asked.

"We think so. The ice was . . . weakened in places. Lines cut in it. Some of the pitch they stole from us, Sabeer said. They cut lines in the ice with it, made weak sections." Allek scratched his neck, and then looked askance at Rialus. "Your people are wicked."

Wonderfully so, Rialus thought. He glanced at Fingel, who dropped her eyes back to the stitch work in her hands.

CHAPTER
FIFTY-ONE

Kelis had not dreamed so vividly in years. He had not slept so long either, so deeply. Unlike other people, he had always been fully aware when he was dreaming. He knew the difference between the functioning of the waking world and the fluid shifting of dream logic. He knew, even while asleep, that in the waking world he was a miserable man with an iron club of a hand, an unwitting traitor who had led enemies to the very heart of his nation. Because of this—and because of the depths of the fatigue that had plunged him back into the dream world—he let himself swim from vision to vision, out of time.

That was why he felt no fear standing on a leviathan's back as it pushed through a furious ocean. He felt no strangeness in the fact that he was not himself, that he was a woman instead. He knew that what separated man from woman was a thin membrane, permeable in ways people's waking minds were afraid of. But he was not. When the beast dove and the waters rushed up over her he did not flinch. She did not claw for the surface or for the light of day. She stayed standing, as if her feet were cemented to the creature. They plunged into the black depths. Luminous shapes swirled around her in the water. Far away first, they came closer and closer until she and the diving whale became the center of a vortex of glowing giants, sliding around one another as fast and numerous as anchovies schooling. It was beautiful.

So was the sight of a sun setting from a sky like none he had seen before, purple hued and hung with floating objects, each of which looked like a child's ball but which was, he knew, a world of its own. He lived through things fantastical and mundane, taking both extremes in with the same equanimity. He walked and loved and lived as himself, as men other than himself, as women, as a version of a child who was he but different than anyone he ever had been. For a time he forgot human shape and ran on four legs and experienced the world through scents that exploded in his mind like bursts of color.

Many of the things he saw he forgot. He did remember that ride on the leviathan's back. He knew even while experiencing it that it would stay with him. There was another thing he would not forget either, for he knew it to have been the purpose of his dreaming, a vision of something that was not yet, but could be. Might be. Having found it, he had no choice but to awake.

He opened his eyes. He lay on his back, the ceiling above him white plaster cut into long rectangles by wooden beams. He stared at them long enough to see the movement of the air against old spiderwebs, to note the cracks in the dry wood. There were shapes there in the grain, elongated faces and eyes contained in knots.

He was in a guest room of the palace. He knew, for he had stayed in such a room before. Whatever had happened while he slept could not be avoided much longer. It waited for him just outside the door, down the corridor. He did not want to move. He did not even want to sit up, for he knew that doing so would mean moving his malformed limb. But he had to. He would rise and dress and walk from here to face what he had to face. He wanted his punishment just as much as he wanted to know the fate of the people important to him.

Only . . . there was the shame of his mangled hand. He did not look at it, but he felt the weight of it there beside him, pressing upon the sheets. He imagined cutting the limb off above the wrist. Then he would be rid of it. He would be one armed, crippled forever, but he was that already. At least he would not have to carry the foulness of the Santoth curse for everyone to see. If there was a knife in the room, he would do it now, right here. If it killed him, no matter. That would be for the best.

He heard a noise. It was just a small sound of a foot pressing against the floor, but hearing it he realized somebody was in the room with him. He turned his head.

Aliver stood, leaning against the wall near the door, staring at nothing at all, lost in thought. Just the sight of him made Kelis's pulse quicken. He wants to be here when I wake, to tell me to my face. He would tell him that none of the kind things he had said back in the room with the queen and the man with the stone eyes and the charlatan and the children had been true. Not the things he said about Kelis, at least. Those had been lies for the others' benefit. Kelis began to close his eyes, knowing it would not help, but wanting his dreams back again.

"Do you remember my laryx hunt?" Aliver asked.

The second the words faded, Kelis doubted that he had heard them. Perhaps he was still asleep.

The prince turned to him. "Do you, Kelis, remember it? I've been thinking about it as you slept. I realized that I'd never spoken to you about it, not truly, I mean. We celebrated together. I accepted the rewards thrown at me. I danced. You did as well. We both danced, didn't we? Younger then, and beautiful. You were, at least. I was too pale to be a handsome Talayan."

He smiled and pushed off the wall. He walked forward a

bit, turned on his heel, stopped. And then, as if the thought just occurred to him, he squatted in the center of the room and bounced on the balls of his feet. He looked to be preparing for a run, building energy in his bunched leg muscles. He tented his fingers together and touched them to his nose.

"And then Thaddeus appeared and my life changed. I thought the laryx hunt marked the change, but that was because by then I thought myself a Talayan. I wanted nothing more than the approval of Talayan men and the love of Talayan women. Thaddeus changed all that. I never made the time to speak to you about what happened. When I could have later, I didn't. And then nothing went as I planned. I want to speak of it now, though, if you'll let me."

Kelis did not know what to make of his energy, his revelry, his tone. Nothing. He remained silent.

Aliver seemed to expect that. He spoke for the both of them. He led Kelis through what he remembered of the hunt. The two of them were in the wild for three weeks before they found the nest of a lone laryx. Only young males ever were alone, those that had left their family group but not found a mate yet. As Kelis stood watch, Aliver fouled the nest. He spat on it and pulled it apart, peed and defecated on it. He left his scent all over the area.

When Kelis saw the beast returning they both moved away a distance to watch. By the cackling yelps it responded with, it felt the insults keenly. The creature snarled and yipped. It was ugly, as all laryx are; misshapenly thick in the chest, stout necked, with small, powerful hind legs. It ran in circles, snout down on the ground and then up in the air, tracking already.

Aliver came in close a few times and twice pricked it with arrows. Neither was enough to truly injure it. Its hide was too thick for arrows. It got its mouth around the shafts and yanked them out. No damage done. But the second one riled it enough to charge, just as Aliver had wished. As he ran before it, Kelis dropped away to the side. His part in the hunt was over.

"Or it was supposed to be," Aliver said. "You were to let me run the thing down alone. But you didn't."

No, Kelis thought, I didn't. And I'm glad I didn't.

Instead of leaving Aliver to his fate, Kelis ran behind the hunted and hunter, following them both across the plains, keeping them at the edge of his capacity to track, just barely in view. During the day he watched the dust kicked up by the laryx's paws. At night Kelis kept track of them by their movement beneath the moonlight. One day into the next, and then on and over again. Three days in motion. Aliver kept the beast on his scent, kept it running, let it see or smell him when its attention wavered, as it grew fatigued. For that was what the run was about: to make the beast so tired it would collapse, exhausted, and receive the spear that would kill it without protest.

"I almost did it right," Aliver said.

Almost, yes. But with a laryx almost is not good enough.

Kelis hid in an outcropping of stones when the laryx first gave up its pursuit and lay down, panting in the shade of a lone acacia tree. Kelis watched, thinking, No, not yet, as Aliver circled back on the beast. No, don't approach from behind it. Make it rise and chase you more. A laryx was never fully exhausted the first time it gave up. It had more in it and was dangerous still. He knew these things, and he knew that Aliver should, too. That's why he held his tongue and stayed hidden.

Aliver glanced at Kelis, and then went back to contemplating the images sheltered beneath the spread of his fingers. "But I was too tired. I let it cloud my judgment, and I let the beast trick me. You know what happened. When I approached to sink my spear in it, thinking it had fallen asleep, the thing opened its eyes and laughed at me. It ran at me and came close to ripping me apart right there. I was just lucky to avoid that first charge. I ran for the tree, jumped into it. I dropped my spear. You remember that, don't you? I dropped my spear to cling to the branches of a tree almost too small to support me."

It had been as Aliver described. Kelis remembered everything. He had seen it with his own eyes, of course, from a different viewpoint. He saw it with fear beating in his heart, more afraid of the prospect of Aliver's death than his own. If he had wished to, he could have admitted that when he ran at the laryx it was not just to distract the beast. It was in the full willingness to offer it his flesh instead of the prince's. The fact that the beast turned toward him without fully charging was just a stroke of good fortune.

It was the moment Aliver needed to come back to himself. He had dropped to the earth, grasped his spear, and sunk it into the beast's side. The laryx spun with all the force of its massive frame, lifting Aliver into the air and tossing him away. This time, though, Aliver kept a grip on his spear, and it ripped out of the beast's hide with a spray of blood. He still had it ready when the laryx lunged at him. This time he sank it in the monster's shoulder. He stood holding it steady, the laryx's mouth bristling with a carnivore's teeth, lips and nose twitching. It even pawed the earth, pushing forward and driving Aliver back. But not enough. The wound in its side was too deep. The hole in its shoulder had severed an artery and cut through enough tendons to weaken it. The laryx died there, so close to Aliver's face that he had only to lean forward to touch his nose to its snout.

"The kill was yours," Kelis said. His first words since he had awoken.

"But it would not have been mine without you."

Kelis fixed his lips in a sour expression, not sure how to deny that.

"Let me tell a few more things. First, you should know that I didn't forget what you did. I didn't fail to understand that you'd saved me. I think, now that I look back on it, that I felt . . . a failure, as if the kill wasn't really mine. I think that's why I agreed to fight Maeander Mein. I'm not saying I knew that it was because of the hunt. I didn't, but how often do we do things without knowing our own reasons? I wanted to make sure I was worthy of all the things given to me—and being asked of me. Foolish, yes? It got me killed."

Kelis started to protest, but Aliver stopped him.

"But here I am again, alive again. I would be a fool twice over not to learn from it. So here's what I think. I think that the laryx was my kill." He let this sit a moment, and then said, "But I needed your help to make it. You watched over me when I needed it. You put your life in danger to save mine. That's what got me out of that tree so fast. I didn't want your death on my hands. See what we have here? We succeeded because we care for each other and risked our lives for each other. It should never have been about doing it alone. When I fought Maeander, I forgot that. I will never do so again. I have you to thank for that. And I have you to thank for bringing Shen to me. Don't make that face."

Kelis did not know what face he was making, but he must have frowned.

"Don't! I know what you are thinking and I don't want to hear a single word of it. Don't tell me anything about your responsibility for bringing the Santoth to Acacia. Don't act like that's your fault. It's bigger than you, Kelis, so don't be so vain. You think the Santoth wouldn't have found a way here without you? They are a sickness that attached itself to something pure—to you and to Shen and to all the labors you and others went through to bring her to me. That is not—and never can or will be—your fault. So don't be the person who wallows in self-pity that way. It's not you, and I couldn't bear it. Such a waste. I need you to march to war with me, not to be sitting here feeling sorry for yourself."

"To war?" Kelis rasped, lifting his metal-flesh hand. "I cannot be a warrior for you. Not with this."

Aliver stepped nearer. His voice dropped, tone softened. "You have a choice. This thing"—he placed his hand over Kelis's metal one—"has become part of your destiny. It doesn't end it; it changes it. Perhaps this is a gift. How can you know? It may be a gift to urge you to return to your destiny. Do you remember the boy you told me you were? The dreamer. You were born with that in your heart. You told me that in dreams you read the future, and that you spoke languages you could not speak when awake and that this gave you joy. So return to it. Don't bemoan the loss of a spear arm. What is that compared to the gifts of a dreamer?"

"I have already had a dream," Kelis heard himself say, "while I slept here."

"Do you remember it?"

"Some things."

"Are they things you could tell me?"

Kelis had to think about that for a while. He knew his answer, but what he had to be slow with was the feeling of hope that rose with it. Could he really be blessed? Could it really be that—after all the things that had come before, and after all the ways his life was and wasn't what he thought it should be—he would still be permitted to return to where he began? To be a dreamer, and find in the sleeping world things that could help the ones he loved in the waking one?

He said, "I dreamed that the queen rode a sea beast into the depths. It gave her no fear, Aliver. It was what she wished."

Aliver sat down on the stool and set a hand on his arm. The two men sat in silence for a long time. Kelis began to fear that he had given the prince ill tidings. He should explain more of the dream, he thought, but that was filled with images that might further seem ill.

"If . . . if the queen is near I could tell her."

"She's not," Aliver said. "Is that all? Did you dream anything else?"

"Yes."

"Then tell it to me."

"I dreamed that you had seven children."

"Did I?" Aliver said. He smiled sadly. "I don't believe that will happen."

"You had seven children other than Shen. I could not see their faces. You walked with them away from me. I could not see your face either. But it was you, and there were seven children with you."

"I'll have to think about that," Aliver said. And then, putting it aside and lifting his voice into a kingly register, "Kelis of Umae, will you march to war with me? I don't need you as a warrior. Not this time. Not ever again. Come with me as a dreamer if you like. Or just come as my friend. Speak to me, as you used to. Puzzle through that dream of seven children with me. Will you do that—be a friend to me? A brother?"

Kelis closed his eyes. He wanted to nod. He wanted to say, *Nothing would mean more to me*, but he still doubted he could be that blessed. Part of him feared that reaching for a future would be just the thing to pull it away from him. He wanted to . . .

"Good," Aliver said, not waiting for his response. "We leave tomorrow."

CHAPTER
FIFTY-TWO

Chafing from the sabotage and accidents, the Auldek halted forward progress for a time. Work crews hewed a thoroughfare through the slabs. The crews labored nonstop, through the short day and long night, lit by pitch lanterns that glowed in the howling white dark. They cut and sawed and melted the ice, creating one wide track, smooth and safe enough for the entire army, the animals, and the slaves to walk on. It took several days, and during the first few the Scav managed to set traps in the ice or pick off lone laborers and scouts. When Menteus Nemré and the sublime motion took up protecting the workers, things progressed more steadily.

A full week after the opening battle, the bulk of the Auldek force slipped through the cleared passage. Rialus watched his own station begin the journey, standing on the ice beside Sabeer one gusty, overcast day. The blizzard had cleared, but it seemed even colder for it. Rialus could not keep from shivering. He had woken several times from nightmares of being trapped within his room as his station broke through the ice and water rushed in a torrent on top of him. He had no wish to see this dream realized during the day.

Menteus Nemré stood a little distance away, legs set wide,

arms crossed, surveying the progress as if he were a king and not a slave. He wore no hood. The wind tugged at his long, knotted mane of white hair, making him look every bit the leonine merging of man and beast that so perfectly embodied his totem.

"Oh, look at that," Sabeer said. "You beauty. You've caught another one."

Thinking she meant Menteus himself in some way, Rialus did not notice at first that a real snow lioness trotted toward him. She skimmed along the thoroughfare at the edge of the enormous wagon and station wheels, oblivious to the rotating danger of them. She carried a corpse in her jaws, held high to keep it from tripping her. Behind her, more feline shapes ran to keep up.

The cat went directly to Menteus. She dropped the body at his feet and circled away as he bent to inspect it. The other lions joined her, milling around, looking expectantly at the warrior. Without going any nearer, Rialus knew the corpse was a Scav. It was clothed just like the other one; bloodstained just like the other one.

Menteus took only a moment. He stood, pressed one of his booted feet against the corpse's side, and kicked it toward the waiting animals. He coughed some command to them, and they pounced on the corpse. They tore into it, clawing at it, growling and snapping at one another.

Rialus looked away, trembling still more.

"My poor chilly boy," Sabeer said, moving in close to blow a plume of warm air in his face. She had not been so near him in days. She slipped her hands inside his hood and rubbed his cheeks. "Rialus silver tongue, what happened to your skin?"

"Frostbite."

"Frostbite? I thought you only stayed in your bed with your slave."

Rialus had explained to her several times before that they

did not have carnal relations. He did not go down that road again. "Still, it—it happened."

Sabeer peered at him a moment, and then touched his cheek with her fingertip. He jerked back. "You're a foolish man, Rialus. You must take better care of yourself. If you don't, we'll have to feed you to the cats. They would like that, considering that you killed one of their number." She smiled and steered him with an arm over his shoulder. "Come, let's go before they seek vengeance on you."

Their walk was short. They stopped at a station that was lined up to enter the ice field. Rialus had seen it before, but had never had reason to visit it or inquire about it. Just one station out of many. A bit smaller than most, its only distinguishing features were the conical gold cap at its pinnacle and the geometry of glass panes that sectioned its roof and sides.

Sabeer entered. Rialus followed. For a moment Rialus did not know why the inside of the place seemed odd. When they reached the top of the winding staircase and came into a dim, dank room, his breath clouding the air in front of him, he realized the station was unheated, unlit except by the dull light that came through the glass panes. Sabeer did nothing about the cold, but she did strike up a spark to get a lamp burning. When she had a flame, she covered it and lengthened it. The room came into highlight and shadow.

Row upon row of shelves lined the walls around them. Tall bookcases crammed with the spines of numerous volumes, or with drawers or doors that folded open. The shelves climbed all the way to the high ceiling of the station, making it one great library, with ladders and narrow walkways scaffolding each level.

"Do you know what's housed here?" Sabeer asked.

"No."

"My heart. My people's history. This collection includes our most sacred records." She set the lamp down on the table and walked along a shelf, perusing the spines. "Individual clans have some of their own collections, but these are the volumes that we hold in trust together. Remember that I told you we can't remember the distant past? This is where we come to be reminded of it. I come, at least. Others can't be bothered. They even let it go unheated since our stores of pitch were depleted. I argued that this should be kept warm, but I lost. They all know how important these records are, but . . . we're preoccupied with other things. As you know. This damp cannot be good for the parchment, don't you think?"

Tossing her long hair out, she looked over her shoulder at him. The lamplight accented the auburn tones of it, and caught in her eyes in an alluring manner. Sometimes, Sabeer was the most beautiful woman he had ever seen. Sometimes, he forgot that she was a different race than he. Sometimes, he wanted her with a hunger made more violent for the ways in which she played with him. She knew as much. Smiling, she said, "Rialus silver tongue, you say things without even speaking. I hear you, though. I hear you."

At her side, he looked through the volumes she found most interesting. Some of them were truly ancient, enough so that Rialus gingerly turned the brittle pages. He read accounts of battles lost to memory, preserved only here, in ink on parchment. In some ways it was no different from looking at old Acacian records, except that he knew the individuals named in these long-past events. Howlk was on the page, and Jàfith with her famed attack on the Wrathic stronghold in Rath Batatt, and Devoth presiding over the terms of the Numreks' exile.

He read of events in Sabeer's life that she knew only from the images and thoughts the words returned to her. She guided him to passages that mentioned her. Shivering and laughing that now *she* was cold, she had them take off their coats. She pulled her stool behind his, scooted up close behind him, and draped the coats over them like blankets. Her inner thighs wrapped snug around him. Leaning forward to point at things on pages, her breasts pressed against his back.

"Not all the records are our own, though. Some of them, Rialus, were written by the Lothan Aklun. The most ancient ones. They gave them to us but would not translate them. At least, they did not offer and we did not ask." She pulled another volume nearer, opened it, and ran her finger over the script. "Perhaps we once could read what they said. We might not have known then that we would forget. I can't say, because I have forgotten. But, Rialus, part of our history is in these Lothan Aklun volumes. Perhaps important things. We can't read them, but you can read their writing, can't you? They were from your nation, I think. Would you translate them for us?"

"Me?" Rialus peered more closely at the pages she had opened to. The letters were looping and antiquated, formal in a way that Acacian no longer was, but it was Acacian. He could read it.

"Who better than you?" Sabeer slid one of her hands across Rialus's thigh. He was aroused already, but the touch of her fingers sent his blood surging. "You know things about us that no other Acacian does. The writing is too complicated for the divine children to translate. It doesn't seem right for them to read things about us that we can't read ourselves. You understand how that could be undesirable. And if you find anything in there that speaks unfavorably about me . . . you'll correct it. Hmmm? It would mean a lot to us if you did this—if you became our chronicler. It would make you an important man, Rialus. Once we have conquered your lands, this will make you a rich man, a man all Auldek will have to respect. Also, it will mean a lot to me."

Rialus tried to stand again.

With her free hand, she turned his face toward hers. She covered his mouth with a kiss. Her lips were softer than he would have imagined. They were unbelievably lush. They were a world, and her tongue, when she slid it through his teeth, was too much for him to bear. She pulled away. "Tell me you'll be our chronicler, Rialus. Tell me and you won't regret it."

❄

That night, he deserted the Auldek army for the second time.

He realized he could as he lay still as death on his bed. He knew what he needed to do in order to face Mena again. Considering the placement of his station near the back of the encampment, there might not be another night as favorable as this one. He could not get the taste of Sabeer out of his mouth. *I can still taste her. Stop it. Stop thinking of her. She is a bitch who would kill you in a heartbeat.* He couldn't stop thinking of her, though, and he hated that he wanted more of her. He would never be able to defy her to her face. He would never be her equal.

So he fled.

When he gauged the hour late enough, he climbed out from under his covers and carefully slipped into his many layers. He tried not to wake Fingel, but it would not matter if he did. She would say nothing. Do nothing. Care not at all about his activities. When he opened his door and felt the rush of frigid air on his face, he glanced back at her cot. Her back was turned to him, as it always had been.

The night was dark, moonless. The wind came and went in savage gusts as he climbed down to the ground. Between the gusts were long, quiet lulls. It was frigidly cold. Despite the temperature, Rialus kept his hood thrown back. He wanted all his senses, and he had them. Every touch of his feet on the ground crunched absurdly loud. It was real earth, frozen just as completely as the ice had been. He kept stopping, thinking the entire camp must have heard him. In the silence he heard motion. Was it the sound of steps or just the play of the wind on the frozen earth?

It doesn't matter, he thought. Just go, fool!

Crouched low, he ran through the shadows of several stations. He looped away from where he knew the rhinos were penned, and soon after he was at the far edge of the encampment, the end farthest away from the Acacians and least guarded. He stopped and looked back. No movement. The stations squatted on the ice, steaming. An antok bellowed. Something groaned on the far side of the camp. He stood long enough that he imagined he could hear Nawth's laments floating across from the ice. That got him moving again.

He had made it away from the camp and down into a dip that ran south. He shuffled fast now, his hood up. Perhaps that was why he did not hear the lioness approach. He just saw her. She crept down the slope in front of him with a feline grace that stopped Rialus in his tracks. The cat froze. She crouched. She moved forward, low to the ground, and then froze again.

Rialus closed his eyes. The thought came to him almost coolly, Kill me fast, you bitch.

When he heard the sound of movement behind him, his eyes snapped open. Another cat? He turned. A heavily furred person rushed toward him. The person raised an arm. Rialus ducked. The person collided with him, throwing something over him at the same time. Rialus saw what happened from his back, sprawled on the ground.

The object—no bigger than a child's ball—bounced once on the ground. It ignited as it sailed up toward the crouched cat. The lioness leaped to one side but not fast enough. The ball exploded in a wide spray of liquid flame. The cat ran writhing and screaming away, a living torch. For a few moments more, at least.

The person grabbed him by the arm and hauled him up. He could not see the person's face, hidden behind a visor, with a hood pulled snug around it. But he recognized the voice.

"Let's go," Fingel said. She tugged him into motion. "Fast."

CHAPTER
FIFTY-THREE

Melio sat on the bench, squashed between Clytus and Kartholomé, with Geena just on the pilot's other side. The bench was too short for all four of them, but it was where a wolf of a man dragging around two hounds had deposited them after the strange events of the clan gathering. Unwashed, bruised, scratched, smeared with dried blood around their wrists and ankles, with staring eyes and faces limp with perplexity, they looked like children rammed together by a callous tutor, being punished for a game that had gotten violently out of control.

"I don't understand anything," Kartholomé said. He had found a comb somewhere. He dragged it through his beard, causing it to frizz in a manner that he would not have liked at all if he'd had a mirror to see it.

The others grunted.

"Not a damn thing." And then, indicating the curving metal slivers that a passing man wore as earrings, Kartholomé asked, "How do you think I'd look with some of those? I feel less myself with only a single hook in. This lobe has healed up, you know?" He caressed the earlobe from which the bone earring had been ripped back when the league ship tried to run them down near the Outer Isles.

Nobody answered him.

"Is that really Dariel?" Melio asked, watching the prince from a distance.

"Of course it is," Geena said.

As ever, Melio could not fathom where she got her certainty. The man they watched in heated discussion with a tight circle of strangely tattooed and accoutred foreigners spoke fluently in a guttural language that sounded like Numrek. His face was spotted like a running cat's from the Talayan plains, and he seemed to have some sort of mark embossed on his forehead. He was one of them. At home amid the strangeness of them. Had Melio not known the man was Dariel—if he had not heard his voice and met his eyes—he would have had no clue to his identity. And that barely helped, for that same man had harangued a chamber filled with the weirdest-looking people Melio had ever seen. Dariel had then been stabbed in the abdomen, a killing slice if ever there was one. Instead of dying, he had shouted out, ripped off his shirt, and displayed himself, bloody and yet unscathed. How could that person be Prince Dariel Akaran? If that was him, what had happened to him? Was he still, somehow, the man Melio had been sent to find?

"How do you know?" Melio whispered.

"His chest," Geena said. "He's got Dariel's physique. And his backside."

Whatever this second, smaller meeting was, it ended abruptly. All the seated participants rose and bowed to one another. The man who might be Dariel spoke a few last words with a woman whose black hair jutted up from her head in featherlike plumes. As she turned away, Dariel seemed to remember the waiting Acacians. He cast about until he spotted them, then rushed over.

Embracing them one by one, he probed their faces, as they did the same to his. Up close it was obvious that he was the prince. The open lips of his smile revealed the spacing of his teeth, a trait Melio never knew he would recognize as Dariel's. And yet there it was. And there was the distinctive ridge of bone high on his nose. The prince named each of them reverently, as if their names held sacred power. "Melio. Clytus. Geena . . . By the Giver, what are you doing here? How are you here? I can't imagine it. Tell me. Tell me!"

For some reason, the others deferred to Melio to answer. "We came to find you," he said. "To rescue you. Corinn sent me, and Clytus and Geena, and Kartholomé."

Dariel grinned as he absorbed that. He said Kartholomé's name a few times, memorizing it, and then he backed a step away, taking them all in. "Well, you found me. Rescued me? Not so much. Would I be boasting if I said I rescued you?"

Thinking about the short, brutal captivity they had suffered at the hands of the gray, tusked people—beatings, interrogations in broken Acacian, threats of their pending horrific deaths—Melio said, "Not at all. I think, really, that we came quite close to having a hard time of it."

Geena barked a laugh, which set the others off as well.

Serious again a moment later, Dariel said, "Oh, there's so much I want to ask you. And so much I want to tell you. I don't know where to start. Also, everything is happening here now."

"I can see that," Clytus said.

"You've no idea what you've dropped into. I may have to ask you to go to war with me."

"A just fight?" Clytus asked.

"Yes, absolutely." Dariel glanced over his shoulder. A woman with facial markings like his own stood waiting for him, looking uneasy. "I have to go now. One of my friends here is hurt. I must see her. We'll talk tonight. All of us. I want to know you, too, Kartholomé. We'll talk each other's ears off as soon as we get a moment. I'll leave you with Birké, to wash up and rest." He indicated the wolf-faced youth. "He is a good friend to me. He'll be one to you very soon."

A half step away, he paused. "Melio, would you come with me? We could speak a little as we walk."

Melio joined him. They walked quickly, part of a small group that cut across courtyards, passing from inside to out and back again, down a mazelike series of corridors that occasionally offered views over a stunning cityscape. As on Acacia, a contingent of guards shadowed Dariel. Not Marah but a motley, deadly serious crew, armed with a hodgepodge assortment of weapons. Judging by the sidelong glances they fixed on him, they did not yet trust Melio to be so near Dariel.

What is going on here?

"How are my sisters?" Dariel asked. "Tell me the last news you had of them."

Melio's attempts at this got him virtually nowhere. So much had happened since Dariel had left the Known World with Sire Neen that each thing he mentioned was predicated on explaining something else. That, in turn, affected something else that he needed to loop away from, enough so that he was soon unsure he was doing anything other than tying them both in troubling knots.

Stopping at the door into which the others entered, Dariel took his arm. "But they lived? When you left, they both lived?"

"Yes. And—" Melio cut himself off. He could not tell Dariel what Corinn had said about Aliver. It might not have been true. It would be cruel to say it now, in the midst of whatever was happening here.

The prince motioned to someone just inside the door that he would only be a moment more. "And what?"

"I can't say it now. Later, when we can truly talk."

Reluctantly, Dariel nodded. He stepped inside. Melio followed him. The entrance opened onto a large living room, filled with silent people. On a wide couch set against the far wall lay a woman, propped on her back, blankets pulled snug across her chest. Her shoulder bulged with bandages. What the injury was Melio could not tell, but that it was grave was obvious. The woman's skin was a light blue. Her eyes were large in their sockets, her cheeks sunken. The woman with the running cat spots had already reached her. She clung to one of the woman's hands, speaking close to her, kissing her face with a passion and sadness that made Melio feel he should look away.

Dariel exhaled a long breath. "Oh, Skylene . . ." Just a whisper. He did not go to her until sometime later, when the spotted woman lifted her head and pointed him out. The blue woman found him and bent her lips up into a weak but sincere smile. On that invitation, Dariel went forward. He kneeled by the spotted woman at the side of the bed and took one of Skylene's hands. He touched her forehead with his own and they spoke close, too quietly for Melio to hear.

Watching them, Melio realized he had forgotten all about doubting this man's identity. He was Dariel Akaran. Somehow, he had found a new family in Ushen Brae, a new conflict that he was at the center of. He had a sense of purpose that positively glowed as if a flame burned inside him. Melio did not yet understand what was going on here, but it felt perfectly right that he had come. Mena would want him here. She would want him fighting beside Dariel, shoulder to shoulder with the same guards that, for the moment, looked at him with suspicion.

I'm with him, Mena. I found him. Now I'll just fight this war with him—whatever that entails—and then I'll bring him home.

※

That night, while Mór and Tam went to another meeting of the clan leaders, the others talked well into the dead hours.

There was so much to tell. It proved impossible to convey any of it in perfect order. Instead, they made a stew together. With Dariel and his friends Anira and Birké and Tunnel on one side of the pot, and the new arrivals ringed around the other, they all tossed in what they could about the situation in the Known World as they knew it, about their voyages across the Gray Slopes, about Dariel's betrayal by Sire Neen, the extermination of the Lothan Aklun, the bloodbath that was the prince's first meeting with the Auldek, the confusion in this city, Avina . . .

It went on and on. When Melio thought the time was right, he offered the tale he'd heard of Aliver's resurrection and of Corinn's confirmation to him that it was true. He just told it plainly, worrying that he was stirring hope for something that sounded too fantastic to be true. Dariel sat with it in silence for a long time, then looked up. "Is she so powerful as that?"

Melio had mentioned the defeat of the Numrek in Teh already. Now he described how it was accomplished. After he had, the others sat through another long silence.

Dariel eventually shook his head. "Not even a year away and one sister's the most powerful sorcerer since Tinhadin, the other is facing the worst invasion in history, and my brother . . . he's defeated death."

"And you—the Rhuin Fá," Tunnel said. "Strange family you have."

Later, visions of the one Dariel called the Sky Watcher, Nâ Gâmen, led Melio into sleep. Against his will he followed the slim man around his mountaintop aerie. He could not help thinking of him with avian features, some blending of him and the injured woman Skylene, perhaps. His version of Nâ Gâmen showed him the way to sleep, walking, explaining to him the unimaginable things that Dariel had just tried to explain.

When Melio woke it was to birds as well. Yellow finches flew through the room in a rush. His eyes fluttered open as they skimmed the ceiling above him, darting away down one of the corridors. It's funny, he thought. In Avina I can never tell whether I'm inside or out. The birds can't either.

Geena lay on the mat beside him, her sleeping warmth curled toward him. He sat up. Around him the others slumbered where they had passed out, on mats and wrapped in light blankets, all of them near the fire pit carved out of the stone floor. The warmth of it had somehow radiated through the stones themselves, fighting back the mild chill of the night.

Dariel sat with his knees pulled up to his chest, watching him. "It's okay," Dariel said when Melio reflectively scooted away from Geena. "I know how she is. She already told me you did nothing to dishonor my sister."

"I never would," Melio said. "I want nothing more than to get back to her alive. We have a child to make, Dariel. She promised me. I want to hold her to it."

"I hope you do. In any event, I'm no one to judge." Dariel poked the coals in the fire, atop which a kettle hung from a thin, delicately constructed framework. "I don't suppose you caught all of what we argued about at the meeting?"

"None of it," Melio said. He rose stiffly and moved closer. One of the hounds pressed against Dariel's hip sniffed in his direction. The other simply stretched. "The lot of you spoke Auldek."

"Well, let's just say I'll have some explaining to do when I get back." He tossed his poking stick into the fire. "You'll know what I mean soon enough."

Melio already had some idea. He had noticed the way Dariel and Anira tended to stay near each other, how she spoke to him in touches on the wrist and back. "When you get back . . . When will that be? I get the feeling you don't plan to leave until you've finished what you've started here." He let his eyes drift around the sleeping forms. "I like these people already. Birké. Tunnel. What kind of name is Tunnel?"

Dariel smiled. He poured a viscous liquid from a carafe into two glasses. He offered one of the glasses to Melio, who took it, squinting warily at what looked, as near as he could tell, like frog's eggs. "The tea's not ready, but try this. It's good. Just try it." He did so himself.

Turning the glass in his fingers, Melio said, "You're at the center of something here. I know that already. I'm surprised you didn't go to the clan leaders meeting last night. I haven't figured out your role here yet."

"Nor have I, entirely. I'm no clan leader, though. Mór is the leader of the Free People. It's for her to speak with her peers, not me. I'm . . . something different."

One of the sleepers stirred. Birké rolled over and then settled again, on his back in a manner that moved his steady breathing toward a snore.

Melio leaned forward and said, "I have to ask: Can we take you home? Now, I mean. There's a league clipper that . . ."

"I've been thinking about that all night," Dariel said. "The things you all told me. It goes around and around in my mind like mad. But no matter how much I want to go home, I can't. I'm already committed here. I allowed this." He ran a finger over the symbol emblazoned on his forehead. Melio almost did the same, wondering at the texture of it. "I wanted this. It's part of me now. And the thing is, Melio, all of this—all of these people—they're part of our story already. If I can, I have to close the circle."

"What circle?"

Dariel frowned as if he did not like hearing his own expression spoken back to him. "Do you know that when I sleep I have dreams in which I speak to people all around Ushen Brae? Individual conversations, with individual people, and yet somehow

I speak with thousands each night. The number is only increasing, and, sometimes, I feel a part of myself—or of Nâ Gâmen—speaking with them even as I move through the world. Even right now, this very moment." Dariel stared at the rim of his glass. His eyes were still, but Melio saw hidden motion in them, as if the surface of his brown irises hid other eyes beneath them, ones that moved in response to things that were not in front of the Dariel sitting here with a glass in his hands. "I can't go home until I'm done," he said. "That's all there is to it. I can't go home *unless* I'm done. One thing depends on the other."

"All right," Melio said. "I had to ask. Corinn would"—he was going to say *skin him alive*, but, considering what he'd seen at Teh, the expression lost its humor—"be displeased with me if I didn't."

Tam and several of the others strode through one of the open doors. Dariel looked up, nodded at them. "Well," he said, "we wouldn't want that, would we?" He pushed upright with the unfolding of his legs and walked to meet them.

A short time later, the entire party, awake and sipping hot tea, listened to the news Tam had gathered. It was more than the dark tattoos under his eyes that made him look tired. "Mór was with the clan leaders all night. She has gone to Skylene now, but she asked me to report to you, Dariel, so that you know what's being proposed. The clans are agreed. They will sign binding declarations of unity. They wish for some autonomy, so that those who want to can retain clan identity, but they all agree to be grouped collectively as the People. They agree to have both clan councils for their own affairs and to send representatives to sit on a council that oversees the People. They will even respect a separate body, the Council of Elders, as another voice in decision making. Dividing up the holdings of Ushen Brae will be complicated, but they have agreed, in principle, to abide the boundaries we've proposed. They've put this in writ-ing."

That's a lot of agreement, Melio thought.

"They've accepted everything we've worked for?" Anira said, pitching it somewhere between a question and exclamation.

"Not exactly," Tam said, "but damn close."

Tunnel took hold of one of his tusks and yanked on it. A strange gesture, but one that seemed to express mirth. "I told you all, the Rhuin Fá would make it so!"

Tam looked away from him, apparently not wanting his offi-cial façade to crumble yet. "They found Dariel very convincing, but it sounded like many of them always had this in their hearts. They just let the wrong voices rule them. Dariel helped give them courage. Not everyone agreed, but those who fought it saw their own people turn against them. Dukish has been stripped of his clan leadership. The Anets did that themselves because he carried a weapon into the gathering."

"And used it," Birké added, scowling.

"By the gathering codes, the clan could be exiled for that. The Anets voted new leaders for themselves and are begging for mercy. They say Dukish deceived them and that they will see to his punishment. The other clan leaders want to know what we wish them to do. Should the entire Anet clan be exiled? Or do we accept that they kill Dukish for his crimes? Or would you have him as a slave, Dariel? They could . . . wound him."

"Wound him?"

"So that he would be a good boy," Tunnel said. "The Auldek had ways of doing that to the troublesome ones. They knew it; we know it."

Dariel had his response ready. "I don't believe we should punish the Anet. We must get beyond that and quickly. If we can—and they can—it will be for the better. The Anet and

Antoks should cede all they grabbed back to the People, and they should swear that their allegiance is to the Free People. They should help us fight the league. Dukish should be imprisoned for now, until the conflict is over and we can decide, in time, what should become of him. This way would be better for as all. No revenge, just justice. That's what I think."

Tam shifted. Melio was not sure how to read the movement, until he grinned. "That's exactly what Mór said when I told her. She wasn't sure you'd agree, though. There are other developments," Tam continued. "Dukish had sent word to Sire Lethel about Dariel."

"They know that Dariel is here?" Clytus asked. "That he's your Rune Fan?"

"Rhuin Fá," Tam said. "Dukish wanted to capture him and serve him up to the league. It would have been the gift that cemented their partnership."

"Ah," Geena said with a smirk, "if they hadn't wanted to do you all in before, they certainly will now."

Looking disgusted, Clytus emptied his tea on the coals. "The damned league . . . We shouldn't have stopped with blowing up the platforms. Should have done it right the first time. Should have squeezed every last one of their pointed heads!" He scowled his way around the gathered faces, lingering on Melio and the others who had come across on the *Slipfin*. He seemed to see what he wanted to in them. He said, "All right, what do we have to do to finish this? Let's get it done."

"Yeah," Kartholomé said, "let's get it done."

"One night and you are willing to fight with us?" Tunnel asked. "I didn't think we were as charming as that."

Geena strolled over, squeezed the man's bulging, gray-hued bicep, and then hung from it. Melio felt a twinge of jealousy. "Don't think of it that way. One night and *you're* willing to help us finish *our* business with the league; that's how I see it. A good deal for us. This is a muscle. Do you all see this thing?"

"If you mean it," Dariel said, looking from Geena to Clytus to Melio, "you fill me with joy. You see, I thought a lot about how to proceed last night. I think I have it, but I do need my brigands to aid me."

"You have us," Clytus said.

"Then we have a fighting chance," Dariel said. "First, let's send the good leagueman a message . . . in Dukish's name."

CHAPTER
FIFTY-FOUR

Aliver and Barad walked side by side on the cobblestone streets that led from the palace down through the various tiers of the city. The prince had asked Barad to accompany him to see off the transport that was to depart that morning, taking Kelis and the last of the soldiers on Acacia to Alecia. Aliver himself would climb aboard his dragon there at the docks. He would lift up and fly away from the island of his birth and from the children he had just parted with. Nothing had ever been harder in his life, but it had to be. And he had to speak a little with this man before parting. He had two questions he wished to ask. This would be the only occasion he had left to do so.

Walking beside the tall, stone-eyed man, Aliver beheld Acacia for what he knew would be the last time. He would never see this view again, never look down at the terraced levels dropping away beneath him. Never again watch the bustle of ships in the great harbor or see that man stepping out of his house or those faces peering from a window or those workmen pausing on that rooftop to watch him pass.

So much of life was now made of *buts* and *nevers* and *cannots* and other words that denied. Despite them, Aliver was not morbid. To every failure he could think of there was a rebuttal.

To each thing he had not done in his life he could respond, *Yes, but think of all I have seen. So much. Who is to say I deserve any more?* To the time he would not have to spend with those he loved he could say, *But if I hadn't had the time I did with them, I would never know how special those moments were.* To thoughts that it was unfair his life would be cut short again, he could reply, *But I've had two lives, two chances. Who else has ever been as fortunate as that?*

He faced his all too few remaining days with a tranquility he had never mastered when the future stretched before him. He would not have predicted that. How much of his life could he have predicted? Very little. He could not have anticipated that upon learning he had a daughter, he would have only one day of life with her. Nor that in that short span he would grow to love the girl. It amazed him how much he loved her. How much he felt that he knew her. Perhaps it was because his mother, Aleera, was behind the girl's eyes, and that his father lived in the corners of her lips. Only hours together, but within them was all the lifetime of parenthood he would ever have. He could be bitter, but doing so would be unjust to what he had just learned. He would not die completely. His death was not his death, not when his daughter lived on.

The prince wore a tunic of black chain mail over a sleeveless vest and long, flowing trousers. The morning was chilly, but he wanted to display the tuvey band that rested snug above his biceps. It did not matter that the enemy was far away. He dressed for the crowds that had gathered to watch him pass. It was early, but the people knew he was to depart this day. Many called to him, bestowing blessings and the Giver's speed on him. Others offered to join the army. An old man said he could not fight but he had once been a blacksmith. He could mend armor, sharpen weapons, and the like. A boy piped up, saying he could cook and tend a fire and carry water. "I'm strong!"

Aliver smiled his thanks to them and declined, telling them

he would remember their offers always. He explained that they had gathered a great host already on the mainland and more were pouring in even yet. "Stay here," he said, "and keep the island secure and proud. Do that for me."

Many asked for news of the queen. Aliver had nothing new to offer them. "She has flown to destroy the Santoth. She will. She is your queen, and she swore to defeat them in your name." The words sounded grandiose to his ears. Too simple a way to put a complex thing. Too buoyed by optimism he could not be entirely swayed by. He still projected the words with the grinning confidence he needed to, and each time he was amazed at the effect. People believed him, or they seemed to, at least. Both were gifts he—and they—needed.

"Barad," Aliver said once they had pulled away a bit and could talk, "I love these people."

"I know. They know it as well, which is what's truly important. It almost softens me on the whole question of the monarchy." He smiled. "Almost. If all monarchs were like you . . . if it were written into the laws that all monarchs must be just like Aliver Akaran in all important matters . . . But they're not all like you, and such a law would not stand longer than it takes to wean a young tyrant from the breast. After you win this war—and after Corinn defeats the Santoth—you two will have to find a way to guide the nation into a different future. I don't say it will be easy, or that you must change everything overnight, but you must put in place a system that lets people decide their own fates. You will do that, won't you?"

Oh, Corinn and I won't do that, Aliver thought. We'll be dead. The people's fate, for better and worse, will be in their own hands. He resisted the urge to confess to Barad, to unburden himself, and ask him to conceive of the fight going on without him and of the world after without him. He pressed it down beneath a clearing of his throat. It would not help anything. Telling anyone would be an indulgence that might do more harm than good. Though he could not have said whom he was beseeching, he thought, Just let me live long enough to finish this. Please.

Out loud, he said, "I wish we had more time to speak of such things, to plan. When the wars are over, will you help our young monarchs into that future?"

Barad did not seem to notice the peculiar wording. "In any way I can, I will."

"Good," Aliver said. "Then there is hope. Does this mean you've forgiven us?"

"I never needed to forgive you. Queen Corinn enslaved us both. For her, forgiveness is a long road. I'm yet only standing on the edge of it."

The prince nodded his acceptance of this.

"I will admit that I do care about your family more than I imagined I could," Barad said. "I still believe that no one family should rule the world, and I will not forget the things Corinn did to me and to the nation. But I cannot feel the anger I wish to."

He paused as a child rushed up to Aliver, offering him a wristband woven from dyed leather. Aliver kneeled and let the girl slip it on.

Watching, Barad said, "I can't imagine the people fighting a war without you. Before, I would have said that these adoring people are deluded by the vintage your sister gave them. That's only part of it, though. Beneath that they see something in you. They need you right now. Without you I don't know what would unite us enough to fight the Auldek. We could be scattered and running, hiding and thinking only of ourselves. Instead, all the people of the world seem content to put aside their differences until this war is over."

They walked for a time, surrounded by well-wishers. Once through them, Aliver asked the first of his two questions. "So, Barad, visionary that you are—how do I defeat this enemy?"

"I'm not a warrior. You know better than I what your family has done in the past." Barad made a fist and smashed it, with force but humor also, into his other palm. "You crush them. Don't you? You kill enough of them so that they have no heart to fight on. You destroy their wealth, their happiness, their capacity to threaten you. You control where they live, how they live, and you take their resources so that they have to come to you for the very things necessary for their survival. You make a myth that explains the rightness of your victory and the wrongness that made the defeated into the defeated." He inhaled a few breaths as if the catalog he had just spoken winded him. "All these things your Acacia has done, and yet none of it made you safe. The Meins came out of defeat a stronger enemy than before you conquered them. The Santoth roar back upon us all now, when we were not even thinking of them. The Auldek come against us because of what? Are they an old or new enemy? They have been devouring our children for generations. Now they want more."

"I know the way things have been," Aliver said. "I ask you to speak of a way things could be."

Barad looked up as they passed through the gate into the lower town, watching the gentle sway of flags above it. Aliver did the same. "Tell me this: Is the world too small for the people that live in it?"

"No," Aliver said.

"Is there too little water and air, wood and food and animals, stones to build with and ore to make tools with? Is there not enough? In the whole of the Known World I mean—not just as measured in any one place."

"Of course there is enough."

"Will any of us live forever?"

"No."

"Need any of us fear death?"

Aliver let his eyes drift over the faces of the people they passed. Young and old, men and women, a child clinging to his mother's leg, a crone with one eye closed as if she were winking at him. "No," he said, "none of us need fear death."

"If all that is as you say, war makes no sense."

"I never said it did."

"Then don't make war."

"I must."

"No, make something different from war. Don't allow your enemies to be enemies. Make them something else, because otherwise they have a power over you that they should not have. If you think in the same ways as the past, you will only get new versions of the past. Think differently. That's what I'm saying."

Exactly, Aliver thought. It was what he had already decided he needed to do. It helped to hear Barad's deep voice expressing the same conclusion. Think differently. That's what I'm learning to do again. Now that he was free inside himself, his visions of what the world could and should be spoke to him with growing urgency. He had been thinking differently when he and Corinn spoke of the souls trapped in the Auldek bodies and when they composed the documents he had in a sealed box already safe in Kohl's saddlebag. He had been thinking differently earlier that day when he met with Delivegu. Aliver sent him on the task unlike any that Corinn had assigned him. The first and last mission Aliver would ever set him on.

A little later they stood on the dock at which the transport was moored. Kelis and Naamen were waiting on the boat. Kelis waved from the deck but did not descend to intrude upon them. Despite the bustling crowds and the din of patriotic songs and the incredible sight of the three dragons perched each on their own cleared section of pier they—and others—knew that the two men were conversing privately.

Aliver stood with a hand resting on a pylon. He and Barad watched the rippling green water below them, the barnacle-encrusted pier fading into the depths below their feet. Crabs worked at their precise harvest, one large claw and one small, coordinated.

"What will you do now?" Aliver asked.

"Is that for me to say?"

Instead of answering, Aliver found a new question. "Barad, do you remember that I spoke to you when you were still in the mines of Kidnaban?"

The man's stone eyes managed to convey surprise. "Of course. Hearing your voice changed my life, Aliver. You gave me purpose. Before I had the words to speak against tyranny, I borrowed yours and learned to speak by juggling them on my tongue. The queen almost took that away from me. Under her spell, I came to doubt that I had ever heard your voice. I came to doubt many things."

"And I had forgotten it myself," Aliver said, "but I have it all back now. I reached out to you because I knew you were the people's conscience. I needed you then. It was good to know that you were there in the mines, among the people, saying all the brilliant, rebellious things you've always said. I still need you, but after what's been done to you I have no right to ask anything of you. Go, if you have a mind to. Do and say what you will all across the world."

A group of soldiers strode by. They bowed their heads to Aliver as they passed. Barad watched them until they began to climb the gangplank to the transport. "I don't know where I would go or what I would say. I have my tongue back, but I am tired, Aliver. I don't have it in me to harangue the masses anymore, not after the speeches I made for your sister. If I were younger, I would go with you. I'd listen to you speak."

"I have a different idea," Aliver said, nervous now as he approached the second question he wanted to ask Barad. "If you want to serve the nation without having to shout above masses or wield a sword . . . how about having a smaller group of pupils? You could stay here with Aaden and Shen."

Barad pulled his head back, studying Aliver as if he needed to adjust his angle to see him clearly. "Aliver . . ."

"Educate them. Speak your mind and tell them every wise thing you know. Explain to them the world as you understand it, so that they can be rulers with their eyes open—and with their hearts and their consciences at the centers of their beings always. Or help them learn to be something other than rulers, if it comes to that."

"Do you mean this?" Barad said after a moment.

"Teach them to think differently. Help them make a better future for themselves and Acacia."

"Shouldn't you do this yourself?"

With all my heart I want that, but I am dead and cannot do it. "If I had the time, I would love to, but I may not have that time. If I don't, will you do it? I have already written a testament giving you complete power over their education."

"And what of the mothers of these children? What would they think of their children being educated by a commoner, a mine worker, a rabble-rousing rebel, a man of—"

"They both approved. Corinn did before she left. Benabe you can ask yourself. Mena, I will tell with my own lips. And Dariel, he may not be of this world anymore. He would approve of this, though. You see? Nobody will stop what you begin."

The man's gaze drifted from Aliver. It seemed to lose itself somewhere in the middle distance of the green depths at their feet. "Corinn approved?" he asked, but Aliver knew it was not so much a question as a statement, one he needed to test out loud to believe. His eyes ground back to the prince's. "I would not lie to them. Not about anything. If I teach, I will teach them that there is a better way than that of monarch and subject. I never believed in that system, Aliver. I still don't."

"I know," Aliver said. "I know what you think about such things. Much of it we are of one mind about."

Barad shook his head. He spoke with an almost angry edge to his voice, almost as if he had not heard Aliver. "You cannot ask this of me and then tie my tongue. I would swallow it first. If I am their tutor, I will dive with them into the royal records. I will show them what your line has done and how. There will be no secrets. If we find horrors, I will hold their hands and face those horrors with them, but I will not lie to them."

"I know."

"Do not tell me that they are only children. War happens to children. Slavery happens to children. The ravages of corruption happen to—"

"I know better than most that children deserve the truth of the world, explained as they can handle it, and reexamined as they grow. I would do the same with them myself. I swear I would. But our history is not all horrors. It's still being written. If you show them what we have done, make sure to show them the things that will make them proud. Let them have that as well. And be kind to them. I know you will, but there is nothing harder for a monarch than to be asked to give back what he thought was his. This new world that you and I want so much, if it comes, it will not be easy for them. I had thought once that I would oversee changes myself. Now I see my work was not about me. It was about helping set the stage for them. I haven't done it all that well, but I'm still trying. Here, please take this for me. Keep it safe." He pulled a chain from around his neck and held it for Barad to take. A key dangled from it. "Keep it for the children, for Mena. When the time comes to offer it to them, you'll know it."

Barad closed his large hand over the chain. His expression deepened. It grew lined and grave even though his stone eyes remained still at the center of it. "You . . . you are not coming back. Aliver, there is a pall around you. Since the coronation, it's been on you and the queen both. I thought it was just sadness, but it's . . ."

"It's the pall of war," Aliver said. He forced his smile to look genuine. "I may as well be cautious. That's all. I may as well leave the children in the hands of a tutor like you. That way, I know they will not face the future blind. You will do it?"

The instant he had the man's affirmation, Aliver bid him farewell. He could look not a moment longer into Barad's stone eyes. Aliver turned away as if his mind had moved on. It hadn't, though. Moments later, though he was aboard the transport, talking with Kelis, shaking hands and patting backs and speaking to the crowd, he fought to contain the emotion of the arrangement he had just made.

And then, back on the pier, he took to the saddle on Kohl's back and looked across at Ilabo on Tij, and at Dram on Thaïs a little farther away. Outfitted for war, they looked like characters of living myth. The dragons wore plates of armor kept in place by a snug lacework of cords. They went laden with packs and supplies, with swords and crossbows strapped into place. The riders wore chain mail tunics like Aliver. As a final touch they pulled snug helmets fashioned to replicate the heads of the mounts they rode. Aliver tugged on a black helm that flared behind his ears in imitation of Kohl's crest feathers.

They all rose into the air at the same moment, propelled upward on the cheers of the onlookers. Kohl roared and Tij answered. Thaïs corkscrewed just above the heads of the crowd, a move that spurred them to even greater applause. For a few moments Aliver forgot the weight of responsibility and loss on him. The scene was too glorious not to fill him with pride. Surging into the air above a beauty of an island, climbing up the terraced levels of the city. Everywhere people waving and shouting for them. Over the palace itself, he saw Shen and Aaden at the balcony of the upper terraces, Rhrenna just behind them. He swooped past them with Kohl tilted to one side so that Aliver hung toward them in the saddle, one arm outstretched as if he were touching them over the distance.

For the first time in his second life, Prince Aliver Akaran went to war.

CHAPTER
FIFTY-FIVE

Breaking camp after the first battle had been a terrible task for Mena's army. They worked through the night, taking no rest, laboring in clothes and armor still smeared with gore. They tended the injured as they went, piling them—the living, the dying, and the dead—on sledges that they dragged toward the broken mangle of shore ice. The Scav had scouted and improved a half-submerged route that proved much more efficient than climbing up and down over the slabs and crevices. Trusting them with a completeness that would have been unimaginable a fortnight earlier, the Acacians followed their lead. They did not stop until they were all out on the frozen ground once more.

Even then the Scav did not rest. They went back into the labyrinth of ice to destroy the route and to set their traps. It was fortunate that they did. Watching from a distance as that Auldek station plunged into the water filled Mena with exhilaration. If only they could have dropped all of them into the depths, let the water and ice cover them, and forget about them. If only they would vanish like the phantoms of a nightmare.

They would not, of course, do any such thing. They rolled and marched, hauled and flew ever onward. They ate each passing mile and bayed to do battle the whole time. Mena refused to meet them again on the field. The Acacians backed across the glacier-scoured contours of the landscape, defensive, cautious, devious. All of it clearly drove the Auldek crazy.

For a time they flew into the Acacian camp on fréketes, ignoring the rain of arrows that always greeted them. Speaking accented Acacian, they hurled insults. They implored the Acacians to fight like true soldiers, threatened that they were only making their nation's fate worse by their cowardice. The fréketes leaped about, crushing people with their feet and snatching others up in their fists. They bit chunks of flesh out of them and spat the meat on the ground. One Auldek leaped from his mount's back and went running through the camp, hacking down anyone he could. If others had followed his example, the slaughter would have been horrible. Fortunately, the rampaging Auldek caught a crossbow bolt in the face. He went down clawing at it. He rose a moment later. His face blood-splattered, he tugged at the arrow as his body jerked and convulsed, unable to pull the bolt free. He managed to climb atop his frékete and took to the air again. After that, such attacks grew less frequent. Heartening, perhaps, except that not even a bolt right through the skull managed to kill these fiends.

That was why Mena pressed her bizarre form of warfare in every way and shape she could imagine, adjusting it daily as the circumstances changed. She once flew a mad gauntlet over the Auldek camp, dodging and dipping, cutting at sharp angles to avoid the fréketes pursuing her. Behind her she trailed a falling snow of sorts, hundreds of short letters on small bits of paper, blowing out of the pack bags she had flipped open. Each note contained a personal entreaty to the quota slaves to desert the Auldek and come over to their own people. Each of them signed with the writer's name, written in their native tongue, with the invitation to bring the note across to the Acacians and be personally welcomed home.

As far as she could tell, the fréketes did not often fly at night. She knew they could because one had done so on the night of the Scav's first fiery attack, but they had never again dropped out of the dark, something Mena had feared. Instead, she owned the dark skies herself. On a night of low cloud she flew in through the mist over their encampment. She circled several times, testing, on edge for the beat of any wing other than Elya's. Nothing.

An hour later she returned with Perrin dangling from Elya's claws. They both dropped to the ground well inside the Auldek encampment. By the time Elya swooped back in to retrieve them, they had slit the throats of five sleeping watchmen and had tossed a sack full of poisoned meat out to steam on the frozen ground. Food for lions, she hoped.

Nor was there anyone in the air to answer her an hour later when she dropped a flaming kettle filled with pitch into one of the pens that held the antoks. She watched the large backs of the creatures from above, the tiny glimmer of the wick falling with the pot. When it hit the ground, the pitch must have splashed out underneath their legs. It ignited in one large sheet beneath them. She stayed above long enough to verify the deadly furnace of kicking, bellowing creatures that she had created. One of them crashed through the pen wall, and in the next instant the creatures were rampaging through the camp, all sizzling hair and flesh.

Confusion. Damage. It must be taking a toll on them. Mena despised it. There was no honor in an assassin's tactics, in making war on animals and supplies. A strange thing to a call a war, really, this running skirmish through the arctic. It was nothing Mena had trained for or read about or studied. Not a style of fighting she had ever imagined. *Fighting* was not even the right word for it, but she did not know what else to call something so deadly. So desperately important. When she doubted her tactics, she had only to think of the lives of her soldiers to remember why she did these things. She had as many reasons for each treachery as she had souls in her army. For them, she would do anything.

Ten days since that first battle. Hundreds of lives lost. The ranks of the injured and incapacitated growing. Mena could not claim that they were winning, but they were not losing either. Since not losing was about as positive a situation as she could envision, she kept her people focused on the small victories they were accumulating. Each slave warrior they killed, any animal they lamed, every carriage or station they crippled, all the delays and inconveniences they created: small victories. On the rare occasions when they killed an Auldek: jubilation. Howlk had died; the frékete Nawth had been taken out of the war. Things that had seemed impossible could be accomplished. If they could keep doing what they were doing . . . If Aliver and his army ever arrived . . .

※

For the second time, Mena found herself standing inside a ring of her officers, interrogating a bedraggled, stammering, nearly frozen Rialus Neptos. This time, however, he brought a companion. The woman stood beside Rialus, unflinching under the men's scrutiny. She wore a full body suit of some sort, so thick it would have hidden her completely, except that in the relative warmth of the tent she had pulled off her hood and stripped back the top of it. She stood with her shoulders and arms exposed, her chest covered by a thin tunic that showed both the sweat around her neck and the outline of her breasts. Meinish, if ever a woman was: gray eyed, delicately featured, with hair so blond it seemed to light the room with its own luminescence. She searched the collected faces with her eyes, touching on Mena briefly before moving on. Her gaze caught on Haleeven.

"Who are you?" Mena asked.

Rialus had been trying to say something, but he jerked to a halt. "Her?" he asked.

"Yes, but I asked her, not you."

"Sh-she doesn't speak much Acacian. Maybe none. I don't know. I never—"

"Meinish, then? Haleeven, speak to her."

He did, and she answered readily enough, her voice calm and deliberate. After a few exchanges, Haleeven said, "She wishes to join us. She was a slave to the Auldek, she says, but only a slave. Never willingly your enemy. She was like Rialus, trapped by the Auldek."

Rialus ceased trembling. His head turned slowly to the woman, and he stared at her. He could not have looked more perplexed.

"She said that?" Edell asked.

"She did."

"What's her name?"

Haleeven asked her. "Fingel. She has served Rialus Neptos since he arrived in Avina, all the way to here."

"We'll have to ask her a thing or two about him, then," Edell said, fixing Rialus with a dry, hostile gaze.

The two Meins talked a little longer. Haleeven screwed up his mouth at something she said. It looked like a grimace, but as he held the expression it showed itself as a smile. "She claims that Rialus is a good man."

"She has reason to think we'd doubt it?"

"He told her as much himself. Rambled on often, even talked in his sleep sometimes."

Rialus actually could look more perplexed, after all. His face reddened, and it was not from the warmth in the tent.

"I really look forward to talking with her at length," Edell said.

Mena could see that there was something more behind her façade. "What else? She has more to say, I think."

Fingel fixed her eyes on Mena for the first extended time. She listened to Haleeven's translation and deliberated her answer by pressing it between her thin lips for a moment. When she answered, Rialus, obviously understanding her Meinish, sat down on a campstool. He stared at her with an expression of complete mystification.

"She represents a contingent of domestic slaves," Haleeven said. "A few hundred of them who want to desert the Auldek. She is a scout to find out if they would be received kindly. She's asking for refuge among us. They'll be coming tonight. She wants to make sure that they are not attacked when they approach."

"She wants us not to attack a few hundred figures walking into our camp in the middle of the night?" Mena asked. "That could be a very foolish thing for us to do."

Haleeven translated. Fingel dug around inside her body suit for a moment, and brought her hand out with a note pinched in her fingers. She offered it to Haleeven and then spoke at length. Haleeven listened a long time before offering his translation. "She says she found this, one of the notes you dropped among them. She's not the only one who hid them and began hoping they were true. She says they will fight any way they can. Those who can will put poison in their masters' kettles. They'll take a few souls out of them. You asked for them to trust you in these notes; she asks that you trust her now as she returns it to you."

The Meinish chieftain handed Mena the note. She rolled it over in her fingers. She let it look like she had to weigh the hazards carefully, but really she was hiding a swell of euphoria. This was what she wanted. This was the beginning of it. If some came now, more would follow soon. "Haleeven, tell her she is very welcome among us. They all are. We'll accept every one of them home. When we have a moment of peace to do so, we'll drop to our knees and ask forgiveness of them. I mean that literally."

"Won't she and Rialus be missed today?" Perrin asked.

"The other slaves will cover for them today. Say Rialus is sick, keep the door to his room closed. They won't be found out today, and tonight they flee."

"Only a couple of hundred?" Edell asked.

Haleeven had the explanation for this already, too. "They kept the conspiracy very tight. They could have gotten more, but it was too risky."

"Any warriors with them?"

Fingel must have understood the question. She guffawed and answered straightaway. "No," Haleeven translated, "those ones will not come over. They are too far up the Auldek's asses. But, she says, they will all suffer from the lack of well-cooked food, laundered clothes." He smiled. "I think she's right."

"A couple of hundred may not be much," Perrin said, "but it's a start. It will put the idea in others' heads."

"Let's hope it's the trickle that starts the flood," Mena said.

For a time the conversation turned to the practical matters of aiding the deserters. Gandrel suggested setting up a distraction like the explosions the Scav created on the first night that Neptos came across. A good idea, Mena thought, but not easy to arrange. The Auldek were more vigilant about patrolling their camp at night—or their lions were. The pitch was guarded particularly well. The small amount the Scav had stolen was all but used up. Mena had a single flame bomb left, and had not decided how best to use it.

Fingel, once she knew what they were discussing, explained

that they had arranged for such a distraction themselves. One of the men who tended the woolly rhinoceroses was going to let them loose after feeding them a concoction that would put fire in their bowels. The creatures would purge themselves in great gouts of excrement. It would be messy, and they would be angry, hard to gain control of. While they rampaged, the others would make their escape.

The officers sat in silence for a moment, all of them, likely, imagining that scene. "There was never a war like this one," Gandrel said. "Or if there was, they didn't write it all down in the official records."

"Maybe we shouldn't either," Edell said.

Looking at Rialus, Mena edged her tone and asked, "This is what you thought would buy your pardon? A few hundred cook slaves and bed servants. I thought you understood that I expected more from you, Rialus."

The man blinked rapidly. He really did look confused.

"Rialus?"

It took him a while, but eventually he managed to say, "I—I brought other information."

"Tell it, then," Mena said, crossing her arms to wait through the long delay of his stammer.

End of Book Three

〰〰〰〰〰〰

Book Four

The
Snow King

CHAPTER
FIFTY-SIX

The hunting lodge of Calfa Ven had once perched on a stone buttress high above the thick woodland of the King's Preserve. The "nest of the mountain condor," as the translation of its Senivalian name went, had catered to Acacian nobility for more than two hundred years. Standing on its balconies with wild valleys stretching out beneath her had been the closest Corinn had come to experiencing flight before her dragons brought it to her for real. It was a place of memories, of long horseback rides, of pastoral opulence, rich meals served by rustic staff, of cordials sipped beside crackling fires, of walks with her father and even images of her mother in health. A place of sunrises and sunsets and the ever-changing play of the light on the crowns of trees and over the granite outcroppings that jutted up like islands amid waves of foliage. It had been here that Corinn had bested Hanish at archery, thinking she hated him at the same time she was falling in love with him.

Now, having just climbed off Po's back along with the ghost of Hanish beside her, she could not even recognize the field in which they had loosed their arrows. The lodge itself had been obliterated. Smashed and scoured clean from its granite foundation, nothing remained of it save the bases of the timbers that had secured the building to the stone. The outbuildings, stables and storehouse: all jumbled piles of lumber, broken and strewn about. The woodland in the valley had been scorched, trees snapped, others uprooted, splintered. Some of the largest trees twisted at bizarre angles, as if they had rendered temporarily molten. Great gashes festered in the earth, smoking, reeking of death. It was like this as far as the eye could see, an enormous scar with the former site of the lodge at its center.

Po cried out in frustration as he flew over the valley. In all that expanse no other living thing moved, nothing for him to hunt. He fled from place to place, chased by evil vapors in the air, uneasy. He wanted to leave, but Corinn did not respond to the wish.

In all of it she recognized the same accursed song that had set worms eating through her flesh. In all of it, Santoth rage. Had she any tears left within her, she would have cried. She took the scene in dry-eyed. She had called this devastation upon the place. What right did she have to cry over it now?

"It is changed, but we knew it would be."

I should not have sent them here.

"You had to send them somewhere," Hanish said. "This place . . . was full of memories for you. For us. It came into your head when you needed to name a destination. You could have chosen much worse places to send them, Corinn." As he talked he walked around her, trying to sift through the ashes with his feet. He did not seem to notice that the toe of his boot did not really push objects about. He left no footprints, touched nothing in the world except for her.

You don't know all of it, Corinn thought to him.

"No, I don't. But still, let's not talk about this." He straightened and took in the desolation of the valley again. "What we should be asking is, where are the Santoth now?"

That's clear enough. They don't exactly walk lightly on the ground.

They're out there. They won't stop searching. Corinn gestured with her chin, indicating the wide world around them. *They've gone in different directions. No doubt some are heading back toward Acacia. We soared so high on the way here. Perhaps we flew over some of them. This is like the rage they experienced when Tinhadin exiled them. They may yet kill many people.*

"That's why we're going to stop them. Call Po back. We should—"

A woman's voice reached them. "Queen Corinn? Is—is that you?"

They both spun around, searching for the speaker. She was so still that Corinn's eyes passed over her, only to snap back a moment later. A woman stood with something gripped to her chest, half hidden behind the rubble of a collapsed wall. She stepped out from behind it. "It is you, isn't it?"

Corinn touched a hand to her cowl, which still hid the lower portion of her face. Realizing that was not a gesture that would serve as an answer here, she nodded.

The woman said something over her shoulder. A second woman emerged. Like the first, she bore a bundle in her arms. Just after, a third head peeked out. She came more reluctantly. As they picked their way forward through the debris, Corinn recognized them both. The first woman: Wren, Dariel's lover. The second, Gurta, Rialus Neptos's recent bride. The third was a girl who worked in the lodge, Peter's daughter. She could not remember her name.

"Steady, Corinn," Hanish said. He stepped up close, one hand at her elbow, one at the small of her back. "They are not ghosts. They live, and so, I think, do the babes they carry."

He was right. The bundles in the women's arms were unmistakable, as was the care with which they cradled them. Corinn felt her breath escape her. She leaned more heavily into Hanish.

"You see?" he asked. "There is still life here."

When Wren reached them, she bowed her head and said, "Your Majesty."

Gurta tried to do the same, but her eyes were round circles that would not leave the queen's face. "What's happening?" she asked. "They came here and destroyed everything. They killed everyone but us. We would not have survived if Bralyn hadn't hidden us. She knew of a cave." She paused, looking from the queen to Wren, a desperate intensity in her eyes. "It was horrible. They . . . I don't know what to call it. They tore the world apart. They stayed for days, raging. They were demons. I know it sounds mad, but look around. Only great evil could do this. Queen Corinn, you should not be here. They may come back. The place may be cursed. It is cursed. I can feel it. Isn't it cursed, Wren?"

The slim woman kept her smoothly lidded eyes on Corinn. She did not seem to be listening to Gurta at all, except that when prompted she did speak. "Queen, how do you come to be here? Alone?"

Corinn shook her head.

Wren misunderstood her. "I saw you ride in. I know that . . . thing out there is yours. But are others coming?"

Hanish said, "Show them."

Corinn did. She pulled down the cowl and tucked it under her chin. All three women drew back, staring, aghast. *Yes, that's the horror of me.* They could not hear her, of course, or see or hear Hanish. Unsure how to proceed, Corinn just stood, looking into the women's faces as if into three mirrors, each of which showed a different reflection.

Wren began the conversation again. "Those ones did this to you, didn't they? The same ones that came here."

Corinn nodded.

"Oh, Queen, I'm sorry. They are so awful. You . . . you're chasing them, aren't you?"

Again, the queen nodded.

"Tell me you are going to destroy them."

Blinking her eyes closed for a moment, Corinn answered with a third nod.

"Good," Wren said. "I don't know how you could possibly do that, but if anybody can, I guess you can. That's what Dariel would say."

At the mention of her brother, Corinn's eyes went to the bundle in the woman's arms. She stepped closer and pulled back the blanket to reveal a tiny child's sleeping face. So small, with thin tendrils of black hair and a fist, a little ball of a fist, clenched just beside its face. "This is my baby," Wren said. "Your niece, if you ever wish to call her so. She was born early. I got ill, bad ill. She wanted out of me. She's all right, though. Small but strong. Like me." The woman smiled.

Corinn almost collapsed. *I got ill, bad ill.* That sentence, next to that smile and beside that child was almost too much for her to stand. She sensed that Po felt her distress and wanted to return to her. She ordered him not to. *Do you see the things I've done, Hanish? I tried to kill this child. I tried to kill this woman, and yet she smiles at me.*

"She has every reason to," he said. "She lives. Her daughter does, too."

"She doesn't have a name yet. I've not had time to think about it. But . . . she's my little girl."

Gurta found her voice again. "I got mine out, too," she said. "I was cursing him for coming, but I'm glad he was out and at the breast before them ones came and did all this. He's got more sense than his father; I can tell that already."

Corinn reached in to see the infant's face. She saw only an ear and a soft, lumpy curve of his head, but she peered in for a long time. She could smell the child, a scent that was sticky with his birthing but somehow lovely all the same. Mostly, though, she listened as Gurta continued her nervous rambling. She sounded more like a maid now than ever. The young woman had annoyed Corinn before. She could not imagine why anymore. Her voice was lovely, kind and warm. Without guile.

Rialus was lucky to have had you.

Touching her back again, Hanish said, "Tell her that so she can hear it. Find a way to talk to them, Corinn. Tell them the things you need to. Time is short."

Reluctantly, she drew back. She rummaged around in one of her saddlebags until she found writing utensils and sheaves of parchment. As the women stood awkwardly beside her, she wrote two notes. One she signed with her royal title and stamped with the Akaran seal, rolled, and tied tight with a strip of ribbon that any official of high rank would recognize. The other was a simpler missive.

When she was finished both, she pressed the rolled document to Wren's breast, indicating that she should hide it somewhere upon her person. The other she offered to them both to read. She had written:

Take this document with you to Acacia. It's an official pass of protection from me. If anyone troubles you, show it to them. Tell them they face my wrath if they harm you. Take it to Acacia, show it at the palace, and ask for my secretary, Rhrenna. Go there and be safe, under Akaran protection. From now and for as long as we can provide it.

Gurta, forgive me for sending Rialus into such danger. I did not know what I was doing. I pray that he gets back to you, and that you live long and raise this child with love.

Wren, I have committed crimes against you. I am too afraid to name them now, and I don't ask you to forgive me. That's too much to ask. But please go to Acacia with my blessing. Declare yourself the mother of Dariel's daughter. If my brother makes it back to you, love him, wed him, be a part of my family.

Go now. Hide yourselves again until I leave and the sorcerers follow me.

When they had both clearly read the messages, they stood, nervous and unsure what to make of them. Gurta said, "You can't fight them by yourself, Your Majesty. Don't do that. Fly home and get others. Get everyone."

In answer, Corinn picked up the quill again. On the back of the missive, she wrote, *I'm not alone. I was before, but I'm not anymore.*

"And need never be again," Hanish said.

※

L̲ater, once the two women had departed and had time to return to their deep hiding place, Corinn opened *The Song of Elenet.* As ever, she heard the song waft up from the pages, winged notes that danced on the breeze, instantly intoxicating.

Do you hear that?

"Of course I do," Hanish said. "I can understand why you like it so much."

Corinn bent forward, eyes closed, breathing the song in through her nose. The music caressed her face, searching the mottled flesh of her sealed mouth with gentle fingers. It wanted to heal her. She could feel it. The song itself—and whatever intelligence somehow lived in it—wished to rewrite the abomination that was the Santoth curse. It was wonderful to sense that sentient wish, but Corinn knew it could not be done. No matter how much of the song she could build within her head, it always had to be released through spoken breath, through open lips and with some resonance of the notes vibrating on her tongue. Even a whisper could do it, as when she whispered Barad's eyes into stone.

But I cannot whisper.

"If I could whisper for you I would," Hanish said.

I know. And she knew he could not. If she had years to be his tutor, perhaps she could have found some way to teach him. He could have been the ghost sorcerer that walked beside her, unseen by any eyes but Barad's. She would have spoken to him with her mind and the song would have danced unheard from his lips. But again there was the trap. She did not have those years. The serpent of her dilemma ate its tail. Her life was a closed ring, tightening each moment.

What a couple we might have been together.

"Corinn, what a couple *we are* together."

Corinn opened her eyes and looked down at the living words. She let them rise up into her eyes with their own power, just as they had done the very first time she looked upon them. That was all she needed to do.

The response came quickly. A bellowing from the west. Followed by a roar from the north. And concussions of rage that passed, soundless, through the air from all around them. The Santoth sensed the touch of her eyes on *The Song.* Just having it alive within her head was enough. She knew they would hear it, just as she knew they were each of them turning toward her, drawn to it.

Hanish said, "I think you've got their attention."

CHAPTER
FIFTY-SEVEN

It all went horribly wrong, and it was her fault. Mena knew it was. She should not have slept. How stupid of her to think she could sleep through a night while others risked their lives. At Perrin's urging, she had left the task of receiving the incoming slave deserters to him. "Greet them in the morning, personally, with all the sincerity of feeling you want," he had said, "but get some rest first." He reasoned that Rialus Neptos had crossed back and forth three times. Surely these slaves—who were cunning if Fingel was anything to judge by—could manage it as well.

Thinking this made it easier for Mena to acquiesce. Sleep she did, harder and longer than she intended. And dream she did as well: of being held tight by Perrin. He clung to her and sought to kiss her mouth. She would not let him. Instead, she placed her lips against his closed eyes. She felt the feather touches of his eyelashes, and there was something wonderful about the ripe curve of his eyeball. That, in her dream state, was permitted. Nothing else.

When she woke to the flute notes that announced the pre-dawn hour, Mena felt in the pit of her stomach that something had gone wrong. She should not have slept so deeply. She should not have dreamed the things she had. Melio's eyes were the only ones she had kissed that way—and that was how it ever should be. The fact that she had slept and dreamed prompted her to kick off her blankets and dress hurriedly.

Perrin collided with her as she came out of her tent. It was dark yet and windy. He was hooded and mittened. She knew him by his stature, though, and his shape.

"What happened?"

"We don't know, Princess. I mean . . . nothing happened. They didn't come. We even had lookouts posted out beyond the barricade. They saw nothing, until just now. Come and see."

Standing atop a sled with her officers, just behind the barricade of wooden spikes, sleds, and other supplies that served as their makeshift protective wall, Mena peered toward the Auldek camp. A barren, rocky expanse separated the two armies, but through a spyglass she could see the enemy's stations steaming in the distance. Something was happening over there. Torches lit the area in front of their camp. In the crimson light Mena could make out shapes moving, structures being shifted, construction work, it seemed, but even through her spyglass she could not figure out what they were building.

"Do you think the deserters were discovered?" Perrin asked.

Mena inhaled, the night air so cold it froze the hair in her nostrils. "Perhaps, but there's something more going on."

※

An hour later the light of dawn, as it finally began to creep in fits and starts across the frozen land's contours, gave her a better idea of what. The structures they had built took on a familiar shape. Simple, solid, tall, and long necked, they reminded Mena of foulthings made of stout wooden beams. "Catapults." She pulled the spyglass from her eye and offered it to Perrin. "They've erected catapults. Big ones."

"About time," Gandrel said. To spite the cold, as he liked to put it, he stood with his hood thrown back, sniffing defiantly to keep his scarred nose from dripping. "I've found these Auldek a bit slow on the uptake, is what I mean. If you'd been on their side, Mena, you'd've finished us by now."

"Let's hope they're not thinking that way." Mena took the spyglass back and lifted it.

"But catapults?" Edell asked. He took off his gloves and tried to rub warmth into his cheeks. "We're not exactly a fortress here. What are they going to . . ."

Through the distorted, circular clarity of the spyglass' view, Mena saw the arm of one of the catapults lever forward abruptly. It looked odd, the silent jerk of motion so far away. "They've shot," she said. The object that surged up from it seemed to come apart as it rose. It broke into pieces that fanned out. She lost sight of them, pulled away the spyglass, and watched like the others, with her naked eyes.

"What are those?" Perrin asked.

Mena realized the answer just before they hit the hard earth. Something in the way each projectile somersaulted and contorted in the air, many limbed and limp as the dead . . . for they were the dead. Bodies. Naked bodies. They hit the ground about a hundred paces out, smacking down with sickening thuds. All that long arc of motion ended in an instant. Some of them split apart and sprayed red mist into the air. Most just landed. The sounds of the impacts followed one another in a quick, dull staccato.

"The deserters were found out," Edell said.

"And this is their punishment?" Perrin asked. "Monsters. They're monsters!" He whispered it first, and then he shouted it. As if in answer, a second rain of falling forms crashed down. Again the staccato of thuds.

A scream yanked Mena around.

Fingel. The woman stood a little distance away, with Rialus beside her. She dropped to her knees, pointing with one arm at the thing they had all already seen. She emitted a sound from somewhere in the tormented center of her. It carried a misleadingly rising tenor, as if she were about to scream or moan, but kept having the foundation of it pulled from under her.

A third catapult hurled its grisly load, ten or so bodies.

"Why are they doing this?" Perrin asked.

The first catapult launched again.

Rialus's voice answered. "They're sending us a message."

The second catapult snapped forward again.

"What message?"

Mena answered, "They would rather be without servants than be betrayed by them."

The Auldek kept it up throughout the day, building scattered piles of hundreds and hundreds of broken, exploded, naked bodies. A battlefield's worth of carnage lofted through the air as a sickening gift. It was as Rialus said: a statement, not an attack.

❋

The attack came that night.

Lookouts sounded the alarm when the Auldek were still out beyond the piles of corpses, riding in atop antoks. Mena—awake this time—jumped out of her cot fully clothed, snatching up the King's Trust. Hearing the alarm horns, the Auldek responded as well. They discarded stealth. They spurred the beasts forward. As Mena reached the barricade, the antoks rushed toward them, bellowing. They plowed through the bodies. They sent the white bears that had come to feast on the frozen meat running, roaring their anger as they did so.

Perceven shouted for archers to man the barricade. Perrin directed the foot soldiers into ranks. Bledas sprinted past, his sword drawn, rallying the confused and groggy. Mena connected with Elya, telling her to stay put, sheltered and hidden.

When the attackers were just a few hundred yards out, the catapults, still in front of their encampment, lobbed balls of flaming pitch instead of bodies. The orbs hurtled upward like shooting stars, bent with the earth's pull, and then plummeted. The catapults this time had been calibrated to send their missiles farther. The first one hit near enough to Mena that the impact knocked her from her feet. The impact area became an instant inferno.

Fly, Elya, Mena thought, hoping the bombardment at least meant the fréketes had been held back. *Get high and stay safe.* Out loud, she shouted, "Ignore them. Ignore the fireballs. Distractions! You can't run from them, so forget them. Look at what else comes!"

Once into the crimson highlights of the fire's glow, the antok riders pulled up their mounts. The beasts halted, churning the turf with their hooves, raking their heads about, impatient for the living blood on the other side of the barricade. The Auldek clinging to them began to leap off. They hit the frozen ground and came up, drawing their weapons. They proceeded forward, leaving the mounts fuming. In their arrogance, Mena realized, the Auldek wanted to do the killing themselves. As far as they were concerned, they did not need the monsters to do it for them.

They were just as tall and fierce as ever, long limbed and fast. They wore dark body suits that covered them entirely, with hoods over their heads, but no obvious armor on them, none of the encumbering bulk of her own troops' thick layers. The Auldek batted away the arrows that hit them as if they were troublesome insects. Even the arrows that struck them in the chest did not stick. Mena saw a heart shot knock an Auldek back. It caused a hitch in his step, but did little more than that.

The arrow hung there until he ripped it away. It had not penetrated at all. It had just caught on his clothing.

"Aim for their faces!" Mena yelled to the archers around her, and then stood on her toes and passed the order over to Perceven on one side and Bledas on the other. "Everyone, aim for their faces!"

Another fireball exploded nearby, flinging out a molten wave of pitch. A man near her got splashed with the stuff, one arm so drenched that it liquefied while he was still on his feet. Other pitch balls landed with powerful whoomps, followed by the horrible splatter of flying liquid and the screams of the burning. They fell everywhere, igniting tents and supplies. The animals worked themselves into a grunting, squealing frenzy. The air, a moment ago ice pure and gelid, filled with the stench of burning pitch, flesh and hair and wood and fabric.

The Auldek reached the Acacians' barricade. The wall, put up and taken down hastily each time they moved their camp, was more a visual gesture than a true fortification. A delay and a nuisance, although for the Auldek it was barely even that. They leaped over it, chopped into it, shoved their way through it. Mena was right there in the front of her troops, yelling for them to attack them as the Auldek came through, while they were encumbered. She hacked at the arm of an Auldek whose feet were caught in a crosshatch of timbers. The man yowled, but the arm did not get sliced through, as she envisioned. She struck again, on his helmet, shoulder, slashing up in the hopes of reaching his face. None of the blows bit. She hacked down on his shoulder with enough force to sever it. In response he buckled beneath the blow for a moment, then surged upright, spouting what must have been Auldek curses.

He was through—and others were through. Instant chaos, at a frantic level immediately different from just moments before.

Her troops behind her surged forward. They became a squirming, struggling press of bodies into which the Auldek cut bloody
paths. Mena got shoved away from the Auldek she had been
fighting, and had to watch as he waded into the soldiers next to
her. Slashing and shouting, the sound of metal striking metal,
shouts of agony and rage and fear, guttural Auldek punching its
way through their Acacian. For a time the battle was such utter
confusion that Mena had no control over anything. She struck
at any Auldek she neared, but she was too hemmed in. Her own
soldiers pushed her into the jumble of the barricade so that she
struggled even to stay upright. This burned away any trace of
fear and left her red hot with anger.

Seeing an opening, she dove for it. With the King's Trust
clenched in her sword hand, she scrambled on all fours beneath
a lattice of wooden beams, along an overturned sled, and then
over another into the clear. Outside the camp now, she ran
along the barricade, trying to work out what they should do.
The Auldek had all passed through already, which meant there
were not so many of them. Only Auldek, and only a small group
of them. She had the sickening thought that they must have
drawn lots or something to win the privilege of this slaughter.

Think, Mena!

They had taken control of the moment, but was fight and
die all that she could respond with? She would not accept
that. She found a clearer section of the barricade, climbed on
a wagon, and got a view. The Auldek rampaged through the
camp. They did not stick to any formation, but ran where they
pleased, swinging their massive swords and axes with a blurred
rapidity that horrified her. They looked like dancers working
through a practiced choreography, except that they were slicing off limbs and sending arcs of blood into the air with every
move. Another sickening thought: that this might be the night

the war ends for her and her army. Had they done enough? Had they delayed and hurt them enough for Corinn and Aliver to be able to defeat them?

Think!

She was just about to call Elya to her when she saw Perrin and another soldier fighting with an Auldek. The monster bore down on them, stepping through the bodies he had already cut down. He slashed and spun. He tossed his sword from one hand to the other and slashed and spun again.

A game, Mena thought. It's a game to him.

It was not a game to Perrin and the young soldier. They barely managed to fend off the Auldek's blows. They kept trying to round the brute, but the Auldek herded them, kept them backing. Perrin tripped once and only avoided getting cut in half because he rolled away, then gained his feet again. In the blurred moment that followed, the young soldier went down. Mena did not see how, but his body fell to the ground, twisted without dignity in a way that only the dead permit. The Auldek celebrated by pumping his fist in the air.

Something in the gesture shot Mena through with recognition. The warrior she thought to be an Auldek—dressed as they were, of the same stature and seemingly just as deadly—was actually a Numrek. Calrach! Mena could not leap down from the wagon fast enough.

She reached Perrin at a sprint, just as he managed to get off an attack. He swung high. Calrach blocked likewise. Mena came around her officer, holding her sword in two hands at mid-height, her left shoulder so near him that she touched his hip. The King's Trust hissed around her and landed exactly where she wanted it, with the full energy of her swing. She expected it to slice into the Numrek's side as far as his spine. Then she would have kicked him with her left foot as she yanked back on the blade, carving it to the side as she did so to maximize the damage. She would have fallen against Perrin and the two of them would have danced back as Calrach followed his guts in their spill to the earth. She saw all this in the rapid screen of her mind's eye. She had seen such visions a thousand times in battle, always able to shape her rage sight so that the reality of it followed. Not so this time.

The sword kicked back against her, torquing her wrists so badly she nearly lost her grip. Damn their armor! Mena thought. I keep forgetting it.

Calrach stumbled back, clutching his side and cursing in a guttural barrage. He frowned at Mena and then grimaced whatever pain the blow had caused into hiding. His sharp features contorted for a moment, then settled. Composed again, Calrach twinned his tongue around Acacian words as if he only wanted to release them after he had strangled them. "Ah, the princess comes to this boy's rescue? Do you hold his thing for him when he pees? I think he would like that."

"I'll happily hold yours," Mena said, "before I slice it off."

Calrach's mouth cracked open, full of mirth and large, even teeth. "None of that, little girl. I have too many uses for my manhood. I have sons to make. Many sons to make. When they are still but babes I will tell them how I killed Princess Mena Akaran with a naked blade. They will like the tale. I know it."

"You'd be dead already if you weren't dressed in that suit," Mena said. "What sort of thing is that for Numrek to wear? I thought you were warriors not afraid to die."

"Warriors enjoy slaughter. Warriors bring pain to others. Warriors find a war. I have done this. All this I will do, and bring joy to myself."

"Fine. Please yourself."

Calrach plucked the devil's forks from his belt, a short, three-pronged metal weapon. Mena knew the weapons from her practice of the Third Form. Calrach was no Bethenri, though, and the King's Trust no normal sword. He stepped forward, brushing back black hair as long and flowing as any Mein's. He gestured casually that he would fight them both at once.

Mena could feel Elya in the air above her, watching, begging to come to her, but she held her back. "I killed Greduc, you know."

"I have heard this but don't believe it."

"I enjoyed it. He and the other Numrek cried like girls."

"I don't think so. But anyway, that doesn't matter. You killed Greduc, but I am not him. I'm Calrach. Calrraaacccchhhhh!" He bellowed the name, then added in a softer, matter-of-fact voice, "Come, let's fight."

Mena and Perrin moved without speaking. They circled to opposite sides of the giant. Calrach turned sideways to them, offering a weapon to each. The princess attacked first. She snapped her sword out. It was a quick motion, intended to catch him off guard, but her blade had hardly moved before he caught it with his devil's forks. He twisted his wrist, pinching her blade between one of the tines and the main stem. He made it look casual, but Mena could feel the strength of his forearm. He released the tension a moment and slid the fork up her blade, testing it even as he looked the other way and parried Perrin's flurry of swordplay.

Savagely, Mena yanked the King's Trust free. She hated the touch of those metal fingers on her sword. She came in again. Calrach called out as he blocked her and Perrin, as he shifted and dodged, high and then low. He spoke Auldek, sounding like he was praising them or teasing them, commenting on their technique like an adult taunting a child. It was infuriating, but he was too fast, too aware of what she or Perrin was going to try next. Mena varied her attacks. She searched for weaknesses. She fought against her instincts and did things surprising even to her. None of it worked, save to amuse the warrior. So frustrated, she forgot that she and Perrin were still living along with him, fighting him—though it took two of them—a draw.

A glob of pitch landed near them. It broke their dance as they all jumped back. Its mother whoomped down a second later, far enough away that they were safe from the splash. The Numrek stepped over the edge of the flaming puddle with a disdainful glance at it, as if it were animal dung. He said something, gesturing with the fingers of his sword hand. He seemed to be explaining that the falling pitch was not his fault. Mena and Perrin circled, keeping him between them.

I've killed Numrek, she said to herself. Don't forget that. "Perrin—I've killed Numrek. This is no Auldek. He has only one life."

"Let's take it, then," Perrin replied.

Calrach did not make that easy for them. "I'm my clan leader!" he shouted. "You know what that means? It means I'm not Greduc. Not Crannog. Who am I?"

A smug bastard who needs to die, Mena thought. And then—why not—she repeated the answer out loud. This was all taking too long, the two of them stuck here fighting one man, when there were so many others. I want you dead, bastard. It should be possible. It should happen right now! So thinking, she swung low, hoping to take out his legs, at least to break them or injure them. Calrach jumped over her blade like a child over a rope. In midair, he caught Perrin's sword in his forks. His toes touched down for a moment, but he leaped again, spinning and landing a kick on Mena's head. Though the force of the blow sent her reeling, she watched Calrach bring his sword down on the flat of Perrin's trapped blade. With a resonant crack, the tip of it twirled away.

Released, Perrin sprawled backward. He landed beside the puddle of burning pitch. He did not rise immediately, and Mena feinted to draw the Numrek's attention. It worked, but it made her head swim. She tried not to show it, but she saw two Cal-rachs. One stepped out of the other and both of them spoke to her in Auldek. She heard that arrogant, boulder-grinding voice doubled. She watched him set two pairs of fists, weapons clenched in them, on his two waists. Two grins.

"Calrach," she said. She had something else to follow it, but forgot it in effort not to stumble. "Calrach . . ."

Behind him two versions of Perrin rose. Calrach noticed them. Both of him turned and rushed toward them. Both of them dropped their devil's forks and cocked their swords far back, two-handed.

"Cal . . ."

The two Perrins turned, both of them holding flaming swords. They snapped out their blades at exactly the same time, in a manner that sent two lines of pitch from the sword through the air, scorching a path right into both Calrachs' faces. They howled, and in howling merged into one. Calrach dropped his sword and wiped at his face, but that only made his hand come away flaming as well. Perrin stared at him, horrified by what he had done, his sword still on fire.

Mena walked forward. She raised her sword and thrust it with both arms and the full weight of her body. The blade pierced Calrach's flaming face, into his skull cavity, and beyond. His head flew back as the point hit the back of his skull. Mena, still dizzy, clamped her gloved hand over the naked blade just in front of his face. She yanked it back and forth, cutting what-ever was inside his skull to scrambled ribbons. He toppled, arms thrashing. Mena went with him, riding his chest all the way to the ground.

She rolled away and lay for a moment on her back. Through panting breaths, she said what she had started to before, with-out knowing that she would finish it: "I killed Greduc. And . . . I killed . . . Calrach."

"Are you hurt?" Perrin asked, as she rose. He still held his broken sword, smoking now and blackened. He looked strangely sheepish, considering the carnage they had just lived through.

Mena shook her head. Regretted it. Flexed her jaw instead. She wiped sweat from her forehead, and then realized too late that she had smeared her face with blood. "Perrin, we're overrun. We must organize a retreat. We'll have to get everyone to head for the stashes we left for the return. Everybody who can make it and all the wounded who . . ."

That was as far as she got before another Auldek strode into view. Mena recognized her immediately. She groaned inside.

Sabeer.

CHAPTER
FIFTY-EIGHT

Once he drew near enough to see that something was amiss, Sire Lethel asked, "What, exactly, is going on here?"

Dariel had never met this particular leagueman, nor had he seen any leagueman in person since the massacre that Sire Neen had dragged him into. Lethel looked just as strange as any of them ever did. His cone-shaped head had been wrapped for this occasion with a silken red fabric. His shoulders were narrow, chest birdlike, and arms so thin it surprised Dariel they carried enough muscle to animate them. The two jagged lines of his eyebrows gave him an expression of almost explosive surprise. Quite a contrast to the grim pucker his lips made.

I know things about your kind that you may not even know yourself, Dariel thought. He had seen a vision of them up in the Sky Mount. Nearly dead. Diseased and insane. Did Lethel even know that it was the Lothan Aklun who had first bound his head and fed him a diet of mist? Probably not. Not with, surely, the clarity of vision that Dariel had: both from what Nâ Gâmen had shown him and because he actually carried some of the Sky Watcher within him. Yes, he was tranquil enough that he let the heat of his resentment for the league roil up just that little bit more. Controlled, calm, satisfying.

Lethel had arrived as scheduled for his meeting with the Anet leader, Dukish. Lethel and his Ishtat strolled into the open-air courtyard quite at ease this time. Lethel approached, his eyes drifting around so casually that they did not settle on Dukish until he was but a few strides from him. At that point, he stuttered to a halt, only then noticing that Dukish was not simply relaxing in the chair, as was his wont. He had been gagged, bound at the wrists and ankles, and set on a stool, not looking relaxed at all. Instead of his trusted Anet and Antok ruffians surrounding him, Mór, Tunnel, Birké, Anira, and Dariel flanked Dukish. Judging by the way Lethel's eyes scanned them all, he was only noticing this just now.

"The situation in Avina has changed somewhat since last you spoke with Dukish," Mór said. Her voice was clipped, official. There was a tension in it, but it was the tension of the control she was keeping over her voice.

Dariel realized how hard this must be for them. All of them had been but children when a leagueman just like this one stripped them of all they knew and changed their lives forever.

"Not more infighting and discord," Lethel said. "Dukish, you assured me you had a firm grasp on Avina. I'm disappointed." Perhaps he was. He tutted at Dukish's misfortune, already putting any sign of surprise behind him. His gaze drifted up and down Mór's lean figure, as appraising as a wealthy customer at a brothel. "You are rather lovely! Do tell me you're the one in charge now. That's an improvement I can acknowledge right away. What do they call you?"

"I am Mór of the Free People. As you were told, Dukish did not—"

"Mór of the Free People!" Lethel exclaimed. He glanced at the Ishtat next him. "We know that name, don't we? The bird woman said something about Mór before we shot her." Turning back to Mór, he added, "How is she faring, by the way? It looked to be a nasty wound. In the chest, wasn't it? We would have looked after her, but your lot bundled her away."

Mór held her anger. She had not introduced herself as Skylene's lover but as Mór of the Free People. She held the dignity of that in her jaw and neck when she said, "As you were told last time, Dukish did not speak for us. He has been deposed, stripped of authority. The disunity he tried to sow in Avina is a thing of the past. We are here only to tell you that Ushen Brae is not a place for you. This is the home of the Free People. We have earned this place, and we will never be slaves again."

Lethel tilted his head back, squinting a little as he took her in. "Oh, I don't know that I would say 'never.' That's rather a long time. Who can say such a thing for certain?"

Glancing around, Lethel seemed to only then realize that a chair had not been set out for him. He motioned an Ishtat closer, whispered something, and then waited as the man stepped forward, hands raised to indicate his harmlessness. He moved to the side of Dukish, which brought him close to the stretch of Tunnel's bare gray chest. He made a visible effort not to look. Instead, he put his hands against Dukish's shoulder and shoved him from the stool. Dukish landed hard on his side, groaning and struggling on the paving stones.

Dariel could not help laughing, though he half hid it behind his hand.

The man lifted the stool and set it down for Lethel to occupy.

"Now, let's get past the bluster, shall we? Is it really you I'm to negotiate with?" he said to Mór. "If so, I'd much rather do it back on my soul vessel. I'd zip you right off the barrier isles. We could talk there. In the baths, perhaps?"

Amusement gone again, Dariel was starting to find Lethel's lecherous remarks aggravating. He inched forward a little bit, itching to enter the conversation.

"There is nothing to negotiate," Mór said.

"There's always something to negotiate. You just haven't thought about it yet. Listen, let's do this. Let's leave Dukish in the past. He's yesterday. I've nothing against dealing with the Free People, especially if—as you say—you really do speak for the whole lot of you here in Avina. How about that?"

"No," Mór said.

Lethel rolled his eyes. "Must you make this difficult? Life would be very much harder for you without us. I mean, honestly, in half a year you could be running your own estates, with staffs of new slaves doing all the work."

"Slavery has no future here."

"You're still not understanding. The league has no desire to enslave *you*. We'll enrich you. You won't be slaves! Nothing of the sort. You'll be masters." He said this last sentence with a flourish and a grin that showed he believed he had won the point.

"You're the one who's thick," Mór said, her voice snapping. "Inside your head, at least. Listen. Ushen Brae is a land of free people now. We are the rightful inhabitants of Avina, and of Ushen Brae. Both the mainland and the barrier isles. The league must leave. If you don't, you'll end as badly as your Sire Neen did."

"Sire Neen? Don't talk about Neen with me. He was a fool. I'm not. Do you know, Dukish made me a gift of Neen's ashes. Thank you for that, Dukish. I smoked them mixed with the water of my mist pipe. Neen was smoother than I would have imagined. Slightly nutty, with a tar undertone that was not entirely pleasant, but soft on the palate despite that. I blew little particles of my uncle out into the world with each exhalation. That's what I think of Neen."

"You have a month to withdraw," Mór said.

One of the Ishtat behind Lethel tried to get his attention,

but the leagueman ignored him. "A moon cycle, you say? What happens after that?"

Edging her words with something like longing, Mór said, "You will find yourself at war with us."

"Do you know how absurd this all sounds?" Lethel looked around as if for support from another, but finding none he came back to himself. "'Rightful inhabitants . . .' Quite absurd, I assure you. Mór of the Free People, this is going nowhere. You'll want to back away from talk of war. Right now, already, just out there on the barrier isles, we have several thousand Ishtat Inspectorate soldiers. Two, three thousand. Something like that." A guard bent and whispered to him. "Three thousand four hundred and ninety nine, I'm told. One unfortunate got knocked in the head—some dock accident. They die much harder on the battlefield. In addition to that—and this you wouldn't know anything about—we have four thousand more troops just recently arrived, all of them trained since birth to kill when we say kill. We have soul vessel transports enough to move all of them, anytime we want, against the tides or winds, with complete control. We could deposit all of them at the wall of Avina at exactly the same moment, if we wished. Consider that before you declare war." He began to cross his arms as if he would give them time to think it through, but then he snapped them out before the gesture was complete. "What makes you think you can wage war on the league? Nobody wages war on the league!"

"I have," Dariel said. He stepped forward, coming around Tunnel's bulk into better view of the leagueman.

Lethel glanced at him, and then away, dismissive. Then back. The thin line of one of his plucked eyebrows expressed his skepticism that the answer to the question was of consequence, but he asked, "Who are you?"

"We've never met," Dariel said, "but I imagine you've cursed my name many times already. I plan to give you reason to do so again."

The eyebrows did not drop, but the face beneath them sobered. "You're not—"

"Prince Dariel Akaran. Hello, Lethel. I know, I've gone a bit native. Tattoos and such. And this—" He gestured at the rune on his forehead. "You would need to have been there to understand. I'm pleased to learn that you weren't on Sire Fen's warship when I dropped a pill in it. Or on the platforms when I blew them up. Or in the soul catcher when I destroyed that. Or on that soul vessel that I set alight down near Sumerled. Why does that please me? Because you're still alive to be killed. I may be afloat in Ushen Brae, but, Lethel"—Dariel bent a little closer; the Ishtat bristled in response—"I still loathe the league. More now than ever."

For the first time, Lethel's face went blank. No readable emotion on it. Neither mirth nor arrogance, nor anything like fear. He said, "I could have my crossbowmen kill you right here and now."

"You probably could," Dariel agreed, "but you wouldn't make it from here alive yourself. You are outnumbered." He nodded that Lethel should take note of all the people who poured into the courtyard as they spoke. "Your Ishtat tried to mention it to you, but you were distracted."

His eyes on the prince, Lethel spoke to Mór. "This man is one of you?"

Mór did not hesitate. "Yes."

"This changes everything." Lethel looked away from Dariel. His cheek twitched, and it was clearly with some effort that he kept emotion from his face. "This man is an enemy of the league. He's a war criminal. A brigand. A murderer. Mór, here are the new terms I offer you. You give me Dariel Akaran. That's it. If you don't, I'll bring armies down upon you. You have no—"

"You can't have Dariel," Mór said. "He's one of us."

"Rhuin Fá!" Tunnel said it first, but others echoed it, both in their group and around the wider circle.

"You've disappointed me," Lethel said, shaking his head. "All of you have, but so be it." He stood and drew himself up. Chin raised, he pronounced, "You leave me no other choice. On behalf of the league, I declare the inhabitants of Ushen Brae enemies. We will settle this through clash of arms. Will you impede us as we depart?"

After glancing at Dariel, Mór said, "No. Go safely. We'll kill you later."

Turning, Lethel said, "You want war? You have it."

"I've never heard sweeter words from a leagueman's mouth," Dariel said.

"He makes good talk sometimes," Tunnel said, watching the group exit. Turning to Dariel, he asked, "Now what? You have a plan, yes?"

✴

Dariel waited until he knew Mór would be away for several hours. She stayed amazingly busy—especially in making their preparations for the league invasion—but she came and went from her chores to check on Skylene so often that he chose his moment carefully. She was crazy with grief. She hid it well, but all who knew her saw it. Skylene was dying, and she was taking Mór's heart with her.

When she went off to the north of the city to oversee the fortifications being built there, he risked it. He went to her dying lover, hoping he would have enough time to accomplish what he had come to believe he could.

Skylene lay as she had when he had first seen her on his

return. Odd that a face already tattooed to sky-blue hue could still look so sickly pale. Or perhaps it was stranger that Dariel no longer saw anything unusual about that color or about a nose altered to resemble an avian beak or about a hairline that included living feathers that sprang right out of her scalp. None of that was strange. It was all Skylene. It was this face that had looked on him with kindness in his first days as a captive here. Skylene, more than anybody, talked him out of ignorance and into a new understanding of the world. She had waked him from childhood and opened his eyes. It was a much gentler maturation than the quota children received, gentler than anyone bearing his family name deserved.

This made it all the more heart wrenching to see how drained she was of life. Her skin sagged into the cavities of her skull, her forehead was slick with perspiration. Even the lids of her closed eyes looked wrong, as if they were too thin and the orbs beneath them too large for the face in which they set. She smelled of death, not just in the festering wound in her chest. The scent seeped from the pores of her skin.

Dariel had closed the door behind him, leaving himself alone with her, and asked her caregivers to allow him some time in solitude with her. Had anyone else been in the room, they would have thought Dariel silent. He wasn't. It's just that the one-sided conversation he carried on with himself went on inside him. *Can we do this?* he asked. *I feel that you're part of me, but I don't know where I begin or end. I don't even know why I believe I can do this. That's why I think it's you telling me that we can do this. Am I right?*

No answer came, but he had not expected it to. Nâ Gâmen was not an active consciousness inside him, not a voice he heard or anything like that. It was more like the life force that had been Nâ Gâmen had been absorbed into Dariel, body and mind and soul. To hear or understand Nâ Gâmen, Dariel needed to listen to himself. The two were one now. *And we always will be.*

"Skylene," he said, and then was not sure what to say. "Skylene, I want to help you. Can I?"

She stirred, but only with discomfort and only for a moment. She had not been awake or conscious for several days. If she were awake, he could have asked for her permission for what he proposed. But if she were awake, she would not have been as gravely ill, and if she were awake, she might give him an answer he did not want to hear. After all, she abhorred the trafficking in spirit energy that the Lothan Aklun had mastered. What he intended was a cousin of that, possible only because part of Nâ Gâmen lived inside him. He had more than a single person's life force inside him. Not much more. His two knife wounds in the gut had depleted him, but Nâ Gâmen's spirit was strong, ancient. It was thicker than other human souls and not so easily depleted.

The taking of souls was a corruption, the most horrible of crimes. That he believed without doubt. Nothing good could come of the theft of life. Not even the soul vessels justified it. But what about giving life, not taking it? That was not a crime. It was an offering he wanted to make. Nâ Gâmen wanted it, too. If he did not, Dariel would never have known such an offering was even possible.

Skylene would not willingly accept even a sliver of Lothan Aklun life force into herself. "But I'm not talking about giving you any of Nâ Gâmen," Dariel said. "Only me. You wouldn't turn that away. You don't find me so repulsive. I hope not, at least."

Another thought followed this—that when Mór loved Skylene in the future she would be loving a little bit of him as well. It made him blush. He brushed it aside. This was not about that. It really wasn't. It was about giving what he could to Skylene. To Mór as well, true enough. But he was giving, not taking.

He lay one hand on Skylene's hot, moist forehead. He

smoothed his fingers back over the plumes of the feathers that were now a part of her hair, and then he set his hand back on her skin. Leaning close, he set his lips just beside hers.

Forgive me, he thought, but I wish you to live. Please live.

He kissed her. With the kiss, he exhaled life out of himself and into her.

Unlike most of the Auldek, Sabeer did not carry a long sword. No battle-ax or halberd. Nothing massive or hooked or pronged. She stood with empty hands, the two long knives sheathed at her waist her only visible weapons. Slim and long limbed, she wore her body suit with an upright grace that was overtly athletic. When she spotted Calrach's motionless body, a look of astonishment transformed her sharp features into softer versions of themselves. Ignoring the two Acacians, she walked to the corpse. She knelt and bent close to him, saying his name and then other words in her language. Judging by the cadence of it: a prayer.

"Mena," Perrin whispered, casting his voice so that the Auldek woman would not hear it, "I'm no coward, but let's . . . go? Let's help the others."

What a reasonable idea, Mena thought. Why can't I think of ideas like that? She said, "Perrin, thank you for fighting with me. That was well fought. Remember how we did it. They may ask for you to document the Form someday. You go now; I'll deal with her. Leave me, and don't come back. Don't bring others here."

"No. Princess . . ."

"That's an order! Take the others and flee. Obey me, Perrin."

Sabeer straightened, rotating to face them as she did so. Sabeer said something. Her tone was casual, like an old friend commenting on the weather.

"But," Perrin said, "what about—"

"Do it," Mena said. Thankful for the moments she had to clear her head, she inhaled and pulled her composure around her like a shawl against the cold. It was not much time, but it would have to do. She said, "It's all right, Perrin. Really, it is. I'll take care of this one."

"No! I can't—"

"Go, right now. That's an order!"

She had to say it several times before he obeyed. I'll need to reprimand him for that later, she thought. Sabeer watched the exchange, patient enough to wait with her hands resting on her hips. Studying her body, her posture, the composed intelligence of her face, Mena thought, This is a woman I could have liked, if I hadn't needed to hate her. She thought, Good that I wrote that note to Melio. It will reach him. That I believe. It wouldn't make sense for it not to.

Bending to one knee, Mena tried to wipe her blade clean on the turf. It did not really work. Calrach's blood had frozen already, etching the fine engravings in a crimson-highlighted black. She stood. Sabeer shook out her arms, making them loose as snakes for a moment. Then she crossed them and unsheathed her knives. She began to say something, lifting one of the curved knives as if she were going to explain her choice of weapon.

"Let's leave off the banter, all right?" Mena asked. "I'm not in the mood for it." She launched at her.

The battle that ensued was more intense than the one with

Calrach. Sabeer had two feet of sinewy, muscular height on Mena, with reach enough that her knives struck like swords. She was incredibly fast. Each time Mena struck, Sabeer deflected the sword with one of her knives, knocking it away or catching the blade at the hilt. Each time her other knife slashed back with a blurred rapidity that Mena could only match by *not* thinking, by not deliberately planning, by not being awed into errors, and certainly not by worrying for her life. She gave her body over to rage, to instinct, and the fury of the blade itself. The King's Trust was savage in its wrath. It screamed as it cut the air. She did not so much direct the blade as follow it. It was not a weapon meant to be deflected, not meant to be caught between those two knives, not meant to slip through the air, missing the body that shifted away from it, not meant to strike angrily into frozen ground. It wanted only to cut.

Breaking away, Mena circled. Sabeer let her, rotating in unison. "This is a race to the cut, bitch. Why don't you finish it, or let me finish it?" Saying this, Mena heard her words from another time, long ago when she was just learning the sword. Back then, to Melio, she said, "I'm sorry, but here's my point: Why dance through fifty moves when a single one will suffice?" It had made sense then, and it still did. And yet, she had already put more than fifty moves behind her.

She wiped at the sweat on her forehead. She blew her nose into her gloved hand and then snapped the snot away.

Sabeer laughed. And then came in again, a whirlwind with both knives cutting circles around her.

✳

Some time later. The two of them balancing on bundles piled atop a line of sledges. Mena backed over the uneven load, saying, "Sabeer, you should die now. You really should. Die now. Die now." She repeated those two words again and again. She fixed on them and drove them into every parry or strike or thrust or dodge. She tried to think only of them, to keep back the other thoughts that clawed at her.

"Die now."

It did not work. For one thing, there was Elya. In flashes she saw the world as Elya did, from above, circling the carnage, watching Mena, wanting to swoop down to her, begging to be allowed to. For another, Melio kept emerging through those two words. She kept seeing him in a part of her mind that was separate from the world around her. She heard him with ears different from the ones filled with the din of death, of explosions and screams and clanging metal. "Where was your fear?" he asked. He was not speaking to her now. He was not even really in her head. She knew that. He was in her past, jogging to stay with her as she left the stick-fighting arena on Vumu ages ago. "Where was your fear?" he had asked. She had answered, "I don't know."

Mena leaped from the sledges, Sabeer just behind her. She sprinted for a time and skidded to a halt. They converged again.

I should have had a better answer for you, she thought. When you said, "Where was your fear?" I should have responded, "I don't have any. I don't know that I love you yet." That would have been the truth. Much better than "I don't know."

Sabeer landed a blow to Mena's cheek with the knob at the base of one of her knives. It was an awkward strike as the two of them slipped by each other. The Auldek swung her blade around. Mena managed to drop beneath it, watching the point trace the air just next to her eye.

I know fear better now. That was another truth.

When a pitch orb exploded near them, Mena fell flat, praying that the splash would take Sabeer out. The Auldek woman fell backward, letting her upper body go horizontal. The spray of pitch scorched right over her. Untouched, she landed on her upper back. She kicked up from there, all back and abdominals and legs, knives still in hands that had not even touched the ground.

Standing a moment, Sabeer crooked a grin at Mena, twisting an admonishment into the expression.

What? Mena thought. I already said I want you dead. I don't care how it happens.

They continued.

✳

On the frozen ground again, the two of them fought, watched by a ring of other Auldek, mostly men. They stood in a loose, blood-splattered circle, taking a break from the slaughter. They talked among themselves as Mena and Sabeer danced death at each other. Occasionally, they tossed a jibe or encouragement or advice at Sabeer; Mena could not tell which.

For her part, the Auldek woman stayed silent. She had left her mirth behind some time ago. Grimly determined, her face glistened with her efforts. Her lips puckered and frowned, puckered and frowned as she struck and parried. Her left cheek twitched. She had yanked back her hood. Her hair, long and auburn, snapped about behind her.

"Die much?" Mena asked, trying to slice the crown of her head off.

Sabeer ducked, and drove an upward thrust with "No!"

"How about trying it?"

"No, you die!" Sabeer said, slashing like she meant it.

She really does want this, Mena thought. She wants me dead more than anything now. Look at her.

To her surprise, her sword finally connected with Sabeer's wrist. But it was not like when she had carved flesh from Larken's arm so effortlessly. This time, nothing happened except that Sabeer spun away spitting curses through her teeth.

Mena wanted to scream at the unfairness of it. If they were fighting on equal terms, Sabeer would be one-handed, in pain, squirting gouts of blood. The fight would be over. She would be dead! And then alive again. *You bitch, you'd be alive again.*

Sabeer shook the pain out of her wrist. She snapped at something one of the watching Auldek had said. She threw out her arms and flung the two knives away. A moment later, she closed her outstretched hand around the hilt of a sword offered her. She twirled it, flexing the wrist that should be useless.

"This really isn't fair," Mena said.

"What is 'fair'?" asked one of the watchers called Devoth. "I don't know this word."

Mena could not tell if he was sincere or joking. The mirth was the same. As Sabeer stood, breathing heavily, Mena spun around, taking in her audience. "I killed Calrach!"

"Yes, but this is not Calrach," Devoth said. "Calrach is the past. Here is Sabeer!"

"No." Mena sheathed the King's Trust. "Calrach is enough for today."

Sabeer shook her head. She said something in Auldek. Mena could not understand a word of it, but the meaning was clear enough. Surrender was not an option she acknowledged. *It's not for me either,* Mena thought, *but not all battles happen on your terms.*

She ran toward Sabeer, five quick steps. She leaped.

The Auldek woman stepped back, more surprised than alarmed. She cocked the sword back, but for once she was not fast enough. Mena kicked her in the face with one foot and pushed off her chest with the other. That was the last contact between them before Elya caught her in midair, cradling Mena tight to her chest, lifting on powerful wingbeats. Mena buried her face in Elya's plumage but only for a few seconds. That's all she had for such things as comfort, relief.

She had lied. Calrach was not enough for today. She wanted more.

※

Moments later, in Elya's saddle and racing over the plain toward the Auldek encampment, Mena clenched an oil lamp full of pitch. Behind her, she left a ruined camp, the tattered remains of her army fleeing into the night as the Auldek danced bloody joy behind them. At least some of them would make it into the dark. Some of them. That was all she hoped for them now, that within a few days some of them would stumble into Mein Tahalian alive. She intended to be with them, but first there was this to take care of.

The lamp's wick glowed red in the night, too buffeted by the wind to actually flame. She flew under the flying pitch orbs, cut through just above the catapults, and saw the fréketes and their riders circling in the air beyond them. She wanted them to see her, to pursue her, to witness what she was there to do. Dodging and weaving among them, she skimmed over the Auldek encampment, searching for the station Rialus had described.

When the traitor had told her about the station that held the Auldek's histories, she had not at first understood why he thought it such important information. A library? Documents and tales from the past? Surely it had no military significance. That was what he thought he could buy his forgiveness with? She had sent him away angrily, on the verge of ordering him back to them once more. That would have been a death sentence, she knew, but she came close to delivering it.

Later, as she lay not sleeping in her tent, she had turned over the things he had said. If the Auldek really did not have any memory of their distant past, how important might those records be for them? She could not imagine not remembering her own life back to her first years of childhood. What would it mean to know that the greater portion of your existence survived only on pieces of parchment? The more she thought about it, the crueler it seemed to imagine destroying those documents. If she did so, the Auldek race would be, effectively, always less than a century old. Before that would be nothing, the tail that connected them to their past cut.

A frékete and rider appeared out of nowhere. Elya spun and dove to avoid him. She came out of the corkscrew so low that she touched her feet to the ground and ran for a moment, wings pulled tight, darting between two stations and circling around one of them. When a kwedeir leaped in front of her, she jumped over it. The beast snapped at her, but she rose above it, slapping it with her tail as she pulled away.

The innocuousness of the station surprised Mena. By the time she found it, she realized she had passed near it on several occasions. It was smaller than the rest. It sat dark along a lane of similarly dark stations. The sight of her and Elya's reflection on the ice-laced glass panes caught her attention. Yes, that's it. The gold cap at its peak, just like Rialus had said. She looped away from it, fréketes behind her, and came back after she had put some distance between them.

She hovered as long as she dared, and then threw the lamp, straight down with all the force and precision she could manage. It twirled end over end, the wick appearing and disappearing. It smashed through the pane of glass. For a moment the inside of the chamber was alight with a wonderful radiance. Mena took in the stacks of shelves, the many volumes, the logs and legends and journals that kept the history of an entire race. It was, in a way, beautiful.

I killed Greduc. I killed Calrach. And I've killed the past.

The flames spread.

CHAPTER
SIXTY

Terribly imprudent," Sire Nathos said as he settled into the elaborate contraption that was his council seat. "I can't wait to ask what you were intending. This will be interesting, Dagon. I'm sure of it."

I was thinking about saving the world from the likes of the Santoth, Dagon thought, aware that in a few moments he would no longer be safe thinking thoughts he wanted kept private.

"And, Grau," Nathos continued, "why would you act without our complete agreement? If you had not hatched your plot to assassinate the bitch and her brother, we would not be so exposed. I can recall nothing like it. Everything we have built is in jeopardy."

Grau was not in a mood to be chastened. He answered in a gruff whisper, "We did what we had to. Nobody could have foreseen the outcome. Dagon, in my opinion, made the best of an unfortunate situation."

One that you caused, in part, Dagon thought.

"You're lucky that some of us have had greater success in our ventures," Nathos said. By that, of course, he meant himself and his vintage. Why he should be so proud of that now Dagon was not sure, but he looked smug. As Nathos settled back and closed his eyes, a smile tickled the corners of his lips. You hardly seem troubled. Perhaps it's you who isn't taking things seriously enough.

Sire Revek called the session into order. "Before I set you to explaining yourself, Sire Dagon," he said, "we should be sure the entire chamber knows just how the calamitous events in the Inner Sea developed and how you acted and why."

Dagon started. He knew he would need to do some explaining, but he did not expect the chairman to begin with him. "Sire," he said, "you have all read my testimony, and Grau's. I delivered it when I arrived this morning and was told everyone would come here prepared. And, with respect, 'calamitous' is hardly the word to—"

"Silence!" Just a word from a frail, thin frame, but with it the chairman stopped him. Resonant echoes of it reverberated through the newly built council chamber on Orlo, the largest of the Outer Isles. Revek had barely more than whispered, but that was all that it took to get heard in here, especially when speaking from the center of the senior leaguemen's circles. Behind his voice, the chairman sent waves of his disquiet resonating through the council chamber. The acoustic structure of the place was sublime, the airflow circulated the mist efficiently, and the sculpted seats in which they reclined seemed to enhance their capacity for subverbal communication. Revek's voice, at least, filled the entirety of Dagon's skull so completely that he felt himself crammed up against the bone. Such a chamber he had never experienced before. Nor had he ever found himself the focus of his brothers' animus. Not what he expected would greet his arrival at the Outer Isles.

"Dagon, you must acknowledge the seriousness of this matter. Reports, testimonies: these are not enough. You single-handedly ended hundreds of years of league occupation of the Known World. You assassinated two monarchs, informed them of their pending deaths while they yet lived, then abandoned league property, ordered other property destroyed, set the vineyards of Prios aflame . . ." Revek sighed in exasperation at the unending extent of it. "The list of things you have to answer for is staggering. Because of it, I move that you provide us access."

Dagon's heart rate had been increasing. On the word *access* it skipped forward into an irregular, syncopated dance of its own choreography. "Access?"

"Just so. You will be probed. You did not see fit to consult us earlier, when you made decisions that affected us all. You will do so now. We will judge you accordingly, and with the wisdom of hindsight. Do any object? Or think this action unwarranted?"

If any did, the cowards and scoundrels leaning back in their seats kept their mouths shut. Had Dagon been one of them, instead of the individual at the center of this scrutiny, he would have been just as silent. Probing was not without its benefits, at least from the point of view of the ones doing the probing. It was rarely called for, but he had enjoyed the unfettered access to other unfortunate leaguemen's minds on several occasions. Nobody would refuse looking into his secret places under the guise of an official inquiry.

Being the one being probed, however, was ghastly. It involved inhaling a liquid distillation of mist, one that inundated your mind in a way that let your fellow leaguemen push inside it and explore your memories at will. It was an ancient process, one that each of them trained for in their youth—both to learn how to penetrate and how to allow penetration. Better the one than the other, Dagon had always thought.

What of Grau? he came very close to saying. *Will he be probed as well?* He did not want to end the possibility of getting aid from that senior leagueman just yet, though. He tried to return the discussion to reason. "We all understand the facts already," he said. "Truly, if you just let me answer each of these points, I'll put your minds at ease. Sire Grau can assist me—"

"I second the chairman's proposal," Sire Nathos intoned.

Several others chorused their assent as well.

Dagon craned around to see back into the dim ranks of reclined leaguemen behind him. "But if you just—"

Sire Grau said, "Let it be done."

Let it be done? "Did you say that, Grau? Let it be—"

"Silence, Dagon!" Sire Revek whisper-shouted. "We will hear from you afterward. The probe will be carried out first. That is our decision. You have no choice but to abide by it."

The litens—special Ishtat officers who normally stayed pasted to the far walls of the chamber—converged on him. They appeared through the mist-thick air as if they had only ever been a step away. Wearing goggles over their eyes and breathing apparatuses over their noses and mouths, they moved with a clearheaded speed that Dagon could not comprehend. They pressed down on his chest, pinned his arms to the arm-rests, and wrapped cords around them so quickly Dagon only realized what they were doing after they had completed the task. He tried to pull free. He could only strain against them. He kicked, but his feet, too, were bound. He shouted, but that ended quickly, too. A liten vised his jaw in a painful finger pinch. The figure stared down at him, eyes unseen behind the green glass that hid them.

Dagon got ahold of himself. He ceased struggling. It was useless and just made him look ridiculous. This situation was absurd, but it was serious. Better that he acquiesce with faith in his rightness, with dignity. That would be the shortest course back to his proper standing. "Of course, Sires," Dagon managed through his nearly immobilized jaw. "My—my mind is yours. I have no fear of . . . being—"

A liten carefully slipped a tube into his nose. Dagon could not help but thrash. He had thought this part amusing when it was happening to someone else, interesting that so much tubing could be shoved and shoved and shoved up a person's nose. Where did it all go? he had wondered. Now he knew. And then the liquid flowed.

In brief moments he had before the liquid mist overcame him, Dagon thrashed around, both in his chair and inside his head, fighting the rush of fear he claimed not to feel. He searched for thoughts that he should somehow banish, but as soon as he found one that was embarrassing or questionable, another popped up like a bubble beside it. And then another. He got nowhere. There was so much to hide, the innocuous just as much as the substantial. He wondered how this was happening. He should have arrived here a hero. A man of action. One of decisive . . .

✸

Being mind-probed by a chamber full of leaguemen, Dagon learned, was unequal parts horrifying, degrading, embarrassing, and enlightening. How much of each depended on the moment in question. Each moment of the examination blurred into spiraling circles, in which he could get no sense of time's progression. He put together a sketchy narrative for himself of how the experience had gone afterward. Even this was putting order to a process that had in truth been like being explored by a swarm of scheming bees.

Early on, his brothers had focused their attention on the Queen's Council meeting that had so disturbed him, the one in which Aliver had appeared in the flesh. They moved forward through his visit to Grau, in which he suggested and then argued for the monarchs' assassinations. An observer at his own dissection, Dagon knew that the memory as he reexperienced it did not match the memory as he recalled it, but he could find no way to voice this.

His brothers watched the coronation through his eyes, turned over his emotions as the monarchs caressed their present, felt his fear as the Santoth changed everything. They looked through his eyes as he searched his library for some way to understand them, and they watched him write the letter that confessed the crime he had helped perpetrate only hours before. They followed him as he fled from Acacia aboard a pleasure yacht in the dead of night, chasing a messenger bird toward Alecia. The voyage surprised him in some particulars. Had fleeing Acacia really wrung him through with as much melancholia as it seemed to? No, not possible! He had not gotten teary at seeing the harbor lights recede in the wake of his boat. He had not been overcome with sadness for the lives of all those poor fools still rafted together, in shock and mourning and confusion now, instead of sharing the euphoria the day had begun with.

Apparently—although he did not remember it this way—a barrage of random memories had assaulted him throughout the short voyage. He revisited old conversations with Leodan Akaran and Thaddeus Clegg, his treacherous, conflicted chancellor. Dagon had not liked either man, so why did it seem like he wished he could have them with him in his cabin, talking through the recent events while sharing a mist pipe? Why recall the time one of the white minks the concubines kept got loose in his quarters, unnerving him as it darted about with its long tail swishing behind it? What use was remembering the time he sat through some banquet with a sore tooth, struggling to hide his discomfort from those around him? What a strange, useless thing to recall. And yet there it was, as vivid in its own way as some of the most crucial moments of his tenure in Acacia.

They lingered with him through the dream he had of the time Corinn arrived in his offices—so young then, beautiful in the newly ripened manner of youth. He had thought cruelly about the work he would have liked to put her mouth to when she caught him off guard. He had to retrace the half-heard words she had spoken, taking a moment to comprehend the audacity of the proposal she was making. She spoke her way into an empire right then and bound Hanish Mein's hands with a few well-conceived words. Not her lover's pawn after all, it turned out.

And that took him to a view of Hanish's face in profile as he stared at one of the palace's golden monkeys. It was an image Dagon saw with such detail it might have been a painting hung on the wall before him. He had hated the man's perfect features, his lover's eyes, and the arrogant grace with which he occupied his body. But what he remembered was wondering if Hanish had any suspicion that the league had often used the monkeys as thieves and messengers. They were clever, easily trained, and seemed to take a certain amount of satisfaction from working covertly. Of course Hanish hadn't known. Nobody on Acacia ever had. Dagon would miss those monkeys. Realizing this made him shake his head at his own mawkishness. He needed the steadying influence of his brothers.

Irrelevant, he thought, and yet some of his brothers seemed fascinated by these things and by the fact that he buried all such thoughts deep when he met with his fellow leaguemen in Alecia. They had all been agitated, both by what had happened during the coronation and by the call for evacuation that Dagon arrived with. He had acted recklessly. There would be a reckoning about it. An investigation. Consequences. Despite the grumbling, they echoed Dagon's orders to their own staff.

See, Dagon thought, they did what I suggested because there was no other choice! I acted. I led. And why was there no mention of Grau's part in all this?

By dawn of the next day they had all fled aboard the largest vessels they could organize on short notice. They sailed south, bristling warning with the manned ballistae hanging from the sides of the ship. In their wake they left abandoned estates and billows of black smoke rising from their offices and libraries, storehouses and estates. Dagon rather liked the images it all left in his mind. It helped sweep away the troublesome memories. Here was something decisive. When the leaguemen abandon a place, they leave scorched earth behind them. Nothing for others to use. No apologies. No regrets.

These portions were not so bad. Much of the probing vindicated him. If it had ended there—and it should have—he would have had no reason to complain. It did not end there, though. He would later wonder just which of his brothers had spent so much time on raking through his childhood like a gardener turning manure into the earth. And who circled around and around his early sexual encounters? What reason was there to tease out small, perverse moments, things at the edge of his life, things inconsequential?

He knew the answer. It could be any of them. And they did it because it amused them. Those things were out of his hands. Only how he handled himself when the probe ended could matter now.

※

Regaining consciousness took much longer than Dagon would have imagined. He slowly came back into his body. He felt the tubes as they were yanked out of his nose, and then the straps on his feet, and later wrists, being untied. Someone wiped spittle from his mouth and tugged at his nose with the same cloth.

He heard one liten ask another if Dagon had soiled himself, and felt the cursory probing of his nether regions that prompted the response, "Not from the back end, at least."

Though his consciousness returned, it took some time before he could so much as open his eyes. He lay there listening to his brothers discuss him. The gurgling of their mist pipes sounded like laughter. If they had spent time discussing the serious matters, they were beyond it now. Sire Grindus joked about the childhood infatuation he had for one of his maids. Sire Pindar increased the mirth by mentioning that he still had the same infatuation, despite the fact the woman must surely be many years a corpse. If the queen knew the sort of things he had pictured her doing, another said, she would have his head. "She would have all our heads," Grindus admitted, to a murmur of laughter that echoed around the chamber.

"Odd the workings of the mind," Sire Nathos said.

"Ah . . ." Dagon said. "Ah, odd . . . indeed."

The others hushed a moment, until Revek said, "I believe he is back among us. Dagon, we have discussed your matter at length. Wake and hear our verdict."

Dagon drew out a handkerchief and dabbed at his face. He ran a hand up over the long cone of his skull, patting his hair into place. That was all the regaining of dignity he managed before Revek continued. Pulling his mouth away from his pipe, he spoke through an exhalation of green mist vapor. "We find you guilty of gross misconduct."

"No!"

"Yes, we do. Why wouldn't we? We know everything that happened. Without a doubt, you committed grave actions without the council's consent. You compounded these with further actions, and then you compelled your fellow leaguemen into actions they had no choice but to agree to. All these things are true. I suggest you close your mouth before letting any of the thoughts in your head slip out of it. Remember, Dagon, that all of us in this chamber have been inside you. We are still, to some degree. So hush. That is a command. For the rest of this council, you will not say a word, on pain of banishment."

Stirring a cloud of mist vapor from in front of his face, Revek peered through it. "So that is the verdict," he said. "As for punishment . . . we are also agreed upon that. You are to forfeit your Rapture tithe. You will keep your rank, but if you ever hope to gain Rapture, you will need to earn a great deal in the coming years. Your tithe will be divided among the sires nearest to Rapture themselves."

This can't be happening. I only did what you all would have. And I did not do it alone. He glanced across the close circle at Grau, but the man had attention only for the chairman.

"Now, let us discuss the future," Revek said. "I know the situation looks dire, but it may not be as bad as all that. We know the ill tidings well enough. Let us share the better news. I'll start." He glanced around, touching each of the faces of the men in the inner circles. "It appears Sires Faleen and Lethel have been doing fine work in Ushen Brae."

Dagon reclined, numb. He knew that what he thought had just happened had, in fact, just happened, but it was too enormous a reversal—and too unwarranted and cruel—for his mind to grasp the whole of it. Despite himself, he listened to Revek's report on Ushen Brae.

The nascent unification of the slaves into some collective state had been nipped. Instead, the slaves had fractured along the very lines of their enslavement. The strongest groups among them were loyal to the league. To aid in the continent's pacification, Sire El had been dispatched with his army. They would ensure that the league secured its position there, should Ushen Brae need to become their base of operations.

Of the fate of the Known World, Revek shrugged and said

that what will be, will be. He did not subscribe to the sort of panic that had taken possession of Dagon's senses. "To those who likewise despair I ask one thing," Sire Revel said, "just one thing and then I will fall silent while the younger among you speak." He let that sit a moment, as if to demonstrate that he was capable of falling silent. "Who is to say that we won't be able to do business with the Santoth when all the confusion dies down? They are sorcerers like Tinhadin was, and we had no difficulty coming to a most agreeable arrangement with him. It could be the same with the Santoth. Better, even, for we now have years of experience on which to set our terms. That, Dagon, is where you erred. Not even a Santoth victory is as calamitous as you seemed to believe."

The phrase "too true" escaped more than one leagueman's lips.

"Bu—" Dagon began, but clipped the word before he completed it. All that he had done, the decisive action he had taken, and this was the thanks he got for it? He wanted to lash out at them all. He could not, though. He realized, listening to the murmuring affirmation and enthusiasm that greeted Revek's "one thing" that, had someone else acted as he had, he would himself be speaking against him. He could not argue because Revek was right. The league had not been in the danger he feared. How could it be? They were the league. It was as simple as that. They rode atop the tides of other nations' follies. They did not—or should not—fall into their traps themselves.

Sire Nathos could not keep the enthusiasm from his voice when he said, "And don't forget the vintage. Brothers, in the coming weeks the supplies of the stuff in the Known World will begin to run out. As our testing has shown, they will grow apathetic. They will lose any lust for life. They will sit down and . . . die. A great many of them will, at least. Imagine the

Santoth newly in charge of the world discovering that their conquered subjects can't be made to work, to eat, to fornicate, or do anything else. The same goes for the Auldek, should they emerge victorious. And the same is true for the Akarans, if by some miracle they hold on to power. All of them will face the same problem—a mass dying that they have no way to remedy." He paused for effect. "Except by reaching out to us. Only we control the process. Only we can make more of the vintage. Sire Dagon was foolish for ordering the warehouse and distillery on Prios destroyed, but we can just rebuild, either here or . . ."

"In Ushen Brae," Grau finished. "I rather fancy one of those Lothan Aklun estates on the barrier isles myself."

"You will have one," Nathos said. "We all will. It's absolutely without risk of failure, brothers. If they balk, we simply let them die. If for any reason we want to prevent that, we can give them the release. Not even the queen ever figured out that we both made the addiction and the cure for it at the same time. It was the cure, really, that took us so long to perfect. Should we want to, we could even give the cure to some and not to others, as suits us." He chuckled. "I'm sorry for showing my mirth, brothers, but we have been too somber up to now. The situation is not so dire, despite Dagon's attempts to make it so."

"True enough," Sire Grau said. "Let us sail through this as ever. When the dust settles, we can make our arrangements with whoever is left. Both the Known World and Ushen Brae will need to be rebuilt, repopulated, controlled. Labor will need to be managed, security provided, goods and services transported. The powerful will need the resources only we can provide them. The weak will again clamor for the illusions and trinkets only we know how to wave before their noses. I think, brothers, that we can look to the future with just as much optimism as ever."

"Easy for you to say," Sire Grindus said. "If I'm not mistaken, you'll be on your way to Rapture now. You and Revek."

"Fate has made that so," Grau acknowledged. "Such is my burden. I may not see it all with you, but I know the future is wonderfully bright."

"Oh . . ." Dagon said. He caught himself before the exhalation became a word. He stretched it out, staring at Grau as he did so. And at Revek. What a fool I am.

CHAPTER
SIXTY-ONE

Having so little time to live, with so much to do, Aliver worked without resting. He did not think about all the weeks he had lounged about the palace in Acacia. Bemoaning the past would do him no good. He had told Corinn not to. He wouldn't either.

Later that very day, he cut away from the other riders and swept down on Kidnaban. He caught Paddel, the head vintner, trying to make his escape on a pleasure yacht loaded to the brim with the riches of his estate. Landing Kohl on the boat's elaborate prow, Aliver shouted over her shoulders and the black flare of her wings, "Paddel, I am Aliver Akaran! I come to you with questions. I will have answers; you will give them now. If not, you will be food for my mount."

Paddel—sweating and faint as he was, constantly touching his bald head and the tattooing meant to replicate hair on it—proved very forthcoming.

That evening in Alecia, Aliver spoke before a late session of the Senate. The things he said were easy for him, the words there on his tongue without hesitation. They were truths as he knew them. He would himself lead the army of Acacia north, up over the Methalian Rim. Hopefully, they would meet Princess

Mena quickly, but in any event they would face the Auldek on the Mein Plateau. "While I live, they will not come down from there," he said. "I pledge you that."

He declared that the league had shown themselves to be traitorous scoundrels, enemies to everyone in the empire. "They've bled us all these years and sipped our blood as if it were wine. You see their abandoned palaces, their warehouses in ashes, and their ships all gone, fled to the Outer Isles? This is all proof that they've been found out. They've run from us, and they are now our enemy just as much as the Auldek are."

He announced to them what he had learned about the vintage. The nation was addicted to the mist once again. They did not even know it, for it came to them in the bottles of wine on every table in the empire and it affected them so mildly that they did not know how much they depended on it. They drank of it every night, an enemy right there in their homes. "It is vile and subtle," he said, "but we cannot save our nation without our full and true minds." He ordered all wine poured out, casks smashed, not one more drop of it consumed. "Friends, let us drink water until this war is concluded. I will do the same. You may find it hard, at first, but I will be with each and every one of you, helping you forward."

He told them that the Santoth had finally revealed their true nature. "They are an evil none of us here can stand against, and if they triumph, all the world will be enslaved to them." He said that only one person could defeat them. Queen Corinn. "Only my sister has sorcery to match theirs. So pray for her. Put behind you now your hatred of her, your jealousy. Put behind you the schemes you have had for grasping power when this war ends. Put it all behind you, and pray to the Giver that she succeeds. If she does not, you have no future anyway."

He admitted that he had a daughter but said she was not to

be a pawn in the war or after it. "The queen and I have agreed to the order of succession. Should anything happen to us, we want these instructions followed." He produced the box, a small metal container that he had carried with him on Kohl. "I have them here, in a locked box that I will leave in the care of the Senate. In this box are my wishes. Corinn's wishes. You need not fear them, for they are just. This box is not to be opened until instructions on succession are needed. The key will be kept in safety. You need not seek it. It will appear when it's needed. Before I leave this in your care I must have something from you: your word that you will abide by our wishes. All of you. Each and every one of you must swear to abide by our wishes. I want your oath on the Senate records." Aliver had smiled then, looking around the chamber at the rapt faces staring at him. "I understand that I am not giving you a say in this. But I am your king."

After saying all this, and after getting each senator's oath to abide by the instructions in the locked box, Aliver left the senators in the chamber speechless. Yes, he spoke the truth, but he did not speak all of it. He had not mentioned that the league, in their treachery, had put numbers on his days of life. If he failed on the Mein Plateau, he would be dead before he had to see the Auldek coming down from it. He did not say that as the people came off the vintage they would lose the will to live, and die because of it. Though he told them Corinn fought on their behalf, he did not say that she had only as many days to succeed as he did, or that she no longer could use *The Song* to aid her, or that she did not intend to return from the mission at all. He knew that the senators who swore to obey the succession plan would not have done so readily if they did not fear him and Corinn and the coming war. And while he told them he would repel the Auldek, he did not say that to him success was no longer the same as what it was for them. Victory could be something else, he believed. No easier to attain—perhaps harder, in truth—but a new way. A better way.

Kohl lifted Aliver away from the city that night. The silence and the sound that is wind in motion, the flapping of massive wings, the creak of Kohl's harness and armor. Far out to his left Thaïs carried Dram. To the east Ilabo rode Tij. The dragons called to one another every now and then. Their sounds were like chirrups stretched out with bass notes, each call ending with an almost flutelike sweetness of tone. Aliver had never heard anything like it.

Dragonsong, he thought. I would never have imagined such a thing.

As he listened to it, the night passed in beauty. The world below them slept beneath a starry sky, farms and villages, rivers and roads and dense patches of woodland. *Love it for what it is*, Aliver told himself. *Love it for being my daughter's world, my nephew's future. Love it for what it is and because it will go on after me.*

Many campfires glowed beneath them, often in clusters. His army. A great migration of soldiers heading north. *Love them for who they are. For them, I cannot fail.*

This thought became the frame inside which he ordered the rest of his life. Inside which he planned and dreamed and worked through the things to come and how he would face every hurdle he could imagine. He had already begun reaching out to people, urging them off the vintage, speaking to them to keep their minds clear, to fill them with his love of life, with purpose. He would not let them die, or waver. Not while he lived. He had done this before, with the Santoth's help, and he believed he could do it again without them. He had only to open his mind, to offer himself to all the people of the Known World, to touch their minds and let them touch his.

As part of his consciousness took root in people's minds,

the sense of connection with them built. Thousands upon thousands of different connections. It was wonderful. Through it, he knew every reason he had to succeed, to end this war, and save all the lives he could. It was not the same as when the Santoth aided him. It was better, the connection his and the peoples' alone. It was a communion shared, even as it was intimate with each individual. It was not even a strain on him. Rather, it felt as if once the connection was established, each person hosted his voice inside himself or herself, keeping alive Aliver's words and praise and hopes for them.

He was still at this at sunrise, when the three dragons left the Eilavan Woodlands and rose over the Methalian Rim. The zigzag path up its heights thronged with his army, climbing. Aliver flew up to the Mein Plateau, skimming low over the great mass of troops already gathered there. He let the army see him and the dragons, and he rejoiced to hear the shouts that rose to greet them. Then he and the other dragon riders pressed on as the climbing sun crept across the land, bringing color to it. And it was later that day, under the brief blaze of the arctic day, that he saw Mena and Elya.

They were under attack.

CHAPTER
SIXTY-TWO

Bad idea, Mena thought. This was a bad idea.

She clung tight to Elya's back as she rose and fell, dipped and twirled and undulated with the contours of the broken, icy terrain. Stone and snow, crevice and outcropping snapped by beneath her at speeds Mena had never experienced before. It might have been exhilarating, except that Elya raced before a snarling pack of fréketes, all baying for her blood. They were so near. Mena had stopped looking back, but she could hear their jaws snap. Several times she felt one of them had clawed at Elya's tail.

Faster, Elya. Come on, girl! Faster!

An hour earlier, back with the ragged remains of her army, Rialus had pointed out Devoth and his frékete mount, Bitten, as they swooped in for another aerial attack. It had seemed like the right strategic move to single him out, as she had done Howlk and Nawth. If she could kill or lame them, perhaps the Auldek would cease their endless pursuit. For headlong pursuit is exactly what her army had faced since the Auldek's nighttime attack. Mena's battered army ran; the Auldek pursued. They rode on their antoks and woolly rhinoceroses and kwedeir. They dropped on them from the air on bellowing fréketes. Her soldiers marched day and night, racing between the food and supplies they had cached during their earlier march northward. But they were not fast enough, or strong enough anymore. They could not pull away, and the Auldek had clearly decided to run them into the ground.

Her soldiers died one by one, trampled or cut down, snatched into the air or impaled. Some simply fell and gave up, the exhaustion and cold too much for them to carry on fighting. Even her officers died. Bledas got trampled by an antok. Perceven won himself honor—and a bloody death—defending a sled packed with the wounded. A group of the divine children ran them down. A man with a lion's mane of white hair cut him with two strokes so fast that Perceven was legless before he even began to topple, and headless by the time his body hit the ground.

Mena watched from a distance, but could do nothing, not even avenge him or the injured, who followed him to the after-death just moments later. If she let this go on, she would not have an army anymore. She was not sure what effect she had expected Calrach's death or the destruction of the Auldek histories to have, but so far all the small victories they had won only seemed to fuel the intensity of the Auldek's rage.

That was why Mena had wanted so badly to buy them a reprieve. She and Elya had flown within shouting distance of the fréketes. Instead of listening to anything she had to say, the beasts converged on her. No talking. No taunting. None of the curious, arrogant bravado of their earlier encounters. They just roared toward her. She had given Elya free rein to flee. Mena simply held on. At least they led the fréketes away from the army. That was something.

The beasts took turns pressing the pursuit. Two or three of them clawed the air behind Elya, as the others flew, resting themselves. Elya performed with agility and speed Mena had not known her capable of. But Elya could not go on much longer. Before them stretched a hilly landscape of dips and rises. Mena glanced back. The frékete that had been behind them had just pulled away. Devoth and Bitten pressed the attack now, coming on with a fresh surge of energy.

Let's get them, Mena thought to Elya. She shaped the thought with anger and defiance, but she knew they had no choice. Any moment now one of those grasping claws would get a firm grip on Elya and pull her from the sky. They had to act first.

They did not get that chance.

While Mena still looked behind, Elya broke her speed and cut to one side. The motion whipped Mena's neck around savagely. A frékete that had lain in hiding for them surged up from a hollow, right in front of them. It raked one of its claws through Elya's thin wing membrane and then down her side. Blood erupted from the wound. The beast's claws cut through the saddle straps. Mena felt her harness go loose and cant off to one side. She barely managed to say atop Elya by clinging to her neck.

Elya skimmed away, so near to the earth that her feet touched down briefly as each hill rose beneath her. That did not last long either. Another frékete and rider dropped from the sky in front of them. Elya snapped her wings in and twisted past them, sleek as a spear. The Auldek's sword sung by Mena's ear, so close. Elya reached another rise, but her feet twisted beneath her. She crashed down on the other side, grinding and rolling, Mena with her in a tangle of harness and webbing and wings. Mena felt the familiar, breath-stealing pain of her shoulder being dislocated, her arm flopping limply.

The frékete and its rider swooped over the rise. Mena tried to grab for her sword hilt with her good arm, but the scabbard had twisted around beneath her and the pain in her shoulder made it hard to control her movements. The frékete touched the ground in a flying run. Mena knew it would reach her before she could draw her weapon. She was still struggling to get the King's Trust free when Elya twisted away from her, found her feet.

Elya leaped over the frékete. He slashed at her, but passed just underneath her—and just above Mena. One of its feet swept so close to the princess that it splattered her face with bits of ripped-up turf. Elya's wings beat the air as she lifted higher, flying backward, tail slapping about, tauntingly close to the frékete's grasping claws. From below, Mena watched the Auldek twist around in his harness, looking at her. He yanked back on his reins with his full body weight, trying to turn the frékete back toward her. The cords pulled taut against the frékete's shoulders, but the creature strained against them. It did not care about following its rider's commands anymore or about Mena. It wanted Elya. The three of them disappeared over the hillcrest, leaving Mena crumpled on the ground, tangled in her harness rigging.

Mena screamed Elya's name, both in her mind and with all her voice. She writhed up and out of the harness and kicked free of it. With her good hand, she gripped the biceps of her dangling arm. She inhaled, clenched her teeth, and then pushed the arm back into place. The pain was dizzying. It took several attempts before she felt the ball of her arm bone slip back into its socket. Once it had, she drew the King's Trust and ran as fast as she could up the slope over which the others had disappeared.

Cresting it, she saw them. Below her in the next depression the frékete fought a snarling duel with Elya. The beast punched and grappled her, landing brutal blows. It was all brawny muscle and weight, sharp claws and bared teeth. Elya writhed with serpentine speed, a hissing tangle of motion. She fought more fiercely than Mena would have thought possible, but she was not made for it, her body too slim and delicate. Her wings hung in useless tatters, her side black with blood. She tried several times to leap away, but the frékete yanked her back down each time.

The Auldek had dismounted to let the beast have its fun. He had started up the rise toward Mena, his sword in hand, but had paused, obviously amused by the fight. He shouted something to the animal. It bellowed in return. It slammed a fist across Elya's jaw. She reeled away, but it grabbed her and pulled her back. It bit down on the long curve of her neck.

"No!"

Mena rushed down the slope, her sword raised, all pain forgotten. The Auldek snapped around. He moved to intercept her. They crashed together, Mena savage in her attack; the Auldek just as furious in repelling it. They went around, the Auldek moving so that she could not see what the frékete was doing to Elya. This drove Mena into a fury of slashing, hacking, thrusting motion faster than any attack she had managed before. The Auldek backed. Mena wanted him dead. Fast. *Now!*

When a roar ripped through the air behind her she feared it was the frékete announcing its kill. The Auldek heard it, too. He looked past her and saw something that surprised him. His eyes left Mena only for a moment. That's all she needed. She hacked his sword hand off at the wrist. As the sword and severed hand dropped, she reached over them and sliced a cut through the Auldek's face. He survived it only by snapping his head back, turning, and running.

A second roar hit Mena's back, this one different from the first, higher and more shrill.

Mena wanted to turn, but she also feared to. She ran after the fleeing Auldek as if blasted forward by a third roar, a low bass note that made the ground tremble.

The Auldek stumbled once. Again, that moment was all Mena needed. She was Maeben now, dropping from the sky, nothing but a screech of mindless rage. At full sprint, she brought the King's Trust up horizontally, her shoulder cocked high. She slammed her foot down on the Auldek's heel. As his step hitched, she dove forward, driving the sword with all her weight and speed. The point of the blade slipped in at the base of the Auldek's skull, cut through, and jutted through his face. Mena nearly ran up the man's back. She kicked off him, yanking the cutting edge up as she did so. His head split in two.

She did not pause to watch him fall. She turned in the air and landed, ready to run back toward Elya. Only then did she see what had so frightened the Auldek.

The sky was alive with dragons.

A brown one hurtled toward the approaching fréketes. The other—nearly as blue as the sky behind it—swept around to attack them from the other side. The brown one roared first, and then the blue one did the same. All the fréketes heard them. They pulled up, hesitating, as their eyes took in the shapes approaching them. Mena saw the dragons cut into the airborne fréketes, scattering them. That was all she saw, for now there was a third dragon. This one became a searing black arrow that shot straight toward Elya and the frékete that held her limp body. The creature—larger than any frékete, dwarfing Elya, with a massive, big-jawed head that was so crimson it could have been on fire—rode in on that rumbling wave of sound, the greatest of the roars.

The frékete holding Elya tossed her down and leaped into flight. The dragon met the frékete that way. At the last moment, the dragon pulled its head back and tossed its claws forward, grabbing and scratching at the very moment of impact. A man leaped from the monster's back. Mena had not even noticed the rider. He slid across a slick stretch of wing membrane and then hit the ground in a jarring roll. The two beasts were carried forward by the dragon's weight and momentum. A writhing ball of wings and tails, teeth and fists, screaming, fighting fury, they disappeared over the hillock.

The man found his feet and spotted Mena. Meeting his gaze, Mena felt her vision blur. She stood swaying, staring, the King's Trust forgotten in her hand. Her eyes followed the man as he rushed toward her. She heard his feet crunching on the snow. She saw the plumes of vapor when he breathed. She knew his face and recognized the joy and concern written in his features. She knew him. She knew him.

"Mena," Aliver said, reaching her in time to catch her before she fell from consciousness, "it's all right. I'm with you."

CHAPTER
SIXTY-THREE

Nualo was the first to appear, called by Corinn's reading from *The Song*. Circling high above the ruined valley of Calfa Ven, she saw the moving tumult of his passage. It began as a disturbance to the east, like a small, dense storm roiling on the horizon and moving at an unnatural speed. She did not know why she knew it was he, except perhaps that his hunger was greater than any of the others', his evil more pronounced.

"How close do we let them get?" Hanish asked.

Close enough, but not too close.

"That could be hard to measure," Hanish said. "There's no ruler for such a thing."

When Nualo was near enough that Corinn could see his tall, elongated form striding up and down the mountains, she turned Po and headed north. They left behind the devastation of Calfa Ven, but there were signs of the Santoth's wandering destruction written across the hills and valleys beneath them. In places it looked like giant versions of the worms that had eaten her mouth had chewed up the earth and then vomited it back in twisted, sickening piles of soil and vegetation and rock. Would the Santoth do this to the entire world? Would studying

The Song move them away from this rage and hunger for destruction, or would it just make them more horrific versions of what they already were? She knew the answers to these questions. The world below her both prompted and confirmed them, over and over again. Whatever had twisted the Santoth had taken them to a state they could not come back from. She hoped the same was not true of herself.

Looking back at Nualo, seeing him shoulder through great pine trees as if they were shrubs, Corinn did not notice how close they flew to another Santoth. Po barked an alarm. The figure climbed up over a buttress of rock on the mountain below them. As soon as he stood with his feet planted, he threw up his arms and bellowed out his garbled version of the song. The notes rushed upward in the form of long, deformed black birds, with eyeless heads stretched eagerly forward from their bodies. They flew without so much as flapping their wings, like darts with only the force of the sorcerer's voice to propel them.

Po twisted and turned as they reached him. He contorted his body as the bird-shaped missiles zipped by. Each of them cried out as it missed, leaving in its wake a scorching burn that fouled the air. The stench of malevolence was so thick Corinn began coughing; a painful, useless gesture that wracked her chest with pain.

"Don't breathe it," Hanish said. "Don't breathe."

Hanish's hands reached around and grasped hers, steadying her. Through her, he pulled the reins to direct Po into a sliding dive away from the sorcerer. The missiles continued to fly past them, but Po kept at his maneuvers even as he banked away, wings pulled tight to edge their speed forward.

One of the birds punched through Po's left wing. It expanded on impact. Its legs and wings and beak all became hooks that tore through the thick membrane. Blood and tissue sprayed from the ragged hole. The barbed bird then sank away beneath them. Po screamed. He yanked the wing in, sending them into a corkscrew dive. Hanish fought to get control, still using Corinn's hands. The spin was too chaotic.

"Corinn!" Hanish called. "I can't . . ."

Corinn reached for the creature's mind. She found it a cauldron overflowing with pain and anger and fear. The wound was worse even than it looked. The touch of the bird's hooks carried the poison of tainted sorcery with it. It ate at Po, burning his wing like flaming oil. The agony of it was driving him mad.

Corinn grasped for the song. She built it inside her head. She conjured the spell she would have used to heal him and shared it with Po. It could not do so, not as she would have liked, but just hearing it in his mind soothed him. She reminded him of who he was, how strong and wonderful. He stretched the wing again, pulling them out of the descent, and flew. The ragged hole remained, loose skin flapping horribly in the wind, but Corinn could feel that he was fighting the poisoned magic, deadening it. And he was beating his wings anyway.

Looking back, Corinn saw the evil bird drifting toward the sorcerer. Dural. That was who it was. He stood calmly, his hands folded, no longer singing, no longer enormous, just a man waiting for the bird to drift back to him. Something about his receding outline gave Corinn his name and brought to mind the face that she had seen him wear back at the Carmelia. Before she looked away, she saw Nualo reach the rock buttress. He, too, had shrunk to normal dimensions. He conferred with Dural, both of them reaching to catch the falling bird.

They have the scent of us, Corinn said. *That's what they just took. They're hunters, and that bird has brought them Po's scent. They can follow us around the world now.*

Hanish responded by pulling his hands away from hers,

giving her the reins again, and wrapping his arms back around her waist. She knew what he was thinking, and loved him for not saying it: better that they have that scent. It would help draw them to her as she led them on. With the part of her mind reserved for Po, she thanked him for it.

Coming on the wide, glimmering snake that was the River Ask, Po rode the air up its course, toward Candovia. All that day they flew. All that day Nualo and Dural trailed them. Toward dusk, another Santoth, Abernis, ran south toward them along the surface of the river. At times he jumped from rock to rock. At others he simply churned across the surface of the water. When he attacked them, he did so with a motion of his hands that scooped water from the river and sent it in a flood up and over them.

As it fell toward them, Corinn knew it was not water any longer. It still sparkled in the air but was more like shards of glass than liquid. The wave of it stretched so wide and moved so quickly that Po could not avoid it. Instead, he beat furiously toward it. As it fell on them, he wrapped his wings around himself, the short lengths of bone in them going loose. They wrapped across his belly and over his back. They covered Corinn and the ghost, and still went farther, wrapping around and around. They punched through the rain of shards like an arrow. Corinn felt Po's agony as the glass slivers cut into him, savage as living things. They cut into his wings, but not deep enough to touch Corinn.

Po's momentum carried him through them. Only then did he snap his wings out and catch the air again. They were even more shredded. Like the previous time, the cuts festered with acid. Like last time, Corinn helped Po fight them, to fly through the pain with yet another Santoth now behind them.

That night they stayed aloft. They saw the lights of Pelos to

the east but stayed far away from that city. Po carved a meandering course, avoiding settlements as much as possible. During
the dark hours Corinn felt other Santoth join the hunters. And
early the next morning, Tenith emerged out of the marshes of
the Lakelands. He hurled the corpses of cranes at them. The
creatures sprang to undead life and surged up toward them. Po
dodged a few. Caught one in his jaws. He snatched it out of the
air and then, with one whiplike snapping of his neck, he sent
it twirling toward the ground. Another he batted away with a
foot. Each touch of them was filled with corruption, but he did
it anyway. He was getting better at this already.

"Corinn," Hanish said, "I've not told you how glad I am that
we have this dragon. And they don't."

Don't tell it to me, Corinn answered. *Tell him.*

Po swung his neck around and gazed at them a moment.
Corinn knew he did so because she asked him to, but it looked
very much as if he had turned to hear Hanish's praise. He
received it gracefully, blinking his large, golden eyes and never
losing the rhythm and strength of his wingbeats.

The Santoth were pulling together now, drawn not just to
her but also back to one another. Corinn kept them as close
to the far horizon as much as she could, watching their numbers grow. They flew out over the northern ocean, and then cut
around the peninsula north of Luana. The Santoth ran across
the waves as if they were moving features of the land. They were
tireless, persistent. They could no more stop pursuing her than
they could choose to stop breathing.

Good, Corinn thought. Good. Hunt me. Hunt me to our
deaths.

Hanish stayed pressed to her the whole time. Often, he spoke
beside her ear, telling her tales like the ones he had that night
he spent with her after she tried to cut herself a new mouth.

He spoke of his childhood, of his brothers. Amazingly, he found humor in even the brutal Meinish winters, in the training that was forced upon him, in the constant need to prove himself to both the living and the dead. Corinn had never shared such stories with him. She had never been able to see the light in the darkness that he did.

Or she had never been able to before.

CHAPTER
SIXTY-FOUR

"You know," Delivegu said, once his gasping breaths had calmed enough to allow it, "I'm not so sure anybody noticed how terribly bold it was of me to bring Kelis and Shen to the palace. I've yet to be thanked properly for it."

Rhrenna lifted her sweat-slicked forehead from his chest. She tossed her head, snapping her hair from her face so that it draped from one naked shoulder. "Why," she asked, "would you think to say that right now?"

"No one has acknowledged it, is all I mean."

"I'm here with you," Rhrenna said. "That should count for something."

From straddling him, she flopped to one side and lay on her back, eyes closed. Delivegu missed the warmth of her immediately. He rolled onto his side and studied her in profile. The almost-too-fine point to her nose, the bones across her shoulders a little too pronounced, her breasts small enough that they all but disappeared when she stretched her arms above her head. In all these ways she was not the type of woman he would usually have fancied. But fancy her he did. Perhaps more than he should.

"Oh, come now, you don't mean to say this bed wrestling

is a thank-you? Am I paid as cheaply as that? In a manner that pleases you so much more than me?"

Rhrenna lifted the arm nearest him and dropped the weight of it over him. "Shut up," she said.

For a time, he did. He liked that she could be so direct. She had been so when she arrived unannounced at his chamber door. Though she had come for seduction, she had not followed any of the routines he was used to. Her light blue eyes had not smoldered. Her lips had not puckered. She had not batted her eyelashes or anything like that. Still, when she said, "I think I'll try you now, if you are prepared for it," he had found that he was—with stunning rapidity—prepared for it.

Lying beside her now, staring at the ceiling, he was so satiated that he did not even mind when Rhrenna began to snore softly. It seemed a little strange to him that she came to him now, when events in the world had taken such a dire turn, when her own mistress was cursed and off somewhere, hunting sorcerers who had already proven themselves more powerful than she. Perhaps Rhrenna was not as devoted to the queen as she had seemed. In a way, the possibility that her loyalty was a carefully calculated deception impressed him as much as if it were real. More so, perhaps.

"Either way, you're besotted, Delivegu," he whispered. "You're growing silly with age."

That got him thinking, with a small measure of concern, about his recent choices. The thing with Kelis and Shen, for example. Stroll into the queen's presence with an illegitimate heir to the throne, one that might very well usurp her own illegitimate heir? Bring along the Talayan who had escorted the Santoth right into the heart of the empire, with catastrophic results? If he had done something like that before the events at the coronation, the queen would have found a way to kill him. Unpleasantly. No doubt employing a man like himself for the task. Nor did he arrange to meet the queen on the stone stair-case, as he once had, to present them both bound and gagged for her secret consideration, interrogation, and disposal. That, based on all the services he had rendered the queen in the past, would have been a reasonable way to proceed.

Why did he choose the first way and not the latter? Because the events at the coronation changed everything. For all he knew, the queen might not have escaped the Carmelia with her powers intact. Surely she had suffered from some curse the Santoth had tossed at her. She might not even be long for this world. If she wasn't, what better than to enter Aliver's service with a golden ticket? Also—dare he even think it?—it felt like the right thing to do. Delivegu had not yet given up on the hope that his role in the world might be measured by things other than hunting down verbose rabble-rousers, poisoning pregnant women, and bedding maidservants and secretaries.

"There's more to me than that," he murmured.

Rhrenna broke from her rhythmic snore for a moment. He watched her until she resumed it, smiling when she did.

Regardless of his reasons, if he judged by what transpired in the library, he had chosen wisely. What was going on with that scarflike thing wrapped around the queen's face he could not have said. Nor could he fathom her silence. Barad the stone-eyed acting as Corinn's mouth, Kelis blubbering like a sleepwalking child, Aliver speaking with an animation Delivegu had never seen in him before: it had been strange stuff all around.

Perhaps he should consider the new mission Aliver had pro-posed before leaving a sort of thanks. At least it indicated that he trusted him, and thought him capable of a task of impor-tance. It was not nearly as interesting as the type of job Corinn had him get up to. And he did not entirely understand what the purpose of it was, but why not go along with it? He had to work for somebody.

I wonder, he thought, if Aliver might be inclined to make me an Agnate? After I've rendered sufficient service, of course. Could he triangulate his former relationship with the queen, his new one with the prince, and his much-improved one with Rhrenna into such an increase in his fortunes? Of course he could. That was what Delivegu Lemardine had always done. He mused on his prospects for a time.

At some point, he realized that Rhrenna's breathing was no longer audible. He turned his head. She still lay in profile, but her eyes were open. Her lips trembled slightly, and a tear escaped the eye nearest him and rushed down toward her ear.

"I dreamed," she said. "I dreamed."

Delivegu waited to hear what she had dreamed, but apparently those two words were full sentences, not the beginning of longer ones.

"I don't know what's going to happen," she continued. "Nothing is right anymore. I read what she wrote to Aaden. It's—" She choked on whatever it was. "I don't want to be without her. I don't want to be alone. She loved me like nobody else did. She gave me life when . . ." That was as far as she got.

Delivegu curled into her. He pulled her into his chest and kissed her eyes closed and smeared her tears away with his lips. He told her she would never be alone. He told her he was with her always. Everything would be all right. He would make sure of it. She would always be loved. He would love her, he said. He already did.

He told her all these things as she sobbed against him, wrapped in the sheets of his bed. And he meant it. By the Giver, he actually meant it all.

✳

He sailed for Aushenia the next morning. He took no joy in leaving Rhrenna. If she had showed any of the emotion that had racked her with sobs during the night, he might well have said something regrettable. Sentimental. Further promises of the type he had thought only lesser men ever made to women. Fortunately, she parted with a businesslike efficiency, wishing him speed on his mission in no more time than it took to roll out of bed, snatch her garments from the floor, and depart while still climbing into them. He lay in bed a moment after the door slammed shut, uneasy with what seemed like a reversal in the role he normally occupied in amorous matters.

"You can't pretend I didn't see into you," he said to his empty chamber. "We both know I did."

What he did not say, but thought, was that perhaps she had seen rather a bit too much into him as well. What he also did not say—and could not quite believe he even found himself thinking—was that he wanted nothing more urgently than to return to her, to have her again, to be with her many more times. To make love, yes, but also to talk; to jest; to see the fit of clothes on her under the play of many different types of light; to be there should she wake crying; perhaps, even, to reveal even more of his intimate thoughts to her.

You're getting soft, Delivegu, he thought.

Ruminating on this as he sailed, Delivegu failed to remember to stop in at Alecia, Manil, or Aos. He could have found diversion in any of these places—social gatherings and flirtation early, more serious drink and fornication later. His friend Yanzen had even left an open invitation for him to stop in at Sigh Saden's rustic estate outside Aos. The senator, having fled the isle of Acacia, divided his staff between Alecia, where he had to conduct senatorial business, and Aos, where he planned to flee if the empire collapsed. Yanzen had promised Delivegu that if he visited, he could deduct from the debt Yanzen owed him by dipping himself into the concubines Saden hid among the household staff. "They'd welcome that stiff rod of yours," he had said.

Yanzen always knew the right things to say to encourage Delivegu.

Inexplicable then, that he sailed right past each port with barely a sideways glance. He landed in Killintich a full two days before schedule, and he found himself riding with King Grae, doing his best to offer the monarch a deference he did not feel. Outside the city, the country was beautiful—woodland and small villages, occasional solitary farms. They rode winding dirt roads through the forest with just a few guards trailing them. Delivegu would have been happiest with silence, but the king was in a more talkative mood.

"We did not expect you so soon," Grae said. He sat easy in his saddle, like one born to horses, which he was. He was just as stone-chiseled handsome as Delivegu remembered. His rustic attire nonetheless wafted a scent of royal luxury, as if the supple leather had been sewn with gold thread and the pockets filled with lavender flowers. He wore his blue eyes as much like jewelry as his turquoise necklace or the subtle diadem that rested on his reddish blond hair.

Delivegu avoided those eyes as much as he could. "I'm on the king's business," he responded. "Best to be prompt."

"'Prompt'? Prompt is not a word I would have associated with the name Delivegu Lemardine," Grae said. He showed a mouthful of straight, white teeth and leaned toward him. "At least, that's not what certain ladies of my acquaintance have said about you. They all attest that there are two things you are gifted at. One is deceitful treachery; the other is . . . Oh, I shouldn't mention it. It's a somewhat more admirable skill, though, even if it's a gift mostly to the whores and maidservants of the world."

He's baiting me, Delivegu thought. It surprised him to hear that the king of Aushenia had been asking anybody about him. For some reason he did not like the idea. It was he who was supposed to know things about others, not the other way around.

It was Grae who had been sent packing from Acacia, spurned by the queen for *his* treachery. The fact that she discovered that treachery had been Delivegu's doing, of course. Apparently the king knew it.

Telling himself to keep his calm, Delivegu shifted the subject. "So, have they been safe in your care? No more unfortunate accidents?"

"Yes, we haven't lost a one of them since the queen sent them here. The ones who were killed were not slaughtered in Aushenia. That happened in Aos. Here they've been taken good care of. All of them."

"How many are there?"

"Seven."

"Seven?"

"I know. Not many to be an entire generation of a race," Grae said. "The queen makes for a . . . challenging adversary. How is she? I've heard all manner of dire things."

"She is the queen," Delivegu said.

"Yes," Grae guffawed, "I'm sure she's that. Off to sort out the Santoth while the rest of us do the same with the Auldek. I suspect we've got the bloodier end of that bargain."

You weren't there. You didn't see them. But he did not want to give Grae anything, so he said, "Is this it?"

On a rise of land coming into view before them stood a squat stone-block building. It was large enough to be a castle, but it was, in truth, a prison.

"Yes, that's our keep," Grae said, straightening to take in the view. "I'm sure you understand the various reasons we did not want to house them in the city. It wasn't one of the queen's stipulations. She asked this of me, and I obliged. They've been perfectly safe here. Safer than they deserve."

"Do they speak Acacian?"

"I suppose. I've not been stopping in to chat with them."

Delivegu noted the edge in the monarch's voice. He rather liked finding it. Beneath his regal demeanor, Grae did chafe at being told to care for these creatures. Feeling a bit like a wet nurse, are you, Your Majesty? "No, I wouldn't imagine you'd have much to say to them. Or they to you."

Once they had both dismounted and had their horses taken from them, Grae led them into the keep on foot. "What are you to do with them?"

"Take them to King Aliver, as instructed."

The Aushenian pondered that for a moment. "I meant what is *he* going to do with them, but I don't suppose it's your place to know that. King Aliver back from the dead . . . By the Giver, the world seems to have turned upside down overnight. You'll have to dine with me this evening. I have many questions for you."

"That's not possible," Delivegu said. "I carry on tonight. I have to see to the details of transporting them."

"Surely, you have an evening to—"

"No, I don't." Delivegu turned toward him, meeting those blue eyes. "As I said, I'm on the king's business. I choose to be prompt."

Grae studied him for a long moment. "You don't seem like the same man I met in Acacia just months ago. You're . . . tamed. Obedient. Fine, don't dine with me. I have no interest in your people anymore. I would say I wish you all the best with your war, but the words would stick on my tongue."

"It may prove to be your war as well," Delivegu pointed out.

"I know more about the Numrek and their kind than you, errand boy. Aushenia took the brunt of the first invasion, or have your people forgotten that? Have they written Aushenguk Fell out of the histories? No matter. We remember. We remember that we fought the Numrek first, with no aid from Acacia. We remember that the Numrek overran our lands while Acacians looked after their own interests. This time, Aushenia will defend its own borders fiercely if need be, but we won't fight your war for you."

They had walked through the keep's main gate, beneath the fortifications, through a second wall and a gate that was cranked up only once they had reached it. As they stepped through, it immediately began to descend again.

"There," Grae said, "they're out at play. We let them spar with wooden swords. What's the harm in it?"

Delivegu saw them then. On the far side of the large enclosure, sparring, just as the king said. Just seven of them. Seven Numrek children of various ages. The only ones still alive after Corinn's massacre of their parents at the Thumb.

"They're yours now," Grae said. "Take them."

CHAPTER
SIXTY-FIVE

Dariel did his best to explain that he had reconsidered how to proceed. Now that he was about to set off, he worried about taking others into danger on a fool's errand. He should go alone. He could handle a small skiff himself. He knew the way to Lithram Len already. If he succeeded at what he had planned, it would not be because he fought his way in. If a league clipper spotted him, it would not matter how many friends he had sitting on the seat beside him. Stealth was what mattered. That he could best achieve alone. This was his mission, after all. If he was wrong or failed at it, they would need each and every able body perched on the walls of Avina.

He might as well have been a youngest child arguing for something before a unified front of older, skeptical siblings. He had felt this way before. They would have none of it. They had discussed Dariel's plan only within a small circle, but Mór still insisted they be cautious. Considering the magnitude of what hinged on Dariel's success, they could not chance some malicious clansman of Dukish's alerting the league somehow.

"Tunnel is with you, Rhuin Fá," the big man said. He tugged on a golden tusk. "That's the way it is. Stop scratching at it."

"And us," Geena said. "You're not going alone in some skiff. Not when we have a right lovely, sleek, fast clipper with your name on it."

"Face it, Dariel," Clytus added. "We're brigands. You can't expect us to stand on a city wall flashing our asses and such. I mean, that's all right for Melio, being Marah and all that, but us? No, not when there's a bit of piracy to get up to."

Even Skylene asked him to see sense. The very fact that she could ask him was miraculous. She woke the evening he breathed life into her. Sometime that night her fever broke, and the next morning she sat up, her skin cool and filled with color. The first thing she did was ask for lentils. Red lentils in a creamy cheese sauce, with long strips of fried onion in it. She ate and ate, and laughed, and asked a thousand questions about the things that she had missed. And here she was, just a couple of days from the edge of death, standing, thin but vibrant, in the late light of the day, holding Mór's arm and asking Dariel to see sense. He had not told her what he had done, and figured he never would. He told no one.

When Birké showed his canines and shrugged, as if to say that he, surely, would not try to say no to Skylene, Dariel did not. He acquiesced without a word more of protest. Tunnel had hefted up his mallets. Clytus tied back his long hair with a band across his forehead, set his hands on his hips, and danced for a few merry moments, preternaturally light on his feet. Kartholomé patted the throwing stars flat against his waist. Geena smiled and batted her eyelashes.

Dariel, loving the buoyancy of the moment, prayed that he knew what he was doing, that he was not leading his friends to certain death and placing the Free People at the mercy of the league.

✳

I think it's safe to say the invasion has begun," Clytus said.

None of the soul vessels churning the waters from the barrier isles toward Avina paid the slightest attention to the single, now terribly old-fashioned clipper moving the other way, propelled only by the power of a favorable breeze. The league had been won over by the wonders that were the soul vessels. And why not? Those vessels cut right into that wind, sleek and glistening, unerringly aimed at their target. Dariel remembered the intoxicating power of having his hands on the steering wheel of one of those ships. It was a hard wheel to let go of. He had counted on that being the case for the leaguemen.

We're right about that, at least, Dariel thought. Of course, if he was wrong about the rest of it, that would be a moot point.

While most of the barge transports would be coming down from Eigg, where the newly arrived army had landed, two of them had sailed for Lithram Len. All on board the *Slipfin* gathered by the bridge to stare at them.

Each transport was its own squat, rectangular island of dull gray, smooth as stone, flat, and largely featureless. Dariel thought them ghostly, dead-looking things, unnatural in the way they shoved through the chop. Both barges thronged with Ishtat soldiers. Thousands of them, from one edge of the structure to another, stood shoulder to shoulder. Here and there towers jutted up. The structures were not the same material as the vessel but were simple wood and stone and leather, obviously recent additions. Other military hardware cluttered them as well. The distance made them hard to discern. The transports may never have been used for warfare before, but the quick outfitting for Sire Lethel's siege of Avina had transformed them most convincingly.

"They moved us on those," Tunnel said, "when we were small. Those took us across to Ushen Brae." He stared a moment longer. "They don't know. Them soldiers, they don't know they're slaves, too."

"Don't start feeling sorry for them," Kartholomé said. He fingered the new earrings that hung in long curves from his lobes. "They'd spit and roast you in a Bocoum minute. Though you wouldn't really taste like pork, would you?"

The large man looked at the brigand, perplexed. He tugged on a tusk.

The harbor of Lithram Len proved a floating labyrinth. Though largely deserted in the wake of the invasion force's departure, it was crowded with the league ships that had been left behind. Dariel and the others tethered the *Slipfin* to a brig well away from the docks. They crammed into the skiff and rowed the rest of the way, navigating a meandering course through the maze of anchored ships. They pulled in below the bow of a large brig. In its shadow, they tied the skiff to the pier and clambered up an old, barnacle-encrusted ladder.

Standing on the long, high pier as the others climbed, Clytus scanned the distant piers, ships, and even the town itself. "We still don't have a plan, do we?"

Dariel said, "If it were just me, I would've worn a disguise. Tried to blend—"

"With that face?" Clytus asked. "I haven't seen too many Ishtat wearing full facial tattoos."

"True enough. They've no fashion sense."

The others continued to bunch around them, nervously looking about. Tunnel came up last. He had looped a strap of leather around his neck and hung his mallets from it. They dangled behind him as he climbed. Gaining the pier, he let the mallets drop, heavy things that dented the wood and stuck to it, pressed down by their weight. A moment later, as everyone watched, he hefted both up and straightened. He stood, surprised to find all eyes on him, holding the mallets out to either side as the muscles of his arms and chest and ridged compartments of his abdomen flexed. "What?"

"I've got the plan," Kartholomé said. He pulled his hand away from the oiled tip of his beard and pointed at Tunnel. "We follow him."

They did. Weapons drawn—bare-chested like Tunnel, open shirted like Clytus and Kartholomé, smiling with unaccountable good humor, like Geena—Dariel and his brigands marched down the pier and into the Lothan Aklun port city of Lithram. Dariel took the vanguard, unsure where his destination was. I'll feel it, he thought. I'll feel it when I'm close.

He thought of Bashar and Cashen, wishing they were with him to help sniff out the place he intended to find. They would not have actually helped, however. The place he searched for was not to be found by scent. Part of him already knew his destination. It was that part of him that had proposed this, vague as it was, to the others. He had not even detailed what he hoped to accomplish here. He had just said that Nâ Gâmen was urging him to go to Lithram. There was something he needed to face there, something important.

They met no one along the waterfront. In the distance several people went about their work, but none was near enough to notice the new arrivals. "Any idea where we're headed?" Clytus asked.

"We could ask that fellow," Geena said, indicating a figure passing between two buildings without noticing them.

Quietly, so the man would not actually hear him, Kartholomé said, "Hey, you know where to find the thing we're looking for? Not sure what it is, but . . ."

"Up there," Dariel said, indicating a narrow structure, the roof of which was just visible rising above the nearer row buildings. "It's over there."

Joking aside, nobody asked him how he knew that. They found a stairway between two of the larger buildings and ascended it, taking the steps a few at a time. Reaching the higher street, they stepped cautiously onto it. Tunnel pointed out that the architecture of the town was nothing like the Lothan Aklun estates he had seen on some of the barrier isles. Though child-hood memories, the images were strong in his mind, as they were in Dariel's. Here the smooth granite stones and the spires atop some buildings looked like the work of laborers, not sorcerers. They did not have long to ponder the differences.

Kartholomé saw them first. He cursed.

A hundred or so paces down the street, a contingent of six Ishtat dashed into view. Judging by their well-armed look of determination, they had been alerted to the group's presence. They pulled up, spotting the intruders. They conferred for a moment. Swords drawn, they fanned out, evenly spaced, clearly disciplined.

"We can handle them," Clytus said to Dariel, drawing his sword. "They can't be the best of the lot. Else they wouldn't be here. They'd be with the invasion."

Kartholomé cursed again. Another group of Ishtat appeared on the far side of them, about the same distance away. The two groups converged, with Dariel's group in the middle.

"We're not so good at sneaking, huh?" Tunnel asked. "Oh well . . ." He stepped toward the first, nearer contingent of soldiers. He paused. "Dariel, I see a passage. What do I do? Go around and over? Or through?"

"Through it," Dariel answered.

Tunnel grinned. "That's the way." He walked at first, but as he came nearer the soldiers he fell into a jog, and then a run. His mallets came up. The careful array of soldiers burst like an explosion had just hit their center. Tunnel had to swing around and come back at them, pressing several up against a building wall. He went to work, mallets hissing savage arcs around him, smashing stone, knocking swords away, and then, when he got serious, smashing bones.

"Go," Clytus said grimly. "Do what you have to. We will, too." He led the charge toward the other group, with Kartholomé just behind him, already snapping his throwing stars into hissing motion.

Geena pulled her knife free. "Go, Dariel!" she said, pointing to the narrow structure Dariel had indicated earlier.

It took great effort for the prince to pull himself away. He hated doing so. He had never left his companions in danger. Hand on the hilt of the Ishtat sword he bore, he almost could not go.

"There's your goal. We'll sort out these ones. Go!" She rushed to join Tunnel. "Go!"

Dariel turned and ran. The entrance of the narrow building stood open. He dashed into it and kept going, stumbling over a low table, reaching out for the wall for support. He kept moving down a long corridor, past adjoining hallways and rooms, not really thinking about where he was going. He just got himself farther and farther from his friends, committing himself to leaving them behind.

Once he was deep enough inside and the clash and shouts of fighting had faded, Dariel paused. All right. Let me do this quickly. He closed his eyes and waited, hoping direction would come to him. When it did, he wasted a few precious seconds realizing it. As ever, Nâ Gâmen did not speak to him as a separate being. He spoke as part of Dariel himself. So the vague feeling that he had to walk down the corridor to the second opening, through it, and down the stairs was not just an idle thought. Remembering this, he opened his eyes and dashed for the opening.

The next several minutes passed in the same manner. Dariel

had to keep reminding himself that his instincts were more than instincts. He was not guessing. He was following a path he already knew, though it only came to him piece by piece. It felt like his knowledge stretched only as far as the light of a candle. As he moved, the illumination did as well. He kept going.

Until he stopped. At some point, just an empty stretch of corridor, he lost the drive to move forward. For a moment the fear that he was lost knifed through him. He breathed. Tried to trust. He leaned his hands against the wall and pushed his weight into it. As before, he thought the action was meaningless until the section of wall turned soft. He pushed right through and emerged into another room.

A small chamber. Four walls and seemingly sealed tight. Just before him, a lean, curving pedestal rose up to waist height. The room was not exactly dark and not exactly light, but he could see what he needed to. The dust was inches thick on the floor. Beneath his feet, it was as soft as carpet, undisturbed until this moment. The league has not found this place yet. They must have scoured the city already and the island after that and farther still, searching without knowing what they were searching for. Here, though, was a relic right here, undiscovered.

I wouldn't have found it either, Dariel thought. Not without help.

Having found it, he stared, hoping Nâ Gâmen was not done helping, for he had no idea what to do now. A framed area on the wall before him glowed with a low luminescence. The frame held no painting or window, and yet it was the center—the purpose—of the chamber. Staring, Dariel saw. Deep inside the wall, which was translucent, lights pulsed and wavered, much like the glowing aquatic life he had seen on special nights at sea. The energy in there was different, though. It changed shape before his eyes. At times it looked like a constellation of stars blooming into life all at once. But then that wasn't right. The lights moved in swirls, tossed and shaped by layers of different currents. In other moments the light came in pulses, like so many heartbeats.

Looking closely at the pedestal's top, he saw a single shape on the flat surface. It looked strangely familiar, but it took him a moment to realize it was an engraving of the same symbol protruding from his forehead.

His fingers tingled.

He had thought the chamber was completely silent, but that was not quite right. He heard something. He craned his head this way and that, sure that there were sounds just out of reach. The sound did not come from inside the room. It did not come from the pedestal. It was not even inside the living wall.

Stepping back, he took in the whole frame. As if in response, the constellation bloomed again. So many lights, all of them pulsing, pulsing. In time with one another. He pressed up close against it. And then he understood. The lights were not within the frame. The lights were not even lights. The wall was simply a way of seeing what they represented. He knew then what this place was and why he had come here. Most important, he knew what he was supposed to do.

He did not question the impulse that came to him. He moved around to the pedestal. He bent forward like a peasant before a king, like the faithful before evidence of his god. He bent forward in reverence and humility, and he touched his forehead to the altar. He placed the rune he wore into the imprint that matched it.

CHAPTER
SIXTY-SIX

"You can't be serious," Mena said. "You can't mean to try that. Not after what they've done."

Aliver almost replied that he was dead serious, but considering the things they had spent the night discussing he did not think the expression would go over well. "I am, Mena," he said. "I do mean to try it. I may be wrong, but it feels right. It feels like it may be the way to cut through to the heart of things. I know it's a hard thing to hear me say, but let's toss it back and forth. If I can't convince you, I won't manage to convince anybody else either."

They had already been at council many hours, sitting together in a shelter made of living bodies. Elya lay at its center, with the long bulk of Kohl curved around her and the two humans. Aliver and Mena sat, wrapped in blankets, with an oil lamp burning between them, heat and light both, such as it was. The night blustered above them, but the spread wings of the dragon covered them, dulling the sound of the wind. An unusual chamber in which to hold a reunion, but it was what the Giver allowed them. Aliver was more thankful for it than he could have expressed.

Mena! He was really seeing Mena again. It took her some

time to stare Aliver into belief, to accept him as real, but he knew her without a doubt. It was truly Mena who had touched his face with her fingers, smearing his tears even as she cried herself. It was Mena who had first been wordlessly amazed, and then had been possessed by a babbling of half-formed sentences and declarations. Aliver had found what threads he could in her words and tied them together. Because of this, Mena—his sister; his young, wise, gifted sister; she who lived both gentle and furious, her faces like two sides of a sword blade, one of peace and one of war—came to believe in him again.

She was leaner than ever, her face gaunt, curls of skin peeling away from her nose and cheeks. Painful-looking crevices lined her lips. She was not the girl he had known in childhood. Nor was she the woman he had later known on the fields of Teh. How very strange their lives had been. How much he loved her, even though fate had kept them apart more years than it had let them be together.

Ilabo and Dram had flown their mounts to meet the tattered remains of Mena's army, to chase back the fréketes and to protect those battered troops as they continued south. They numbered only a fraction of the souls the princess had set out with. By the time they arrived, they would be even fewer than they had been the day before. Mena, delirious with pain and fatigue, battered by the sight of Elya's horrible wounds and the shock of Aliver's appearance, had stilled only after Ilabo had sworn to guide her army to safety.

"You're not alone out here anymore," Aliver had said.

There, with the sleeping mother and daughter sheltering them, they worked through many things of import. When they did begin to talk, everything came out in a rush: all the events on Acacia, the truth of things Corinn had done, the arrival of Shen and the Santoth, the events at the Carmelia, the curse on Corinn's mouth, and the changes they all went through in the days just afterward. So much. Aliver confessed the death sentence that he and Corinn were under. He thought it best to reveal this right away, before Mena grew too accustomed to him being among the living again.

The many things Mena told him in return were troubling. Her hatred of the Auldek blazed in her eyes. The hardest of the things Aliver had to explain was that he wanted to make peace with them. But that was the truth, so he said it.

"You can't be serious," Mena repeated. "They nearly killed Elya. They would have, if you hadn't arrived. If they had . . . if they had, I would have gone mad. I would have killed every one of them, each and every soul I'd have—"

"Mena, I did arrive. Elya is not dead. I don't want you dead either. I don't want thousands upon thousands more dead— which will happen if we keep fighting."

The look she gave him was a glare, but he thought the lamplight exaggerated her anger. He hoped so, for the wildness in her eyes was nothing he had seen in her before. She said, "I hate them. There is no way to make peace with them."

"What if I find a way? Would you consider it?"

"They *ate* the villagers of Tavirith. That can't be undone. It can't be forgiven."

"I know," Aliver said, "but perhaps the way to move forward is to find peace without forgiveness. Or to find forgiveness in peace. Not to forget anything but to put first the lives of those still living. Mena, you're arguing with me, but everything you've done up here was for the same cause. In all your decisions I see you trying to keep your soldiers alive. That's what I'm proposing. If we ask the thousands who are still climbing up the Methalian Rim to run to their deaths, they'll do it. If we do that, they'll understand it. It will be the same as what our family has asked of them for generations. Maybe their sheer numbers will tire the Auldek's arms or dull their blades. But what then?

Won't that be defeat? What world will there be for any of them afterward?"

Mena closed her eyes. "They won't let you."

"You may be right, but I have to try."

"They want us all enslaved."

Aliver reached over the lamp and set a hand on her blanketed knee. "That they cannot have. I'm not talking about giving in to them. No concessions. No defeat. I'm talking about finding a peace that doesn't destroy us all. Help me do that. Tell me everything you know about them. Help me find their souls. It's that I'll have to speak to."

"How can you even think that's possible?"

"I am Aliver," he said. He lifted his hand to her chin, nudging her head up so that she looked at the thin smile he offered her. "I've been given a second chance. I can't fail this time. I won't."

✳

That resolve was what drove his soul up out of his body two nights later. After hours upon hours of talking with his sister, after caring for Mena and seeing Elya's wounds miraculously heal as the creature slept, after seeing the first of his troops arriving in force, after flying out to greet Mena's battered forces, even after speaking for a time to Rialus Neptos, the traitor who had proved a treasure trove of information about the invaders . . . After all that, when it was time to sleep, Aliver lay down for the busy night's work he had ahead of him.

He had seen Devoth flying atop his mount when he saved Mena. She had identified him. Aliver used those images to pull his spirit out of his body and to send it after the Auldek. His version of dream travel may or may not have been akin to what Corinn had attempted, or to what Hanish Mein had used to commune both with his undead ancestors and with others among the living. Likely, it came to Aliver easily because of the years he had spent as a spirit dispersed throughout the world, floating. Separating his soul from his body proved not difficult. Perhaps his body had already begun the dying that would soon make his release complete.

He had barely fallen into the rhythm of sleep before he rose above his growing war camp. He surveyed the tents and supplies and animals, the slumbering forms and the many campfires for a time, but only until he got his bearings. Then he set his mind on Devoth. Aliver's spirit floated north. Slowly at first, then gaining speed until the dark, cold world of the plateau rushed by beneath him, gray-white under the moon's light.

He reached the Auldek camp, coming upon its steaming masses, bodies and beasts and fires. The towers seemed like mountains on the undulating landscape. Their numbers might have daunted him, but he had not the time to consider them. Before he knew it, his soul found the station it needed and punched, soundless and without force of impact, through the structure's wall. Inside, a large, sumptuous room, the walls hung with swords and axes, with tapestries depicting cityscapes and mountain ranges and vistas not of the Known World. A lamp burned low on a table, but even without it he would have been able to see. Light was within him. It illumined the room around him and also flowed through his vision. He came to stillness at the foot of a bed. Standing there for a while, Aliver's glow built in the room until he could see the shape beneath the covers.

"Devoth," Aliver called. "You are Devoth, aren't you? Chieftain of the Lvin. Get up. I know you speak my tongue."

The shape in the bed went from lying down to sitting up in one flash of motion. His reaction was so immediate he might have been lying in wait for the moment. His eyes found Aliver's wavering form, and his face expressed the depths of his confusion and fear. He sprang from the bed. He snatched for a battle-ax racked on the wall and whirled around with a savage swing that would have cut a man in half at the waist.

Or it would have if he had managed this same motion as a physical body and if Aliver had been there in the flesh also. Instead, the Auldek's body lay still beneath the blankets, just as motionless as before. The ax that Devoth had grasped for hung as it had, not disturbed at all. Devoth's spirit swung around after the blow he had tried to make.

"You can't defeat me that way," Aliver said, once Devoth had looked back at him, still now, and even more terrified. "I'm a ghost, you see. I'm one who went to the afterdeath and returned. I've pulled you out of your body so that we may speak."

"Who are you?" Devoth rasped, his accent thick on the Acacian words.

"Aliver Akaran."

"No, that one has gone. Do not lie to me!"

Aliver crossed his glowing arms. "Look at me, Devoth. Do I look like any man you have ever known? I am vapor and light. I am one who is dead and who also lives. Look at me and decide for yourself."

He stood, letting the warrior take him in. At the same time, he studied Devoth. There was something about his spirit that confused Aliver. He could see the Auldek's features, versions of his body made of glowing light. But his form held more than just his features. There were others beneath that outer skin of spirit light. The longer Devoth held still, the more Aliver could see the others move.

Quota children.

"What?" Devoth asked. He circled around the bed, trying to pull several weapons down, clearly hating it each time his hands passed like vapor through the wood and steel. "What have you done to me?"

"Nothing yet," Aliver said. "We are just talking. When I release you, you can return to your body."

Devoth shook his head. He tried to climb back onto the bed, but he was terrified at how he sank into the blankets, both having purchase and yet passing through them. Part of the world but not.

"Look at me," Aliver said. The Auldek did. All the other spirits within him did as well. How many incorporeal faces were layered there? Aliver could not tell, but he could see them. And they could see and hear him. "I have come with an army that dwarfs yours. All the people of the Known World are united against you. They pour onto this plateau like a river running uphill. We will overrun you. I have come to tell you to turn back now. Go back to your own lands, and we will not pursue you."

For the first time, Devoth's spirit seemed to regain some composure. He said slowly, drawing the word out, "Nooo."

"You've made a mistake in coming here, one that will destroy your people if you don't return to your own lands. Think about this: you forget the past. I know this about you. You forget the past, which is why you brought that collection of records with you. What will you do now that it's gone? You have lost so much already. So much cannot be regained, but if you continue with this war, you will lose yourselves completely. What will you tell your grandchildren? Nothing, because you'll have forgotten. Your grandchildren won't know the truth of where you came from. They won't see your cities in their minds or know the view over Avina or understand the beauty of Ushen Brae. They won't see Lvinreth or Amratseer. You say you want to die back into your true souls and age and die again. Good. Do so. That's the natural order. But if you do it here, your grandchildren's children will know nothing of what it means to be Auldek. Do you hear what I'm saying? You are already a defeated people. It's up to you, now, to decide the depths of that defeat. Stay and war with us—and you will destroy yourselves."

"Your sister is an evil one," Devoth said. "That much is true. To burn our records . . ." His spirit form spat, though nothing came of the gesture. "But it is not as you say. We can have Acacia, and we can journey back to Ushen Brae. We know the way now. We can have both places. Why not? The future is an Auldek future. The entire world Auldek. When you are defeated, nobody will be able to stop us, so why not an Auldek world?"

Behind the clear words that Devoth spoke, Aliver could hear other voices. They were soundless, like screams on the other side of thick glass. They had substance, but he had to learn how to hear them.

Aliver answered, "Because we can make a peace between us that will honor us both."

Devoth's smile showed a glimmer of confidence. "That's what you want? Only that? Now I know this is a trick. No, no, no," Devoth said, chuckling. "You have no terms for me. Your world is ours. You may send your army against us, but they will die. We are a great host. There are as many divine children fighting for us as there are Acacians in your army. And we have sublime motion. We could send only our slaves and they could harvest your army for us."

"But they are *slaves*, Devoth."

The spirits trapped inside him clamored about the truth of this. They so clearly heard him. Aliver tried harder to hear them as well. He pressed his consciousness up against that unseen and intangible barrier, listening from a place that had nothing to do with sound.

"They are loyal. Your speech is a trick, and I am not afraid of it."

"You have not heard my terms."

"There are none that I need hear."

Aliver closed his spirit eyes and stilled himself completely. He heard. The words and thoughts and emotions bloomed inside him. They were children's thoughts. Raw and youthful, filled with life and scared, trapped, begging for him. They spoke their names to him. There was a boy called Nik, and another named Drü. A girl, Hanna, cried out to him, so beseechingly it was hard for Aliver not to open his eyes and let it show. Erin and Allis, Ravi . . . So many names. Each of them belonging not to Devoth but to an individual who should have lived a true life.

I'm so sorry, Aliver thought. They could not hear this, but he thought it more than once.

"I present my terms anyway," Aliver said, opening his eyes. He spoke slowly, doing his best to ensure that the Auldek would understand him. "You and all the other Auldek with you will release your quota slaves from bondage. You will tell them they are free to do as they please. You will send them all across to our camp, so that my people can speak to them and make sure they are acting on their free will, whatever they choose. You Auldek will abandon this war. You will turn your stations around and go home, shedding no more blood in the Known World. You will make a solemn oath that when you return to Ushen Brae you will not punish the people living there. Every Auldek will make this oath, calling on your totem deities as witnesses. Such an oath would be unbreakable, right?"

"If it were made, yes."

"We may send ships to retrieve the people in your lands, but they are free. If they choose to live in Ushen Brae, you will have to find a way to live with them. We will have your oath on that."

At first, Devoth had listened with incredulity. As Aliver talked, he craned his head to hear better. By the time he finished, Devoth's spirit had begun to smile. "Is that all? And what will you give us in return?"

There was nothing like sincerity in the question, but Aliver answered it as if there had been. The entrapped children had begun to name where they were born. They seemed to fear he did not believe them. They threw memories at him, emotions, images of what home was to them. Under the bombardment, Aliver could barely keep track of his interaction with Devoth. It took all his concentration to do so.

"We will do four things for you," he said. "First, we will give you peace without fear of retribution. Our past will be our past. Though we will not forget your crimes, we will not hold them hard in our hearts." The children screamed for him not to forget their crimes. They were not past, they said. They were entrapped now!

"Very kind of you."

"Yes. Second, we will allow you to leave without interference. Nobody will hunt your backs. I will not haunt you anymore. Third, we will put into your hands the Numrek children."

"Numrek children?"

"Yes, those who still live. My sister captured them but did not kill them. There are not many, but they could be the start of your future, of the generations to come. We will give you that gift."

"Is that it?"

"There is a fourth thing."

"Yes? Is it the best thing?"

"It may be."

"Tell it, then."

"I will, but not tonight. I will tell it to you in person, on the field south of here when our forces meet. Talk to me then, Devoth. You and all the other Auldek. Come to me in front of your army, with all your great host behind you. Then I will tell the fourth thing. But now, go back to your slumber. Wake in the morning and remember what I said. Go, sleep, Devoth."

For a second it seemed the Auldek would fight the order,

that he had something else to say, but the command was strong. His spirit slid back toward the body beneath the blankets. Aliver saw the trapped souls being pulled back with him. He heard them, shouting without sound, pleading with him. The sight of their anguished faces was heartbreaking, but he waited until the final moment to do what he had planned. He felt there was only one moment that he could achieve what he wanted to.

Just as Devoth's spirit began to sink back into the skin of his body, Aliver rushed forward. He swept through the Auldek with his arms outstretched, filled with love and shame and grief and hope, asking forgiveness for those who came before him. He grabbed for the children's' souls.

And he pulled them all free.

CHAPTER
SIXTY-SEVEN

A cave on an outcropping of rock at the very edge of the Outer Isles, out beyond Thrain and Palishdock. The dark of a cloud-heavy night. The air and sea in furious struggle. Not a place many would choose to rest, and yet that was what Corinn and Hanish knew they had to do. Atop Po, they had ranged over hundreds of miles, gathering sorcerers all along the way. They had pushed Po to great speed over the sea, leaving the Santoth far behind, but not so far that they would not catch up with them soon. Though he showed not the slightest indication of needing it, Po had earned a rest, such as it was. Having furled his wings, the dragon perched sentinel above them, still as the wet stone and just as black. Corinn hoped that his wounds were healing. She thought so. The turmoil in his mind had grown calm. Damaged, yes, but resolved.

She did her best to always keep a part of her mind speaking to him, and to the other dragons. They were each of them faithful to her, but she could feel their desire for freedom. When she was gone, no other would be able to keep them tamed.

He will warn us, Corinn said, *if they come faster than we expect.*

Hanish stood at the mouth of the cave, gazing out into the night as if he were keeping his own watch. "I know he will," he responded. "I'm not doubting him. Just looking is all. Just look-ing."

The leaning rock walls around them provided the only shelter from the heaving of waves and the wind. A small fire cast their only light. Corinn fed it with things her servants had packed into her saddlebags: a tent and its bamboo poles; thick, hard crackers that burned as well as wood and that she could not eat anyway; rolls of parchment she would never now need; the leather bags themselves. *My servants: what would they think to see me now?* Though she took warmth from the fire, she knew she could have sat in the damp chill and not been affected by it. Just as she had gone days now with no food or drink. She was as empty as she had ever been, and yet she went on, feeding on the goal she had set herself.

To Hanish, she sent the thought, *We have them all behind us.*

"You're sure of it?"

Yes. I can't tell you how many they are. Their number never sets in my mind, but I can feel that they're all together. They have a different energy. It hums at the same tune now, with only one purpose.

"Catching us?"

Exactly.

"We have the scoundrels just where we want them, then," Hanish said, turning back toward Corinn and the fire. "Ha-ha! Take that!" He swiped at the air with an exaggerated flourish that made Corinn smile. Or that made her know she would have smiled, had it been possible. He came away from the cave mouth and settled himself beside the fire. He rubbed his hands together and held them, palm out, toward the flames.

Old habits, Corinn thought to herself, *are hard to break.*

Hanish said, "I guess that's it, then. We have a few hours. Until dawn, perhaps. Then it's nothing but the Gray Slopes for us. Have you any way of calling this worm of yours?"

I won't need to. It can hear The Song *even more clearly than the*

Santoth. It has been telling me as much for years. I just didn't listen. I suspect it already knows we're coming.

"Ah. So the worm is expecting us," Hanish said. "I guess it's not the first time either of us has had dealings with worms."

No, but this one I like better than senators and leaguemen. It's not like anything else. It doesn't really talk to me. That's not quite right. It's more like the way I communicate with Po. It thinks to me. It's very old, Hanish. I think it's something the Giver made when the world was still new, before Elenet, before any of the creatures of the land. It has a quiet mind. It's gentle, except that it knows the Giver's tongue is not for us to speak. That's one thing that matters to it.

"And what, exactly, happens when we find this creature? You've not filled me in on the specifics yet."

I don't know, Corinn said. This was not entirely the truth. She did know. The worm itself had shown her what was to happen in images that she had once thought of as nightmares. Now, those same images were the exact fate she sought. They were not, however, things she could say. Not even to Hanish. *I think we just have to find it,* she said. *The rest will come with that.*

"All right, love," Hanish said, "the rest will come with that. You should sleep now if you can. Even just a little. This next flight will be long. Come."

He indicated that she could rest her head on his lap. She did so, and, without prompting, he began to talk. Corinn lay, watching the play of the firelight on the cave wall, marveling that even now—with everything that had happened and was happening—she was still learning more about how to love this man. How was it possible that she could rest her head on a ghost's lap and learn of things he had never told her while he lived? How could she feel the warmth of him, the texture of his tunic against her cheek, the weight of his hand where it rested on her shoulder? She tried to listen to his tales, but after a while what she truly did was listen to the sound of his voice. How she liked his voice. It managed to be truthful but at the same time denied that life was anything less than a grand amusement. Corinn breathed him in, wishing she had some of his equanimity herself, wondering if this was how she gained it, by having him complete her.

Later, after Hanish had fallen silent, thinking her asleep, Corinn remembered another dream. It had nothing to do with the worm. She had only had it once, on the morning that she had worked three acts of magic, including bringing Aliver back from the dead. In the dream, she had been riding in a carriage down from Calfa Ven. When Aaden became unwell, she stepped out and walked the path to avoid smelling his stink. Aliver and then Hanish had walked beside her for a time, and then both of them had rolled into somersaults and become leaves that blew away on the breeze. For some reason, she had whistled a tune for them.

She asked, *Are you real?*

He still sat as before, stroked her hair slowly, as if counting the strands one by one. "Yes, of course."

Are you sure you love me?

"Corinn, you're the single woman who has ever had all my heart. You did in life and you still did in death, and you will do forever."

Why? Asking it, she was not seeking praise, not looking for false comfort. She really meant the question. At times, thinking of all the mistakes she had made, she thought herself unlovable. Unworthy of anybody's trust. She had proven herself that so many times, in so many ways.

"Who knows why anybody loves anybody? I love you for the things I love about you. I love you for the things I hate about you. I think, Corinn, that you love me as well; me, the one who would've killed you. Don't ask me to make sense of it, and I won't ask you. My heart is yours for as long as you want it. Do you want it?"

Yes.

"Then it's yours. In life and in the afterdeath. Glad that's decided."

He leaned forward and kissed the damaged skin where her mouth should have been. Though she knew he was but a ghost, a vapor that no other eyes except Barad's could see, she still loved his touch. There in that small cave at the edge of the Gray Slopes, with her eyes closed, it seemed each of his kisses glowed with golden warmth, each of them a pulse of light in the midst of an ocean of darkness.

✳

As the sun broke over the eastern horizon later that morning and cast crimson highlights over the gray waves, Po spread his wings and lifted the couple into the sky again. Gaining height, they saw their pursuers. They still ran atop the surface of the water, rising and falling with the swells. Unrelenting.

Po turned and headed west. Before them stretched nothing at all except moving mountains of water, and the rest of their lives.

CHAPTER
SIXTY-EIGHT

As soon as the vessel cleared the quay, Lethel called to his pilot, "Let's go." He sat on a seat he had ordered specially constructed. It perched high on the sleek ship's deck, the perfect vantage from which to watch the Lothan Aklun vessel devour whatever distance he set it toward. "Make it fast," he shouted as he pulled tight the straps across his waist.

The pilot backed out, as silently as if by sail power, and yet without any sails or oars or poles. The boat moved with a power infused into every portion of the craft. It spun atop the water and surged forward, into a curving arc that bore them away from the estate Lethel had claimed on one of the craggier barrier isles. It moved north around the island, then turned west.

When the open stretch of the Inner Sea came into view, the vessel raced, smacking and leaping across the waves with a speed like nothing Lethel had ever experienced. He clung to his chair, roaring with laughter each time the spray fanned over him. He liked speed very much. In no time at all, the league-man's hair was a disheveled bird's nest blown back behind his pointed cranium. He clutched his skullcap in his hands, riding high on the exhilaration of the journey.

When they joined the invasion fleet, the great mass of soul

vessels plowed toward Avina. Lethel had his pilot zip among the barges and larger ships at breathtaking speeds. He could not help himself. He laughed idiotically. Every spray of water that fell over him, or any expected turn that yanked his body one way or another, caused him to throw back his head in uncontrolled hilarity. To think that the league had avoided military campaigns all these years! What a waste.

As far as Lethel was concerned, this invasion was a lark. They could not lose. The outcome was obvious. They had the troops. Ishtat by the thousands. Sire El's trained army of quota slaves. They had the means to deposit these troops anywhere they wished. Everything just as he had told Dariel Akaran and Mór of the Free People. The only thing for him to do, really, was to enjoy it.

The pilot pushed them through a narrow, choppy gap between two barges. Their ship squeezed past them and shot out ahead of the armada. The coastline of Avina stretched before him. It shone bright in the morning light. The city's drab seawall crawled with life.

The Free People out to defend themselves, Lethel thought. How charming.

They raced toward the shoreline. The pilot pressed the speed so unrelentingly that Lethel let go of his cap and gripped the seat beneath him. His cap flew away in the wind. The pilot wrenched the boat to the left at what must have been the last possible moment. Water sprayed up from the side of the boat, drenching the breakwater and washing well up onto the quay that ran along the base of the city's walls. The flat stone ledge would make a wonderful platform on which to deposit their soldiers. The boat sped along it, sending up a spray of water the whole way. The speed was such that Lethel's eyes watered in the wind. He still managed to look up at the figures on the wall beside them. A few of the figures threw stones at him, but none of them gauged the speed right.

In response, Lethel waved a chastising finger at them.

❋

A little later, back out toward the rear of the fleet now, he sat watching from a safe distance. He spotted the large schooner that Sires Faleen and El had chosen for the occasion. At least, he thought he should call it a schooner. It hardly looked like one in his understanding of the term, but for pure size and carrying capacity he thought the term fit. Multistoried, outfitted for pleasure, the ship crawled with Ishtat guards, staffers, hangers-on, and concubines. El, when he arrived with his army, had done the leaguemen the service of bringing a great number of these with him. Most of them, it seemed, hung about the upper decks of the schooner.

"They're hardly even paying attention," Lethel muttered. He waved a hand, trying to catch someone's attention so that he could point at the attack, which had commenced. He did not try for long. The proceedings proved too interesting to be distracted from them.

The barges approached the shore first. Though massive, packed with soldiers and ballistae, battering rams and movable towers, their draft was so shallow they could press right up to the quay, with the water beneath them only on the height of three or four men. It would be as if the barges had simply added a wide extension to the shoreline, one filled to the brim with soldiers.

The barges halted a little distance from the quay. The large ballistae, with their mortar-punching missiles, cranked back. When they shot, the barbed bolts flew with blurred speed. They slammed into the stone walls with explosive thuds, sinking deep and sending shards of rubble into the air. Each bolt was attached to a length of rope trailing back toward the barges. More and more of the missiles struck home. Soldiers fastened the trailing end to anchors jutting from the barges. Then they reloaded and shot still more missiles.

The fools on the wall hunkered down. They cowered each time a missile sent up clouds of debris. "Do you know nothing?" Lethel asked. Having been briefed just the previous day on how the attack would proceed, he knew that it was not the impact of weapons they had to fear. It was what they did next.

Once enough of the bolts were set, the ballistae stopped firing. Normally, Lethel had learned, winches would crank back on those ropes. The lines, going taut, would pull the missiles, which in turn would cause the barbed points of them to expand inside the stone, pulling down sections of the wall for the invaders to clamor over into the city. Normally, this winching was a slow process, dangerous for the attackers because of the tension in the ropes and the possibility of mechanical failure. But these were not normal circumstances.

Today, the barges simply backed away from the shore. The ropes went from drooping lengths to straight, taut cords. All along the expanse of the wall, Lethel watched the chaos that ensued through a small spyglass. In some spots single blocks crashed down. In others the wall buckled and weakened before the prong fell free. Whole sections of wall crumbled toward the sea in an avalanche of stone blocks, debris, and screaming Free People.

Lethel set down his spyglass and clapped his hands. He yanked it up to view again. Where was Dariel Akaran along that wall? Where was Mór or the bird woman or anybody else he recognized? The confusion was considerable. He could not make sense of what the defenders were doing, like so many ants responding to the destructive pressure of a boy's foot. Swarm-ing, running in circles. He thought of calling for a larger spy-glass, but with the pitching of the boat he would not be able to keep anyone in focus.

The barges approached the wall for a second round. As with the first, the poor defenders could do nothing but scurry about or cower. The walls came tumbling down. As they should. They were unforgivably ugly. The Lothan Aklun, having feared the sea, had looked away from it. They left the shoreline drab and unfinished. Not a façade at all, the wall more resembled the dingy rear of a city. Let the entire thing fall. The league would redesign the coastline to wonderful effect. Avina would become one of the world's premier trading cities, a powerhouse for a nation that the league would rebuild to suit them.

Why am I so far back? Lethel wondered. He shouted over his shoulder for the pilot to move them in.

The boat closed some of the distance so that he had an improved view when the barges pushed forward a third time. They smacked right up against the quay, stopped dead there. The first contingent of soldiers jumped the narrow gap. They poured onto the platform and clambered over the rubble. The defenders, to their credit, rushed down to meet them. They seemed, in their exuberance, to forget that they were supposed to stay safely in the city. They brought the fight out to the quay itself.

Only the early ranks of the troops could engage, but that was perfect. The first ashore would batter the defenders into bloody heaps until they surrendered or fled. Lethel rather hoped they would do the latter. Let them run through the city streets, Ishtat in pursuit. Slaughter every last one of them, for all he cared. They did not need them. In the coming years, the league could repopulate the city as they saw fit, just as they would rebuild it to suit them. Crumbled walls, massacred rebels. It was all messy at the moment, but to build a sturdy foundation one always began with a bit of demolition.

Lethel still could not find the Akaran. He did focus in on one individual who seemed to be directing the defense, but it was not Dariel. His hair was darker than the prince's, an unruly mop clinging to his head. After pointing and shouting and gesticulating for a time, he dove down into the mêlée below the wall.

Lethel assumed that the sound, when he first noticed it, was coming from the besieged city itself. He had experienced an earthquake once while staying along the Talayan coast, and the strangeness in the air reminded him of the odd moments that preceded the earth shaking. He yanked the spyglass up, expecting to see the entirety of the wall come tumbling down or something like that.

It did not. The fighting just continued.

What happened next did not so much frighten Lethel as perplex him to his core. The humming grew louder. He wrinkled his forehead, making the thin slashes of his plucked eyebrows into two squiggles. The fighting figures stopped. They must have heard it, too. And then the sea . . . it went flat. Not calm, but completely flat. The entire undulating surface of the water became as featureless as polished stone. Lethel saw this all clearly, especially when his vantage point shifted.

He soared up from the deck, so fast he left his gasp at water level. His seat came with him, ripped free of the vessel. He hung in the air with a view of the sea beneath him. Craning his head around, he saw that all the thousands of soldiers on the transports likewise floated in the air. The leaguemen and staffers and concubines turned circles, their arms and legs waving about them in a slow pantomime of panic.

How unusual, Lethel thought, sure that nothing like this had been included in his briefing.

There followed a moment of stillness, and then the world changed. The soul vessels concussed with a sudden explosion of pressure, except that it was not really an explosion. It was soundless. There was no flame or smoke, no flying debris. Only a flash and ripple in the fabric of the world. In an instant, the vessels all disappeared. Lethel's ship vanished beneath him, as did the frigates and schooners and brigs, as did all the barges. They just ceased to be. Just afterward all the hovering people—thousands of them—splashed down into the sea.

As he hit the surface, losing control of his bodily functions on impact, Lethel was certain this had not been mentioned in his briefing. Nobody had said anything about this.

CHAPTER

SIXTY-NINE

The next couple of days brought a steady inflow of troops coming onto the plateau. Not just soldiers, the new arrivals included the young and the old, women, bakers and cooks, merchants offering their wares, laborers offering their bodies for whatever work needed to be done. It looked, gloriously, as if the people of the empire all came to aid the war effort, bringing whatever they could with them. Aliver had known from his connection to them that this was happening. As he spoke to them about why and how to overcome the addiction to the vintage, he challenged them not to lose their sense of purpose. Clearly, they had not.

Elder Anath, and Sinper and Ioma Ou of Bocoum appeared. They came riding in a covered carriage that looked most out of place on the plateau, among the dreary disarray of a growing war camp. They petitioned for a meeting with Aliver. The king allowed it, but he kept it brief. He could see these men wanted only to ingratiate themselves with him, to play up their role in getting Shen back to him, and find some way to turn all this turmoil to their benefit.

Aliver gave them nothing. Once he was gone they would grab for power and influence through their connection with

Shen. He had already done the best he could to leave a legacy behind him, in that locked box back in Alecia. He gave Rialus Neptos more of his time, for the things he had to say had more bearing on his present actions. Beyond that, he decided to speak to no one but those he needed to help him end this war.

The Auldek approached as well. Before them, fréketes swooped through the air, calling taunts from a distance. They did not come very close. The dragons had only to lift off the ground to drive them back. The invading army crept over the horizon one morning, and by midday had paused to make their camp. That was it. They were in place. The tundra between them would be their battlefield. The meeting Aliver had arranged with Devoth would happen tomorrow, before the two hosts, both of them ready for battle.

When Kelis arrived, tired from running across the mainland, his friend Naamen with him, Aliver could not have been more ready for them.

"I need your help," Aliver said. "Each of you, I need you to fight with me in a way you have not before."

He stood before the small group he had summoned to meet him: Mena, Kelis, Naamen, Perrin, Haleeven, Rialus. "What I say here is, for now, to stay among this company. I am going to ask something of you that few others would understand, and I'm going to ask it for a goal not many would imagine possible. Mena knows what I intend. She is a skeptic, which I understand. Still, she helped me choose each of you for this. Mena herself has dream-talked with her sister's spirit before. Perrin, Mena tells me you don't know this, but you were kind enough to offer your body as a spirit vessel."

The young officer could not have looked more perplexed.

"Corinn also reached you, Rialus, over a great distance. You must be sensitive to the spirit world. Kelis, you were born with powers over dreams, with gifts outside the waking world. Naamen, few people have spent as much time with sorcery in the air around them as you, and, Haleeven, I believe your people for generations knew much about conversing with the dead."

The old Mein nodded.

"It's those traits in each of you that I want to use. Before I tell you what I want us to do, I should tell you why I want us to do it." He sat down to be closer to the others. "I am going to make peace with the Auldek."

"No!" Rialus barked. And then, surprised by his own outburst, asked much more quietly. "What . . . did you say?"

Aliver repeated it. He saw exactly the concern and doubt he had expected—and which he had received from Mena as well. As with her, he took some time to explain himself, making it clear that he did not mean surrender or defeat in any way. He intended for both sides to gain much more in the agreement than they would lose by continuing to fight.

By the time he finished, the concern and doubt had moved around on all their faces. It remained, but in differing proportions on each of them. Rialus was, again, the first to find his tongue. "Your Majesty, this . . . this cannot happen. Even if we offer it, they will never accept. You don't know them as I do. They are fearless. Ruthless. They have no respect for life. Not their own or anybody's. I saw them eat human flesh!"

"Why did they eat flesh, Rialus?"

"I told you!" Shocked again by his outburst, he said, "Your Majesty, I explained earlier. They thought it would make them fertile. They wanted to have children. They are so obsessed with—"

"With life? That's what they're obsessed with. They are not casual about life. They hunger for it. More than anything else they want to be parents. Wouldn't you say that?"

Rialus thought for a moment. He seemed reluctant about the

answer he came up with. "Yes, but they want war and conquest, murder just as much. They are vile. Just vile!"

"They are not 'just vile.' There is more to them than that. If you cannot see that, then you have only one of two choices: destroy them or be destroyed by them. I want more than two choices. Rialus, you yourself told me the Auldek once built magnificent cities. You said they sing poems of love and tell tales of valor. You said that they trained birds to dance about them, to land even in their mouths! You said that in their country eating human flesh was a crime. And you said, Rialus, that you were certain that their codes of honor mean more to them than ours do to us. I'm sorry to use your own testimony against you, but the race you described to me was not entirely vile. And the part of it that is most vile—the ways they use our people as slaves, body and soul . . . that is something we partnered with them on."

Rialus shook his head. "I pray you destroy them all."

"I pray for something better," Aliver said.

Mena's young officer Perrin spoke for the first time. "If we do make peace with them, what's to stop them from becoming our enemies again sometime? They've suffered coming over here. We made sure of it." He glanced down at his hands, which were wrapped with layers of new bandages. Frostbite, suffered on the long run south with the Auldek tormenting them. He had lost parts of all his fingers. He knew something about suffering, though it barely showed on his boyish face.

What a group we are, Aliver thought. Perrin with his hands two bandaged mallets. Kelis with one hand part flesh and part metal. Naamen, born with one stunted arm, small of stature. Rialus, sniffling through his peeling nose, his eyes darting about, nervous as a mouse. Haleeven, once an enemy, now a grave face watching him from the back of the small group. And

Mena, bruised and battered, her shoulder wrapped and arm in a sling, ready to shake free of it and bring up a sword again at a moment's notice. An extraordinary group . . .

"But what about in ten years?" Perrin asked. "Twenty? Who is to say they won't come at us again? I would not want future generations to have to face them because we didn't."

"Nor would I. But it may also be that a future generation will find them to be friends. I am an idealist, Perrin. Have you heard that about me?"

The young man smiled. Nodded.

"What else can I do but provide the possibility of us all finding our better natures?"

Haleeven, sitting behind most of the others, said, "I can testify that such a thing is possible. Enemies may become friends." Lest he sound wistful, he carried on more sharply, "But will our soldiers accept this? All these people, they've come to fight, haven't they?"

"They came to live. They came because living meant they might have to fight. It's the peace they want, though, not the war that precedes it. If we can end this honorably, of course, the troops will support it. Perhaps in the future some will find cowardice in the act, but I hope they will see inspiration instead. Mena and Rialus—perhaps you as well, Perrin, Haleeven— think that the Auldek will accept nothing but victory on their terms. Right now, today, that's probably true. But by tomorrow, if you help me, I believe we can have them thinking differently. Will you help me?"

As nobody objected, Aliver explained it as best he could.

❋

They think you're crazy," Mena said, once the others had exhausted their questions, talked it all through, and then walked, mystified, out into the fading day.

Aliver smiled. "Yes, but they will get past that soon. Before I got here, they thought you were the crazy one." He caught the first scent of the dinner stew. That made him smile as well. He could count the time he had left alive on his fingers and toes, and yet he still knew hunger when his belly was empty.

"How is Elya?" he asked.

Mena nodded. "Much better. I think she is healed as much as she is going to. She is strong everywhere except the wing that the frékete chewed on. I'm not sure why. I think she could heal it if she wanted to, but . . . I don't know. I may be imagining it. I may be thinking of myself instead, but I feel like the intent of the wound is what she fears. It was too malicious. She was not meant to be attacked like that."

"With time?" Aliver asked.

"She will heal that, too. Yes, I think so. We will have to be far from here, though."

"Has she warmed to her children?"

"No," Mena said. "I know she recognizes them. She stares at them. They approach often, but she hisses them away. They're so much bigger than she, but they fear her. Corinn took them from her. I don't know if I can forgive her for that."

Aliver closed his eyes. He nodded and exhaled a breath and said, "I know."

With the hand of her good arm, Mena rubbed her injured shoulder. It, too, was healed she said, but only as healed as it could be. That arm had tried to leave her body several times already, the first when she was a girl being pummeled by the surf in Vumu, hand clenched around a sword too heavy for her to even lift at that point. The shoulder was healed by Elya's touch, but that did not mean it had not been damaged by time and abuse.

"Mena," Aliver said, "I am going to die."

"You told me that already, but I don't need to believe it until it happens. Sire Dagon is a liar. I would not trust him to tell me whether it was snowing outside or not."

"You've changed, Mena. Before you came up here, you would not have talked of snow. You would have said, 'I would not trust him to tell me whether it was raining outside or not.' We knew so little of snow on Acacia. Just that one time, really. That's the only snow I remember."

He cleared his throat, then coughed for a bit. By the time he quieted the memory had passed. "I can feel it. Believe me. I've been to death already. I know what it feels like as it approaches. I'm not scared. I do wish I had—"

He stopped himself. Cut the words with the side of his hand and pushed them away with the flat of it. "It's hard not to talk of regrets, but I won't. Waste of time, regret." He sat forward and took her hands in his. "Mena, I am constantly asking myself if I could live in a world in which the Auldek are at peace with us. Can I find a way to get beyond the crimes they've done and the suffering they've caused? Can I do all the things that come after this war ends in peace between us? It's not easy to imagine." He looked at her a long moment. "When I ask these things, the answer I come back with is yes. Yes. Of course yes. I would be a fool to let even one more good person die if he or she didn't have to. That's what tyrants do, not kings.

"The thing is, I won't be living in that world. So then I ask the same questions, but thinking about the world you'll live on in, and Aaden and Shen. Do you know what happens to my answer? It changes. It becomes an even firmer yes. I don't just think you *could* live in that world. I think you *should*. I think it will be a world to be proud of."

"That's a lot to ask of me."

"Mena, it's not the only thing I'm going to ask of you. Both Corinn and I, we expect a great deal from you."

L/ater that night, Aliver once more rose up from his sleeping body. He floated through the top of his tent and hovered in the air above it. For a time he paused there alone, the world quiet around him, save wolves howling somewhere in the distance.

He knew he was not alone when he heard Mena's voice, saying that she was here.

A little later, Haleeven found them, and then Perrin, glowing bright as he moved toward them. Soon, they were all there with him. Beautiful spirit selves, pure energy and light, hovering about the earth.

"All right," Aliver said. "Come harvesting with me. Come, you will like this work. Remember, we are not killing. We are setting innocents free. Come harvesting souls with me." So saying, he led them north, toward the sleeping Auldek.

CHAPTER
SEVENTY

Amazing, Corinn thought, how different one wave can look from another. She would never have believed it before, but after days on the wing, with only water beneath them, she began to see waves that seethed and waves that crested, ones that bulged in soft mounds and others that cut like blades, some smooth and black as stone, others foaming and hissing. Some cut diagonally against the others. Some changed their character and shading right before her eyes. And some rose like mountain peaks, so vast that they changed the air currents above them and had Po struggling to maintain his course.

The Range, Corinn thought. Dariel saw this before I did.

Amazing also how much the sea thronged with life. Yes, there were great lifeless and gray swaths of sea. But so, too, were there times when schools of fish rose to the surface in such massive numbers they became the world. She watched shoals of silverfish paint swirls and shimmers, dancing as predators cut through them. For the greater part of a morning, they flew over floating islands of sea fronds, so thick that creatures lived atop them, running from Po's shadow like tiny antelopes. One night the glow of life under the sea outdid the shining of the stars. And once she watched the illuminated outlines of a pod of whales, large and ghostly, moving with a stately grace.

At the back edge of all this wonder ran their hunters, pressing ever onward. Sometimes they, too, seemed like giants, striding ocean miles with each step. But other times they were only men, tiny men in an ocean that dwarfed them. Po stayed beyond the reach of their sorcery, but Corinn heard them speaking to her. For a time they tried to convince her to stop running. They must have the book, but once they did they claimed they would heal her, make her mouth right. They would study *The Song* with her.

Though she knew better, there was something powerfully persuasive about them. Strange how narrow the line between their warm, soothing voices and their evil truth was. The intent behind both was the same, strong in a way that had a similar essence. She never let herself believe them. It helped that Hanish was there whispering warnings, keeping her true to her course.

Eventually, they dropped the pretense and taunted her instead. They would never tire, they said. She had already failed. She had already led them back into the world. She could not stand against them. She was not Tinhadin. She had not his strength. She had not his *mouth*. They would chase her right around the world if they had to. She could not outfly them. They would catch her tomorrow, or the next day. But they would catch her.

The Song *is ours! It's already ours. Your days are few.*

She did not know if they said that because they knew about the poison in her, or because they intended to make sure of that themselves. She gave them no response. Hanish did not even talk anymore. He just rested his chin on her shoulder and watched the same watery world that she did. That was all right. There was nothing more to say. They just flew.

※

$\widetilde{A}$nd then came the day they were searching for. The sea beneath them suddenly thronged with creatures. One moment it was empty. The next, white leviathans clamored at the surface. Hundreds of them. Enormous creatures that she had only seen in paintings, paintings that at the time she had assumed were touched by fancy.

"Sea wolves," Hanish said.

Po did not like them. At first he roared at them, thinking them some new curse of the Santoths'. Corinn calmed him. Careful not to let him see the images she had of what was to come, she had him bank into a wide circle, looping around and around above the water.

"Why are you doing that?"

I dreamed it.

"Ah." She knew that Hanish had a quip to follow, but he held it in.

I dreamed it. Since that was so, she did the only thing she could. She did what had been shown to her already in the dream. She flew that circle, taking Po lower and lower as she did. Each time she came around, she saw the Santoth on the horizon but closing on them. They had not been part of the dream, but they would be part of the reality.

The sea wolves did something Hanish found very strange. "What in the Giver's name?" he murmured. Corinn expected it, though. They copied Po's circular motion. They drew tighter, going around and around beneath them. They swam with a strange pulsing motion, twisting over one another, ghostly white, tentacled, with eyes that watched the dragon fly above them. Hard to separate one from another. The tighter they got, the more that became the case.

They are his searchers, Corinn said. *That's all they were ever doing, searching for* The Song of Elenet *anytime ships passed near them.*

By the time Po's wingtip skimmed the surface they were so close together there was no water visible between them. And when Corinn asked Po to land on them, the bodies of the strange leviathans congealed together, forming a circular, flat surface on which to land. It took some convincing to get the dragon to do it. In the end, he did it only because she promised him he could fly away as soon as she and Hanish were down.

Po's feet danced across the surface. It was flat, and strangely smooth, but it was made of great, sea-crusted white bodies, entwined tentacles, and large eyes that stared up at them. Po only stayed touching them for the time it took for Corinn to gather *The Song of Elenet* from a saddlebag and climb down. Then he lifted into the air, barking as he did so. It was a strange noise, one she had not heard him make before. For some reason, she knew what it meant. He was telling her to be quick. He did not like this place and wanted to go.

Hanish stood beside her. "What now, Corinn?"

Now we call for the worm.

She had wondered how he would respond to this. When he did, she knew he had done so perfectly. "All right. I hope it's quick." He dipped his head in the direction of the Santoth, who were tall figures now, slashing the air as they ran, sending sprays of water up from their feet.

Corinn held the book out before her. She ran her palms over the aged leather of its cover. Her fingers caressed the frayed leaves of its pages. As she did so, she felt the creature wake. He was somewhere far below them, embedded in the depths of the ocean floor. *Come, I've brought it.* What it sent back to her was not an image or a clear thought, certainly not words. It was a feeling. It was the sensation of a massive body peeling away from the bottom, turning upward in the blackness and writhing in great sweeps of its gargantuan length.

It's coming. She opened her eyes. The first thing she saw was Hanish, standing just before her, his gray eyes there to meet her gaze. *I could not have done this without you.*

"You could have," he said, "but I'm glad you didn't have to."

The Santoth were much nearer. They stood even taller, their elongated forms stretching far up into sky. Their churning arms cut through the clouds. She could hear them now, singing themselves faster and faster, hungrier than ever for the book that was so near.

Corinn opened it and, pulling her gaze away from the sorcerers, she began to read. The song bloomed inside her. It twined and danced about her. It wrapped her and Hanish in ribbons of energy. It sped the Santoth on, and it snapped through the tail of the creature below them, driving it upward.

When the Santoth reached them, it looked as if they would arrive in massive stature, stamping the strange platform down into the water. They held to that size until the last moment. Po had to pull back, roaring at them. Just as their feet touched the sea wolves, the Santoth shrank. The entire stretched length of their bodies pulled in, so that they stepped onto the platform the size of normal men. Cloaked, dull figures, old and ravaged by time and evil and desolation. Their eyes bulged and trembled with intensity.

"Give it to me." Nualo extended his hand. "Give it to me!"

Looking at his cracked, aged hand, Corinn realized what the last thing Leeka had tried to say to her and Aliver was. *They cannot take it from me. I have to give it to them.* They stood there, ranked in front of her, like starving men before a feast she held in her hands . . . and they could do nothing.

For a sliver of a moment Corinn rejoiced. If they could not

take it from her, she could keep it! They did not have the power over her that they claimed. She could . . .

And then that brief madness was gone. She could not keep it. She had not the life to use it anymore, and, even now, surrounded by the threads of beauty that still swam around her, she knew the song should not be sung by any human mouth. Never again.

You cannot have it, she said. *None of us can. This ends now. Here.*

Nualo's face bunched with rage. He raked up a curse from deep within him, but before he could utter it, the worm arrived. As when she had envisioned it swallowing the whole of the isle of Acacia, the creature's mouth was enormous. It emerged under a great swell of seawater, a wide ring that took in everything: the sea wolves, the people standing on them, the sea around them. The mouth rose around them all. It stretched upward, stories upon stories tall, a wall so dripping with water and encrusted with barnacles and hanging with tendrils of seaweed that Corinn could only take in the vastness of it with no greater understanding of exactly what it was. The strong, aquatic smell of it drenched the air. And still it rose.

The Santoth tried to leap away. They roared their anger and slashed out with their foul sorcery. Nualo clawed for the book, begging Corinn to give it to him. She yanked it from his grasp when the sea wolves beneath him fell away. He splashed down among them, bellowing curses. The sea wolves loosed their tight weave and sent the sorcerers down to thrash among their tentacles and the great rolling heave of their bodies. Only the sea wolves directly beneath Corinn stayed together.

The queen pressed the book to her chest and looked at Hanish. He stared back. He reached out and took one of her hands. The two of them stood like that, the only stillness in all that great commotion. His mouth opened as if to say something. But instead of speaking he smiled. Of all the things he could have said and done, that smile was perfect. It was sad, resigned, and yet also confident. Somehow, it conveyed that this was as it had to be, the best of all possible outcomes. It said that what they went to now was nothing to fear.

Then the creature's mouth closed around them all. It stopped its upward thrust and slowly, heavily, fell back into the sea. Above the churning froth into which it sank, the dragon Po circled for a time, crying out his distress. Circling, as the sea went calm beneath him, as the waves rolled on, and the wind, until there was nothing but the sea.

CHAPTER
SEVENTY-ONE

Standing alone in the dressing room he had been provided, Dariel listened to the murmur of the gathering crowd. He could not help but remember the multitude of voices he had sensed inside that glowing wall on Lithram Len. It was the same sound in so many ways, except that here, out in the main courtyard of Avina, the masses gathered in exuberant joy. They had mouths to speak with, hands to clap, free will to move themselves through the world. They had life to rejoice in, now more than ever.

Such had not been the case with the spirits trapped through the sorcery that encased them in that wall and somehow connected them to all the accursed soul vessels. Dariel did not expect to ever understand it entirely. He hoped he wouldn't. Understanding the sorcery was the very thing that drove the Lothan Aklun to acts of revenge that had enslaved the entire world—themselves along with it—for generations. Better just to know that his bow of reverence had placed the raised rune on his forehead into the engraving meant to receive it. His living tissue touched that strange, glowing matter. A key. That was what Nâ Gâmen had given him. A key that unlocked that cage of souls, freeing all the spirits that the Lothan Aklun had used to power their vessels. The moment it was done, the glowing wall had gone dark. Silent. Motionless. He had felt a concussion of energy, but it had come from elsewhere. In that small chamber, the cage of souls simply ceased to be, and the enslaved vanished into freedom.

"I freed them," Dariel said. "Or . . . you freed them." That was another thing that he was going to have to learn to live with: that he and Nâ Gâmen would share his soul for as long as they both lived on inside Dariel's mortal body. Acknowledging that, Dariel said, "*We* freed them."

Bashar brushed his leg. He stroked the hound. Still a pup, but tall enough already that Dariel did not need to bend to reach him. All lean muscle and bone. Hunters. The ridge running against the grain up his back bristled stronger than ever. He looked at Cashen, who lay watching them. The pup thumped his tail. Considering the massive pads of their paws, Dariel had finally come to believe Birké had not exaggerated. The hounds would be enormous, and they would be there soon.

Dariel repeated, "We freed them."

"Yes," a voice said, "we did." Mór stood in the open doorway, in silhouette against the light behind her. Dariel could not see her face, but he knew her form and her voice. She walked in, more beautiful now as the lamplight illuminated her. "You look good in these clothes." She reached for the collar of his new linen cloak, tugged it around a bit, seemed to like it even better. "Are you ready?"

Dariel said he was, but Mór did not move to lead him to the meeting being held in his honor. She stared at his face, tattooed just like hers. She stared at his forehead, which no longer had the rune embossed on it. His skin was as smooth as it had been before the Sky Watcher took the stylus to it. The key, once used, vanished along with the soul vessels.

"At least you'll always have these Shivith markings," Mór said.

"And I'll never forget who drew them under my skin," Dariel responded. "Rather painful, as I recall."

Mór ducked her head a moment, laughed. "We've come a long way, Dariel Akaran. I'll tell you something." She leaned in a little closer and whispered. "I am a woman who finds beauty first in other women. That is just the way I am. But if I did like men . . . I might come to you to explore it."

Dariel was glad she pulled back. His face had flushed, and he feared if she kept studying him so closely his cheek might start to twitch.

"I never told you what Nâ Gâmen told me at the Sky Mount," Mór said, strolling away and running her finger across a nearby desk. "I didn't doubt him, but I didn't want to accept it, either. First, he said you had a destiny here. He said your story, whether it ended well or ill, would be the story of our nation as well. I told him I despised the blood in your veins. Do you know what he told me?"

"What?"

"That it was your Akaran blood that made greatness in you possible. I thought that was foolishness, but the more I've thought about the many things he showed me, the more I believe he could not complete his work without an Akaran's blessing. Does that sound right?"

Dariel nodded.

Mór did as well. "The second thing . . . was that he confirmed that my brother's spirit force was still inside Devoth. Buried deep, he said. It was close to his true self. I had always thought my memory of that was true, and it was." She picked up a stylus and felt the grain of the wooden handle. "He said that if I went in search of him—to kill him—I might succeed, but that I might not get back to Ushen Brae. He said I could have revenge or a future among the People. He did not think that I could have both."

She hit the stylus against the palm of one hand for a time. Stopped. Glanced down and seemed surprised that she even held it.

"Which do you want more?"

"I wanted each more than the other, but I had sworn to fight for the Free People. I thought that once we had won I would track Devoth to the ends of the earth and cut each soul out of him until I found Ravi. I would have done it."

"I believe that."

"I would have, but now I don't have to. Ravi's been released."

"Released? How do you know?"

"I felt it happen. I always felt his life force, Dariel. Every day since he was taken from me I've known that he still lived, trapped. You once called me cranky. You would be, too, if you had to live with that." She tossed the stylus back onto the desk. "Anyway, I felt his soul go free. I don't know how it happened. I don't know if Devoth is dead. I only know that it was a different thing from what you did with the soul vessels. Somehow, over there in your lands, Ravi found peace."

❈

In the high hall a short time later, Mór led Dariel to the gathered Council of Elders. Yoen and the other elders stood waiting for him. They had arrived the day before, having trekked all the way from the Sky Isle on the news that Dariel had been accepted as the Rhuin Fá. Little did they know that as they journeyed, a short, crucial war would unfold. Little did they know they would arrive in a city rejoicing, with the league defeated at the moment that the soul vessels vanished. A great number of the invaders had drowned, but others were plucked from the water, prisoners now locked away and awaiting their fate.

Mór waved Dariel into the circle of elders. He stood, feeling awkward before them. He knew them all, if only from his brief time at the Sky Isle. Perhaps it was the new garments. It had been some time since he had worn clean clothes with sharp creases and fine stitching. Or maybe it was the crowd gathered in the squares just below them. He could hear them even better now, the sound drifting through the large, open balcony windows at the far end of the room. It was heady stuff to be a hero to so many people.

Heady enough to make young Spratling nervous, Dariel thought.

It might also be that the chamber contained a solemn air he had not expected. Everyone gazed at him: the elders near at hand; Mór and Skylene, Tunnel and Birké and all the People he had become so close to here in Ushen Brae. A little farther back stood Melio and Clytus, Geena, and the others who had come so far to find him. All of them safe and well, largely unscarred by the skirmishes they had fought so that he could complete his part in this story. They stared at him, too. He got the feeling everyone knew something that he did not.

"I have a story to tell you," Yoen said. He spoke to Dariel, but he lifted his voice for everyone to hear. "It's a true story. True stories do not always make the best ones, but this one is pretty good. Many, many years ago, hundreds of years, during the early days of the Free People's settlement at the Sky Lake—" He cut in on himself to say, "This was before my time, in case you are wondering."

He waited as the polite laughter faded. He was just as frail looking as before, his hair still disheveled, in contrast to the care taken with his long robe. His limp had increased, the product, no doubt, of the journey. He leaned heavily on his cane.

"One day, a Lothan Aklun found the settlement," he continued. "The People were shocked, because no Lothan Aklun had ever come searching for them before. Not even the Auldek had ranged that far. They need not have been alarmed, though. The

Lothan Aklun was not hunting them. He was on a mission. He told them that he had come to hate his people's ways. He was taking his quota children—both those inside him and those living through their years beside him—up into seclusion in Rath Batatt. You know this man. It was Nâ Gâmen.

"Before he went, he gave the villagers something. He took from his wrist a bracelet made of pure, precious gold. He said that it was not actually a bracelet. It was an armband that had been worn by the first quota child he had come to love as his own. I called it a tuvey band, though in truth it was just a child's trinket. He gave it to us, and he also gave us a sapling from a tree of your lands, Dariel. An acacia tree. He planted the tree, and slipped the band around it. He told those Free People that one day the quota trade would end. One day, a person would come to us who had the power to change everything. A good person. A kingly person. A man or a woman with a pure heart and noble intent. This person would have the power to release our trapped spirits. He said that on that day—when we knew this person had arrived—we should build a great fire around that tree. A beacon to announce the freeing of the world. When it died down, we were to retrieve the band from the ashes and see if it still held its shape.

"We did as he asked us to. We left the band around the trunk of that small tree, waiting for the day we could build that fire. A lovely idea, but it did not go as anyone wished. The wait was to be longer than we could have known. Not a lifetime or two. Many more than that. That sapling became a tree. Generations lived and died. The tree got thicker, stretched taller. Years passed. The ring grew tight around the trunk, and then the tree lifted the ring into the air. Still longer it took, so long that the tree swallowed the band and grew around it. The band went hidden for generations. The world turned so long that I was born, and you were as well, Dariel, and everyone else in this room and out in the courtyard there."

The old man pointed to the great balcony that opened above the gathered crowd. He had been strolling in circles as he talked, his eyes drifting, gentle everywhere they touched. They came back to Dariel now. "Do you know the tree I'm speaking of?"

Remembering the sacred acacia he had seen from the hillside above the village by the Sky Lake, Dariel nodded.

"Before we came here, we burned it. We believed in you, Dariel Akaran. It appears that we were right to. And look what we found in the ashes . . ."

Yoen had paused behind a small table, atop which a simple box sat. Dariel had not noticed it before. Yoen opened it, reached in, and lifted out a thin circlet of twisted gold. He walked toward Dariel, holding it high for all to see. "It began as a child's armband," he said. "Now it looks rather more like a crown."

He paused before Dariel. The band was but a simple circlet. No stones set in it. No engravings. The only feature enhancing the gold beauty of it was the waves that years inside the tree must have bent into it.

"It's beautiful," the prince said.

Yoen agreed. "None here dispute it. You are our savior, Dariel. You are the one who came to free us. The Rhuin Fá. This band is yours to do with as you wish. I hope that you do something wise with it." He pushed the band from his fingers into Dariel's.

"This is not for me. It's too precious."

"We believe it is yours. It was always yours. You may even slip it atop your head, if you wish, and ask the people to accept your leadership. I believe they would."

Holding the warped and stretched band—a child's bracelet that had grown inside an acacia tree—Dariel absorbed what was being offered. It was there in the curves of the band. It was in Yoen's eyes. Looking around the circle of elders and beyond them to his companions—both the new ones and the old—they all waited for him. It was up to him to say whether he wanted to ask the People to make him king of Ushen Brae. The headiness of this dizzied him. He stood with his mind racing out across the great continent he had only seen a portion of. He thought about the glowing ruins of Amratseer and the jagged peaks of Rath Batatt and the wild rapids of the Sheeven Lek. He remembered names of places he had heard of but had never seen. By the Giver, he might rebuild the ancient city of Lvinreth. He had never seen it, but the notion of a white-rocked city carved into the far north, a place where snow lions roamed the streets beside people . . . It took his breath away. He could be king, and he could create a culture different from anything in the Known World. Better. Fairer. A dream of a nation like one Aliver might have imagined. Perhaps one day he and Birké would climb into Rath Batatt. With Bashar and Cashen they would go hunting, wandering until they found whatever wonders lay beyond that range of mountains.

It would be a magnificent life.

Only . . . He searched out Melio's face, saw him watching, concern on his features. Clytus as well. Geena. Even Kartholomé. If they had not come for him he might have answered Yoen differently. He might have grasped for a magnificent life in Ushen Brae. But they had come, and that life could not be. They had come to take him home, to Acacia, to Wren. If she lived and he could get back to her, he would never let her go again. Never. He had to go back. He had to sail with Melio beside him, hoping that the future included him being uncle to the child Melio wanted to have with Mena.

"No, I can't accept this." He looked around at the silent people watching him. "I love the Free People," he said. "I have learned to love Ushen Brae, and I could not be more thankful for the gifts you've given me. But"—his gaze settled on Mór—"I must go home." He walked to Mór and pushed the crown into her hands. "If this is mine to do with what I wish, I give it to Mór. Why not a queen instead of a king? A mother for the nation. Go ask the crowd what they think of that."

When Mór looked down, stunned by the treasure in her hands, Dariel turned and walked away. In the hush, his steps sounded loud on the marble slabs. He did not look back, though he badly wanted to. He wanted to see Mór stepping into the light of day, crown in hand, to ask the People to name their future. He pictured it in his mind. He saw it that way, and walked with the vision in his mind's eye, knowing it was a fine vision, a truly fine vision.

He was into the hallway and down it some ways before his steps slowed. He wanted to go back. What was he doing? He loved this place! If he had come here under different terms, he might have stayed forever. But he had been away from home too long. He did not want to forget the ones he loved over there. No, he had to go. He had to go home.

He got a few steps farther before he heard the eruption of cheers from the square. He kept walking, embarrassed lest anybody see the tears suddenly washing his face. A good effort, but he did not get far. He stopped again. He leaned against a wall and watched the world go liquid. He was not even sure why he was crying, whether it was for this place or the other, whether from sadness or joy. He listened to the hush and burst of cheers, to the gaps during which one or another person spoke. He could not hear what they were saying, but he was happy for them. The Free People were becoming a nation. The children who had been stolen had finally—

"Dariel!"

He began to walk again, but with blurred vision he was not sure which columned passage would take him out.

Anira caught up to him as he hesitated. He tried to turn his face from view. She caught his chin. "Has anyone told you what Rhuin Fá means?" she asked. "They did not say so before because it might have affected your decisions. You had to be pure, and to do what you would of your own accord."

The moment she said this, Dariel realized that he did know what the title meant. He just had not thought about it since Nâ Gâmen gifted him with the Lothan Aklun language. He knew, though. He knew before Anira even said it.

"Dariel, it means 'the one who closes the circle.'" She shook him gently. She moved her face close to his and kissed him. It was not a sensual gesture. It was just a gift between two friends. "Do you hear me? The one who closes the circle. Rhuin Fá, do you hear them? They're calling for you. I think some of them want to go home with you. I think . . . many of them want to go home with you. They want a big, big league boat. They want you to captain it, and to take them home."

CHAPTER
SEVENTY-TWO

They're not bad young ones," Delivegu said. "Didn't talk much at first, but they loosened up as we traveled. Get them talking about warfare and they'll chew your ear off. I mean that literally." He mussed the unruly black hair of the boy beside him.

Aliver smiled at the gesture. There was a fatherly sincerity to it that he had to acknowledge. He had always thought Delivegu a swaggering braggart, though he had not managed to say so while still bound by Corinn's magic. Delivegu still had a swagger, but he had done what Aliver requested. He had reached them last night, in time, perhaps, for his mission to make a difference in what happened today.

"Thank you, Delivegu," Aliver said. "You have done well."

The Numrek children stood in a nervous cluster around the Senivalian. The eldest was in his early teens, the youngest looked to be five or six. Aliver could not be sure if their ages matched their appearance, but he thought so. He saw in the older boys the flame of newfound rebelliousness, in the younger children, the staring eyes of ones so frightened by the world that they could not look away from it even for a moment. They were just children. His enemy's children, but still just children.

He counted seven of them, just like the number in Kelis's dream. He recalled that Kelis had called them his children. He had dreamed that Aliver had seven children. Here they were. He thought, What if Shen had been captured like this? Aaden? It was not a far-fetched thought. In a world in which the Auldek fought this war to victory, his own dear ones would be at the mercy of his enemies, as these were.

"I mean you no harm," Aliver said. "I know harm was done to you. I think, perhaps, that you saw what my sister did to your parents back in Teh. I am sorry for that. I hope that you live long lives, and that the years as they pass blur that memory. I can't undo it any more than you can undo the crimes that drove the queen to feel the wrath she did that day. Do you know why she was so angry? Because your parents conspired to kill her son. That, more than anything, drove her to the madness you watched. I understand that madness, but I want no part of it myself. I have a child, too."

That last statement stopped him. Whatever he was going to follow it with flew out of his mind. He sat a moment looking from one child's face to another's, searching for what he had been about to say. He did not find it. "I have a child, too" was not the beginning of a thought. It was the conclusion of it.

"Would you like to see Ushen Brae?" Aliver asked.

It took some time to get them to respond, with Delivegu helping. All of them eventually said they did want to see Ushen Brae.

"It's a foreign land to you, and it won't be as it was when your parents left." This they did not have any response to. Why should they? They did not know Ushen Brae. They did know Acacia, though, and this place had not been kind to them. "If the Auldek will have you, would you go to them?"

The answers came back faster this time. Yes, of course they would.

Rising, Aliver moved toward the tent flap. He paused at it, and said, "I will try to send you home. It's not up to me, but I will try."

※

The mass of troops collected a few hundred paces behind them was an impressive force. Aliver only glanced at them, though. He had no desire to see the thousands of warriors and hundreds of beasts and machines of war arrayed against him. His own army had grown just as massive. The united humanity of the Known World stood rank upon rank behind him, people from all the provinces, with all their various languages and traits and characteristics. They would fight and die today, just as the Auldek forces would. For different reasons, but with the same ferocity. Corinn's dragons would take to the air; the fréketes would do the same. This day could become an unimaginable, bloody conflagration. The wood was all stacked. The torch had only to be touched to the fuel. Or not.

So he kept his attention on the delegation just in front of him. Devoth, Sabeer, and the other clan chieftains stood a few strides away. Aliver had only seen them as spirit people, glowing and transparent. Still, he knew the figures who stood before him now were not as they had been but a few days ago. The defiance in Devoth's laugh just a few nights before, the confidence, the certainty of knowing that death was far removed from them: it was all gone. Their faces looked haggard, stunned. Their eyes drooped with fatigue.

Mena stared at them as if she did not even recognize them. Behind him and his sister, Aliver had brought a small contingent, the handful who had done the spirit work with him the night before. It fell to him to complete this, to succeed or fail, but it felt very good to have those trusted friends behind him. Both groups were unarmed, having set their weapons on the ground before drawing near each other. If the Auldek attacked them, he and his people would die. Again, if that happened, he would have failed, and there would be nothing more he could do about it.

Devoth spoke first. "What have you done to us?" he asked, speaking Acacian.

"Nothing unjust," Aliver said. He spoke without a hint of bravado. Without derision or anger, managing to sound both firm and empathetic. It was not a tone of voice he had to work hard to master. It was simply how he felt. "You awoke the other morning feeling different, didn't you? You didn't speak of it to the others because you felt weak. You felt frightened in a way you never have before. Or, at least, a way you don't remember ever having felt before."

"No," Devoth grumbled. Though his eyes were savage, his *no* came out strangely passive. He denied it. He also wanted to hear more. The others did as well.

"You were alone then," Aliver continued, "but when all the Auldek woke this morning they felt the same as you. They might not have said as much. I know you are a proud people. And what could you say, when you could not explain why the world feels different to you today from yesterday? I can explain it, for I had a hand in it. Do you want to know what we've done to you?"

"We have already asked you to tell us," Sabeer said.

"Has Devoth told you of the peace that I proposed?"

"Yes," Sabeer answered.

"Have you also heard it in your dreams—from me or from one of these here behind me?" The silence they responded with was answer enough. "The peace I offered is still what I offer today. I swear to it before my god, the Giver, who I believe created this world. The visitors that you had in your dreams, they were also real. They took my message to you; they also took something from you. They took back what you never should have stolen. They took from you, and released into death, the souls you had eaten. That's why the world feels different to you today. Today, you have all woken up mortal. You have only the life you were born with inside you. Only that single, transparent, fragile soul stands between you and the afterdeath."

The other Auldek stared at him, their faces like masks. They looked, standing so still and vacant, like they were already dead. Aliver almost smiled. *You would think I'd killed you already. I haven't. I'm the one counting down his last breaths. Hurry, let's complete this.*

"You have stolen our lives from us?" Devoth whispered.

"No, you stole them from the children we sent you. Your sin was taking them inside yourself; ours was sending them to you in the first place. These last nights we worked to end both your sin and ours."

"You stole from us," Devoth said.

"We made you Auldek again!" Aliver said. "You don't even remember what you used to be. Once, you were mortal. You don't remember that, but back then—before you sold yourselves to the Lothan Aklun—you were truly Auldek. You lived and died. You married and had children. I know these things about you. Rialus Neptos told you of us; he also told us of you."

Devoth did not glance at the thin Acacian. Sabeer did, though. She pinned him with her eyes. Without even turning, Aliver knew Rialus squirmed beneath the gaze.

"You loved life and feared death and that is what living is! Life is given to us only as a temporary thing. All of us who can think know we live on borrowed time. That's the beauty of it. We have to live now, for it will soon be gone. You lost that, and then you forgot that you lost it. We have given it back to you. It's a gift from us to you. I know that you intended to die back to your true soul here in the Known World. That's part of what you came for. You would have killed or enslaved us first, but I cannot allow that. So take the gifts we have given you. Leave the rest. Leave the old crimes. Leave the new ones you would have committed. Leave it and go home. Take with you a future in which you can live true again. Your mission here will not be a failure. This is not defeat, Devoth. You came to find a way to live again. You came to become fertile. You came to end your life as slavers and become your true selves again. All that you can have. Let me show you what that future can look like."

Aliver turned before they could respond. He shouted something back to his army, and a moment later several soldiers moved aside. The Numrek children walked through the gap left open for them. The seven figures proceeded forward cautiously. Aliver beckoned to them. "Come! Let your uncles and aunts see you. Come!"

When the children reached them, they stood awkwardly, out from the Acacians, and yet reluctant to go any nearer the Auldek. Sabeer said something to the children in Auldek. Several of them responded. She motioned them forward with her fingers. A man to one side of her squatted down and beckoned them with his arms. The children drifted closer, until near enough that the adults touched them. They began speaking rapidly to them, different adults asking different children questions. They squeezed them on the shoulders and pulled them into embraces and cupped their faces in their palms.

Allek, the Numrek who had come in his father's place, pushed his way through his elders and called to one of the younger girls. Seeing him, she broke from the woman who was stroking her hair and ran to him. She jumped into his embrace and the young man turned away, trying to hide the heaving sobs that wracked his chest.

Aliver gave them a few moments, and then said, "I told you I would provide these children to you. Here they are. Take them. Take them home to your lands and teach them how to be Auldek. I believe that will give both you and them great joy."

"We have not said we accept your terms," Devoth said. He had been gazing, enraptured, in a young man's face. He straightened, hardening his expression.

"No, but that's because I have not told you the last aspect of my terms. I told you I would reveal it now, so I will." Aliver lifted his chin and indicated the vast array of troops that made up Devoth's army. "Those soldiers and slaves who fight for you—I want you to let them decide their lives from now on. They may return to Ushen Brae with you, or they are welcome among us. There will be no punishment for the fighting that came before today. You'll tell them this. If you don't, we will tell them that all of you Auldek are mortal." He paused, letting the significance of that grow inside them. "You may think they love you and are loyal to you, but I think it's more that they fear you. They think you're invincible. That's what keeps them standing behind you. If they knew that you were just as mortal as they, they would not look at you with slave eyes anymore. That one there. What is his name?"

Aliver picked out a Lvin slave, one who stood out before a contingent of the divine children. He stared, his chin raised almost as if he were sniffing the air. His face was white as snow, framed by the thick locks of white hair that made him seem truly half snow lion, just as regal, even more deadly.

Rialus answered, "Menteus Nemré."

"What do you think that one would do if he knew one blow of his sword could end you? I suspect I know the answer, but should we ask him? We could call him over and hear what he thinks."

"We gave him a good life," Devoth said. The old certainty,

which had already slipped out of him along with his souls, had escaped him now entirely. He spoke, but he did not even seem to believe himself. "You don't know how much we gave him."

"You did not give him freedom," Aliver said. He stared at Menteus Nemré. The man had noticed. He stared back. "You did not give him the respect an equal deserves. I suspect he would like that more than anything else. I suspect they would all want that. I may be wrong, Devoth, but I believe that if I shouted the truth of your mortality to them right now, you would not have one army facing you. You would find two surrounding you. I suspect that your own army would slaughter you with more relish than anyone standing behind me."

Aliver brought his eyes back to Devoth and asked, "Should I ask them?"

※

Later that day, after Devoth said no, he did not want Aliver to ask Menteus Nemré or any of the divine children that question, after he had conferred with the rest of the Auldek and brought back the answer Aliver had longed to hear, after he had listened to all the oaths to peace that he could and when he believed it had really, truly been achieved, with protection for any Acacians remaining in Ushen Brae as well, Aliver asked if Mena would accept the rest. There was still a long line of Auldek waiting to accept the peace. It would take some time.

She said she would complete the work. She took his hand as he rose and held it a time, as if she were rehearsing the words she would say to him. In the end, she only repeated, "I will complete this."

Aliver parted with her casually, as if he just wished to go outside and walk among the troops. He did that. There was much rejoicing among them, and he wanted to feel some of it. But when he felt the fingers of death brush his shoulder, he did not run from them. They had been near for a long time, and he could not possibly begrudge them their due now, not after the day they had just allowed him to complete. His time had come. He hoped that Mena would not be angry with him for not saying a more formal good-bye, but he thought she would know that he had been doing that with every action he took since being freed from Corinn's spell. Better that she take over from him, as that was what the future held for her anyway.

He walked for as long as he could, greeting soldiers and touching hands, until he managed to slip down a quiet lane of tents. He lay down on a cot under a shelter. And then, on second thought, he rose and pulled the cot out underneath the sky. He watched the heavy blanket of clouds, so near to them in the darkening sky. When the first snowflakes began to fall, he closed his eyes and felt their cold, delicate kisses on his cheeks. On his eyelids and lips.

He opened his eyes once more, stirred by a commotion near at hand. He heard Po's roar come down from up above. He saw the dragon's dark shadow pass above, and then heard the answering calls from his siblings. His eyes almost fluttered closed, but then a man yelled. There came the crash of something being knocked over, and then a series of snaps, the clink of metal rings and grunts of agitation.

Aliver understood what was happening before he knew why he understood. Po flew riderless above, calling on his kin to join him. The other three were tearing off their harnesses. He heard their wings unfurl, that loud concussion of clicking that was like nothing else in the world, and then swoosh as those great wings grabbed the air and lifted them upward. He heard the panic in people's voices, but he did not feel it. Corinn had written, *As long as I live they will be true to us.* After that, she said, they would be different. Listening to them chatter to one another as they rose into the snow-heavy night, Aliver knew that change had begun, and he knew that his sister had gone before him to the afterdeath.

"Corinn . . ." He had been so consumed by his own work, that he had almost forgotten her battle with the Santoth. He remembered it now, and knew that she had been triumphant.

Eyes closed again, he lay there a long time, feeling the snow build a blanket atop him, thanking his sister. It was not just her saving the world from the Santoth that he was grateful for. He thanked her for himself, for allowing him to know, in the end, that she was wonderful, that he loved her completely, without reservation. As a brother should.

A little later he stopped feeling the snow. He stopped feeling anything. He had a thought that would have made him laugh, except he no longer had the lips to laugh with. Aliver Akaran, he thought, look what you've done. You've made it so that they're going to start calling you the Snow King again. He did not really mind. He had always liked the ring of the name. Before, he just had not deserved it. Now, perhaps he had earned it.

CHAPTER
SEVENTY-THREE

The flutes played the noon hour. They started high in Acacia, at the top of the palace, and then the tune cascaded down toward the lower town. Beautiful. A sound that Mena had never really believed she would hear again. She stood on the balcony of Corinn's offices, amazed at the view of the island in the brilliance of the spring light. How was it even possible that a sound so wonderful lived in this world, in the same one that had just been filled with the din of war, with arctic winds howling and men and women crying in pain and rage? It did not seem possible that the images that had comprised her life the last half year could be real if this was real; or that the view out across the spires and down toward the glistening sea could be anything but a dream if that other version of life was a reality. She would need to spend a great deal of time coming to terms with this and finding a way to face it alone.

She was home, but Aliver was not. Corinn never would be. Dariel and Melio had gone out of the Known World and nobody could say a word about their fate. She was alone. At least Aliver's body worked its slow way home, escorted by the army that loved him. His body, encased in a simple casket, took one last meandering trip around the Mainland. Mena hoped Aliver would have welcomed that. She thought he would. She thought he would like it very much that his body was being carried the entire way on the shoulders of former slaves who had just weeks before stood in the army that opposed him. So many of them had chosen to stay and had begged for the honor of bearing Aliver home to Acacia. There was a rightness to that, a closing of very old wrongs.

Yes, she thought. He would have liked that very much.

Hearing someone enter, Mena stepped back into the room. Rhrenna, her sister's former secretary, stood at attention, a collection of papers held to her chest. She bowed her blond head. "I have news," she said, "from Alecia."

Of course she did. Rhrenna had nothing if not news. Since Mena's return to the island a few days before, the Meinish woman had acted as if she were Mena's personal assistant. She had been a great help, really, leading the princess through her own palace as if she were a visitor new to it. Perhaps she was. Perhaps she had not come back the same and would never feel the same. Or perhaps, with Aliver and Corinn both gone, Acacia itself was not the same.

"I would rather you had news from the Other Lands," Mena said. "One fair word about Dariel or Melio would be all the news I need for some time."

"Still nothing from there, I'm afraid. This news, though . . . Your Majesty, perhaps you should sit down."

Rhrenna had been nothing but courteous to her. She had not called her Majesty before, though.

"Why, do I look so ill as that?" Mena glanced down at the dress she wore, and nearly started. A dress! A garment of light cotton that flowed all the way to the stone floor, pressed and clean, embroidered with gold thread. This will take some getting used to, she thought. It had been a good thing for her to return directly to Acacia on Elya. She needed time to remember how not to be at war, how to wear a dress and wake in a mild clime and not think constantly about the lives that depended on each decision she made.

"You look very well," Rhrenna said. "It's just . . . the decrees were opened and read before the Senate. They . . . may surprise you."

The secretary had her attention now. Not knowing how to read her face, Mena felt a tingling of fear, familiar trepidation. "What's happened?"

"It's not anything that you expected." Rhrenna looked around the empty room. "I feel like somebody should be here with us when I say this."

"Just speak it."

"Aliver and Corinn . . . have made you queen."

Mena stared at her.

"They both conceded that their children, being illegitimate, should not inherit the throne. That's how they explained it, at least. You are the only direct, legitimate heir. Only you are married, with the potential to produce a legal heir." Rhrenna paused, searching Mena to see if she acknowledged that logic. "The Senate agreed. They've reratified the decrees already. They had no choice. They had already accepted the decrees Aliver gave them in a locked box. Remember I told you about that? He did that before he flew to meet you. And now, considering the way the people love the Snow King, nobody disputes his and Corinn's wishes. You are to be queen of Acacia. Nobody opposes it."

And what if I oppose it? Mena thought.

"There's more."

Of course there is.

"You should read it yourself."

The secretary offered it, but Mena made no move to accept it. After a moment, Rhrenna continued. "Aliver and Corinn have called for an alliance of nations, not an empire. They called it the Sacred Band." She stopped again. "Do you really want me to—"

"Rhrenna, just tell me, please!"

"It's a plan to be implemented over time," Rhrenna said, skimming the pages. "Right now, you are to be queen of the empire. You are to oversee the five provinces as they each form governments. In ten years—or after ten of peace, calm, if all is going well—they gain self-governance. They'll still be within the empire, I think. But after twenty years the nations are to become truly independent. There are details. More to it than that, but that's the thrust of it. Eventually, Acacia will be one nation among others. Among equals." She set the papers down on the desk. "Now that I think about it, I can see why the senators wouldn't want to interfere with this. Self-rule. You know how many new kings that will make?"

What a grand confusion that will be, Mena thought. But even as she thought it she felt lifted on a tide of relief. It was right. A confusion, but confusion that would no longer rest on a single pair of shoulders. Hers. They trapped me and freed me at the same time. Aliver, you did say you were going to ask a lot of me. Now I understand. Or, I'm starting to.

❋

Later that afternoon, Mena gathered Aaden and Shen from their lesson with Barad. They took it up at the same open-air classroom in which she and her siblings had received lessons from Jason. Mena ushered them away quickly, thanking Barad but not wanting to stay too long with the memories of the place, or with him. Not that she could escape memories in the palace. Barad's eyes, though, saw into one. Yet another thing she would have to get accustomed to. Another topic on which she would need to slowly come to trust her older siblings' wisdom.

The children were unusually quiet as they walked. Only when they reached Elya's terrace and heard the creature chirrup a greeting did they find voice to ask about what Barad must have told them.

"Is it true?" Aaden asked.

"Many things are true. Which one are you asking about?"

"You're to be the queen," Shen answered. She did that sometimes, and Aaden did the same for her, finishing each other's thoughts as they shared them.

Like twins, Mena thought, looking at them. A pale-skinned boy with light eyes; a brown-skinned girl with dark ones. So different, and yet not. Not for the first time since joining them, she wondered what her child by Melio would have looked like. It was too difficult a thought, though. She pushed it away, knowing that she faced a lifetime of wishing she had had that child with him when she had the chance.

"That's what I've been told," Mena said. "I never planned that. I don't . . . know what it means, really. I don't know." She looked at the two of them helplessly. "I'm sorry, but it's too new. I just don't know."

"Melio will be king," Aaden said, "when he comes back."

Mena had not had time to consider that. Melio Sharratt, a king. Love him as she did, that was rather hard to imagine. "Let's pray he comes back, then."

"I always do," Aaden said. "Every morning, I ask the Giver to let Dariel and Melio return."

The boy turned his face away. He watched Elya preen, pretending to be fascinated. Mena knew better. She heard the emotion trying to crawl over his last words. She almost said that she said the same prayers herself. She wanted Melio back beside her so much she walked with a perpetual emptiness inside. It had been there throughout the war, but she noticed it much more acutely now that she was home. Finding Wren here on Acacia when she returned, with a wee babe whom she had named Corinn in her arms, made things both better and worse. Mena was so pleased to be an aunt a third time, so pleased to know that Dariel lived on in the child, and that Corinn would be honored by her as well. What a father Dariel would have been! She could not imagine anyone better suited to it. Instead, though, it was the likes of Rialus Neptos who would soon be arriving back to meet his daughter for the first time. Maybe he would make a good father, too. Mena could not say. Despite the animus she might always feel for him, he had played a part in saving the nation.

How very strange, the turning of fate.

Shen said, "My mother is happy. She said this means I won't have to worry about being queen."

"Would you have worried about it?"

The girl caught the question on her lips and paused to consider it. "I'd rather you did it."

"Me, too," Aaden said, glancing back. "Don't tell Mother I . . ." The words fell from his mouth and dropped out of the air, the sentence unfinished. He began to turn away again, but his aunt did not let him.

"Oh, dear, come," Mena said. She pulled Aaden in, hugging him tight, and then looked up and motioned with her fingers that Shen should join the embrace. Arms around both of them, she whispered, "You two are good friends now, aren't you? That would make your parents happy. It makes me happy. Listen, the world surprises us all. Me as much as you. It even surprised Corinn and Aliver. Again and again it finds ways to surprise. It makes things tough sometimes. That's what it's been lately. But it won't always be so hard. We've come through so much. We really have."

"Aunt, what will become of us?" Shen asked.

Mena drew back to see her niece's face. "What a question to

ask! I don't know the future, child. I only know what's been, and what I wish will be. And even then I know that I'll never even really understand what's been. It confounds me all the time. Nor will what I wish to be ever come to pass exactly as I imagine."

Shen crossed her eyes. It was such an unexpected, bizarre gesture that at first it alarmed Mena. When the girl's eyes popped back to normal, Mena saw it for the joke it was. Smiling, she agreed, "You're right. Life is confusing enough to make you go cross-eyed."

"But what do you imagine?" Aaden asked. "I know—it won't happen just perfectly—but still. Tell us."

"You would have me lay the future before you, made only of my hopes and fears?" Both children nodded. "All right. Here . . ." Mena took a seat on a couch and motioned for the children to do the same. She had one sit on either side of her, turned them so that they rested their heads on her lap. Elya stopped preening to watch them.

Mena looked up and away from them all. "What I imagine is that you will live magnificent lives," she said, "and that you will live lives of quiet disappointment. You won't be able to explain why, but there will always be some failures. You will strive for greatness and justice, and you will help to make our nation wondrous. I'm counting on that. Don't let me down. You will both be great, but you will also fail at many of the things dearest to you, and people—even ones you love—will disappoint you. You will know great loves and you will have dear friends and you will be part of the great tree of Akaran. You will never be alone. And yet some of those you hold dearest will betray you, or envy you, or covet the things they perceive you to have that they do not. At times—even within a throng of people, despite the noise and clamor of attention—you will feel strangely lost. You will find gifts that are special to you, but you will never understand why such things were thrust upon you. You may curse the world for always, always spinning, never pausing, and yet this motion will be the music to which you dance. In the end, I hope, you will come to feel that none of the life you led could have been any different, any better or worse. You will find meaning in accepting many things you cannot understand or change. And if you live a long life, you'll grow tired and that will be all right, because you will have done the best you could during your lives."

Aaden shifted his head as if to look up at her, but Mena stilled him with her palm and pressed him gently back against her knee.

"You will take into the future all that ever has been for us. You will take your mothers and your fathers. You will take all that was Acacia, and all that was Talay, and all that was Mein, and you will take more than that—gifts and memories beyond measure. All of it lives inside you. Because of you, the days to come will be better than the days before this one."

Mena paused. She flexed her fingers where they touched the two children. "At least, that is how I imagine it. I may be wrong. I am not so old myself. Some say the greater portion of my life is before me. But, dear ones, that's the future I imagine for you. I wish that it were more, and yet I also know it to be a vast thing, beyond what you can imagine now." She paused again, unsure how they would respond, if they would be saddened unduly. She did not want that, but she could not lie to them.

She was surprised, then, by the calm with which they answered.

"Let that be so," Shen said.

And a moment later, Aaden echoed, "Yes, let that be so."

After a silence, Shen said, "Mena?"

"Yes, love?"

But it was Aaden who answered, "You've said many of the

things that my mother wrote me in her letter. Shen read it, too. Did you read it, Mena?"

"No."

"Funny," Aaden said, "because she wrote the same thing. Almost."

"Only 'almost'? What did she say that was different?"

Shen responded. "She wrote all that, and then she said that it was our job to make it better than that. When we're grown, she said, we should make it better in ways she could not imagine."

"We will," Aaden said.

Mena closed her eyes. She tilted her head up slightly, as if she needed to scent the air. When she opened her eyes she was glad the children couldn't see the tears that escaped them. She was glad her hand—that was a gentle weight on their heads—could just as easily hold them in place. She said, "Of course you will. That's what you were born for."

End of Book Four

Epilogue

Sire Dagon lingered on the dock after the others had departed the ceremony. He stepped out of the shadow of the *Enrapture* and stood gazing at the ship. There it was, the new home of His Eminence, the Enraptured Sire Grau. Stacked stories upon stories tall, the *Enrapture* was not the largest league brig, but it was the most revered, the most sacred. It never docked longer than a few days, never filed a plan of sail, and for most of each year it kept no contact whatsoever with the rest of league society. It floated the world's seas, followed the currents. It rose and fell with the tides. All the time it did so, the enraptured leaguemen housed within it lived in a state of unending bliss. Sire Grau, having just joined them, had an eternity of floating, dreaming paradise stretching before him.

The bastard, Dagon thought. You lying, conniving bastard. I hope the vessel sinks!

He glanced around to make sure nobody heard his thoughts. He would never let such venom escape him in council, but he was not in council now. The leaguemen and Ishtat and workers draining away toward the town paid him no heed. He wished he did not have to hide his thoughts, as he just had throughout the ceremony. He had stood beside his brothers through the pomp of Grau's Rapture, watching Grau climb into the casing that was to be his lasting paradise, watching as the casing was winched up into the vessel. Dagon had even intoned the sacred songs, honoring the sire for the life of service he had lived. Complete rubbish. Why would anyone think I'd have anything but hatred for him anyway? He's ruined me.

Thanks to Grau and his plotting, Dagon was a failure. Having been forced to forfeit his Rapture tithe—part of which went to conclude Grau's payments—Dagon would never live long enough to earn admittance. The lowliest young league novice in the outer circles of the council had a brighter future than he.

Dagon did not follow the others. He strolled out to the far end of the dock, looking to the west and also south across the open expanse of water. He set a hand on a pylon, a thick stump of wood that he knew was actually the very tip of a massive tree, one that extended far down into the depths of the deep-water dock. A brig caught his eye in the distance, coming in from the west. One of the large ones most often used for crossing the Gray Slopes. He did not recall a brig's return being planned, but his mind had been on other matters recently.

He tried to take some comfort from being able to absorb the news of the world from the safety of Orlo. Tumultuous events were best studied from a safe distance. He much preferred mulling over the Known World's turmoil while inhaling the sea breeze blowing in from the west, watching the sun slide toward the watery horizon, as he was doing now. He even took some satisfaction in finding himself somewhat vindicated by recent events. "Who among you, brothers," he had asked at the last council meeting, "would prefer being prisoner in the Inner Sea to being free leaguemen perched between the two continents?" The answering silence had been gratifying, regardless of the grumbling undertone hidden just beneath it.

Watching the brig come in and waiting for the sun to dive into the horizon, he stood cataloging what he knew of recent events. For one, Queen Corinn was no more. Nobody knew what had happened to her, but she never returned from the confrontation with the Santoth. Dead, gone, and good riddance.

Her dragon, Po, circled high over the isle of Acacia one evening, but he never landed. He flew north and gathered his siblings. All four of them ripped off their harnesses and lofted into the air, roaring themselves into freedom. Wild, monstrous freedom. Elya, their mother, could do nothing to restrain them, though she stayed true to Mena.

Aliver had managed to arrange a truce with the Auldek. He even sent them home with his blessing, the Numrek orphans, and a box of children's toys. Or so went the joke making the rounds among the leaguemen. The vintage had not proved to have the deadly apathetic withdrawals their trials had suggested. That, the people claimed, was Aliver's doing, the same magical connection with the masses he had employed to help them off the mist during the war with Hanish Mein. The people went on. And then the king had promptly lain down and died! Dagon had tried to win some credit for that, but—injustice!—it all fell on Grau. None of the blame, all of the credit. Hail Grau!

Dagon lofted a bit of phlegm into the air, watched it splat on the water below. It floated until the gaping oval of some fish's mouth opened below it and sucked it in. The brig was near enough now that Dagon expected it to furl its mainsail. There were sailors up in the rigging, but whatever they were doing it was not tending the sails. Perhaps it was not going to dock at Orlo at all. On to Thrain, maybe.

Then there was all the business about Mena becoming queen. A neat maneuver for her—it avoided all sorts of unpleasant manipulation of the two illegitimate children. The leaguemen were unsure whether the crown had been thrust upon her, or whether she had arranged it for herself. Mena had never seemed interested in rule, but Akarans—especially Akaran women— had proved surprising before.

As for the whole notion of a "Sacred Band" of independent nations . . . Aliver's work, obviously. Nathos doubted that it would result in anything but a new round of wars, but Revek had offered that it might actually be for the best. It made for an entire continent of individual monarchs, all of them new, even Mena. The potential for the league to enrich themselves exploiting them was considerable.

Tired as the thought made Dagon, he had to admit it was true. The league would worm its way back into the commerce of the Known World. The Sires Faleen, El, and Lethel surely had hold on Ushen Brae by now. The Auldek might be marching back that way even now, but they were not to be feared anymore. Not really. For many in the league—the Raptured, of course, and the young as well—the future remained bright.

"For yourself, Dagon, not so . . ."

He paused midsentence, realizing that the brig really had not lessened its speed at all. It grew larger by the second, plowing through the water most recklessly. It was sure to pass too close to the docks. Shouts of alarm confirmed that others thought this, too. Dagon could hear the strange, almost inaudible hiss of the prow cutting through the water. He started to back away.

He paused when he saw the sailors in the rigging release a flag. As it rolled out, and then snapped full, Dagon felt the color drain from his face. He knew it immediately. How could he not? He had lived years beneath it on Acacia. The Tree of Akaran, the black shape of an acacia tree against a yellow sunburst. Unmistakable, even if it lacked the perfect craftsmanship of the flag that flew atop the palace. It made no sense. A joke of some sort? Had one of the sires gone mad on the voyage home?

A figure waved and shouted from the deck. Dagon ignored him, searching for the conical head that would distinguish a fellow leagueman.

"Sire Dagon!" the person yelled. "Sire Dagon!"

Dagon squinted him into sharper focus. The man moved along the deck as the ship slipped past. Others crowded the deck, shouting and waving also. But the single figure held Dagon's attention now. As he ran, others leaped out of the way. He was in a state of mad euphoria, pointing to his chest and gesturing in the air. "Look at me! You see me?" Though Dagon could not make out his features, he could see that the man wore a smile as radiant as the sun. Watching him, Dagon failed to heed the warning shouted by those around him.

The wave thrown up by the ship's prow hit Dagon with a force that knocked him off his feet and sent him sprawling, sliding across the pier, grasping for something to hold on to. He slammed into a pylon. His breath escaped him, and for a few moments the tide of water held him in place, wrapped around the plug of wood. By the time he gained his feet again, breathless, sopping wet, and bareheaded, the brig was almost past the pier.

"It's me, your friend Dariel Akaran," the madman on the brig shouted. "It's Spratling. I'm in a hurry now. Can't stop and chat. Too much good news to spread. I'll come back soon and settle our business!"

The stern of the brig cleared the pier. As it carried on, Dagon lost sight of the prince for a moment. Then he appeared once more, looking out from the rear deck. He yelled, "Tell your brothers that Spratling is back! And he's brought friends!" He pointed at the bulky figure beside him, a gray man who climbed upon the railing, turned around, dropped his trousers, and wiggled his buttocks over the stern.

As the ship charged away, Dagon barely heard the commotion of the others rushing around him and the leaguemen pouring out onto the pier to watch the ship as it carried on to the east. He sat down on a pylon. He went to take off his cap and hold it on his lap, but he did not have a cap. He glanced around for it, and then gave up and watched the vanishing brig. He could have thought a thousand things, but what came to him was something small, something that Grau had said back in Alecia. How had he worded it? He had said . . . *What use is going to Rapture if it all comes crashing down in a few years?*

Sire Dagon chuckled. What use indeed? he thought. What use indeed?

In a perverse way, despite the unfortunate magnitude of what had just been revealed, he felt a little better than he had just a moment before. He wondered if he might gain entrance to the Rapture vessel just long enough to find Grau's chamber. He would knock on his casing and say, "I hate to wake you, brother, but guess what? Guess what . . . ?"

The End

ACKNOWLEDGMENTS

This trilogy was a long journey, both for me and for those who helped along the way. I would like to thank everyone I thanked in the previous volumes. For this one in particular, I have to begin with Gudrun, my first reader, the one who approved the novel before anyone else did, the one who made me believe in it. I had some great beta readers this time: Allison Hartman Adams, Hannah Strom-Martin, and Erin Underwood all made the book better than it would have been without them. Carola Strang and all the team at Le Pré aux clercs in France were wonderfully encouraging; and Gerry Howard and Sloan Harris worked through many trials and tribulations with me as we brought this home. Thank you all.

The Acacia Trilogy

"David Anthony Durham has serious chops. I can't
wait to read whatever he writes next."
—George R. R. Martin

ACACIA
Book One: The War with the Mein

Born into generations of prosperity, the four royal children of the Akaran dynasty know little of the world
outside their opulent island paradise. But when an assassin
strikes at the heart of their power, their lives are changed
forever. Forced to flee to distant corners and separated
against their will, the children must navigate a web of hidden allegiances, ancient magic, foreign invaders, and illicit
trade that will challenge their very notion of who they are.
As they come to understand their true purpose in life, the
fate of the world lies in their hands.

Fiction/Fantasy

THE OTHER LANDS
Book Two of the Acacia Trilogy

A few years have passed since Queen Corinn usurped control of the Known World—and she now rules with an iron
fist. With plans to expand her empire, she sends her brother, Dariel, on an exploratory mission across the sea to The
Other Lands. There, he discovers an alliance of tribes that
have no interest in being ruled by Queen Corinn and the
Akarans. In fact, Dariel's arrival ignites a firestorm that
once more exposes the Known World to a massive invasion, one unlike anything they have yet faced.

Fiction/Fantasy

GABRIEL'S STORY

When Gabriel Lynch moves with his mother and brother from a brownstone in Baltimore to a dirt-floor hovel on a homestead in Kansas, he is not pleased. He does not dislike his new stepfather, a former slave, but he has no desire to submit to a life of drudgery and toil. So he joins up with a motley crew headed for Texas only to be sucked into an ever-westward wandering replete with a mindless violence he can neither abet nor avoid—a terrifying trek he penitently fears may never allow for a safe return.

Fiction/Literature

PRIDE OF CARTHAGE

This epic retelling of the legendary Carthaginian military leader's assault on the Roman empire begins in ancient Spain, where Hannibal Barca sets out with tens of thousands of soldiers and 30 elephants. After conquering the Roman city of Saguntum, Hannibal wages his campaign through the outposts of the empire, shrewdly befriending peoples disillusioned by Rome and, with dazzling tactics, outwitting the opponents who believe the land route he has chosen is impossible. Yet Hannibal's armies must take brutal losses as they pass through the Pyrenees mountains and make a winter crossing of the Alps before descending to the great tests at Cannae and Rome itself.

Fiction/Literature

WALK THROUGH DARKNESS

When he learns that his pregnant wife has been spirited off to a distant city, William responds as any man might— he drops everything to pursue her. But as a fugitive slave in antebellum America, he must run a terrifying gauntlet, eluding the many who would re-enslave him while learning to trust the few who dare to aid him on his quest.

Fiction/Literature

ANCHOR BOOKS
Available wherever books are sold.
www.randomhouse.com